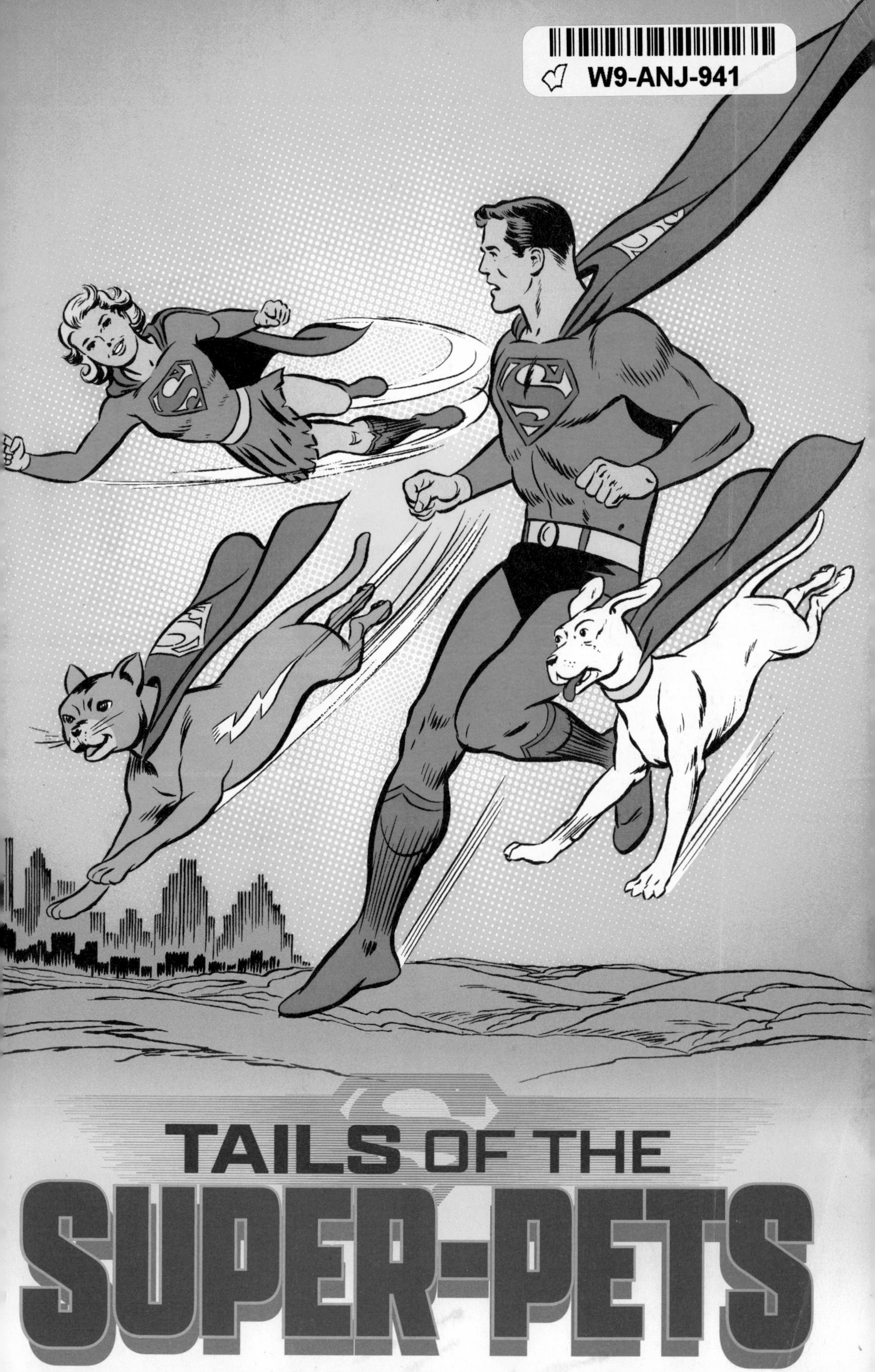

TAILS OF THE SUPER-PETS

TAILS OF THE
SUPER-PETS

Robert Bernstein Otto Binder Leo Dorfman Bill Finger
Edmond Hamilton William Moulton Marston Jim Shooter Jerry Siegel
Writers

Pete Costanza John Forte Ramona Fradon
Jim Mooney George Papp Harry G. Peter Curt Swan
Pencillers

Sy Barry Stan Kaye Ramona Fradon George Klein
Sheldon Moldoff Jim Mooney George Papp Charles Paris Harry G. Peter
Inkers

Collected Edition Cover by **Curt Swan** and **Stan Kaye**

Whitney Ellsworth
Sheldon Mayer
Jack Schiff
Mort Weisinger
Editors – Original Series
Kristy Quinn
Editor – Collected Edition
Steve Cook
Design Director – Books
Curtis King Jr.
Publication Design
Christy Sawyer
Publication Production

Marie Javins
Editor-in-Chief, DC Comics

Anne DePies
Senior VP – General Manager
Jim Lee
Publisher & Chief Creative Officer
Don Falletti
VP – Manufacturing Operations & Workflow Management
Lawrence Ganem
VP – Talent Services
Alison Gill
Senior VP – Manufacturing & Operations
Jeffrey Kaufman
VP – Editorial Strategy & Programming
Nick J. Napolitano
VP – Manufacturing Administration & Design
Nancy Spears
VP – Revenue

TAILS OF THE SUPER-PETS

Published by DC Comics. Compilation and all new material
Copyright © 2022 DC Comics. All Rights Reserved. Originally
published in single magazine form in *Action Comics* 261, 266,
277, 292-293, *Adventure Comics* 210, 256, 293, 322, 364,
Batman 125, *Superboy* 76, *Superman* 176, and *Wonder Woman*
23. Copyright © 1947, 1955, 1958, 1959, 1960, 1961, 1962,
1964, 1965, and 1968 DC Comics. All Rights Reserved. All
characters, their distinctive likenesses, and related elements
featured in this publication are trademarks of DC Comics.
The stories, characters, and incidents featured in this publication
are entirely fictional. DC Comics does not read or accept
unsolicited submissions of ideas, stories, or artwork.
DC – a WarnerMedia Company.

DC Comics, 2900 West Alameda Ave., Burbank, CA 91505
Printed by LSC Communications, Owensville, MO, USA. 3/25/22.
First Printing. ISBN: 978-1-77951-339-7

Library of Congress Cataloging-in-Publication Data is available.

TABLE OF CONTENTS

The comics reprinted in this volume were produced in a time when racism played a larger role in society and popular culture both consciously and unconsciously. They are presented here without alteration for historical reference.

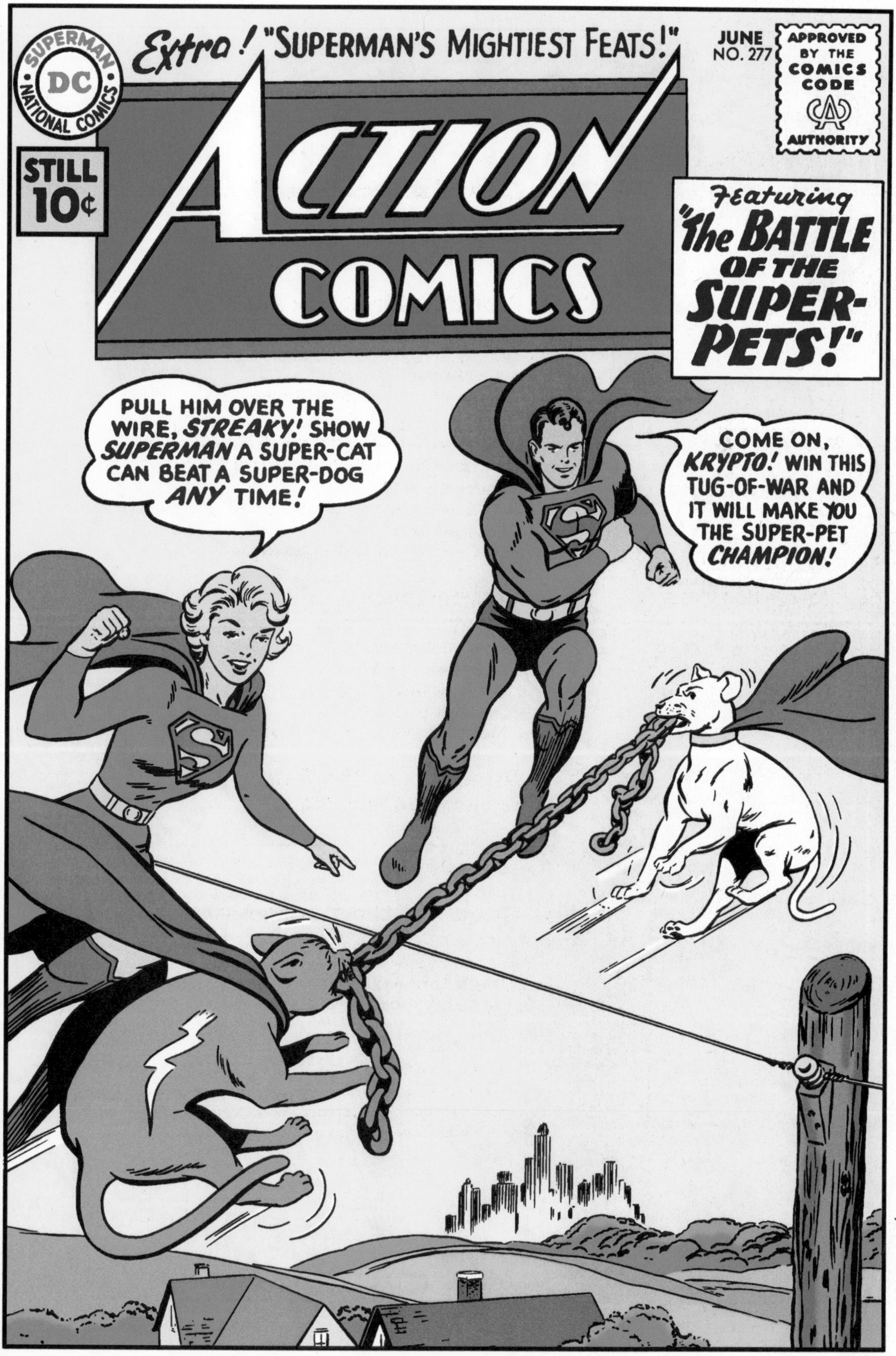

Extra! "SUPERMAN'S MIGHTIEST FEATS!"
SUPERMAN
DC
NATIONAL COMICS
JUNE
NO. 277
APPROVED BY THE COMICS CODE AUTHORITY
STILL 10¢
ACTION COMICS
Featuring "The BATTLE OF THE SUPER-PETS!"
PULL HIM OVER THE WIRE, STREAKY! SHOW SUPERMAN A SUPER-CAT CAN BEAT A SUPER-DOG ANY TIME!
COME ON, KRYPTO! WIN THIS TUG-OF-WAR AND IT WILL MAKE YOU THE SUPER-PET CHAMPION!

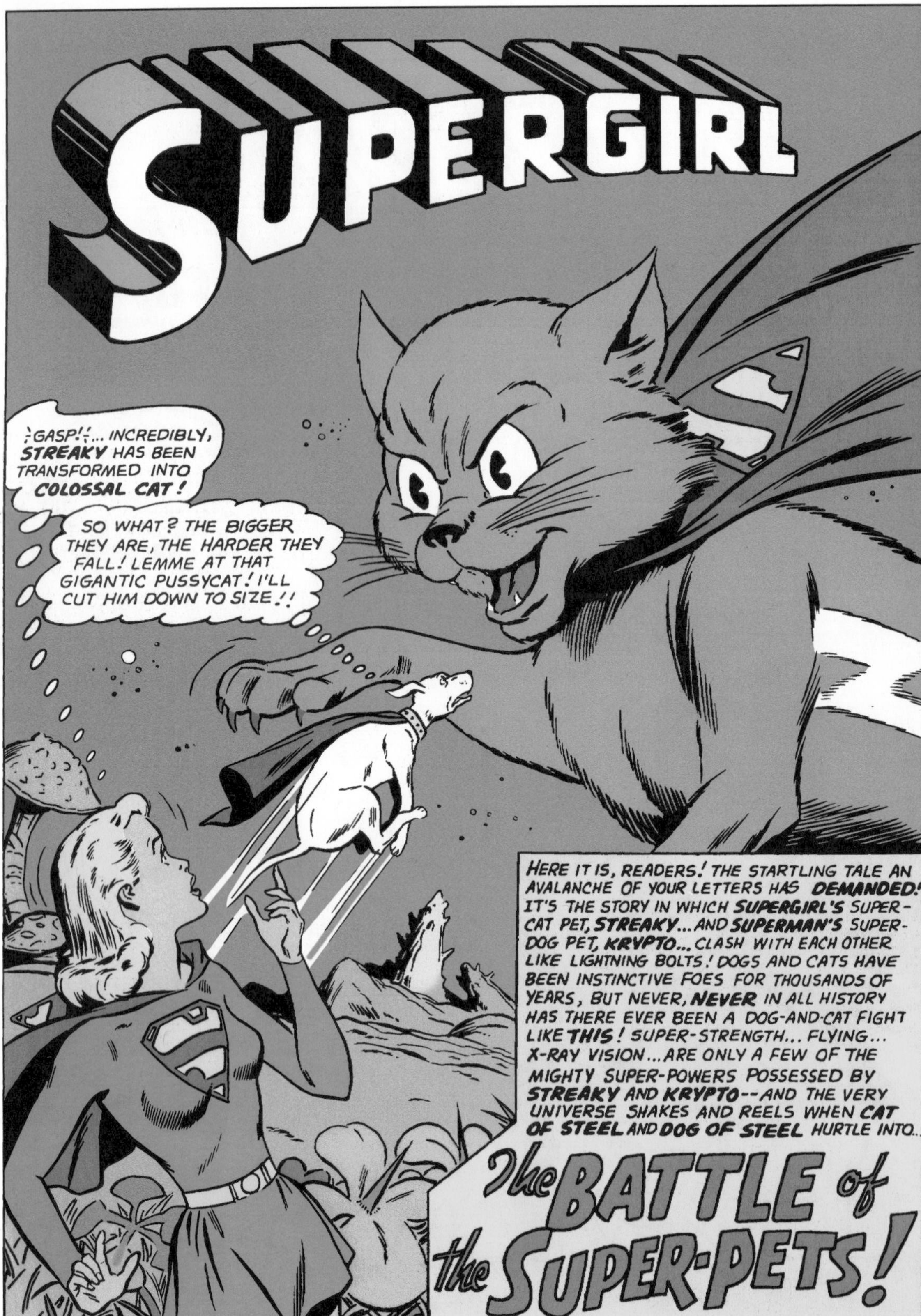
SUPERGIRL
¡GASP!¡... INCREDIBLY, STREAKY HAS BEEN TRANSFORMED INTO COLOSSAL CAT!
SO WHAT? THE BIGGER THEY ARE, THE HARDER THEY FALL! LEMME AT THAT GIGANTIC PUSSYCAT! I'LL CUT HIM DOWN TO SIZE!!
HERE IT IS, READERS! THE STARTLING TALE AN AVALANCHE OF YOUR LETTERS HAS DEMANDED! IT'S THE STORY IN WHICH SUPERGIRL'S SUPER-CAT PET, STREAKY... AND SUPERMAN'S SUPER-DOG PET, KRYPTO... CLASH WITH EACH OTHER LIKE LIGHTNING BOLTS! DOGS AND CATS HAVE BEEN INSTINCTIVE FOES FOR THOUSANDS OF YEARS, BUT NEVER, NEVER IN ALL HISTORY HAS THERE EVER BEEN A DOG-AND-CAT FIGHT LIKE THIS! SUPER-STRENGTH... FLYING... X-RAY VISION... ARE ONLY A FEW OF THE MIGHTY SUPER-POWERS POSSESSED BY STREAKY AND KRYPTO--AND THE VERY UNIVERSE SHAKES AND REELS WHEN CAT OF STEEL AND DOG OF STEEL HURTLE INTO...
The BATTLE of the SUPER-PETS!

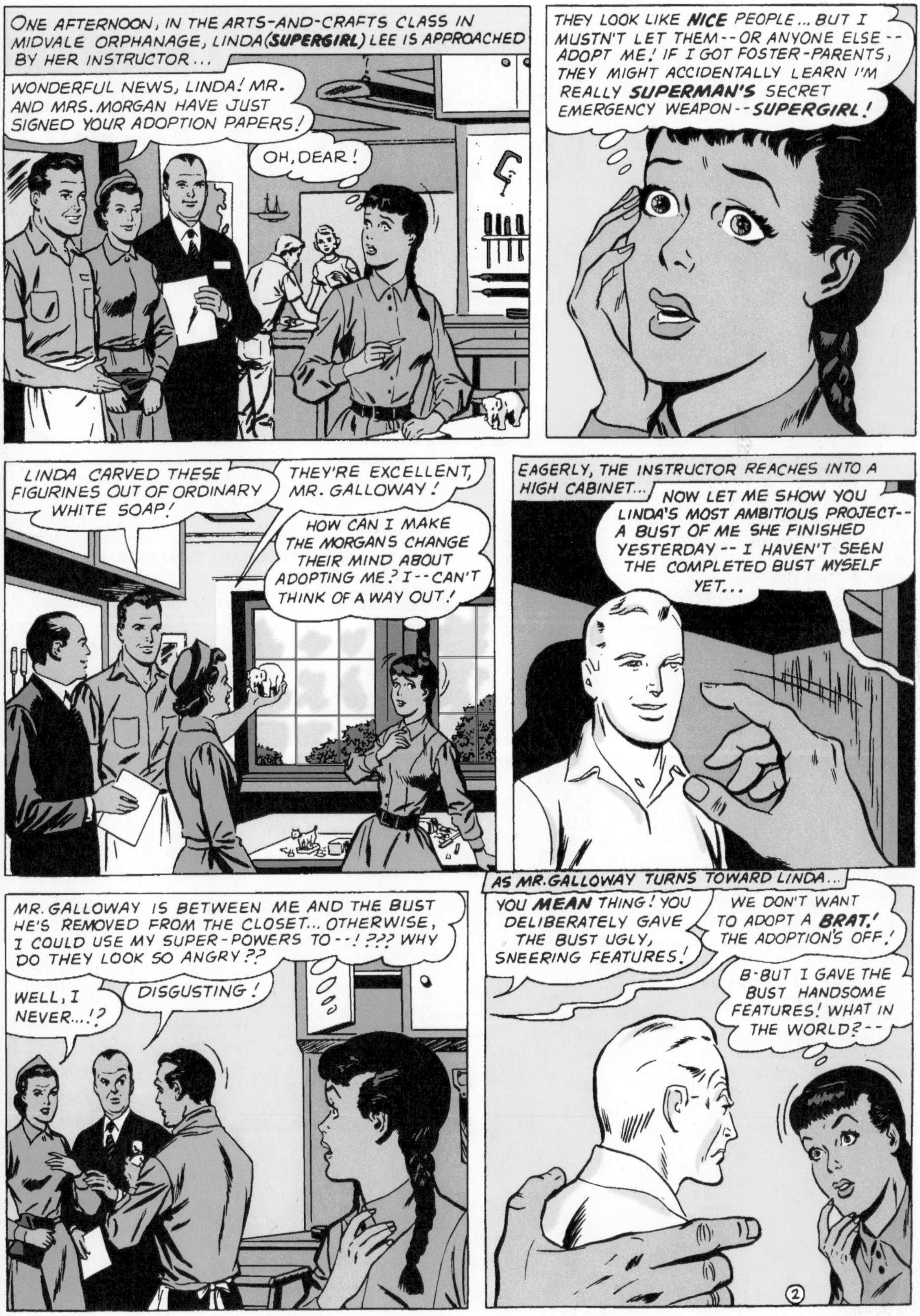
ONE AFTERNOON, IN THE ARTS-AND-CRAFTS CLASS IN MIDVALE ORPHANAGE, LINDA (SUPERGIRL) LEE IS APPROACHED BY HER INSTRUCTOR...
WONDERFUL NEWS, LINDA! MR. AND MRS. MORGAN HAVE JUST SIGNED YOUR ADOPTION PAPERS!
OH, DEAR!
THEY LOOK LIKE NICE PEOPLE... BUT I MUSTN'T LET THEM--OR ANYONE ELSE--ADOPT ME! IF I GOT FOSTER-PARENTS, THEY MIGHT ACCIDENTALLY LEARN I'M REALLY SUPERMAN'S SECRET EMERGENCY WEAPON--SUPERGIRL!
LINDA CARVED THESE FIGURINES OUT OF ORDINARY WHITE SOAP!
THEY'RE EXCELLENT, MR. GALLOWAY!
HOW CAN I MAKE THE MORGANS CHANGE THEIR MIND ABOUT ADOPTING ME? I--CAN'T THINK OF A WAY OUT!
EAGERLY, THE INSTRUCTOR REACHES INTO A HIGH CABINET...
NOW LET ME SHOW YOU LINDA'S MOST AMBITIOUS PROJECT--A BUST OF ME SHE FINISHED YESTERDAY--I HAVEN'T SEEN THE COMPLETED BUST MYSELF YET...
MR. GALLOWAY IS BETWEEN ME AND THE BUST HE'S REMOVED FROM THE CLOSET... OTHERWISE, I COULD USE MY SUPER-POWERS TO--! ??? WHY DO THEY LOOK SO ANGRY??
WELL, I NEVER...!?
DISGUSTING!
AS MR. GALLOWAY TURNS TOWARD LINDA...
YOU MEAN THING! YOU DELIBERATELY GAVE THE BUST UGLY, SNEERING FEATURES!
WE DON'T WANT TO ADOPT A BRAT! THE ADOPTION'S OFF!
B-BUT I GAVE THE BUST HANDSOME FEATURES! WHAT IN THE WORLD?--
2

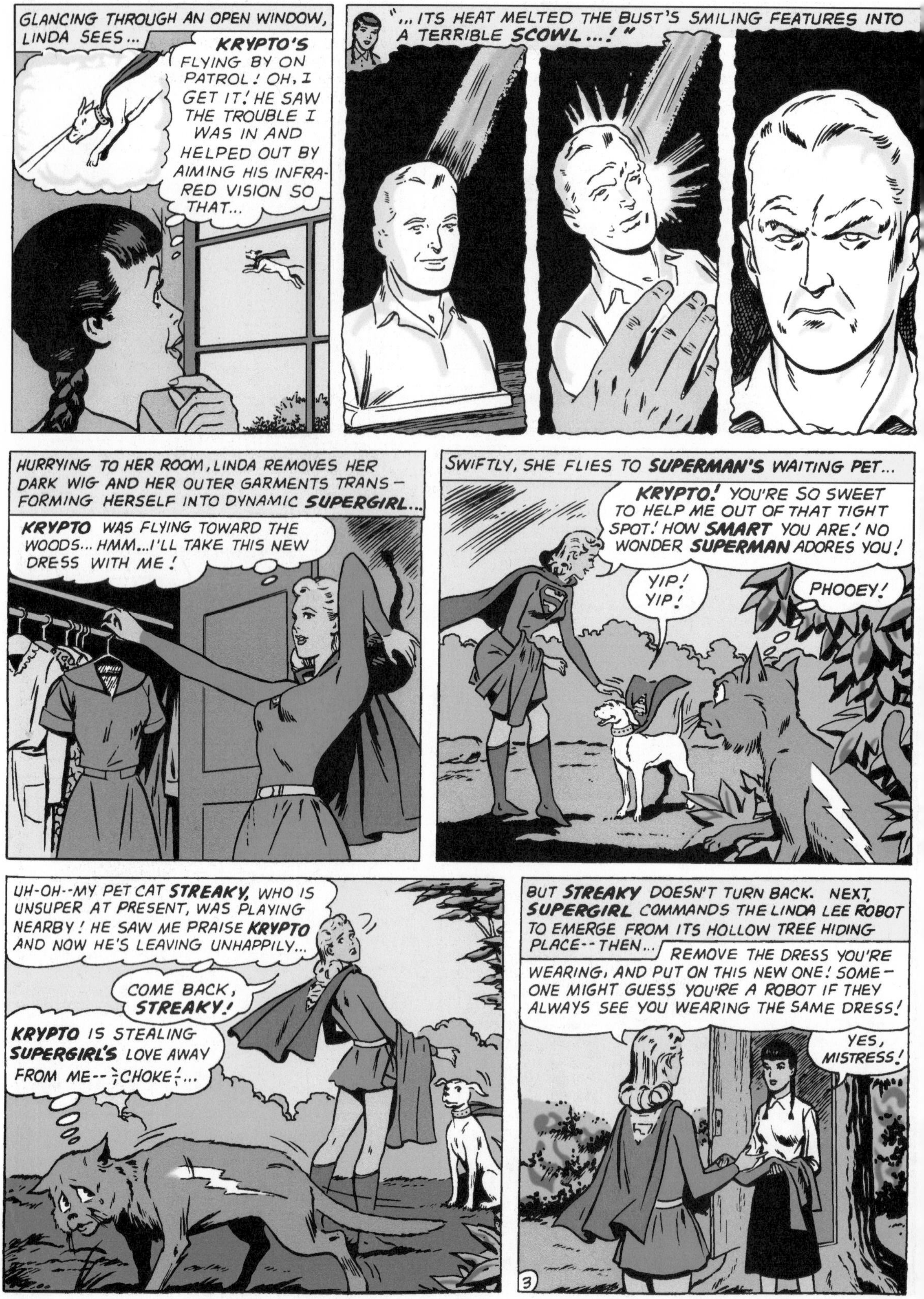
GLANCING THROUGH AN OPEN WINDOW, LINDA SEES...
KRYPTO'S FLYING BY ON PATROL! OH, I GET IT! HE SAW THE TROUBLE I WAS IN AND HELPED OUT BY AIMING HIS INFRA-RED VISION SO THAT...
"...ITS HEAT MELTED THE BUST'S SMILING FEATURES INTO A TERRIBLE SCOWL...!"
HURRYING TO HER ROOM, LINDA REMOVES HER DARK WIG AND HER OUTER GARMENTS TRANS-FORMING HERSELF INTO DYNAMIC SUPERGIRL...
KRYPTO WAS FLYING TOWARD THE WOODS... HMM... I'LL TAKE THIS NEW DRESS WITH ME!
SWIFTLY, SHE FLIES TO SUPERMAN'S WAITING PET...
KRYPTO! YOU'RE SO SWEET TO HELP ME OUT OF THAT TIGHT SPOT! HOW SMART YOU ARE! NO WONDER SUPERMAN ADORES YOU!
YIP! YIP!
PHOOEY!
UH-OH--MY PET CAT STREAKY, WHO IS UNSUPER AT PRESENT, WAS PLAYING NEARBY! HE SAW ME PRAISE KRYPTO AND NOW HE'S LEAVING UNHAPPILY...
COME BACK, STREAKY!
KRYPTO IS STEALING SUPERGIRL'S LOVE AWAY FROM ME-- ;CHOKE;...
BUT STREAKY DOESN'T TURN BACK. NEXT, SUPERGIRL COMMANDS THE LINDA LEE ROBOT TO EMERGE FROM ITS HOLLOW TREE HIDING PLACE--THEN...
REMOVE THE DRESS YOU'RE WEARING, AND PUT ON THIS NEW ONE! SOME-ONE MIGHT GUESS YOU'RE A ROBOT IF THEY ALWAYS SEE YOU WEARING THE SAME DRESS!
YES, MISTRESS!
3

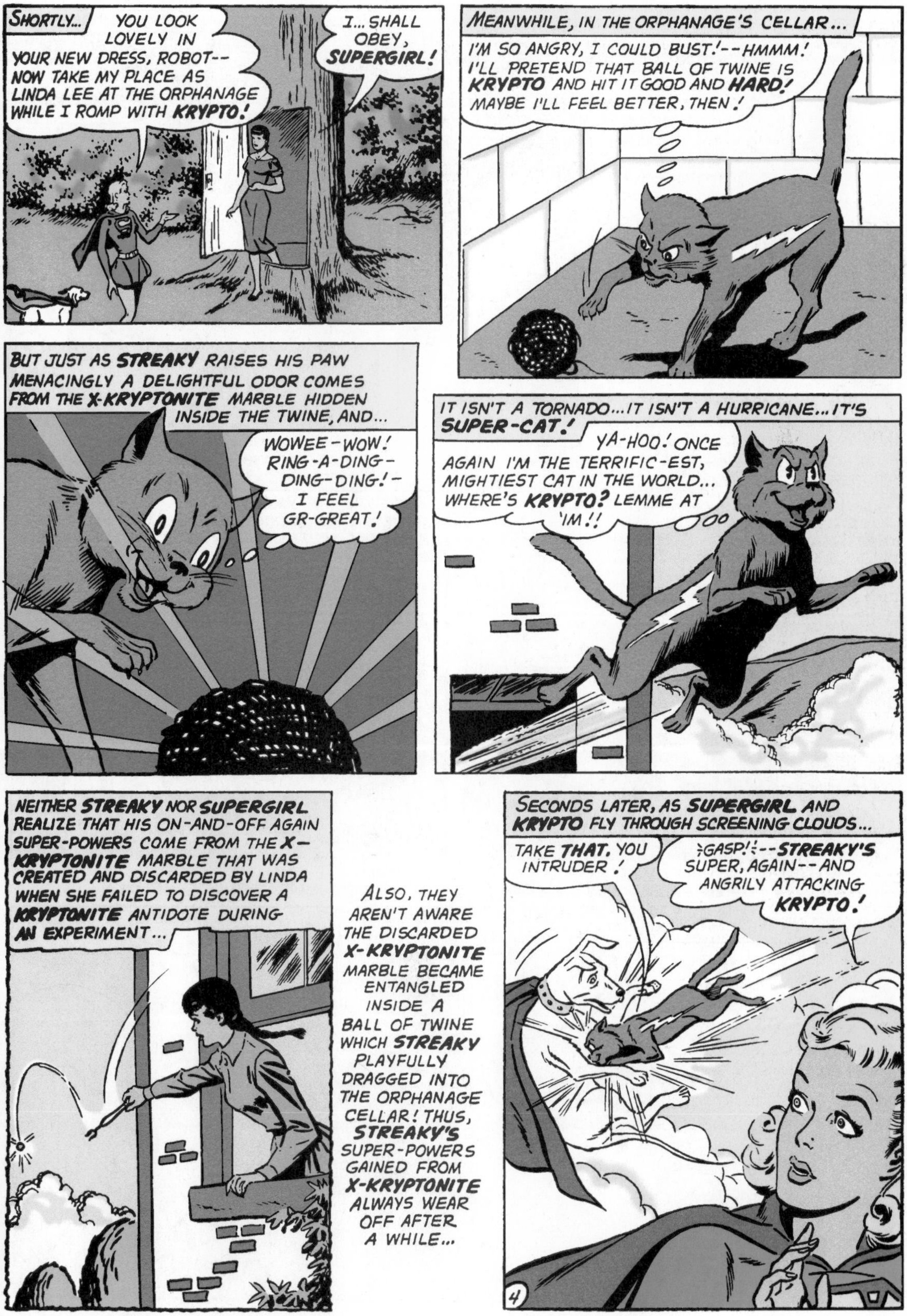
SHORTLY...
YOU LOOK LOVELY IN YOUR NEW DRESS, ROBOT-- NOW TAKE MY PLACE AS LINDA LEE AT THE ORPHANAGE WHILE I ROMP WITH KRYPTO!
I...SHALL OBEY, SUPERGIRL!
MEANWHILE, IN THE ORPHANAGE'S CELLAR...
I'M SO ANGRY, I COULD BUST!--HMMM! I'LL PRETEND THAT BALL OF TWINE IS KRYPTO AND HIT IT GOOD AND HARD! MAYBE I'LL FEEL BETTER, THEN!
BUT JUST AS STREAKY RAISES HIS PAW MENACINGLY A DELIGHTFUL ODOR COMES FROM THE X-KRYPTONITE MARBLE HIDDEN INSIDE THE TWINE, AND...
WOWEE-WOW! RING-A-DING-DING-DING!-I FEEL GR-GREAT!
IT ISN'T A TORNADO...IT ISN'T A HURRICANE...IT'S SUPER-CAT!
YA-HOO! ONCE AGAIN I'M THE TERRIFIC-EST, MIGHTIEST CAT IN THE WORLD... WHERE'S KRYPTO? LEMME AT 'IM!!
NEITHER STREAKY NOR SUPERGIRL REALIZE THAT HIS ON-AND-OFF AGAIN SUPER-POWERS COME FROM THE X-KRYPTONITE MARBLE THAT WAS CREATED AND DISCARDED BY LINDA WHEN SHE FAILED TO DISCOVER A KRYPTONITE ANTIDOTE DURING AN EXPERIMENT...
ALSO, THEY AREN'T AWARE THE DISCARDED X-KRYPTONITE MARBLE BECAME ENTANGLED INSIDE A BALL OF TWINE WHICH STREAKY PLAYFULLY DRAGGED INTO THE ORPHANAGE CELLAR! THUS, STREAKY'S SUPER-POWERS GAINED FROM X-KRYPTONITE ALWAYS WEAR OFF AFTER A WHILE...
SECONDS LATER, AS SUPERGIRL AND KRYPTO FLY THROUGH SCREENING CLOUDS...
TAKE THAT, YOU INTRUDER!
GASP!--STREAKY'S SUPER, AGAIN--AND ANGRILY ATTACKING KRYPTO!
4

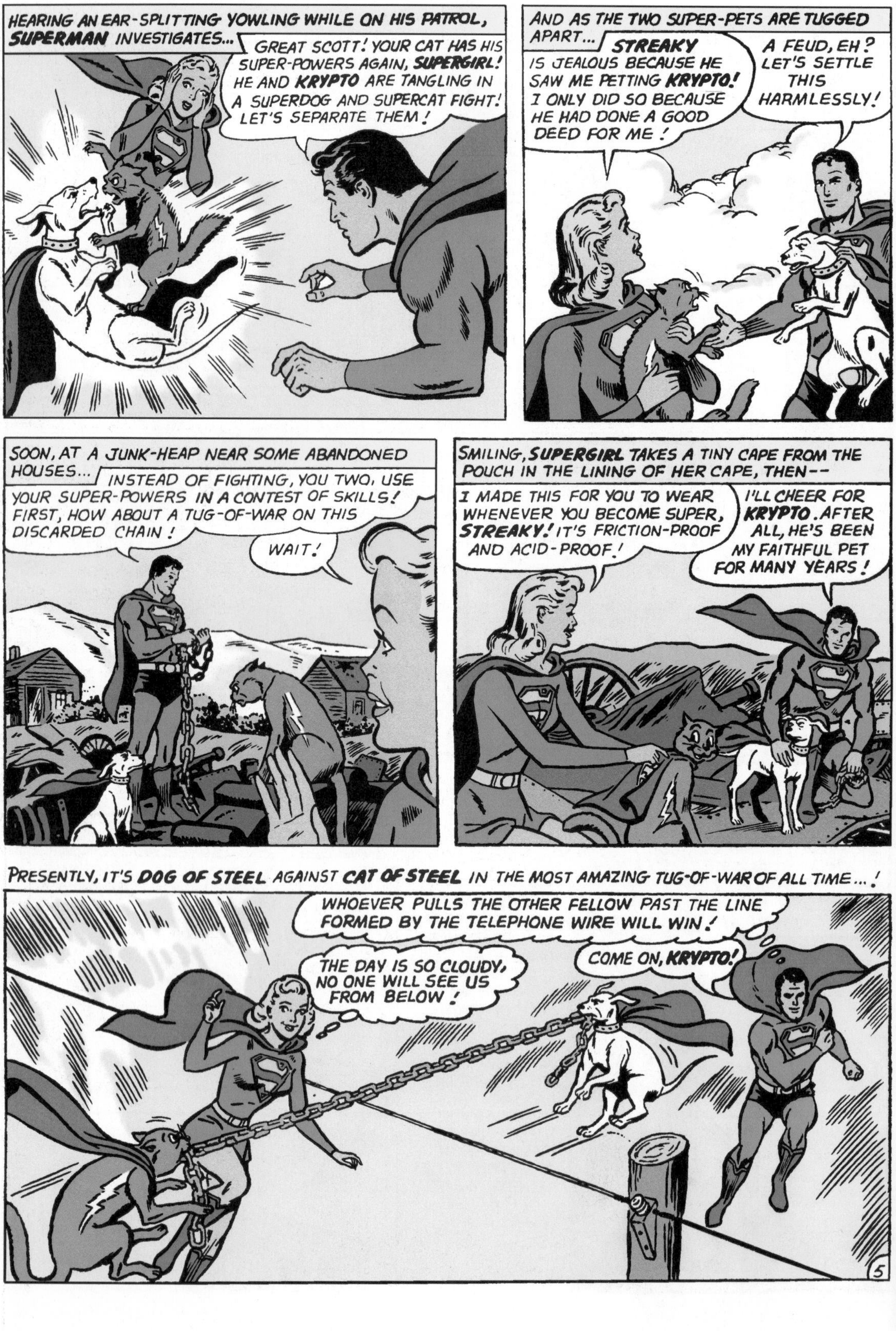
HEARING AN EAR-SPLITTING YOWLING WHILE ON HIS PATROL, SUPERMAN INVESTIGATES...
GREAT SCOTT! YOUR CAT HAS HIS SUPER-POWERS AGAIN, SUPERGIRL! HE AND KRYPTO ARE TANGLING IN A SUPERDOG AND SUPERCAT FIGHT! LET'S SEPARATE THEM!
AND AS THE TWO SUPER-PETS ARE TUGGED APART...
STREAKY IS JEALOUS BECAUSE HE SAW ME PETTING KRYPTO! I ONLY DID SO BECAUSE HE HAD DONE A GOOD DEED FOR ME!
A FEUD, EH? LET'S SETTLE THIS HARMLESSLY!
SOON, AT A JUNK-HEAP NEAR SOME ABANDONED HOUSES...
INSTEAD OF FIGHTING, YOU TWO, USE YOUR SUPER-POWERS IN A CONTEST OF SKILLS! FIRST, HOW ABOUT A TUG-OF-WAR ON THIS DISCARDED CHAIN!
WAIT!
SMILING, SUPERGIRL TAKES A TINY CAPE FROM THE POUCH IN THE LINING OF HER CAPE, THEN--
I MADE THIS FOR YOU TO WEAR WHENEVER YOU BECOME SUPER, STREAKY! IT'S FRICTION-PROOF AND ACID-PROOF!
I'LL CHEER FOR KRYPTO. AFTER ALL, HE'S BEEN MY FAITHFUL PET FOR MANY YEARS!
PRESENTLY, IT'S DOG OF STEEL AGAINST CAT OF STEEL IN THE MOST AMAZING TUG-OF-WAR OF ALL TIME...!
WHOEVER PULLS THE OTHER FELLOW PAST THE LINE FORMED BY THE TELEPHONE WIRE WILL WIN!
THE DAY IS SO CLOUDY, NO ONE WILL SEE US FROM BELOW!
COME ON, KRYPTO!
5

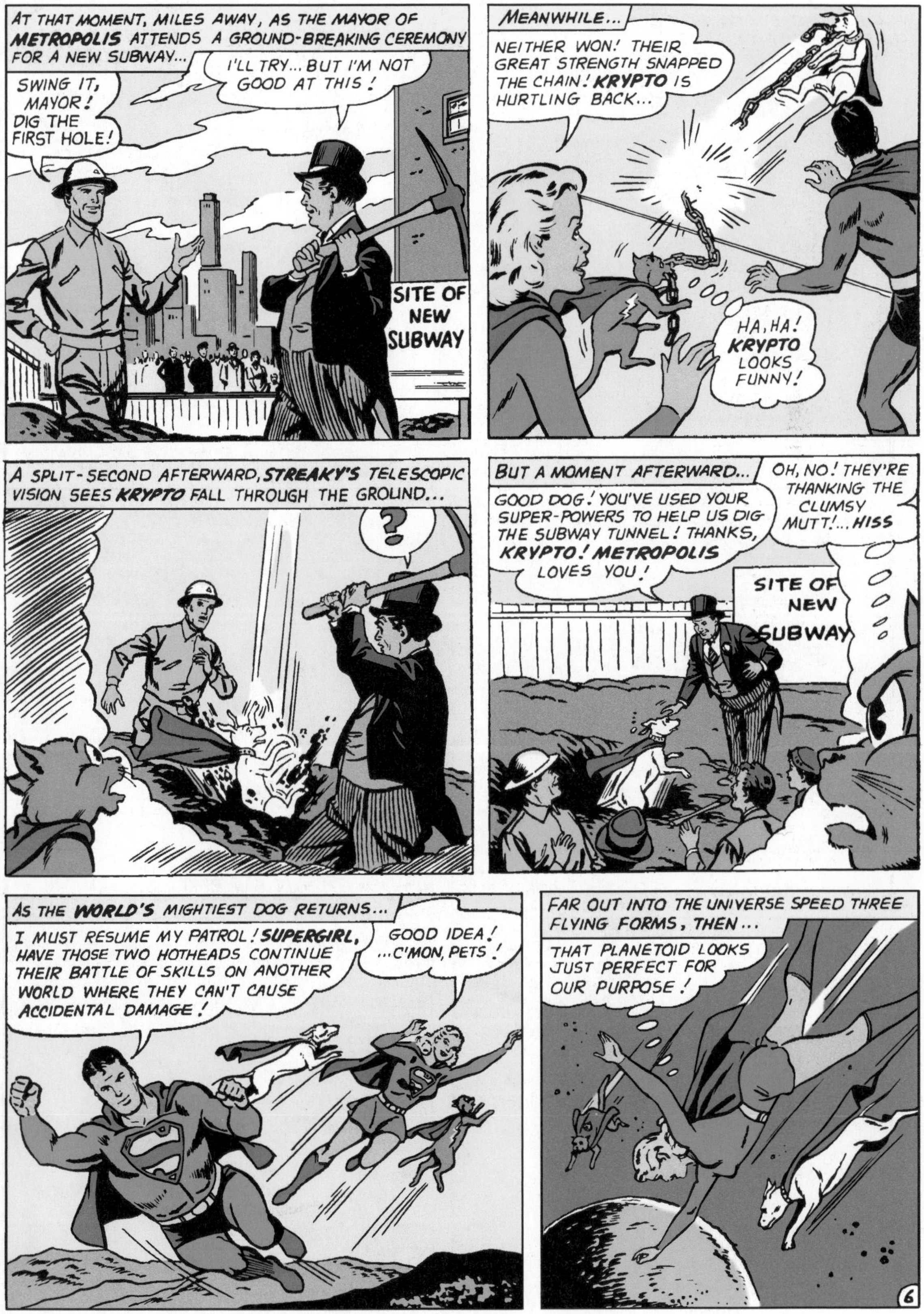
AT THAT MOMENT, MILES AWAY, AS THE MAYOR OF METROPOLIS ATTENDS A GROUND-BREAKING CEREMONY FOR A NEW SUBWAY...
SWING IT, MAYOR! DIG THE FIRST HOLE!
I'LL TRY... BUT I'M NOT GOOD AT THIS!
SITE OF NEW SUBWAY
MEANWHILE...
NEITHER WON! THEIR GREAT STRENGTH SNAPPED THE CHAIN! KRYPTO IS HURTLING BACK...
HA, HA! KRYPTO LOOKS FUNNY!
A SPLIT-SECOND AFTERWARD, STREAKY'S TELESCOPIC VISION SEES KRYPTO FALL THROUGH THE GROUND...
?
BUT A MOMENT AFTERWARD...
GOOD DOG! YOU'VE USED YOUR SUPER-POWERS TO HELP US DIG THE SUBWAY TUNNEL! THANKS, KRYPTO! METROPOLIS LOVES YOU!
OH, NO! THEY'RE THANKING THE CLUMSY MUTT!... HISS
SITE OF NEW SUBWAY
AS THE WORLD'S MIGHTIEST DOG RETURNS...
I MUST RESUME MY PATROL! SUPERGIRL, HAVE THOSE TWO HOTHEADS CONTINUE THEIR BATTLE OF SKILLS ON ANOTHER WORLD WHERE THEY CAN'T CAUSE ACCIDENTAL DAMAGE!
GOOD IDEA! ...C'MON, PETS!
FAR OUT INTO THE UNIVERSE SPEED THREE FLYING FORMS, THEN...
THAT PLANETOID LOOKS JUST PERFECT FOR OUR PURPOSE!
6

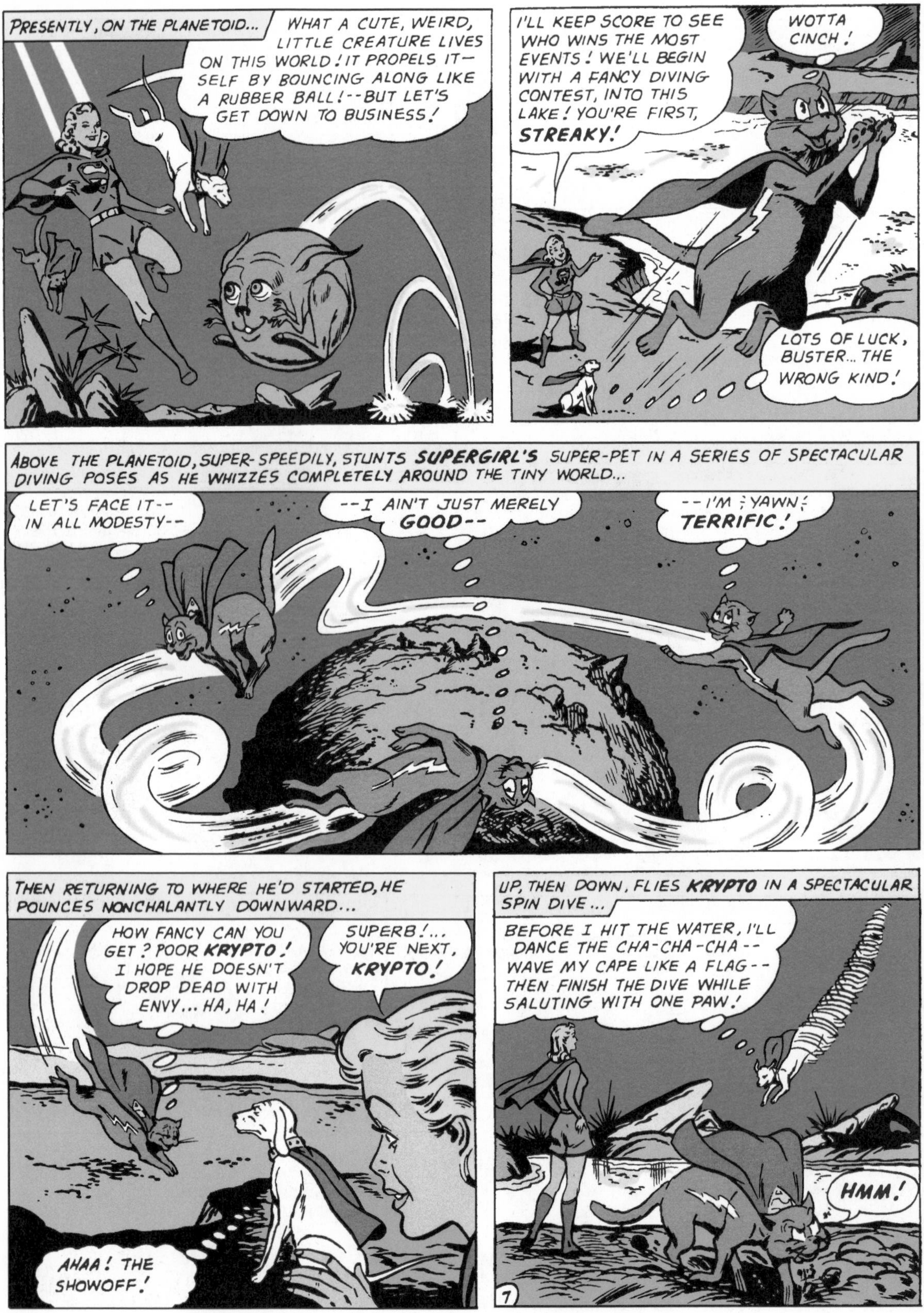

PRESENTLY, ON THE PLANETOID...
WHAT A CUTE, WEIRD, LITTLE CREATURE LIVES ON THIS WORLD! IT PROPELS IT-SELF BY BOUNCING ALONG LIKE A RUBBER BALL!--BUT LET'S GET DOWN TO BUSINESS!
I'LL KEEP SCORE TO SEE WHO WINS THE MOST EVENTS! WE'LL BEGIN WITH A FANCY DIVING CONTEST, INTO THIS LAKE! YOU'RE FIRST, STREAKY!
WOTTA CINCH!
LOTS OF LUCK, BUSTER... THE WRONG KIND!
ABOVE THE PLANETOID, SUPER-SPEEDILY, STUNTS SUPERGIRL'S SUPER-PET IN A SERIES OF SPECTACULAR DIVING POSES AS HE WHIZZES COMPLETELY AROUND THE TINY WORLD...
LET'S FACE IT-- IN ALL MODESTY--
--I AIN'T JUST MERELY GOOD--
--I'M ;YAWN; TERRIFIC!
THEN RETURNING TO WHERE HE'D STARTED, HE POUNCES NONCHALANTLY DOWNWARD...
HOW FANCY CAN YOU GET? POOR KRYPTO! I HOPE HE DOESN'T DROP DEAD WITH ENVY... HA, HA!
SUPERB!... YOU'RE NEXT, KRYPTO!
AHAA! THE SHOWOFF!
UP, THEN DOWN, FLIES KRYPTO IN A SPECTACULAR SPIN DIVE...
BEFORE I HIT THE WATER, I'LL DANCE THE CHA-CHA-CHA-- WAVE MY CAPE LIKE A FLAG-- THEN FINISH THE DIVE WHILE SALUTING WITH ONE PAW!
HMM!
7

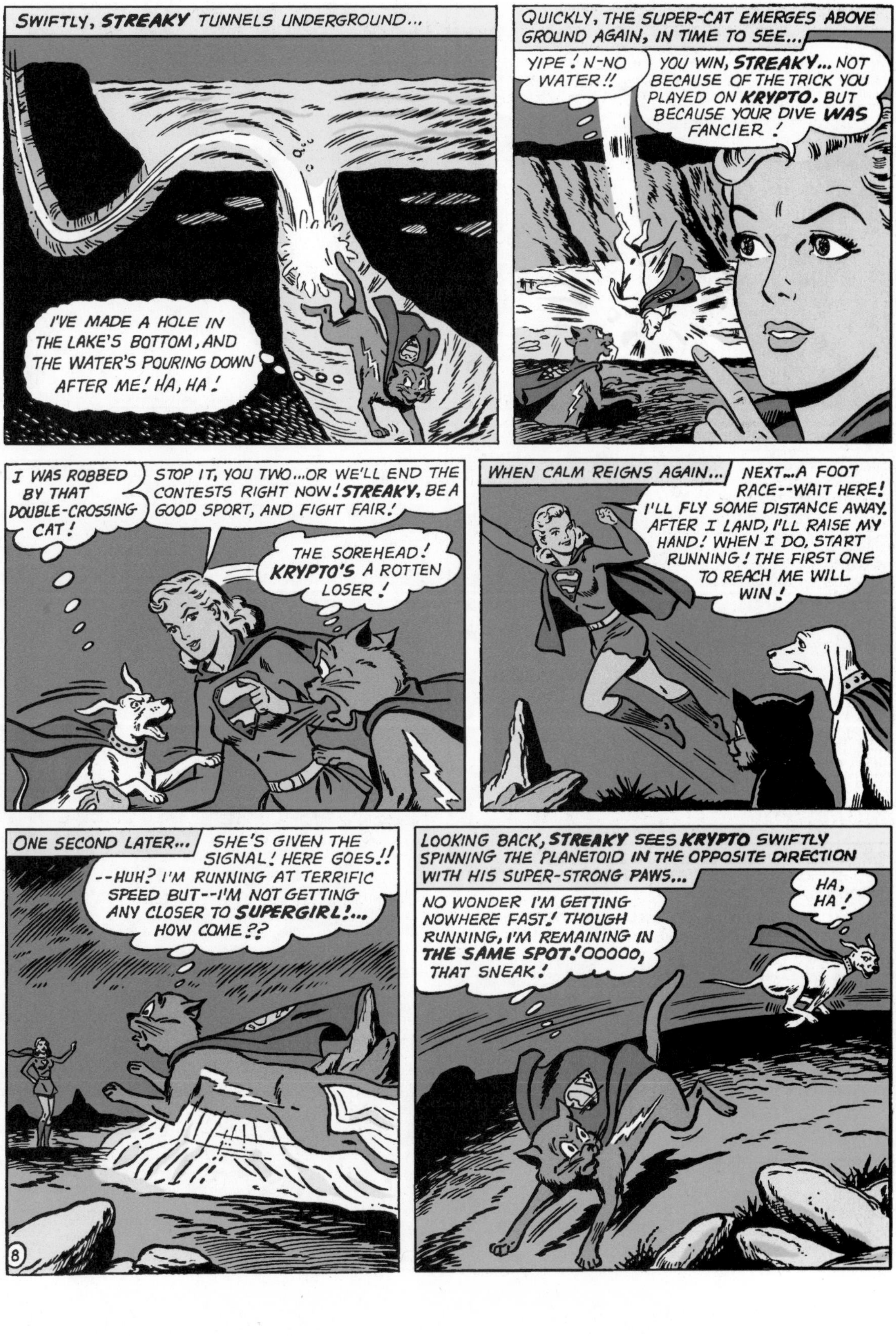

SWIFTLY, STREAKY TUNNELS UNDERGROUND...
I'VE MADE A HOLE IN THE LAKE'S BOTTOM, AND THE WATER'S POURING DOWN AFTER ME! HA, HA!
QUICKLY, THE SUPER-CAT EMERGES ABOVE GROUND AGAIN, IN TIME TO SEE...
YIPE! N-NO WATER!!
YOU WIN, STREAKY... NOT BECAUSE OF THE TRICK YOU PLAYED ON KRYPTO, BUT BECAUSE YOUR DIVE WAS FANCIER!
I WAS ROBBED BY THAT DOUBLE-CROSSING CAT!
STOP IT, YOU TWO...OR WE'LL END THE CONTESTS RIGHT NOW! STREAKY, BE A GOOD SPORT, AND FIGHT FAIR!
THE SOREHEAD! KRYPTO'S A ROTTEN LOSER!
WHEN CALM REIGNS AGAIN...
NEXT...A FOOT RACE--WAIT HERE! I'LL FLY SOME DISTANCE AWAY. AFTER I LAND, I'LL RAISE MY HAND! WHEN I DO, START RUNNING! THE FIRST ONE TO REACH ME WILL WIN!
ONE SECOND LATER...
SHE'S GIVEN THE SIGNAL! HERE GOES!! --HUH? I'M RUNNING AT TERRIFIC SPEED BUT--I'M NOT GETTING ANY CLOSER TO SUPERGIRL!... HOW COME??
8
LOOKING BACK, STREAKY SEES KRYPTO SWIFTLY SPINNING THE PLANETOID IN THE OPPOSITE DIRECTION WITH HIS SUPER-STRONG PAWS...
NO WONDER I'M GETTING NOWHERE FAST! THOUGH RUNNING, I'M REMAINING IN THE SAME SPOT! OOOOO, THAT SNEAK!
HA, HA!

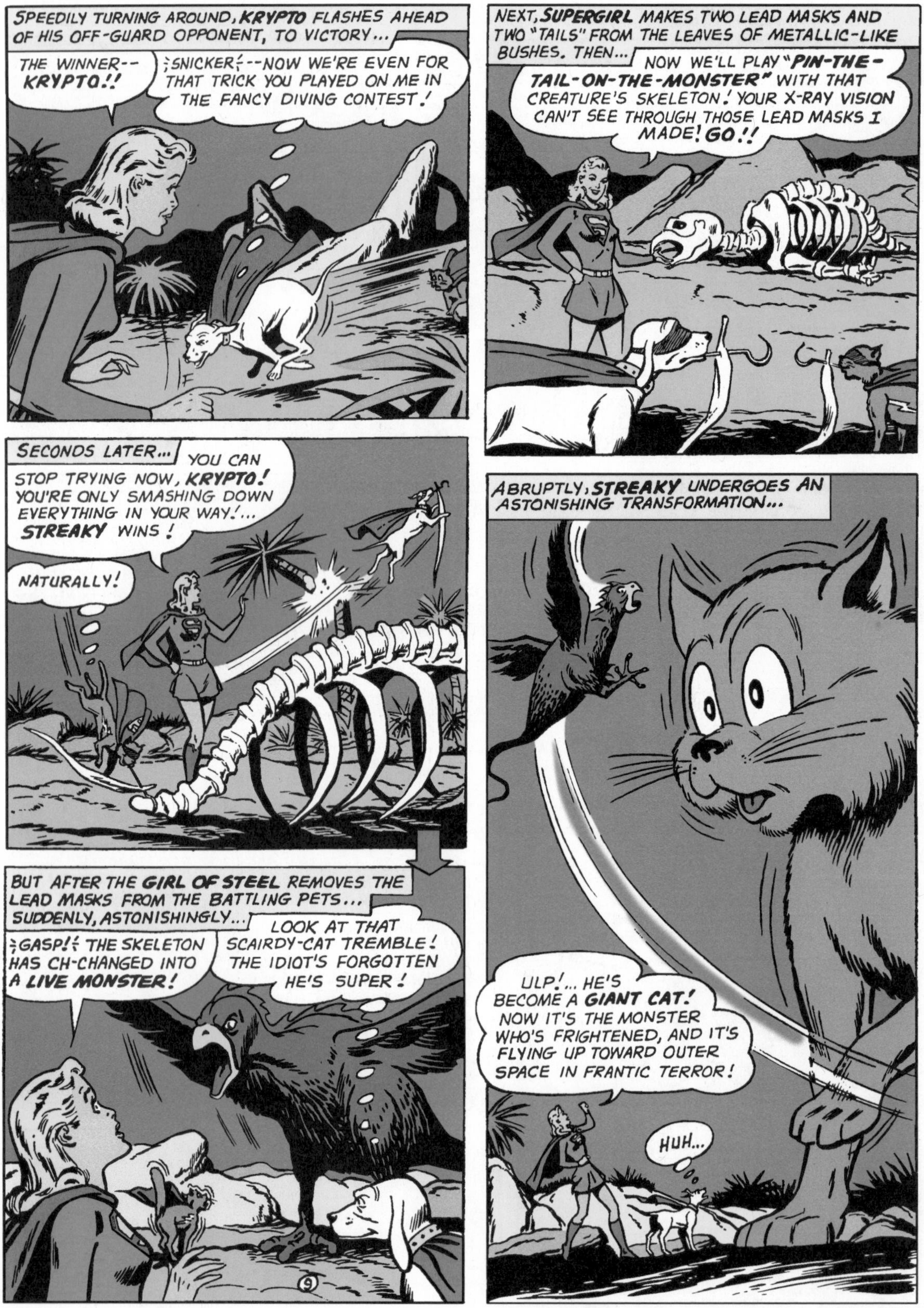
SPEEDILY TURNING AROUND, KRYPTO FLASHES AHEAD OF HIS OFF-GUARD OPPONENT, TO VICTORY...
THE WINNER-- KRYPTO!!
¡SNICKER¡--NOW WE'RE EVEN FOR THAT TRICK YOU PLAYED ON ME IN THE FANCY DIVING CONTEST!
NEXT, SUPERGIRL MAKES TWO LEAD MASKS AND TWO "TAILS" FROM THE LEAVES OF METALLIC-LIKE BUSHES. THEN...
NOW WE'LL PLAY "PIN-THE-TAIL-ON-THE-MONSTER" WITH THAT CREATURE'S SKELETON! YOUR X-RAY VISION CAN'T SEE THROUGH THOSE LEAD MASKS I MADE! GO!!
SECONDS LATER...
YOU CAN STOP TRYING NOW, KRYPTO! YOU'RE ONLY SMASHING DOWN EVERYTHING IN YOUR WAY!... STREAKY WINS!
NATURALLY!
BUT AFTER THE GIRL OF STEEL REMOVES THE LEAD MASKS FROM THE BATTLING PETS... SUDDENLY, ASTONISHINGLY...
¡GASP!¡ THE SKELETON HAS CH-CHANGED INTO A LIVE MONSTER!
LOOK AT THAT SCAIRDY-CAT TREMBLE! THE IDIOT'S FORGOTTEN HE'S SUPER!
9
ABRUPTLY, STREAKY UNDERGOES AN ASTONISHING TRANSFORMATION...
ULP!... HE'S BECOME A GIANT CAT! NOW IT'S THE MONSTER WHO'S FRIGHTENED, AND IT'S FLYING UP TOWARD OUTER SPACE IN FRANTIC TERROR!
HUH...

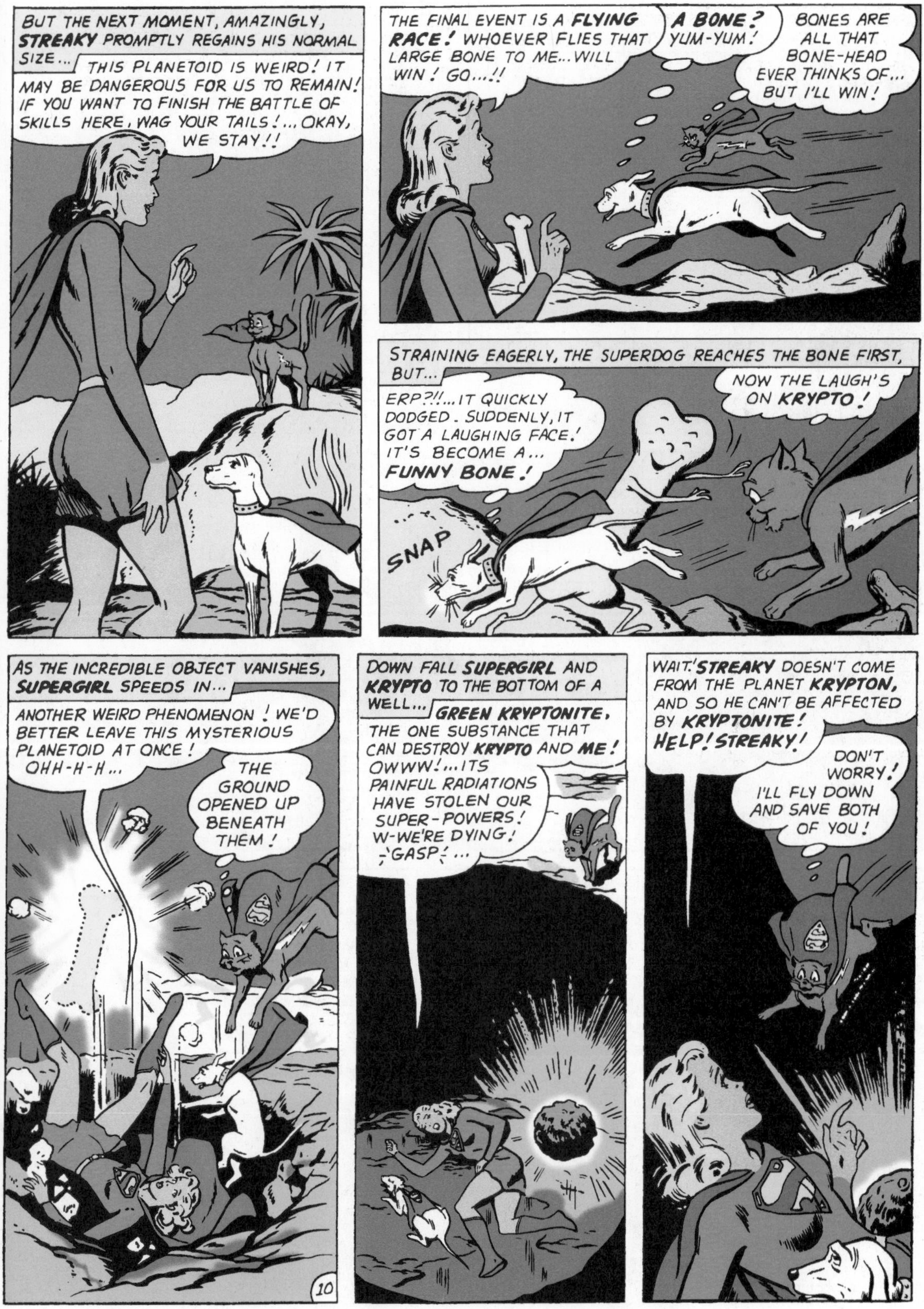
BUT THE NEXT MOMENT, AMAZINGLY, STREAKY PROMPTLY REGAINS HIS NORMAL SIZE...
THIS PLANETOID IS WEIRD! IT MAY BE DANGEROUS FOR US TO REMAIN! IF YOU WANT TO FINISH THE BATTLE OF SKILLS HERE, WAG YOUR TAILS!... OKAY, WE STAY!!
THE FINAL EVENT IS A FLYING RACE! WHOEVER FLIES THAT LARGE BONE TO ME... WILL WIN! GO...!!
A BONE? YUM-YUM!
BONES ARE ALL THAT BONE-HEAD EVER THINKS OF... BUT I'LL WIN!
STRAINING EAGERLY, THE SUPERDOG REACHES THE BONE FIRST, BUT...
ERP?!!... IT QUICKLY DODGED. SUDDENLY, IT GOT A LAUGHING FACE! IT'S BECOME A... FUNNY BONE!
NOW THE LAUGH'S ON KRYPTO!
SNAP
AS THE INCREDIBLE OBJECT VANISHES, SUPERGIRL SPEEDS IN...
ANOTHER WEIRD PHENOMENON! WE'D BETTER LEAVE THIS MYSTERIOUS PLANETOID AT ONCE! OHH-H-H...
THE GROUND OPENED UP BENEATH THEM!
10
DOWN FALL SUPERGIRL AND KRYPTO TO THE BOTTOM OF A WELL...
GREEN KRYPTONITE, THE ONE SUBSTANCE THAT CAN DESTROY KRYPTO AND ME! OWWW!... ITS PAINFUL RADIATIONS HAVE STOLEN OUR SUPER-POWERS! W-WE'RE DYING! -GASP-...
WAIT! STREAKY DOESN'T COME FROM THE PLANET KRYPTON, AND SO HE CAN'T BE AFFECTED BY KRYPTONITE! HELP! STREAKY!
DON'T WORRY! I'LL FLY DOWN AND SAVE BOTH OF YOU!

BUT AS **STREAKY** HITS BOTTOM...

MEOWRR!

HE YELPED PAINFULLY! OH, NO--HE MUST HAVE JUST **LOST** HIS ON-AGAIN-OFF-AGAIN SUPER-POWERS! WE'RE ...DOOMED--; SOB!; OH, HOW I **WISH** THE **KRYPTONITE** DIDN'T HARM US...

UNEXPECTEDLY...

KRYPTO AND I FEEL-- **FINE!**--THE **KRYPTONITE** DOESN'T AFFECT US ANY MORE! THE PAINS ARE GONE AND OUR SUPER-POWERS HAVE RETURNED!

WHAT'S THIS? MY SUPER-HEARING DETECTS THE SOUND OF MACHINERY WORKING! I'LL START TUNNELING!

WHHIIIIBRRR!!

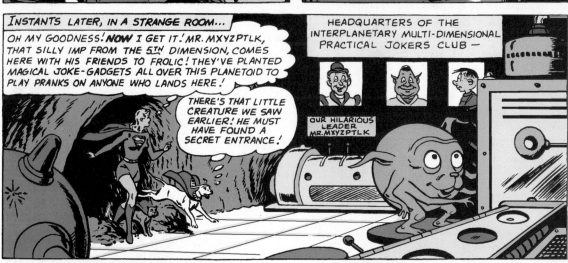

INSTANTS LATER, IN A STRANGE ROOM...

OH MY GOODNESS! **NOW** I GET IT! MR. MXYZPTLK, THAT SILLY IMP FROM **THE 5TH** DIMENSION, COMES HERE WITH HIS FRIENDS TO FROLIC! THEY'VE PLANTED MAGICAL JOKE-GADGETS ALL OVER THIS PLANETOID TO PLAY PRANKS ON ANYONE WHO LANDS HERE!

THERE'S THAT LITTLE CREATURE WE SAW EARLIER! HE MUST HAVE FOUND A SECRET ENTRANCE!

HEADQUARTERS OF THE INTERPLANETARY MULTI-DIMENSIONAL PRACTICAL JOKERS CLUB--

OUR HILARIOUS LEADER MR. MXYZPTLK

THAT TINY CREATURE, PLAYING WITH THE CONTROL-BOARD'S LEVERS, UNWITTINGLY CAUSED THE PRANKS THAT SHOCKED US!... THE **KRYPTONITE** DIDN'T HARM US, AFTER I **WISHED** IT WOULDN'T, BECAUSE WE HAD FALLEN INTO A MAGIC **WISHING WELL!**

GROWTH RAY

SHRINKING RAY

SKELETON CREATURE GAG

FUNNY-BONE GAG

MAGIC WISHING WELL

11

SOON, ON THE PLANETOID'S SURFACE...

WISHING WELL, I WISH THE **GREEN KRYPTONITE** BELOW TO CHANGE INTO HARMLESS **FALSE KRYPTONITE**--FOREVER! MY SUPER-VISION REVEALS THE WISH WORKED! HMMM... PERHAPS MR. MXYZPTLK STORED THE **KRYPTONITE** THERE FOR USE AGAINST **SUPERMAN** SOMEDAY!

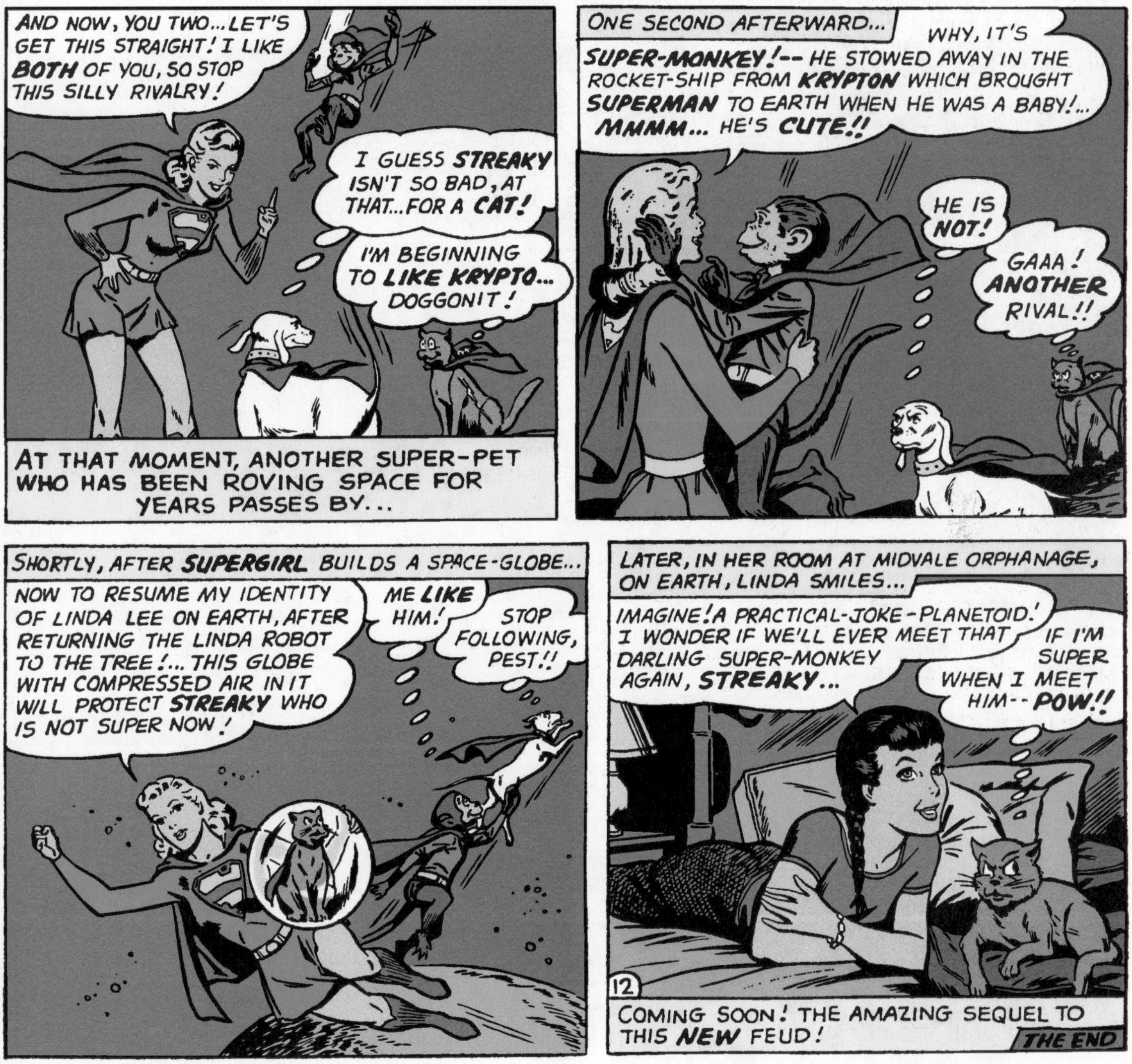
AND NOW, YOU TWO...LET'S GET THIS STRAIGHT! I LIKE BOTH OF YOU, SO STOP THIS SILLY RIVALRY!
I GUESS STREAKY ISN'T SO BAD, AT THAT...FOR A CAT!
I'M BEGINNING TO LIKE KRYPTO... DOGGONIT!
AT THAT MOMENT, ANOTHER SUPER-PET WHO HAS BEEN ROVING SPACE FOR YEARS PASSES BY...
ONE SECOND AFTERWARD...
WHY, IT'S SUPER-MONKEY!-- HE STOWED AWAY IN THE ROCKET-SHIP FROM KRYPTON WHICH BROUGHT SUPERMAN TO EARTH WHEN HE WAS A BABY!... MMMM... HE'S CUTE!!
HE IS NOT!
GAAA! ANOTHER RIVAL!!
SHORTLY, AFTER SUPERGIRL BUILDS A SPACE-GLOBE...
NOW TO RESUME MY IDENTITY OF LINDA LEE ON EARTH, AFTER RETURNING THE LINDA ROBOT TO THE TREE!... THIS GLOBE WITH COMPRESSED AIR IN IT WILL PROTECT STREAKY WHO IS NOT SUPER NOW!
ME LIKE HIM!
STOP FOLLOWING, PEST!!
LATER, IN HER ROOM AT MIDVALE ORPHANAGE, ON EARTH, LINDA SMILES...
IMAGINE! A PRACTICAL-JOKE-PLANETOID! I WONDER IF WE'LL EVER MEET THAT DARLING SUPER-MONKEY AGAIN, STREAKY...
IF I'M SUPER WHEN I MEET HIM--POW!!
12
COMING SOON! THE AMAZING SEQUEL TO THIS NEW FEUD!
THE END

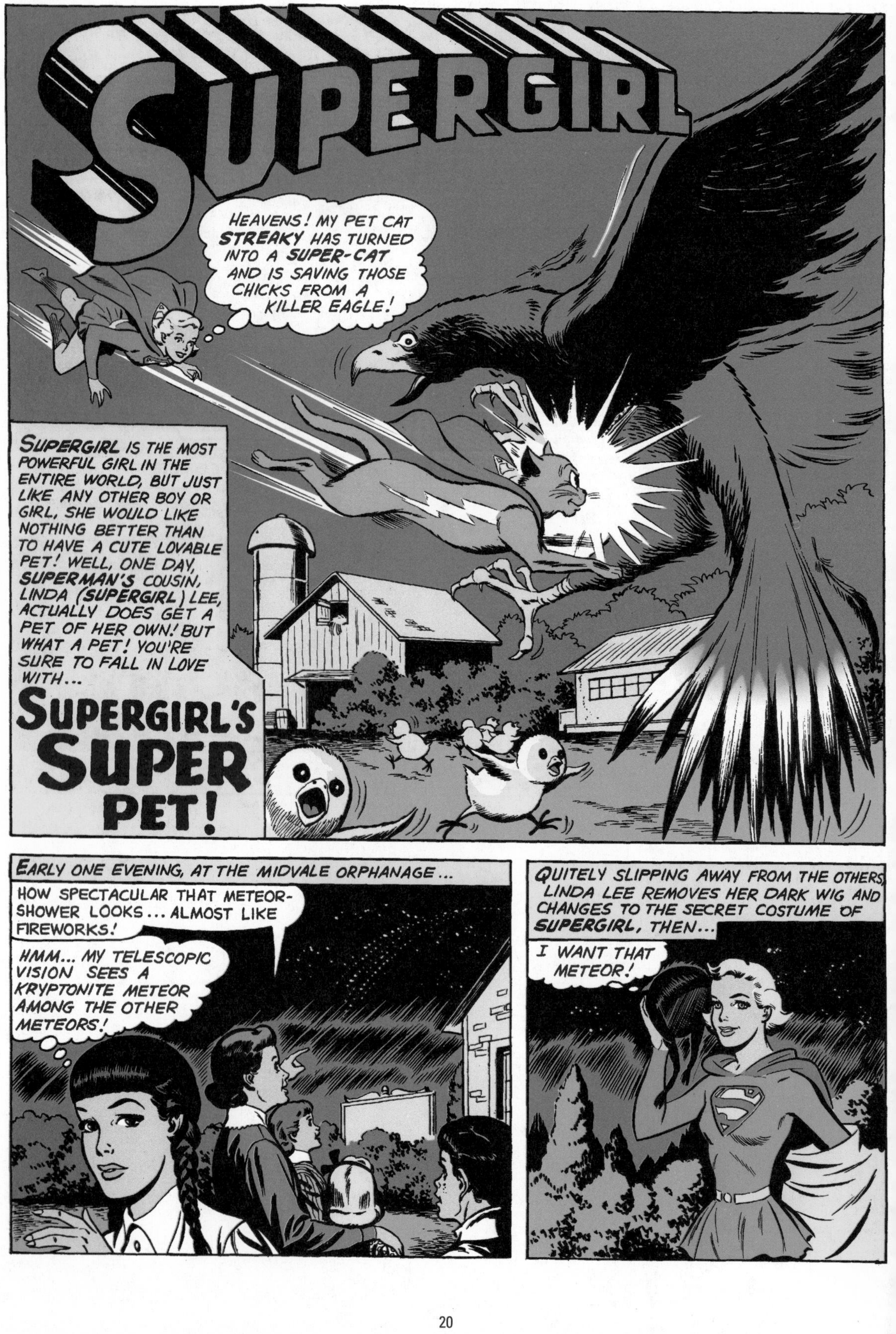
SUPERGIRL
HEAVENS! MY PET CAT STREAKY HAS TURNED INTO A SUPER-CAT AND IS SAVING THOSE CHICKS FROM A KILLER EAGLE!
SUPERGIRL IS THE MOST POWERFUL GIRL IN THE ENTIRE WORLD, BUT JUST LIKE ANY OTHER BOY OR GIRL, SHE WOULD LIKE NOTHING BETTER THAN TO HAVE A CUTE LOVABLE PET! WELL, ONE DAY, SUPERMAN'S COUSIN, LINDA (SUPERGIRL) LEE, ACTUALLY DOES GET A PET OF HER OWN! BUT WHAT A PET! YOU'RE SURE TO FALL IN LOVE WITH...
SUPERGIRL'S SUPER PET!
EARLY ONE EVENING, AT THE MIDVALE ORPHANAGE...
HOW SPECTACULAR THAT METEOR-SHOWER LOOKS... ALMOST LIKE FIREWORKS!
HMM... MY TELESCOPIC VISION SEES A KRYPTONITE METEOR AMONG THE OTHER METEORS!
QUITELY SLIPPING AWAY FROM THE OTHERS, LINDA LEE REMOVES HER DARK WIG AND CHANGES TO THE SECRET COSTUME OF SUPERGIRL, THEN...
I WANT THAT METEOR!

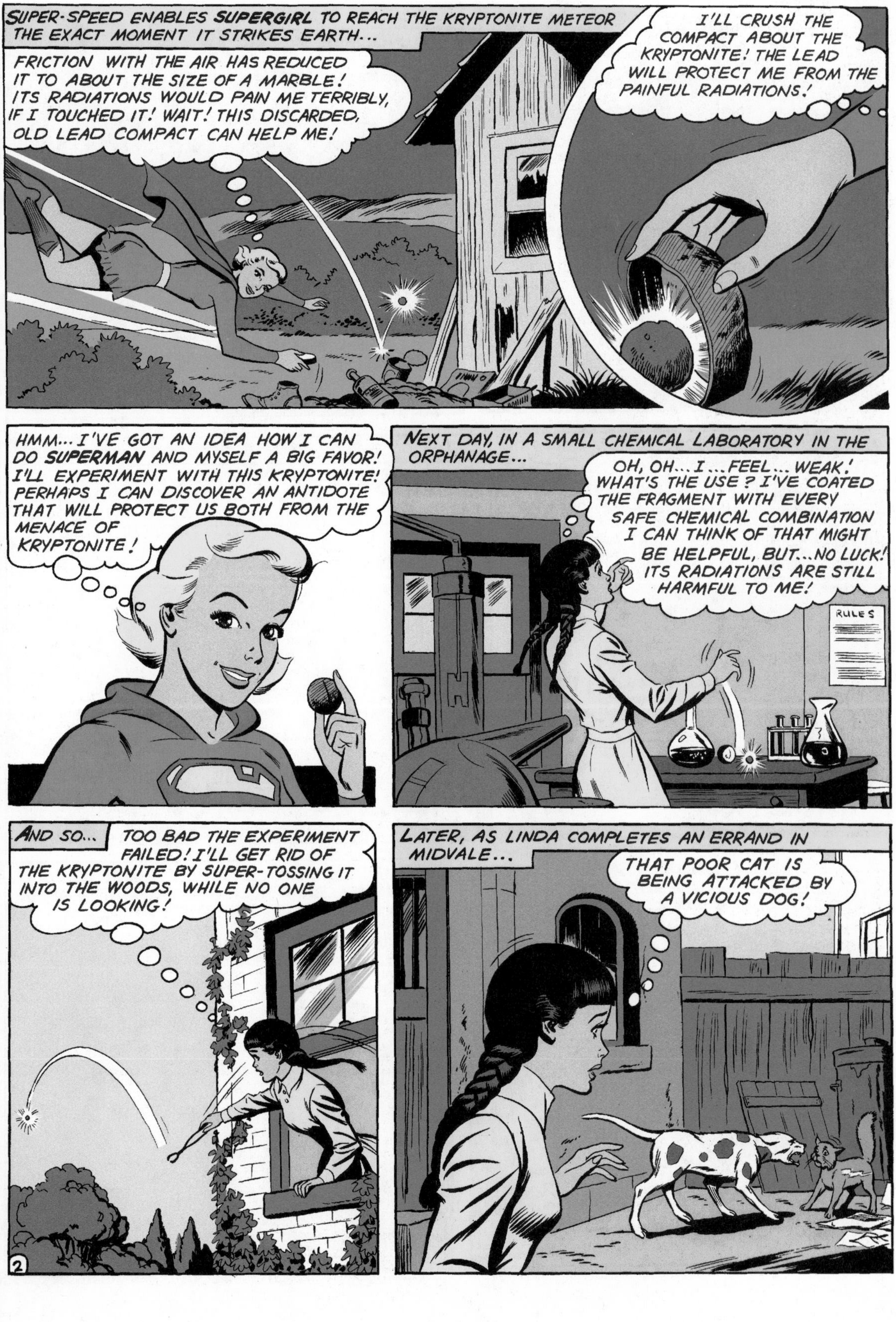
SUPER-SPEED ENABLES SUPERGIRL TO REACH THE KRYPTONITE METEOR THE EXACT MOMENT IT STRIKES EARTH...
FRICTION WITH THE AIR HAS REDUCED IT TO ABOUT THE SIZE OF A MARBLE! ITS RADIATIONS WOULD PAIN ME TERRIBLY, IF I TOUCHED IT! WAIT! THIS DISCARDED, OLD LEAD COMPACT CAN HELP ME!
I'LL CRUSH THE COMPACT ABOUT THE KRYPTONITE! THE LEAD WILL PROTECT ME FROM THE PAINFUL RADIATIONS!
HMM... I'VE GOT AN IDEA HOW I CAN DO SUPERMAN AND MYSELF A BIG FAVOR! I'LL EXPERIMENT WITH THIS KRYPTONITE! PERHAPS I CAN DISCOVER AN ANTIDOTE THAT WILL PROTECT US BOTH FROM THE MENACE OF KRYPTONITE!
NEXT DAY, IN A SMALL CHEMICAL LABORATORY IN THE ORPHANAGE...
OH, OH... I... FEEL... WEAK! WHAT'S THE USE? I'VE COATED THE FRAGMENT WITH EVERY SAFE CHEMICAL COMBINATION I CAN THINK OF THAT MIGHT BE HELPFUL, BUT... NO LUCK! ITS RADIATIONS ARE STILL HARMFUL TO ME!
RULES
AND SO...
TOO BAD THE EXPERIMENT FAILED! I'LL GET RID OF THE KRYPTONITE BY SUPER-TOSSING IT INTO THE WOODS, WHILE NO ONE IS LOOKING!
2
LATER, AS LINDA COMPLETES AN ERRAND IN MIDVALE...
THAT POOR CAT IS BEING ATTACKED BY A VICIOUS DOG!

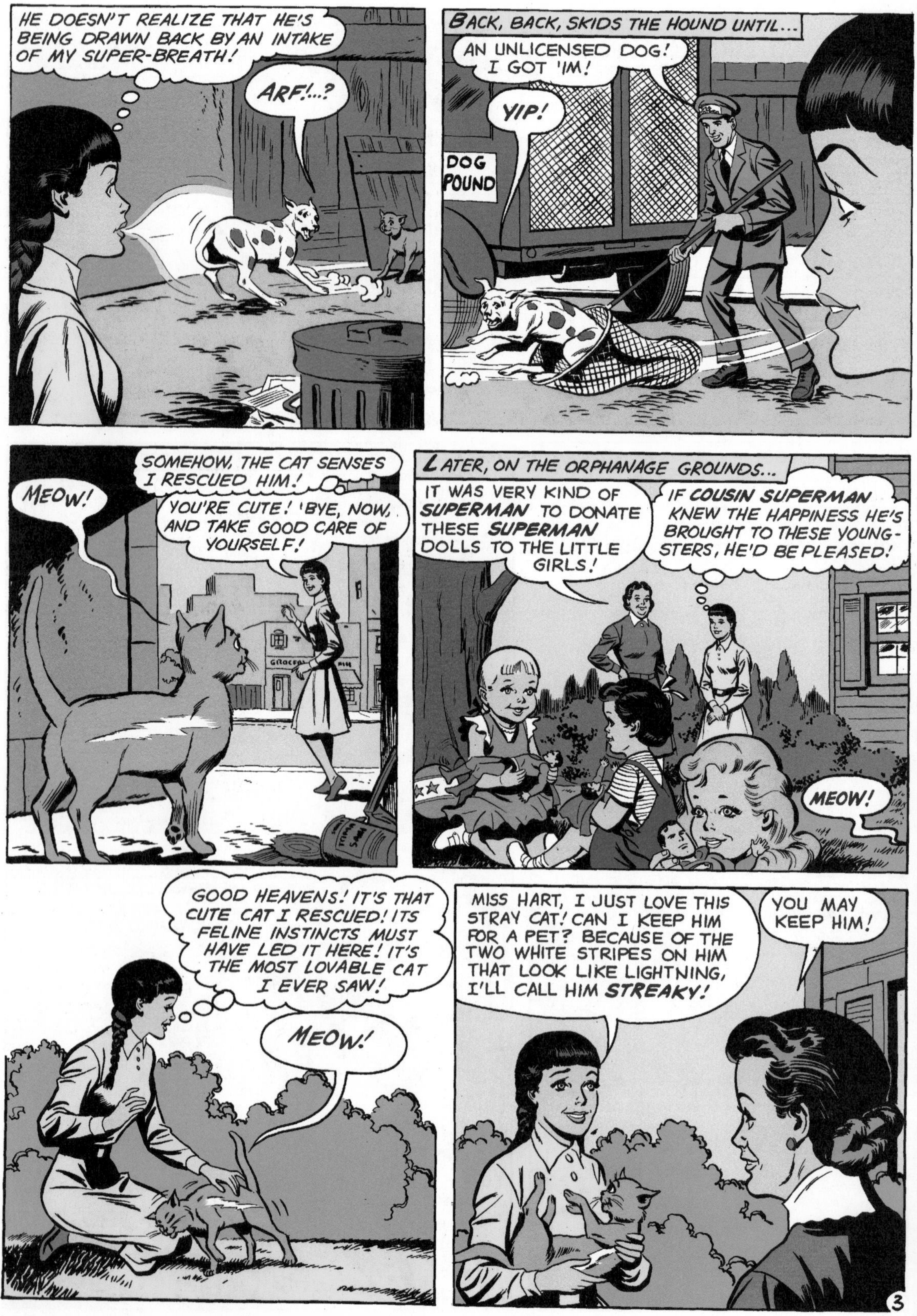
HE DOESN'T REALIZE THAT HE'S BEING DRAWN BACK BY AN INTAKE OF MY SUPER-BREATH!
ARF!...?
BACK, BACK, SKIDS THE HOUND UNTIL...
AN UNLICENSED DOG! I GOT 'IM!
YIP!
DOG POUND
SOMEHOW, THE CAT SENSES I RESCUED HIM!
MEOW!
YOU'RE CUTE! 'BYE, NOW, AND TAKE GOOD CARE OF YOURSELF!
LATER, ON THE ORPHANAGE GROUNDS...
IT WAS VERY KIND OF SUPERMAN TO DONATE THESE SUPERMAN DOLLS TO THE LITTLE GIRLS!
IF COUSIN SUPERMAN KNEW THE HAPPINESS HE'S BROUGHT TO THESE YOUNGSTERS, HE'D BE PLEASED!
MEOW!
GOOD HEAVENS! IT'S THAT CUTE CAT I RESCUED! ITS FELINE INSTINCTS MUST HAVE LED IT HERE! IT'S THE MOST LOVABLE CAT I EVER SAW!
MEOW!
MISS HART, I JUST LOVE THIS STRAY CAT! CAN I KEEP HIM FOR A PET? BECAUSE OF THE TWO WHITE STRIPES ON HIM THAT LOOK LIKE LIGHTNING, I'LL CALL HIM STREAKY!
YOU MAY KEEP HIM!
3

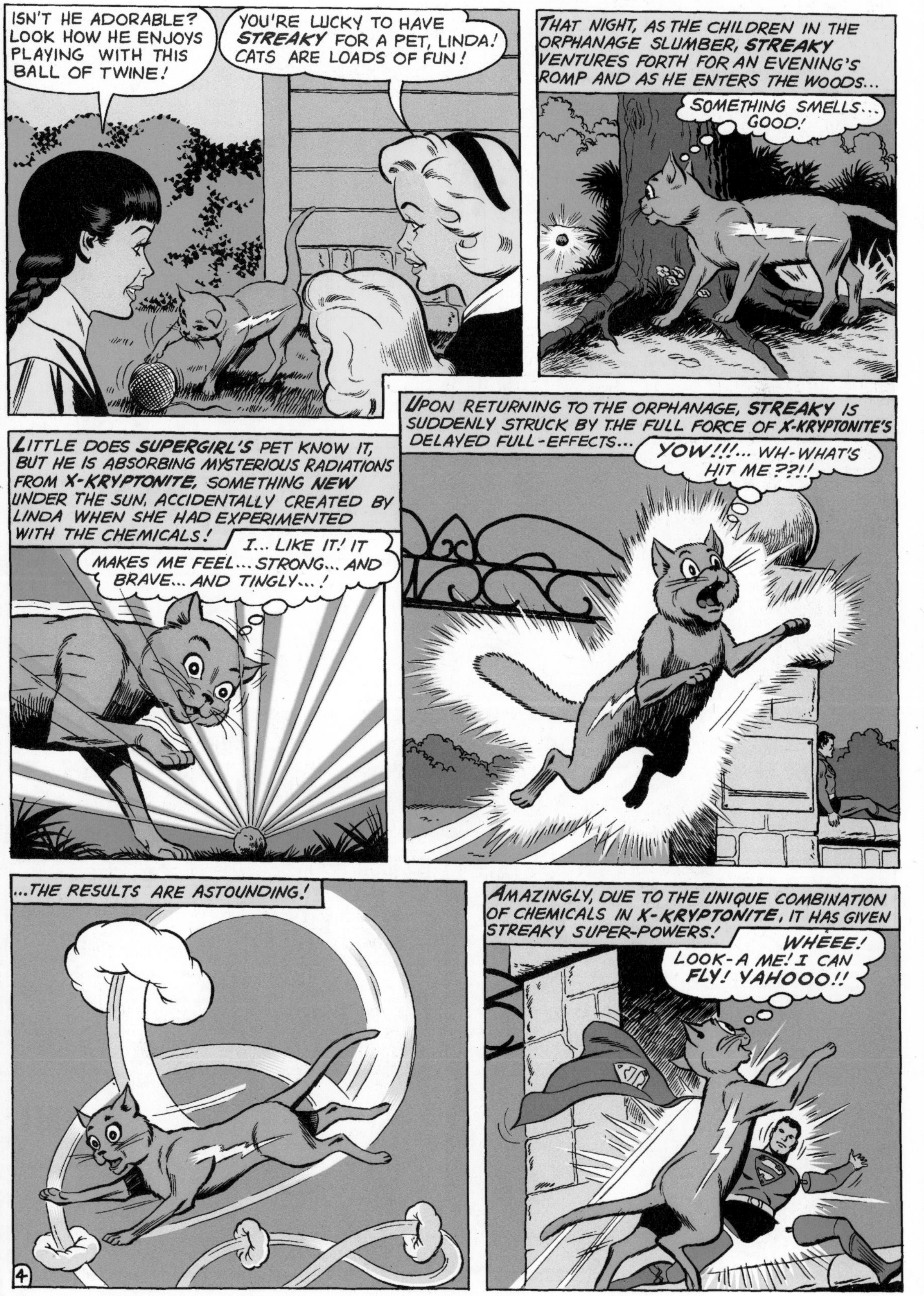
ISN'T HE ADORABLE? LOOK HOW HE ENJOYS PLAYING WITH THIS BALL OF TWINE!
YOU'RE LUCKY TO HAVE STREAKY FOR A PET, LINDA! CATS ARE LOADS OF FUN!
THAT NIGHT, AS THE CHILDREN IN THE ORPHANAGE SLUMBER, STREAKY VENTURES FORTH FOR AN EVENING'S ROMP AND AS HE ENTERS THE WOODS...
SOMETHING SMELLS... GOOD!
LITTLE DOES SUPERGIRL'S PET KNOW IT, BUT HE IS ABSORBING MYSTERIOUS RADIATIONS FROM X-KRYPTONITE, SOMETHING NEW UNDER THE SUN, ACCIDENTALLY CREATED BY LINDA WHEN SHE HAD EXPERIMENTED WITH THE CHEMICALS!
I... LIKE IT! IT MAKES ME FEEL... STRONG... AND BRAVE... AND TINGLY...!
UPON RETURNING TO THE ORPHANAGE, STREAKY IS SUDDENLY STRUCK BY THE FULL FORCE OF X-KRYPTONITE'S DELAYED FULL-EFFECTS...
YOW!!!... WH-WHAT'S HIT ME??!!
...THE RESULTS ARE ASTOUNDING!
AMAZINGLY, DUE TO THE UNIQUE COMBINATION OF CHEMICALS IN X-KRYPTONITE, IT HAS GIVEN STREAKY SUPER-POWERS!
WHEEE! LOOK-A ME! I CAN FLY! YAHOOO!!
4

AS **STREAKY** ROCKETS THROUGH THE AIR, THE CAPE FROM THE SHATTERED **SUPERMAN** DOLL DROPS DOWN OVER HIS HEAD, SNUGLY INTO PLACE!

GET ME, I'M A SUPER-CAT! GEE, IF ONLY SOME OF MY OLD PALS COULD SEE ME NOW! I FEEL SUPER-STRONG!! I'LL BET THERE'S HARDLY ANYTHING I CAN'T DO! YIPEEEEE!

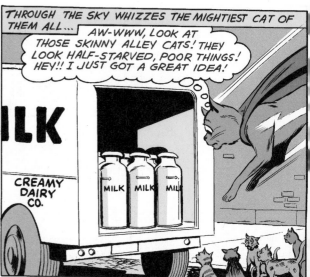

THROUGH THE SKY WHIZZES THE MIGHTIEST CAT OF THEM ALL...

AW-WWW, LOOK AT THOSE SKINNY ALLEY CATS! THEY LOOK HALF-STARVED, POOR THINGS! HEY!! I JUST GOT A GREAT IDEA!

ZIPPING UNDER THE MILK-TRUCK'S FRONT BUMPER, **STREAKY** LEAPS POWERFULLY UPWARD, AND...

IT'S "FREE MILK FOR STARVING CATS DAY"!!!

CLANG!

HA! HA! ENJOY YOURSELVES, PALS! THE DRINKS ARE ON **STREAKY**!

DELIGHTED WITH HIS GOOD DEED, **STREAKY** SPEEDS OFF...

IMPOSSIBLE! THOSE CATS COULDN'T POSSIBLY HAVE TIPPED OVER THOSE HEAVY MILK-CANS, THEMSELVES!

SAY, I COULD MAKE A CAREER OUT OF THIS! I COULD BECOME STREAKY THE SUPER CAT, FAMOUS SUPER-RESCUER OF DOWNTRODDEN KITTENS!

5

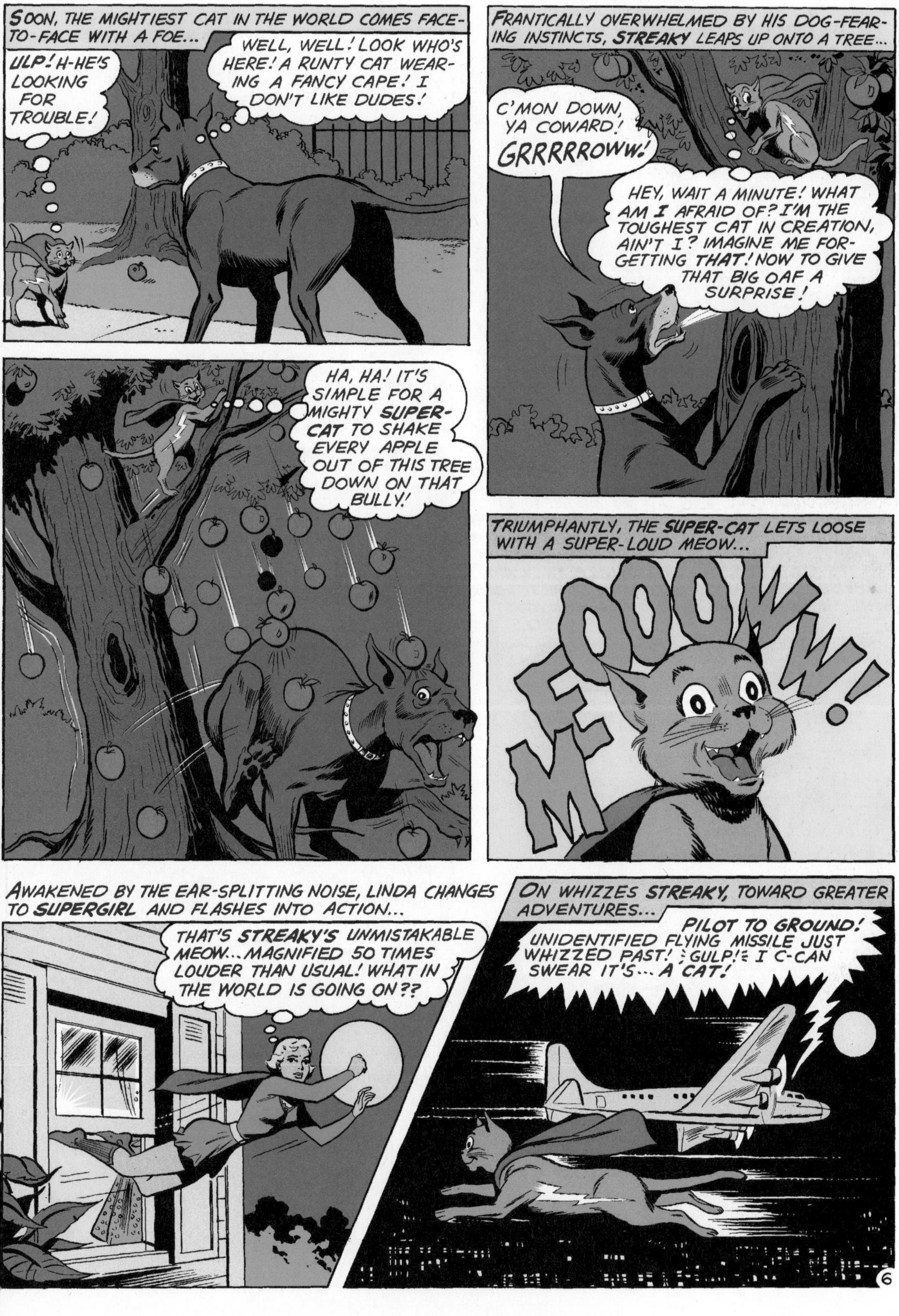
SOON, THE MIGHTIEST CAT IN THE WORLD COMES FACE-TO-FACE WITH A FOE...
ULP! H-HE'S LOOKING FOR TROUBLE!
WELL, WELL! LOOK WHO'S HERE! A RUNTY CAT WEARING A FANCY CAPE! I DON'T LIKE DUDES!
FRANTICALLY OVERWHELMED BY HIS DOG-FEARING INSTINCTS, STREAKY LEAPS UP ONTO A TREE...
C'MON DOWN, YA COWARD! GRRRRROWW!
HEY, WAIT A MINUTE! WHAT AM I AFRAID OF? I'M THE TOUGHEST CAT IN CREATION, AIN'T I? IMAGINE ME FORGETTING THAT! NOW TO GIVE THAT BIG OAF A SURPRISE!
HA, HA! IT'S SIMPLE FOR A MIGHTY SUPER-CAT TO SHAKE EVERY APPLE OUT OF THIS TREE DOWN ON THAT BULLY!
TRIUMPHANTLY, THE SUPER-CAT LETS LOOSE WITH A SUPER-LOUD MEOW...
MEOOOWW!
AWAKENED BY THE EAR-SPLITTING NOISE, LINDA CHANGES TO SUPERGIRL AND FLASHES INTO ACTION...
THAT'S STREAKY'S UNMISTAKABLE MEOW...MAGNIFIED 50 TIMES LOUDER THAN USUAL! WHAT IN THE WORLD IS GOING ON??
ON WHIZZES STREAKY, TOWARD GREATER ADVENTURES...
PILOT TO GROUND! UNIDENTIFIED FLYING MISSILE JUST WHIZZED PAST! GULP! I C-CAN SWEAR IT'S... A CAT!
6

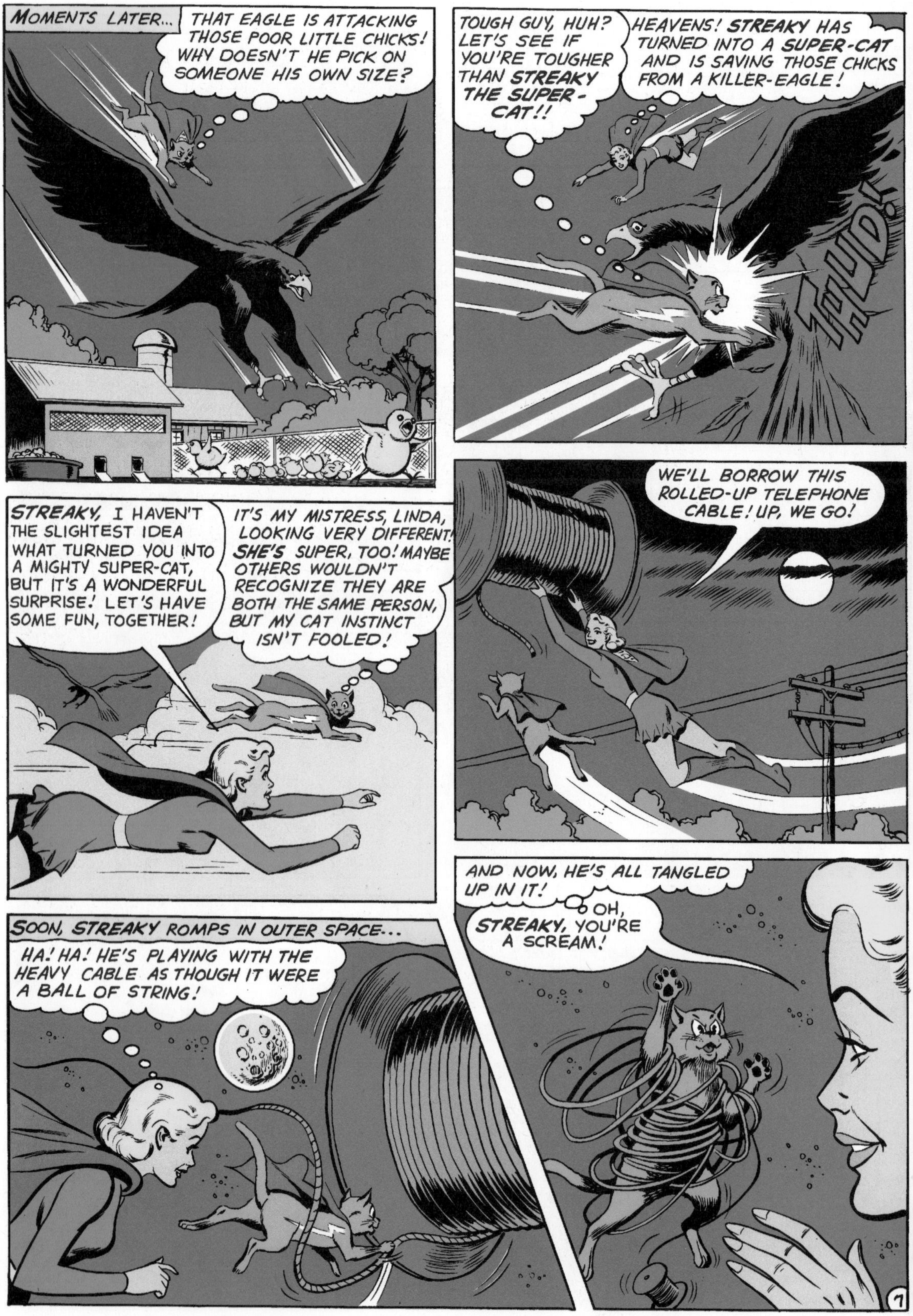
MOMENTS LATER...
THAT EAGLE IS ATTACKING THOSE POOR LITTLE CHICKS! WHY DOESN'T HE PICK ON SOMEONE HIS OWN SIZE?
TOUGH GUY, HUH? LET'S SEE IF YOU'RE TOUGHER THAN STREAKY THE SUPER-CAT!!
HEAVENS! STREAKY HAS TURNED INTO A SUPER-CAT AND IS SAVING THOSE CHICKS FROM A KILLER-EAGLE!
THUD!
STREAKY, I HAVEN'T THE SLIGHTEST IDEA WHAT TURNED YOU INTO A MIGHTY SUPER-CAT, BUT IT'S A WONDERFUL SURPRISE! LET'S HAVE SOME FUN, TOGETHER!
IT'S MY MISTRESS, LINDA, LOOKING VERY DIFFERENT! SHE'S SUPER, TOO! MAYBE OTHERS WOULDN'T RECOGNIZE THEY ARE BOTH THE SAME PERSON, BUT MY CAT INSTINCT ISN'T FOOLED!
WE'LL BORROW THIS ROLLED-UP TELEPHONE CABLE! UP, WE GO!
SOON, STREAKY ROMPS IN OUTER SPACE...
HA! HA! HE'S PLAYING WITH THE HEAVY CABLE AS THOUGH IT WERE A BALL OF STRING!
AND NOW, HE'S ALL TANGLED UP IN IT!
OH, STREAKY, YOU'RE A SCREAM!
7

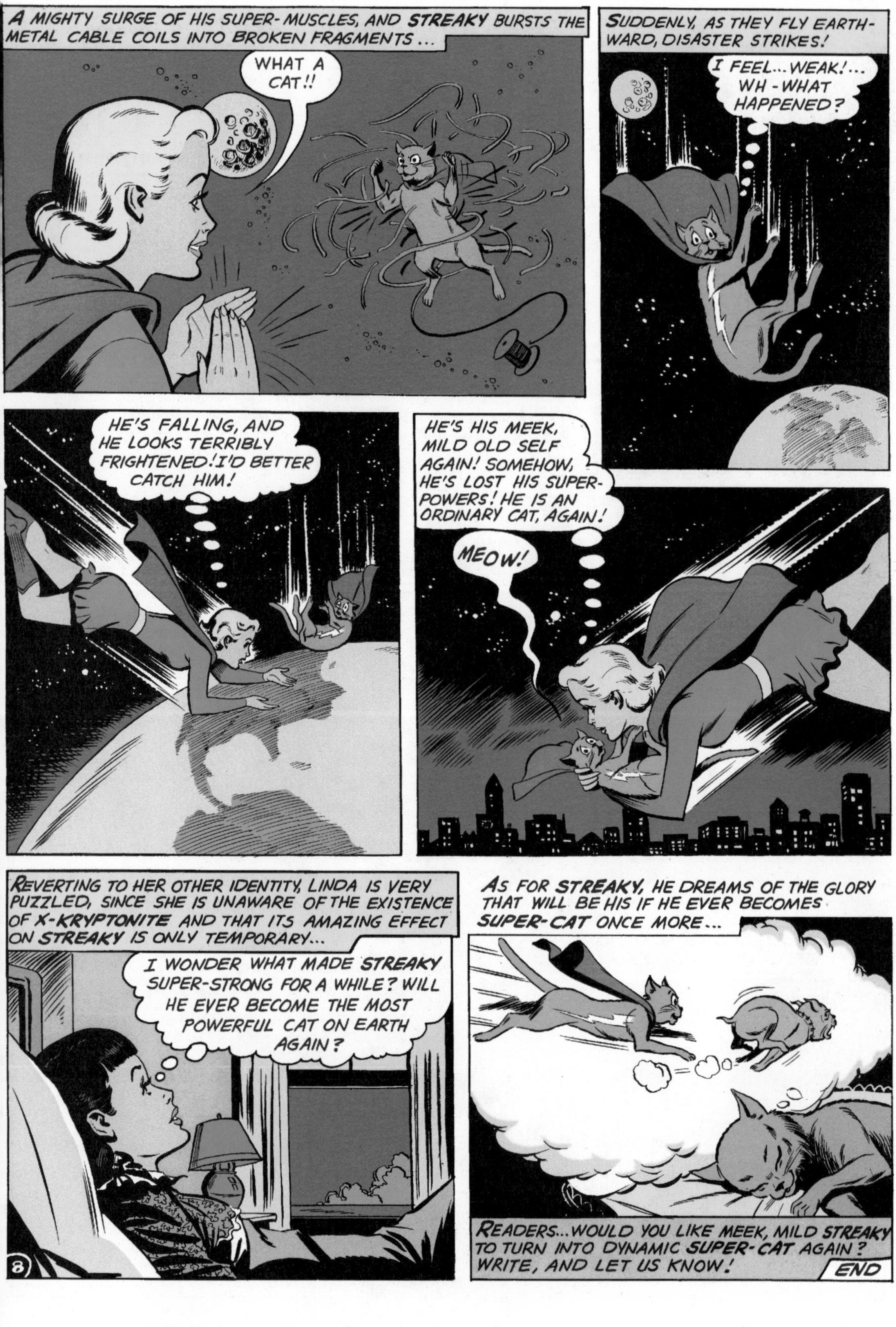

A MIGHTY SURGE OF HIS SUPER-MUSCLES, AND STREAKY BURSTS THE METAL CABLE COILS INTO BROKEN FRAGMENTS...
WHAT A CAT!!
SUDDENLY, AS THEY FLY EARTHWARD, DISASTER STRIKES!
I FEEL...WEAK!... WH-WHAT HAPPENED?
HE'S FALLING, AND HE LOOKS TERRIBLY FRIGHTENED! I'D BETTER CATCH HIM!
HE'S HIS MEEK, MILD OLD SELF AGAIN! SOMEHOW, HE'S LOST HIS SUPER-POWERS! HE IS AN ORDINARY CAT, AGAIN!
MEOW!
REVERTING TO HER OTHER IDENTITY, LINDA IS VERY PUZZLED, SINCE SHE IS UNAWARE OF THE EXISTENCE OF X-KRYPTONITE AND THAT ITS AMAZING EFFECT ON STREAKY IS ONLY TEMPORARY...
I WONDER WHAT MADE STREAKY SUPER-STRONG FOR A WHILE? WILL HE EVER BECOME THE MOST POWERFUL CAT ON EARTH AGAIN?
8
AS FOR STREAKY, HE DREAMS OF THE GLORY THAT WILL BE HIS IF HE EVER BECOMES SUPER-CAT ONCE MORE...
READERS...WOULD YOU LIKE MEEK, MILD STREAKY TO TURN INTO DYNAMIC SUPER-CAT AGAIN? WRITE, AND LET US KNOW!
END

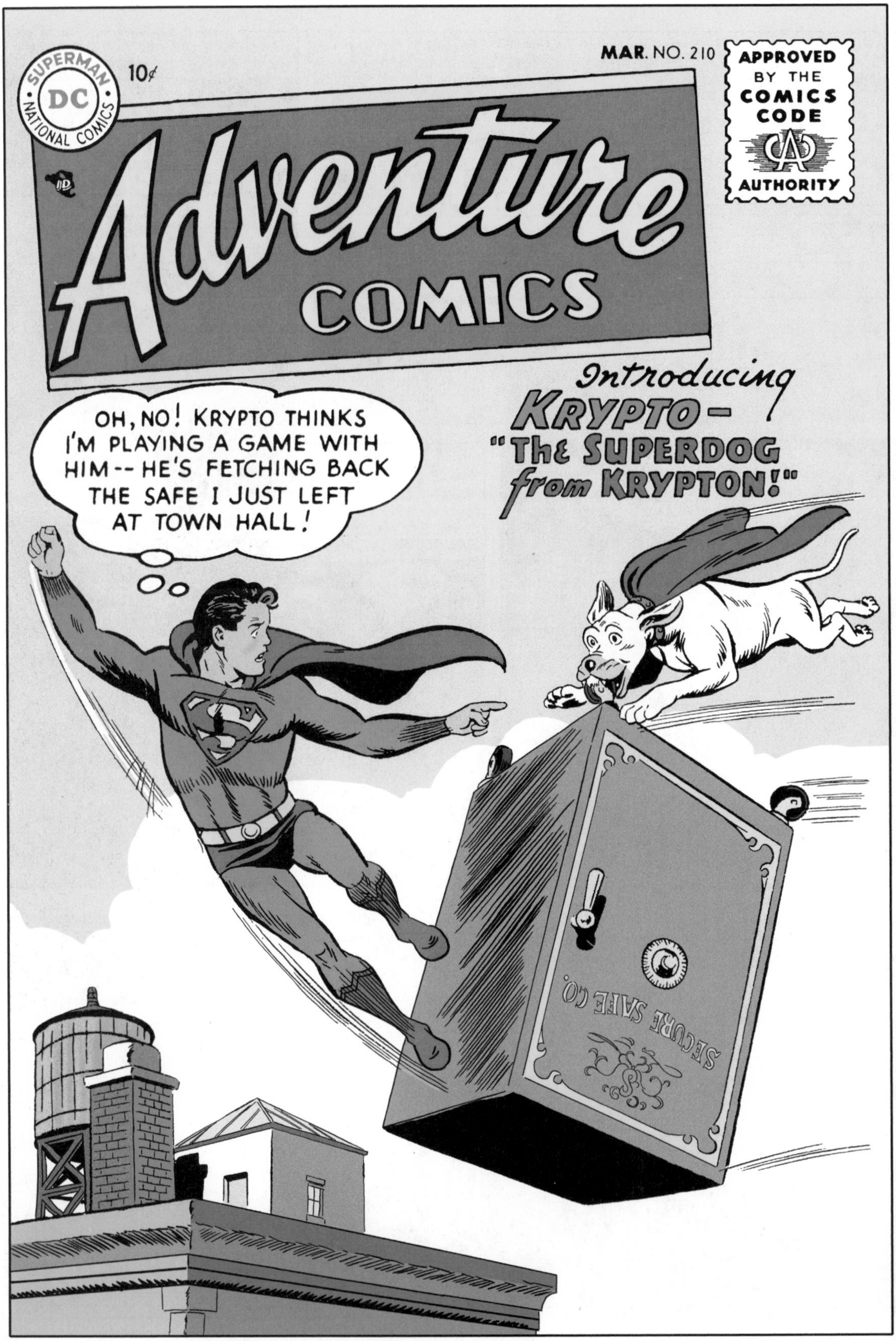
SUPERMAN DC NATIONAL COMICS
10¢
MAR. NO. 210
APPROVED BY THE COMICS CODE AUTHORITY
Adventure COMICS
Introducing KRYPTO - "The SUPERDOG from KRYPTON!"
OH, NO! KRYPTO THINKS I'M PLAYING A GAME WITH HIM -- HE'S FETCHING BACK THE SAFE I JUST LEFT AT TOWN HALL!
SECURE SAFE CO.

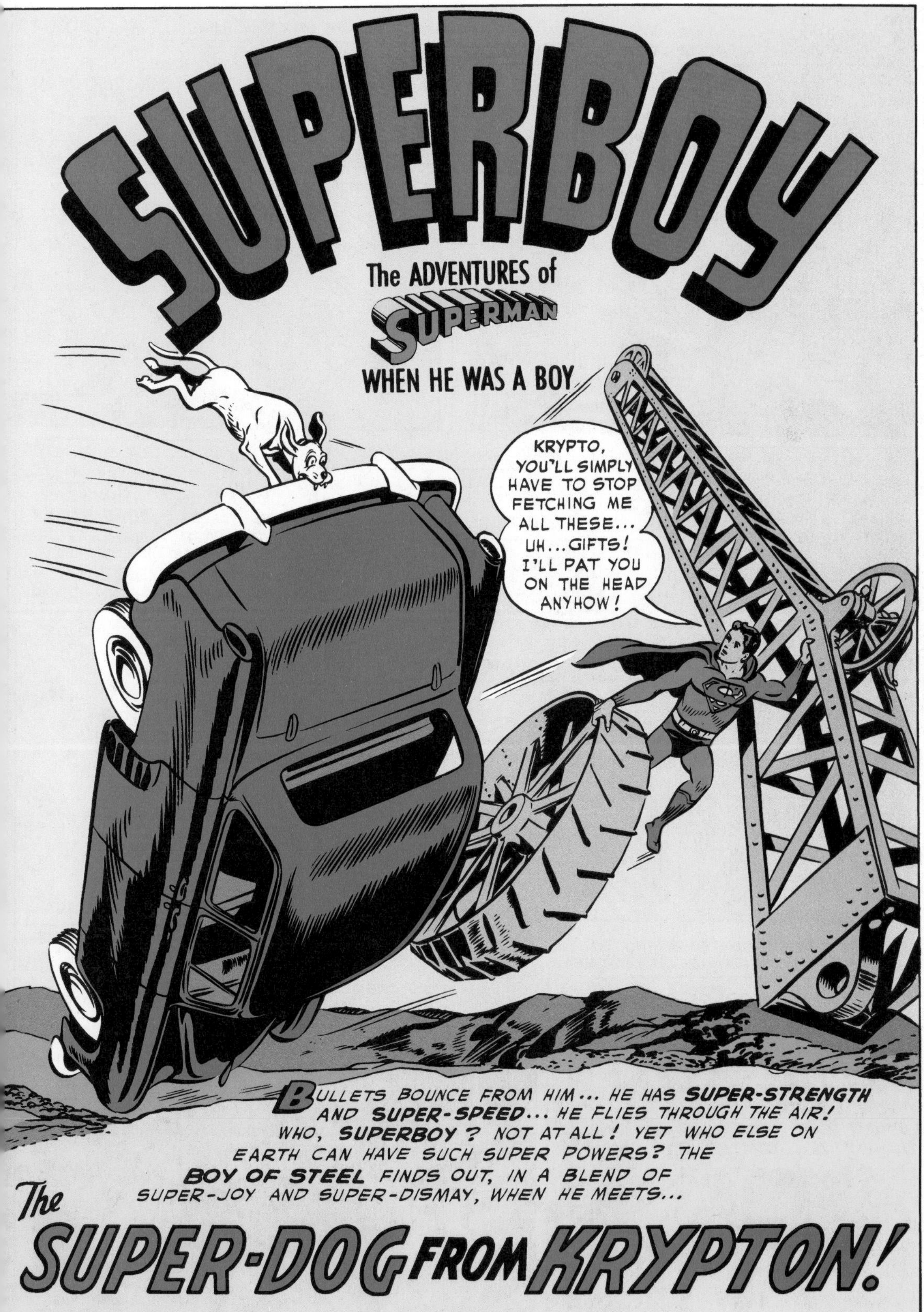
SUPERBOY
The ADVENTURES of
SUPERMAN
WHEN HE WAS A BOY
KRYPTO, YOU'LL SIMPLY HAVE TO STOP FETCHING ME ALL THESE... UH...GIFTS! I'LL PAT YOU ON THE HEAD ANYHOW!
BULLETS BOUNCE FROM HIM... HE HAS SUPER-STRENGTH AND SUPER-SPEED... HE FLIES THROUGH THE AIR! WHO, SUPERBOY? NOT AT ALL! YET WHO ELSE ON EARTH CAN HAVE SUCH SUPER POWERS? THE BOY OF STEEL FINDS OUT, IN A BLEND OF SUPER-JOY AND SUPER-DISMAY, WHEN HE MEETS...
The SUPER-DOG FROM KRYPTON!

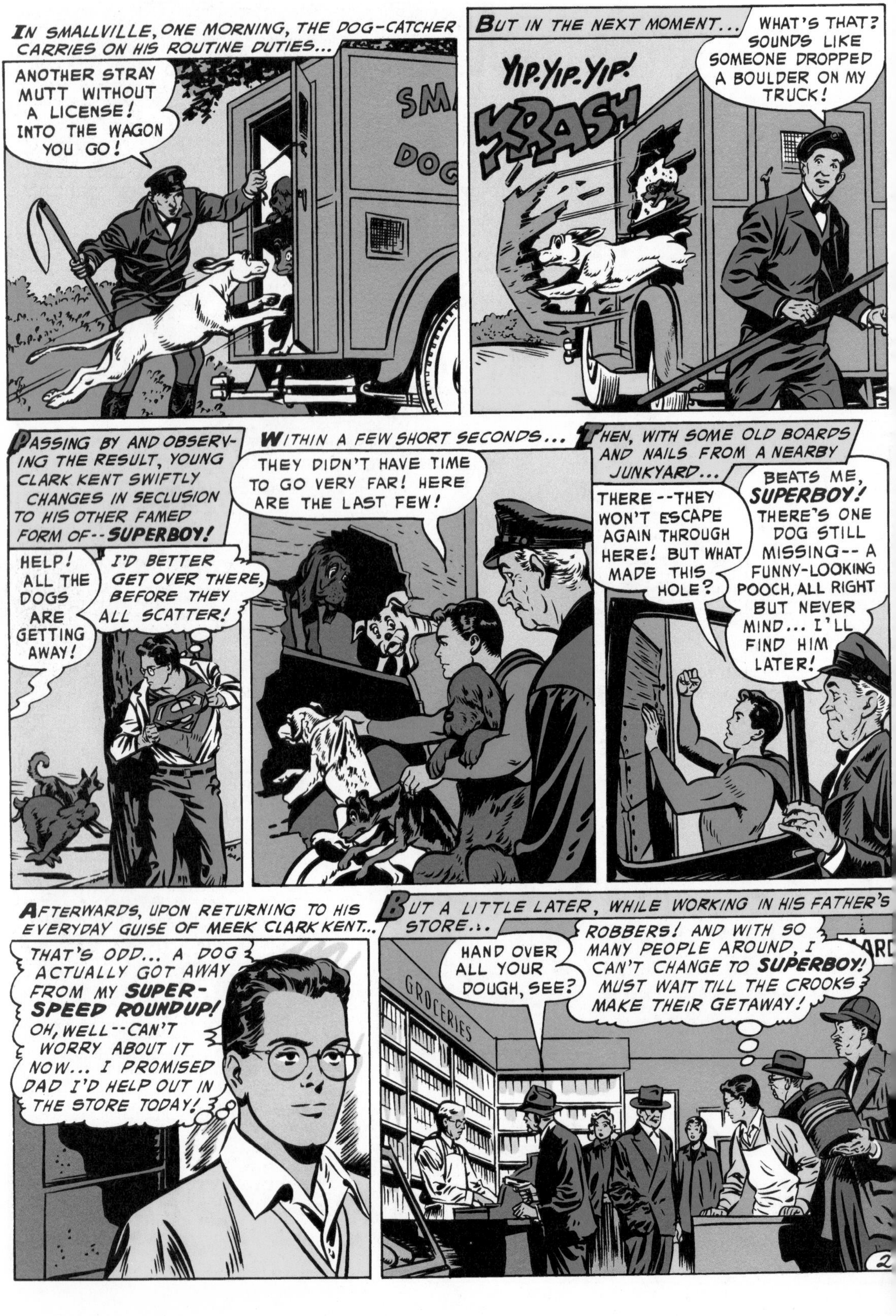
IN SMALLVILLE, ONE MORNING, THE DOG-CATCHER CARRIES ON HIS ROUTINE DUTIES...
ANOTHER STRAY MUTT WITHOUT A LICENSE! INTO THE WAGON YOU GO!
BUT IN THE NEXT MOMENT...
YIP-YIP-YIP!
KRASH
WHAT'S THAT? SOUNDS LIKE SOMEONE DROPPED A BOULDER ON MY TRUCK!
PASSING BY AND OBSERVING THE RESULT, YOUNG CLARK KENT SWIFTLY CHANGES IN SECLUSION TO HIS OTHER FAMED FORM OF--SUPERBOY!
HELP! ALL THE DOGS ARE GETTING AWAY!
I'D BETTER GET OVER THERE, BEFORE THEY ALL SCATTER!
WITHIN A FEW SHORT SECONDS...
THEY DIDN'T HAVE TIME TO GO VERY FAR! HERE ARE THE LAST FEW!
THEN, WITH SOME OLD BOARDS AND NAILS FROM A NEARBY JUNKYARD...
THERE--THEY WON'T ESCAPE AGAIN THROUGH HERE! BUT WHAT MADE THIS HOLE?
BEATS ME, SUPERBOY! THERE'S ONE DOG STILL MISSING--A FUNNY-LOOKING POOCH, ALL RIGHT BUT NEVER MIND... I'LL FIND HIM LATER!
AFTERWARDS, UPON RETURNING TO HIS EVERYDAY GUISE OF MEEK CLARK KENT...
THAT'S ODD... A DOG ACTUALLY GOT AWAY FROM MY SUPER-SPEED ROUNDUP! OH, WELL--CAN'T WORRY ABOUT IT NOW... I PROMISED DAD I'D HELP OUT IN THE STORE TODAY!
BUT A LITTLE LATER, WHILE WORKING IN HIS FATHER'S STORE...
GROCERIES
HAND OVER ALL YOUR DOUGH, SEE?
ROBBERS! AND WITH SO MANY PEOPLE AROUND, I CAN'T CHANGE TO SUPERBOY! MUST WAIT TILL THE CROOKS MAKE THEIR GETAWAY!
2

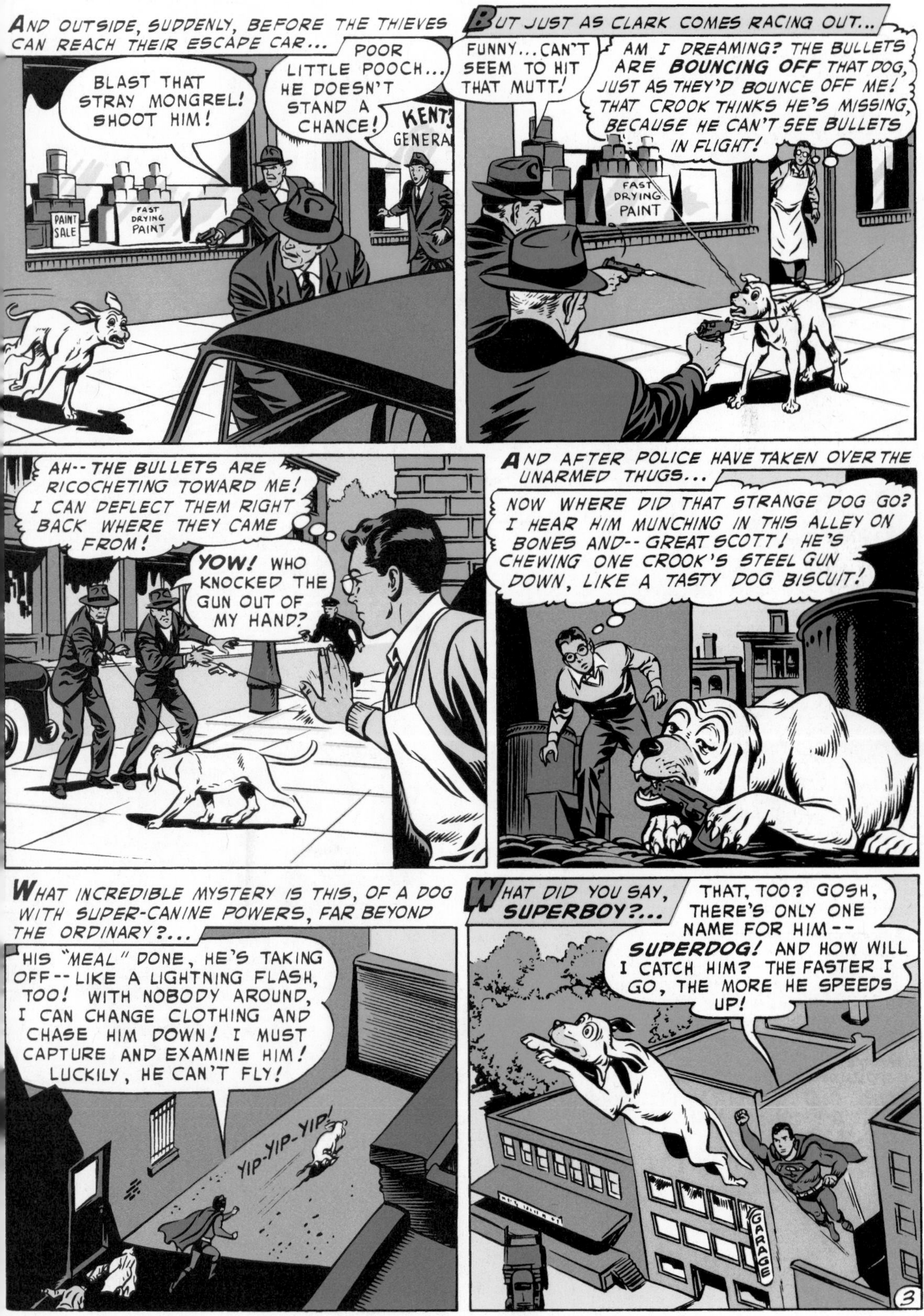
AND OUTSIDE, SUDDENLY, BEFORE THE THIEVES CAN REACH THEIR ESCAPE CAR...
BLAST THAT STRAY MONGREL! SHOOT HIM!
POOR LITTLE POOCH... HE DOESN'T STAND A CHANCE!
KENT'S GENERAL
PAINT SALE
FAST DRYING PAINT
BUT JUST AS CLARK COMES RACING OUT...
FUNNY... CAN'T SEEM TO HIT THAT MUTT!
AM I DREAMING? THE BULLETS ARE BOUNCING OFF THAT DOG, JUST AS THEY'D BOUNCE OFF ME! THAT CROOK THINKS HE'S MISSING, BECAUSE HE CAN'T SEE BULLETS IN FLIGHT!
FAST DRYING PAINT
AH-- THE BULLETS ARE RICOCHETING TOWARD ME! I CAN DEFLECT THEM RIGHT BACK WHERE THEY CAME FROM!
YOW! WHO KNOCKED THE GUN OUT OF MY HAND?
AND AFTER POLICE HAVE TAKEN OVER THE UNARMED THUGS...
NOW WHERE DID THAT STRANGE DOG GO? I HEAR HIM MUNCHING IN THIS ALLEY ON BONES AND-- GREAT SCOTT! HE'S CHEWING ONE CROOK'S STEEL GUN DOWN, LIKE A TASTY DOG BISCUIT!
WHAT INCREDIBLE MYSTERY IS THIS, OF A DOG WITH SUPER-CANINE POWERS, FAR BEYOND THE ORDINARY?...
HIS "MEAL" DONE, HE'S TAKING OFF-- LIKE A LIGHTNING FLASH, TOO! WITH NOBODY AROUND, I CAN CHANGE CLOTHING AND CHASE HIM DOWN! I MUST CAPTURE AND EXAMINE HIM! LUCKILY, HE CAN'T FLY!
YIP-YIP-YIP!
WHAT DID YOU SAY, SUPERBOY?...
THAT, TOO? GOSH, THERE'S ONLY ONE NAME FOR HIM-- SUPERDOG! AND HOW WILL I CATCH HIM? THE FASTER I GO, THE MORE HE SPEEDS UP!
GARAGE
3

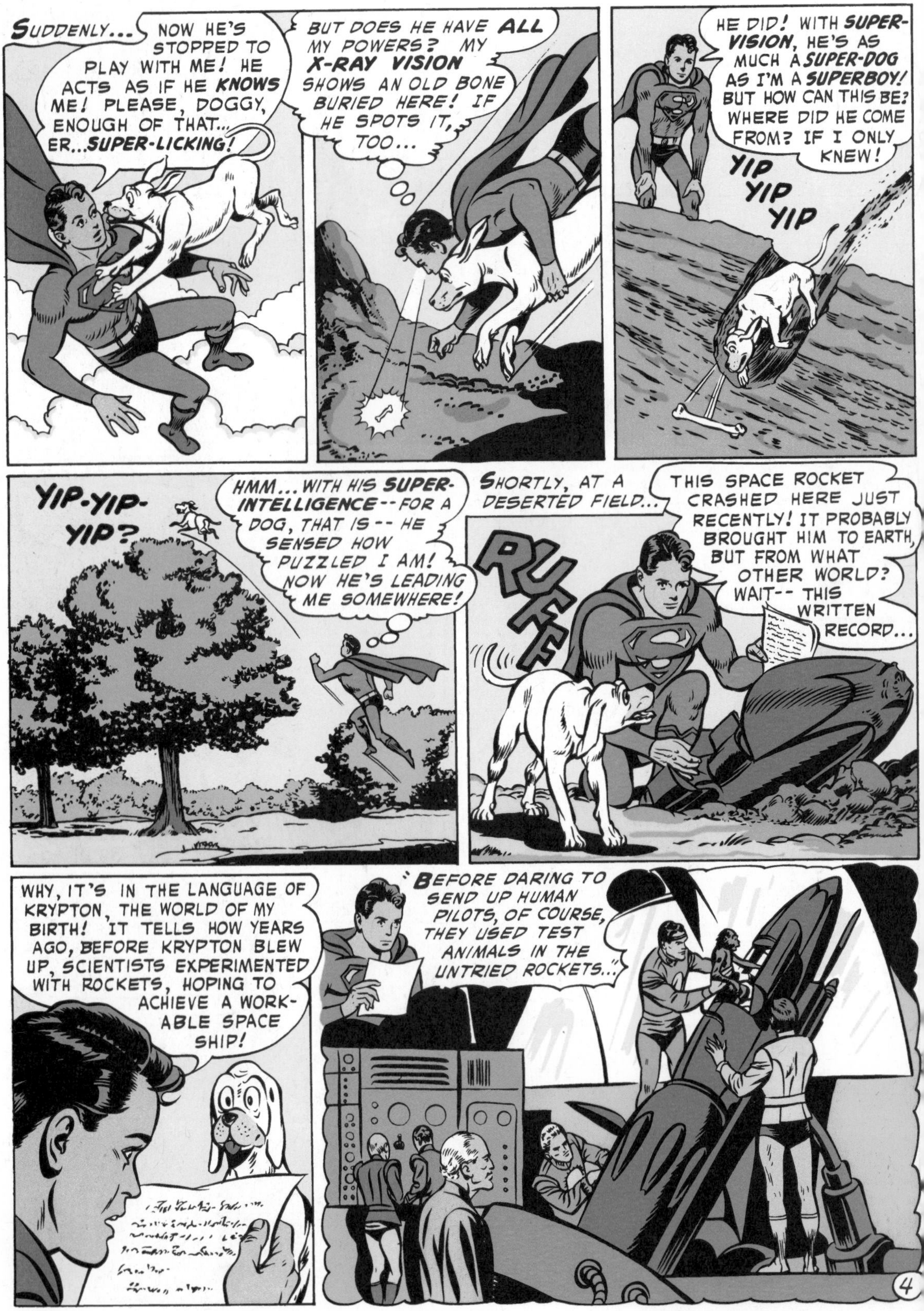
SUDDENLY...
NOW HE'S STOPPED TO PLAY WITH ME! HE ACTS AS IF HE KNOWS ME! PLEASE, DOGGY, ENOUGH OF THAT... ER...SUPER-LICKING!
BUT DOES HE HAVE ALL MY POWERS? MY X-RAY VISION SHOWS AN OLD BONE BURIED HERE! IF HE SPOTS IT, TOO...
HE DID! WITH SUPER-VISION, HE'S AS MUCH A SUPER-DOG AS I'M A SUPERBOY! BUT HOW CAN THIS BE? WHERE DID HE COME FROM? IF I ONLY KNEW!
YIP YIP YIP
YIP-YIP-YIP?
HMM... WITH HIS SUPER-INTELLIGENCE--FOR A DOG, THAT IS--HE SENSED HOW PUZZLED I AM! NOW HE'S LEADING ME SOMEWHERE!
SHORTLY, AT A DESERTED FIELD...
THIS SPACE ROCKET CRASHED HERE JUST RECENTLY! IT PROBABLY BROUGHT HIM TO EARTH, BUT FROM WHAT OTHER WORLD? WAIT-- THIS WRITTEN RECORD...
RUFF
WHY, IT'S IN THE LANGUAGE OF KRYPTON, THE WORLD OF MY BIRTH! IT TELLS HOW YEARS AGO, BEFORE KRYPTON BLEW UP, SCIENTISTS EXPERIMENTED WITH ROCKETS, HOPING TO ACHIEVE A WORKABLE SPACE SHIP!
"BEFORE DARING TO SEND UP HUMAN PILOTS, OF COURSE, THEY USED TEST ANIMALS IN THE UNTRIED ROCKETS..."
4

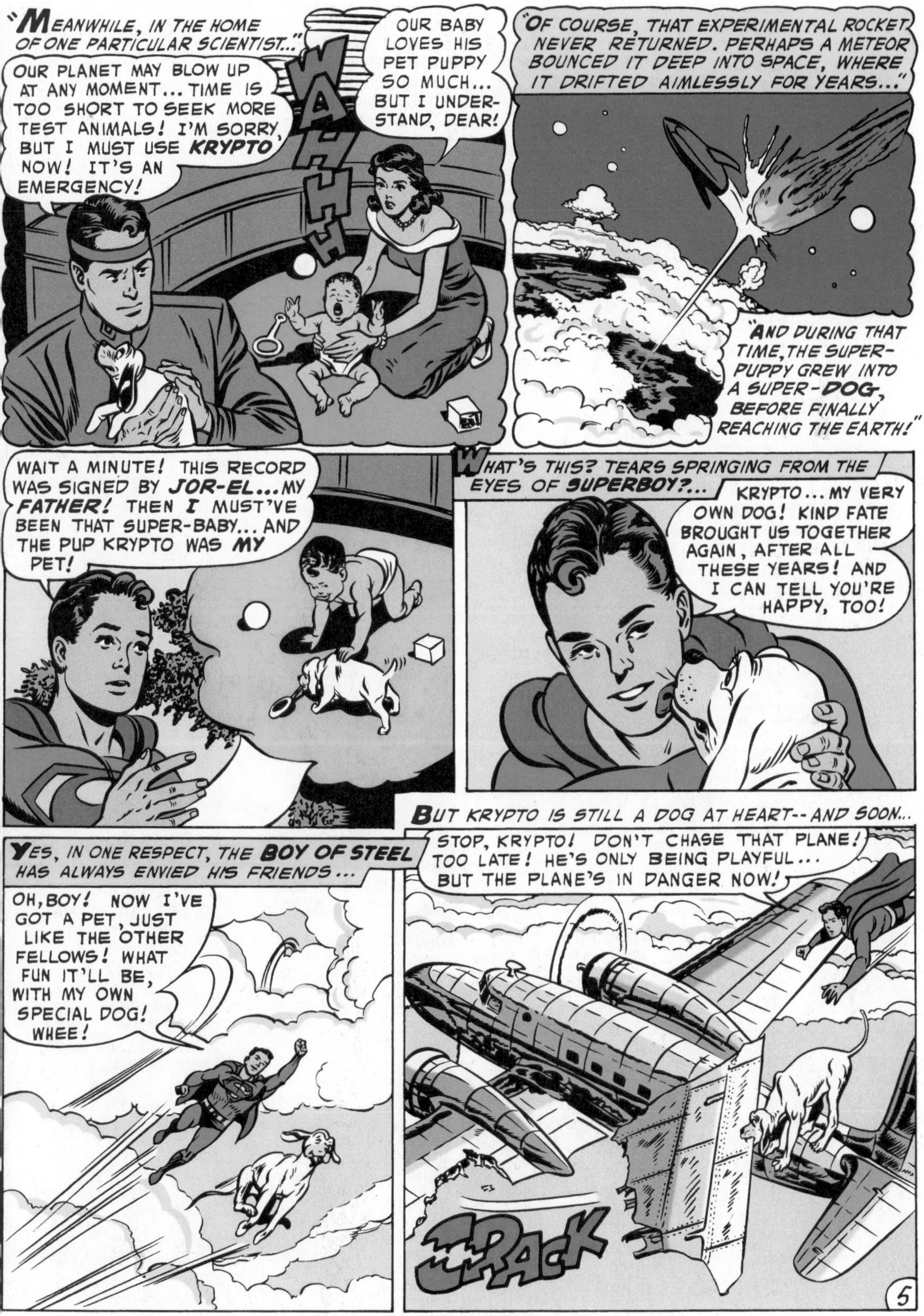
"MEANWHILE, IN THE HOME OF ONE PARTICULAR SCIENTIST..."
OUR PLANET MAY BLOW UP AT ANY MOMENT... TIME IS TOO SHORT TO SEEK MORE TEST ANIMALS! I'M SORRY, BUT I MUST USE KRYPTO NOW! IT'S AN EMERGENCY!
WAHHHH
OUR BABY LOVES HIS PET PUPPY SO MUCH... BUT I UNDERSTAND, DEAR!
"OF COURSE, THAT EXPERIMENTAL ROCKET NEVER RETURNED. PERHAPS A METEOR BOUNCED IT DEEP INTO SPACE, WHERE IT DRIFTED AIMLESSLY FOR YEARS..."
"AND DURING THAT TIME, THE SUPER-PUPPY GREW INTO A SUPER-DOG, BEFORE FINALLY REACHING THE EARTH!"
WAIT A MINUTE! THIS RECORD WAS SIGNED BY JOR-EL... MY FATHER! THEN I MUST'VE BEEN THAT SUPER-BABY... AND THE PUP KRYPTO WAS MY PET!
WHAT'S THIS? TEARS SPRINGING FROM THE EYES OF SUPERBOY?...
KRYPTO... MY VERY OWN DOG! KIND FATE BROUGHT US TOGETHER AGAIN, AFTER ALL THESE YEARS! AND I CAN TELL YOU'RE HAPPY, TOO!
YES, IN ONE RESPECT, THE BOY OF STEEL HAS ALWAYS ENVIED HIS FRIENDS...
OH, BOY! NOW I'VE GOT A PET, JUST LIKE THE OTHER FELLOWS! WHAT FUN IT'LL BE, WITH MY OWN SPECIAL DOG! WHEE!
BUT KRYPTO IS STILL A DOG AT HEART-- AND SOON...
STOP, KRYPTO! DON'T CHASE THAT PLANE! TOO LATE! HE'S ONLY BEING PLAYFUL... BUT THE PLANE'S IN DANGER NOW!
CRACK
5

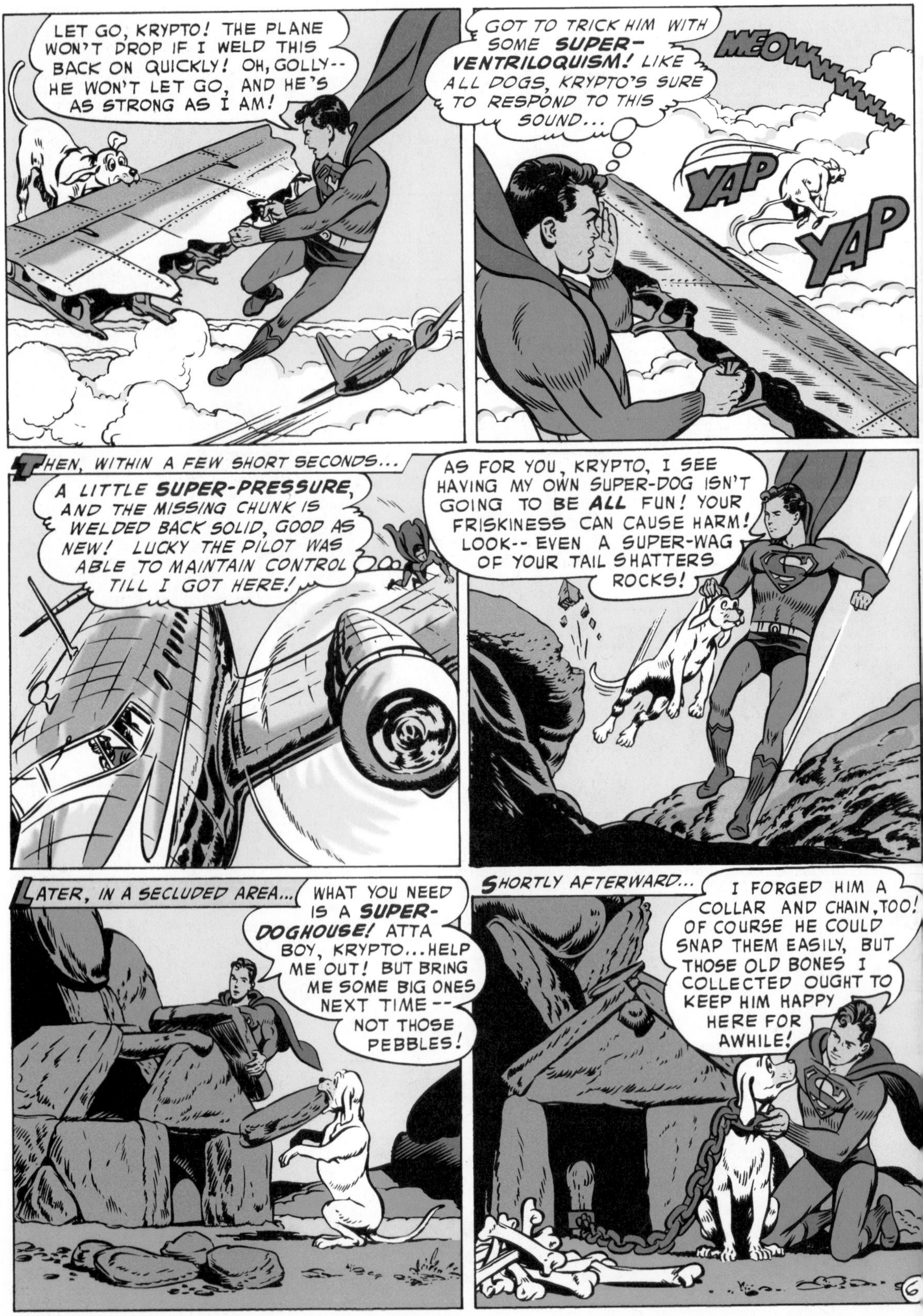

LET GO, KRYPTO! THE PLANE WON'T DROP IF I WELD THIS BACK ON QUICKLY! OH, GOLLY-- HE WON'T LET GO, AND HE'S AS STRONG AS I AM!
GOT TO TRICK HIM WITH SOME SUPER-VENTRILOQUISM! LIKE ALL DOGS, KRYPTO'S SURE TO RESPOND TO THIS SOUND...
MEOWWWWWW
YAP
YAP
THEN, WITHIN A FEW SHORT SECONDS...
A LITTLE SUPER-PRESSURE, AND THE MISSING CHUNK IS WELDED BACK SOLID, GOOD AS NEW! LUCKY THE PILOT WAS ABLE TO MAINTAIN CONTROL TILL I GOT HERE!
AS FOR YOU, KRYPTO, I SEE HAVING MY OWN SUPER-DOG ISN'T GOING TO BE ALL FUN! YOUR FRISKINESS CAN CAUSE HARM! LOOK-- EVEN A SUPER-WAG OF YOUR TAIL SHATTERS ROCKS!
LATER, IN A SECLUDED AREA...
WHAT YOU NEED IS A SUPER-DOGHOUSE! ATTA BOY, KRYPTO...HELP ME OUT! BUT BRING ME SOME BIG ONES NEXT TIME-- NOT THOSE PEBBLES!
SHORTLY AFTERWARD...
I FORGED HIM A COLLAR AND CHAIN, TOO! OF COURSE HE COULD SNAP THEM EASILY, BUT THOSE OLD BONES I COLLECTED OUGHT TO KEEP HIM HAPPY HERE FOR AWHILE!
6

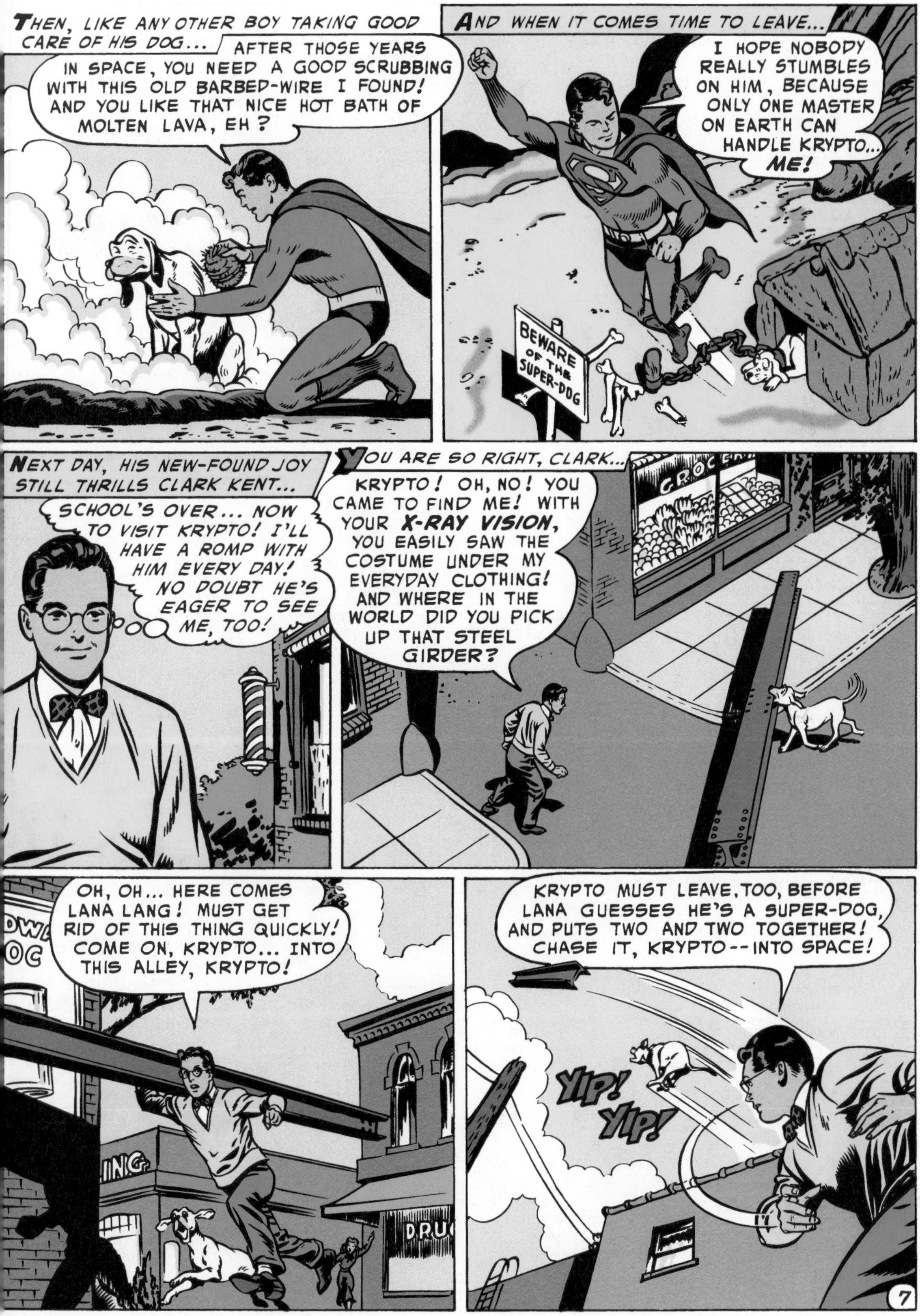
THEN, LIKE ANY OTHER BOY TAKING GOOD CARE OF HIS DOG...
AFTER THOSE YEARS IN SPACE, YOU NEED A GOOD SCRUBBING WITH THIS OLD BARBED-WIRE I FOUND! AND YOU LIKE THAT NICE HOT BATH OF MOLTEN LAVA, EH?
AND WHEN IT COMES TIME TO LEAVE...
I HOPE NOBODY REALLY STUMBLES ON HIM, BECAUSE ONLY ONE MASTER ON EARTH CAN HANDLE KRYPTO... ME!
BEWARE OF THE SUPER-DOG
NEXT DAY, HIS NEW-FOUND JOY STILL THRILLS CLARK KENT...
SCHOOL'S OVER... NOW TO VISIT KRYPTO! I'LL HAVE A ROMP WITH HIM EVERY DAY! NO DOUBT HE'S EAGER TO SEE ME, TOO!
YOU ARE SO RIGHT, CLARK...
KRYPTO! OH, NO! YOU CAME TO FIND ME! WITH YOUR X-RAY VISION, YOU EASILY SAW THE COSTUME UNDER MY EVERYDAY CLOTHING! AND WHERE IN THE WORLD DID YOU PICK UP THAT STEEL GIRDER?
OH, OH... HERE COMES LANA LANG! MUST GET RID OF THIS THING QUICKLY! COME ON, KRYPTO... INTO THIS ALLEY, KRYPTO!
KRYPTO MUST LEAVE, TOO, BEFORE LANA GUESSES HE'S A SUPER-DOG, AND PUTS TWO AND TWO TOGETHER! CHASE IT, KRYPTO--INTO SPACE!
YIP! YIP!
7

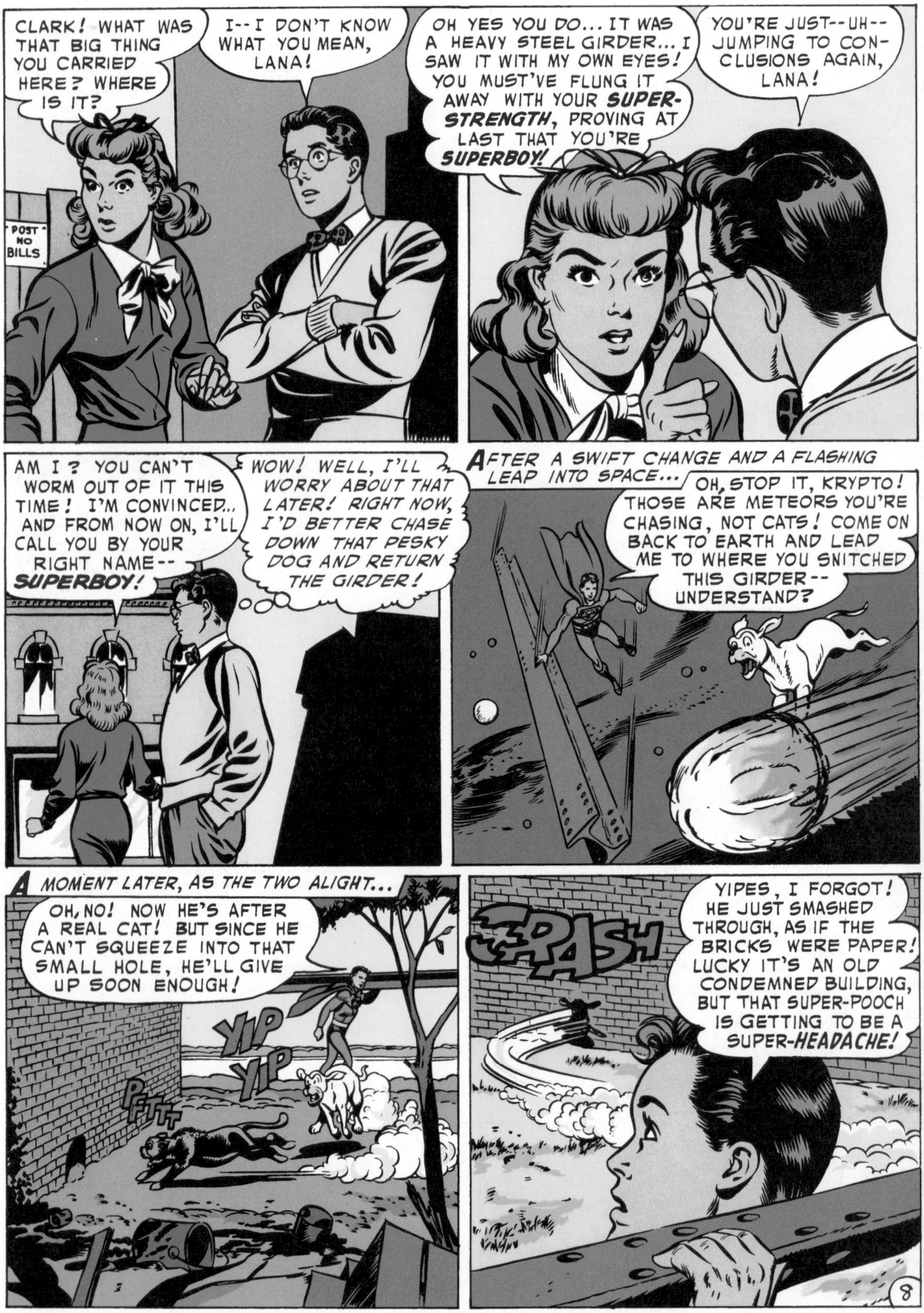

CLARK! WHAT WAS THAT BIG THING YOU CARRIED HERE? WHERE IS IT?
I-- I DON'T KNOW WHAT YOU MEAN, LANA!
POST NO BILLS
OH YES YOU DO... IT WAS A HEAVY STEEL GIRDER... I SAW IT WITH MY OWN EYES! YOU MUST'VE FLUNG IT AWAY WITH YOUR SUPER-STRENGTH, PROVING AT LAST THAT YOU'RE SUPERBOY!
YOU'RE JUST-- UH-- JUMPING TO CONCLUSIONS AGAIN, LANA!
AM I? YOU CAN'T WORM OUT OF IT THIS TIME! I'M CONVINCED... AND FROM NOW ON, I'LL CALL YOU BY YOUR RIGHT NAME-- SUPERBOY!
WOW! WELL, I'LL WORRY ABOUT THAT LATER! RIGHT NOW, I'D BETTER CHASE DOWN THAT PESKY DOG AND RETURN THE GIRDER!
AFTER A SWIFT CHANGE AND A FLASHING LEAP INTO SPACE...
OH, STOP IT, KRYPTO! THOSE ARE METEORS YOU'RE CHASING, NOT CATS! COME ON BACK TO EARTH AND LEAD ME TO WHERE YOU SNITCHED THIS GIRDER-- UNDERSTAND?
A MOMENT LATER, AS THE TWO ALIGHT...
OH, NO! NOW HE'S AFTER A REAL CAT! BUT SINCE HE CAN'T SQUEEZE INTO THAT SMALL HOLE, HE'LL GIVE UP SOON ENOUGH!
YIP
YIP
PFTTT
CRASH
YIPES, I FORGOT! HE JUST SMASHED THROUGH, AS IF THE BRICKS WERE PAPER! LUCKY IT'S AN OLD CONDEMNED BUILDING, BUT THAT SUPER-POOCH IS GETTING TO BE A SUPER-HEADACHE!
8

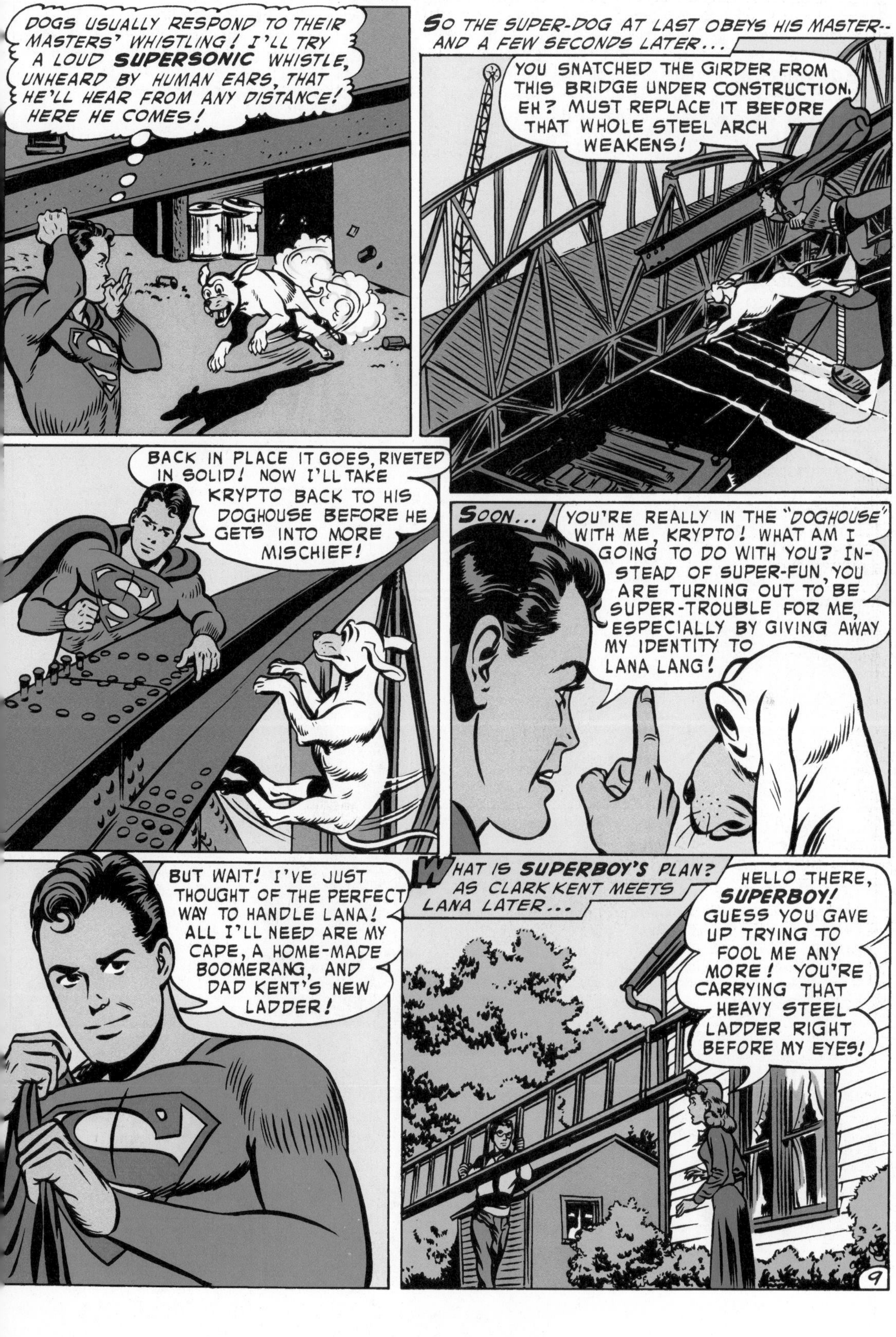
DOGS USUALLY RESPOND TO THEIR MASTERS' WHISTLING! I'LL TRY A LOUD SUPERSONIC WHISTLE, UNHEARD BY HUMAN EARS, THAT HE'LL HEAR FROM ANY DISTANCE! HERE HE COMES!
SO THE SUPER-DOG AT LAST OBEYS HIS MASTER-- AND A FEW SECONDS LATER...
YOU SNATCHED THE GIRDER FROM THIS BRIDGE UNDER CONSTRUCTION, EH? MUST REPLACE IT BEFORE THAT WHOLE STEEL ARCH WEAKENS!
BACK IN PLACE IT GOES, RIVETED IN SOLID! NOW I'LL TAKE KRYPTO BACK TO HIS DOGHOUSE BEFORE HE GETS INTO MORE MISCHIEF!
SOON...
YOU'RE REALLY IN THE "DOGHOUSE" WITH ME, KRYPTO! WHAT AM I GOING TO DO WITH YOU? INSTEAD OF SUPER-FUN, YOU ARE TURNING OUT TO BE SUPER-TROUBLE FOR ME, ESPECIALLY BY GIVING AWAY MY IDENTITY TO LANA LANG!
BUT WAIT! I'VE JUST THOUGHT OF THE PERFECT WAY TO HANDLE LANA! ALL I'LL NEED ARE MY CAPE, A HOME-MADE BOOMERANG, AND DAD KENT'S NEW LADDER!
WHAT IS SUPERBOY'S PLAN? AS CLARK KENT MEETS LANA LATER...
HELLO THERE, SUPERBOY! GUESS YOU GAVE UP TRYING TO FOOL ME ANY MORE! YOU'RE CARRYING THAT HEAVY STEEL LADDER RIGHT BEFORE MY EYES!
9

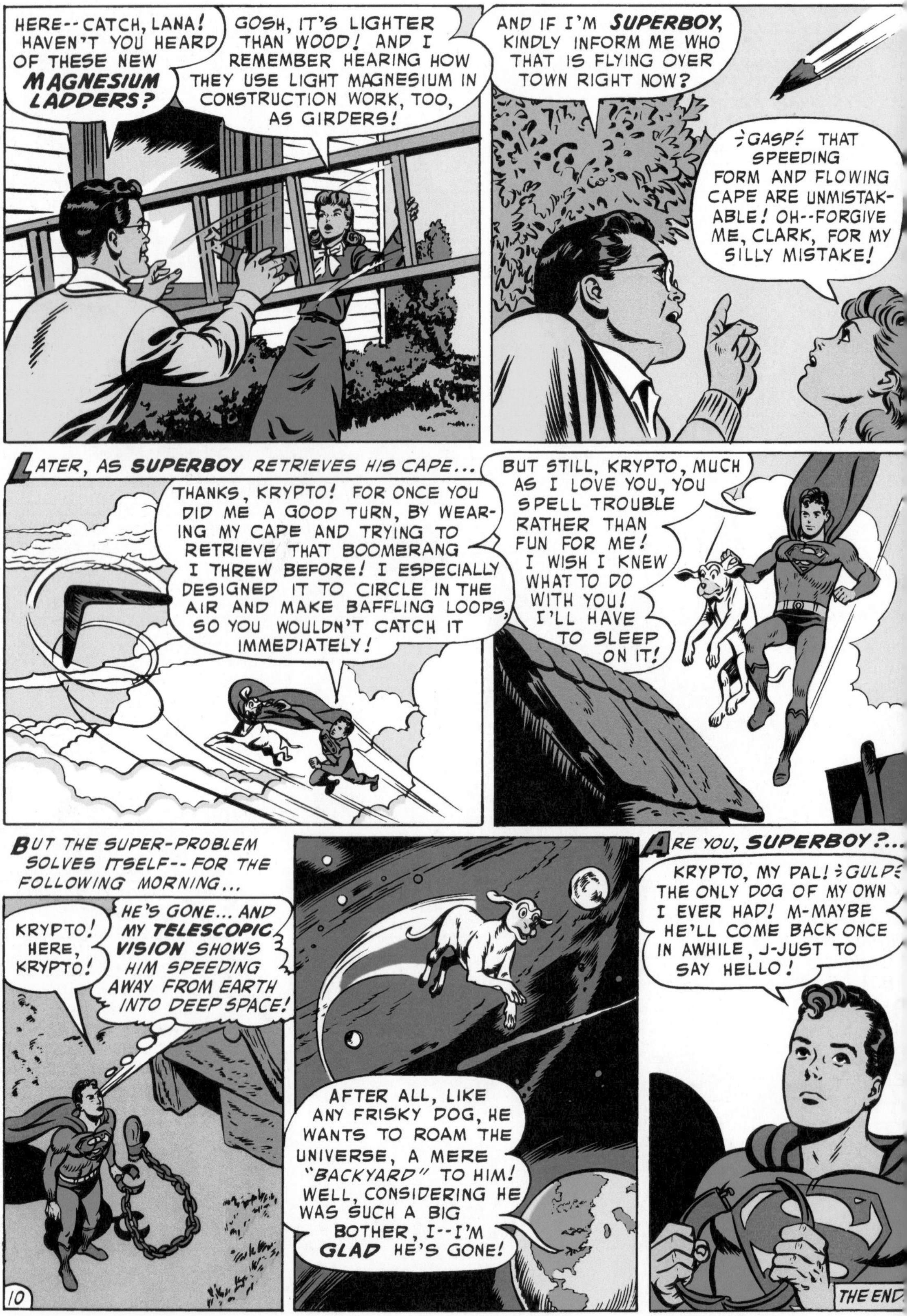
HERE--CATCH, LANA! HAVEN'T YOU HEARD OF THESE NEW MAGNESIUM LADDERS?
GOSH, IT'S LIGHTER THAN WOOD! AND I REMEMBER HEARING HOW THEY USE LIGHT MAGNESIUM IN CONSTRUCTION WORK, TOO, AS GIRDERS!
AND IF I'M SUPERBOY, KINDLY INFORM ME WHO THAT IS FLYING OVER TOWN RIGHT NOW?
GASP THAT SPEEDING FORM AND FLOWING CAPE ARE UNMISTAKABLE! OH--FORGIVE ME, CLARK, FOR MY SILLY MISTAKE!
LATER, AS SUPERBOY RETRIEVES HIS CAPE...
THANKS, KRYPTO! FOR ONCE YOU DID ME A GOOD TURN, BY WEARING MY CAPE AND TRYING TO RETRIEVE THAT BOOMERANG I THREW BEFORE! I ESPECIALLY DESIGNED IT TO CIRCLE IN THE AIR AND MAKE BAFFLING LOOPS, SO YOU WOULDN'T CATCH IT IMMEDIATELY!
BUT STILL, KRYPTO, MUCH AS I LOVE YOU, YOU SPELL TROUBLE RATHER THAN FUN FOR ME! I WISH I KNEW WHAT TO DO WITH YOU! I'LL HAVE TO SLEEP ON IT!
BUT THE SUPER-PROBLEM SOLVES ITSELF--FOR THE FOLLOWING MORNING...
KRYPTO! HERE, KRYPTO!
HE'S GONE... AND MY TELESCOPIC VISION SHOWS HIM SPEEDING AWAY FROM EARTH INTO DEEP SPACE!
10
AFTER ALL, LIKE ANY FRISKY DOG, HE WANTS TO ROAM THE UNIVERSE, A MERE "BACKYARD" TO HIM! WELL, CONSIDERING HE WAS SUCH A BIG BOTHER, I--I'M GLAD HE'S GONE!
ARE YOU, SUPERBOY?...
KRYPTO, MY PAL! GULP THE ONLY DOG OF MY OWN I EVER HAD! M-MAYBE HE'LL COME BACK ONCE IN AWHILE, J-JUST TO SAY HELLO!
THE END

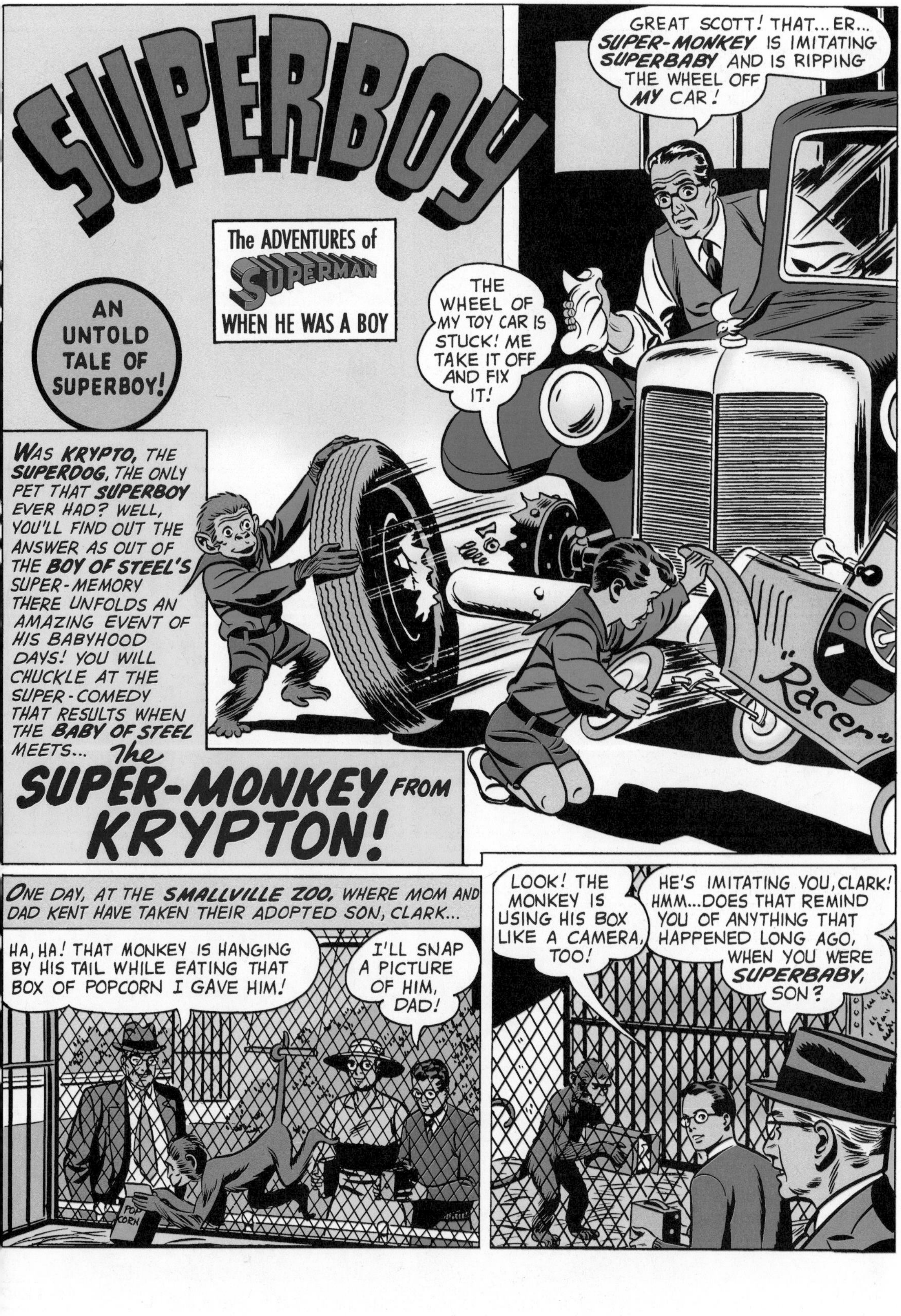
SUPERBOY
The ADVENTURES of SUPERMAN WHEN HE WAS A BOY
AN UNTOLD TALE OF SUPERBOY!
WAS KRYPTO, THE SUPERDOG, THE ONLY PET THAT SUPERBOY EVER HAD? WELL, YOU'LL FIND OUT THE ANSWER AS OUT OF THE BOY OF STEEL'S SUPER-MEMORY THERE UNFOLDS AN AMAZING EVENT OF HIS BABYHOOD DAYS! YOU WILL CHUCKLE AT THE SUPER-COMEDY THAT RESULTS WHEN THE BABY OF STEEL MEETS... The
SUPER-MONKEY FROM KRYPTON!
GREAT SCOTT! THAT... ER... SUPER-MONKEY IS IMITATING SUPERBABY AND IS RIPPING THE WHEEL OFF MY CAR!
THE WHEEL OF MY TOY CAR IS STUCK! ME TAKE IT OFF AND FIX IT!
"Racer"
ONE DAY, AT THE SMALLVILLE ZOO, WHERE MOM AND DAD KENT HAVE TAKEN THEIR ADOPTED SON, CLARK...
HA, HA! THAT MONKEY IS HANGING BY HIS TAIL WHILE EATING THAT BOX OF POPCORN I GAVE HIM!
I'LL SNAP A PICTURE OF HIM, DAD!
POP CORN
LOOK! THE MONKEY IS USING HIS BOX LIKE A CAMERA, TOO!
HE'S IMITATING YOU, CLARK! HMM... DOES THAT REMIND YOU OF ANYTHING THAT HAPPENED LONG AGO, WHEN YOU WERE SUPERBABY, SON?

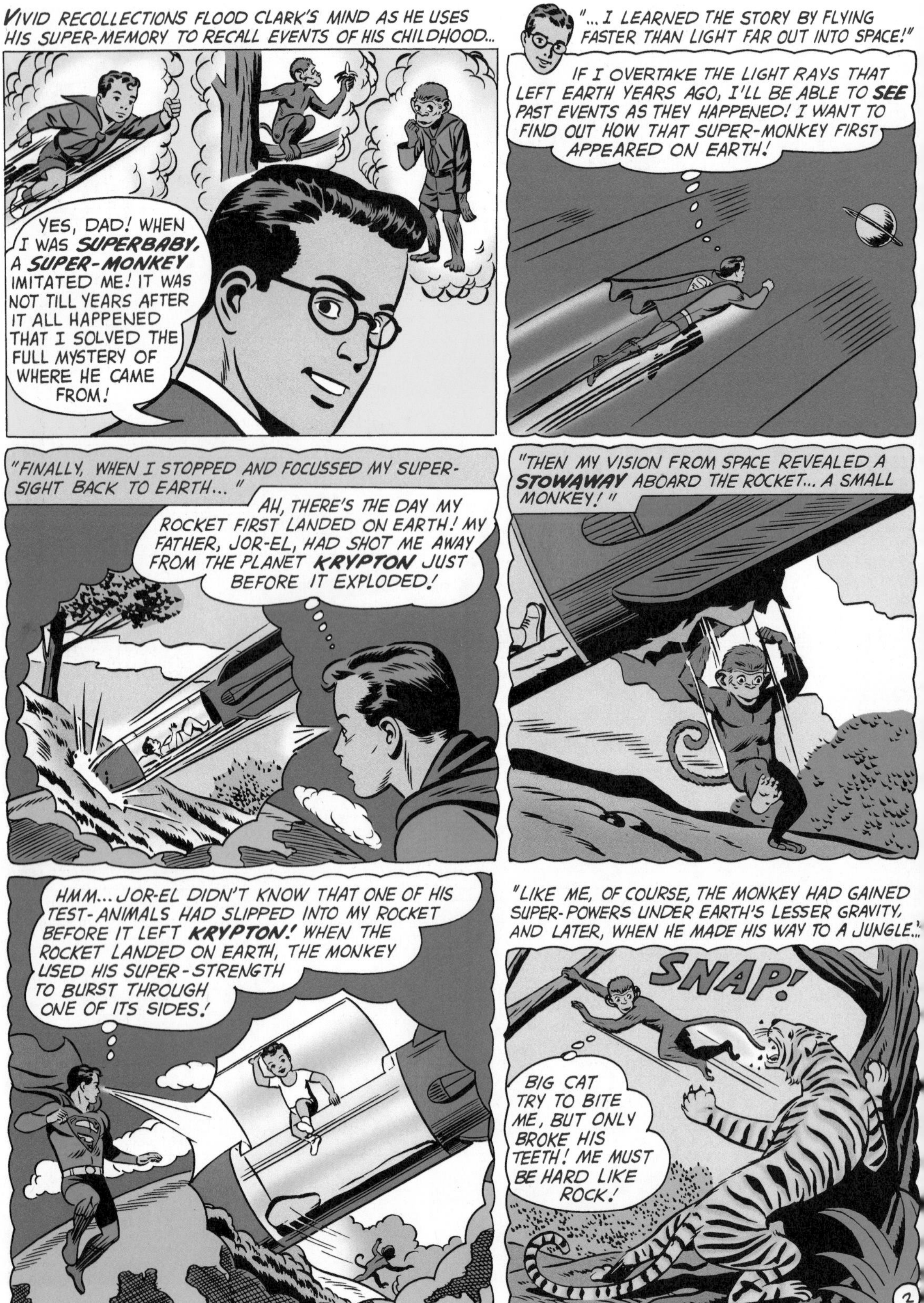
VIVID RECOLLECTIONS FLOOD CLARK'S MIND AS HE USES HIS SUPER-MEMORY TO RECALL EVENTS OF HIS CHILDHOOD...
YES, DAD! WHEN I WAS SUPERBABY, A SUPER-MONKEY IMITATED ME! IT WAS NOT TILL YEARS AFTER IT ALL HAPPENED THAT I SOLVED THE FULL MYSTERY OF WHERE HE CAME FROM!
"...I LEARNED THE STORY BY FLYING FASTER THAN LIGHT FAR OUT INTO SPACE!"
IF I OVERTAKE THE LIGHT RAYS THAT LEFT EARTH YEARS AGO, I'LL BE ABLE TO SEE PAST EVENTS AS THEY HAPPENED! I WANT TO FIND OUT HOW THAT SUPER-MONKEY FIRST APPEARED ON EARTH!
"FINALLY, WHEN I STOPPED AND FOCUSSED MY SUPER-SIGHT BACK TO EARTH..."
AH, THERE'S THE DAY MY ROCKET FIRST LANDED ON EARTH! MY FATHER, JOR-EL, HAD SHOT ME AWAY FROM THE PLANET KRYPTON JUST BEFORE IT EXPLODED!
"THEN MY VISION FROM SPACE REVEALED A STOWAWAY ABOARD THE ROCKET... A SMALL MONKEY!"
HMM...JOR-EL DIDN'T KNOW THAT ONE OF HIS TEST-ANIMALS HAD SLIPPED INTO MY ROCKET BEFORE IT LEFT KRYPTON! WHEN THE ROCKET LANDED ON EARTH, THE MONKEY USED HIS SUPER-STRENGTH TO BURST THROUGH ONE OF ITS SIDES!
"LIKE ME, OF COURSE, THE MONKEY HAD GAINED SUPER-POWERS UNDER EARTH'S LESSER GRAVITY, AND LATER, WHEN HE MADE HIS WAY TO A JUNGLE..."
SNAP!
BIG CAT TRY TO BITE ME, BUT ONLY BROKE HIS TEETH! ME MUST BE HARD LIKE ROCK!
2

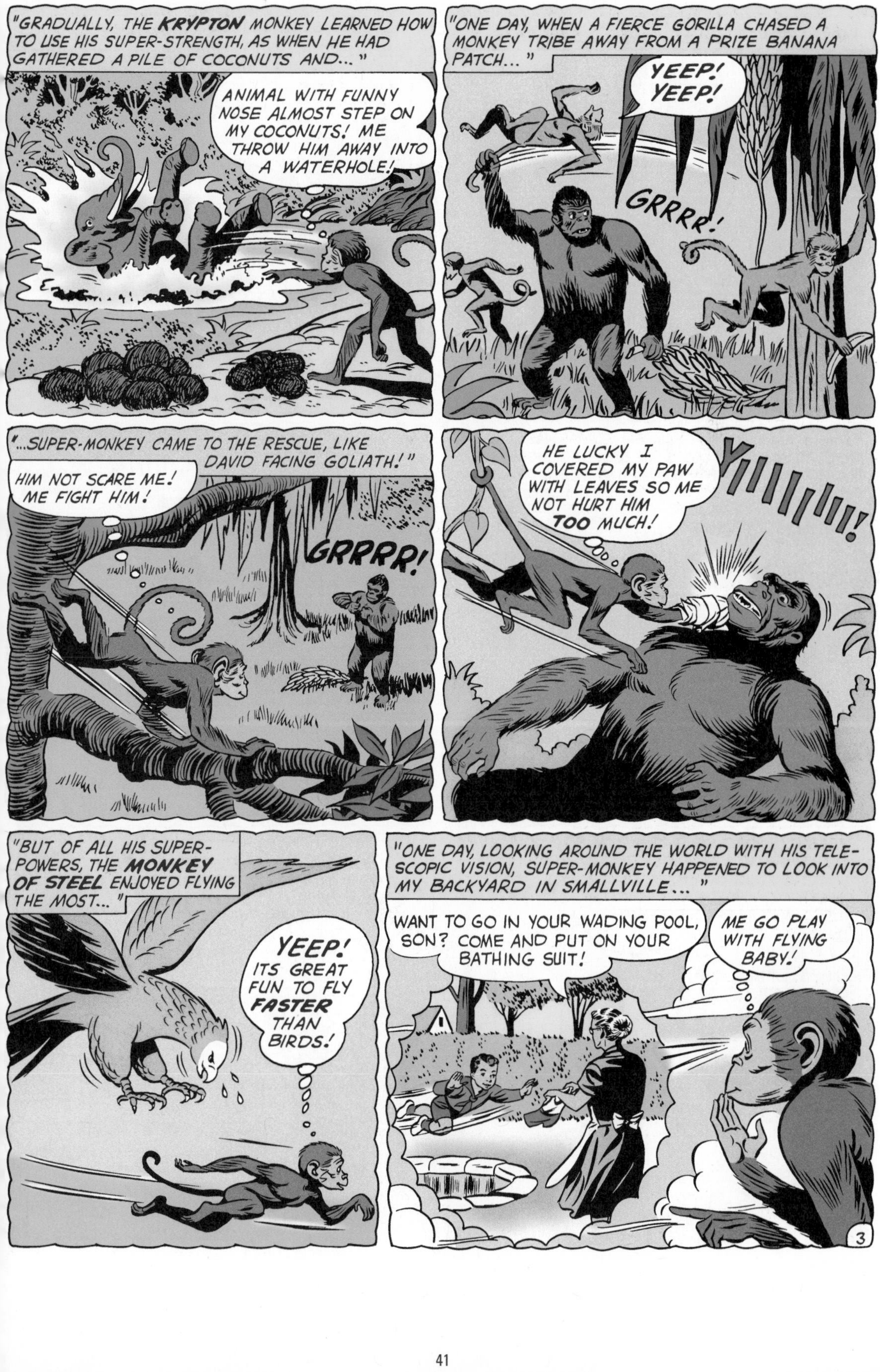

"GRADUALLY, THE KRYPTON MONKEY LEARNED HOW TO USE HIS SUPER-STRENGTH, AS WHEN HE HAD GATHERED A PILE OF COCONUTS AND..."
ANIMAL WITH FUNNY NOSE ALMOST STEP ON MY COCONUTS! ME THROW HIM AWAY INTO A WATERHOLE!
"ONE DAY, WHEN A FIERCE GORILLA CHASED A MONKEY TRIBE AWAY FROM A PRIZE BANANA PATCH..."
YEEP! YEEP!
GRRRR!
"...SUPER-MONKEY CAME TO THE RESCUE, LIKE DAVID FACING GOLIATH!"
HIM NOT SCARE ME! ME FIGHT HIM!
GRRRR!
HE LUCKY I COVERED MY PAW WITH LEAVES SO ME NOT HURT HIM TOO MUCH!
YIIIIIII!
"BUT OF ALL HIS SUPER-POWERS, THE MONKEY OF STEEL ENJOYED FLYING THE MOST..."
YEEP! ITS GREAT FUN TO FLY FASTER THAN BIRDS!
"ONE DAY, LOOKING AROUND THE WORLD WITH HIS TELE-SCOPIC VISION, SUPER-MONKEY HAPPENED TO LOOK INTO MY BACKYARD IN SMALLVILLE..."
WANT TO GO IN YOUR WADING POOL, SON? COME AND PUT ON YOUR BATHING SUIT!
ME GO PLAY WITH FLYING BABY!
3

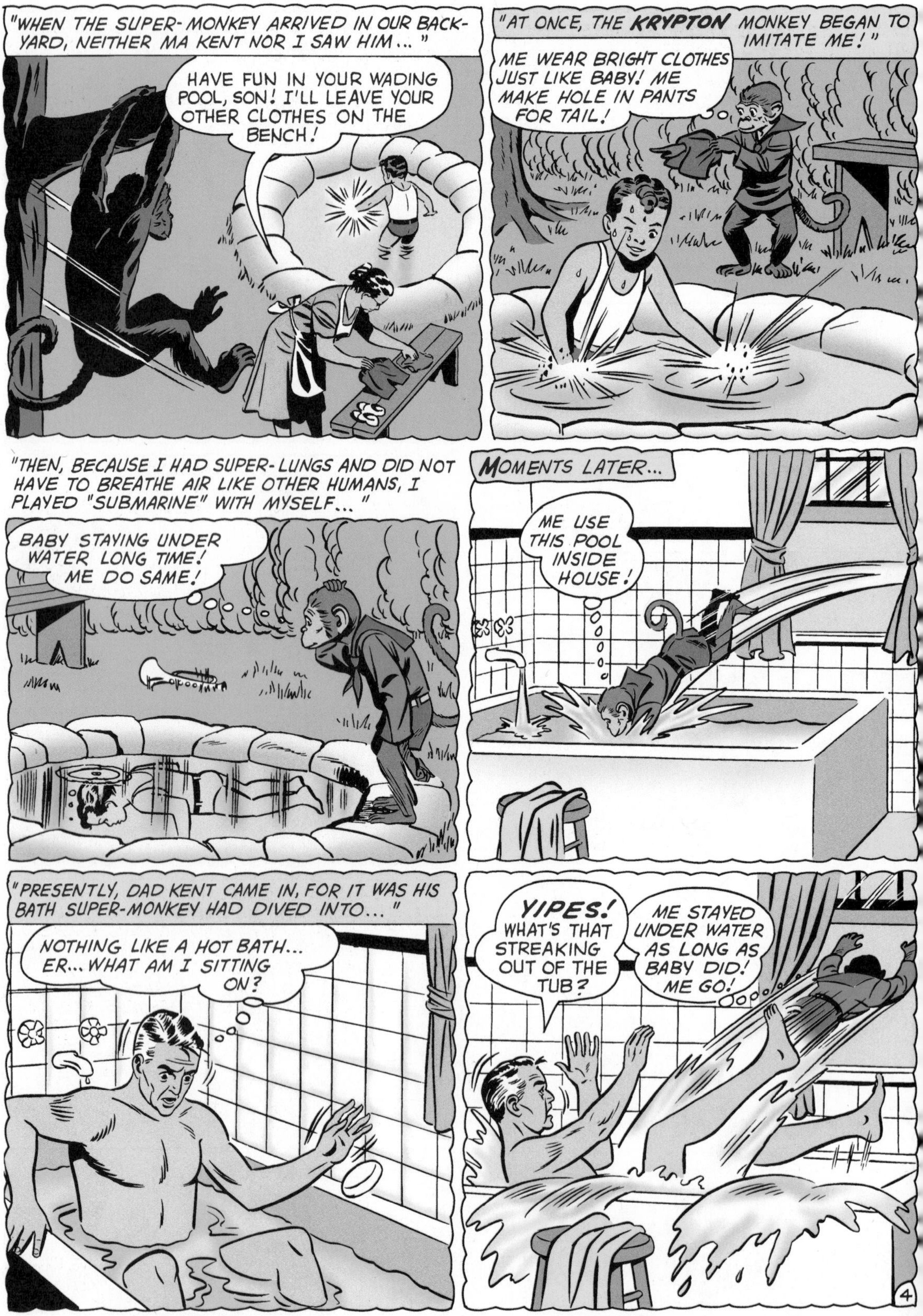
"WHEN THE SUPER-MONKEY ARRIVED IN OUR BACK-YARD, NEITHER MA KENT NOR I SAW HIM..."
HAVE FUN IN YOUR WADING POOL, SON! I'LL LEAVE YOUR OTHER CLOTHES ON THE BENCH!
"AT ONCE, THE KRYPTON MONKEY BEGAN TO IMITATE ME!"
ME WEAR BRIGHT CLOTHES JUST LIKE BABY! ME MAKE HOLE IN PANTS FOR TAIL!
"THEN, BECAUSE I HAD SUPER-LUNGS AND DID NOT HAVE TO BREATHE AIR LIKE OTHER HUMANS, I PLAYED "SUBMARINE" WITH MYSELF..."
BABY STAYING UNDER WATER LONG TIME! ME DO SAME!
MOMENTS LATER...
ME USE THIS POOL INSIDE HOUSE!
"PRESENTLY, DAD KENT CAME IN, FOR IT WAS HIS BATH SUPER-MONKEY HAD DIVED INTO..."
NOTHING LIKE A HOT BATH... ER... WHAT AM I SITTING ON?
YIPES! WHAT'S THAT STREAKING OUT OF THE TUB?
ME STAYED UNDER WATER AS LONG AS BABY DID! ME GO!
4

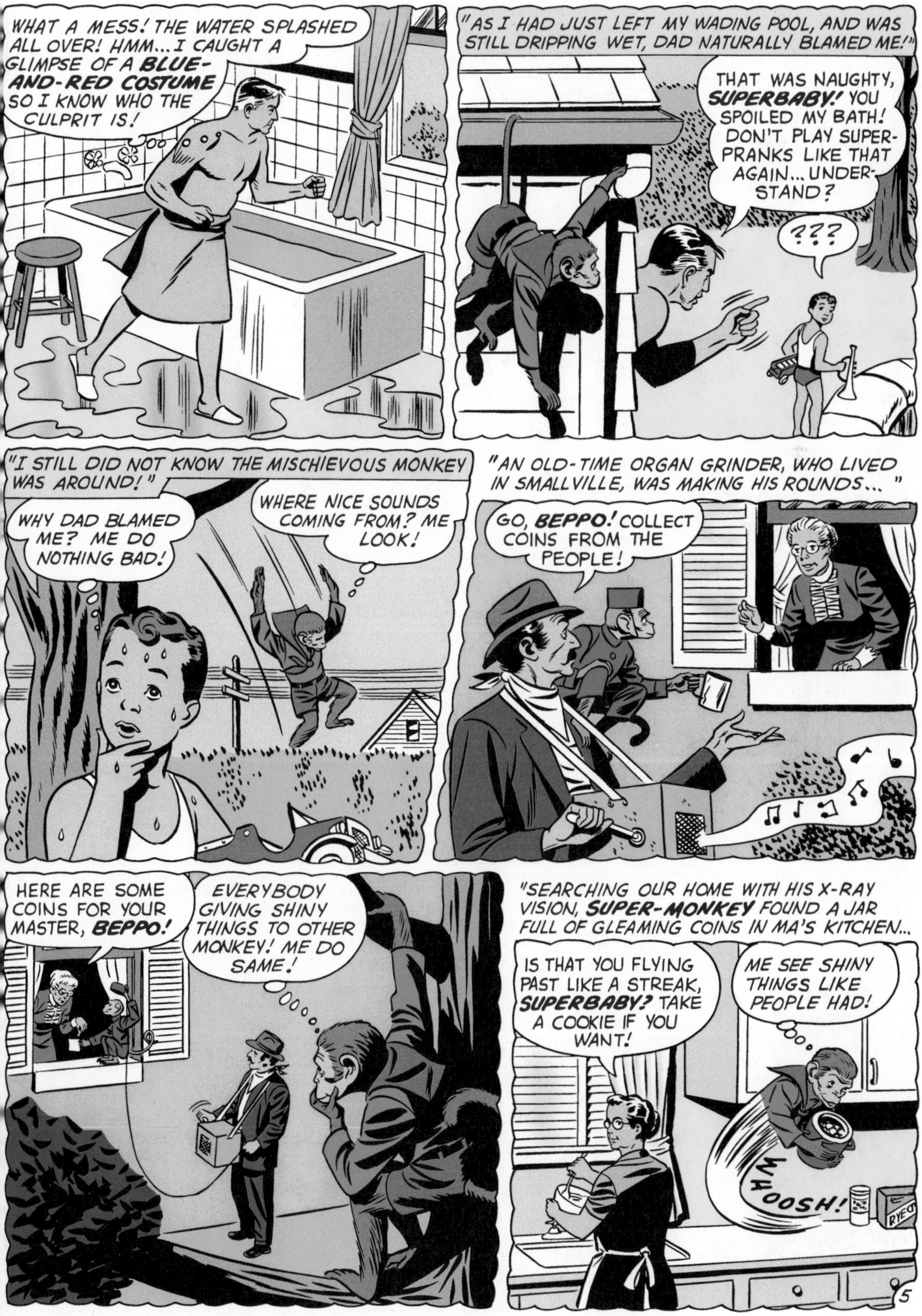
WHAT A MESS! THE WATER SPLASHED ALL OVER! HMM... I CAUGHT A GLIMPSE OF A BLUE-AND-RED COSTUME SO I KNOW WHO THE CULPRIT IS!
"AS I HAD JUST LEFT MY WADING POOL, AND WAS STILL DRIPPING WET, DAD NATURALLY BLAMED ME!"
THAT WAS NAUGHTY, SUPERBABY! YOU SPOILED MY BATH! DON'T PLAY SUPER-PRANKS LIKE THAT AGAIN... UNDERSTAND?
???
"I STILL DID NOT KNOW THE MISCHIEVOUS MONKEY WAS AROUND!"
WHY DAD BLAMED ME? ME DO NOTHING BAD!
WHERE NICE SOUNDS COMING FROM? ME LOOK!
"AN OLD-TIME ORGAN GRINDER, WHO LIVED IN SMALLVILLE, WAS MAKING HIS ROUNDS..."
GO, BEPPO! COLLECT COINS FROM THE PEOPLE!
HERE ARE SOME COINS FOR YOUR MASTER, BEPPO!
EVERYBODY GIVING SHINY THINGS TO OTHER MONKEY! ME DO SAME!
"SEARCHING OUR HOME WITH HIS X-RAY VISION, SUPER-MONKEY FOUND A JAR FULL OF GLEAMING COINS IN MA'S KITCHEN...
IS THAT YOU FLYING PAST LIKE A STREAK, SUPERBABY? TAKE A COOKIE IF YOU WANT!
ME SEE SHINY THINGS LIKE PEOPLE HAD!
WHOOSH!
5

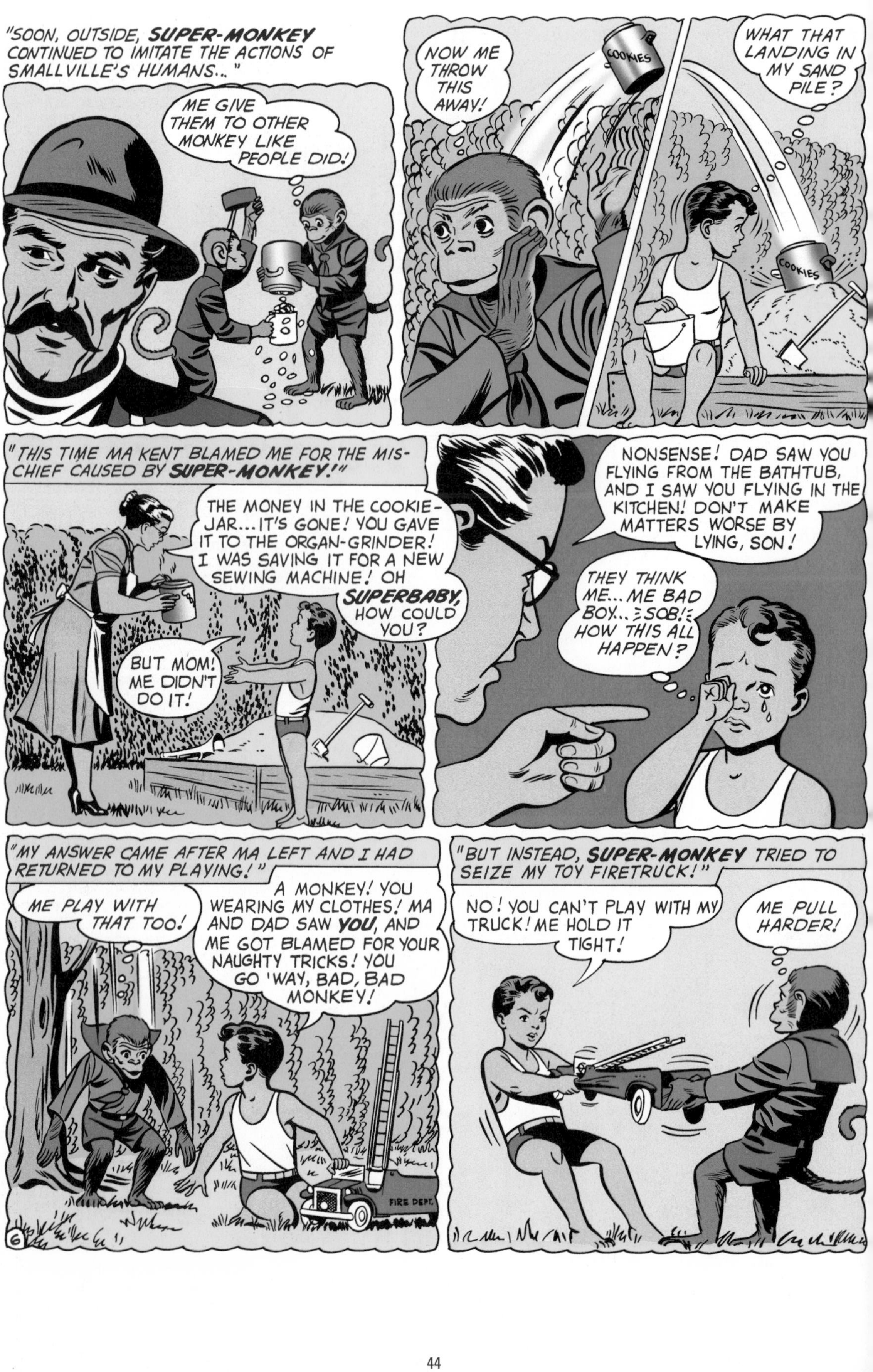
"SOON, OUTSIDE, SUPER-MONKEY CONTINUED TO IMITATE THE ACTIONS OF SMALLVILLE'S HUMANS..."
ME GIVE THEM TO OTHER MONKEY LIKE PEOPLE DID!
NOW ME THROW THIS AWAY!
COOKIES
WHAT THAT LANDING IN MY SAND PILE?
COOKIES
"THIS TIME MA KENT BLAMED ME FOR THE MISCHIEF CAUSED BY SUPER-MONKEY!"
THE MONEY IN THE COOKIE-JAR... IT'S GONE! YOU GAVE IT TO THE ORGAN-GRINDER! I WAS SAVING IT FOR A NEW SEWING MACHINE! OH SUPERBABY, HOW COULD YOU?
BUT MOM! ME DIDN'T DO IT!
NONSENSE! DAD SAW YOU FLYING FROM THE BATHTUB, AND I SAW YOU FLYING IN THE KITCHEN! DON'T MAKE MATTERS WORSE BY LYING, SON!
THEY THINK ME... ME BAD BOY... SOB! HOW THIS ALL HAPPEN?
"MY ANSWER CAME AFTER MA LEFT AND I HAD RETURNED TO MY PLAYING!"
ME PLAY WITH THAT TOO!
A MONKEY! YOU WEARING MY CLOTHES! MA AND DAD SAW YOU, AND ME GOT BLAMED FOR YOUR NAUGHTY TRICKS! YOU GO 'WAY, BAD, BAD MONKEY!
FIRE DEPT.
6
"BUT INSTEAD, SUPER-MONKEY TRIED TO SEIZE MY TOY FIRETRUCK!"
NO! YOU CAN'T PLAY WITH MY TRUCK! ME HOLD IT TIGHT!
ME PULL HARDER!

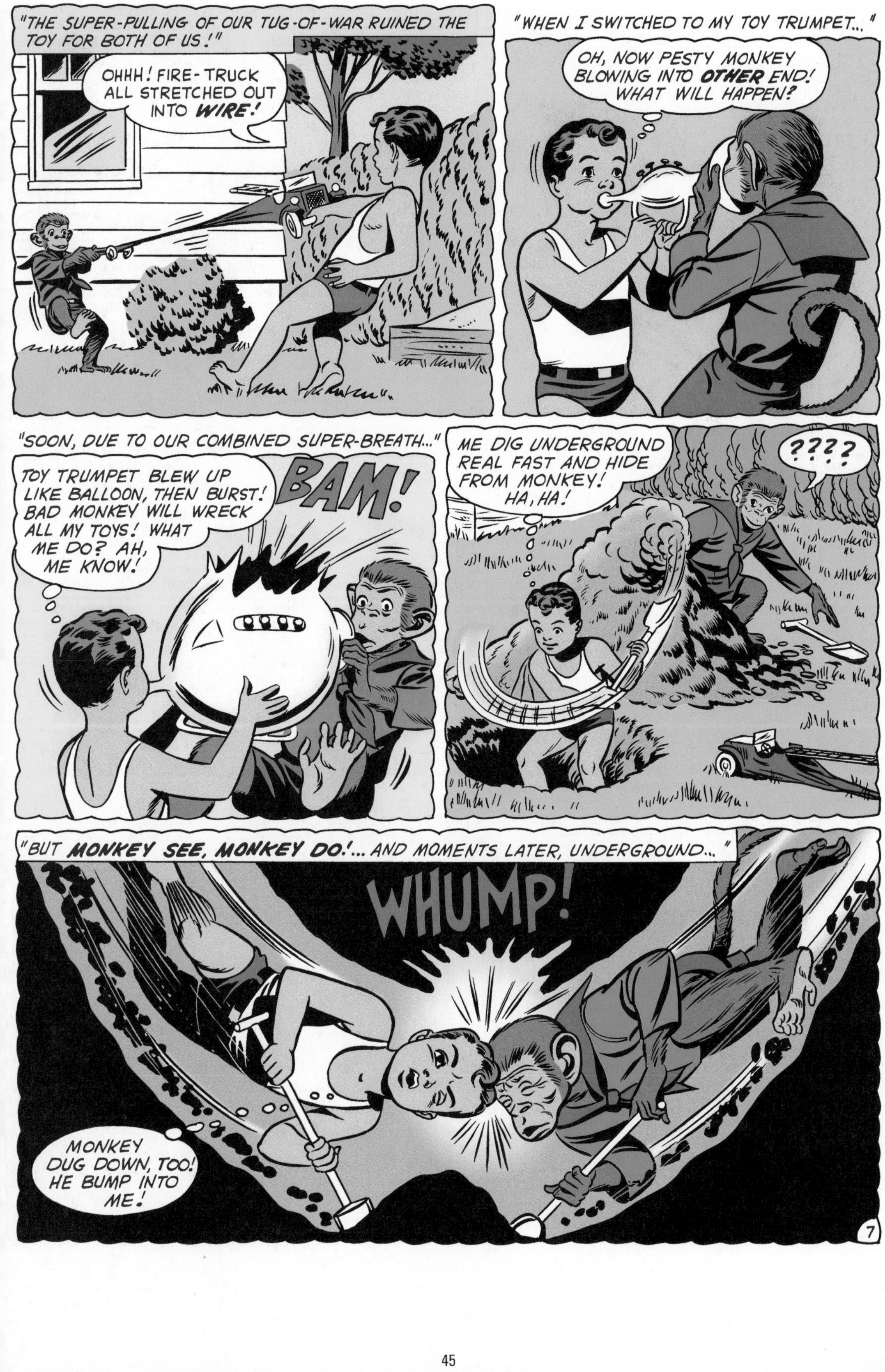
"THE SUPER-PULLING OF OUR TUG-OF-WAR RUINED THE TOY FOR BOTH OF US!"
OHHH! FIRE-TRUCK ALL STRETCHED OUT INTO WIRE!
"WHEN I SWITCHED TO MY TOY TRUMPET..."
OH, NOW PESTY MONKEY BLOWING INTO OTHER END! WHAT WILL HAPPEN?
"SOON, DUE TO OUR COMBINED SUPER-BREATH..."
TOY TRUMPET BLEW UP LIKE BALLOON, THEN BURST! BAD MONKEY WILL WRECK ALL MY TOYS! WHAT ME DO? AH, ME KNOW!
BAM!
ME DIG UNDERGROUND REAL FAST AND HIDE FROM MONKEY! HA, HA!
????
"BUT MONKEY SEE, MONKEY DO!... AND MOMENTS LATER, UNDERGROUND..."
WHUMP!
MONKEY DUG DOWN, TOO! HE BUMP INTO ME!
7

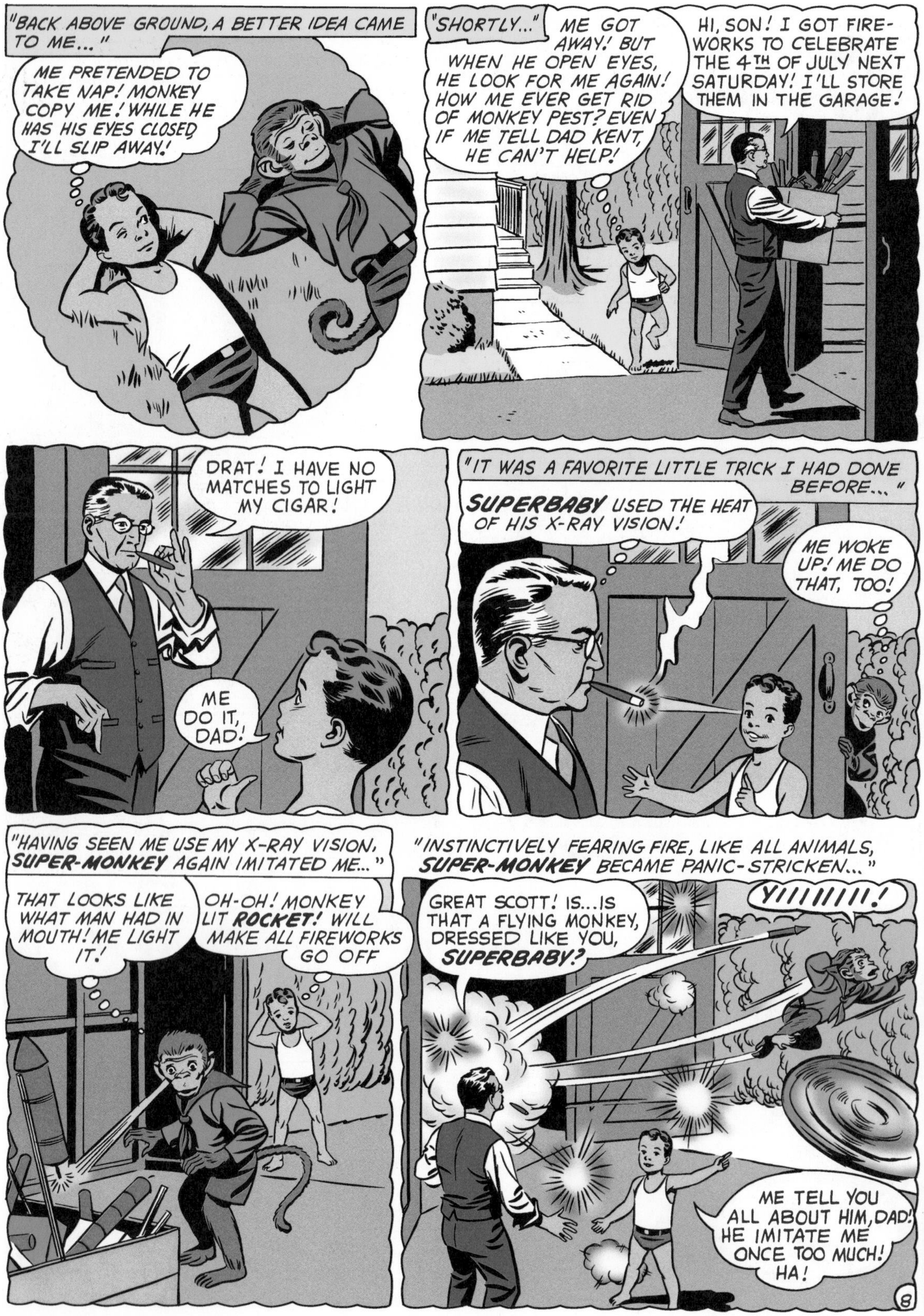
"BACK ABOVE GROUND, A BETTER IDEA CAME TO ME..."
ME PRETENDED TO TAKE NAP! MONKEY COPY ME! WHILE HE HAS HIS EYES CLOSED I'LL SLIP AWAY!
"SHORTLY..."
ME GOT AWAY! BUT WHEN HE OPEN EYES, HE LOOK FOR ME AGAIN! HOW ME EVER GET RID OF MONKEY PEST? EVEN IF ME TELL DAD KENT, HE CAN'T HELP!
HI, SON! I GOT FIRE-WORKS TO CELEBRATE THE 4TH OF JULY NEXT SATURDAY! I'LL STORE THEM IN THE GARAGE!
DRAT! I HAVE NO MATCHES TO LIGHT MY CIGAR!
ME DO IT, DAD!
"IT WAS A FAVORITE LITTLE TRICK I HAD DONE BEFORE..."
SUPERBABY USED THE HEAT OF HIS X-RAY VISION!
ME WOKE UP! ME DO THAT, TOO!
"HAVING SEEN ME USE MY X-RAY VISION, SUPER-MONKEY AGAIN IMITATED ME..."
THAT LOOKS LIKE WHAT MAN HAD IN MOUTH! ME LIGHT IT!
OH-OH! MONKEY LIT ROCKET! WILL MAKE ALL FIREWORKS GO OFF
"INSTINCTIVELY FEARING FIRE, LIKE ALL ANIMALS, SUPER-MONKEY BECAME PANIC-STRICKEN..."
GREAT SCOTT! IS...IS THAT A FLYING MONKEY, DRESSED LIKE YOU, SUPERBABY?
YIIIIIIII!
ME TELL YOU ALL ABOUT HIM, DAD! HE IMITATE ME ONCE TOO MUCH! HA!
8

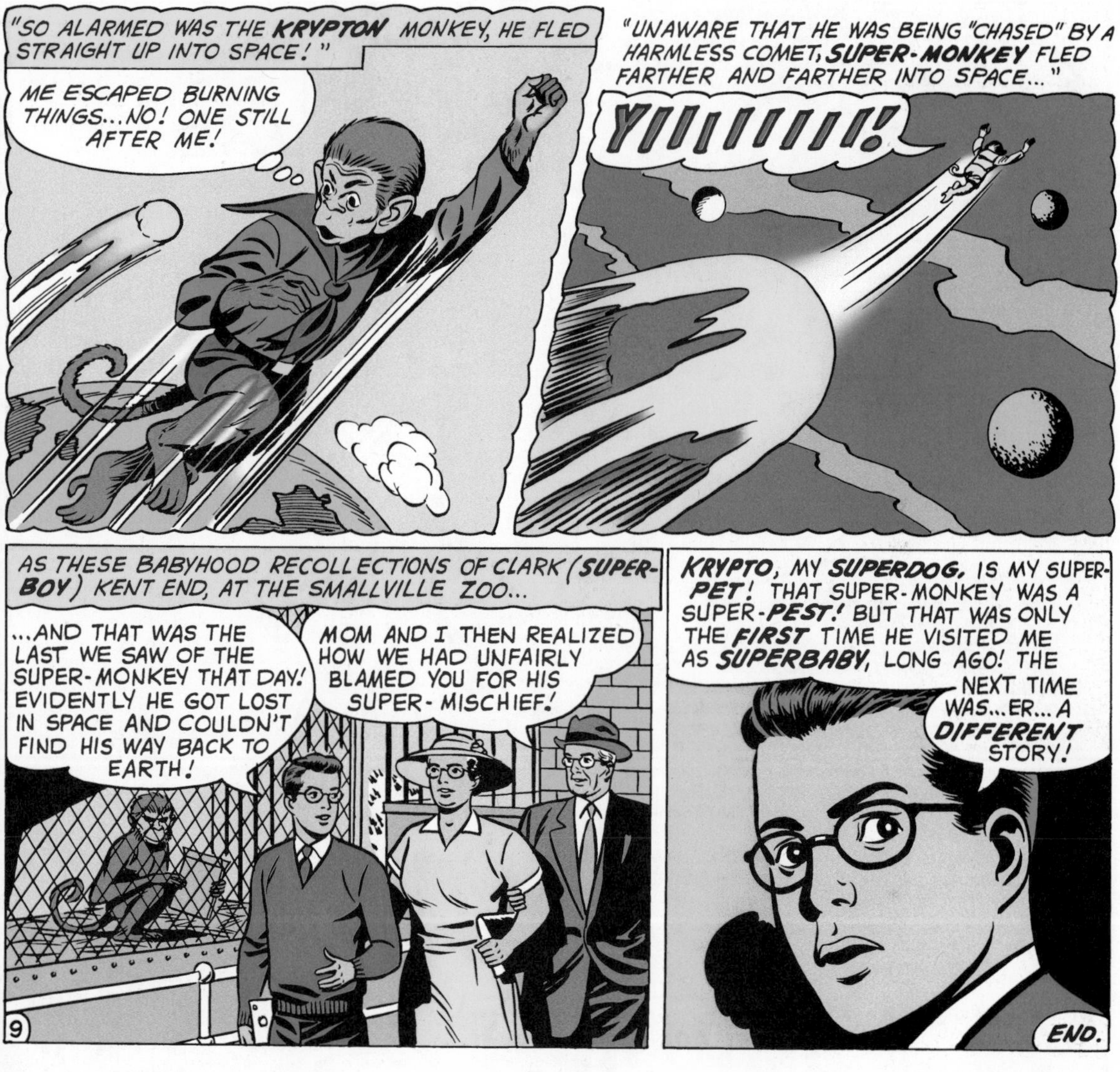
"SO ALARMED WAS THE KRYPTON MONKEY, HE FLED STRAIGHT UP INTO SPACE!"
ME ESCAPED BURNING THINGS...NO! ONE STILL AFTER ME!
"UNAWARE THAT HE WAS BEING "CHASED" BY A HARMLESS COMET, SUPER-MONKEY FLED FARTHER AND FARTHER INTO SPACE..."
YIIIIIIII!
AS THESE BABYHOOD RECOLLECTIONS OF CLARK (SUPERBOY) KENT END, AT THE SMALLVILLE ZOO...
...AND THAT WAS THE LAST WE SAW OF THE SUPER-MONKEY THAT DAY! EVIDENTLY HE GOT LOST IN SPACE AND COULDN'T FIND HIS WAY BACK TO EARTH!
MOM AND I THEN REALIZED HOW WE HAD UNFAIRLY BLAMED YOU FOR HIS SUPER-MISCHIEF!
9
KRYPTO, MY SUPERDOG, IS MY SUPER-PET! THAT SUPER-MONKEY WAS A SUPER-PEST! BUT THAT WAS ONLY THE FIRST TIME HE VISITED ME AS SUPERBABY, LONG AGO! THE NEXT TIME WAS...ER...A DIFFERENT STORY!
END.

SUPERGIRL

SUPER-HORSE, I DON'T KNOW YOUR NAME, OR WHERE YOU CAME FROM, BUT YOU CAME ALONG JUST IN TIME TO SAVE ME FROM THE KRYPTONITE RAYS OF THOSE ENEMY ALIENS!

IMAGINE IT! A **MAGNIFICENT STALLION** APPEARING OUT OF NOWHERE TO FLASH ACROSS THE SKY AT **SUPER-SPEED**. A GALLANT CHARGER WHOSE **IRON HOOFS** CAN LEVEL MOUNTAINS, WHOSE SILKEN HIDE IS **INVULNERABLE** TO THE DEADLIEST OF WEAPONS! **IMPOSSIBLE,** YOU SAY! NO SUCH SUPER-HORSE EXISTS,... YET, THESE ARE THE POWERS OF THE **FANTASTIC STEED** FATED TO BE **SUPERGIRL'S** COMPANION AS SHE BATTLES AGAINST THE FORCES OF CRIME AND EVIL! WHAT IS THE ORIGIN OF THIS AMAZING HORSE? HOW DID HE GAIN HIS INCREDIBLE SUPER-POWERS? WHAT MYSTERIOUS MISSION BRINGS HIM TO **SUPERGIRL'S** SIDE? EVEN **SUPERGIRL** HERSELF IS BAFFLED BY THE EERIE MYSTERY OF...

the SUPER-STEED of STEEL!

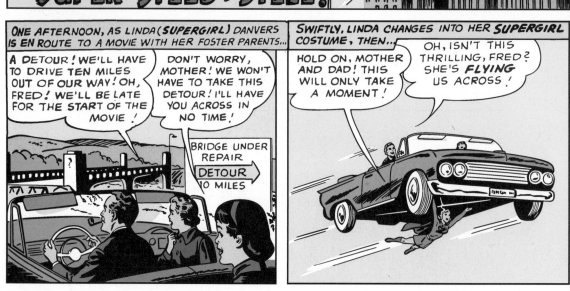

ONE AFTERNOON, AS LINDA (**SUPERGIRL**) DANVERS IS EN ROUTE TO A MOVIE WITH HER FOSTER PARENTS...

A DETOUR! WE'LL HAVE TO DRIVE TEN MILES OUT OF OUR WAY! OH, FRED! WE'LL BE LATE FOR THE START OF THE MOVIE!

DON'T WORRY, MOTHER! WE WON'T HAVE TO TAKE THIS DETOUR! I'LL HAVE YOU ACROSS IN NO TIME!

BRIDGE UNDER REPAIR
DETOUR
10 MILES

SWIFTLY, LINDA CHANGES INTO HER **SUPERGIRL** COSTUME, THEN...

HOLD ON, MOTHER AND DAD! THIS WILL ONLY TAKE A MOMENT!

OH, ISN'T THIS THRILLING, FRED? SHE'S **FLYING** US ACROSS!

SOON THE HAPPY DANVERS FAMILY RESUMES ITS JOURNEY...

WE'RE THE **LUCKIEST PARENTS** ALIVE TO HAVE **SUPERGIRL** AS A DAUGHTER!

I COULD JUST BURST WITH PRIDE TELLING FRIENDS OUR LINDA IS **SUPERGIRL**... BUT WE MUST KEEP IT A SECRET!

¡CHOKE!¡ MOM... DAD, YOU'RE SO SWEET TO ME!

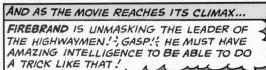

AND AS THE MOVIE REACHES ITS CLIMAX...

FIREBRAND IS UNMASKING THE LEADER OF THE HIGHWAYMEN!¡ GASP!¡ HE MUST HAVE AMAZING INTELLIGENCE TO BE ABLE TO DO A TRICK LIKE THAT!

AT THE MOVIE... THAT'S THE FAMOUS WONDER HORSE, **FIREBRAND**! HE'S CARRYING THAT COWBOY STAR ACROSS A CHASM AS EASILY AS I CARRIED OUR FAMILY CAR ACROSS THAT BROKEN BRIDGE!

THAT NIGHT, IN HER ROOM, AS LINDA RETIRES...

I KEEP THINKING ABOUT **FIREBRAND**! OH, WOULDN'T IT BE EXCITING IF I COULD HAVE A WONDER HORSE **FOR MY OWN**? THE FUN WE COULD HAVE TOGETHER! GOSH, JUST THINKING ABOUT IT GIVES ME GOOSE FLESH! I HOPE I CAN FALL ASLEEP TONIGHT!

SURE ENOUGH, LINDA'S RESTLESS SLEEP IS DISTURBED BY A STRANGE DREAM...

REPEATING THE BULLETIN! ATTENTION ALL LISTENERS! AN ALIEN SPACE-FLEET IS ATTACKING **METROPOLIS**! CIVILIANS ARE ORDERED TO EVACUATE THE CITY AT ONCE!

OMIGOSH!

THE ALIEN RAIDERS ARE DESTROYING **METROPOLIS'** TALLEST SKYSCRAPERS! **CALLING SUPERMAN**! IF YOU ARE WITHIN REACH, RESPOND TO THIS EMERGENCY **AT ONCE**!

SUPERMAN CAN'T ANSWER THAT CALL! HE'S OFF IN A DISTANT GALAXY! I'LL HAVE TO TACKLE THIS JOB MYSELF!

②

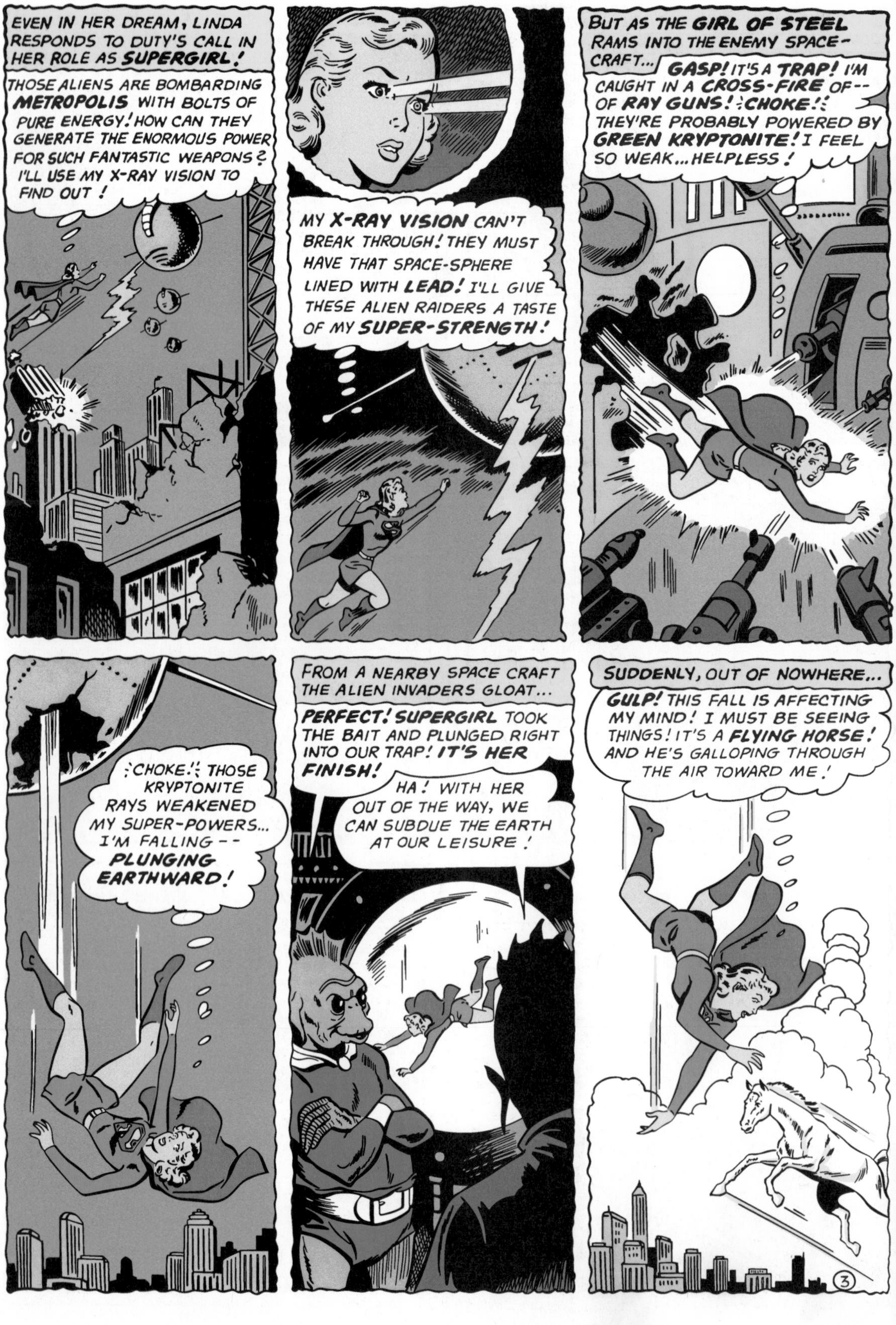
EVEN IN HER DREAM, LINDA RESPONDS TO DUTY'S CALL IN HER ROLE AS SUPERGIRL!
THOSE ALIENS ARE BOMBARDING METROPOLIS WITH BOLTS OF PURE ENERGY! HOW CAN THEY GENERATE THE ENORMOUS POWER FOR SUCH FANTASTIC WEAPONS? I'LL USE MY X-RAY VISION TO FIND OUT!
MY X-RAY VISION CAN'T BREAK THROUGH! THEY MUST HAVE THAT SPACE-SPHERE LINED WITH LEAD! I'LL GIVE THESE ALIEN RAIDERS A TASTE OF MY SUPER-STRENGTH!
BUT AS THE GIRL OF STEEL RAMS INTO THE ENEMY SPACE-CRAFT...
GASP! IT'S A TRAP! I'M CAUGHT IN A CROSS-FIRE OF-- OF RAY GUNS! CHOKE! THEY'RE PROBABLY POWERED BY GREEN KRYPTONITE! I FEEL SO WEAK... HELPLESS!
CHOKE! THOSE KRYPTONITE RAYS WEAKENED MY SUPER-POWERS... I'M FALLING-- PLUNGING EARTHWARD!
FROM A NEARBY SPACE CRAFT THE ALIEN INVADERS GLOAT...
PERFECT! SUPERGIRL TOOK THE BAIT AND PLUNGED RIGHT INTO OUR TRAP! IT'S HER FINISH!
HA! WITH HER OUT OF THE WAY, WE CAN SUBDUE THE EARTH AT OUR LEISURE!
SUDDENLY, OUT OF NOWHERE...
GULP! THIS FALL IS AFFECTING MY MIND! I MUST BE SEEING THINGS! IT'S A FLYING HORSE! AND HE'S GALLOPING THROUGH THE AIR TOWARD ME!
3

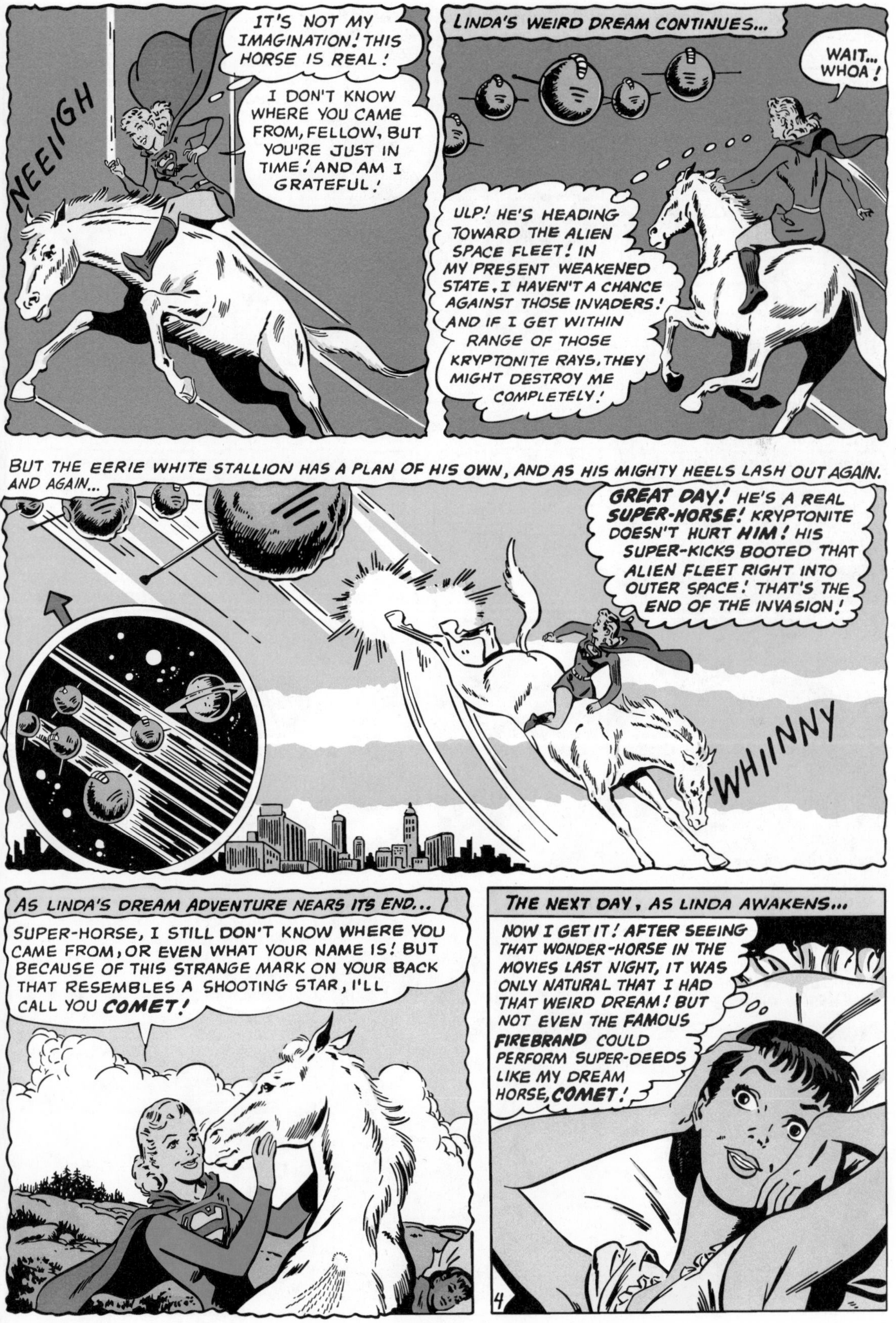

IT'S NOT MY IMAGINATION! THIS HORSE IS REAL!
I DON'T KNOW WHERE YOU CAME FROM, FELLOW, BUT YOU'RE JUST IN TIME! AND AM I GRATEFUL!
NEEIGH
LINDA'S WEIRD DREAM CONTINUES...
WAIT... WHOA!
ULP! HE'S HEADING TOWARD THE ALIEN SPACE FLEET! IN MY PRESENT WEAKENED STATE, I HAVEN'T A CHANCE AGAINST THOSE INVADERS! AND IF I GET WITHIN RANGE OF THOSE KRYPTONITE RAYS, THEY MIGHT DESTROY ME COMPLETELY!
BUT THE EERIE WHITE STALLION HAS A PLAN OF HIS OWN, AND AS HIS MIGHTY HEELS LASH OUT AGAIN. AND AGAIN...
GREAT DAY! HE'S A REAL SUPER-HORSE! KRYPTONITE DOESN'T HURT HIM! HIS SUPER-KICKS BOOTED THAT ALIEN FLEET RIGHT INTO OUTER SPACE! THAT'S THE END OF THE INVASION!
WHIINNY
AS LINDA'S DREAM ADVENTURE NEARS ITS END...
SUPER-HORSE, I STILL DON'T KNOW WHERE YOU CAME FROM, OR EVEN WHAT YOUR NAME IS! BUT BECAUSE OF THIS STRANGE MARK ON YOUR BACK THAT RESEMBLES A SHOOTING STAR, I'LL CALL YOU COMET!
THE NEXT DAY, AS LINDA AWAKENS...
NOW I GET IT! AFTER SEEING THAT WONDER-HORSE IN THE MOVIES LAST NIGHT, IT WAS ONLY NATURAL THAT I HAD THAT WEIRD DREAM! BUT NOT EVEN THE FAMOUS FIREBRAND COULD PERFORM SUPER-DEEDS LIKE MY DREAM HORSE, COMET!
4

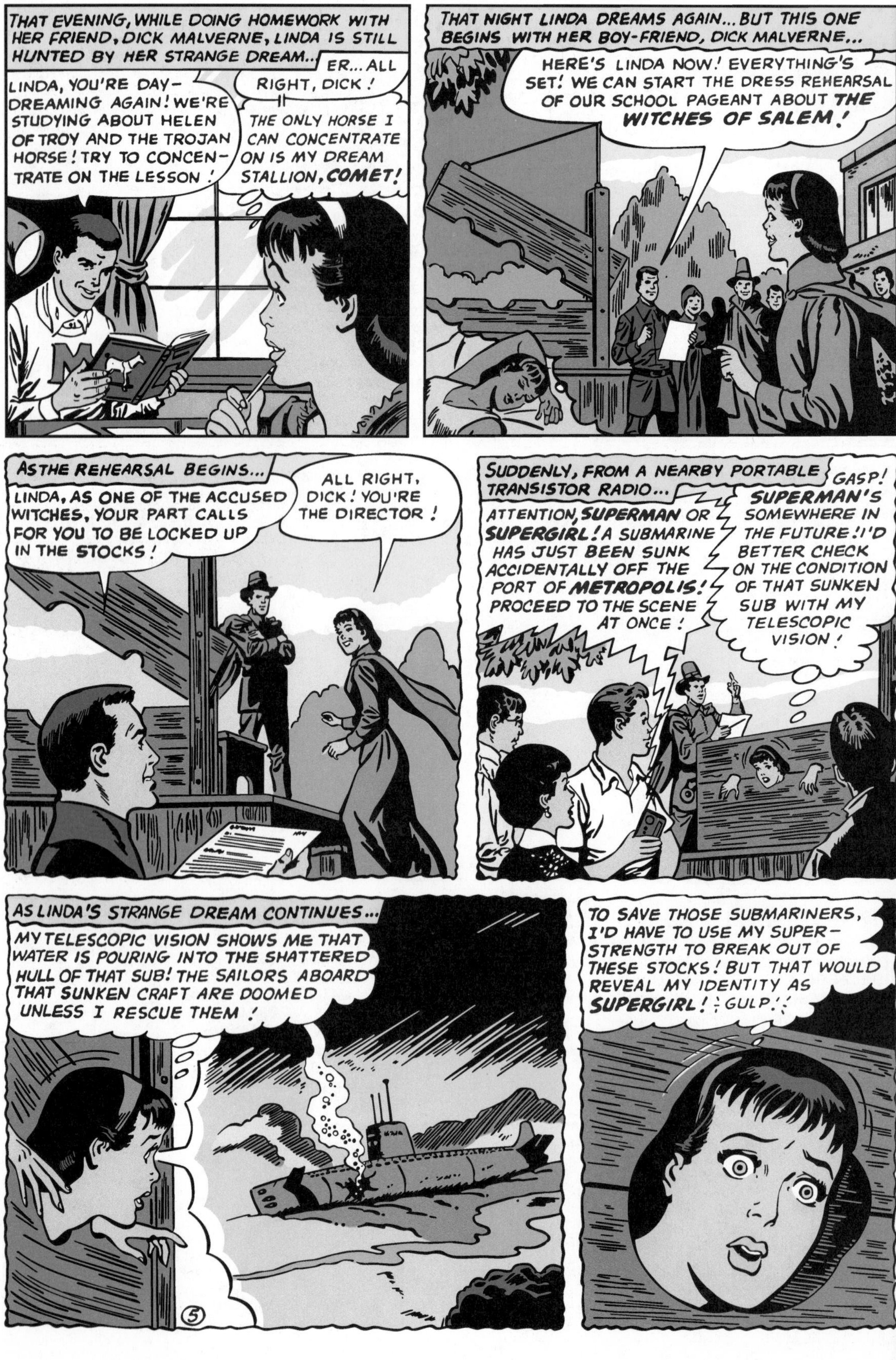
THAT EVENING, WHILE DOING HOMEWORK WITH HER FRIEND, DICK MALVERNE, LINDA IS STILL HUNTED BY HER STRANGE DREAM...
LINDA, YOU'RE DAY-DREAMING AGAIN! WE'RE STUDYING ABOUT HELEN OF TROY AND THE TROJAN HORSE! TRY TO CONCENTRATE ON THE LESSON!
ER... ALL RIGHT, DICK!
THE ONLY HORSE I CAN CONCENTRATE ON IS MY DREAM STALLION, COMET!
THAT NIGHT LINDA DREAMS AGAIN... BUT THIS ONE BEGINS WITH HER BOY-FRIEND, DICK MALVERNE...
HERE'S LINDA NOW! EVERYTHING'S SET! WE CAN START THE DRESS REHEARSAL OF OUR SCHOOL PAGEANT ABOUT THE WITCHES OF SALEM!
AS THE REHEARSAL BEGINS...
LINDA, AS ONE OF THE ACCUSED WITCHES, YOUR PART CALLS FOR YOU TO BE LOCKED UP IN THE STOCKS!
ALL RIGHT, DICK! YOU'RE THE DIRECTOR!
SUDDENLY, FROM A NEARBY PORTABLE TRANSISTOR RADIO...
ATTENTION, SUPERMAN OR SUPERGIRL! A SUBMARINE HAS JUST BEEN SUNK ACCIDENTALLY OFF THE PORT OF METROPOLIS! PROCEED TO THE SCENE AT ONCE!
GASP! SUPERMAN'S SOMEWHERE IN THE FUTURE! I'D BETTER CHECK ON THE CONDITION OF THAT SUNKEN SUB WITH MY TELESCOPIC VISION!
AS LINDA'S STRANGE DREAM CONTINUES...
MY TELESCOPIC VISION SHOWS ME THAT WATER IS POURING INTO THE SHATTERED HULL OF THAT SUB! THE SAILORS ABOARD THAT SUNKEN CRAFT ARE DOOMED UNLESS I RESCUE THEM!
5
TO SAVE THOSE SUBMARINERS, I'D HAVE TO USE MY SUPER-STRENGTH TO BREAK OUT OF THESE STOCKS! BUT THAT WOULD REVEAL MY IDENTITY AS SUPERGIRL! GULP!

AT THAT MOMENT, THE AMAZING WHITE STALLION APPEARS IN LINDA'S DREAM...

GASP! IT'S *COMET!* HE'S PLUNGING DOWN INTO THE OCEAN'S DEPTHS TO SAVE THAT SUBMARINE! ITS IMMENSE WATER PRESSURE DOESN'T BOTHER HIM! HE'S TERRIFIC!

COMET USES HIS SUPER-STRENGTH TO DRAG THE SUB TO SAFETY!

GOOD BOY, *COMET!* THAT'S A SUPER-DEED IF I EVER SAW ONE! AND HE'S DONE ME A SUPER-FAVOR BY ALLOWING ME TO KEEP MY IDENTITY A SECRET!

WITH HER TELESCOPIC VISION, LINDA WATCHES *COMET* FLY AWAY, THEN...

SPECIAL BULLETIN! THE SUBMARINE HAS BEEN SAVED! SOME UNKNOWN HERO DRAGGED THE STRICKEN CRAFT ASHORE! OFFICIALS BELIEVE THE HEROIC DEED WAS BY *SUPERMAN* OR *SUPERGIRL!*

COMET WAS THE REAL HERO! BUT HE'S TOO MODEST TO TAKE THE CREDIT!

AT DAWN, AS LINDA AWAKENS...

GOOD GRIEF! THAT'S THE *SECOND* DREAM I HAD ABOUT THAT SUPER-STALLION, *COMET!* GOSH! I'M EVEN CALLING HIM BY NAME NOW! IT'S ALMOST AS IF MY DREAM-HORSE WAS *REAL!*

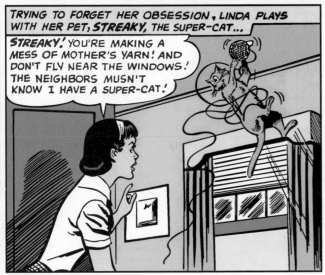

TRYING TO FORGET HER OBSESSION, LINDA PLAYS WITH HER PET, *STREAKY,* THE SUPER-CAT...

STREAKY! YOU'RE MAKING A MESS OF MOTHER'S YARN! AND DON'T FLY NEAR THE WINDOWS! THE NEIGHBORS MUSN'T KNOW I HAVE A SUPER-CAT!

BUT LINDA'S THOUGHTS INEVITABLY TURN TO *COMET...*

STREAKY! YOU'RE A LITTLE DICKENS! WHY DON'T YOU LEARN TO BEHAVE? SIGH! YOU SHOULD LEARN TO USE YOUR SUPER-POWERS TO DO USEFUL THINGS THE WAY *COMET* DOES!

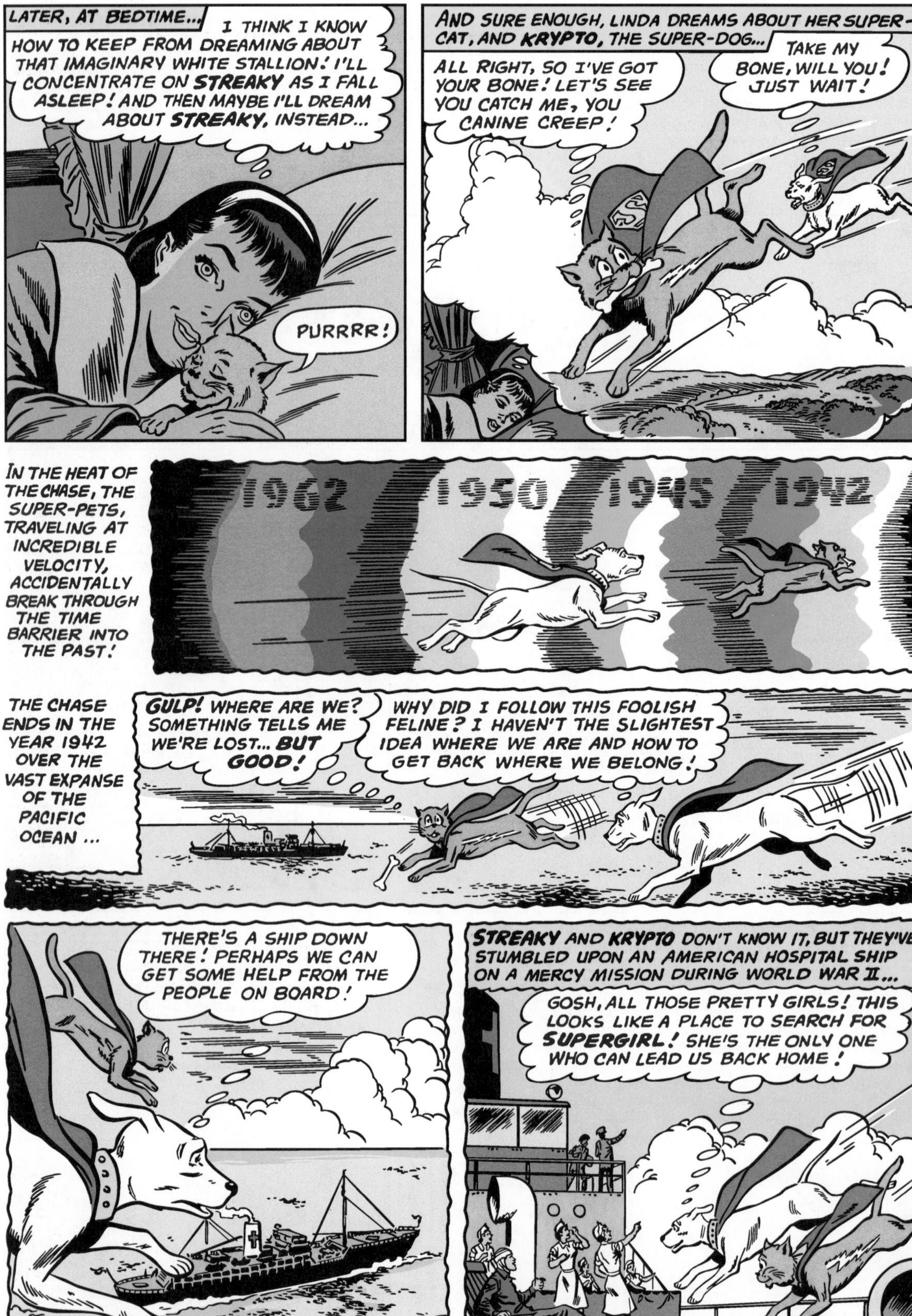
LATER, AT BEDTIME...
I THINK I KNOW HOW TO KEEP FROM DREAMING ABOUT THAT IMAGINARY WHITE STALLION! I'LL CONCENTRATE ON STREAKY AS I FALL ASLEEP! AND THEN MAYBE I'LL DREAM ABOUT STREAKY, INSTEAD...
PURRRR!
AND SURE ENOUGH, LINDA DREAMS ABOUT HER SUPER-CAT, AND KRYPTO, THE SUPER-DOG...
ALL RIGHT, SO I'VE GOT YOUR BONE! LET'S SEE YOU CATCH ME, YOU CANINE CREEP!
TAKE MY BONE, WILL YOU! JUST WAIT!
IN THE HEAT OF THE CHASE, THE SUPER-PETS, TRAVELING AT INCREDIBLE VELOCITY, ACCIDENTALLY BREAK THROUGH THE TIME BARRIER INTO THE PAST!
1962
1950
1945
1942
THE CHASE ENDS IN THE YEAR 1942 OVER THE VAST EXPANSE OF THE PACIFIC OCEAN...
GULP! WHERE ARE WE? SOMETHING TELLS ME WE'RE LOST... BUT GOOD!
WHY DID I FOLLOW THIS FOOLISH FELINE? I HAVEN'T THE SLIGHTEST IDEA WHERE WE ARE AND HOW TO GET BACK WHERE WE BELONG!
THERE'S A SHIP DOWN THERE! PERHAPS WE CAN GET SOME HELP FROM THE PEOPLE ON BOARD!
7
STREAKY AND KRYPTO DON'T KNOW IT, BUT THEY'VE STUMBLED UPON AN AMERICAN HOSPITAL SHIP ON A MERCY MISSION DURING WORLD WAR II...
GOSH, ALL THOSE PRETTY GIRLS! THIS LOOKS LIKE A PLACE TO SEARCH FOR SUPERGIRL! SHE'S THE ONLY ONE WHO CAN LEAD US BACK HOME!

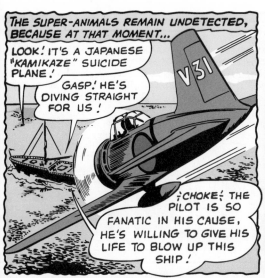

THE SUPER-ANIMALS REMAIN UNDETECTED, BECAUSE AT THAT MOMENT...

LOOK! IT'S A JAPANESE "KAMIKAZE" SUICIDE PLANE!

GASP! HE'S DIVING STRAIGHT FOR US!

¡CHOKE! THE PILOT IS SO FANATIC IN HIS CAUSE, HE'S WILLING TO GIVE HIS LIFE TO BLOW UP THIS SHIP!

BUT AT THAT CRITICAL MOMENT, A MIGHTY STALLION SMASHES THROUGH THE TIME-BARRIER...

WAIT! LOOK UP THERE, ABOVE THAT "KAMIKAZE" PLANE! DO YOU SEE WHAT I SEE?

IT'S A HORSE! A FLYING WHITE STALLION! HE'S HEADING FOR THE PLANE!

IT'S COMET, THE SUPER-HORSE OF LINDA'S WEIRD DREAMS... AND AT SUPER-SPEED, HE INTERCEPTS THE ATTACKING PLANE...

WE MUST BE SEEING THINGS! THAT JAPANESE PLANE STRUCK THE FLYING HORSE AND JUST DISINTEGRATED!

AS LINDA'S DREAM ENDS, THE SUPER-STALLION COMPLETES HIS MISSION, GUIDING KRYPTO AND STREAKY BACK INTO THE YEAR 1962...

THE NEXT MORNING, AS LINDA AWAKENS...

THOSE CONSTANT DREAMS ABOUT A WHITE SUPER-STALLION ARE BEGINNING TO WORRY ME! I'VE GOT TO FIND SOME WAY OF GETTING THAT IMAGINARY HORSE OUT OF MY MIND!

AND THAT AFTERNOON, FATE COMES TO LINDA'S RESCUE...

LINDA, I'VE GOT A WEEK'S VACATION COMING TO ME! I'M PLANNING TO TAKE IT NEXT WEEK, WHEN THE SCHOOL INTERSESSION BEGINS!

WE'RE PLANNING A TRIP, DEAR! WHERE WOULD YOU LIKE TO GO? THE MOUNTAINS? THE SEA SHORE?

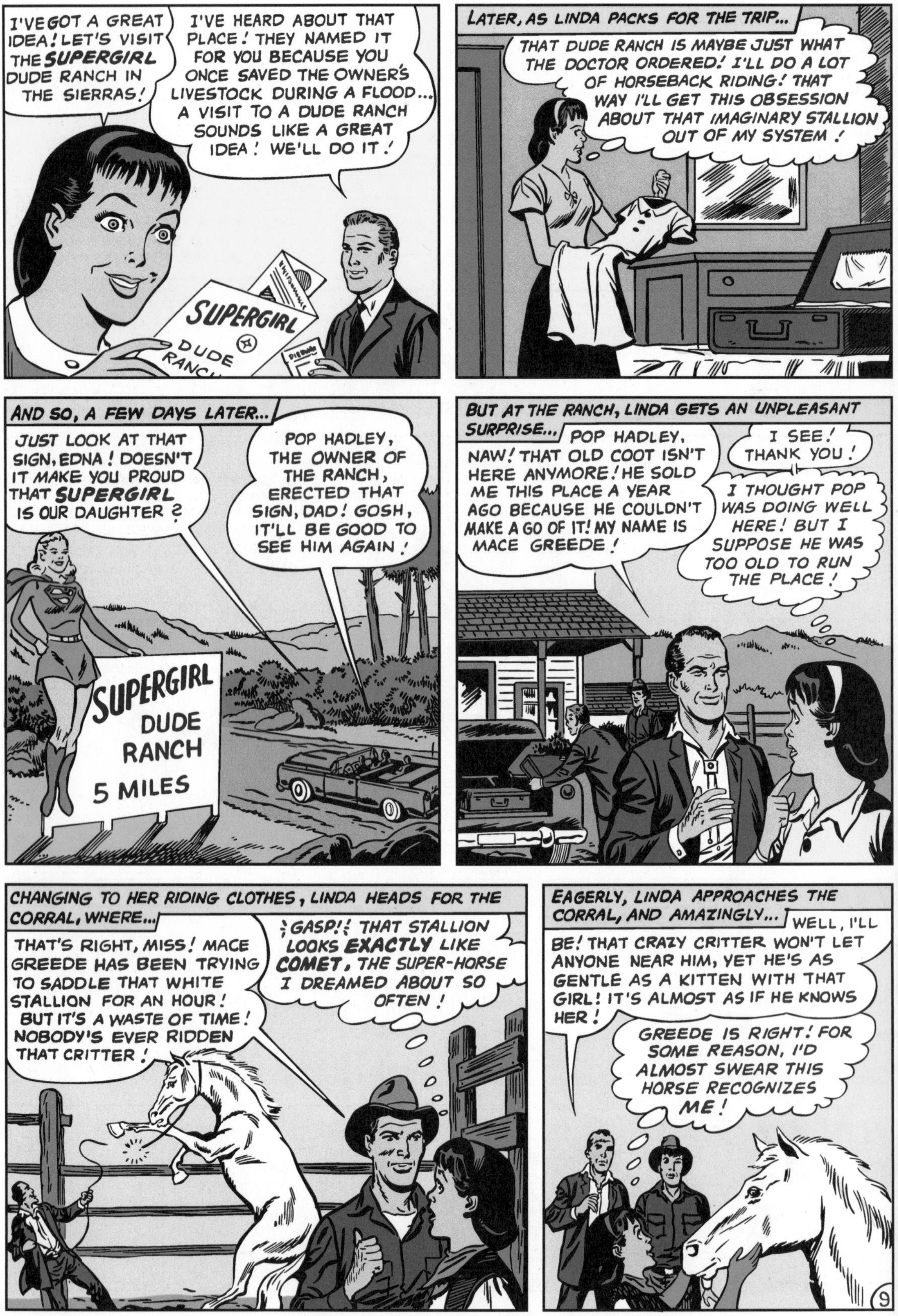
I'VE GOT A GREAT IDEA! LET'S VISIT THE SUPERGIRL DUDE RANCH IN THE SIERRAS!
I'VE HEARD ABOUT THAT PLACE! THEY NAMED IT FOR YOU BECAUSE YOU ONCE SAVED THE OWNER'S LIVESTOCK DURING A FLOOD... A VISIT TO A DUDE RANCH SOUNDS LIKE A GREAT IDEA! WE'LL DO IT!
SUPERGIRL DUDE RANCH
LATER, AS LINDA PACKS FOR THE TRIP...
THAT DUDE RANCH IS MAYBE JUST WHAT THE DOCTOR ORDERED! I'LL DO A LOT OF HORSEBACK RIDING! THAT WAY I'LL GET THIS OBSESSION ABOUT THAT IMAGINARY STALLION OUT OF MY SYSTEM!
AND SO, A FEW DAYS LATER...
JUST LOOK AT THAT SIGN, EDNA! DOESN'T IT MAKE YOU PROUD THAT SUPERGIRL IS OUR DAUGHTER?
POP HADLEY, THE OWNER OF THE RANCH, ERECTED THAT SIGN, DAD! GOSH, IT'LL BE GOOD TO SEE HIM AGAIN!
SUPERGIRL DUDE RANCH 5 MILES
BUT AT THE RANCH, LINDA GETS AN UNPLEASANT SURPRISE...
POP HADLEY. NAW! THAT OLD COOT ISN'T HERE ANYMORE! HE SOLD ME THIS PLACE A YEAR AGO BECAUSE HE COULDN'T MAKE A GO OF IT! MY NAME IS MACE GREEDE!
I SEE! THANK YOU!
I THOUGHT POP WAS DOING WELL HERE! BUT I SUPPOSE HE WAS TOO OLD TO RUN THE PLACE!
CHANGING TO HER RIDING CLOTHES, LINDA HEADS FOR THE CORRAL, WHERE...
THAT'S RIGHT, MISS! MACE GREEDE HAS BEEN TRYING TO SADDLE THAT WHITE STALLION FOR AN HOUR! BUT IT'S A WASTE OF TIME! NOBODY'S EVER RIDDEN THAT CRITTER!
GASP! THAT STALLION LOOKS EXACTLY LIKE COMET, THE SUPER-HORSE I DREAMED ABOUT SO OFTEN!
EAGERLY, LINDA APPROACHES THE CORRAL, AND AMAZINGLY...
WELL, I'LL BE! THAT CRAZY CRITTER WON'T LET ANYONE NEAR HIM, YET HE'S AS GENTLE AS A KITTEN WITH THAT GIRL! IT'S ALMOST AS IF HE KNOWS HER!
GREEDE IS RIGHT! FOR SOME REASON, I'D ALMOST SWEAR THIS HORSE RECOGNIZES ME!
9

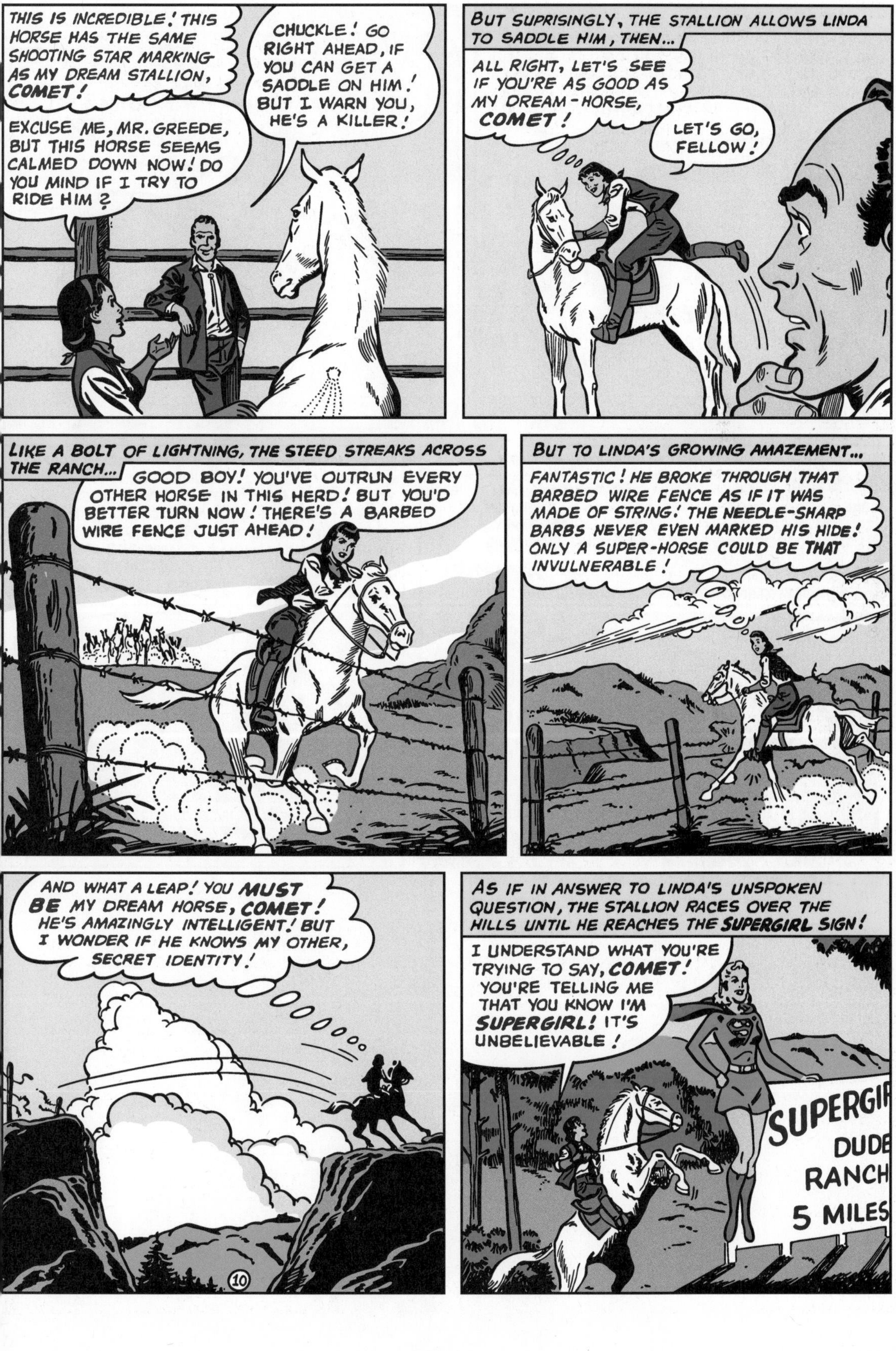
THIS IS INCREDIBLE! THIS HORSE HAS THE SAME SHOOTING STAR MARKING AS MY DREAM STALLION, COMET!
EXCUSE ME, MR. GREEDE, BUT THIS HORSE SEEMS CALMED DOWN NOW! DO YOU MIND IF I TRY TO RIDE HIM?
CHUCKLE! GO RIGHT AHEAD, IF YOU CAN GET A SADDLE ON HIM! BUT I WARN YOU, HE'S A KILLER!
BUT SUPRISINGLY, THE STALLION ALLOWS LINDA TO SADDLE HIM, THEN...
ALL RIGHT, LET'S SEE IF YOU'RE AS GOOD AS MY DREAM-HORSE, COMET!
LET'S GO, FELLOW!
LIKE A BOLT OF LIGHTNING, THE STEED STREAKS ACROSS THE RANCH...
GOOD BOY! YOU'VE OUTRUN EVERY OTHER HORSE IN THIS HERD! BUT YOU'D BETTER TURN NOW! THERE'S A BARBED WIRE FENCE JUST AHEAD!
BUT TO LINDA'S GROWING AMAZEMENT...
FANTASTIC! HE BROKE THROUGH THAT BARBED WIRE FENCE AS IF IT WAS MADE OF STRING! THE NEEDLE-SHARP BARBS NEVER EVEN MARKED HIS HIDE! ONLY A SUPER-HORSE COULD BE THAT INVULNERABLE!
AND WHAT A LEAP! YOU MUST BE MY DREAM HORSE, COMET! HE'S AMAZINGLY INTELLIGENT! BUT I WONDER IF HE KNOWS MY OTHER, SECRET IDENTITY!
10
AS IF IN ANSWER TO LINDA'S UNSPOKEN QUESTION, THE STALLION RACES OVER THE HILLS UNTIL HE REACHES THE SUPERGIRL SIGN!
I UNDERSTAND WHAT YOU'RE TRYING TO SAY, COMET! YOU'RE TELLING ME THAT YOU KNOW I'M SUPERGIRL! IT'S UNBELIEVABLE!
SUPERGIR
DUDE
RANCH
5 MILES

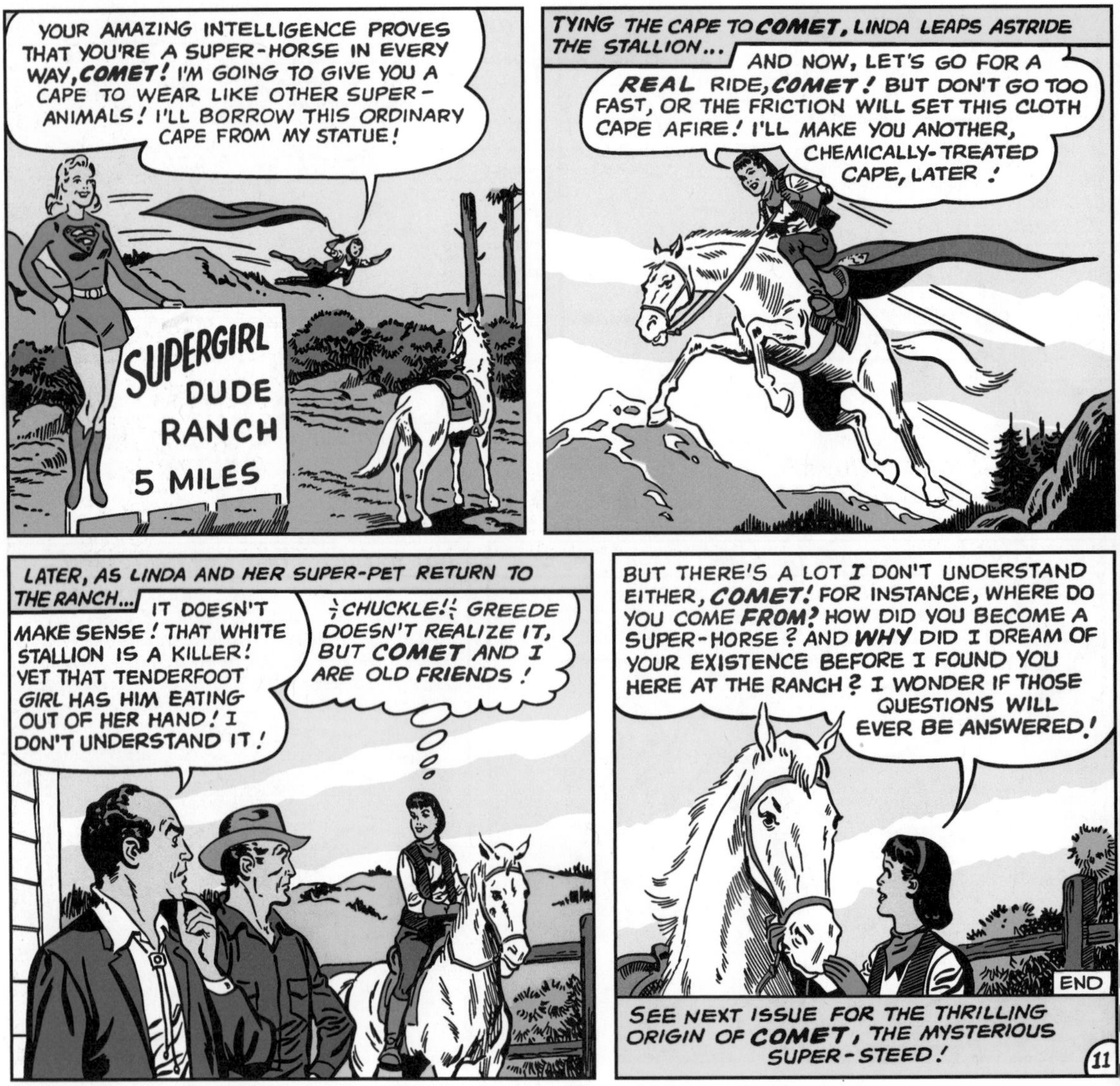

YOUR AMAZING INTELLIGENCE PROVES THAT YOU'RE A SUPER-HORSE IN EVERY WAY, COMET! I'M GOING TO GIVE YOU A CAPE TO WEAR LIKE OTHER SUPER-ANIMALS! I'LL BORROW THIS ORDINARY CAPE FROM MY STATUE!
SUPERGIRL DUDE RANCH 5 MILES
TYING THE CAPE TO COMET, LINDA LEAPS ASTRIDE THE STALLION...
AND NOW, LET'S GO FOR A REAL RIDE, COMET! BUT DON'T GO TOO FAST, OR THE FRICTION WILL SET THIS CLOTH CAPE AFIRE! I'LL MAKE YOU ANOTHER, CHEMICALLY-TREATED CAPE, LATER!
LATER, AS LINDA AND HER SUPER-PET RETURN TO THE RANCH...
IT DOESN'T MAKE SENSE! THAT WHITE STALLION IS A KILLER! YET THAT TENDERFOOT GIRL HAS HIM EATING OUT OF HER HAND! I DON'T UNDERSTAND IT!
CHUCKLE! GREEDE DOESN'T REALIZE IT, BUT COMET AND I ARE OLD FRIENDS!
BUT THERE'S A LOT I DON'T UNDERSTAND EITHER, COMET! FOR INSTANCE, WHERE DO YOU COME FROM? HOW DID YOU BECOME A SUPER-HORSE? AND WHY DID I DREAM OF YOUR EXISTENCE BEFORE I FOUND YOU HERE AT THE RANCH? I WONDER IF THOSE QUESTIONS WILL EVER BE ANSWERED!
END
SEE NEXT ISSUE FOR THE THRILLING ORIGIN OF COMET, THE MYSTERIOUS SUPER-STEED!
11

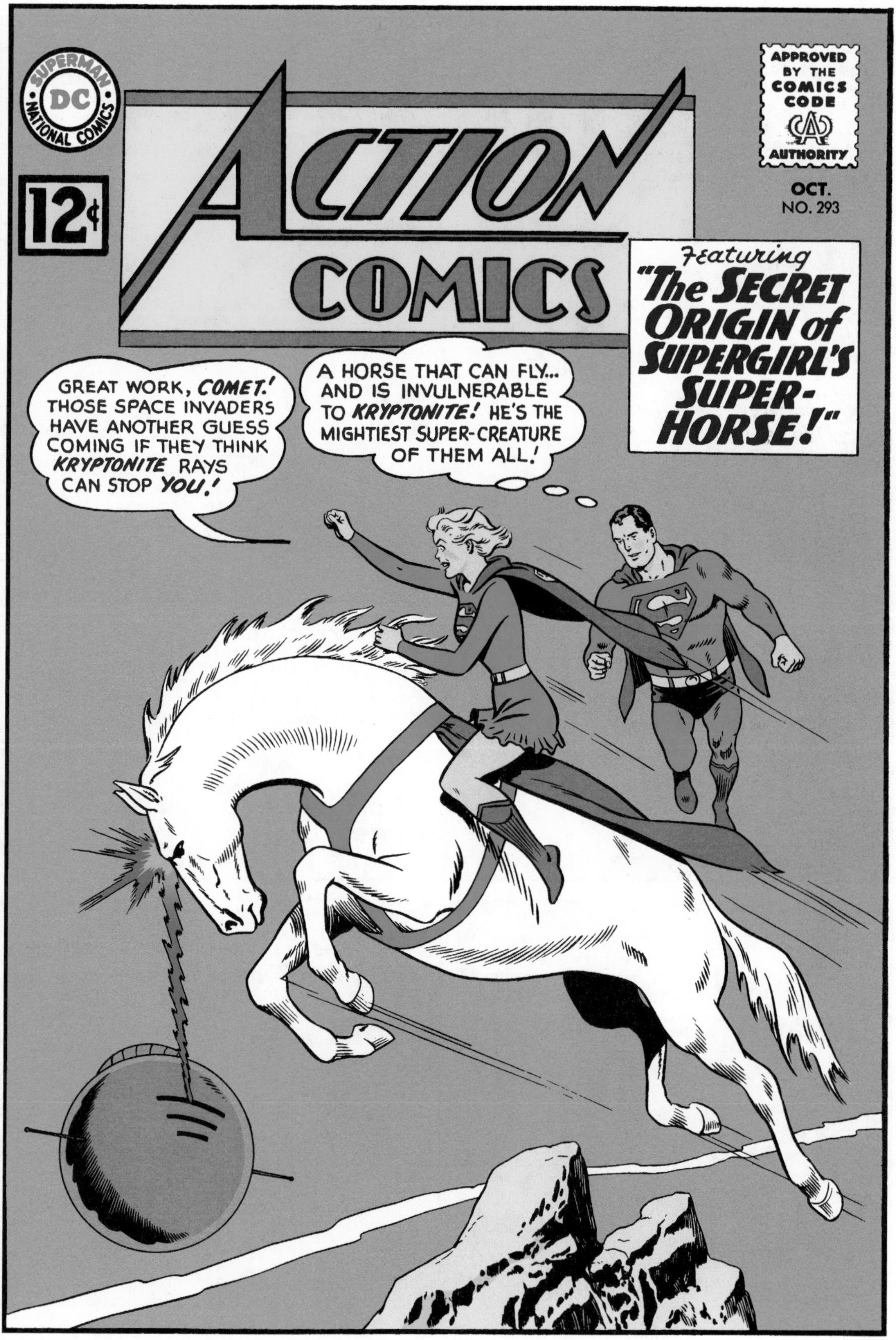
SUPERMAN DC NATIONAL COMICS
12¢
ACTION COMICS
APPROVED BY THE COMICS CODE AUTHORITY
OCT. NO. 293
Featuring "The SECRET ORIGIN of SUPERGIRL'S SUPER-HORSE!"
GREAT WORK, COMET! THOSE SPACE INVADERS HAVE ANOTHER GUESS COMING IF THEY THINK KRYPTONITE RAYS CAN STOP YOU!
A HORSE THAT CAN FLY... AND IS INVULNERABLE TO KRYPTONITE! HE'S THE MIGHTIEST SUPER-CREATURE OF THEM ALL!

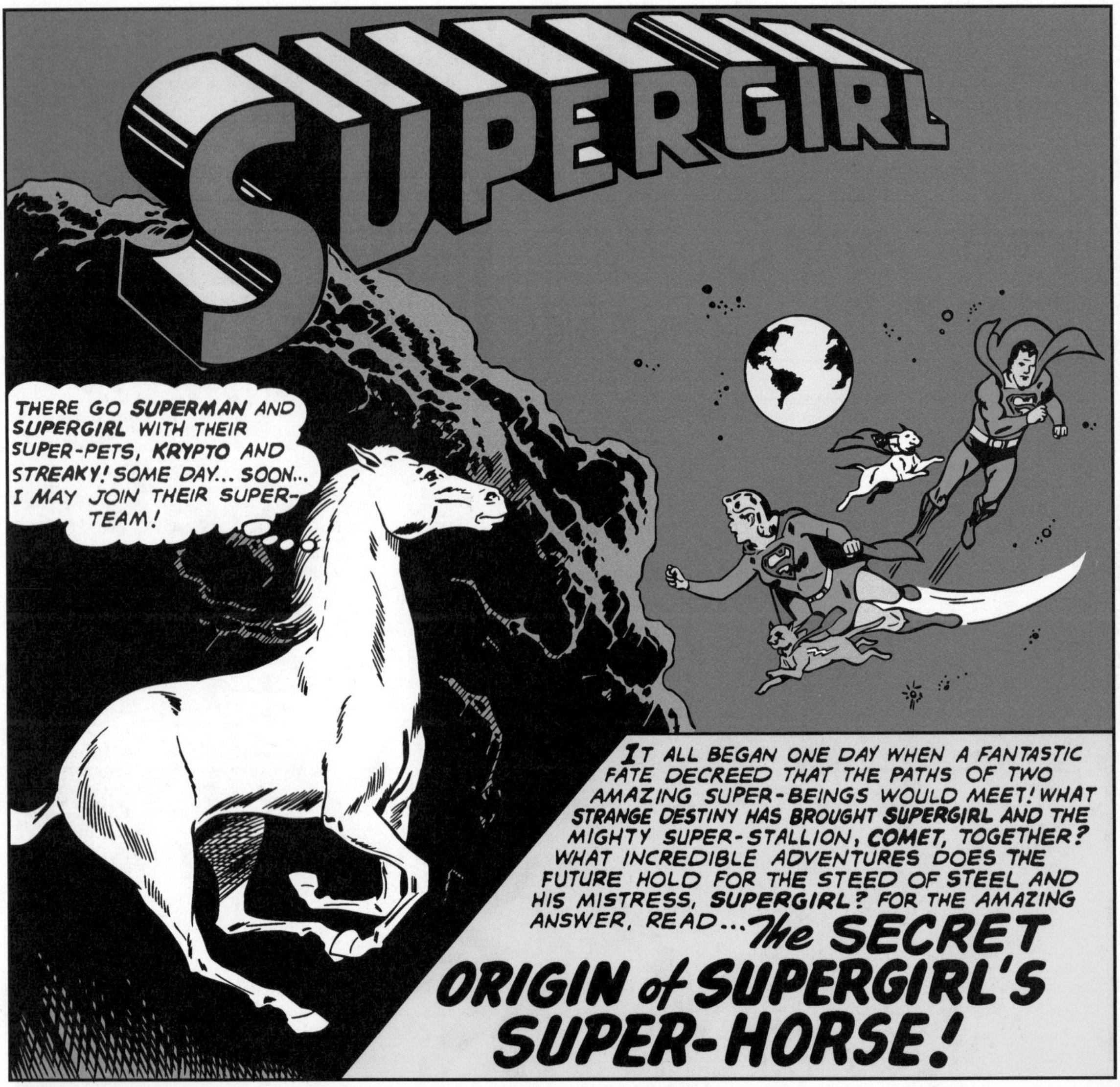
SUPERGIRL
THERE GO SUPERMAN AND SUPERGIRL WITH THEIR SUPER-PETS, KRYPTO AND STREAKY! SOME DAY... SOON... I MAY JOIN THEIR SUPER-TEAM!
IT ALL BEGAN ONE DAY WHEN A FANTASTIC FATE DECREED THAT THE PATHS OF TWO AMAZING SUPER-BEINGS WOULD MEET! WHAT STRANGE DESTINY HAS BROUGHT SUPERGIRL AND THE MIGHTY SUPER-STALLION, COMET, TOGETHER? WHAT INCREDIBLE ADVENTURES DOES THE FUTURE HOLD FOR THE STEED OF STEEL AND HIS MISTRESS, SUPERGIRL? FOR THE AMAZING ANSWER, READ...
The SECRET ORIGIN of SUPERGIRL'S SUPER-HORSE!

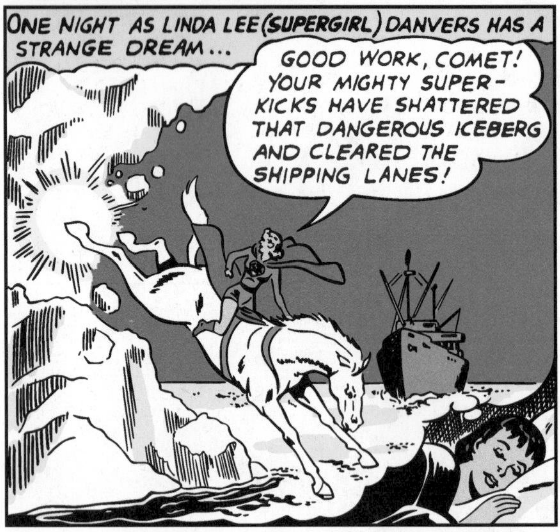
ONE NIGHT AS LINDA LEE (SUPERGIRL) DANVERS HAS A STRANGE DREAM...
GOOD WORK, COMET! YOUR MIGHTY SUPER-KICKS HAVE SHATTERED THAT DANGEROUS ICEBERG AND CLEARED THE SHIPPING LANES!

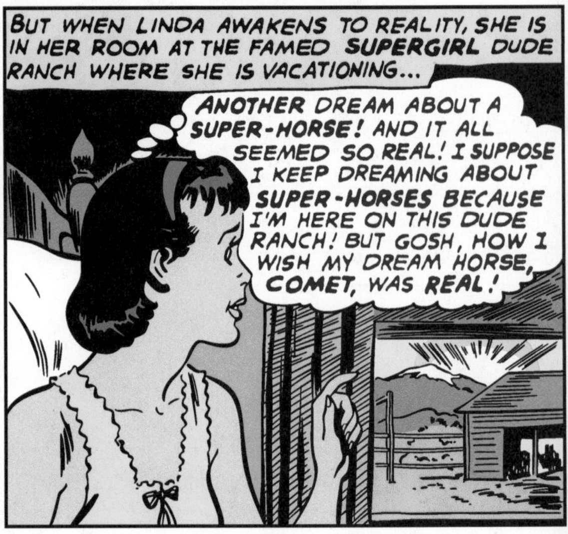
BUT WHEN LINDA AWAKENS TO REALITY, SHE IS IN HER ROOM AT THE FAMED SUPERGIRL DUDE RANCH WHERE SHE IS VACATIONING...
ANOTHER DREAM ABOUT A SUPER-HORSE! AND IT ALL SEEMED SO REAL! I SUPPOSE I KEEP DREAMING ABOUT SUPER-HORSES BECAUSE I'M HERE ON THIS DUDE RANCH! BUT GOSH, HOW I WISH MY DREAM HORSE, COMET, WAS REAL!

BUT JUST THEN AN EERIE FIGURE STREAKS THROUGH THE MORNING SKY!...

IT'S *COMET!* THEN HE'S MORE THAN JUST A DREAM! HE'S *REAL!* YES! I REMEMBER NOW! I FOUND HIM HERE AT THE *SUPERGIRL* RANCH! I EVEN *RODE* HIM!

AS THE SUPER-STALLION SWOOPS TO EARTH...

NOBODY ELSE SAW HIM FLYING BUT *ME!* HE'S JOINING THE OTHER HORSES IN THE CORRAL! OH, THIS IS SO *EXCITING!* I'LL GO DOWN AND VISIT HIM AS SOON AS I DRESS!

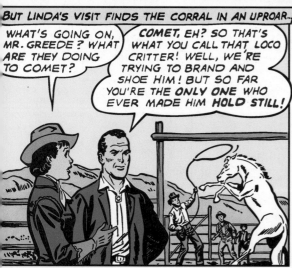

BUT LINDA'S VISIT FINDS THE CORRAL IN AN UPROAR...

WHAT'S GOING ON, MR. GREEDE? WHAT ARE THEY DOING TO COMET?

COMET, EH? SO THAT'S WHAT YOU CALL THAT *LOCO CRITTER!* WELL, WE'RE TRYING TO BRAND AND SHOE HIM! BUT SO FAR YOU'RE THE *ONLY ONE* WHO EVER MADE HIM *HOLD STILL!*

BETTER LET ME HANDLE COMET, MR. GREEDE! I'LL TAKE CARE OF EVERYTHING!

¡GULP!¡ IF THEY TRY TO BURN HIS HIDE OR DRIVE A NAIL IN HIS HOOF THEY'LL FIND OUT *COMET IS INVULNERABLE!* I'VE GOT TO PREVENT THAT!

THINK *YOU* CAN SHOE AND BRAND THAT WILD CRITTER, EH? YOU'RE WELCOME TO TRY!

WORKING SWIFTLY, LINDA SHIELDS HER MOVEMENTS FROM THE ONLOOKERS AS THE MIGHTY STALLION HOLDS STILL...

GREEDE THINKS I'M NAILING THESE SHOES INTO PLACE! ACTUALLY, I'M USING MY *HEAT-VISION* TO MELT THEM AROUND THE EDGE OF COMET'S HOOFS!

CLANG! CLANG!

THEN, WITH LIGHT PUFFS OF HER SUPER-BREATH, LINDA RAISES A CLOUD OF SMOKE FROM THE BRANDING FIRE...

EXCUSE THE SMOKE, GENTLEMEN! I'M TRYING TO HEAT UP THIS *BRANDING IRON* A LITTLE MORE!

¡CHUCKLE!¡ THAT'S JUST ENOUGH SMOKE TO SCREEN ME.. WHILE I "BRAND" COMET!

COUGH! COUGH!

2

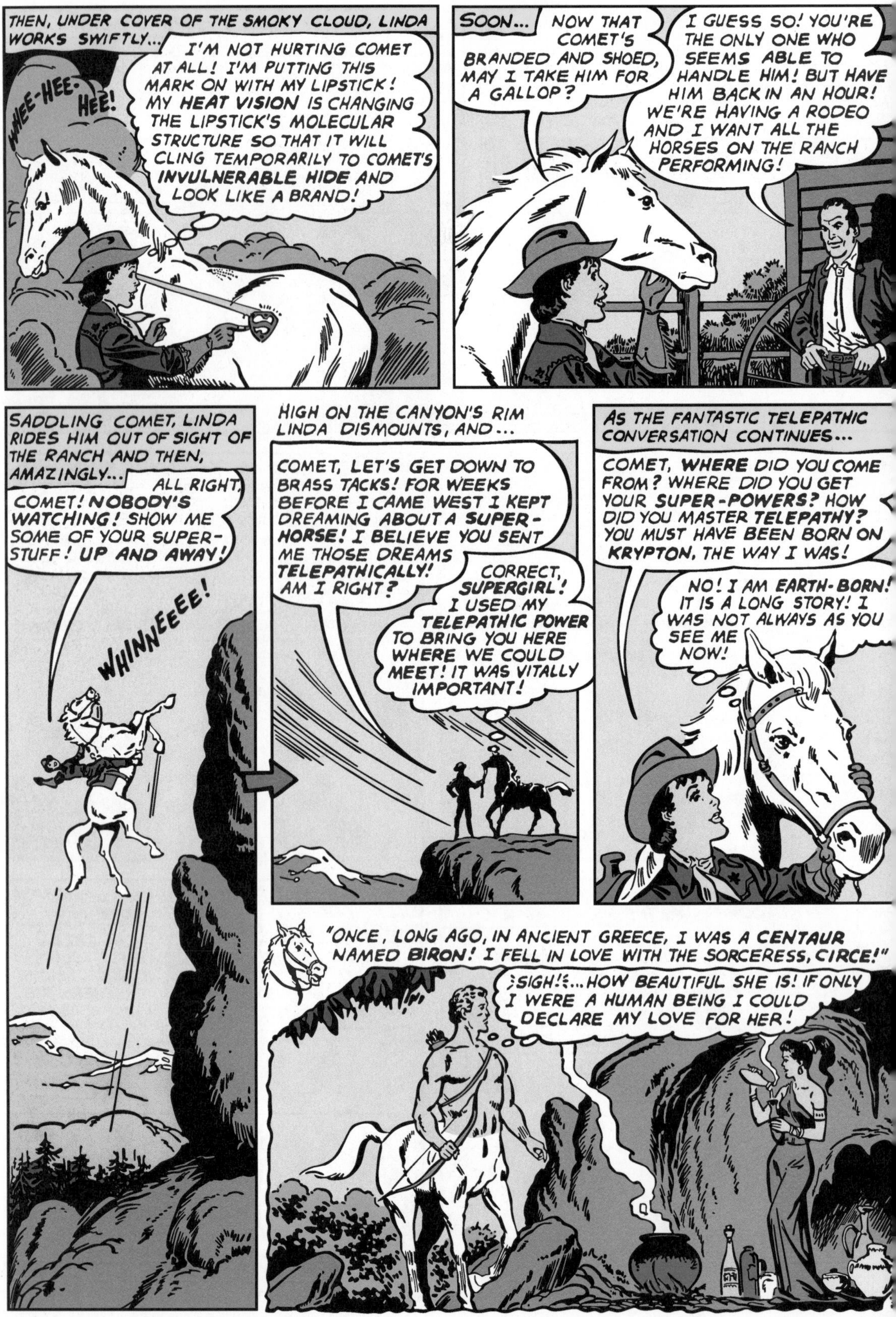

THEN, UNDER COVER OF THE SMOKY CLOUD, LINDA WORKS SWIFTLY...
I'M NOT HURTING COMET AT ALL! I'M PUTTING THIS MARK ON WITH MY LIPSTICK! MY HEAT VISION IS CHANGING THE LIPSTICK'S MOLECULAR STRUCTURE SO THAT IT WILL CLING TEMPORARILY TO COMET'S INVULNERABLE HIDE AND LOOK LIKE A BRAND!
WHEE-HEE-HEE!
SOON...
NOW THAT COMET'S BRANDED AND SHOED, MAY I TAKE HIM FOR A GALLOP?
I GUESS SO! YOU'RE THE ONLY ONE WHO SEEMS ABLE TO HANDLE HIM! BUT HAVE HIM BACK IN AN HOUR! WE'RE HAVING A RODEO AND I WANT ALL THE HORSES ON THE RANCH PERFORMING!
SADDLING COMET, LINDA RIDES HIM OUT OF SIGHT OF THE RANCH AND THEN, AMAZINGLY...
ALL RIGHT, COMET! NOBODY'S WATCHING! SHOW ME SOME OF YOUR SUPER-STUFF! UP AND AWAY!
WHINNEEEE!
HIGH ON THE CANYON'S RIM LINDA DISMOUNTS, AND...
COMET, LET'S GET DOWN TO BRASS TACKS! FOR WEEKS BEFORE I CAME WEST I KEPT DREAMING ABOUT A SUPER-HORSE! I BELIEVE YOU SENT ME THOSE DREAMS TELEPATHICALLY! AM I RIGHT?
CORRECT, SUPERGIRL! I USED MY TELEPATHIC POWER TO BRING YOU HERE WHERE WE COULD MEET! IT WAS VITALLY IMPORTANT!
AS THE FANTASTIC TELEPATHIC CONVERSATION CONTINUES...
COMET, WHERE DID YOU COME FROM? WHERE DID YOU GET YOUR SUPER-POWERS? HOW DID YOU MASTER TELEPATHY? YOU MUST HAVE BEEN BORN ON KRYPTON, THE WAY I WAS!
NO! I AM EARTH-BORN! IT IS A LONG STORY! I WAS NOT ALWAYS AS YOU SEE ME NOW!
"ONCE, LONG AGO, IN ANCIENT GREECE, I WAS A CENTAUR NAMED BIRON! I FELL IN LOVE WITH THE SORCERESS, CIRCE!"
SIGH!...HOW BEAUTIFUL SHE IS! IF ONLY I WERE A HUMAN BEING I COULD DECLARE MY LOVE FOR HER!

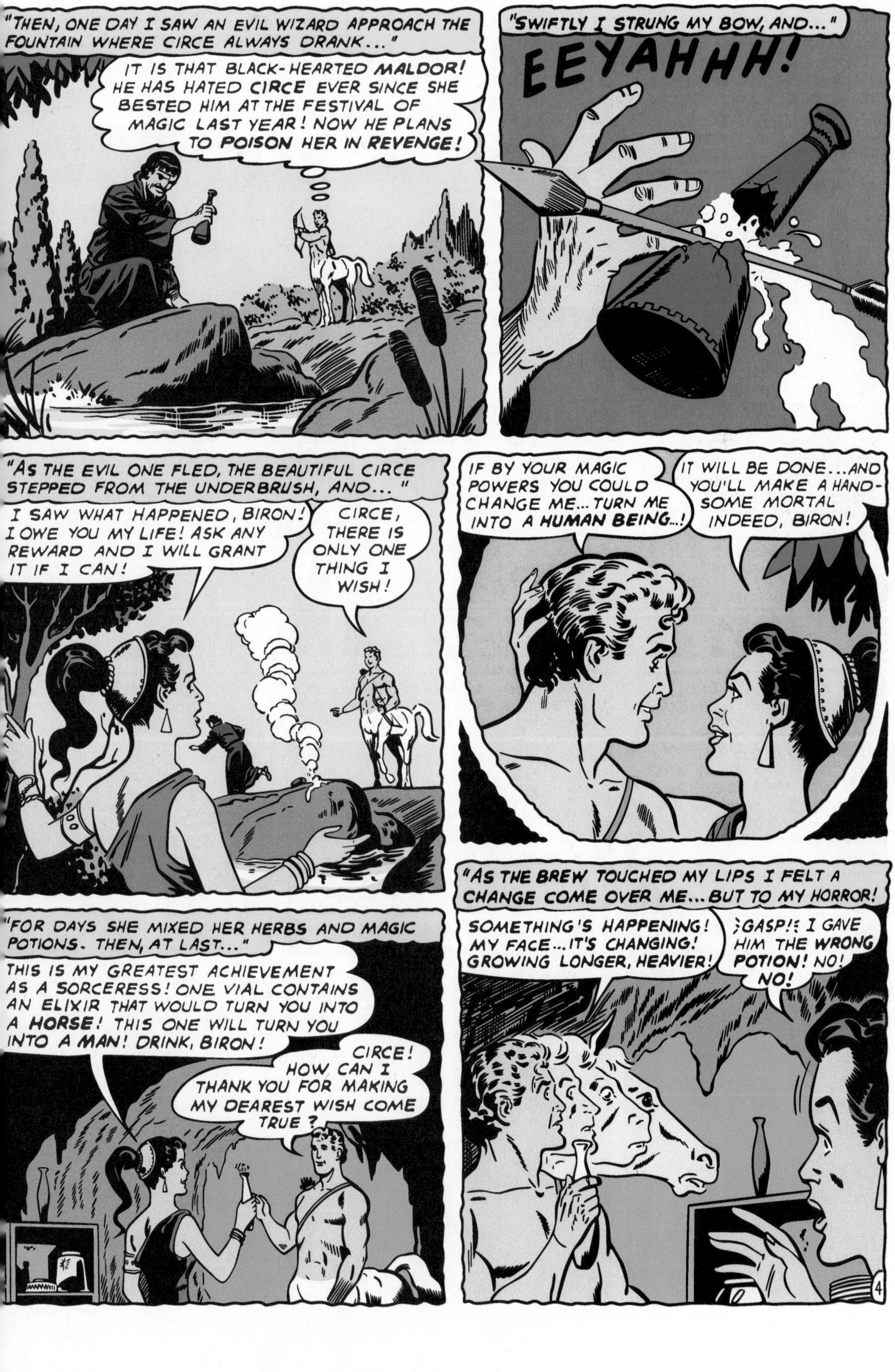
"THEN, ONE DAY I SAW AN EVIL WIZARD APPROACH THE FOUNTAIN WHERE CIRCE ALWAYS DRANK..."
IT IS THAT BLACK-HEARTED MALDOR! HE HAS HATED CIRCE EVER SINCE SHE BESTED HIM AT THE FESTIVAL OF MAGIC LAST YEAR! NOW HE PLANS TO POISON HER IN REVENGE!
"SWIFTLY I STRUNG MY BOW, AND..."
EEYAHHH!
"AS THE EVIL ONE FLED, THE BEAUTIFUL CIRCE STEPPED FROM THE UNDERBRUSH, AND..."
I SAW WHAT HAPPENED, BIRON! I OWE YOU MY LIFE! ASK ANY REWARD AND I WILL GRANT IT IF I CAN!
CIRCE, THERE IS ONLY ONE THING I WISH!
IF BY YOUR MAGIC POWERS YOU COULD CHANGE ME... TURN ME INTO A HUMAN BEING...!
IT WILL BE DONE... AND YOU'LL MAKE A HANDSOME MORTAL INDEED, BIRON!
"FOR DAYS SHE MIXED HER HERBS AND MAGIC POTIONS. THEN, AT LAST..."
THIS IS MY GREATEST ACHIEVEMENT AS A SORCERESS! ONE VIAL CONTAINS AN ELIXIR THAT WOULD TURN YOU INTO A HORSE! THIS ONE WILL TURN YOU INTO A MAN! DRINK, BIRON!
CIRCE! HOW CAN I THANK YOU FOR MAKING MY DEAREST WISH COME TRUE?
"AS THE BREW TOUCHED MY LIPS I FELT A CHANGE COME OVER ME... BUT TO MY HORROR!
SOMETHING'S HAPPENING! MY FACE... IT'S CHANGING! GROWING LONGER, HEAVIER!
GASP! I GAVE HIM THE WRONG POTION! NO! NO!
4

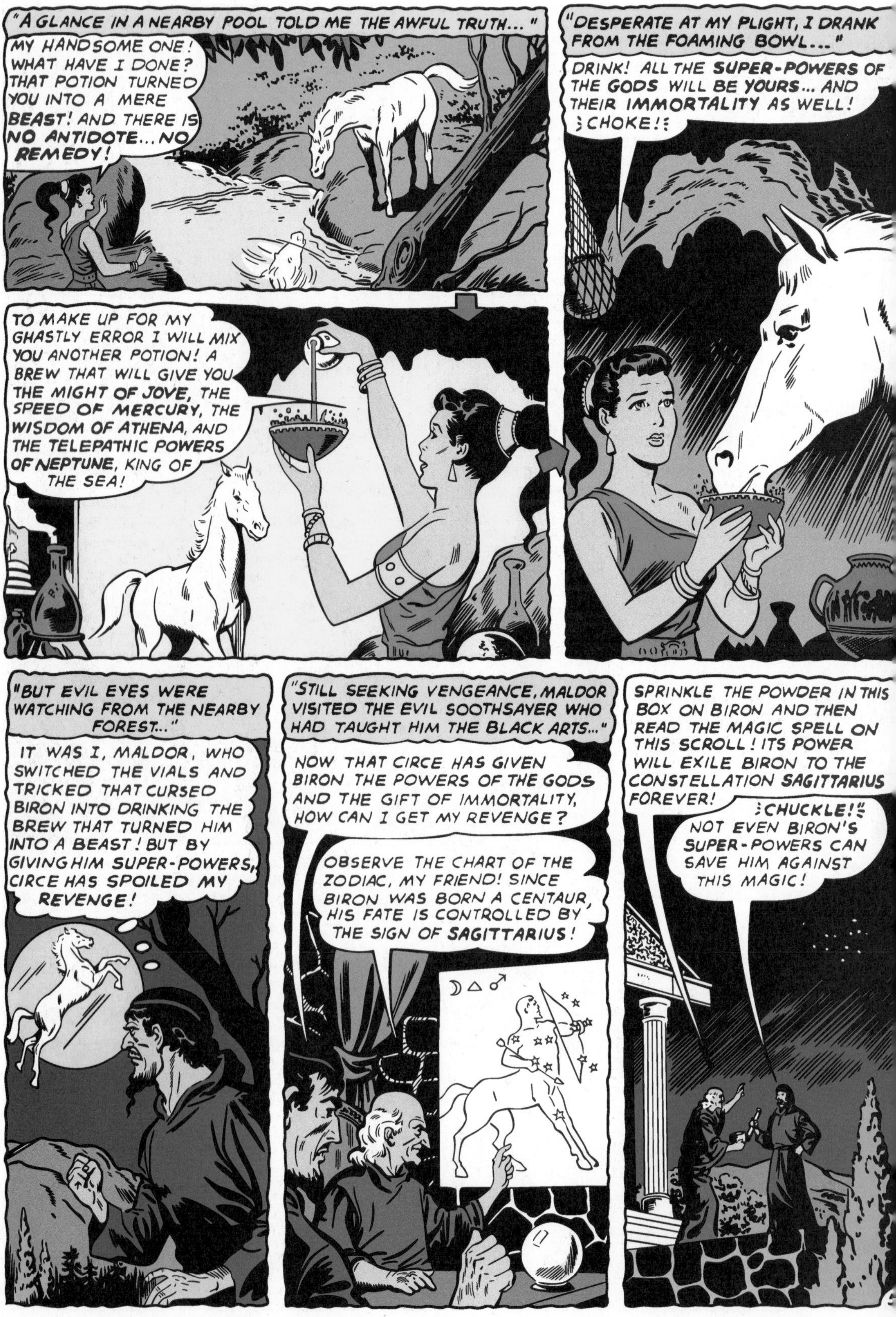
"A GLANCE IN A NEARBY POOL TOLD ME THE AWFUL TRUTH..."
MY HANDSOME ONE! WHAT HAVE I DONE? THAT POTION TURNED YOU INTO A MERE BEAST! AND THERE IS NO ANTIDOTE... NO REMEDY!
TO MAKE UP FOR MY GHASTLY ERROR I WILL MIX YOU ANOTHER POTION! A BREW THAT WILL GIVE YOU THE MIGHT OF JOVE, THE SPEED OF MERCURY, THE WISDOM OF ATHENA, AND THE TELEPATHIC POWERS OF NEPTUNE, KING OF THE SEA!
"DESPERATE AT MY PLIGHT, I DRANK FROM THE FOAMING BOWL..."
DRINK! ALL THE SUPER-POWERS OF THE GODS WILL BE YOURS... AND THEIR IMMORTALITY AS WELL!
CHOKE!
"BUT EVIL EYES WERE WATCHING FROM THE NEARBY FOREST..."
IT WAS I, MALDOR, WHO SWITCHED THE VIALS AND TRICKED THAT CURSED BIRON INTO DRINKING THE BREW THAT TURNED HIM INTO A BEAST! BUT BY GIVING HIM SUPER-POWERS, CIRCE HAS SPOILED MY REVENGE!
"STILL SEEKING VENGEANCE, MALDOR VISITED THE EVIL SOOTHSAYER WHO HAD TAUGHT HIM THE BLACK ARTS..."
NOW THAT CIRCE HAS GIVEN BIRON THE POWERS OF THE GODS AND THE GIFT OF IMMORTALITY, HOW CAN I GET MY REVENGE?
OBSERVE THE CHART OF THE ZODIAC, MY FRIEND! SINCE BIRON WAS BORN A CENTAUR, HIS FATE IS CONTROLLED BY THE SIGN OF SAGITTARIUS!
SPRINKLE THE POWDER IN THIS BOX ON BIRON AND THEN READ THE MAGIC SPELL ON THIS SCROLL! ITS POWER WILL EXILE BIRON TO THE CONSTELLATION SAGITTARIUS FOREVER!
CHUCKLE!
NOT EVEN BIRON'S SUPER-POWERS CAN SAVE HIM AGAINST THIS MAGIC!

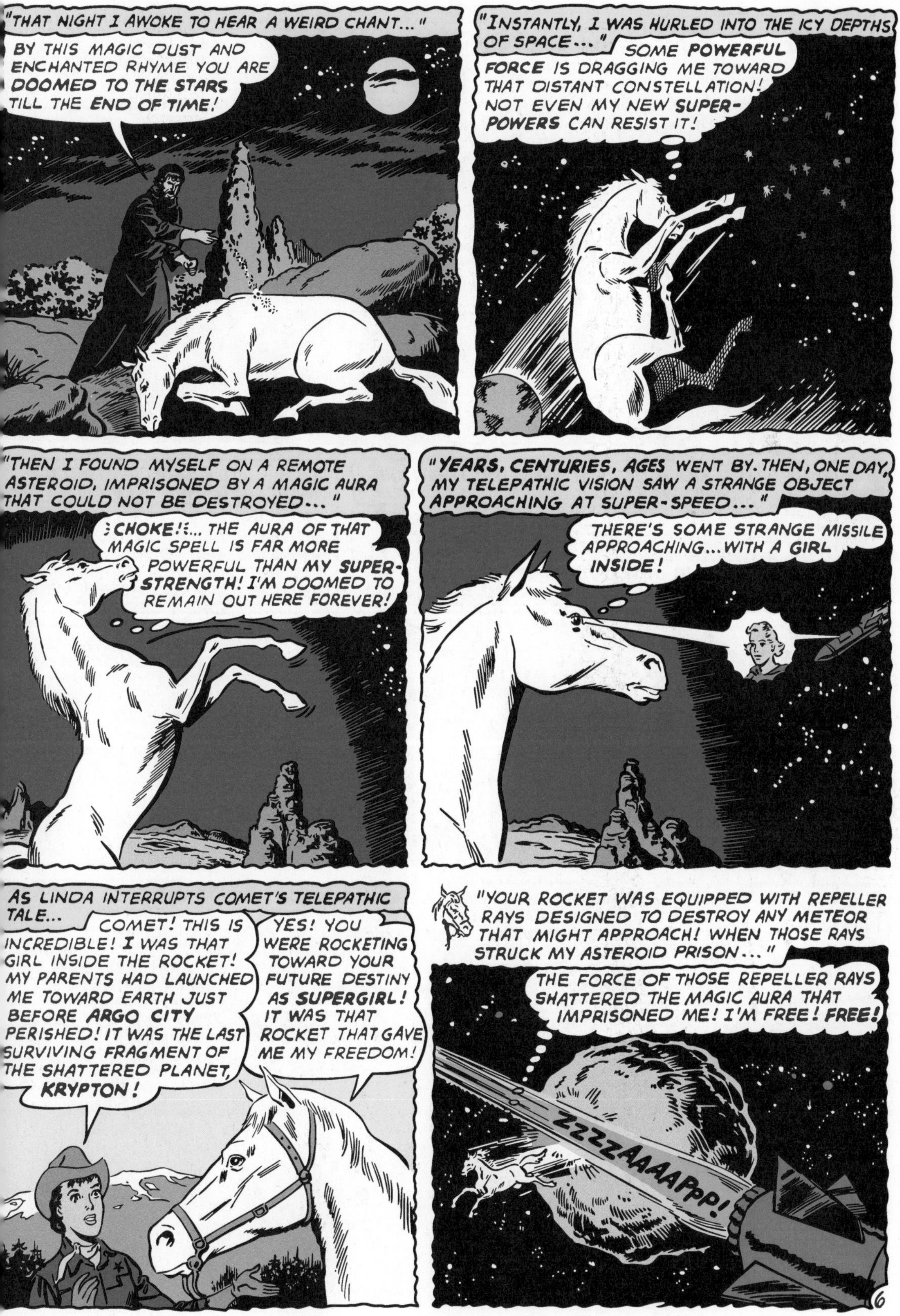
"THAT NIGHT I AWOKE TO HEAR A WEIRD CHANT..."
BY THIS MAGIC DUST AND ENCHANTED RHYME YOU ARE DOOMED TO THE STARS TILL THE END OF TIME!
"INSTANTLY, I WAS HURLED INTO THE ICY DEPTHS OF SPACE..."
SOME POWERFUL FORCE IS DRAGGING ME TOWARD THAT DISTANT CONSTELLATION! NOT EVEN MY NEW SUPER-POWERS CAN RESIST IT!
"THEN I FOUND MYSELF ON A REMOTE ASTEROID, IMPRISONED BY A MAGIC AURA THAT COULD NOT BE DESTROYED..."
CHOKE!... THE AURA OF THAT MAGIC SPELL IS FAR MORE POWERFUL THAN MY SUPER-STRENGTH! I'M DOOMED TO REMAIN OUT HERE FOREVER!
"YEARS, CENTURIES, AGES WENT BY. THEN, ONE DAY, MY TELEPATHIC VISION SAW A STRANGE OBJECT APPROACHING AT SUPER-SPEED..."
THERE'S SOME STRANGE MISSILE APPROACHING...WITH A GIRL INSIDE!
AS LINDA INTERRUPTS COMET'S TELEPATHIC TALE...
COMET! THIS IS INCREDIBLE! I WAS THAT GIRL INSIDE THE ROCKET! MY PARENTS HAD LAUNCHED ME TOWARD EARTH JUST BEFORE ARGO CITY PERISHED! IT WAS THE LAST SURVIVING FRAGMENT OF THE SHATTERED PLANET, KRYPTON!
YES! YOU WERE ROCKETING TOWARD YOUR FUTURE DESTINY AS SUPERGIRL! IT WAS THAT ROCKET THAT GAVE ME MY FREEDOM!
"YOUR ROCKET WAS EQUIPPED WITH REPELLER RAYS DESIGNED TO DESTROY ANY METEOR THAT MIGHT APPROACH! WHEN THOSE RAYS STRUCK MY ASTEROID PRISON..."
THE FORCE OF THOSE REPELLER RAYS SHATTERED THE MAGIC AURA THAT IMPRISONED ME! I'M FREE! FREE!
ZZZZZAAAAPPP!
6

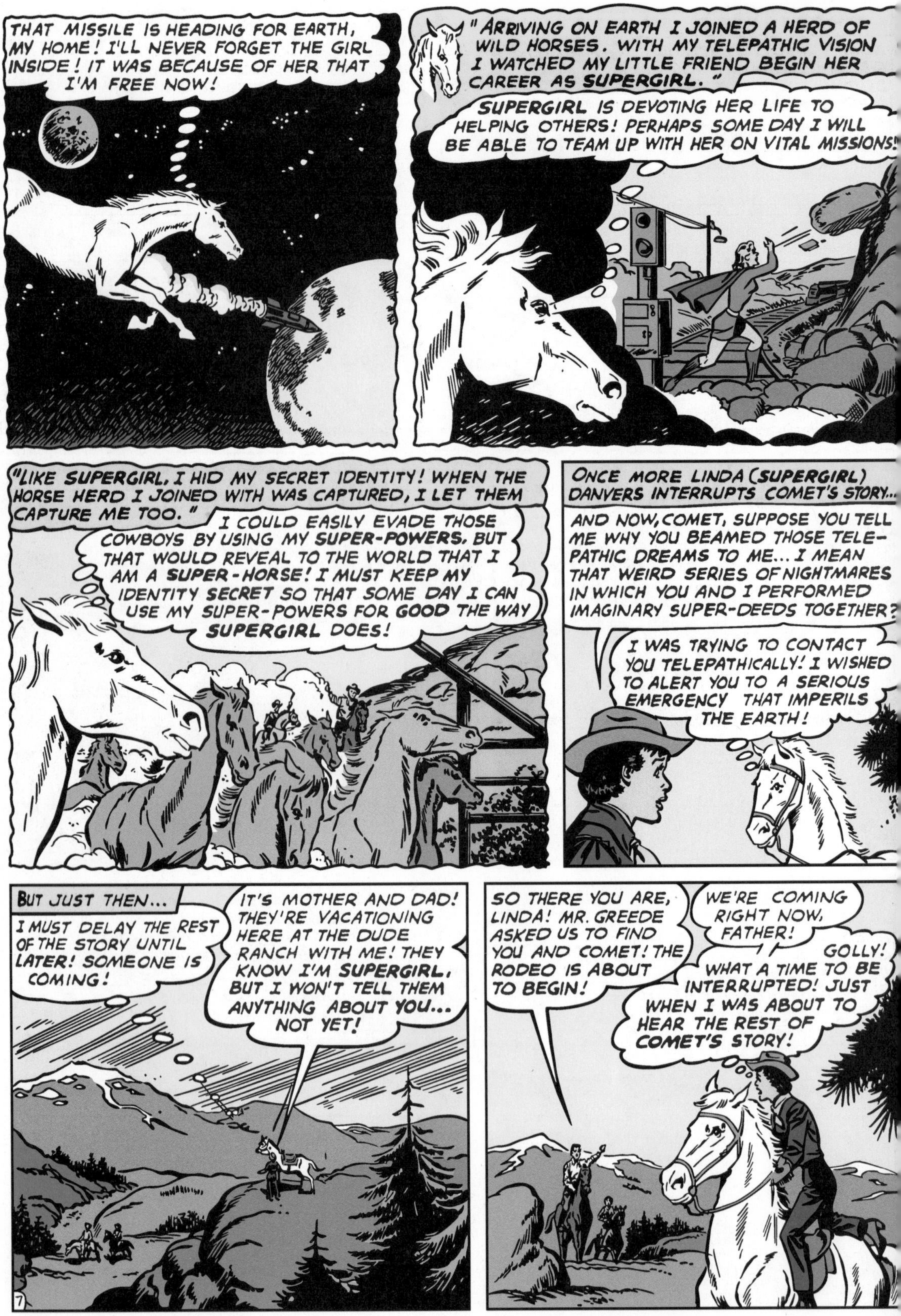
THAT MISSILE IS HEADING FOR EARTH, MY HOME! I'LL NEVER FORGET THE GIRL INSIDE! IT WAS BECAUSE OF HER THAT I'M FREE NOW!
"ARRIVING ON EARTH I JOINED A HERD OF WILD HORSES. WITH MY TELEPATHIC VISION I WATCHED MY LITTLE FRIEND BEGIN HER CAREER AS SUPERGIRL."
SUPERGIRL IS DEVOTING HER LIFE TO HELPING OTHERS! PERHAPS SOME DAY I WILL BE ABLE TO TEAM UP WITH HER ON VITAL MISSIONS!
"LIKE SUPERGIRL, I HID MY SECRET IDENTITY! WHEN THE HORSE HERD I JOINED WITH WAS CAPTURED, I LET THEM CAPTURE ME TOO."
I COULD EASILY EVADE THOSE COWBOYS BY USING MY SUPER-POWERS, BUT THAT WOULD REVEAL TO THE WORLD THAT I AM A SUPER-HORSE! I MUST KEEP MY IDENTITY SECRET SO THAT SOME DAY I CAN USE MY SUPER-POWERS FOR GOOD THE WAY SUPERGIRL DOES!
ONCE MORE LINDA (SUPERGIRL) DANVERS INTERRUPTS COMET'S STORY...
AND NOW, COMET, SUPPOSE YOU TELL ME WHY YOU BEAMED THOSE TELE-PATHIC DREAMS TO ME... I MEAN THAT WEIRD SERIES OF NIGHTMARES IN WHICH YOU AND I PERFORMED IMAGINARY SUPER-DEEDS TOGETHER?
I WAS TRYING TO CONTACT YOU TELEPATHICALLY! I WISHED TO ALERT YOU TO A SERIOUS EMERGENCY THAT IMPERILS THE EARTH!
BUT JUST THEN...
I MUST DELAY THE REST OF THE STORY UNTIL LATER! SOMEONE IS COMING!
IT'S MOTHER AND DAD! THEY'RE VACATIONING HERE AT THE DUDE RANCH WITH ME! THEY KNOW I'M SUPERGIRL, BUT I WON'T TELL THEM ANYTHING ABOUT YOU... NOT YET!
7
SO THERE YOU ARE, LINDA! MR. GREEDE ASKED US TO FIND YOU AND COMET! THE RODEO IS ABOUT TO BEGIN!
WE'RE COMING RIGHT NOW, FATHER!
GOLLY! WHAT A TIME TO BE INTERRUPTED! JUST WHEN I WAS ABOUT TO HEAR THE REST OF COMET'S STORY!

SOON, AT THE RANCH RODEO, AS STARTLED ONLOOKERS WATCH...

AND LINDA LEE DANVERS, RIDING COMET, WINS THE BARREL JUMP WITH A LEAP OF 12 BARRELS!

¡CHUCKLE!¡ THEY DON'T KNOW IT, BUT COMET COULD LEAP ACROSS THE ROCKIES WITH ONE JUMP!

RODEO

THEN, AT THE OBEDIENCE CONTEST...

JEHOSHAPHAT! SHE'S GOT THAT CRAZY CRITTER, COMET, EATING OUT OF HER HAND! LOOK! HE'S BOWING LIKE A DUDE!

GREAT WORK, COMET! GREEDE DOESN'T KNOW IT, BUT YOU'RE FOLLOWING MY EVERY COMMAND BY MEANS OF TELEPATHY!

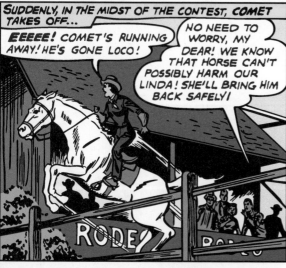

SUDDENLY, IN THE MIDST OF THE CONTEST, COMET TAKES OFF...

EEEEE! COMET'S RUNNING AWAY! HE'S GONE LOCO!

NO NEED TO WORRY, MY DEAR! WE KNOW THAT HORSE CAN'T POSSIBLY HARM OUR LINDA! SHE'LL BRING HIM BACK SAFELY!

RODE... RO...

MOMENTS LATER, AS LINDA AND COMET PAUSE IN THE SHELTER OF A NEARBY MESA...

I GOT YOUR TELEPATHIC WARNING, COMET, AND MY TELESCOPIC VISION CONFIRMED IT! AN ALIEN SPACESHIP IS ATTACKING THE PACIFIC WORLD'S FAIR! WE'LL HAVE TO GO INTO ACTION AT ONCE!

HOW CAN THEY GENERATE THE ENORMOUS POWER FOR SUCH FANTASTIC WEAPONS? ULP! MY X-RAY VISION CAN'T BREAK THROUGH THAT SPACE-SPHERE! IT MUST BE LINED WITH LEAD!

SWIFTLY CHANGING TO HER SUPERGIRL COSTUME, AND ALSO SUPPLYING ONE FOR COMET...

HURRY, COMET! THOSE ALIENS ARE USING BOLTS OF PURE ENERGY TO SHATTER EVERY STRUCTURE IN THEIR PATH! WE'D BETTER MOVE FAST BEFORE THEY DESTROY THE ENTIRE FAIR!

WHINNNEEE

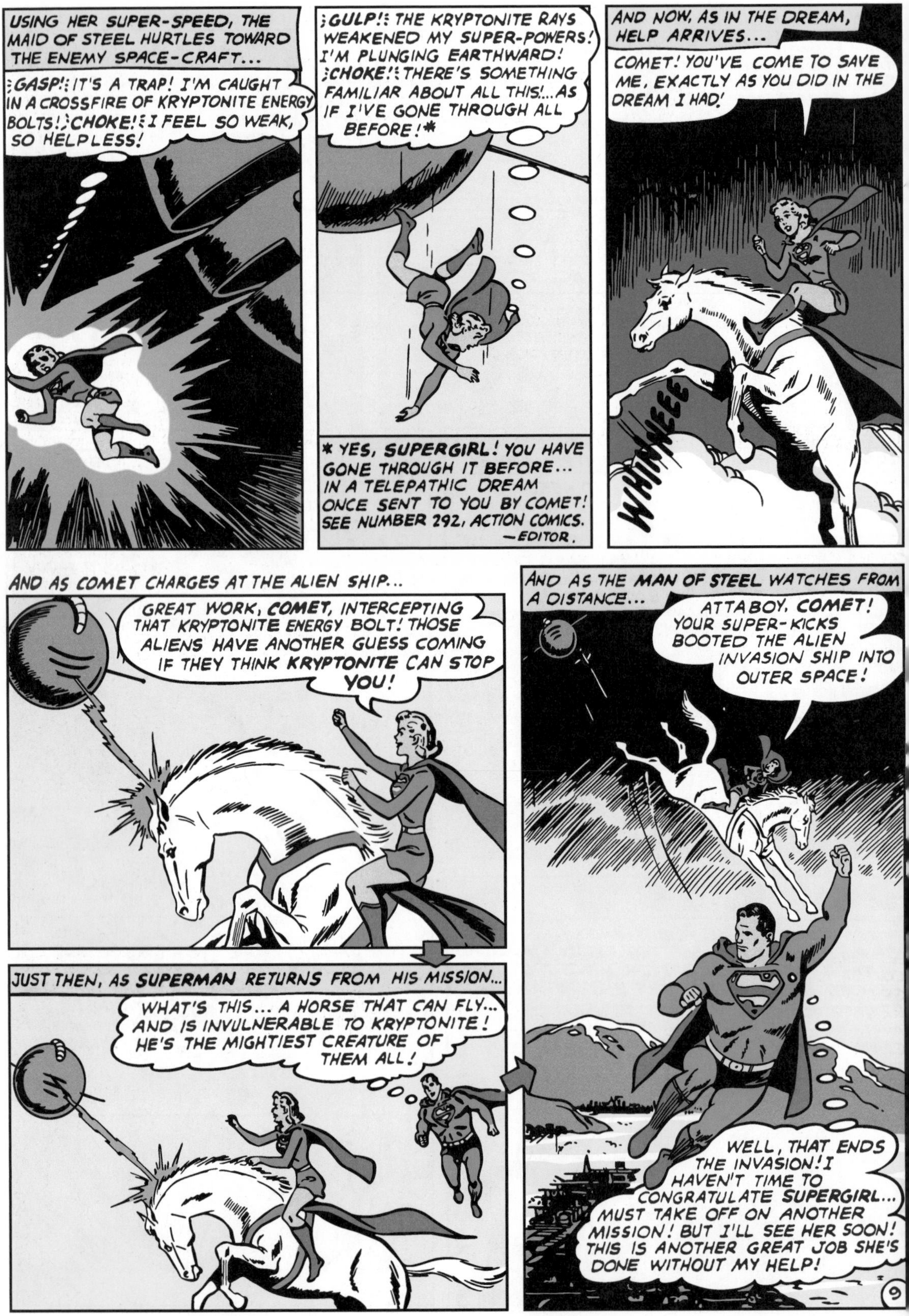
USING HER SUPER-SPEED, THE MAID OF STEEL HURTLES TOWARD THE ENEMY SPACE-CRAFT...
;GASP!; IT'S A TRAP! I'M CAUGHT IN A CROSSFIRE OF KRYPTONITE ENERGY BOLTS!;CHOKE!; I FEEL SO WEAK, SO HELPLESS!
;GULP!; THE KRYPTONITE RAYS WEAKENED MY SUPER-POWERS! I'M PLUNGING EARTHWARD! ;CHOKE!; THERE'S SOMETHING FAMILIAR ABOUT ALL THIS!...AS IF I'VE GONE THROUGH ALL BEFORE!*
* YES, SUPERGIRL! YOU HAVE GONE THROUGH IT BEFORE... IN A TELEPATHIC DREAM ONCE SENT TO YOU BY COMET! SEE NUMBER 292, ACTION COMICS. —EDITOR.
AND NOW, AS IN THE DREAM, HELP ARRIVES...
COMET! YOU'VE COME TO SAVE ME, EXACTLY AS YOU DID IN THE DREAM I HAD!
WHINNEEE
AND AS COMET CHARGES AT THE ALIEN SHIP...
GREAT WORK, COMET, INTERCEPTING THAT KRYPTONITE ENERGY BOLT! THOSE ALIENS HAVE ANOTHER GUESS COMING IF THEY THINK KRYPTONITE CAN STOP YOU!
JUST THEN, AS SUPERMAN RETURNS FROM HIS MISSION...
WHAT'S THIS... A HORSE THAT CAN FLY... AND IS INVULNERABLE TO KRYPTONITE! HE'S THE MIGHTIEST CREATURE OF THEM ALL!
AND AS THE MAN OF STEEL WATCHES FROM A DISTANCE...
ATTABOY, COMET! YOUR SUPER-KICKS BOOTED THE ALIEN INVASION SHIP INTO OUTER SPACE!
WELL, THAT ENDS THE INVASION! I HAVEN'T TIME TO CONGRATULATE SUPERGIRL... MUST TAKE OFF ON ANOTHER MISSION! BUT I'LL SEE HER SOON! THIS IS ANOTHER GREAT JOB SHE'S DONE WITHOUT MY HELP!
9

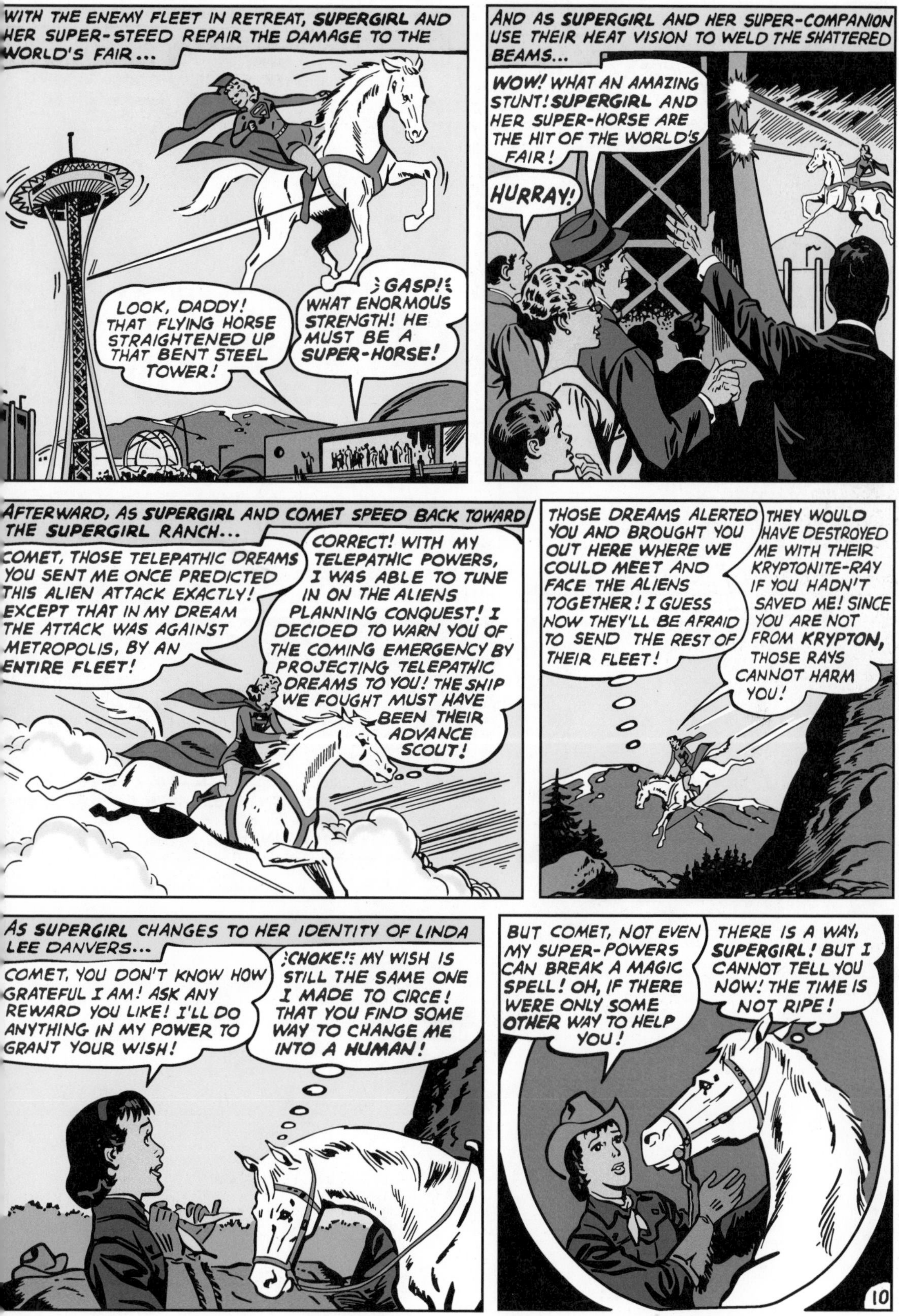
WITH THE ENEMY FLEET IN RETREAT, SUPERGIRL AND HER SUPER-STEED REPAIR THE DAMAGE TO THE WORLD'S FAIR...
LOOK, DADDY! THAT FLYING HORSE STRAIGHTENED UP THAT BENT STEEL TOWER!
GASP! WHAT ENORMOUS STRENGTH! HE MUST BE A SUPER-HORSE!
AND AS SUPERGIRL AND HER SUPER-COMPANION USE THEIR HEAT VISION TO WELD THE SHATTERED BEAMS...
WOW! WHAT AN AMAZING STUNT! SUPERGIRL AND HER SUPER-HORSE ARE THE HIT OF THE WORLD'S FAIR!
HURRAY!
AFTERWARD, AS SUPERGIRL AND COMET SPEED BACK TOWARD THE SUPERGIRL RANCH...
COMET, THOSE TELEPATHIC DREAMS YOU SENT ME ONCE PREDICTED THIS ALIEN ATTACK EXACTLY! EXCEPT THAT IN MY DREAM THE ATTACK WAS AGAINST METROPOLIS, BY AN ENTIRE FLEET!
CORRECT! WITH MY TELEPATHIC POWERS, I WAS ABLE TO TUNE IN ON THE ALIENS PLANNING CONQUEST! I DECIDED TO WARN YOU OF THE COMING EMERGENCY BY PROJECTING TELEPATHIC DREAMS TO YOU! THE SHIP WE FOUGHT MUST HAVE BEEN THEIR ADVANCE SCOUT!
THOSE DREAMS ALERTED YOU AND BROUGHT YOU OUT HERE WHERE WE COULD MEET AND FACE THE ALIENS TOGETHER! I GUESS NOW THEY'LL BE AFRAID TO SEND THE REST OF THEIR FLEET!
THEY WOULD HAVE DESTROYED ME WITH THEIR KRYPTONITE-RAY IF YOU HADN'T SAVED ME! SINCE YOU ARE NOT FROM KRYPTON, THOSE RAYS CANNOT HARM YOU!
AS SUPERGIRL CHANGES TO HER IDENTITY OF LINDA LEE DANVERS...
COMET, YOU DON'T KNOW HOW GRATEFUL I AM! ASK ANY REWARD YOU LIKE! I'LL DO ANYTHING IN MY POWER TO GRANT YOUR WISH!
CHOKE! MY WISH IS STILL THE SAME ONE I MADE TO CIRCE! THAT YOU FIND SOME WAY TO CHANGE ME INTO A HUMAN!
BUT COMET, NOT EVEN MY SUPER-POWERS CAN BREAK A MAGIC SPELL! OH, IF THERE WERE ONLY SOME OTHER WAY TO HELP YOU!
THERE IS A WAY, SUPERGIRL! BUT I CANNOT TELL YOU NOW! THE TIME IS NOT RIPE!
10

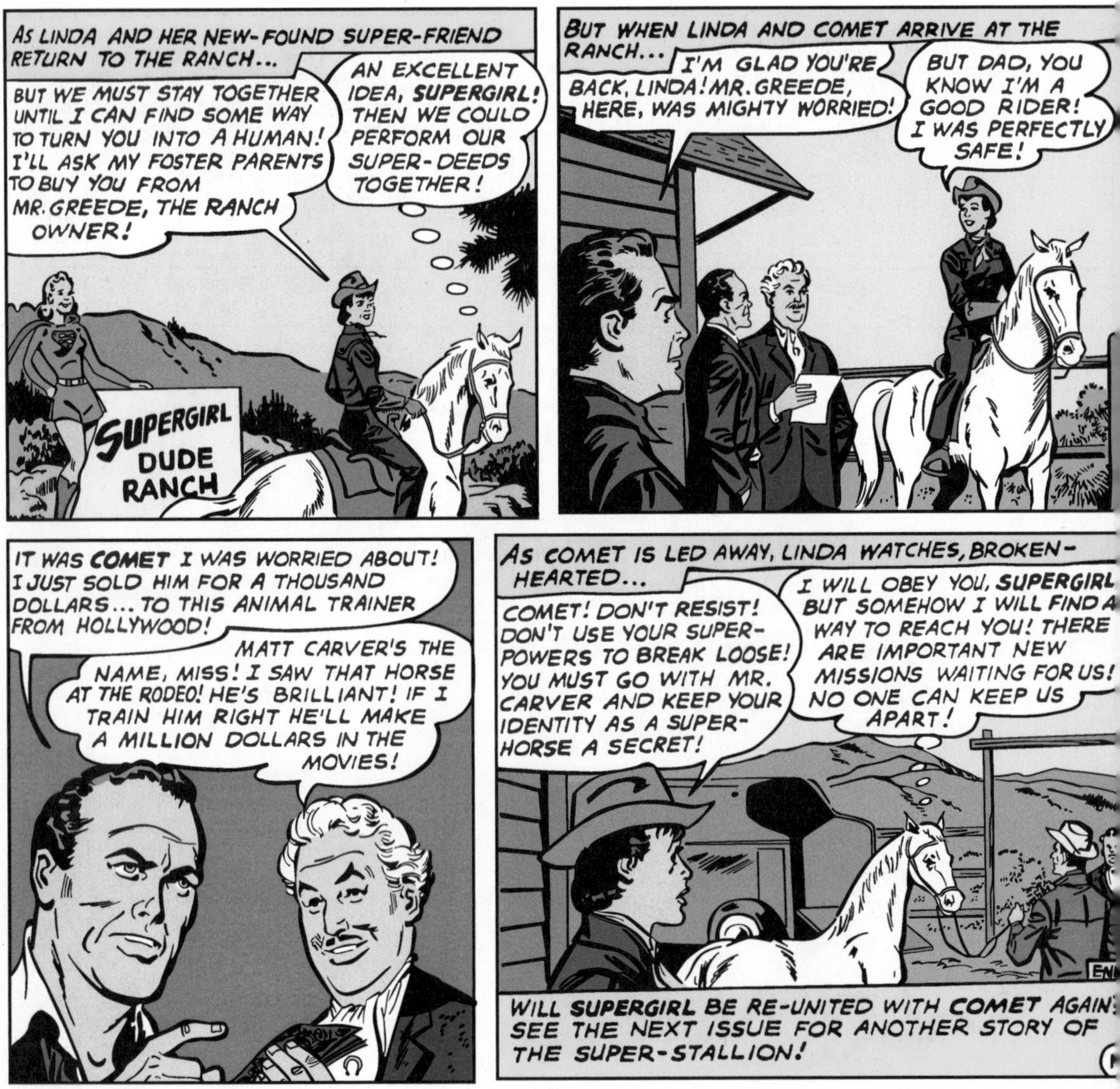
AS LINDA AND HER NEW-FOUND SUPER-FRIEND RETURN TO THE RANCH...
BUT WE MUST STAY TOGETHER UNTIL I CAN FIND SOME WAY TO TURN YOU INTO A HUMAN! I'LL ASK MY FOSTER PARENTS TO BUY YOU FROM MR. GREEDE, THE RANCH OWNER!
AN EXCELLENT IDEA, SUPERGIRL! THEN WE COULD PERFORM OUR SUPER-DEEDS TOGETHER!
SUPERGIRL DUDE RANCH
BUT WHEN LINDA AND COMET ARRIVE AT THE RANCH...
I'M GLAD YOU'RE BACK, LINDA! MR. GREEDE, HERE, WAS MIGHTY WORRIED!
BUT DAD, YOU KNOW I'M A GOOD RIDER! I WAS PERFECTLY SAFE!
IT WAS COMET I WAS WORRIED ABOUT! I JUST SOLD HIM FOR A THOUSAND DOLLARS... TO THIS ANIMAL TRAINER FROM HOLLYWOOD!
MATT CARVER'S THE NAME, MISS! I SAW THAT HORSE AT THE RODEO! HE'S BRILLIANT! IF I TRAIN HIM RIGHT HE'LL MAKE A MILLION DOLLARS IN THE MOVIES!
AS COMET IS LED AWAY, LINDA WATCHES, BROKEN-HEARTED...
COMET! DON'T RESIST! DON'T USE YOUR SUPER-POWERS TO BREAK LOOSE! YOU MUST GO WITH MR. CARVER AND KEEP YOUR IDENTITY AS A SUPER-HORSE A SECRET!
I WILL OBEY YOU, SUPERGIRL BUT SOMEHOW I WILL FIND A WAY TO REACH YOU! THERE ARE IMPORTANT NEW MISSIONS WAITING FOR US! NO ONE CAN KEEP US APART!
WILL SUPERGIRL BE RE-UNITED WITH COMET AGAIN? SEE THE NEXT ISSUE FOR ANOTHER STORY OF THE SUPER-STALLION!

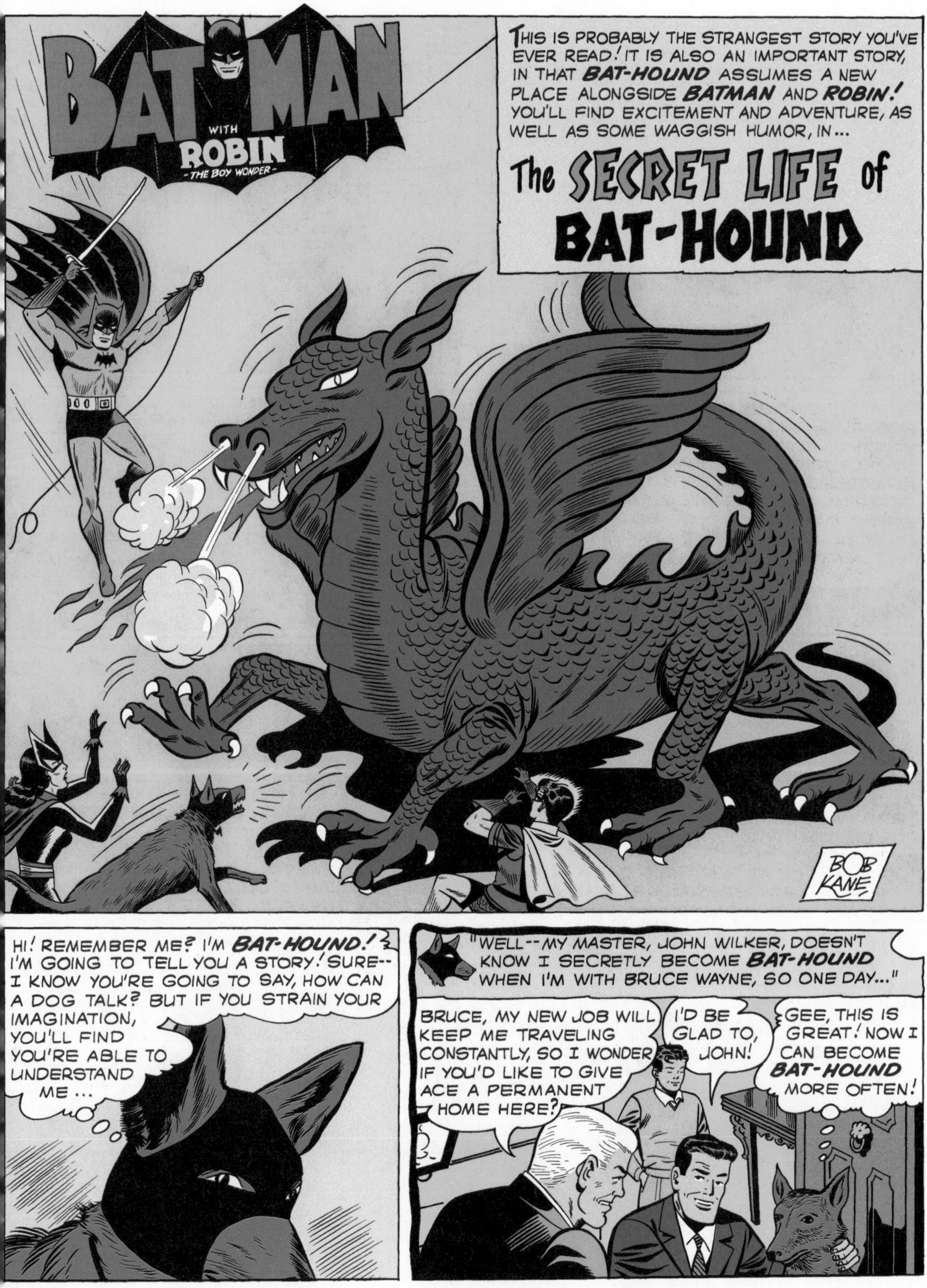
BATMAN WITH ROBIN -THE BOY WONDER-
THIS IS PROBABLY THE STRANGEST STORY YOU'VE EVER READ! IT IS ALSO AN IMPORTANT STORY, IN THAT BAT-HOUND ASSUMES A NEW PLACE ALONGSIDE BATMAN AND ROBIN! YOU'LL FIND EXCITEMENT AND ADVENTURE, AS WELL AS SOME WAGGISH HUMOR, IN...
The SECRET LIFE of BAT-HOUND
BOB KANE
HI! REMEMBER ME? I'M BAT-HOUND! I'M GOING TO TELL YOU A STORY! SURE-- I KNOW YOU'RE GOING TO SAY, HOW CAN A DOG TALK? BUT IF YOU STRAIN YOUR IMAGINATION, YOU'LL FIND YOU'RE ABLE TO UNDERSTAND ME ...
"WELL--MY MASTER, JOHN WILKER, DOESN'T KNOW I SECRETLY BECOME BAT-HOUND WHEN I'M WITH BRUCE WAYNE, SO ONE DAY..."
BRUCE, MY NEW JOB WILL KEEP ME TRAVELING CONSTANTLY, SO I WONDER IF YOU'D LIKE TO GIVE ACE A PERMANENT HOME HERE?
I'D BE GLAD TO, JOHN!
GEE, THIS IS GREAT! NOW I CAN BECOME BAT-HOUND MORE OFTEN!

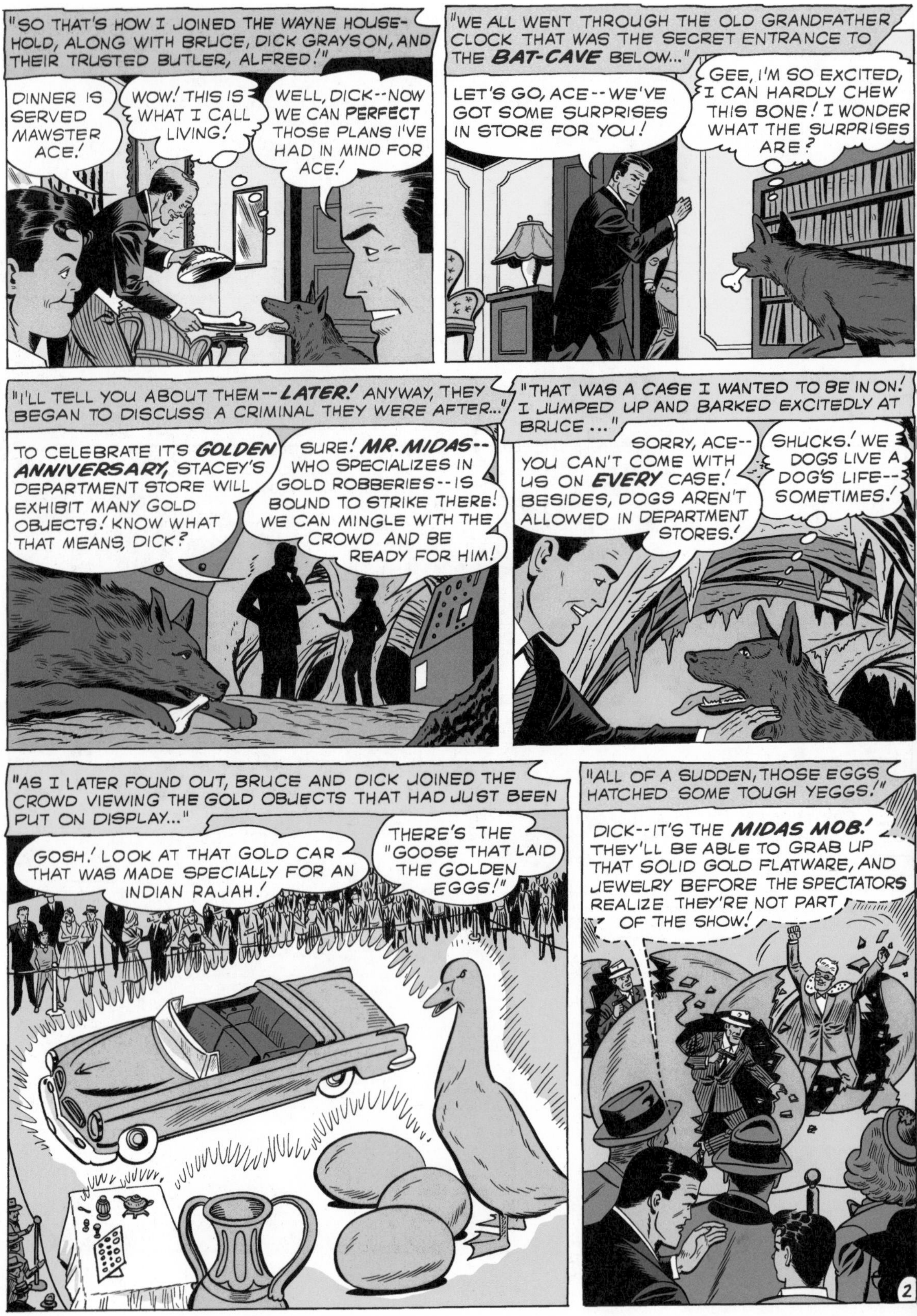
"SO THAT'S HOW I JOINED THE WAYNE HOUSEHOLD, ALONG WITH BRUCE, DICK GRAYSON, AND THEIR TRUSTED BUTLER, ALFRED!"
DINNER IS SERVED MAWSTER ACE!
WOW! THIS IS WHAT I CALL LIVING!
WELL, DICK--NOW WE CAN PERFECT THOSE PLANS I'VE HAD IN MIND FOR ACE!
"WE ALL WENT THROUGH THE OLD GRANDFATHER CLOCK THAT WAS THE SECRET ENTRANCE TO THE BAT-CAVE BELOW..."
LET'S GO, ACE--WE'VE GOT SOME SURPRISES IN STORE FOR YOU!
GEE, I'M SO EXCITED, I CAN HARDLY CHEW THIS BONE! I WONDER WHAT THE SURPRISES ARE?
"I'LL TELL YOU ABOUT THEM--LATER! ANYWAY, THEY BEGAN TO DISCUSS A CRIMINAL THEY WERE AFTER..."
TO CELEBRATE ITS GOLDEN ANNIVERSARY, STACEY'S DEPARTMENT STORE WILL EXHIBIT MANY GOLD OBJECTS! KNOW WHAT THAT MEANS, DICK?
SURE! MR. MIDAS--WHO SPECIALIZES IN GOLD ROBBERIES--IS BOUND TO STRIKE THERE! WE CAN MINGLE WITH THE CROWD AND BE READY FOR HIM!
"THAT WAS A CASE I WANTED TO BE IN ON! I JUMPED UP AND BARKED EXCITEDLY AT BRUCE..."
SORRY, ACE--YOU CAN'T COME WITH US ON EVERY CASE! BESIDES, DOGS AREN'T ALLOWED IN DEPARTMENT STORES!
SHUCKS! WE DOGS LIVE A DOG'S LIFE--SOMETIMES!
"AS I LATER FOUND OUT, BRUCE AND DICK JOINED THE CROWD VIEWING THE GOLD OBJECTS THAT HAD JUST BEEN PUT ON DISPLAY..."
GOSH! LOOK AT THAT GOLD CAR THAT WAS MADE SPECIALLY FOR AN INDIAN RAJAH!
THERE'S THE "GOOSE THAT LAID THE GOLDEN EGGS!"
"ALL OF A SUDDEN, THOSE EGGS HATCHED SOME TOUGH YEGGS!"
DICK--IT'S THE MIDAS MOB! THEY'LL BE ABLE TO GRAB UP THAT SOLID GOLD FLATWARE, AND JEWELRY BEFORE THE SPECTATORS REALIZE THEY'RE NOT PART OF THE SHOW!
2

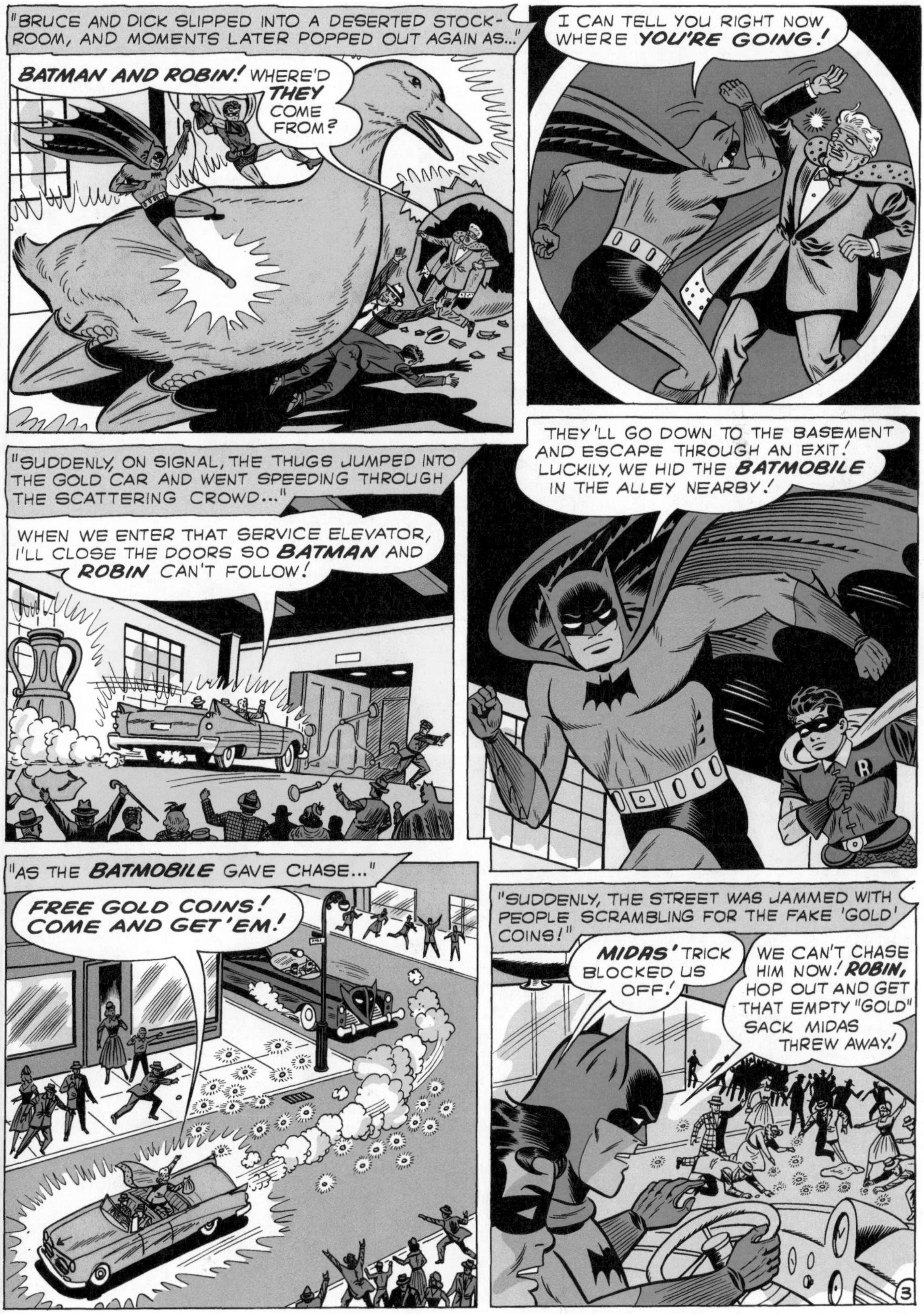
"BRUCE AND DICK SLIPPED INTO A DESERTED STOCK-ROOM, AND MOMENTS LATER POPPED OUT AGAIN AS..."
BATMAN AND ROBIN! WHERE'D THEY COME FROM?
I CAN TELL YOU RIGHT NOW WHERE YOU'RE GOING!
"SUDDENLY, ON SIGNAL, THE THUGS JUMPED INTO THE GOLD CAR AND WENT SPEEDING THROUGH THE SCATTERING CROWD..."
WHEN WE ENTER THAT SERVICE ELEVATOR, I'LL CLOSE THE DOORS SO BATMAN AND ROBIN CAN'T FOLLOW!
THEY'LL GO DOWN TO THE BASEMENT AND ESCAPE THROUGH AN EXIT! LUCKILY, WE HID THE BATMOBILE IN THE ALLEY NEARBY!
"AS THE BATMOBILE GAVE CHASE..."
FREE GOLD COINS! COME AND GET 'EM!
"SUDDENLY, THE STREET WAS JAMMED WITH PEOPLE SCRAMBLING FOR THE FAKE 'GOLD' COINS!"
MIDAS' TRICK BLOCKED US OFF!
WE CAN'T CHASE HIM NOW! ROBIN, HOP OUT AND GET THAT EMPTY "GOLD" SACK MIDAS THREW AWAY!
3

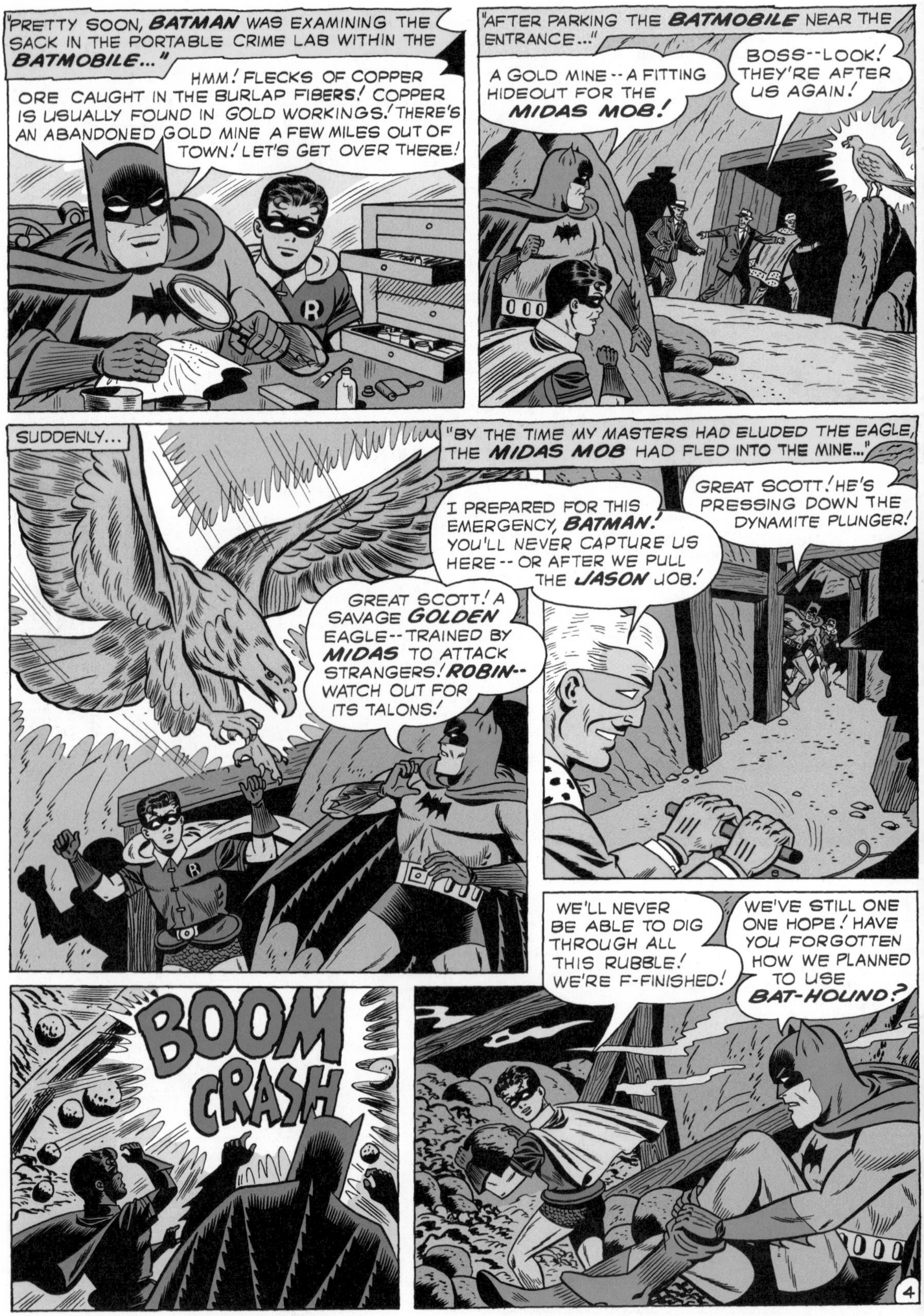
"PRETTY SOON, BATMAN WAS EXAMINING THE SACK IN THE PORTABLE CRIME LAB WITHIN THE BATMOBILE..."
HMM! FLECKS OF COPPER ORE CAUGHT IN THE BURLAP FIBERS! COPPER IS USUALLY FOUND IN GOLD WORKINGS! THERE'S AN ABANDONED GOLD MINE A FEW MILES OUT OF TOWN! LET'S GET OVER THERE!
"AFTER PARKING THE BATMOBILE NEAR THE ENTRANCE..."
A GOLD MINE -- A FITTING HIDEOUT FOR THE MIDAS MOB!
BOSS--LOOK! THEY'RE AFTER US AGAIN!
SUDDENLY...
GREAT SCOTT! A SAVAGE GOLDEN EAGLE--TRAINED BY MIDAS TO ATTACK STRANGERS! ROBIN--WATCH OUT FOR ITS TALONS!
"BY THE TIME MY MASTERS HAD ELUDED THE EAGLE, THE MIDAS MOB HAD FLED INTO THE MINE..."
I PREPARED FOR THIS EMERGENCY, BATMAN! YOU'LL NEVER CAPTURE US HERE -- OR AFTER WE PULL THE JASON JOB!
GREAT SCOTT! HE'S PRESSING DOWN THE DYNAMITE PLUNGER!
BOOM
CRASH
WE'LL NEVER BE ABLE TO DIG THROUGH ALL THIS RUBBLE! WE'RE F-FINISHED!
WE'VE STILL ONE ONE HOPE! HAVE YOU FORGOTTEN HOW WE PLANNED TO USE BAT-HOUND?
4

Panel 1: *BATMAN'S* HOLLOW BOOT HEEL CONTAINED A TINY RADIO THAT TRANSMITTED A SIGNAL WHEN HE FLIPPED THE SWITCH...

Panel 2: "THE SIGNAL REACHED A TINY RECEIVER CONCEALED INSIDE MY COLLAR--AND IT COULD ONLY BE HEARD BY ME BECAUSE IT WAS ABOVE THE RANGE OF THE HUMAN EAR!"

BATMAN--HE'S IN TROUBLE AND NEEDS ME!

BEEP! BEEP!

Panel 3: "I BOLTED DOWN TO THE *BAT-CAVE*-- AND SLIPPED INTO MY MASK, HELD BY A GADGET *BATMAN* HAD DEVISED..."

I SHOULD GET SOMEONE TO GO WITH ME! ALFRED?--NO, THIS IS HIS NIGHT OUT! WHO CAN I GET? I KNOW...

Panel 4: "I STREAKED TO THE HOUSE OF *BATMAN'S* FRIEND, *KATHY KANE*"...

BAT-HOUND!

GOOD THING I KNOW SHE'S BATWOMAN! I HOPE SHE REALIZES ALL MY BARKING MEANS I WANT HER TO FOLLOW ME!

ARRF! ARRRF!

Panel 5: "AFTER A SWIFT CHANGE TO HER COSTUME, SHE ACCOMPANIED ME ON THE TRAIL OF THE RADIO-BEAMED SIGNAL..."

THE SIGNAL'S STRONGER NOW! I'M GOING IN THE RIGHT DIRECTION!

BEEP! BEEP!

Panel 6: "WHEN WE REACHED THE CAVE-IN, *BATWOMAN* REALIZED WHAT HAD HAPPENED AND DUG THEM OUT WITH A NEARBY STEAM SHOVEL..."

...SO IT WAS THE *MIDAS MOB* THAT IMPRISONED YOU! WHERE ARE THEY NOW?

MIDAS SAID HE WAS GOING TO DO THE *"JASON JOB"*--WHICH MEANS HE'LL TRY TO STEAL *"THE GOLDEN FLEECE!"*

Panel 7: BUT THAT'S ONLY A GREEK LEGEND -- JASON HAD TO RECOVER A GOLDEN RAM'S FLEECE, WHICH WAS GUARDED BY A DRAGON!

A MOVIE IS BEING MADE OF IT--AND AS A PUBLICITY STUNT, A FLEECE MADE OF PURE GOLD IS BEING USED!

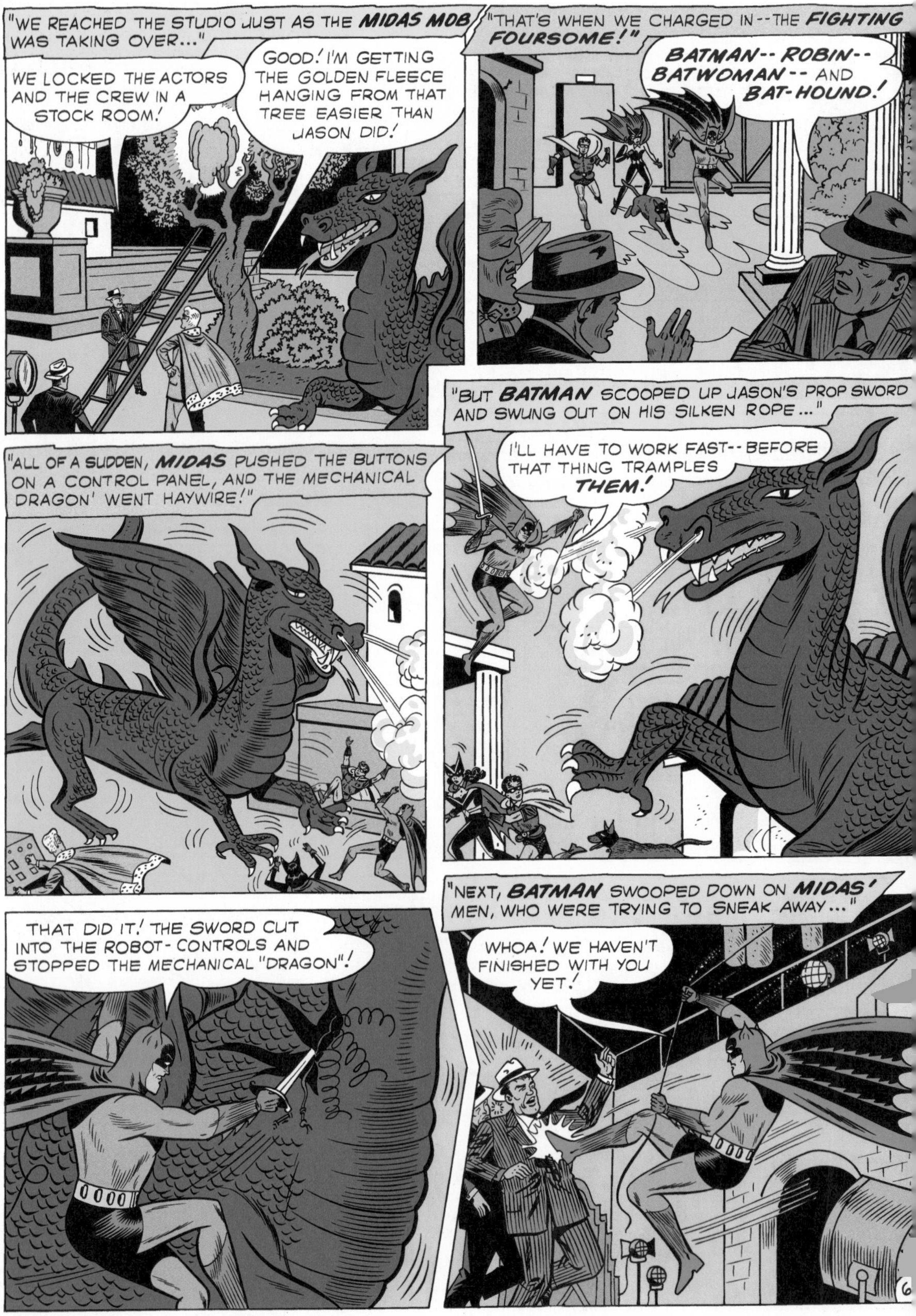
"WE REACHED THE STUDIO JUST AS THE MIDAS MOB WAS TAKING OVER..."
WE LOCKED THE ACTORS AND THE CREW IN A STOCK ROOM!
GOOD! I'M GETTING THE GOLDEN FLEECE HANGING FROM THAT TREE EASIER THAN JASON DID!
"THAT'S WHEN WE CHARGED IN--THE FIGHTING FOURSOME!"
BATMAN--ROBIN--BATWOMAN--AND BAT-HOUND!
"ALL OF A SUDDEN, MIDAS PUSHED THE BUTTONS ON A CONTROL PANEL, AND THE MECHANICAL 'DRAGON' WENT HAYWIRE!"
"BUT BATMAN SCOOPED UP JASON'S PROP SWORD AND SWUNG OUT ON HIS SILKEN ROPE..."
I'LL HAVE TO WORK FAST--BEFORE THAT THING TRAMPLES THEM!
THAT DID IT! THE SWORD CUT INTO THE ROBOT-CONTROLS AND STOPPED THE MECHANICAL "DRAGON"!
"NEXT, BATMAN SWOOPED DOWN ON MIDAS' MEN, WHO WERE TRYING TO SNEAK AWAY..."
WHOA! WE HAVEN'T FINISHED WITH YOU YET!
6

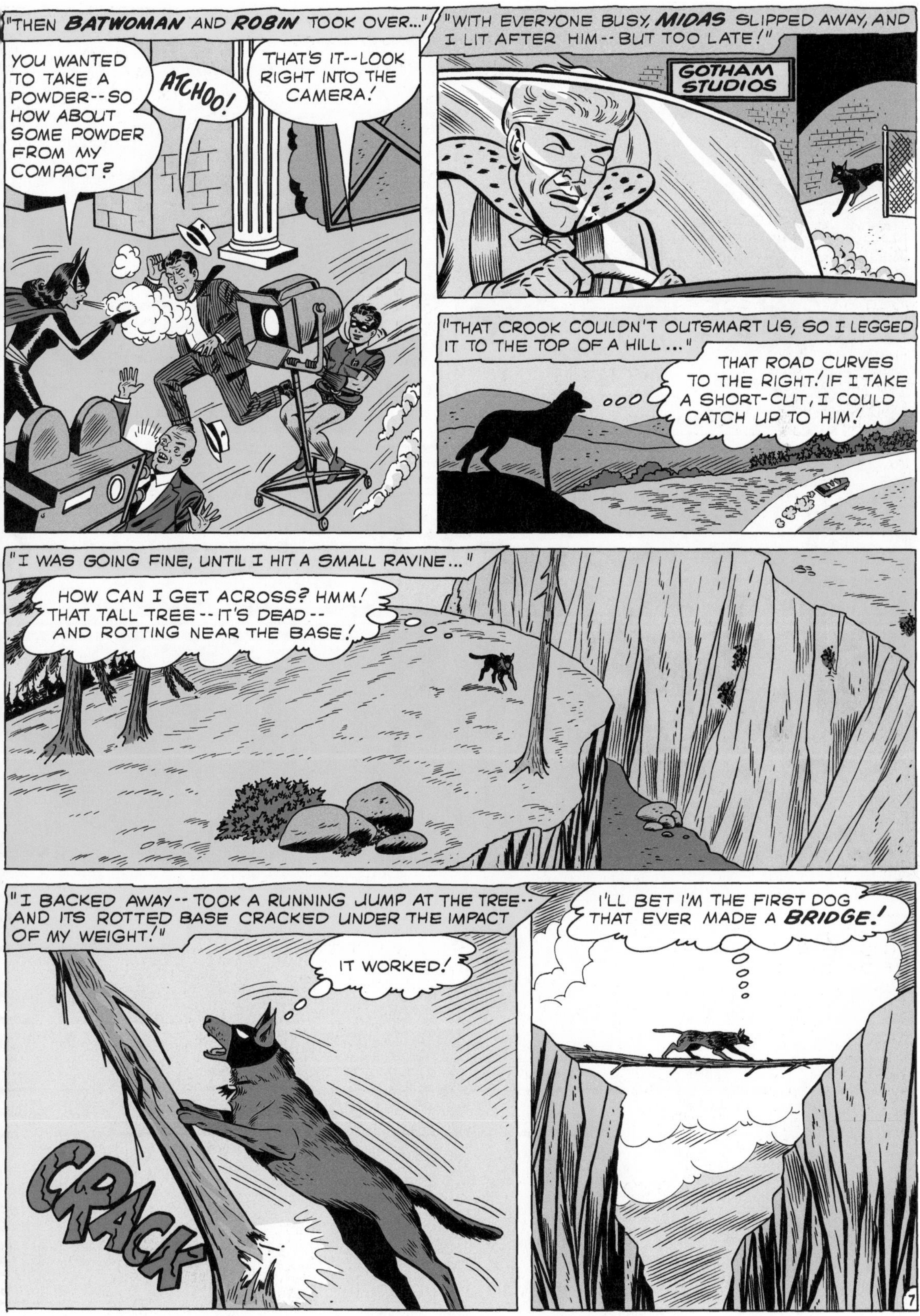
"THEN BATWOMAN AND ROBIN TOOK OVER..."
YOU WANTED TO TAKE A POWDER--SO HOW ABOUT SOME POWDER FROM MY COMPACT?
ATCHOO!
THAT'S IT--LOOK RIGHT INTO THE CAMERA!
"WITH EVERYONE BUSY, MIDAS SLIPPED AWAY, AND I LIT AFTER HIM--BUT TOO LATE!"
GOTHAM STUDIOS
"THAT CROOK COULDN'T OUTSMART US, SO I LEGGED IT TO THE TOP OF A HILL..."
THAT ROAD CURVES TO THE RIGHT! IF I TAKE A SHORT-CUT, I COULD CATCH UP TO HIM!
"I WAS GOING FINE, UNTIL I HIT A SMALL RAVINE..."
HOW CAN I GET ACROSS? HMM! THAT TALL TREE--IT'S DEAD--AND ROTTING NEAR THE BASE!
"I BACKED AWAY--TOOK A RUNNING JUMP AT THE TREE--AND ITS ROTTED BASE CRACKED UNDER THE IMPACT OF MY WEIGHT!"
IT WORKED!
CRACK
I'LL BET I'M THE FIRST DOG THAT EVER MADE A BRIDGE!
7

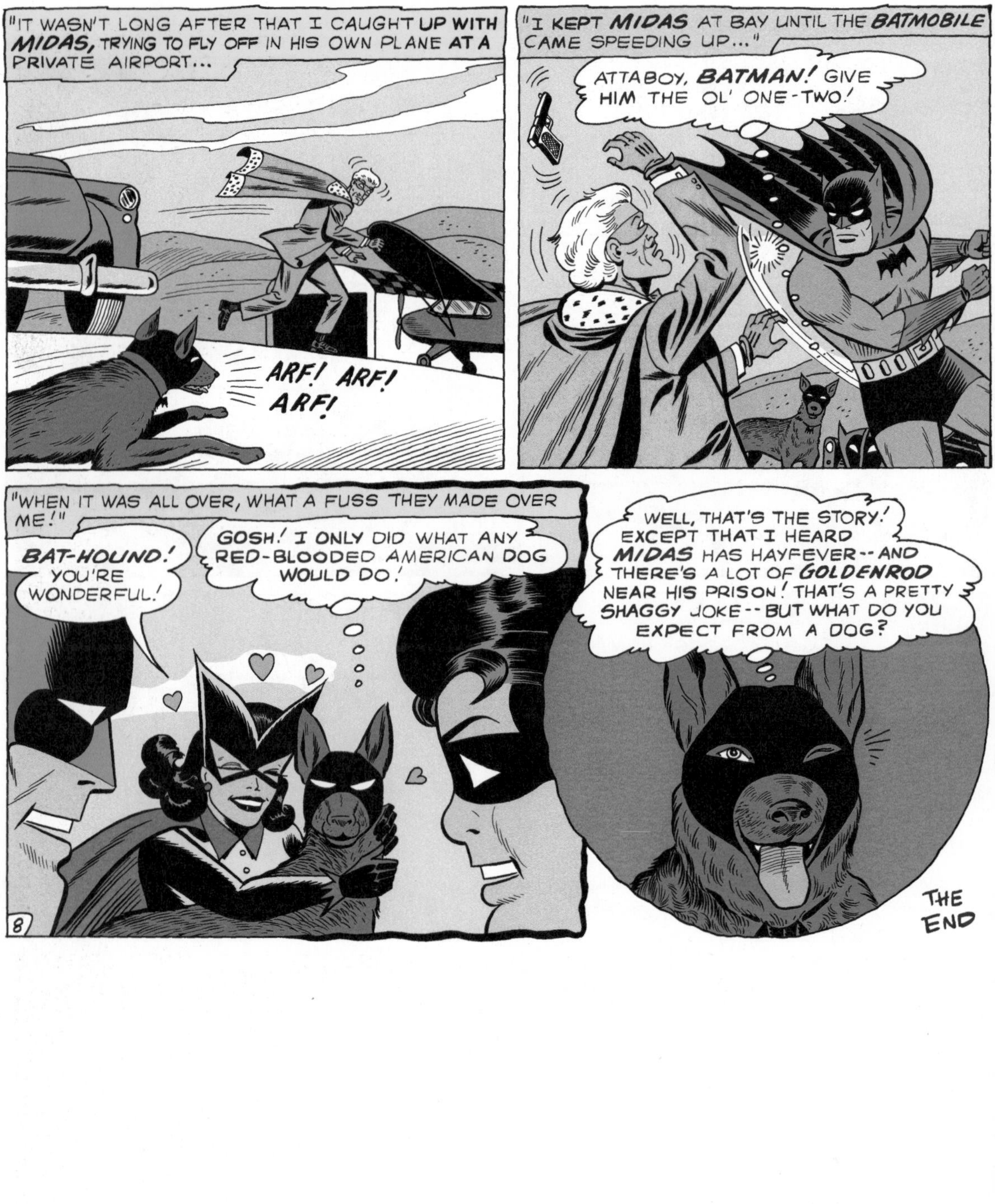
"IT WASN'T LONG AFTER THAT I CAUGHT UP WITH MIDAS, TRYING TO FLY OFF IN HIS OWN PLANE AT A PRIVATE AIRPORT...
ARF! ARF! ARF!
"I KEPT MIDAS AT BAY UNTIL THE BATMOBILE CAME SPEEDING UP..."
ATTABOY, BATMAN! GIVE HIM THE OL' ONE-TWO!
"WHEN IT WAS ALL OVER, WHAT A FUSS THEY MADE OVER ME!"
BAT-HOUND! YOU'RE WONDERFUL!
GOSH! I ONLY DID WHAT ANY RED-BLOODED AMERICAN DOG WOULD DO!
8
WELL, THAT'S THE STORY! EXCEPT THAT I HEARD MIDAS HAS HAYFEVER--AND THERE'S A LOT OF GOLDENROD NEAR HIS PRISON! THAT'S A PRETTY SHAGGY JOKE--BUT WHAT DO YOU EXPECT FROM A DOG?
THE END

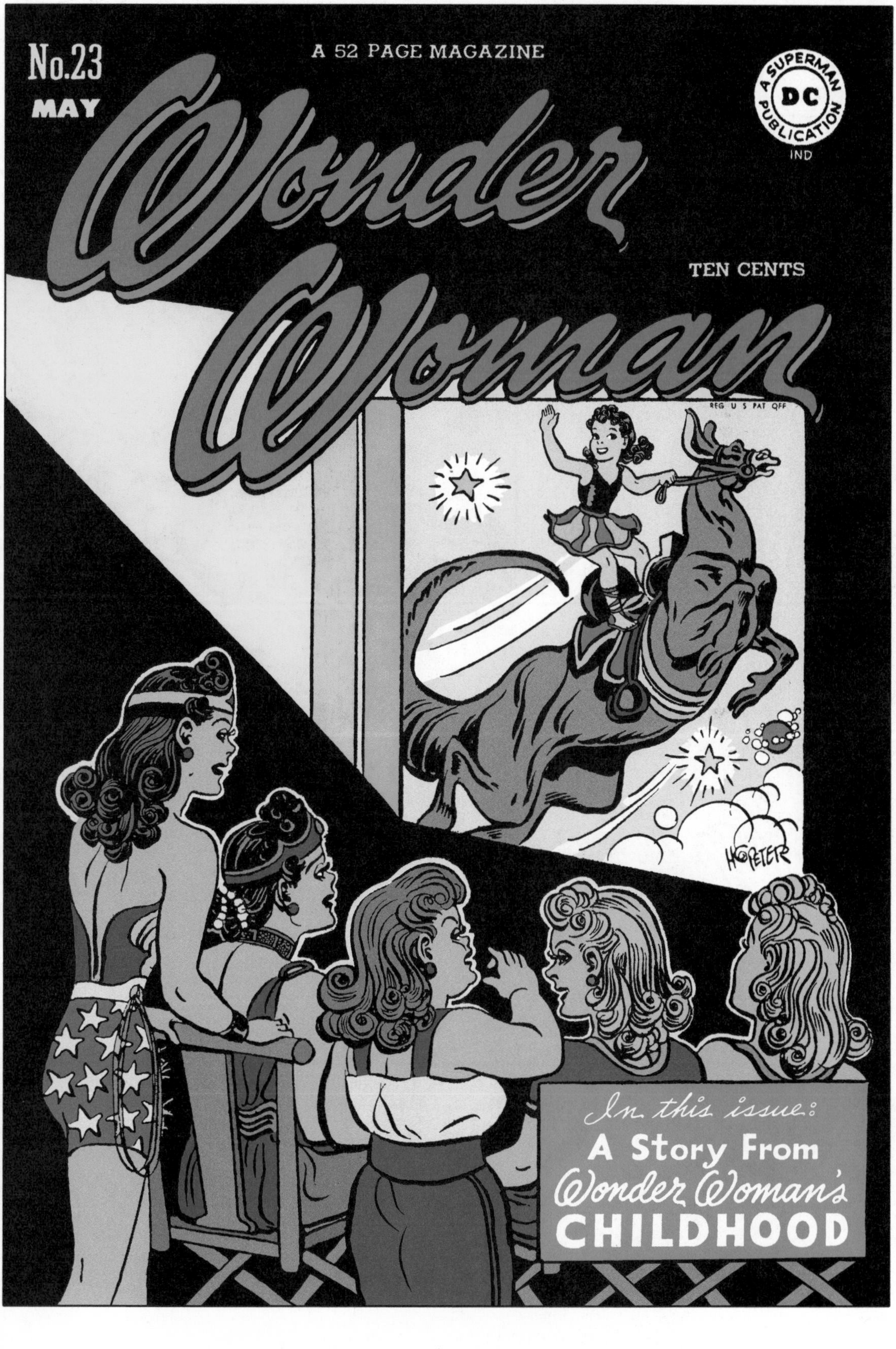
No.23
MAY
A 52 PAGE MAGAZINE
A SUPERMAN DC PUBLICATION
IND
Wonder Woman
TEN CENTS
REG U S PAT OFF
H G PETER
In this issue:
A Story From
Wonder Woman's
CHILDHOOD

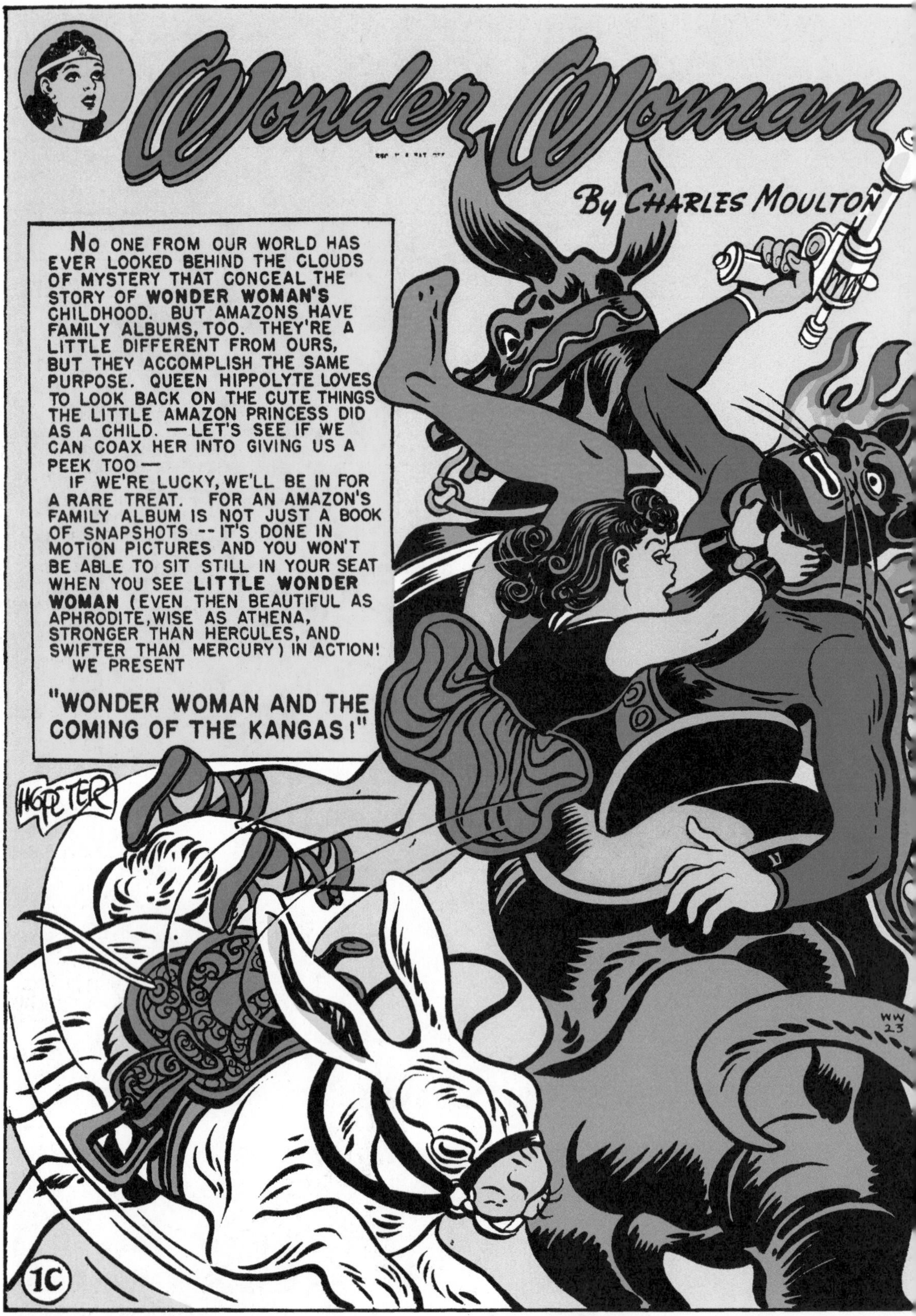

Wonder Woman
By Charles Moulton
No one from our world has ever looked behind the clouds of mystery that conceal the story of WONDER WOMAN'S childhood. But Amazons have family albums, too. They're a little different from ours, but they accomplish the same purpose. Queen Hippolyte loves to look back on the cute things the little Amazon princess did as a child. — Let's see if we can coax her into giving us a peek too —
If we're lucky, we'll be in for a rare treat. For an Amazon's family album is not just a book of snapshots -- it's done in motion pictures and you won't be able to sit still in your seat when you see LITTLE WONDER WOMAN (even then beautiful as Aphrodite, wise as Athena, stronger than Hercules, and swifter than Mercury) in action!
We present
"WONDER WOMAN AND THE COMING OF THE KANGAS!"
1C

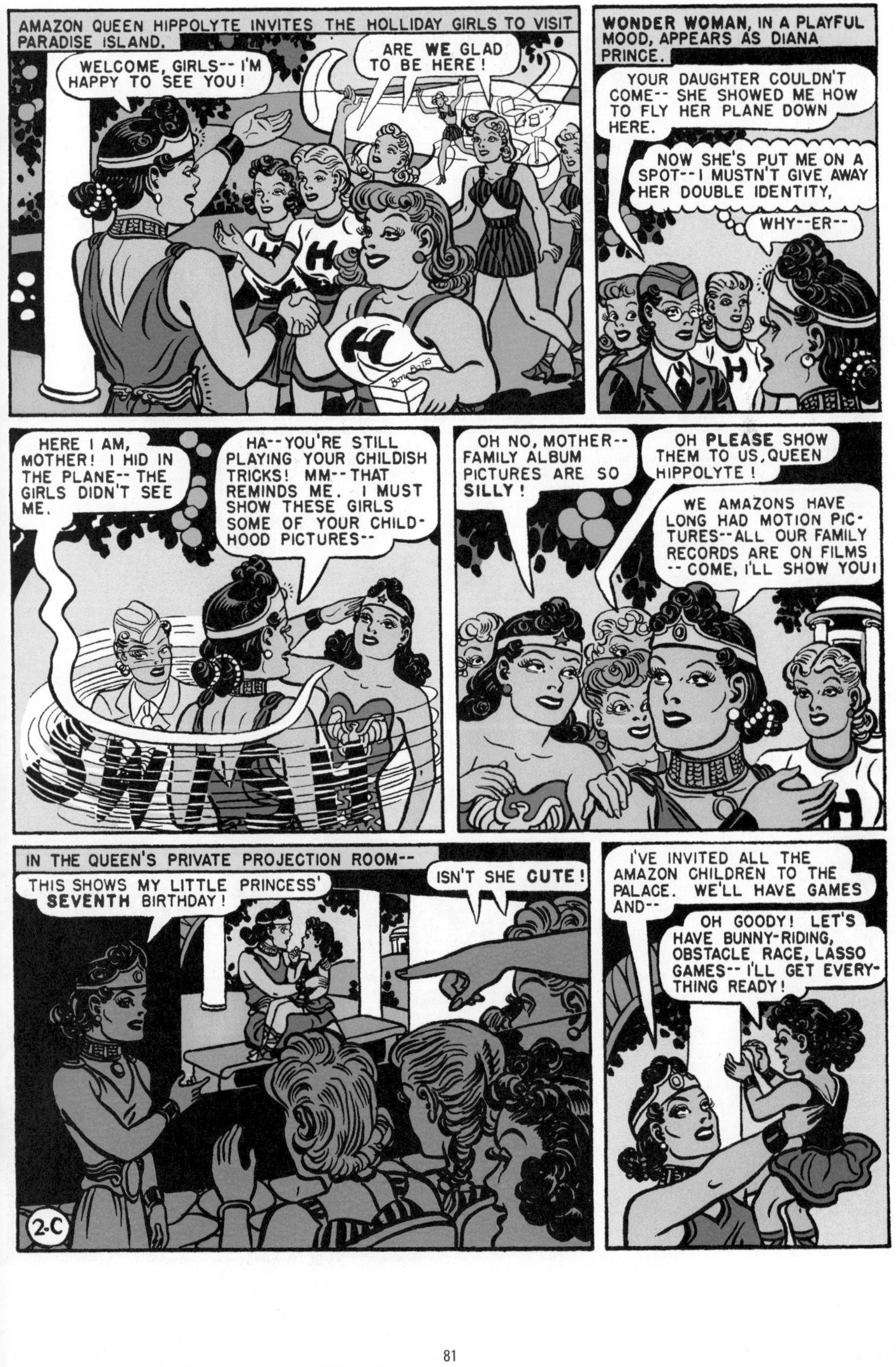

AMAZON QUEEN HIPPOLYTE INVITES THE HOLLIDAY GIRLS TO VISIT PARADISE ISLAND.
WELCOME, GIRLS-- I'M HAPPY TO SEE YOU!
ARE WE GLAD TO BE HERE!
WONDER WOMAN, IN A PLAYFUL MOOD, APPEARS AS DIANA PRINCE.
YOUR DAUGHTER COULDN'T COME-- SHE SHOWED ME HOW TO FLY HER PLANE DOWN HERE.
NOW SHE'S PUT ME ON A SPOT--I MUSTN'T GIVE AWAY HER DOUBLE IDENTITY,
WHY--ER--
HERE I AM, MOTHER! I HID IN THE PLANE-- THE GIRLS DIDN'T SEE ME.
HA--YOU'RE STILL PLAYING YOUR CHILDISH TRICKS! MM--THAT REMINDS ME. I MUST SHOW THESE GIRLS SOME OF YOUR CHILDHOOD PICTURES--
SWISH
OH NO, MOTHER-- FAMILY ALBUM PICTURES ARE SO SILLY!
OH PLEASE SHOW THEM TO US, QUEEN HIPPOLYTE!
WE AMAZONS HAVE LONG HAD MOTION PICTURES--ALL OUR FAMILY RECORDS ARE ON FILMS --COME, I'LL SHOW YOU!
IN THE QUEEN'S PRIVATE PROJECTION ROOM--
THIS SHOWS MY LITTLE PRINCESS' SEVENTH BIRTHDAY!
ISN'T SHE CUTE!
2-C
I'VE INVITED ALL THE AMAZON CHILDREN TO THE PALACE. WE'LL HAVE GAMES AND--
OH GOODY! LET'S HAVE BUNNY-RIDING, OBSTACLE RACE, LASSO GAMES-- I'LL GET EVERYTHING READY!

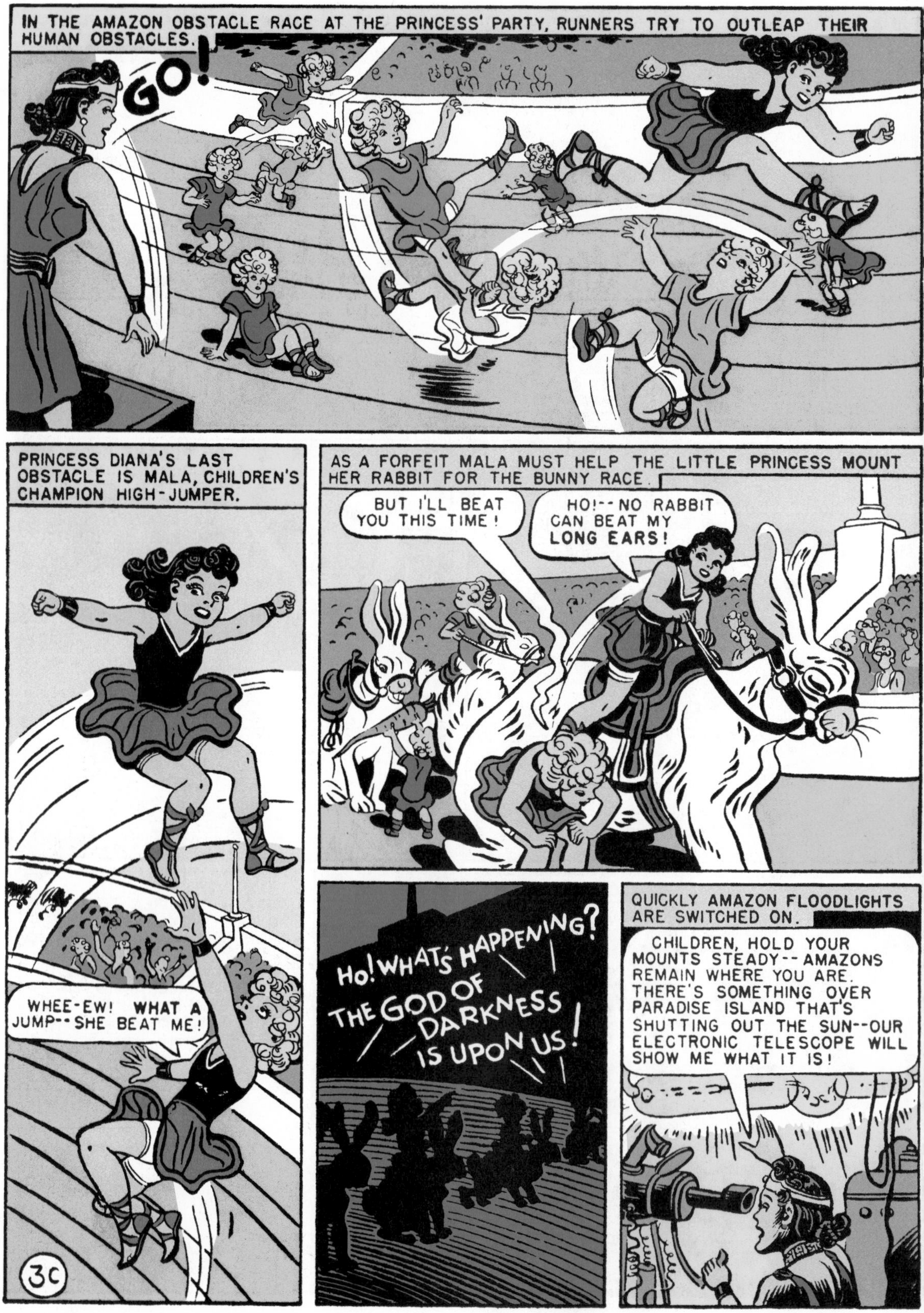
IN THE AMAZON OBSTACLE RACE AT THE PRINCESS' PARTY, RUNNERS TRY TO OUTLEAP THEIR HUMAN OBSTACLES.
GO!
PRINCESS DIANA'S LAST OBSTACLE IS MALA, CHILDREN'S CHAMPION HIGH-JUMPER.
WHEE-EW! WHAT A JUMP--SHE BEAT ME!
3C
AS A FORFEIT MALA MUST HELP THE LITTLE PRINCESS MOUNT HER RABBIT FOR THE BUNNY RACE.
BUT I'LL BEAT YOU THIS TIME!
HO!--NO RABBIT CAN BEAT MY LONG EARS!
HO! WHAT'S HAPPENING?
THE GOD OF DARKNESS IS UPON US!
QUICKLY AMAZON FLOODLIGHTS ARE SWITCHED ON.
CHILDREN, HOLD YOUR MOUNTS STEADY--AMAZONS REMAIN WHERE YOU ARE. THERE'S SOMETHING OVER PARADISE ISLAND THAT'S SHUTTING OUT THE SUN--OUR ELECTRONIC TELESCOPE WILL SHOW ME WHAT IT IS!

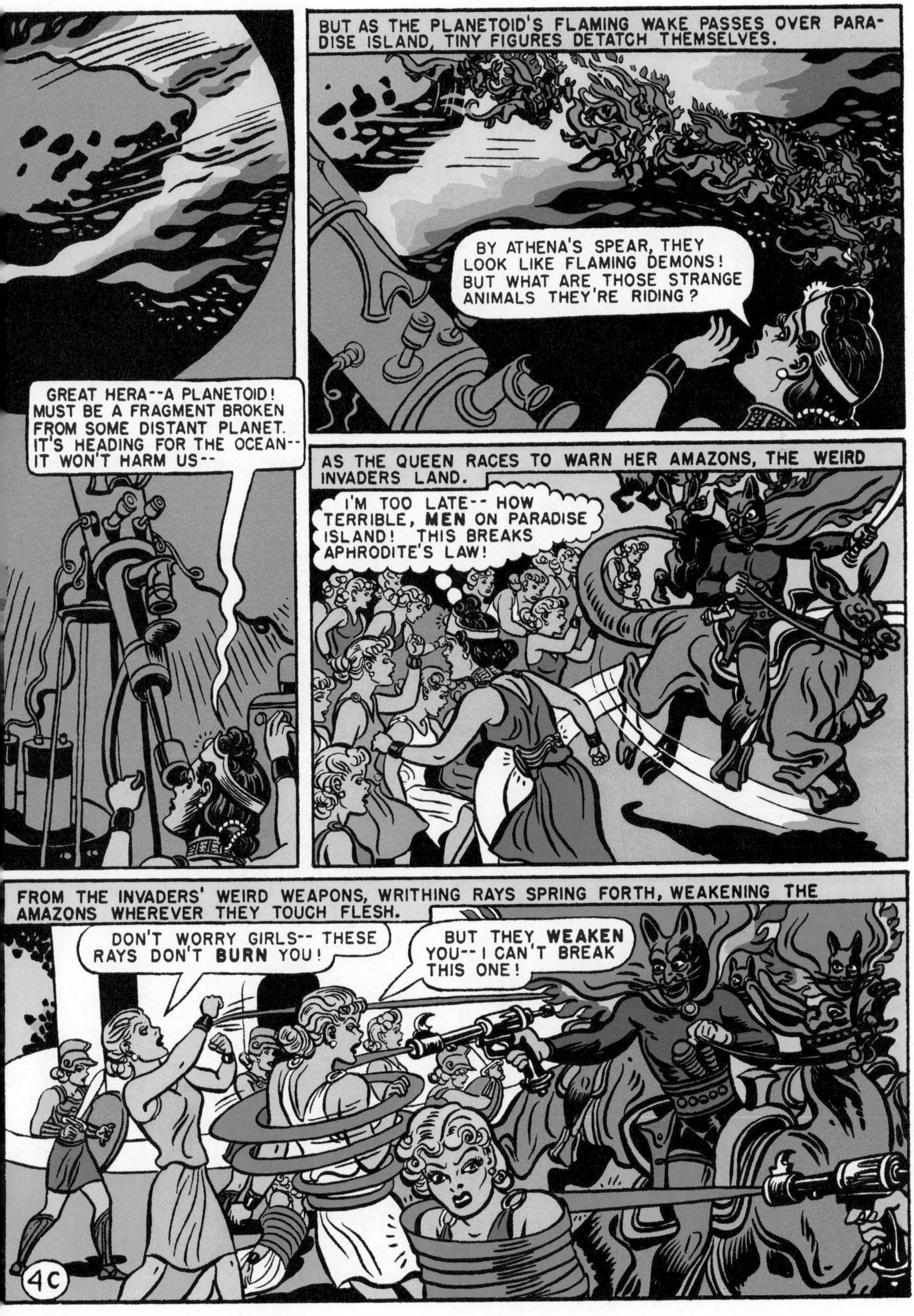

GREAT HERA--A PLANETOID! MUST BE A FRAGMENT BROKEN FROM SOME DISTANT PLANET. IT'S HEADING FOR THE OCEAN--IT WON'T HARM US--
BUT AS THE PLANETOID'S FLAMING WAKE PASSES OVER PARADISE ISLAND, TINY FIGURES DETATCH THEMSELVES.
BY ATHENA'S SPEAR, THEY LOOK LIKE FLAMING DEMONS! BUT WHAT ARE THOSE STRANGE ANIMALS THEY'RE RIDING?
AS THE QUEEN RACES TO WARN HER AMAZONS, THE WEIRD INVADERS LAND.
I'M TOO LATE-- HOW TERRIBLE, **MEN** ON PARADISE ISLAND! THIS BREAKS APHRODITE'S LAW!
FROM THE INVADERS' WEIRD WEAPONS, WRITHING RAYS SPRING FORTH, WEAKENING THE AMAZONS WHEREVER THEY TOUCH FLESH.
DON'T WORRY GIRLS-- THESE RAYS DON'T **BURN** YOU!
BUT THEY **WEAKEN** YOU--I CAN'T BREAK THIS ONE!
4C

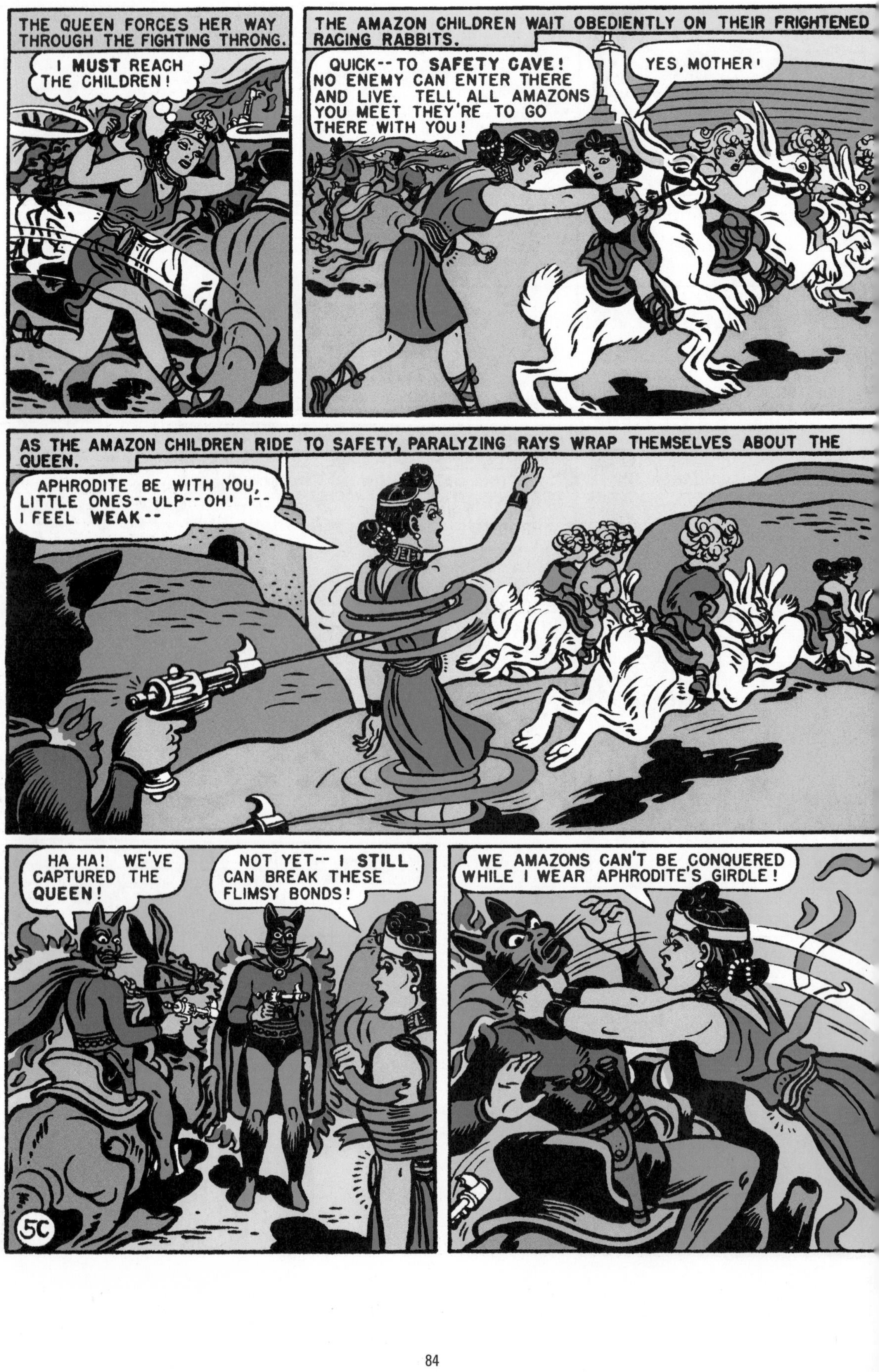
THE QUEEN FORCES HER WAY THROUGH THE FIGHTING THRONG.
I MUST REACH THE CHILDREN!
THE AMAZON CHILDREN WAIT OBEDIENTLY ON THEIR FRIGHTENED RACING RABBITS.
QUICK-- TO SAFETY CAVE! NO ENEMY CAN ENTER THERE AND LIVE. TELL ALL AMAZONS YOU MEET THEY'RE TO GO THERE WITH YOU!
YES, MOTHER!
AS THE AMAZON CHILDREN RIDE TO SAFETY, PARALYZING RAYS WRAP THEMSELVES ABOUT THE QUEEN.
APHRODITE BE WITH YOU, LITTLE ONES-- ULP-- OH! I-- I FEEL WEAK--
HA HA! WE'VE CAPTURED THE QUEEN!
NOT YET-- I STILL CAN BREAK THESE FLIMSY BONDS!
5C
WE AMAZONS CAN'T BE CONQUERED WHILE I WEAR APHRODITE'S GIRDLE!

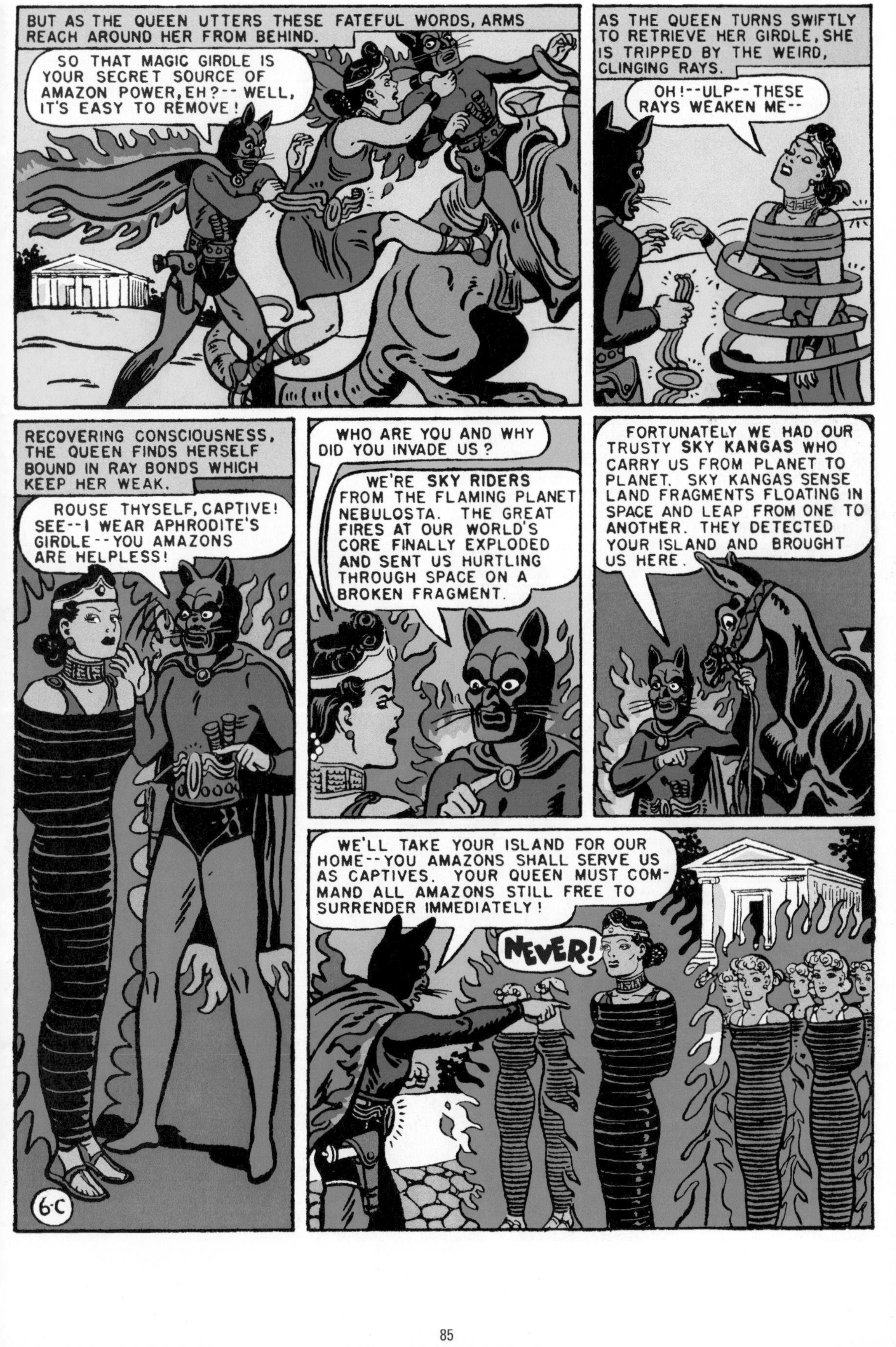

BUT AS THE QUEEN UTTERS THESE FATEFUL WORDS, ARMS REACH AROUND HER FROM BEHIND.
SO THAT MAGIC GIRDLE IS YOUR SECRET SOURCE OF AMAZON POWER, EH?-- WELL, IT'S EASY TO REMOVE!
AS THE QUEEN TURNS SWIFTLY TO RETRIEVE HER GIRDLE, SHE IS TRIPPED BY THE WEIRD, CLINGING RAYS.
OH!--ULP--THESE RAYS WEAKEN ME--
RECOVERING CONSCIOUSNESS, THE QUEEN FINDS HERSELF BOUND IN RAY BONDS WHICH KEEP HER WEAK.
ROUSE THYSELF, CAPTIVE! SEE--I WEAR APHRODITE'S GIRDLE--YOU AMAZONS ARE HELPLESS!
6-C
WHO ARE YOU AND WHY DID YOU INVADE US?
WE'RE SKY RIDERS FROM THE FLAMING PLANET NEBULOSTA. THE GREAT FIRES AT OUR WORLD'S CORE FINALLY EXPLODED AND SENT US HURTLING THROUGH SPACE ON A BROKEN FRAGMENT.
FORTUNATELY WE HAD OUR TRUSTY SKY KANGAS WHO CARRY US FROM PLANET TO PLANET. SKY KANGAS SENSE LAND FRAGMENTS FLOATING IN SPACE AND LEAP FROM ONE TO ANOTHER. THEY DETECTED YOUR ISLAND AND BROUGHT US HERE.
WE'LL TAKE YOUR ISLAND FOR OUR HOME--YOU AMAZONS SHALL SERVE US AS CAPTIVES. YOUR QUEEN MUST COMMAND ALL AMAZONS STILL FREE TO SURRENDER IMMEDIATELY!
NEVER!

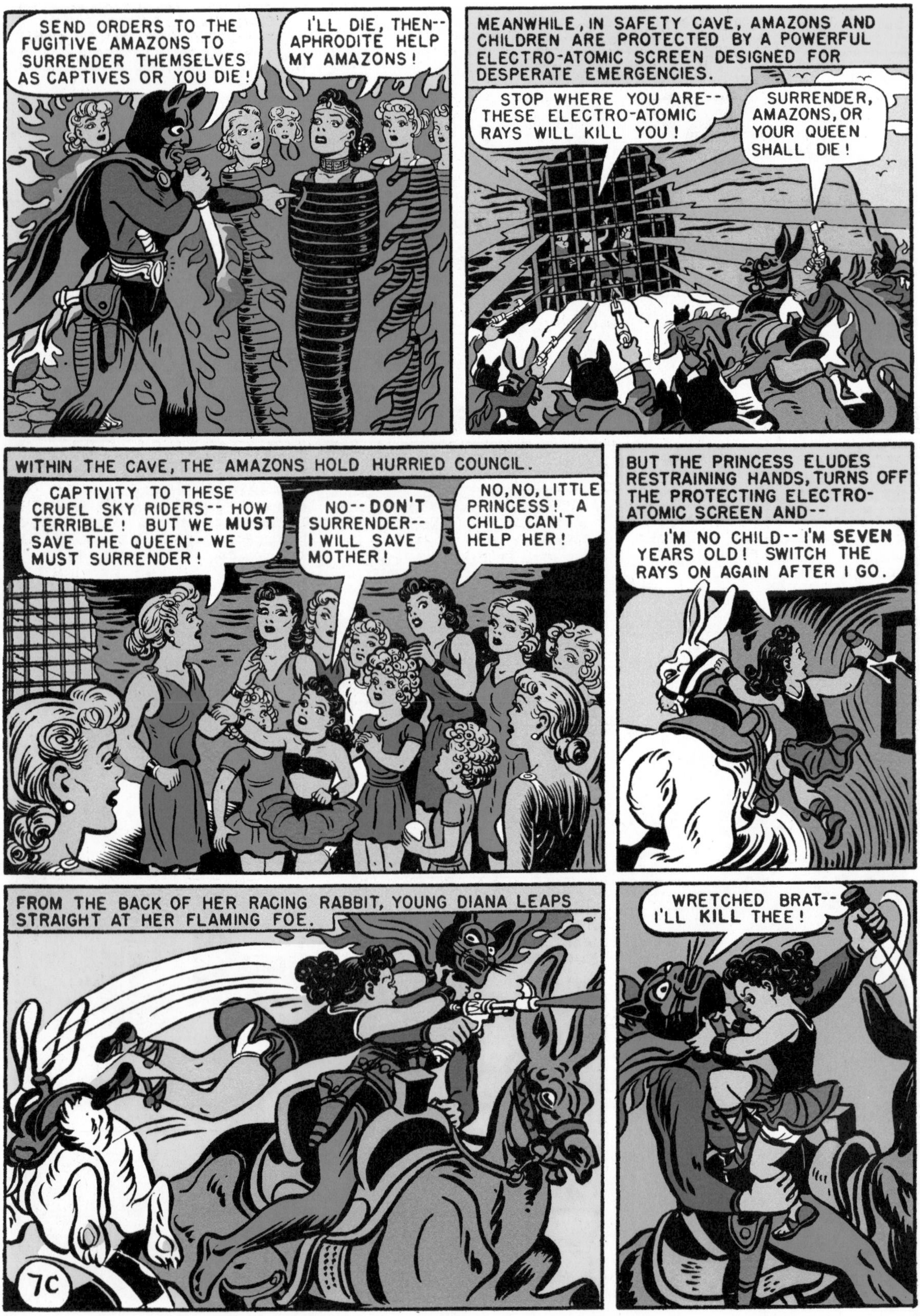
SEND ORDERS TO THE FUGITIVE AMAZONS TO SURRENDER THEMSELVES AS CAPTIVES OR YOU DIE!
I'LL DIE, THEN-- APHRODITE HELP MY AMAZONS!
MEANWHILE, IN SAFETY CAVE, AMAZONS AND CHILDREN ARE PROTECTED BY A POWERFUL ELECTRO-ATOMIC SCREEN DESIGNED FOR DESPERATE EMERGENCIES.
STOP WHERE YOU ARE-- THESE ELECTRO-ATOMIC RAYS WILL KILL YOU!
SURRENDER, AMAZONS, OR YOUR QUEEN SHALL DIE!
WITHIN THE CAVE, THE AMAZONS HOLD HURRIED COUNCIL.
CAPTIVITY TO THESE CRUEL SKY RIDERS-- HOW TERRIBLE! BUT WE MUST SAVE THE QUEEN-- WE MUST SURRENDER!
NO-- DON'T SURRENDER-- I WILL SAVE MOTHER!
NO, NO, LITTLE PRINCESS! A CHILD CAN'T HELP HER!
BUT THE PRINCESS ELUDES RESTRAINING HANDS, TURNS OFF THE PROTECTING ELECTRO-ATOMIC SCREEN AND--
I'M NO CHILD-- I'M SEVEN YEARS OLD! SWITCH THE RAYS ON AGAIN AFTER I GO.
FROM THE BACK OF HER RACING RABBIT, YOUNG DIANA LEAPS STRAIGHT AT HER FLAMING FOE.
7C
WRETCHED BRAT-- I'LL KILL THEE!

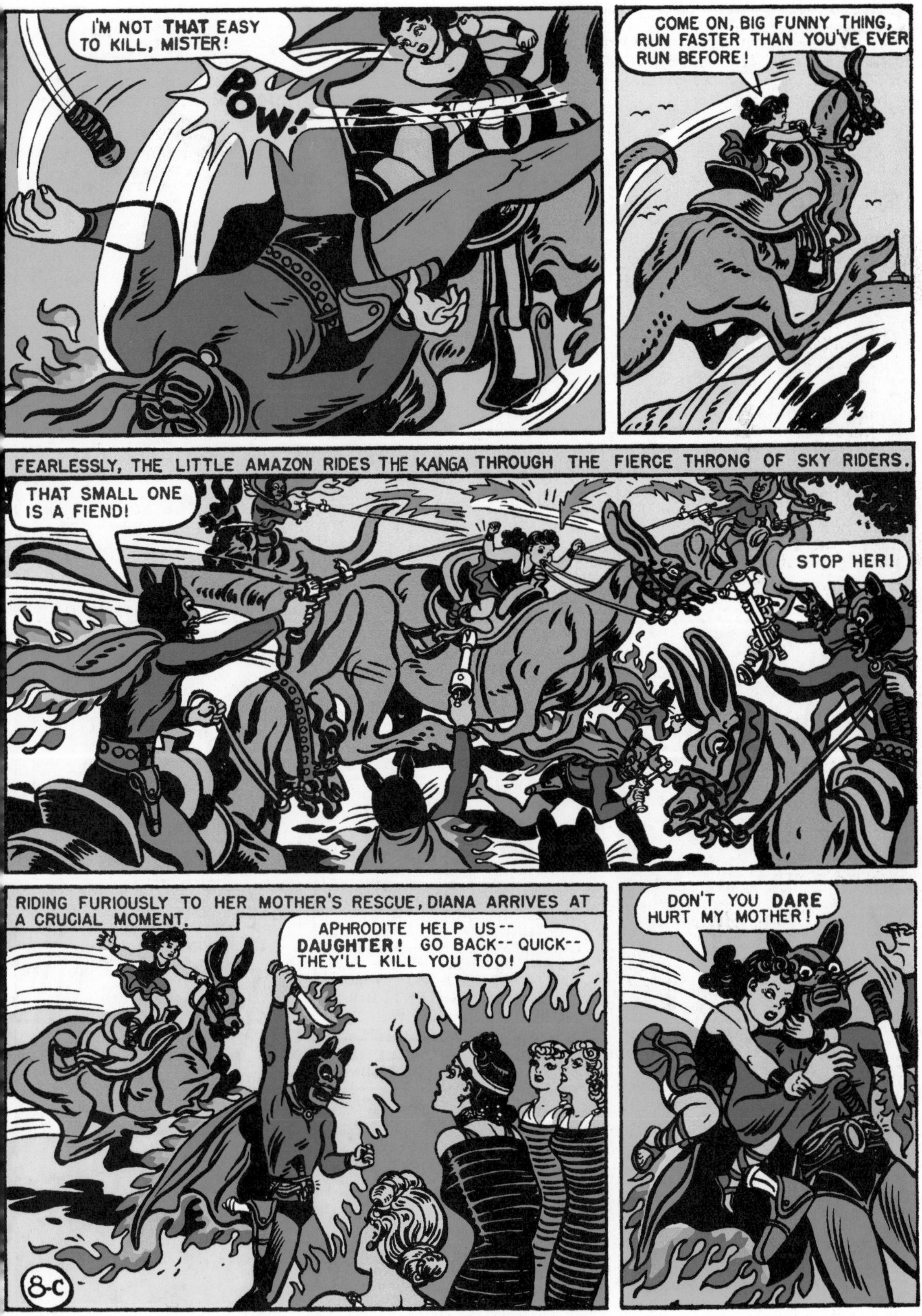

I'M NOT THAT EASY TO KILL, MISTER!
POW!
COME ON, BIG FUNNY THING, RUN FASTER THAN YOU'VE EVER RUN BEFORE!
FEARLESSLY, THE LITTLE AMAZON RIDES THE KANGA THROUGH THE FIERCE THRONG OF SKY RIDERS.
THAT SMALL ONE IS A FIEND!
STOP HER!
RIDING FURIOUSLY TO HER MOTHER'S RESCUE, DIANA ARRIVES AT A CRUCIAL MOMENT.
APHRODITE HELP US-- DAUGHTER! GO BACK-- QUICK-- THEY'LL KILL YOU TOO!
8-C
DON'T YOU DARE HURT MY MOTHER!

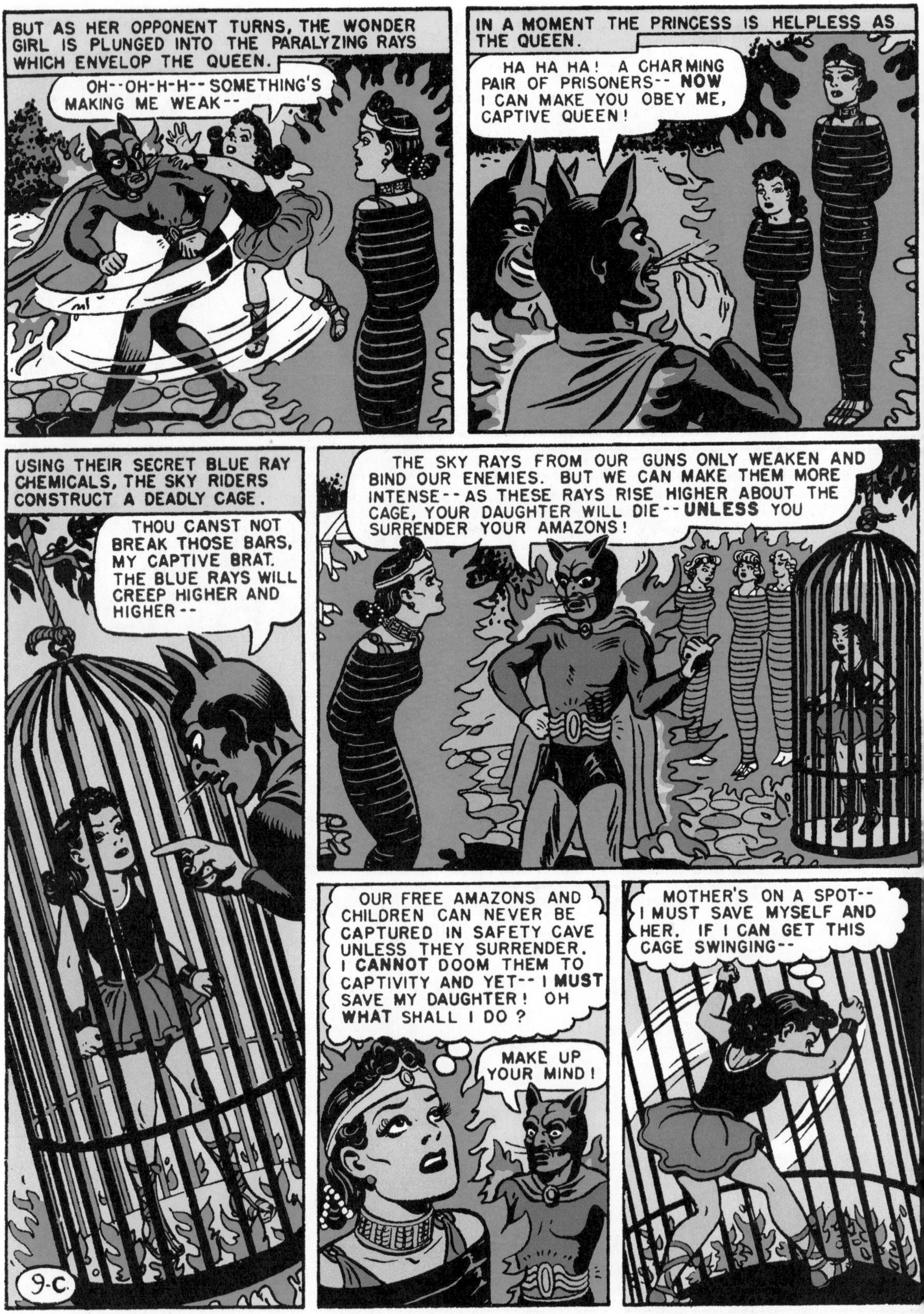
BUT AS HER OPPONENT TURNS, THE WONDER GIRL IS PLUNGED INTO THE PARALYZING RAYS WHICH ENVELOP THE QUEEN.
OH--OH-H-H--SOMETHING'S MAKING ME WEAK--
IN A MOMENT THE PRINCESS IS HELPLESS AS THE QUEEN.
HA HA HA! A CHARMING PAIR OF PRISONERS-- **NOW** I CAN MAKE YOU OBEY ME, CAPTIVE QUEEN!
USING THEIR SECRET BLUE RAY CHEMICALS, THE SKY RIDERS CONSTRUCT A DEADLY CAGE.
THOU CANST NOT BREAK THOSE BARS, MY CAPTIVE BRAT. THE BLUE RAYS WILL CREEP HIGHER AND HIGHER--
9-C.
THE SKY RAYS FROM OUR GUNS ONLY WEAKEN AND BIND OUR ENEMIES. BUT WE CAN MAKE THEM MORE INTENSE--AS THESE RAYS RISE HIGHER ABOUT THE CAGE, YOUR DAUGHTER WILL DIE--**UNLESS** YOU SURRENDER YOUR AMAZONS!
OUR FREE AMAZONS AND CHILDREN CAN NEVER BE CAPTURED IN SAFETY CAVE UNLESS THEY SURRENDER. I **CANNOT** DOOM THEM TO CAPTIVITY AND YET-- I **MUST** SAVE MY DAUGHTER! OH **WHAT** SHALL I DO?
MAKE UP YOUR MIND!
MOTHER'S ON A SPOT-- I MUST SAVE MYSELF AND HER. IF I CAN GET THIS CAGE SWINGING--

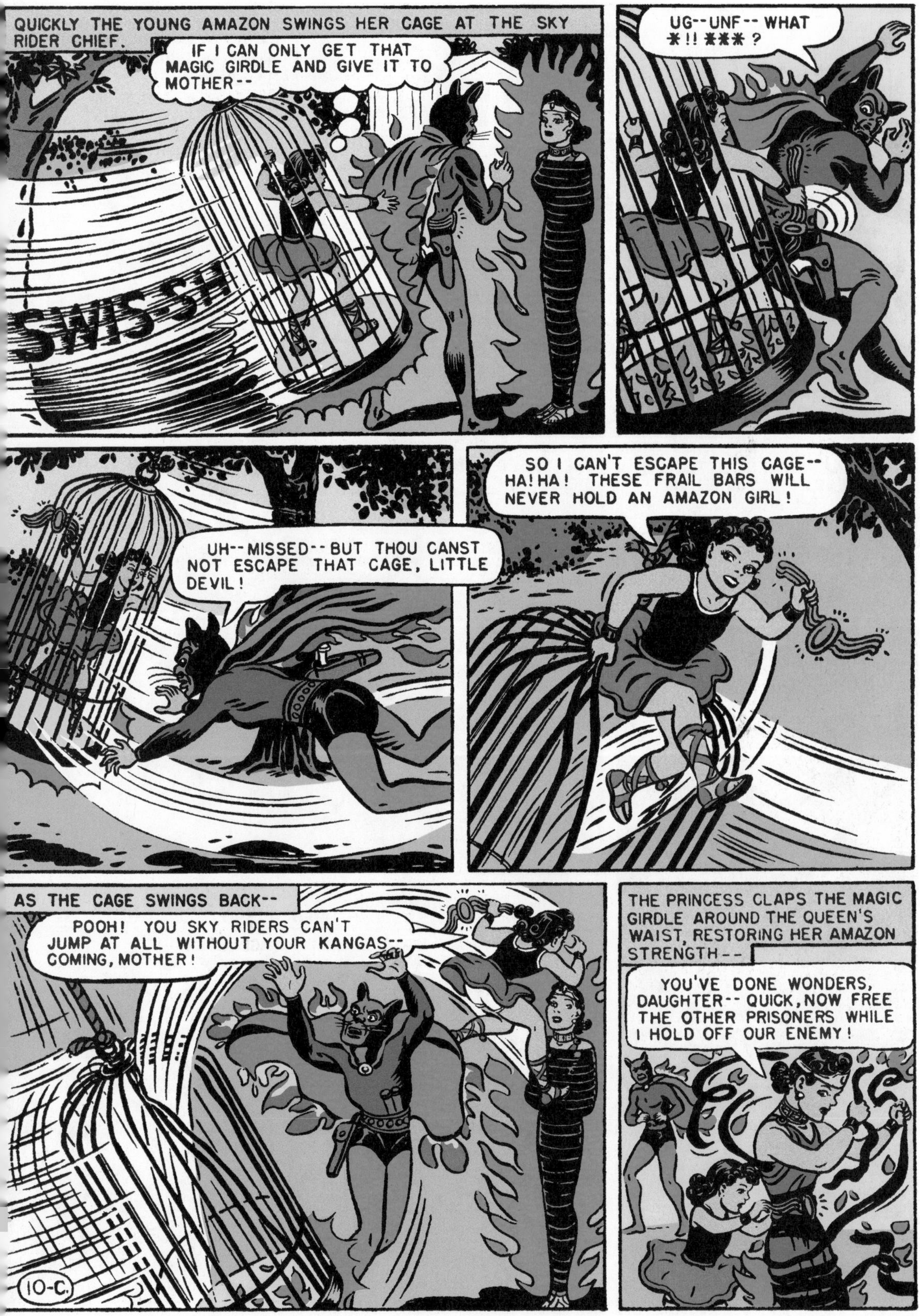
QUICKLY THE YOUNG AMAZON SWINGS HER CAGE AT THE SKY RIDER CHIEF.
IF I CAN ONLY GET THAT MAGIC GIRDLE AND GIVE IT TO MOTHER--
SWIS-SH
UG--UNF--WHAT *!! *** ?
UH--MISSED--BUT THOU CANST NOT ESCAPE THAT CAGE, LITTLE DEVIL!
SO I CAN'T ESCAPE THIS CAGE--HA! HA! THESE FRAIL BARS WILL NEVER HOLD AN AMAZON GIRL!
AS THE CAGE SWINGS BACK--
POOH! YOU SKY RIDERS CAN'T JUMP AT ALL WITHOUT YOUR KANGAS--COMING, MOTHER!
10-C.
THE PRINCESS CLAPS THE MAGIC GIRDLE AROUND THE QUEEN'S WAIST, RESTORING HER AMAZON STRENGTH--
YOU'VE DONE WONDERS, DAUGHTER--QUICK, NOW FREE THE OTHER PRISONERS WHILE I HOLD OFF OUR ENEMY!

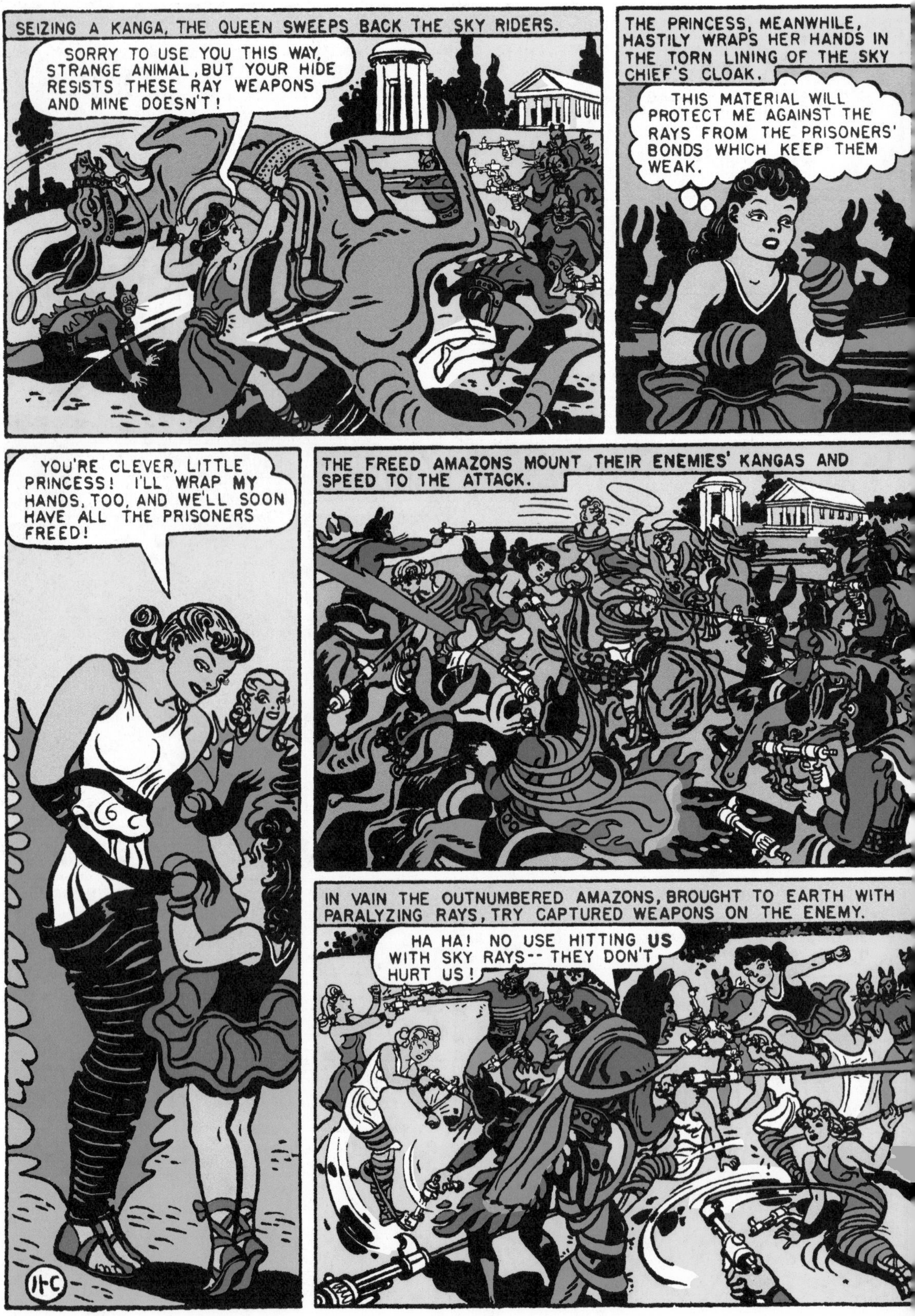

SEIZING A KANGA, THE QUEEN SWEEPS BACK THE SKY RIDERS.
SORRY TO USE YOU THIS WAY, STRANGE ANIMAL, BUT YOUR HIDE RESISTS THESE RAY WEAPONS AND MINE DOESN'T!
THE PRINCESS, MEANWHILE, HASTILY WRAPS HER HANDS IN THE TORN LINING OF THE SKY CHIEF'S CLOAK.
THIS MATERIAL WILL PROTECT ME AGAINST THE RAYS FROM THE PRISONERS' BONDS WHICH KEEP THEM WEAK.
YOU'RE CLEVER, LITTLE PRINCESS! I'LL WRAP MY HANDS, TOO, AND WE'LL SOON HAVE ALL THE PRISONERS FREED!
11-C
THE FREED AMAZONS MOUNT THEIR ENEMIES' KANGAS AND SPEED TO THE ATTACK.
IN VAIN THE OUTNUMBERED AMAZONS, BROUGHT TO EARTH WITH PARALYZING RAYS, TRY CAPTURED WEAPONS ON THE ENEMY.
HA HA! NO USE HITTING US WITH SKY RAYS-- THEY DON'T HURT US!

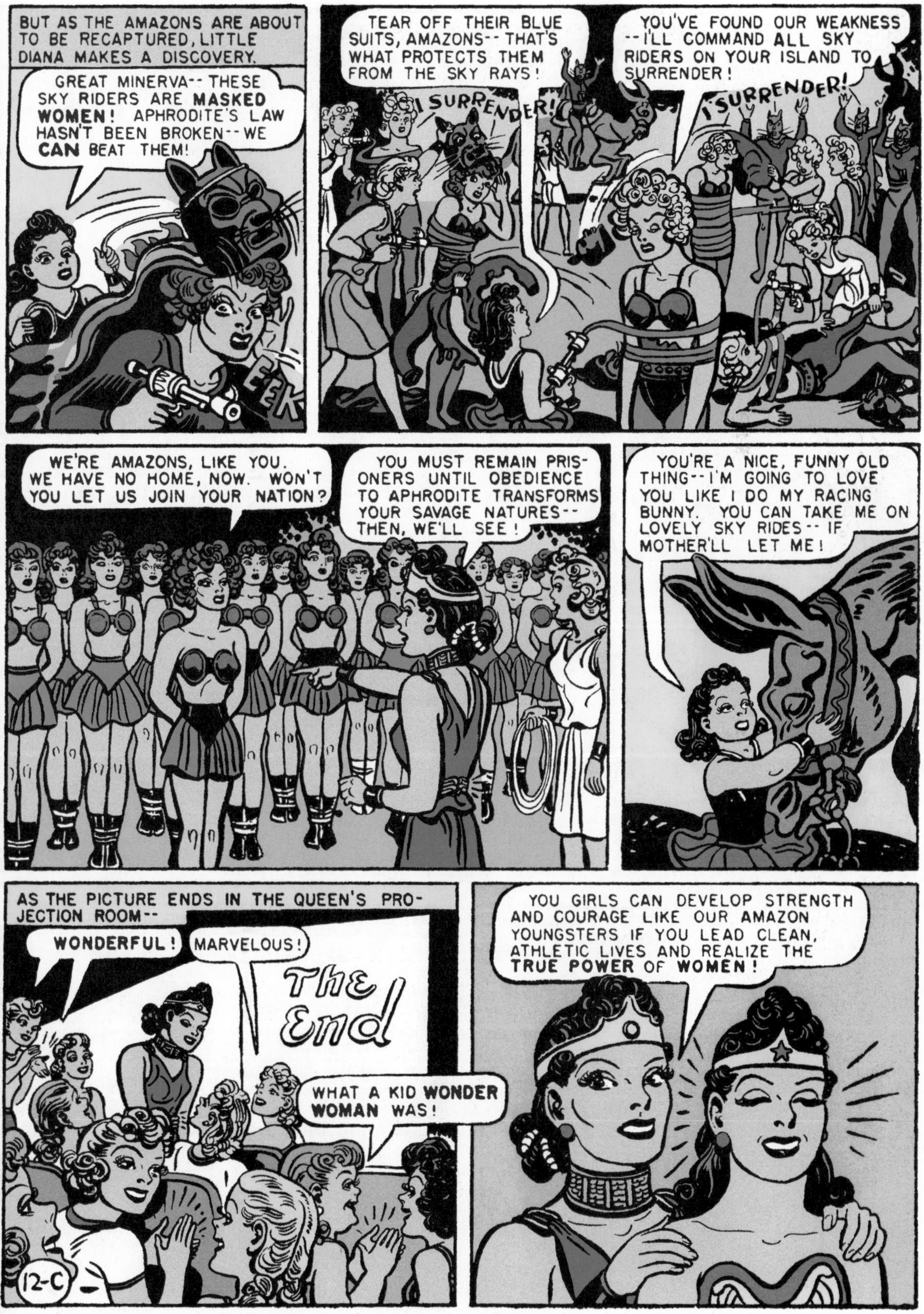
BUT AS THE AMAZONS ARE ABOUT TO BE RECAPTURED, LITTLE DIANA MAKES A DISCOVERY.
GREAT MINERVA-- THESE SKY RIDERS ARE **MASKED WOMEN**! APHRODITE'S LAW HASN'T BEEN BROKEN-- WE **CAN** BEAT THEM!
EEK
TEAR OFF THEIR BLUE SUITS, AMAZONS-- THAT'S WHAT PROTECTS THEM FROM THE SKY RAYS!
I SURRENDER!
YOU'VE FOUND OUR WEAKNESS --I'LL COMMAND **ALL** SKY RIDERS ON YOUR ISLAND TO SURRENDER!
I SURRENDER!
WE'RE AMAZONS, LIKE YOU. WE HAVE NO HOME, NOW. WON'T YOU LET US JOIN YOUR NATION?
YOU MUST REMAIN PRISONERS UNTIL OBEDIENCE TO APHRODITE TRANSFORMS YOUR SAVAGE NATURES-- THEN, WE'LL SEE!
YOU'RE A NICE, FUNNY OLD THING-- I'M GOING TO LOVE YOU LIKE I DO MY RACING BUNNY. YOU CAN TAKE ME ON LOVELY SKY RIDES-- IF MOTHER'LL LET ME!
AS THE PICTURE ENDS IN THE QUEEN'S PROJECTION ROOM--
WONDERFUL!
MARVELOUS!
The End
WHAT A KID **WONDER WOMAN** WAS!
12-C
YOU GIRLS CAN DEVELOP STRENGTH AND COURAGE LIKE OUR AMAZON YOUNGSTERS IF YOU LEAD CLEAN, ATHLETIC LIVES AND REALIZE THE **TRUE POWER** OF **WOMEN**!

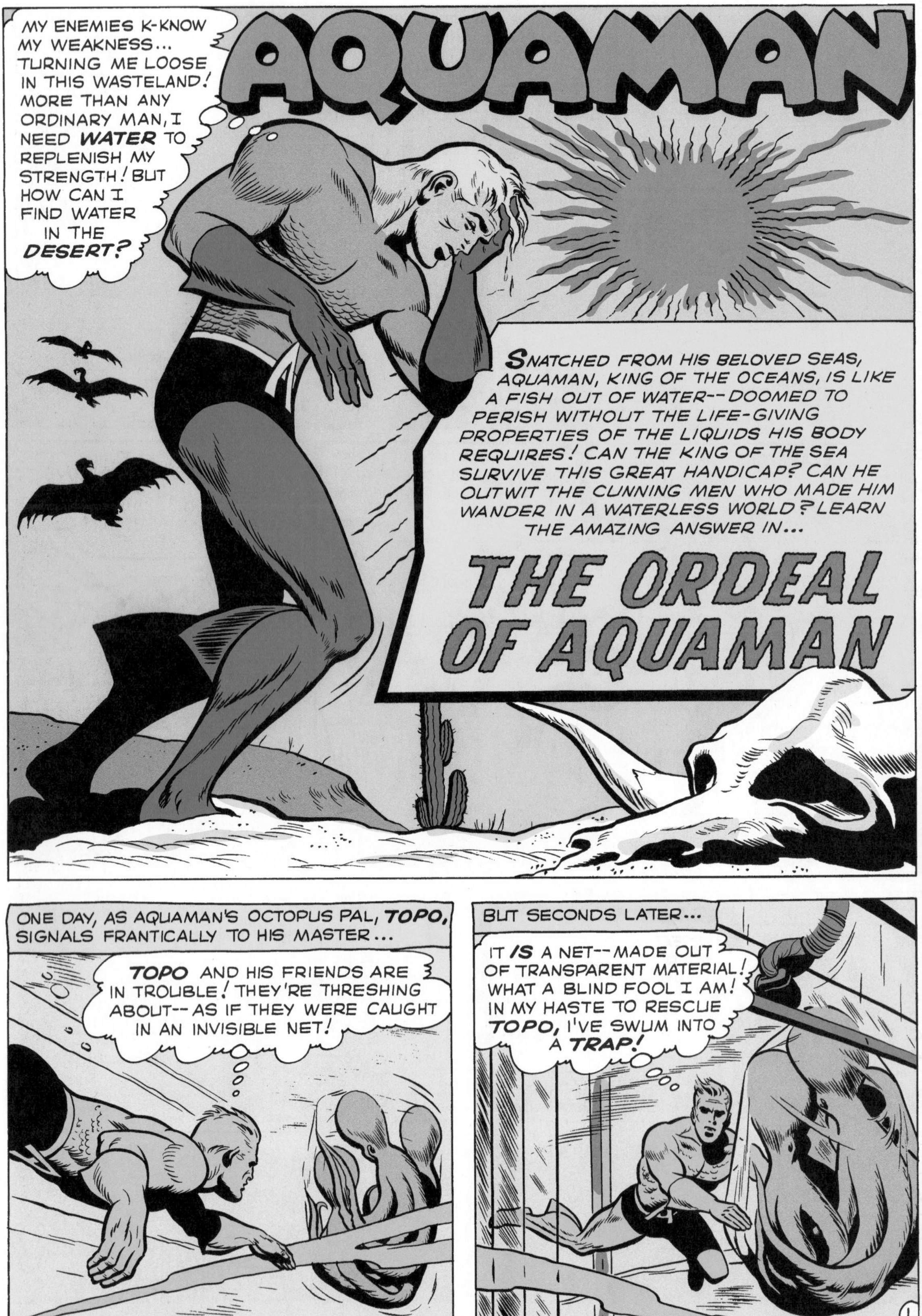
AQUAMAN
MY ENEMIES K-KNOW MY WEAKNESS... TURNING ME LOOSE IN THIS WASTELAND! MORE THAN ANY ORDINARY MAN, I NEED WATER TO REPLENISH MY STRENGTH! BUT HOW CAN I FIND WATER IN THE DESERT?
SNATCHED FROM HIS BELOVED SEAS, AQUAMAN, KING OF THE OCEANS, IS LIKE A FISH OUT OF WATER--DOOMED TO PERISH WITHOUT THE LIFE-GIVING PROPERTIES OF THE LIQUIDS HIS BODY REQUIRES! CAN THE KING OF THE SEA SURVIVE THIS GREAT HANDICAP? CAN HE OUTWIT THE CUNNING MEN WHO MADE HIM WANDER IN A WATERLESS WORLD? LEARN THE AMAZING ANSWER IN...
THE ORDEAL OF AQUAMAN
ONE DAY, AS AQUAMAN'S OCTOPUS PAL, TOPO, SIGNALS FRANTICALLY TO HIS MASTER...
TOPO AND HIS FRIENDS ARE IN TROUBLE! THEY'RE THRESHING ABOUT--AS IF THEY WERE CAUGHT IN AN INVISIBLE NET!
BUT SECONDS LATER...
IT IS A NET--MADE OUT OF TRANSPARENT MATERIAL! WHAT A BLIND FOOL I AM! IN MY HASTE TO RESCUE TOPO, I'VE SWUM INTO A TRAP!
1

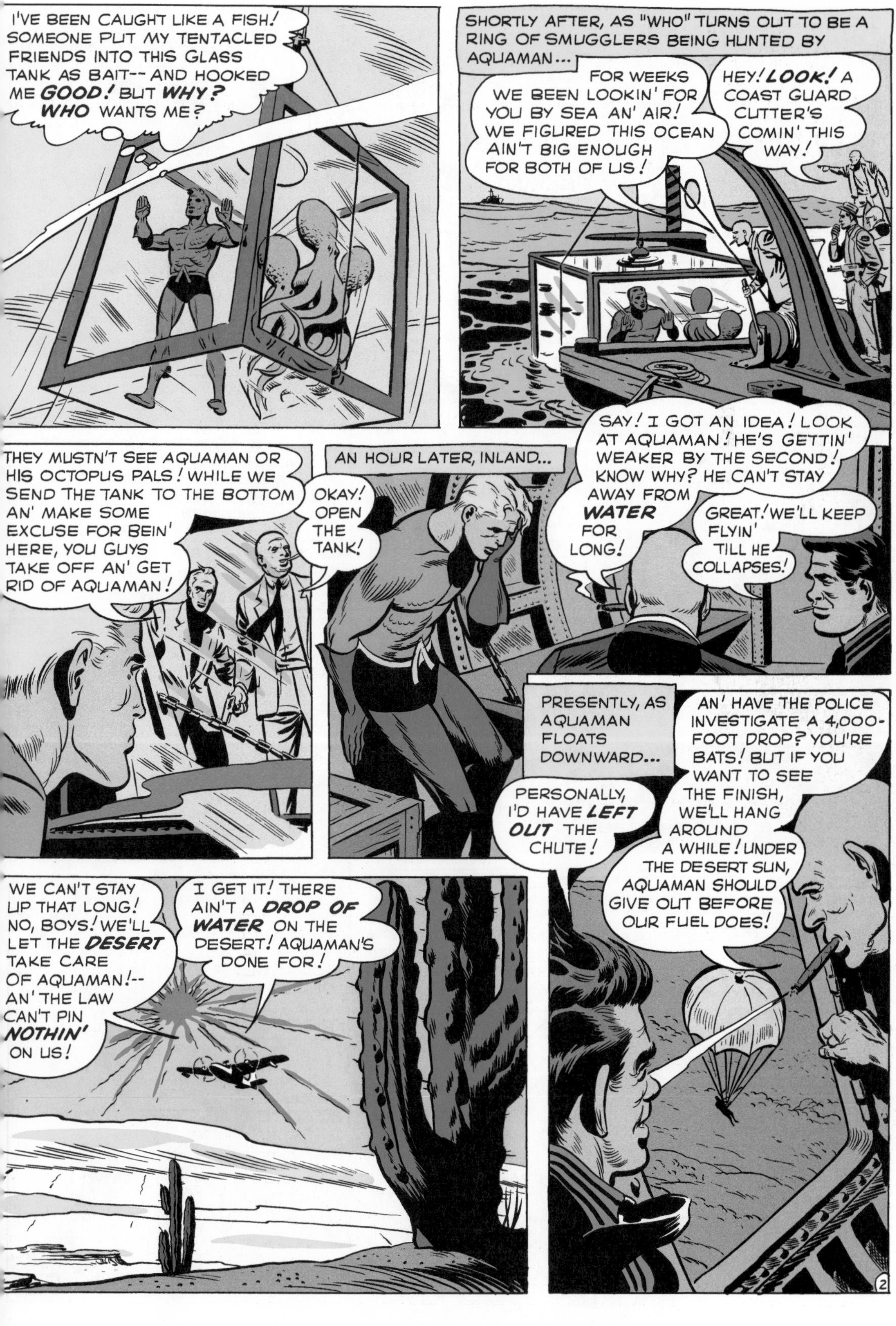
I'VE BEEN CAUGHT LIKE A FISH! SOMEONE PUT MY TENTACLED FRIENDS INTO THIS GLASS TANK AS BAIT-- AND HOOKED ME GOOD! BUT WHY? WHO WANTS ME?
SHORTLY AFTER, AS "WHO" TURNS OUT TO BE A RING OF SMUGGLERS BEING HUNTED BY AQUAMAN...
FOR WEEKS WE BEEN LOOKIN' FOR YOU BY SEA AN' AIR! WE FIGURED THIS OCEAN AIN'T BIG ENOUGH FOR BOTH OF US!
HEY! LOOK! A COAST GUARD CUTTER'S COMIN' THIS WAY!
THEY MUSTN'T SEE AQUAMAN OR HIS OCTOPUS PALS! WHILE WE SEND THE TANK TO THE BOTTOM AN' MAKE SOME EXCUSE FOR BEIN' HERE, YOU GUYS TAKE OFF AN' GET RID OF AQUAMAN!
AN HOUR LATER, INLAND...
OKAY! OPEN THE TANK!
SAY! I GOT AN IDEA! LOOK AT AQUAMAN! HE'S GETTIN' WEAKER BY THE SECOND! KNOW WHY? HE CAN'T STAY AWAY FROM WATER FOR LONG!
GREAT! WE'LL KEEP FLYIN' TILL HE COLLAPSES!
WE CAN'T STAY UP THAT LONG! NO, BOYS! WE'LL LET THE DESERT TAKE CARE OF AQUAMAN!-- AN' THE LAW CAN'T PIN NOTHIN' ON US!
I GET IT! THERE AIN'T A DROP OF WATER ON THE DESERT! AQUAMAN'S DONE FOR!
PRESENTLY, AS AQUAMAN FLOATS DOWNWARD...
PERSONALLY, I'D HAVE LEFT OUT THE CHUTE!
AN' HAVE THE POLICE INVESTIGATE A 4,000-FOOT DROP? YOU'RE BATS! BUT IF YOU WANT TO SEE THE FINISH, WE'LL HANG AROUND A WHILE! UNDER THE DESERT SUN, AQUAMAN SHOULD GIVE OUT BEFORE OUR FUEL DOES!
2

FIVE MINUTES LATER, AS AQUAMAN EXHAUSTEDLY REMOVES THE PARACHUTE...

THOSE SMUGGLERS KNOW MY WEAKNESS! IF I DON'T FIND WATER SOON I'M A GONER! BUT WHERE CAN I F-FIND WATER IN THE *DESERT?*

W-WHERE SHOULD I LOOK? IN WHAT DIRECTION? I KNOW THE DESERT IS *WATERLESS*... AND YET, I CAN'T JUST G-GIVE UP! I'VE GOT TO KEEP MOVING... AND HOPING...

I *MUST* FIND WATER! I *MUST!*

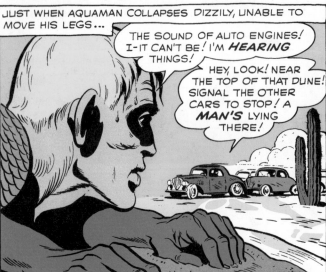

JUST WHEN AQUAMAN COLLAPSES DIZZILY, UNABLE TO MOVE HIS LEGS...

THE SOUND OF AUTO ENGINES! I-IT CAN'T BE! I'M *HEARING* THINGS!

HEY, LOOK! NEAR THE TOP OF THAT DUNE! SIGNAL THE OTHER CARS TO STOP! A *MAN'S* LYING THERE!

SOON, AS AN ANXIOUS GROUP OF RACING DRIVERS SURROUND AQUAMAN.

WE'RE RACING ACROSS THE DESERT'S ONLY HIGHWAY! WE'RE TRAVELING LIGHT! WE HAVEN'T GOT THE WATER YOU NEED!

Y-YOU'RE WRONG! THERE'S WATER IN YOUR *RADIATORS!* DRAIN THEM-- AND LET THE WATER COOL A LITTLE! QUICKLY!

BUT EVEN AS AQUAMAN WATCHES THE RACING CARS SPEED OFF.

I-I SPOKE TOO SOON! THIS BLAZING SUN DRIES THE MOISTURE RIGHT OUT OF MY BODY! I M-MIGHT BE IN TROUBLE *BEFORE* I REACH THAT TOWN!

USING A DRIVER'S SHIRT KNOTTED AT THE ENDS FOR A BASIN, AQUAMAN REVIVES HIMSELF...

THE NEAREST TOWN IS FIVE MILES BACK AT THE FRINGE OF THE DESERT! I'LL DRIVE YOU THERE EVEN THOUGH IT MEANS DISQUALIFYING MYSELF IN THE RACE!

NO, THANKS! I'M REVIVED NOW! I CAN GET THERE MYSELF!

MEANWHILE, 5,000 FEET ABOVE AQUAMAN...

AQUAMAN *F-FOUND* WATER! HE'S MOVIN' ON! IF HE REACHES CIVILIZATION, HE'LL FIND ENOUGH WATER TO BE HIS OLD SELF AGAIN! HE'LL TELL THE POLICE ABOUT US!

DON'T GET JITTERY! I GOT AN IDEA!

NOT LONG AFTER, AS THE SEAPLANE PLUNKS DOWN ON A WATER RESERVOIR...

WE TIMED THIS LANDING PERFECTLY! WE'RE ALMOST OUT OF GAS!

FORGET THE GAS! WE MUST GET AQUAMAN! WE'LL TURN OFF EVERY VALVE, EVERY WATER MAIN! NOT ONE TRICKLE OF WATER WILL FLOW INTO TOWN FROM THIS *RESERVOIR!*

THREE HOURS LATER, AS THE EX-KING OF THE SEAS STAGGERS INTO TOWN...

W-WATER! I MUST HAVE WATER! QUICK... BEFORE I PASS OUT!

SURE, AQUAMAN! WE'VE GOT ALL THE WATER YOU WANT! I'LL JUST TURN THE FAUCET ON, AND...

THE SAME WATERLESS CONDITION PREVAILS EVERYWHERE, AS THE AMAZED POPULATION TRIES ONE SOURCE AFTER ANOTHER...

JUMPIN' CACTUS! THERE ISN'T A DROP OF WATER IN TOWN -- AND WE'LL NEVER REPAIR THE TROUBLE IN TIME! -- AQUAMAN WON'T LAST THAT LONG!

W-WAIT! CARRY ME INTO THAT BUILDING! IT'S MY ONLY CHANCE!

SKATING RINK
INDOOR AND OUTDOOR SKA

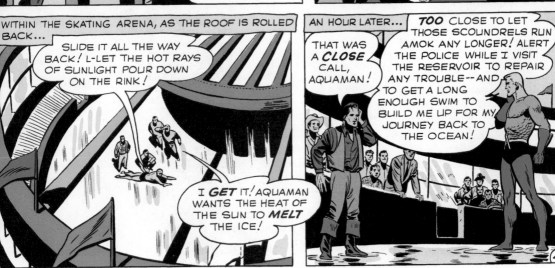

WITHIN THE SKATING ARENA, AS THE ROOF IS ROLLED BACK...

SLIDE IT ALL THE WAY BACK! L-LET THE HOT RAYS OF SUNLIGHT POUR DOWN ON THE RINK!

I *GET* IT! AQUAMAN WANTS THE HEAT OF THE SUN TO *MELT* THE ICE!

AN HOUR LATER...

THAT WAS A *CLOSE* CALL, AQUAMAN!

TOO CLOSE TO LET THOSE SCOUNDRELS RUN AMOK ANY LONGER! ALERT THE POLICE WHILE I VISIT THE RESERVOIR TO REPAIR ANY TROUBLE -- AND TO GET A LONG ENOUGH SWIM TO BUILD ME UP FOR MY JOURNEY BACK TO THE OCEAN!

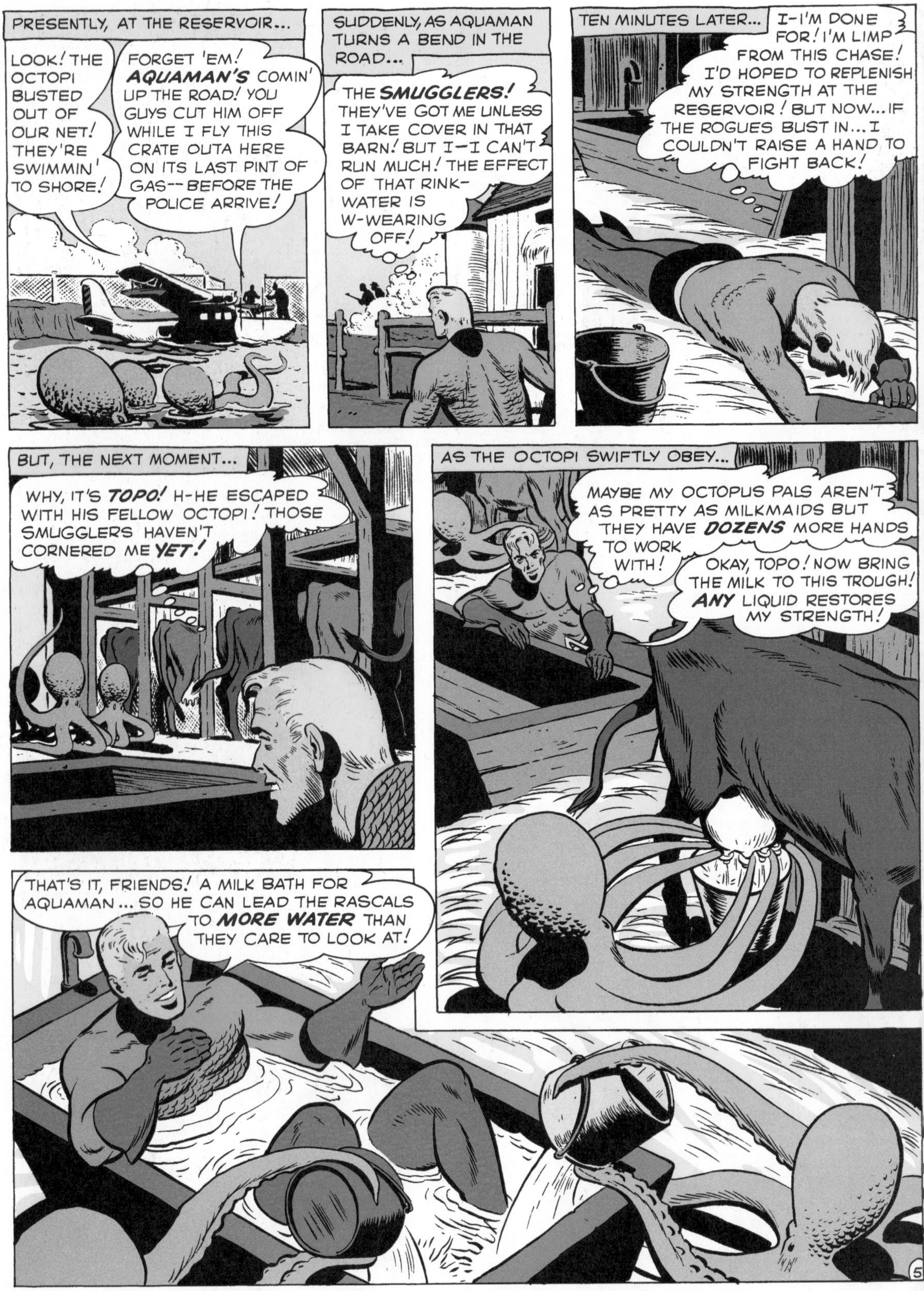
PRESENTLY, AT THE RESERVOIR...
LOOK! THE OCTOPI BUSTED OUT OF OUR NET! THEY'RE SWIMMIN' TO SHORE!
FORGET 'EM! AQUAMAN'S COMIN' UP THE ROAD! YOU GUYS CUT HIM OFF WHILE I FLY THIS CRATE OUTA HERE ON ITS LAST PINT OF GAS-- BEFORE THE POLICE ARRIVE!
SUDDENLY, AS AQUAMAN TURNS A BEND IN THE ROAD...
THE SMUGGLERS! THEY'VE GOT ME UNLESS I TAKE COVER IN THAT BARN! BUT I--I CAN'T RUN MUCH! THE EFFECT OF THAT RINK-WATER IS W-WEARING OFF!
TEN MINUTES LATER...
I-I'M DONE FOR! I'M LIMP FROM THIS CHASE! I'D HOPED TO REPLENISH MY STRENGTH AT THE RESERVOIR! BUT NOW...IF THE ROGUES BUST IN...I COULDN'T RAISE A HAND TO FIGHT BACK!
BUT, THE NEXT MOMENT...
WHY, IT'S TOPO! H-HE ESCAPED WITH HIS FELLOW OCTOPI! THOSE SMUGGLERS HAVEN'T CORNERED ME YET!
AS THE OCTOPI SWIFTLY OBEY...
MAYBE MY OCTOPUS PALS AREN'T AS PRETTY AS MILKMAIDS BUT THEY HAVE DOZENS MORE HANDS TO WORK WITH!
OKAY, TOPO! NOW BRING THE MILK TO THIS TROUGH! ANY LIQUID RESTORES MY STRENGTH!
THAT'S IT, FRIENDS! A MILK BATH FOR AQUAMAN... SO HE CAN LEAD THE RASCALS TO MORE WATER THAN THEY CARE TO LOOK AT!
5

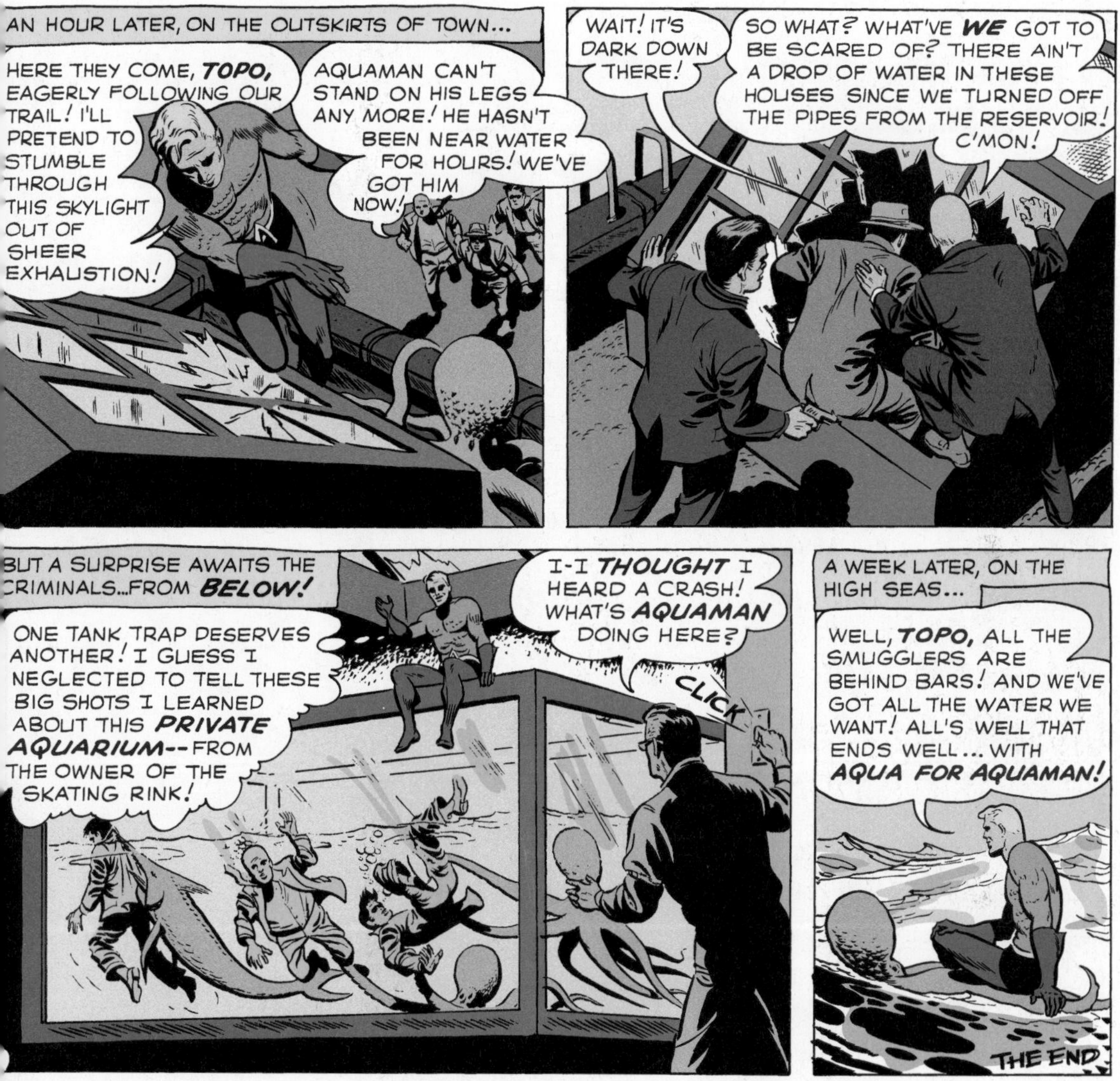
AN HOUR LATER, ON THE OUTSKIRTS OF TOWN...
HERE THEY COME, TOPO, EAGERLY FOLLOWING OUR TRAIL! I'LL PRETEND TO STUMBLE THROUGH THIS SKYLIGHT OUT OF SHEER EXHAUSTION!
AQUAMAN CAN'T STAND ON HIS LEGS ANY MORE! HE HASN'T BEEN NEAR WATER FOR HOURS! WE'VE GOT HIM NOW!
WAIT! IT'S DARK DOWN THERE!
SO WHAT? WHAT'VE WE GOT TO BE SCARED OF? THERE AIN'T A DROP OF WATER IN THESE HOUSES SINCE WE TURNED OFF THE PIPES FROM THE RESERVOIR! C'MON!
BUT A SURPRISE AWAITS THE CRIMINALS...FROM BELOW!
ONE TANK TRAP DESERVES ANOTHER! I GUESS I NEGLECTED TO TELL THESE BIG SHOTS I LEARNED ABOUT THIS PRIVATE AQUARIUM--FROM THE OWNER OF THE SKATING RINK!
I-I THOUGHT I HEARD A CRASH! WHAT'S AQUAMAN DOING HERE?
CLICK
A WEEK LATER, ON THE HIGH SEAS...
WELL, TOPO, ALL THE SMUGGLERS ARE BEHIND BARS! AND WE'VE GOT ALL THE WATER WE WANT! ALL'S WELL THAT ENDS WELL... WITH AQUA FOR AQUAMAN!
THE END

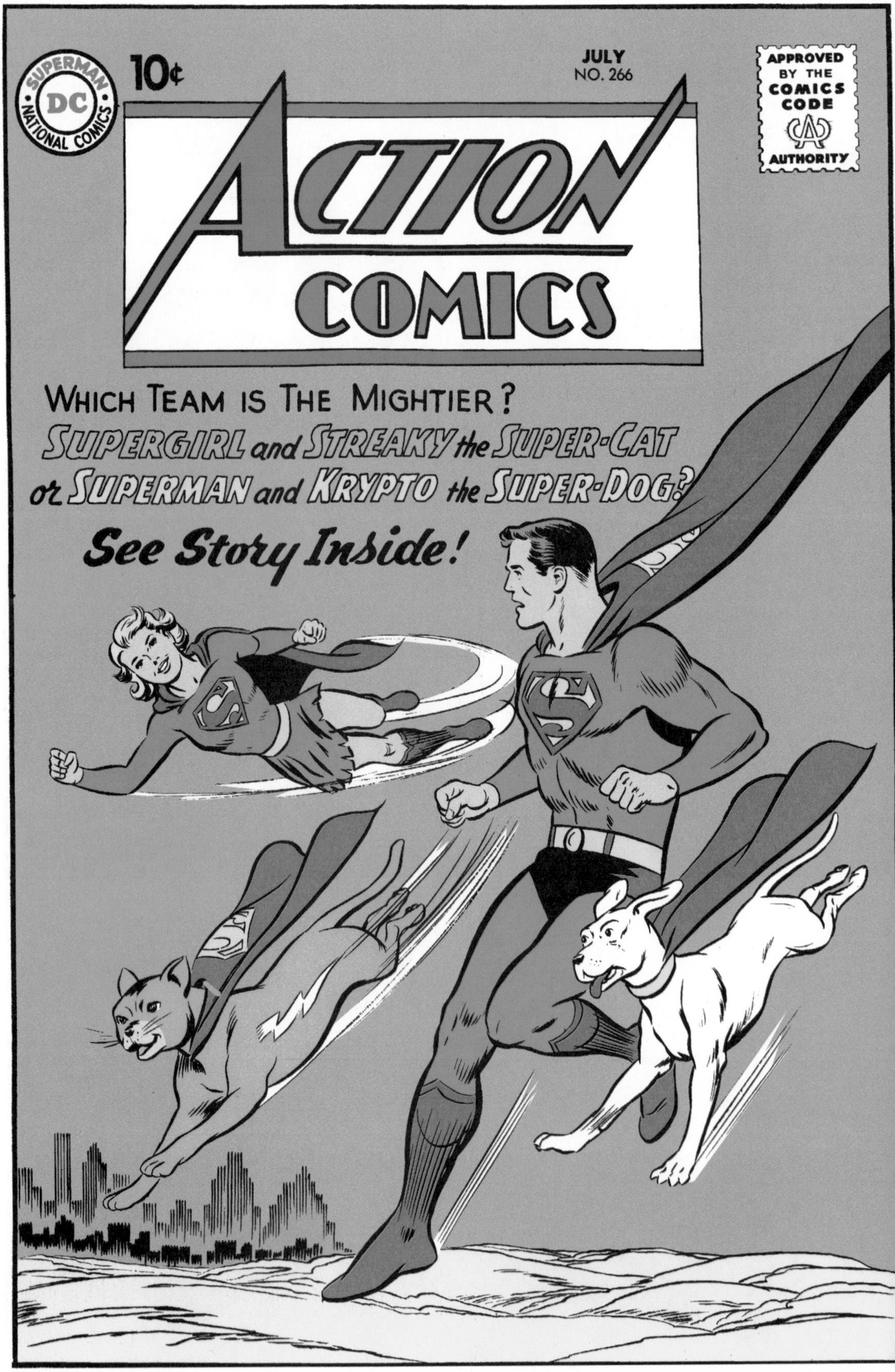

SUPERMAN
DC
NATIONAL COMICS
10¢
JULY
NO. 266
APPROVED BY THE COMICS CODE AUTHORITY
ACTION COMICS
WHICH TEAM IS THE MIGHTIER?
SUPERGIRL and STREAKY the SUPER-CAT
or SUPERMAN and KRYPTO the SUPER-DOG?
See Story Inside!

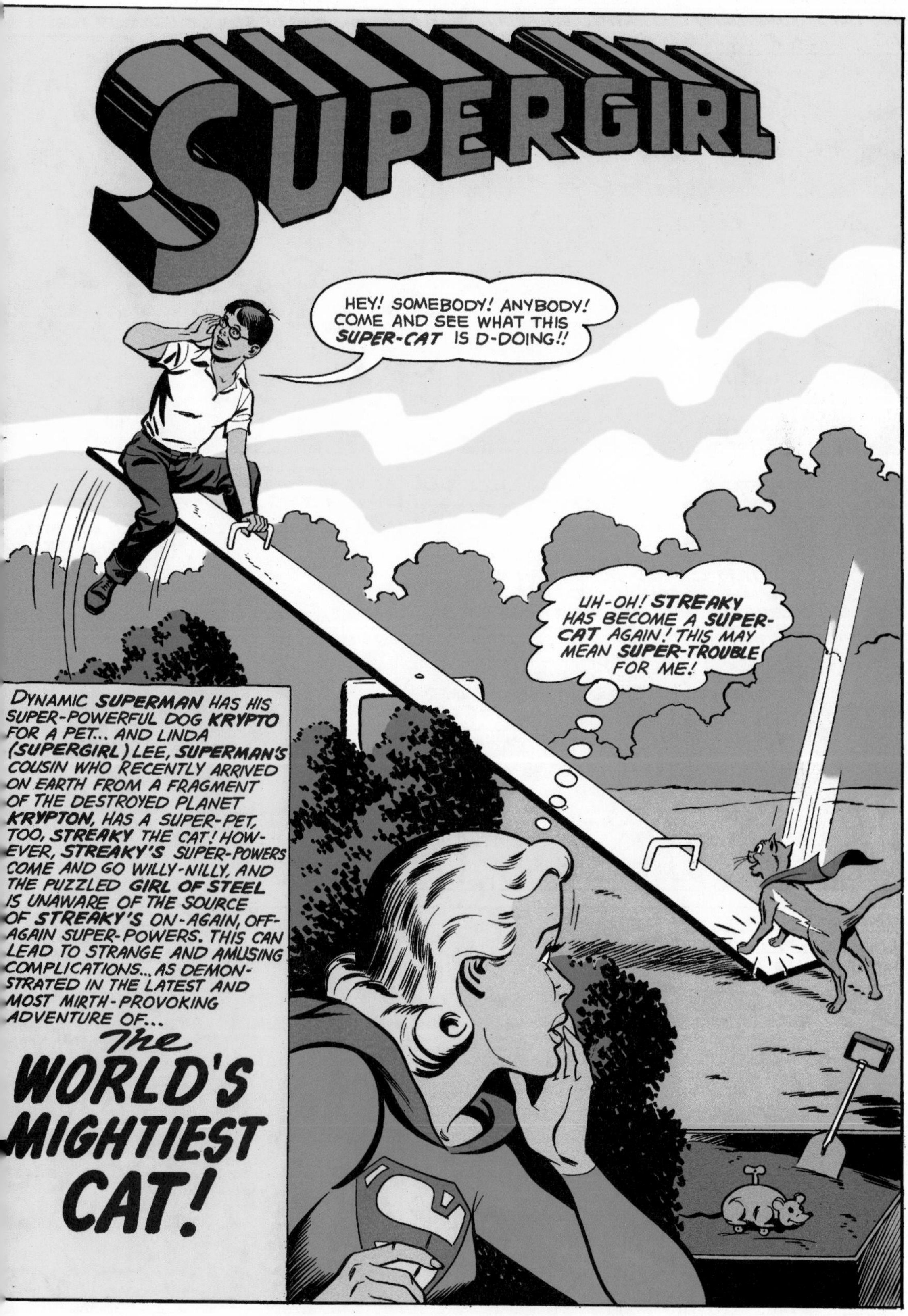
SUPERGIRL
HEY! SOMEBODY! ANYBODY! COME AND SEE WHAT THIS SUPER-CAT IS D-DOING!!
UH-OH! STREAKY HAS BECOME A SUPER-CAT AGAIN! THIS MAY MEAN SUPER-TROUBLE FOR ME!
DYNAMIC SUPERMAN HAS HIS SUPER-POWERFUL DOG KRYPTO FOR A PET... AND LINDA (SUPERGIRL) LEE, SUPERMAN'S COUSIN WHO RECENTLY ARRIVED ON EARTH FROM A FRAGMENT OF THE DESTROYED PLANET KRYPTON, HAS A SUPER-PET, TOO, STREAKY THE CAT! HOWEVER, STREAKY'S SUPER-POWERS COME AND GO WILLY-NILLY, AND THE PUZZLED GIRL OF STEEL IS UNAWARE OF THE SOURCE OF STREAKY'S ON-AGAIN, OFF-AGAIN SUPER-POWERS. THIS CAN LEAD TO STRANGE AND AMUSING COMPLICATIONS... AS DEMONSTRATED IN THE LATEST AND MOST MIRTH-PROVOKING ADVENTURE OF...
The WORLD'S MIGHTIEST CAT!

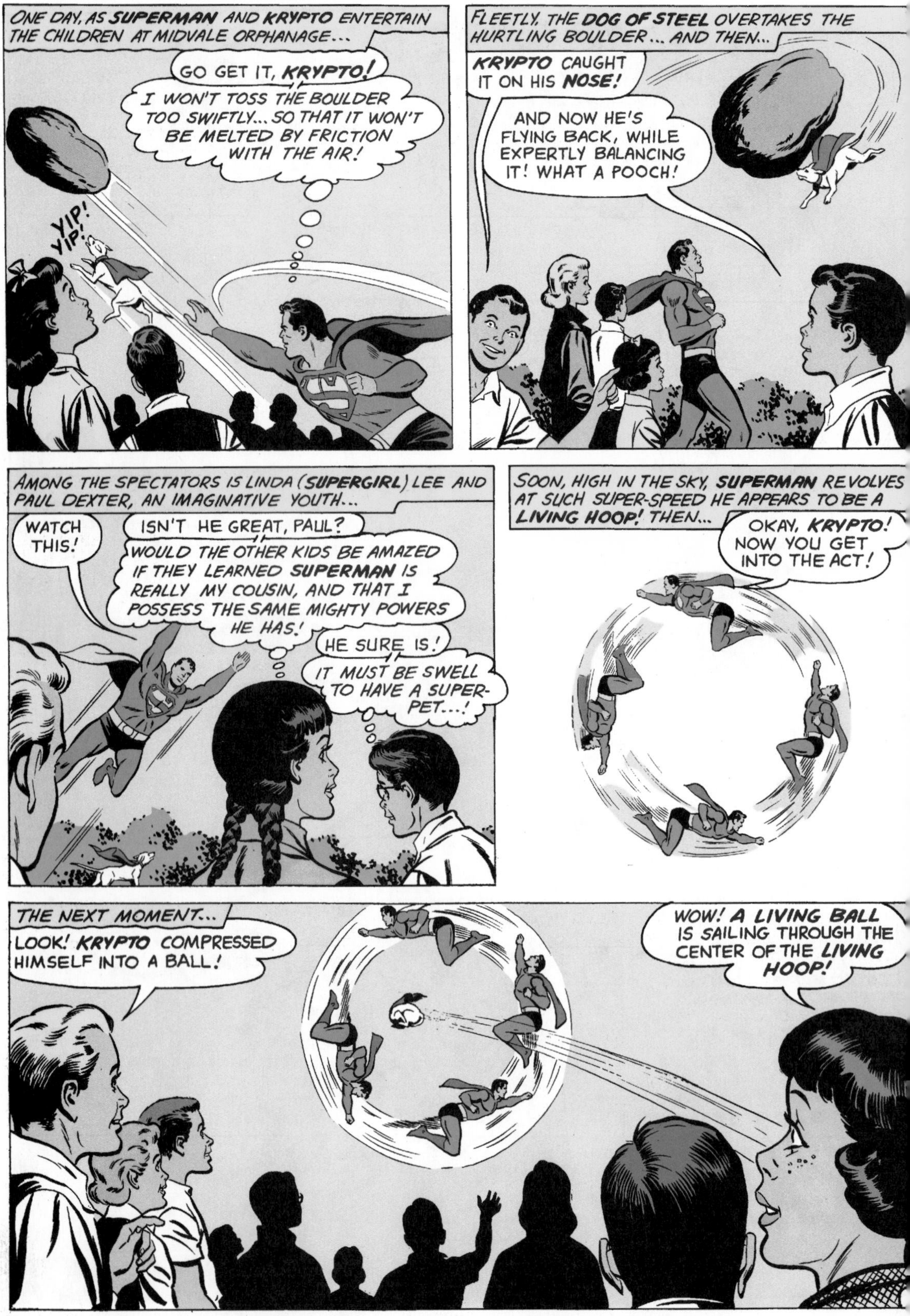
ONE DAY, AS SUPERMAN AND KRYPTO ENTERTAIN THE CHILDREN AT MIDVALE ORPHANAGE...
GO GET IT, KRYPTO!
I WON'T TOSS THE BOULDER TOO SWIFTLY... SO THAT IT WON'T BE MELTED BY FRICTION WITH THE AIR!
YIP! YIP!
FLEETLY, THE DOG OF STEEL OVERTAKES THE HURTLING BOULDER... AND THEN...
KRYPTO CAUGHT IT ON HIS NOSE!
AND NOW HE'S FLYING BACK, WHILE EXPERTLY BALANCING IT! WHAT A POOCH!
AMONG THE SPECTATORS IS LINDA (SUPERGIRL) LEE AND PAUL DEXTER, AN IMAGINATIVE YOUTH...
WATCH THIS!
ISN'T HE GREAT, PAUL?
WOULD THE OTHER KIDS BE AMAZED IF THEY LEARNED SUPERMAN IS REALLY MY COUSIN, AND THAT I POSSESS THE SAME MIGHTY POWERS HE HAS!
HE SURE IS!
IT MUST BE SWELL TO HAVE A SUPER-PET...!
SOON, HIGH IN THE SKY, SUPERMAN REVOLVES AT SUCH SUPER-SPEED HE APPEARS TO BE A LIVING HOOP! THEN...
OKAY, KRYPTO! NOW YOU GET INTO THE ACT!
THE NEXT MOMENT...
LOOK! KRYPTO COMPRESSED HIMSELF INTO A BALL!
WOW! A LIVING BALL IS SAILING THROUGH THE CENTER OF THE LIVING HOOP!

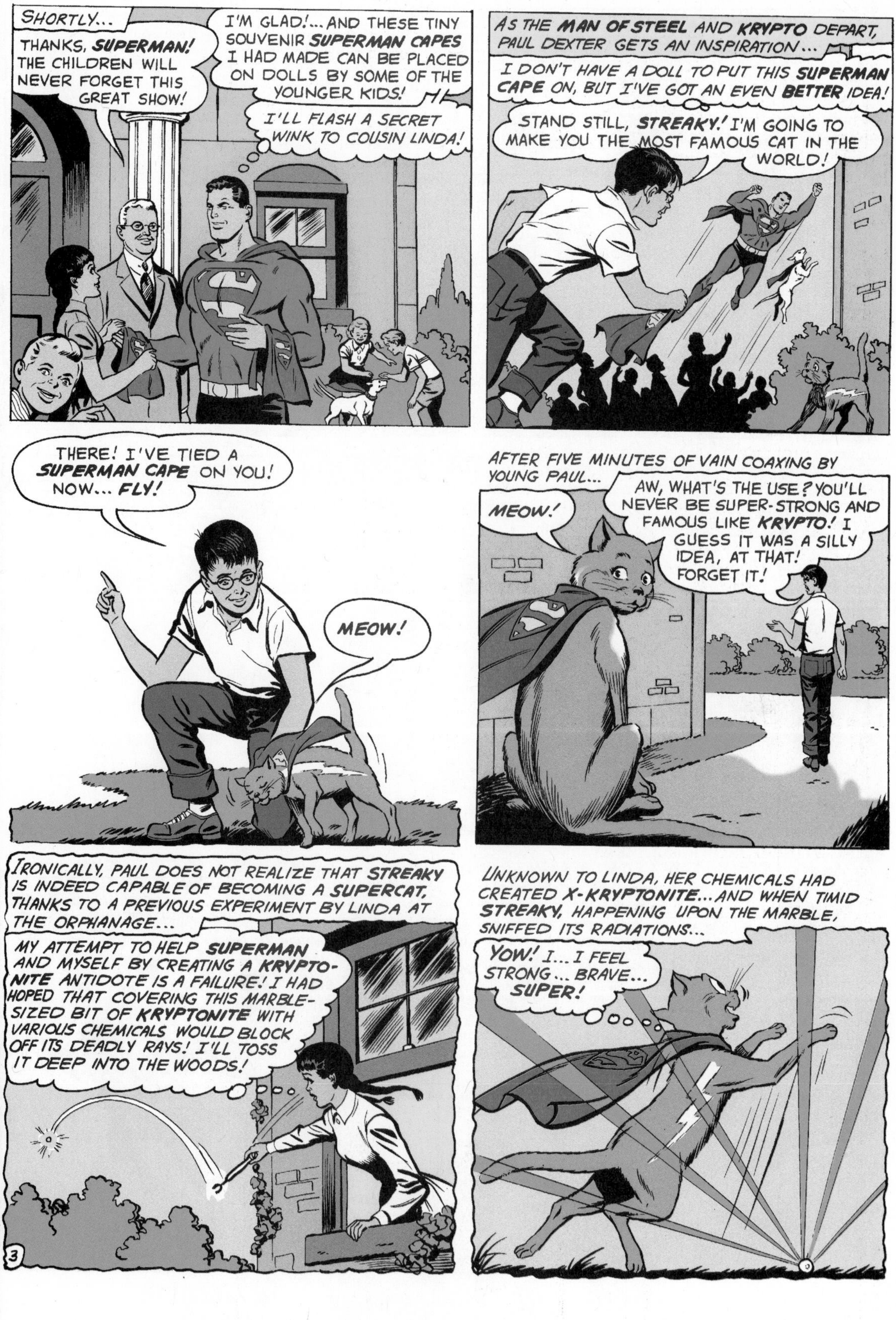

SHORTLY...
THANKS, SUPERMAN! THE CHILDREN WILL NEVER FORGET THIS GREAT SHOW!
I'M GLAD!... AND THESE TINY SOUVENIR SUPERMAN CAPES I HAD MADE CAN BE PLACED ON DOLLS BY SOME OF THE YOUNGER KIDS!
I'LL FLASH A SECRET WINK TO COUSIN LINDA!
AS THE MAN OF STEEL AND KRYPTO DEPART, PAUL DEXTER GETS AN INSPIRATION...
I DON'T HAVE A DOLL TO PUT THIS SUPERMAN CAPE ON, BUT I'VE GOT AN EVEN BETTER IDEA!
STAND STILL, STREAKY! I'M GOING TO MAKE YOU THE MOST FAMOUS CAT IN THE WORLD!
THERE! I'VE TIED A SUPERMAN CAPE ON YOU! NOW... FLY!
MEOW!
AFTER FIVE MINUTES OF VAIN COAXING BY YOUNG PAUL...
MEOW!
AW, WHAT'S THE USE? YOU'LL NEVER BE SUPER-STRONG AND FAMOUS LIKE KRYPTO! I GUESS IT WAS A SILLY IDEA, AT THAT! FORGET IT!
IRONICALLY, PAUL DOES NOT REALIZE THAT STREAKY IS INDEED CAPABLE OF BECOMING A SUPERCAT, THANKS TO A PREVIOUS EXPERIMENT BY LINDA AT THE ORPHANAGE...
MY ATTEMPT TO HELP SUPERMAN AND MYSELF BY CREATING A KRYPTONITE ANTIDOTE IS A FAILURE! I HAD HOPED THAT COVERING THIS MARBLE-SIZED BIT OF KRYPTONITE WITH VARIOUS CHEMICALS WOULD BLOCK OFF ITS DEADLY RAYS! I'LL TOSS IT DEEP INTO THE WOODS!
3
UNKNOWN TO LINDA, HER CHEMICALS HAD CREATED X-KRYPTONITE... AND WHEN TIMID STREAKY, HAPPENING UPON THE MARBLE, SNIFFED ITS RADIATIONS...
YOW! I... I FEEL STRONG... BRAVE... SUPER!

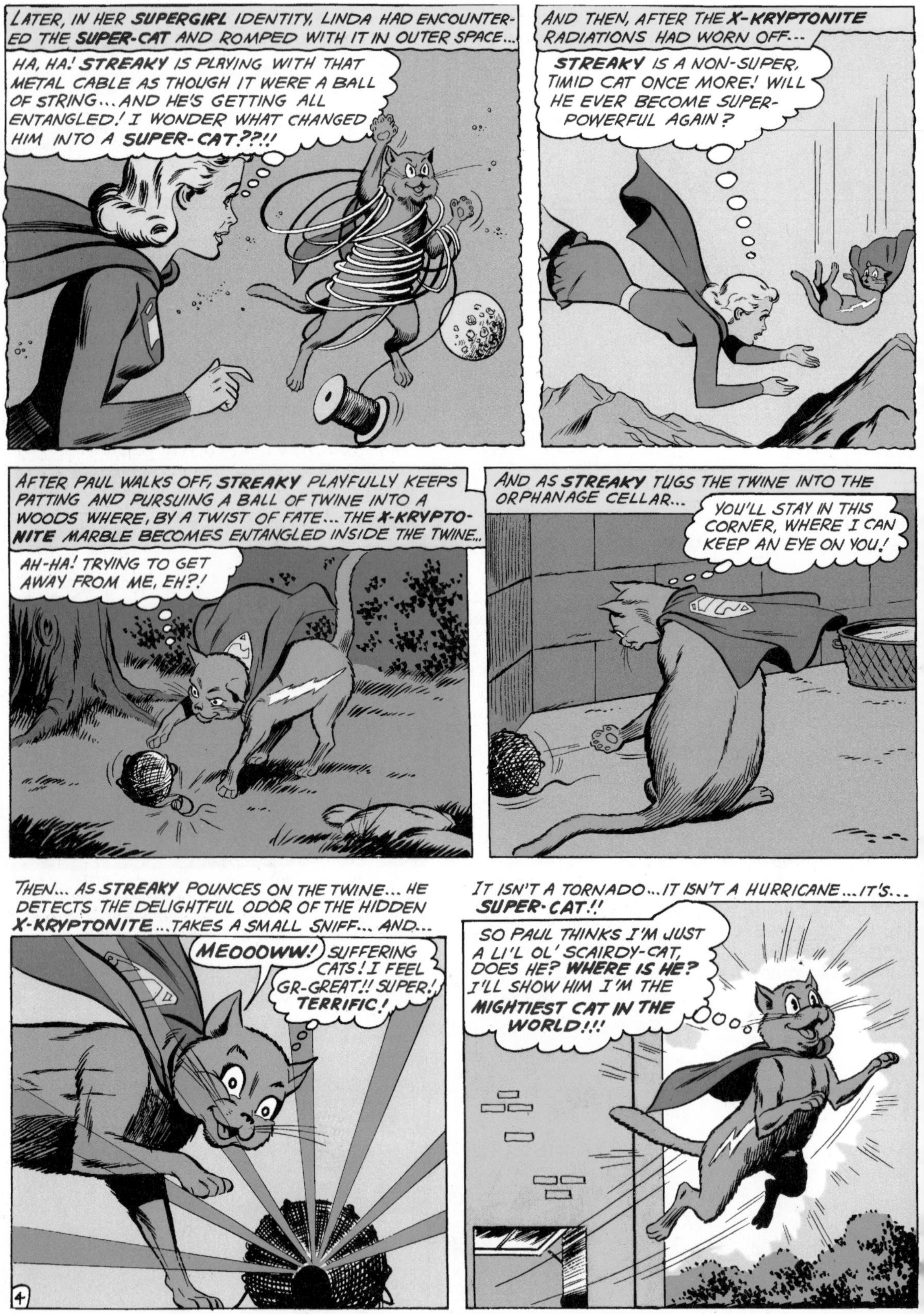
LATER, IN HER SUPERGIRL IDENTITY, LINDA HAD ENCOUNTERED THE SUPER-CAT AND ROMPED WITH IT IN OUTER SPACE...
HA, HA! STREAKY IS PLAYING WITH THAT METAL CABLE AS THOUGH IT WERE A BALL OF STRING... AND HE'S GETTING ALL ENTANGLED! I WONDER WHAT CHANGED HIM INTO A SUPER-CAT??!!
AND THEN, AFTER THE X-KRYPTONITE RADIATIONS HAD WORN OFF...
STREAKY IS A NON-SUPER, TIMID CAT ONCE MORE! WILL HE EVER BECOME SUPER-POWERFUL AGAIN?
AFTER PAUL WALKS OFF, STREAKY PLAYFULLY KEEPS PATTING AND PURSUING A BALL OF TWINE INTO A WOODS WHERE, BY A TWIST OF FATE... THE X-KRYPTONITE MARBLE BECOMES ENTANGLED INSIDE THE TWINE...
AH-HA! TRYING TO GET AWAY FROM ME, EH?!
AND AS STREAKY TUGS THE TWINE INTO THE ORPHANAGE CELLAR...
YOU'LL STAY IN THIS CORNER, WHERE I CAN KEEP AN EYE ON YOU!
THEN... AS STREAKY POUNCES ON THE TWINE... HE DETECTS THE DELIGHTFUL ODOR OF THE HIDDEN X-KRYPTONITE...TAKES A SMALL SNIFF... AND...
MEOOOWW!
SUFFERING CATS! I FEEL GR-GREAT!! SUPER! TERRIFIC!
4
IT ISN'T A TORNADO...IT ISN'T A HURRICANE...IT'S... SUPER-CAT!!
SO PAUL THINKS I'M JUST A LI'L OL' SCAIRDY-CAT, DOES HE? WHERE IS HE? I'LL SHOW HIM I'M THE MIGHTIEST CAT IN THE WORLD!!!

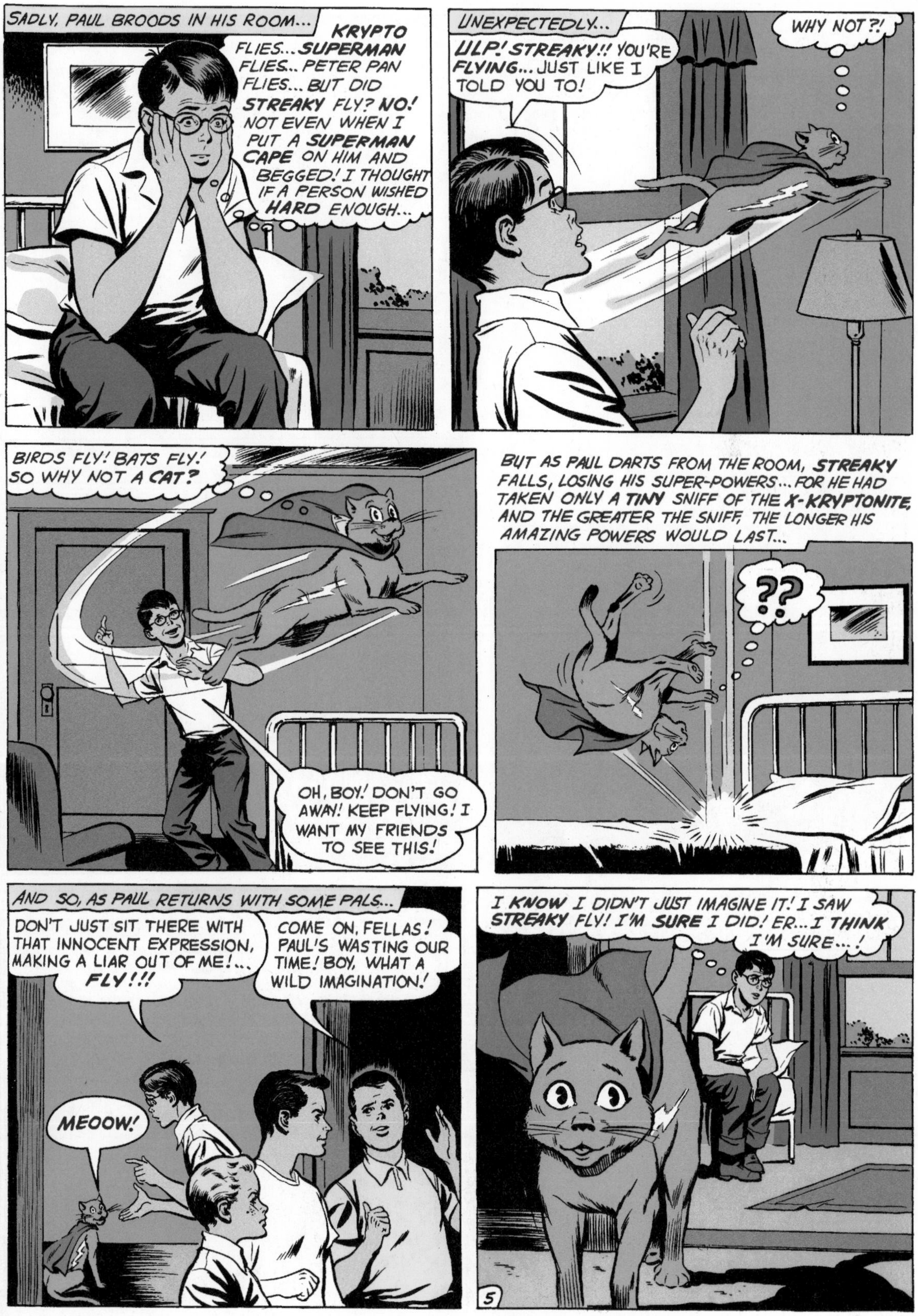
SADLY, PAUL BROODS IN HIS ROOM...
KRYPTO FLIES...SUPERMAN FLIES... PETER PAN FLIES... BUT DID STREAKY FLY? NO! NOT EVEN WHEN I PUT A SUPERMAN CAPE ON HIM AND BEGGED! I THOUGHT IF A PERSON WISHED HARD ENOUGH...
UNEXPECTEDLY...
ULP! STREAKY!! YOU'RE FLYING... JUST LIKE I TOLD YOU TO!
WHY NOT?!
BIRDS FLY! BATS FLY! SO WHY NOT A CAT?
OH, BOY! DON'T GO AWAY! KEEP FLYING! I WANT MY FRIENDS TO SEE THIS!
BUT AS PAUL DARTS FROM THE ROOM, STREAKY FALLS, LOSING HIS SUPER-POWERS... FOR HE HAD TAKEN ONLY A TINY SNIFF OF THE X-KRYPTONITE, AND THE GREATER THE SNIFF, THE LONGER HIS AMAZING POWERS WOULD LAST...
??
AND SO, AS PAUL RETURNS WITH SOME PALS...
DON'T JUST SIT THERE WITH THAT INNOCENT EXPRESSION, MAKING A LIAR OUT OF ME!... FLY!!!
COME ON, FELLAS! PAUL'S WASTING OUR TIME! BOY, WHAT A WILD IMAGINATION!
MEOOW!
I KNOW I DIDN'T JUST IMAGINE IT! I SAW STREAKY FLY! I'M SURE I DID! ER...I THINK I'M SURE...!
5

RETURNING TO THE CELLAR, **STREAKY** PLAYS WITH THE TWINE AGAIN... THIS TIME TAKING DEEP, POWERFUL SNIFFS THAT HAVE A LONG-LASTING EFFECT...

WHEE-EE! I...FEEL **SUPER!** WHERE'S PAUL? I'VE GOT TO SEE THAT BOY! CHEER HIM UP! HE LOOKED UNHAPPY!

AS **STREAKY** REJOINS THE IMAGINATIVE YOUTH...

OH, SO YOU'RE BACK! I'LL GIVE YOU ANOTHER CHANCE! CARRY THAT HEAVY LAMP ACROSS THE ROOM!

I'LL DO IT! MAYBE IT WILL MAKE HIM HAPPY!

BUT AS **SUPER-CAT** LIFTS THE FLOOR LAMP...

WOW! HIS SUPER-STRONG TEETH BIT CLEAR THROUGH THE METAL BAR! HE SLICED THE ELECTRIC WIRES, TOO, AND THE ELECTRICITY DOESN'T HURT HIM A BIT! WAIT'LL MY FRIENDS SEE **THIS!**

PRESENTLY, LINDA (**SUPERGIRL**) LEE OVERHEARS PAUL'S EXCITED CONVERSATION WITH HIS FRIENDS...

I KNOW IT SOUNDS CRAZY, BUT **STREAKY** BIT A LAMP IN TWO, AND THE ELECTRICITY DIDN'T HURT HIM! COME... I'LL **PROVE** IT!

I'LL CHECK WITH MY SUPER-VISION! OH-OH! **STREAKY HAS** BECOME A **SUPER-CAT** AGAIN! I SEE HIM CHASING HIS TAIL, AT SUPER-SPEED!

SUPER-SWIFTLY, LINDA REMOVES HER DARK, PIG-TAILED WIG AND HER OUTER GARMENTS, TRANS-FORMING HERSELF INTO DYNAMIC **SUPERGIRL**...

I'VE GOT TO CONCEAL **STREAKY'S** SUPER-POWERS BEFORE HE DOES SOMETHING THAT MAY GIVE AWAY **MY** SUPER-SECRET!

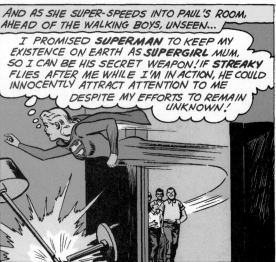

AND AS SHE SUPER-SPEEDS INTO PAUL'S ROOM, AHEAD OF THE WALKING BOYS, UNSEEN...

I PROMISED **SUPERMAN** TO KEEP MY EXISTENCE ON EARTH AS **SUPERGIRL** MUM, SO I CAN BE HIS SECRET WEAPON! IF **STREAKY** FLIES AFTER ME WHILE I'M IN ACTION, HE COULD INNOCENTLY ATTRACT ATTENTION TO ME DESPITE MY EFFORTS TO REMAIN UNKNOWN!

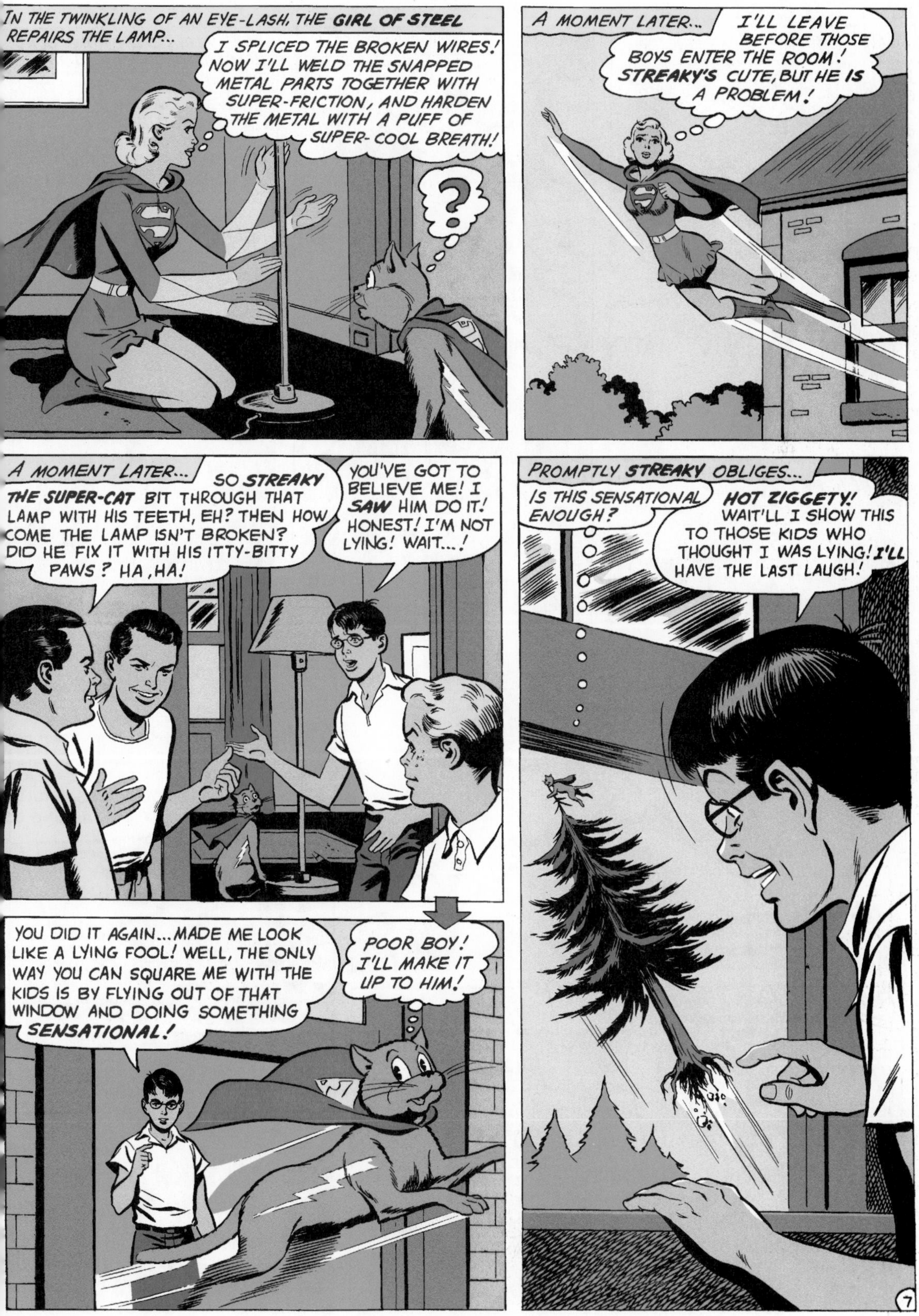
IN THE TWINKLING OF AN EYE-LASH, THE GIRL OF STEEL REPAIRS THE LAMP...
I SPLICED THE BROKEN WIRES! NOW I'LL WELD THE SNAPPED METAL PARTS TOGETHER WITH SUPER-FRICTION, AND HARDEN THE METAL WITH A PUFF OF SUPER-COOL BREATH!
?
A MOMENT LATER...
I'LL LEAVE BEFORE THOSE BOYS ENTER THE ROOM! STREAKY'S CUTE, BUT HE IS A PROBLEM!
A MOMENT LATER...
SO STREAKY THE SUPER-CAT BIT THROUGH THAT LAMP WITH HIS TEETH, EH? THEN HOW COME THE LAMP ISN'T BROKEN? DID HE FIX IT WITH HIS ITTY-BITTY PAWS? HA, HA!
YOU'VE GOT TO BELIEVE ME! I SAW HIM DO IT! HONEST! I'M NOT LYING! WAIT...!
YOU DID IT AGAIN... MADE ME LOOK LIKE A LYING FOOL! WELL, THE ONLY WAY YOU CAN SQUARE ME WITH THE KIDS IS BY FLYING OUT OF THAT WINDOW AND DOING SOMETHING SENSATIONAL!
POOR BOY! I'LL MAKE IT UP TO HIM!
PROMPTLY STREAKY OBLIGES...
IS THIS SENSATIONAL ENOUGH?
HOT ZIGGETY! WAIT'LL I SHOW THIS TO THOSE KIDS WHO THOUGHT I WAS LYING! I'LL HAVE THE LAST LAUGH!
7

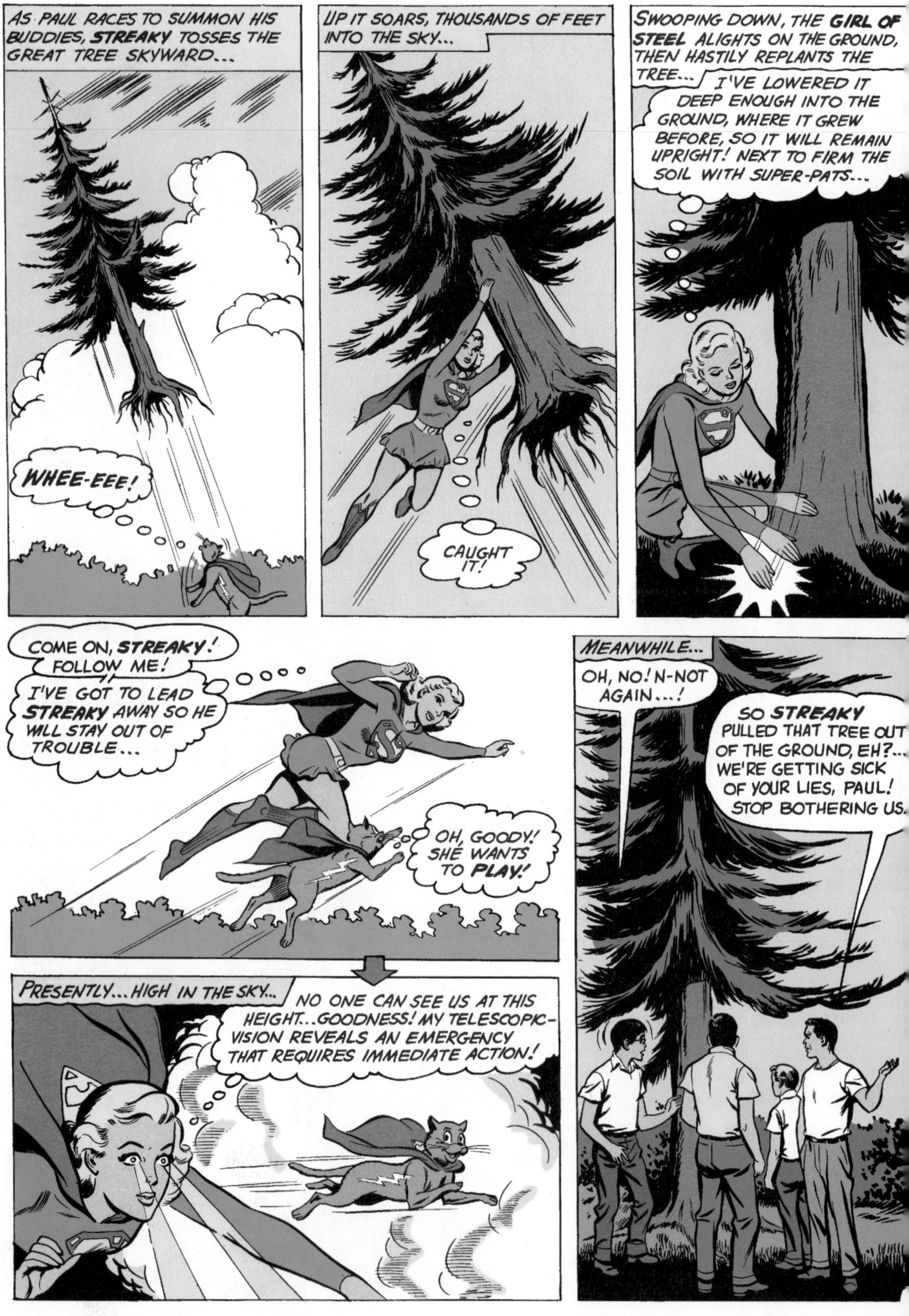
AS PAUL RACES TO SUMMON HIS BUDDIES, STREAKY TOSSES THE GREAT TREE SKYWARD...
WHEE-EEE!
UP IT SOARS, THOUSANDS OF FEET INTO THE SKY...
CAUGHT IT!
SWOOPING DOWN, THE GIRL OF STEEL ALIGHTS ON THE GROUND, THEN HASTILY REPLANTS THE TREE...
I'VE LOWERED IT DEEP ENOUGH INTO THE GROUND, WHERE IT GREW BEFORE, SO IT WILL REMAIN UPRIGHT! NEXT TO FIRM THE SOIL WITH SUPER-PATS...
COME ON, STREAKY! FOLLOW ME!
I'VE GOT TO LEAD STREAKY AWAY SO HE WILL STAY OUT OF TROUBLE...
OH, GOODY! SHE WANTS TO PLAY!
MEANWHILE...
OH, NO! N-NOT AGAIN...!
SO STREAKY PULLED THAT TREE OUT OF THE GROUND, EH?... WE'RE GETTING SICK OF YOUR LIES, PAUL! STOP BOTHERING US.
PRESENTLY...HIGH IN THE SKY...
NO ONE CAN SEE US AT THIS HEIGHT...GOODNESS! MY TELESCOPIC-VISION REVEALS AN EMERGENCY THAT REQUIRES IMMEDIATE ACTION!

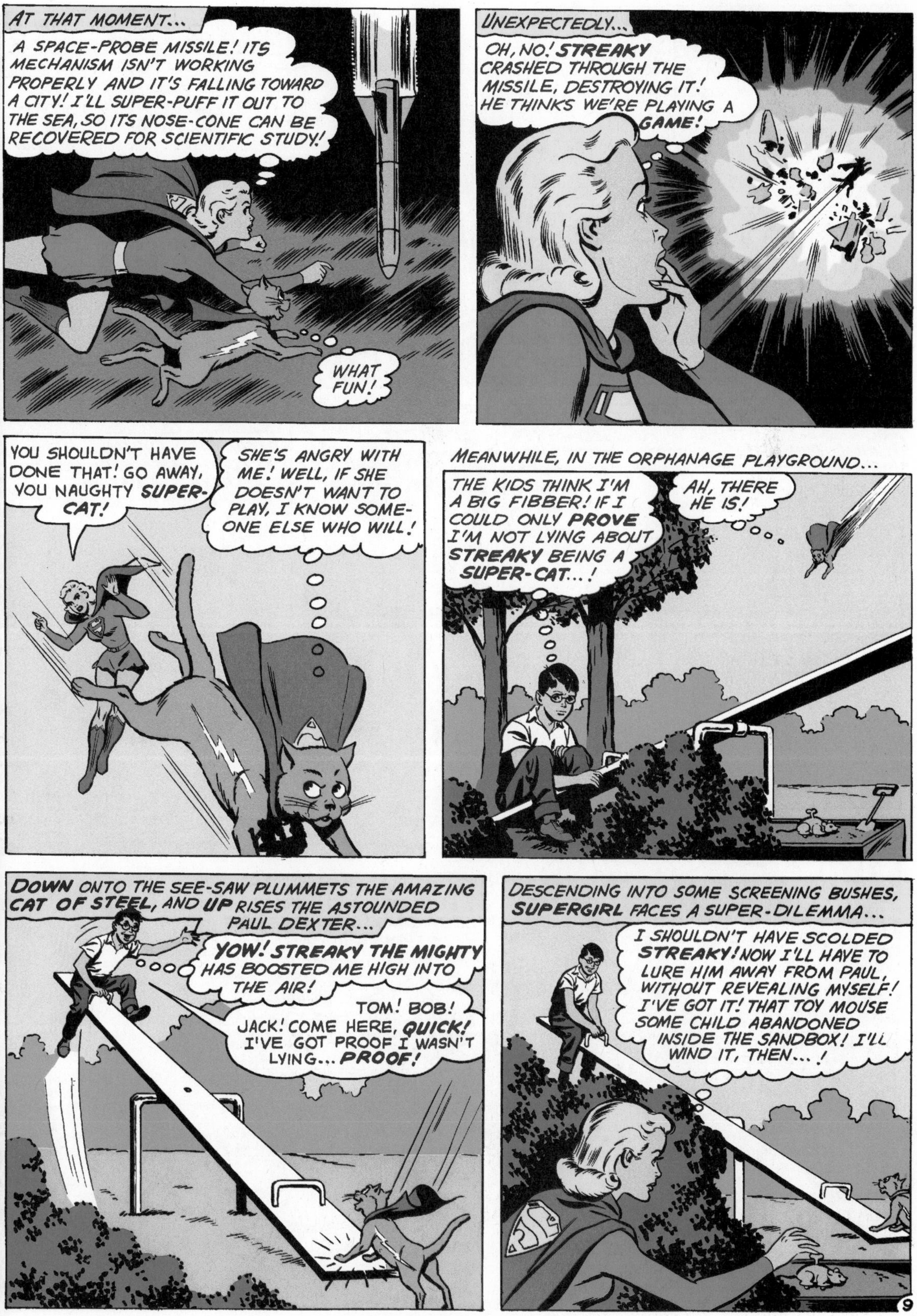
AT THAT MOMENT...
A SPACE-PROBE MISSILE! ITS MECHANISM ISN'T WORKING PROPERLY AND IT'S FALLING TOWARD A CITY! I'LL SUPER-PUFF IT OUT TO THE SEA, SO ITS NOSE-CONE CAN BE RECOVERED FOR SCIENTIFIC STUDY!
WHAT FUN!
UNEXPECTEDLY...
OH, NO! STREAKY CRASHED THROUGH THE MISSILE, DESTROYING IT! HE THINKS WE'RE PLAYING A GAME!
YOU SHOULDN'T HAVE DONE THAT! GO AWAY, YOU NAUGHTY SUPER-CAT!
SHE'S ANGRY WITH ME! WELL, IF SHE DOESN'T WANT TO PLAY, I KNOW SOME-ONE ELSE WHO WILL!
MEANWHILE, IN THE ORPHANAGE PLAYGROUND...
THE KIDS THINK I'M A BIG FIBBER! IF I COULD ONLY PROVE I'M NOT LYING ABOUT STREAKY BEING A SUPER-CAT...!
AH, THERE HE IS!
DOWN ONTO THE SEE-SAW PLUMMETS THE AMAZING CAT OF STEEL, AND UP RISES THE ASTOUNDED PAUL DEXTER...
YOW! STREAKY THE MIGHTY HAS BOOSTED ME HIGH INTO THE AIR!
TOM! BOB! JACK! COME HERE, QUICK! I'VE GOT PROOF I WASN'T LYING... PROOF!
DESCENDING INTO SOME SCREENING BUSHES, SUPERGIRL FACES A SUPER-DILEMMA...
I SHOULDN'T HAVE SCOLDED STREAKY! NOW I'LL HAVE TO LURE HIM AWAY FROM PAUL, WITHOUT REVEALING MYSELF! I'VE GOT IT! THAT TOY MOUSE SOME CHILD ABANDONED INSIDE THE SANDBOX! I'LL WIND IT, THEN...!
9

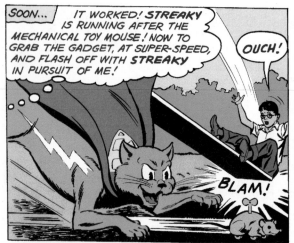

SOON... IT WORKED! **STREAKY** IS RUNNING AFTER THE MECHANICAL TOY MOUSE! NOW TO GRAB THE GADGET, AT SUPER-SPEED, AND FLASH OFF WITH **STREAKY** IN PURSUIT OF ME!

OUCH!

BLAM!

THUS, SECONDS LATER, AS PAUL'S FRIENDS ARRIVE ON THE SCENE, AGAIN HE HAS NO PROOF TO SHOW THEM...

BUT I TELL YOU... **STREAKY** RAISED ME HIGH ON MY END OF THE SEE-SAW, THEN LET ME DROP!

IS THAT SO? LET'S ALL GO AND TELL THE SUPERINTENDENT ABOUT IT!

MEANWHILE, AS **SUPERGIRL** SWIFTLY FLASHES ABOVE THE PLANET EARTH, PURSUED BY HER PLAYFUL **SUPER-CAT**...

MY TELESCOPIC-VISION REVEALS TROUBLE BELOW, IN AN AFRICAN JUNGLE!

DOWN SWOOPS THE **GIRL OF STEEL**, FOLLOWED BY **SUPER-CAT**...

CAPTIVE WILD ANIMALS ESCAPED FROM A SAFARI AND ARE ATTACKING A NATIVE VILLAGE!

NEXT MOMENT...

I'LL HANDLE THE ELEPHANT AND GORILLA, **STREAKY!** YOU TAKE CARE OF THOSE BIG CATS!

LET ME AT THOSE BULLIES!

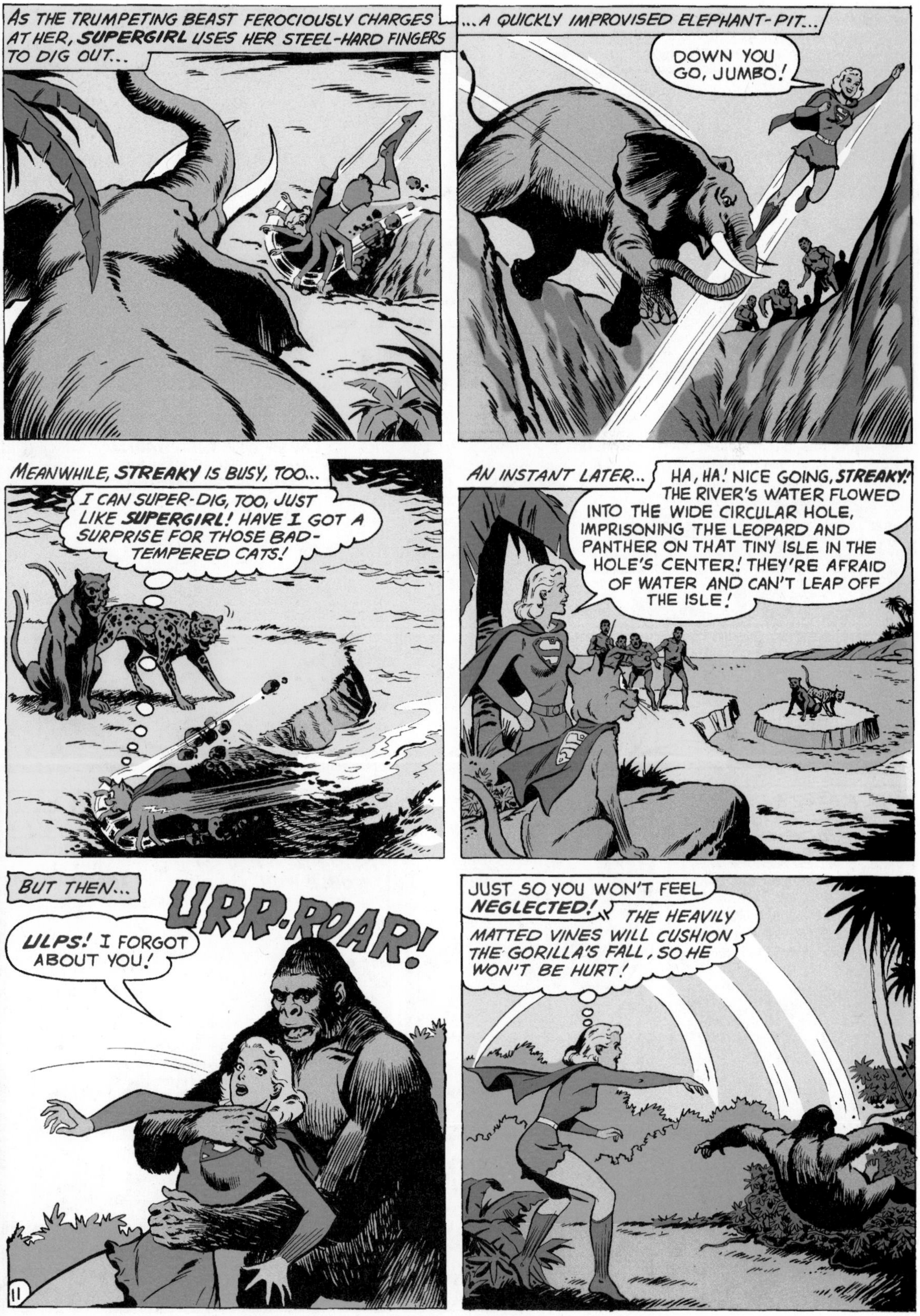

AS THE TRUMPETING BEAST FEROCIOUSLY CHARGES AT HER, SUPERGIRL USES HER STEEL-HARD FINGERS TO DIG OUT...
...A QUICKLY IMPROVISED ELEPHANT-PIT...
DOWN YOU GO, JUMBO!
MEANWHILE, STREAKY IS BUSY, TOO...
I CAN SUPER-DIG, TOO, JUST LIKE SUPERGIRL! HAVE I GOT A SURPRISE FOR THOSE BAD-TEMPERED CATS!
AN INSTANT LATER...
HA, HA! NICE GOING, STREAKY! THE RIVER'S WATER FLOWED INTO THE WIDE CIRCULAR HOLE, IMPRISONING THE LEOPARD AND PANTHER ON THAT TINY ISLE IN THE HOLE'S CENTER! THEY'RE AFRAID OF WATER AND CAN'T LEAP OFF THE ISLE!
BUT THEN...
URR-ROAR!
ULPS! I FORGOT ABOUT YOU!
11
JUST SO YOU WON'T FEEL NEGLECTED!
THE HEAVILY MATTED VINES WILL CUSHION THE GORILLA'S FALL, SO HE WON'T BE HURT!

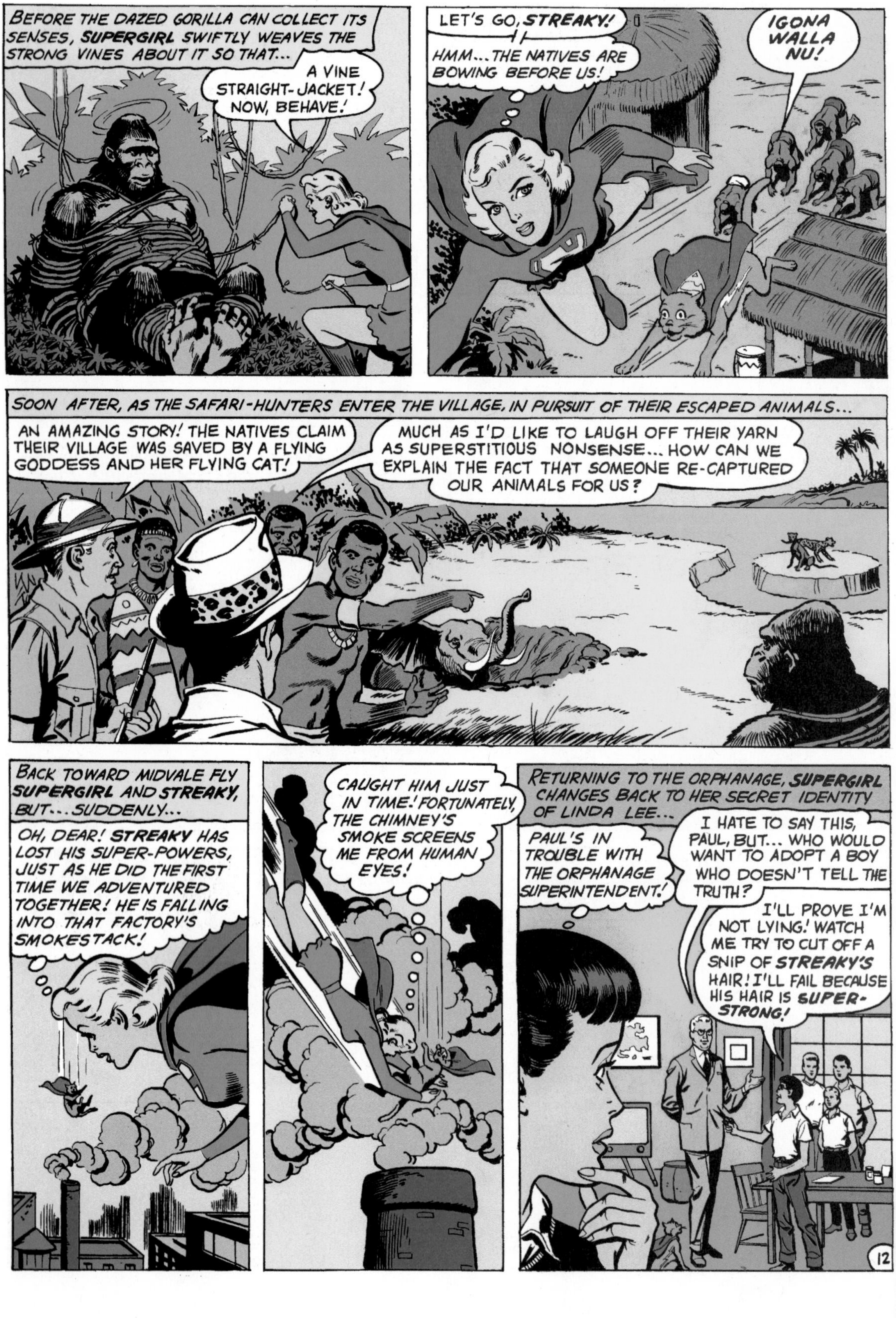
BEFORE THE DAZED GORILLA CAN COLLECT ITS SENSES, SUPERGIRL SWIFTLY WEAVES THE STRONG VINES ABOUT IT SO THAT...
A VINE STRAIGHT-JACKET! NOW, BEHAVE!
LET'S GO, STREAKY!
HMM... THE NATIVES ARE BOWING BEFORE US!
IGONA WALLA NU!
SOON AFTER, AS THE SAFARI-HUNTERS ENTER THE VILLAGE, IN PURSUIT OF THEIR ESCAPED ANIMALS...
AN AMAZING STORY! THE NATIVES CLAIM THEIR VILLAGE WAS SAVED BY A FLYING GODDESS AND HER FLYING CAT!
MUCH AS I'D LIKE TO LAUGH OFF THEIR YARN AS SUPERSTITIOUS NONSENSE... HOW CAN WE EXPLAIN THE FACT THAT SOMEONE RE-CAPTURED OUR ANIMALS FOR US?
BACK TOWARD MIDVALE FLY SUPERGIRL AND STREAKY, BUT... SUDDENLY...
OH, DEAR! STREAKY HAS LOST HIS SUPER-POWERS, JUST AS HE DID THE FIRST TIME WE ADVENTURED TOGETHER! HE IS FALLING INTO THAT FACTORY'S SMOKESTACK!
CAUGHT HIM JUST IN TIME! FORTUNATELY, THE CHIMNEY'S SMOKE SCREENS ME FROM HUMAN EYES!
RETURNING TO THE ORPHANAGE, SUPERGIRL CHANGES BACK TO HER SECRET IDENTITY OF LINDA LEE...
PAUL'S IN TROUBLE WITH THE ORPHANAGE SUPERINTENDENT!
I HATE TO SAY THIS, PAUL, BUT... WHO WOULD WANT TO ADOPT A BOY WHO DOESN'T TELL THE TRUTH?
I'LL PROVE I'M NOT LYING! WATCH ME TRY TO CUT OFF A SNIP OF STREAKY'S HAIR! I'LL FAIL BECAUSE HIS HAIR IS SUPER-STRONG!
12

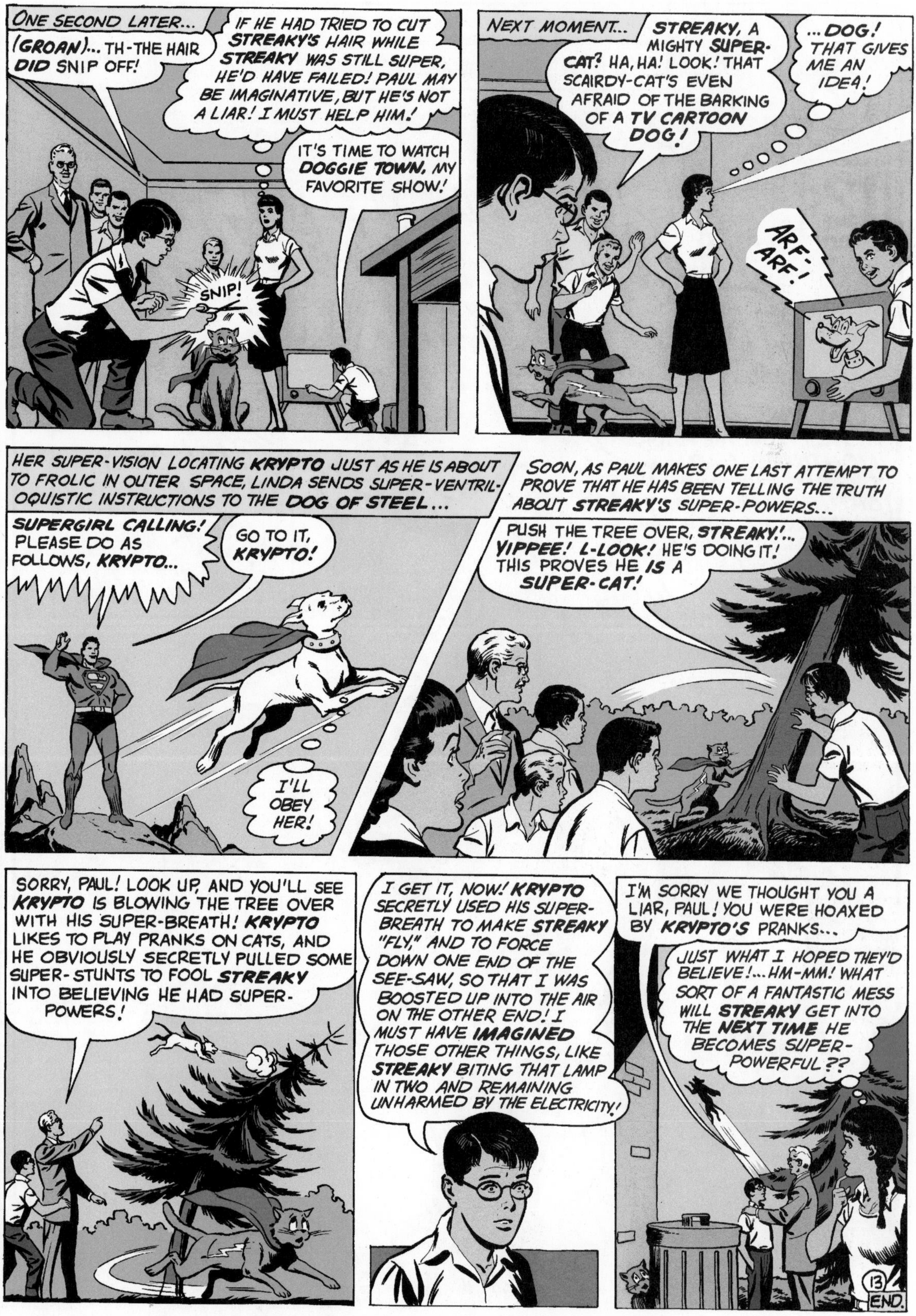
ONE SECOND LATER...
(GROAN)... TH-THE HAIR DID SNIP OFF!
IF HE HAD TRIED TO CUT STREAKY'S HAIR WHILE STREAKY WAS STILL SUPER, HE'D HAVE FAILED! PAUL MAY BE IMAGINATIVE, BUT HE'S NOT A LIAR! I MUST HELP HIM!
IT'S TIME TO WATCH DOGGIE TOWN, MY FAVORITE SHOW!
SNIP!
NEXT MOMENT...
STREAKY, A MIGHTY SUPER-CAT? HA, HA! LOOK! THAT SCAIRDY-CAT'S EVEN AFRAID OF THE BARKING OF A TV CARTOON DOG!
...DOG! THAT GIVES ME AN IDEA!
ARF! ARF!
HER SUPER-VISION LOCATING KRYPTO JUST AS HE IS ABOUT TO FROLIC IN OUTER SPACE, LINDA SENDS SUPER-VENTRILOQUISTIC INSTRUCTIONS TO THE DOG OF STEEL...
SUPERGIRL CALLING! PLEASE DO AS FOLLOWS, KRYPTO...
GO TO IT, KRYPTO!
I'LL OBEY HER!
SOON, AS PAUL MAKES ONE LAST ATTEMPT TO PROVE THAT HE HAS BEEN TELLING THE TRUTH ABOUT STREAKY'S SUPER-POWERS...
PUSH THE TREE OVER, STREAKY!... YIPPEE! L-LOOK! HE'S DOING IT! THIS PROVES HE IS A SUPER-CAT!
SORRY, PAUL! LOOK UP, AND YOU'LL SEE KRYPTO IS BLOWING THE TREE OVER WITH HIS SUPER-BREATH! KRYPTO LIKES TO PLAY PRANKS ON CATS, AND HE OBVIOUSLY SECRETLY PULLED SOME SUPER-STUNTS TO FOOL STREAKY INTO BELIEVING HE HAD SUPER-POWERS!
I GET IT, NOW! KRYPTO SECRETLY USED HIS SUPER-BREATH TO MAKE STREAKY "FLY," AND TO FORCE DOWN ONE END OF THE SEE-SAW, SO THAT I WAS BOOSTED UP INTO THE AIR ON THE OTHER END! I MUST HAVE IMAGINED THOSE OTHER THINGS, LIKE STREAKY BITING THAT LAMP IN TWO AND REMAINING UNHARMED BY THE ELECTRICITY!
I'M SORRY WE THOUGHT YOU A LIAR, PAUL! YOU WERE HOAXED BY KRYPTO'S PRANKS...
JUST WHAT I HOPED THEY'D BELIEVE!... HM-MM! WHAT SORT OF A FANTASTIC MESS WILL STREAKY GET INTO THE NEXT TIME HE BECOMES SUPER-POWERFUL??
13
END.

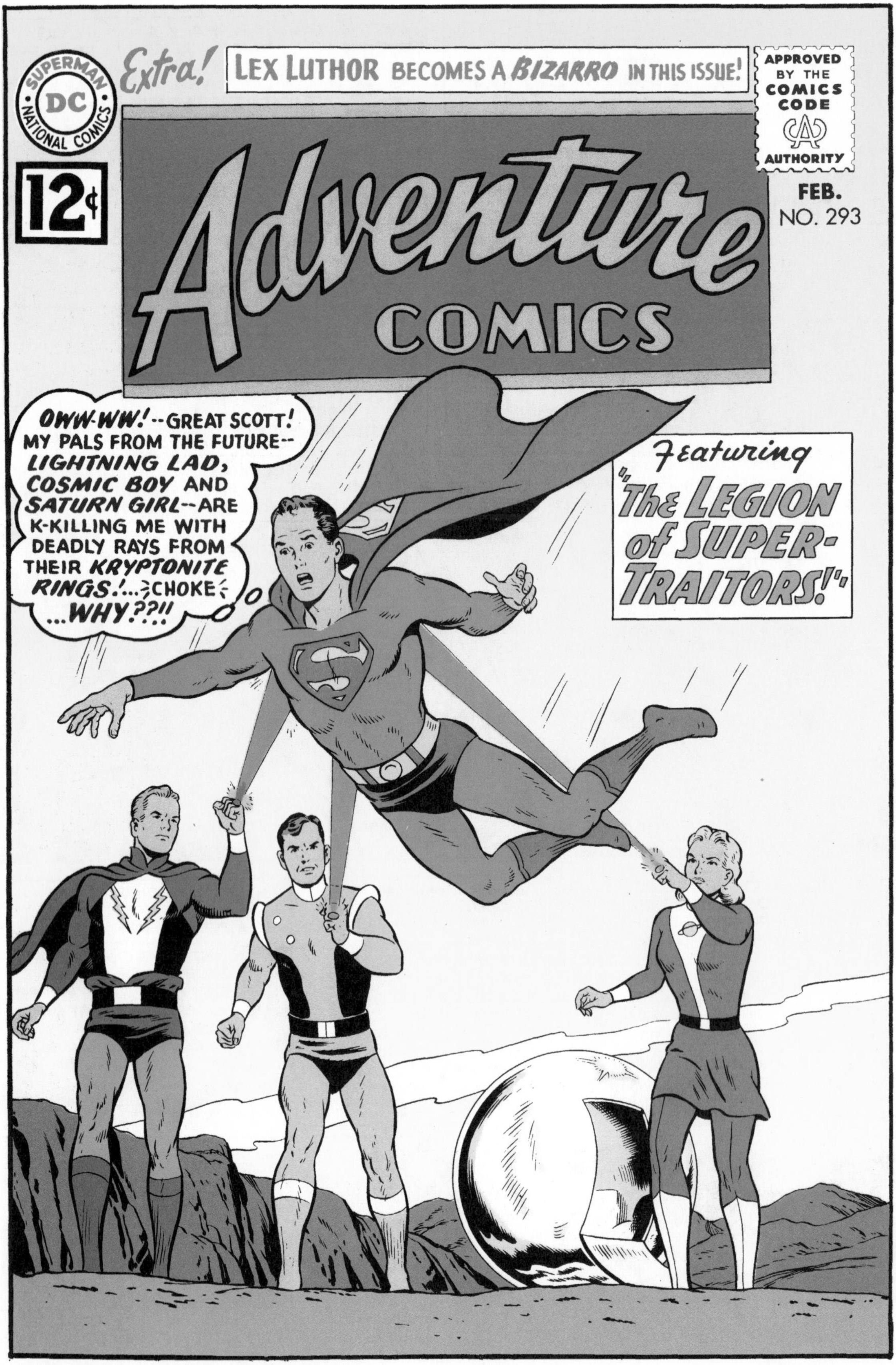
Extra!
LEX LUTHOR BECOMES A BIZARRO IN THIS ISSUE!
SUPERMAN DC NATIONAL COMICS
12¢
APPROVED BY THE COMICS CODE AUTHORITY
FEB.
NO. 293
Adventure COMICS
OWW-WW! --GREAT SCOTT! MY PALS FROM THE FUTURE-- LIGHTNING LAD, COSMIC BOY AND SATURN GIRL--ARE K-KILLING ME WITH DEADLY RAYS FROM THEIR KRYPTONITE RINGS!...CHOKE ...WHY??!!
Featuring "The LEGION of SUPER-TRAITORS!"

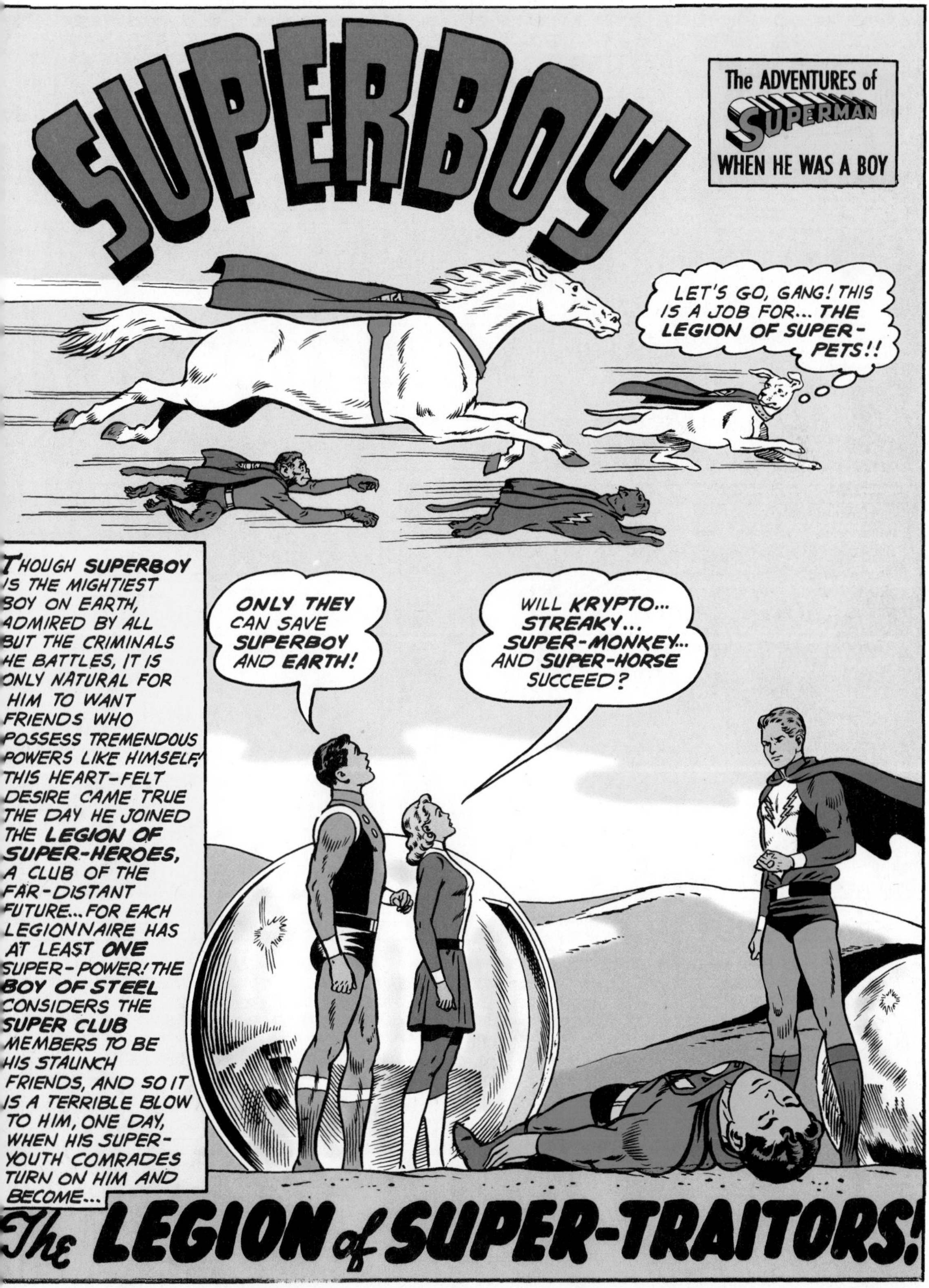
SUPERBOY
The ADVENTURES of SUPERMAN WHEN HE WAS A BOY
LET'S GO, GANG! THIS IS A JOB FOR... THE LEGION OF SUPER-PETS!!
THOUGH SUPERBOY IS THE MIGHTIEST BOY ON EARTH, ADMIRED BY ALL BUT THE CRIMINALS HE BATTLES, IT IS ONLY NATURAL FOR HIM TO WANT FRIENDS WHO POSSESS TREMENDOUS POWERS LIKE HIMSELF! THIS HEART-FELT DESIRE CAME TRUE THE DAY HE JOINED THE LEGION OF SUPER-HEROES, A CLUB OF THE FAR-DISTANT FUTURE...FOR EACH LEGIONNAIRE HAS AT LEAST ONE SUPER-POWER! THE BOY OF STEEL CONSIDERS THE SUPER CLUB MEMBERS TO BE HIS STAUNCH FRIENDS, AND SO IT IS A TERRIBLE BLOW TO HIM, ONE DAY, WHEN HIS SUPER-YOUTH COMRADES TURN ON HIM AND BECOME...
ONLY THEY CAN SAVE SUPERBOY AND EARTH!
WILL KRYPTO... STREAKY... SUPER-MONKEY... AND SUPER-HORSE SUCCEED?
The LEGION of SUPER-TRAITORS!

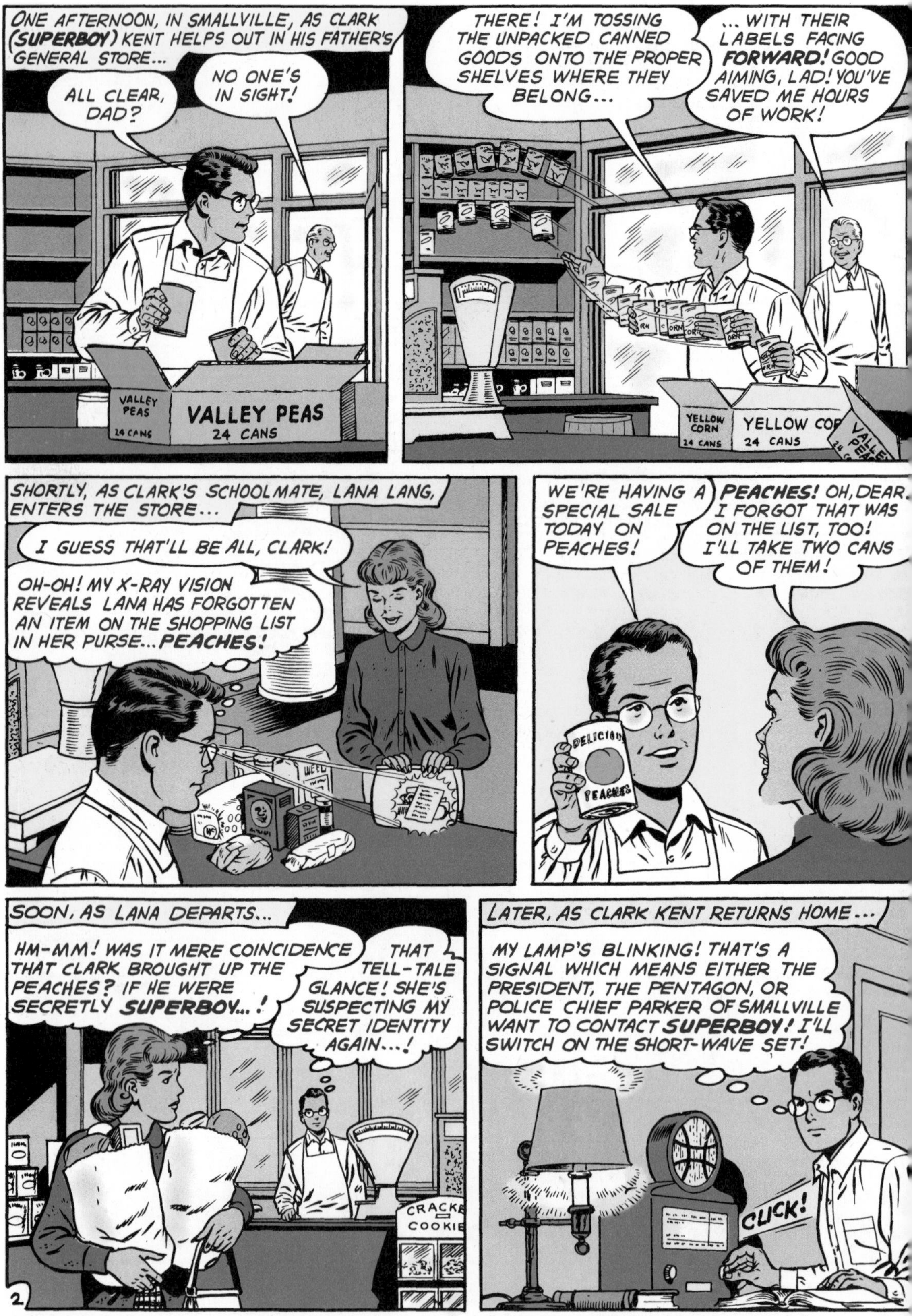
ONE AFTERNOON, IN SMALLVILLE, AS CLARK (SUPERBOY) KENT HELPS OUT IN HIS FATHER'S GENERAL STORE...
ALL CLEAR, DAD?
NO ONE'S IN SIGHT!
VALLEY PEAS 24 CANS
VALLEY PEAS 24 CANS
THERE! I'M TOSSING THE UNPACKED CANNED GOODS ONTO THE PROPER SHELVES WHERE THEY BELONG...
...WITH THEIR LABELS FACING FORWARD! GOOD AIMING, LAD! YOU'VE SAVED ME HOURS OF WORK!
YELLOW CORN 24 CANS
YELLOW CO 24 CANS
SHORTLY, AS CLARK'S SCHOOLMATE, LANA LANG, ENTERS THE STORE...
I GUESS THAT'LL BE ALL, CLARK!
OH-OH! MY X-RAY VISION REVEALS LANA HAS FORGOTTEN AN ITEM ON THE SHOPPING LIST IN HER PURSE... PEACHES!
WE'RE HAVING A SPECIAL SALE TODAY ON PEACHES!
PEACHES! OH, DEAR. I FORGOT THAT WAS ON THE LIST, TOO! I'LL TAKE TWO CANS OF THEM!
DELICIOUS PEACHES
SOON, AS LANA DEPARTS...
HM-MM! WAS IT MERE COINCIDENCE THAT CLARK BROUGHT UP THE PEACHES? IF HE WERE SECRETLY SUPERBOY...!
THAT TELL-TALE GLANCE! SHE'S SUSPECTING MY SECRET IDENTITY AGAIN...!
CRACKE COOKIE
2
LATER, AS CLARK KENT RETURNS HOME...
MY LAMP'S BLINKING! THAT'S A SIGNAL WHICH MEANS EITHER THE PRESIDENT, THE PENTAGON, OR POLICE CHIEF PARKER OF SMALLVILLE WANT TO CONTACT SUPERBOY! I'LL SWITCH ON THE SHORT-WAVE SET!
CLICK!

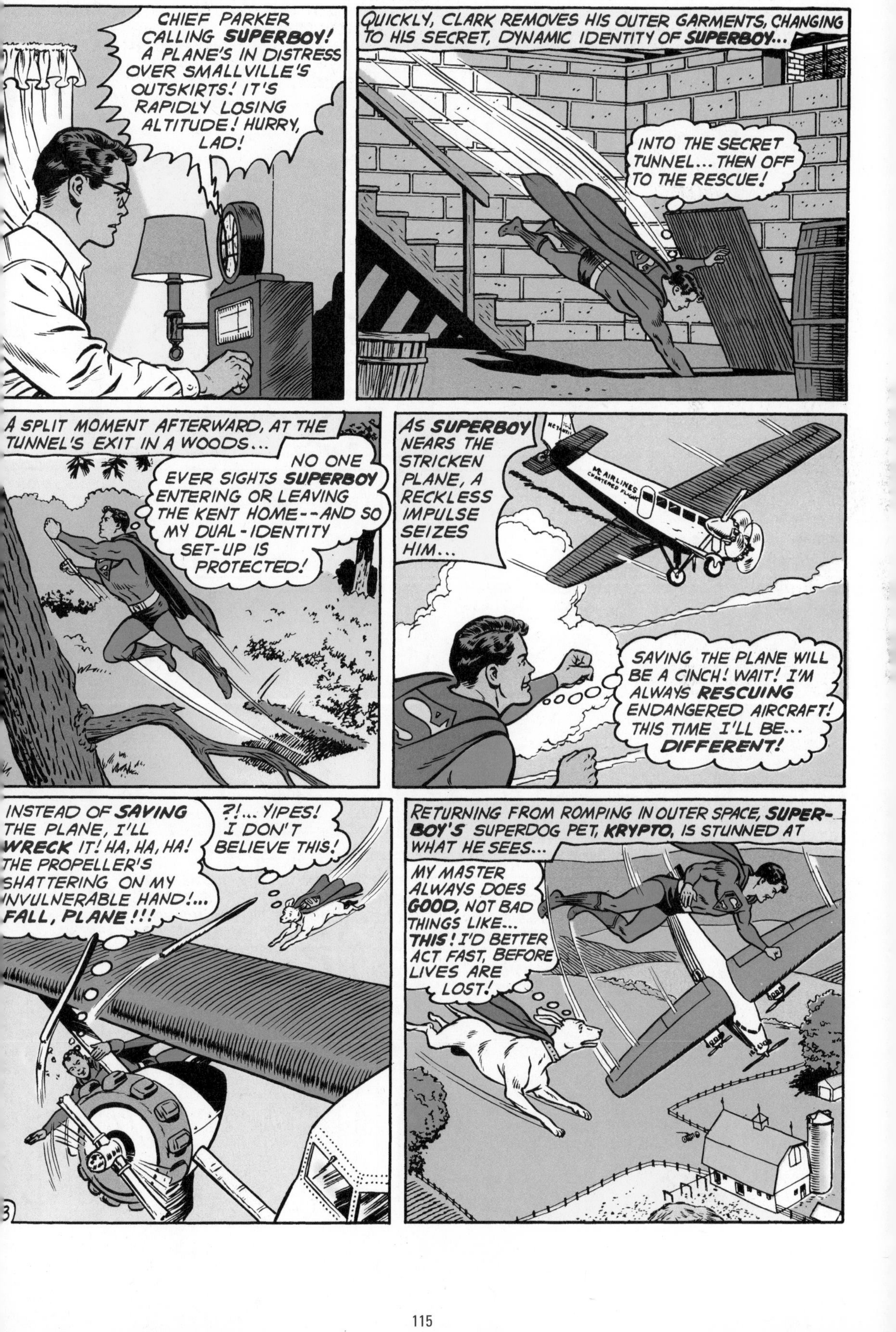
CHIEF PARKER CALLING SUPERBOY! A PLANE'S IN DISTRESS OVER SMALLVILLE'S OUTSKIRTS! IT'S RAPIDLY LOSING ALTITUDE! HURRY, LAD!
QUICKLY, CLARK REMOVES HIS OUTER GARMENTS, CHANGING TO HIS SECRET, DYNAMIC IDENTITY OF SUPERBOY...
INTO THE SECRET TUNNEL... THEN OFF TO THE RESCUE!
A SPLIT MOMENT AFTERWARD, AT THE TUNNEL'S EXIT IN A WOODS...
NO ONE EVER SIGHTS SUPERBOY ENTERING OR LEAVING THE KENT HOME--AND SO MY DUAL-IDENTITY SET-UP IS PROTECTED!
AS SUPERBOY NEARS THE STRICKEN PLANE, A RECKLESS IMPULSE SEIZES HIM...
SAVING THE PLANE WILL BE A CINCH! WAIT! I'M ALWAYS RESCUING ENDANGERED AIRCRAFT! THIS TIME I'LL BE... DIFFERENT!
INSTEAD OF SAVING THE PLANE, I'LL WRECK IT! HA, HA, HA! THE PROPELLER'S SHATTERING ON MY INVULNERABLE HAND!... FALL, PLANE!!!
?!... YIPES! I DON'T BELIEVE THIS!
RETURNING FROM ROMPING IN OUTER SPACE, SUPERBOY'S SUPERDOG PET, KRYPTO, IS STUNNED AT WHAT HE SEES...
MY MASTER ALWAYS DOES GOOD, NOT BAD THINGS LIKE... THIS! I'D BETTER ACT FAST, BEFORE LIVES ARE LOST!

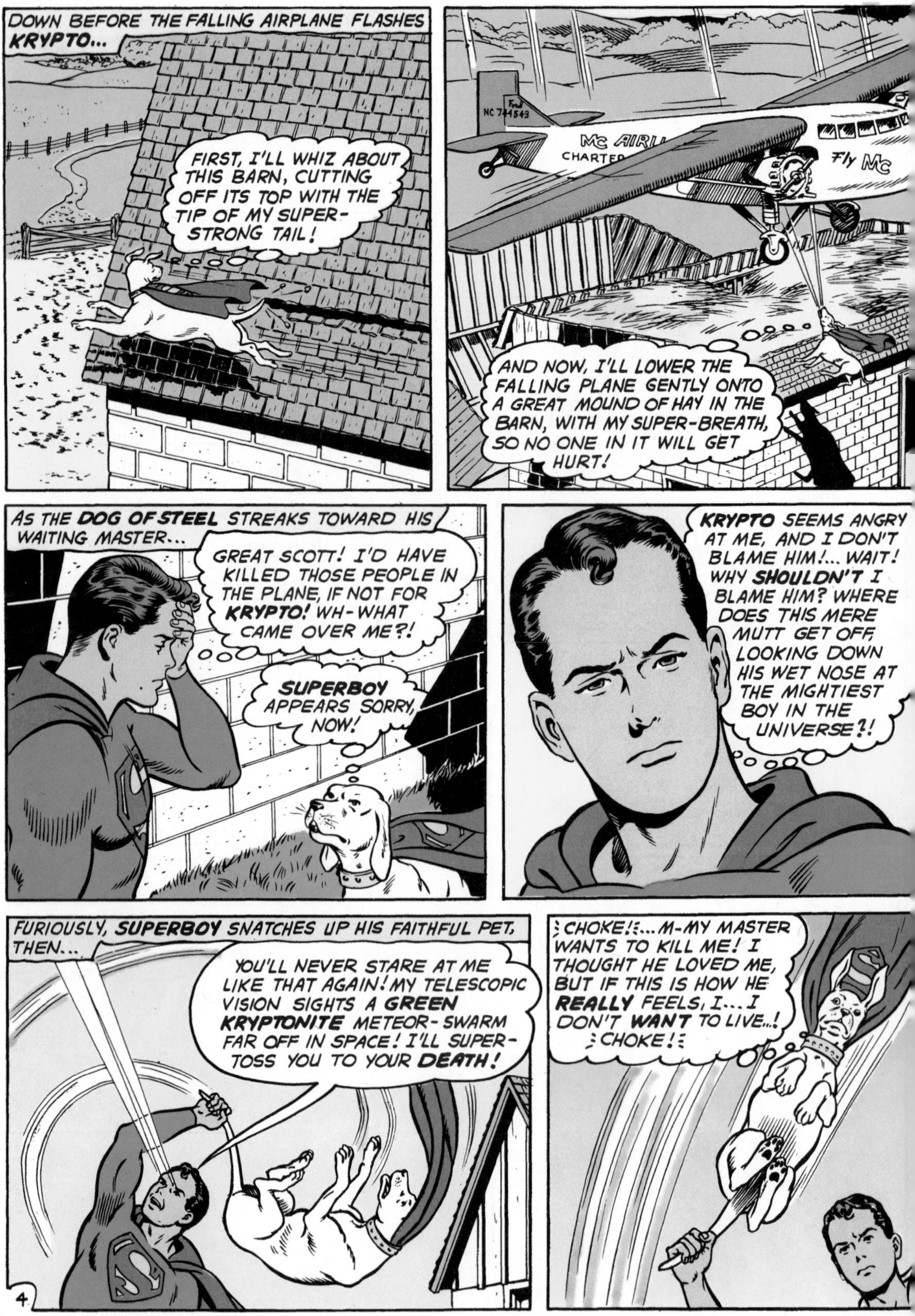
DOWN BEFORE THE FALLING AIRPLANE FLASHES KRYPTO...
FIRST, I'LL WHIZ ABOUT THIS BARN, CUTTING OFF ITS TOP WITH THE TIP OF MY SUPER-STRONG TAIL!
NC 744543
MC AIRL
CHARTER
Fly MC
AND NOW, I'LL LOWER THE FALLING PLANE GENTLY ONTO A GREAT MOUND OF HAY IN THE BARN, WITH MY SUPER-BREATH, SO NO ONE IN IT WILL GET HURT!
AS THE DOG OF STEEL STREAKS TOWARD HIS WAITING MASTER...
GREAT SCOTT! I'D HAVE KILLED THOSE PEOPLE IN THE PLANE, IF NOT FOR KRYPTO! WH-WHAT CAME OVER ME?!
SUPERBOY APPEARS SORRY, NOW!
KRYPTO SEEMS ANGRY AT ME, AND I DON'T BLAME HIM!... WAIT! WHY SHOULDN'T I BLAME HIM? WHERE DOES THIS MERE MUTT GET OFF, LOOKING DOWN HIS WET NOSE AT THE MIGHTIEST BOY IN THE UNIVERSE?!
FURIOUSLY, SUPERBOY SNATCHES UP HIS FAITHFUL PET, THEN...
YOU'LL NEVER STARE AT ME LIKE THAT AGAIN! MY TELESCOPIC VISION SIGHTS A GREEN KRYPTONITE METEOR-SWARM FAR OFF IN SPACE! I'LL SUPER-TOSS YOU TO YOUR DEATH!
4
CHOKE!... M-MY MASTER WANTS TO KILL ME! I THOUGHT HE LOVED ME, BUT IF THIS IS HOW HE REALLY FEELS, I... I DON'T WANT TO LIVE...! CHOKE!

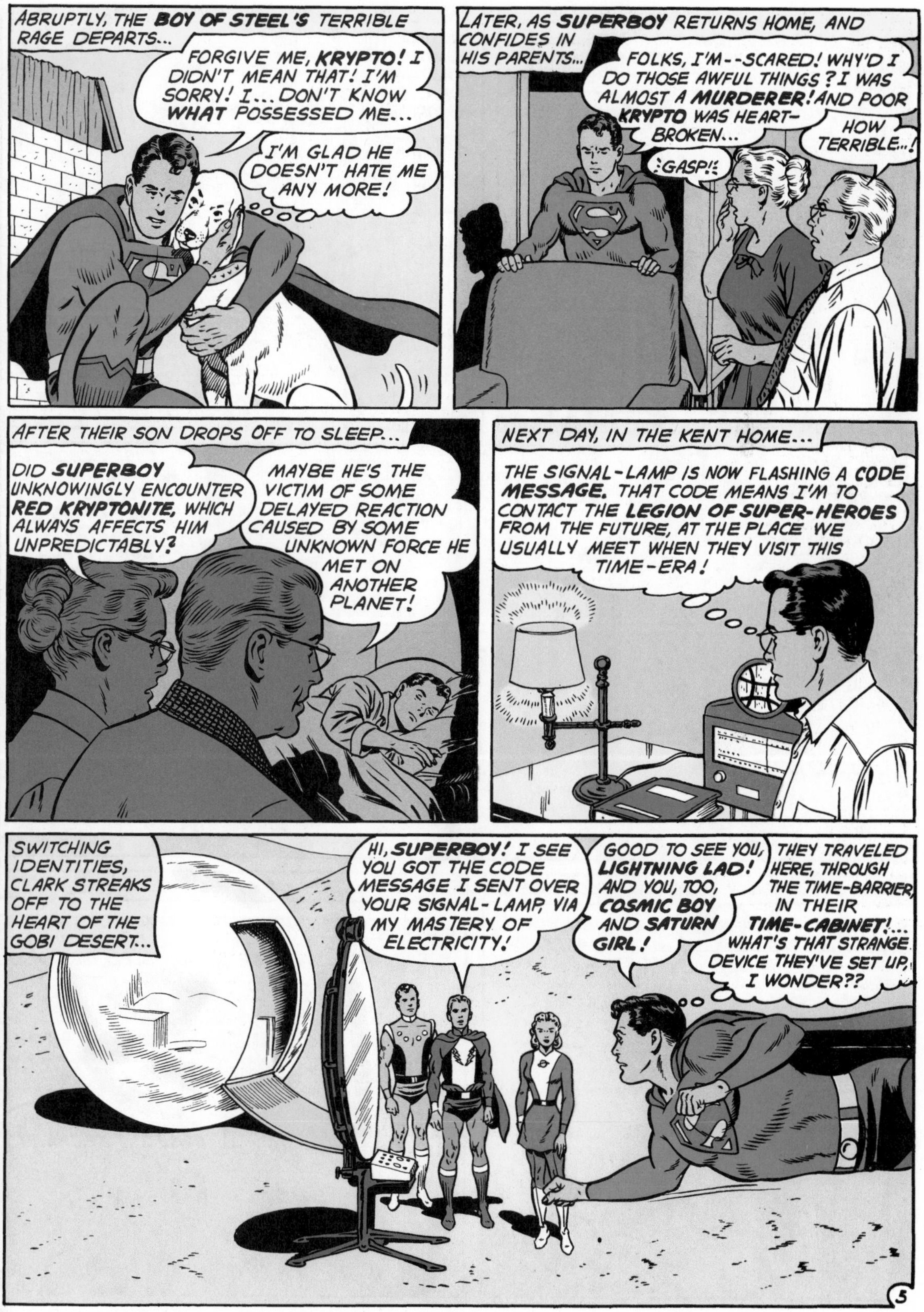
ABRUPTLY, THE BOY OF STEEL'S TERRIBLE RAGE DEPARTS...
FORGIVE ME, KRYPTO! I DIDN'T MEAN THAT! I'M SORRY! I... DON'T KNOW WHAT POSSESSED ME...
I'M GLAD HE DOESN'T HATE ME ANY MORE!
LATER, AS SUPERBOY RETURNS HOME, AND CONFIDES IN HIS PARENTS...
FOLKS, I'M--SCARED! WHY'D I DO THOSE AWFUL THINGS? I WAS ALMOST A MURDERER! AND POOR KRYPTO WAS HEART-BROKEN...
GASP!
HOW TERRIBLE...!
AFTER THEIR SON DROPS OFF TO SLEEP...
DID SUPERBOY UNKNOWINGLY ENCOUNTER RED KRYPTONITE, WHICH ALWAYS AFFECTS HIM UNPREDICTABLY?
MAYBE HE'S THE VICTIM OF SOME DELAYED REACTION CAUSED BY SOME UNKNOWN FORCE HE MET ON ANOTHER PLANET!
NEXT DAY, IN THE KENT HOME...
THE SIGNAL-LAMP IS NOW FLASHING A CODE MESSAGE. THAT CODE MEANS I'M TO CONTACT THE LEGION OF SUPER-HEROES FROM THE FUTURE, AT THE PLACE WE USUALLY MEET WHEN THEY VISIT THIS TIME-ERA!
SWITCHING IDENTITIES, CLARK STREAKS OFF TO THE HEART OF THE GOBI DESERT...
HI, SUPERBOY! I SEE YOU GOT THE CODE MESSAGE I SENT OVER YOUR SIGNAL-LAMP, VIA MY MASTERY OF ELECTRICITY!
GOOD TO SEE YOU, LIGHTNING LAD! AND YOU, TOO, COSMIC BOY AND SATURN GIRL!
THEY TRAVELED HERE, THROUGH THE TIME-BARRIER, IN THEIR TIME-CABINET!... WHAT'S THAT STRANGE DEVICE THEY'VE SET UP, I WONDER??
5

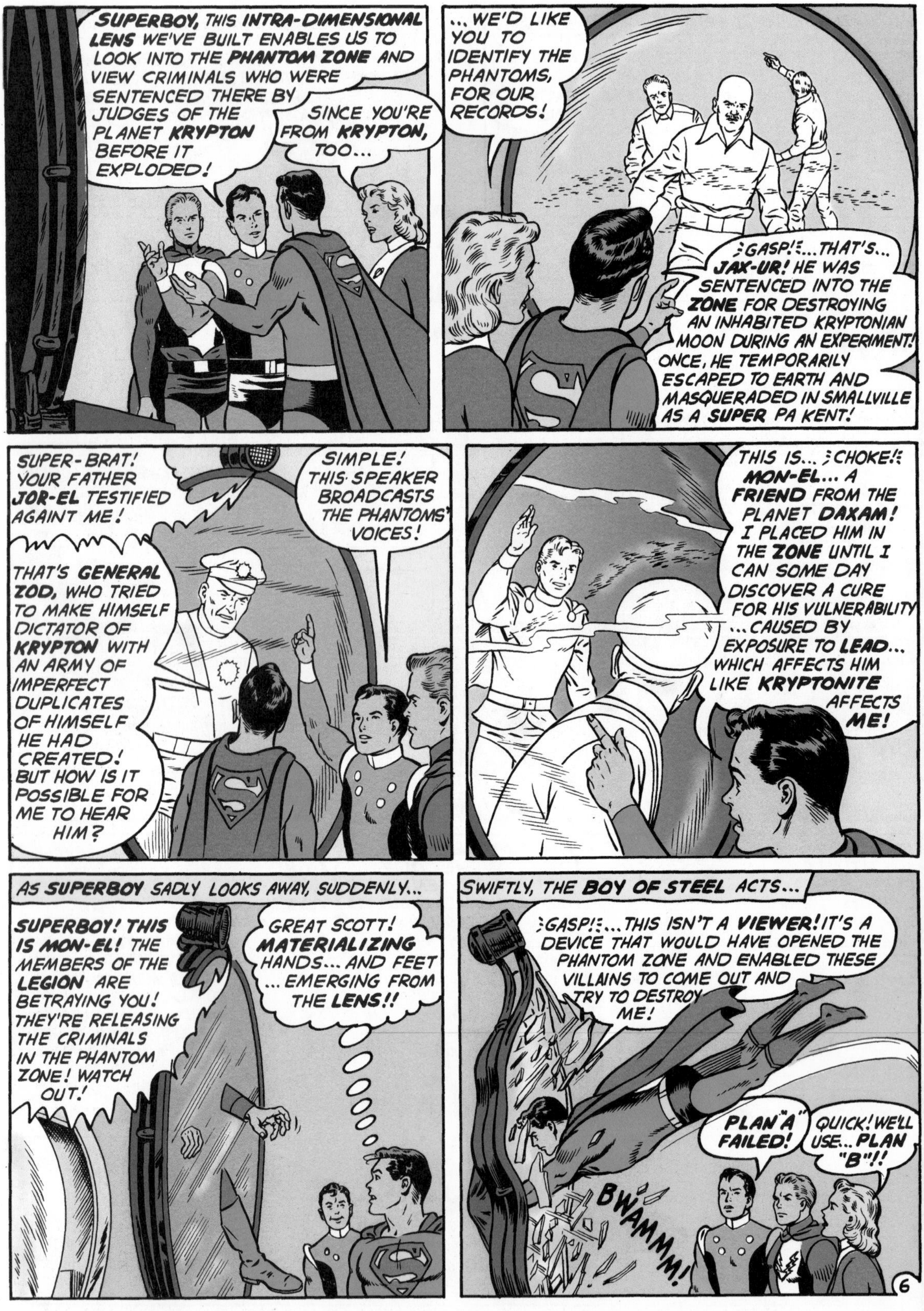
SUPERBOY, THIS INTRA-DIMENSIONAL LENS WE'VE BUILT ENABLES US TO LOOK INTO THE PHANTOM ZONE AND VIEW CRIMINALS WHO WERE SENTENCED THERE BY JUDGES OF THE PLANET KRYPTON BEFORE IT EXPLODED!
SINCE YOU'RE FROM KRYPTON, TOO...
...WE'D LIKE YOU TO IDENTIFY THE PHANTOMS, FOR OUR RECORDS!
GASP! ...THAT'S... JAX-UR! HE WAS SENTENCED INTO THE ZONE FOR DESTROYING AN INHABITED KRYPTONIAN MOON DURING AN EXPERIMENT! ONCE, HE TEMPORARILY ESCAPED TO EARTH AND MASQUERADED IN SMALLVILLE AS A SUPER PA KENT!
SUPER-BRAT! YOUR FATHER JOR-EL TESTIFIED AGAINT ME!
SIMPLE! THIS SPEAKER BROADCASTS THE PHANTOMS' VOICES!
THAT'S GENERAL ZOD, WHO TRIED TO MAKE HIMSELF DICTATOR OF KRYPTON WITH AN ARMY OF IMPERFECT DUPLICATES OF HIMSELF HE HAD CREATED! BUT HOW IS IT POSSIBLE FOR ME TO HEAR HIM?
THIS IS... CHOKE! MON-EL... A FRIEND FROM THE PLANET DAXAM! I PLACED HIM IN THE ZONE UNTIL I CAN SOME DAY DISCOVER A CURE FOR HIS VULNERABILITY ...CAUSED BY EXPOSURE TO LEAD... WHICH AFFECTS HIM LIKE KRYPTONITE AFFECTS ME!
AS SUPERBOY SADLY LOOKS AWAY, SUDDENLY...
SUPERBOY! THIS IS MON-EL! THE MEMBERS OF THE LEGION ARE BETRAYING YOU! THEY'RE RELEASING THE CRIMINALS IN THE PHANTOM ZONE! WATCH OUT!
GREAT SCOTT! MATERIALIZING HANDS... AND FEET ... EMERGING FROM THE LENS!!
SWIFTLY, THE BOY OF STEEL ACTS...
GASP! ...THIS ISN'T A VIEWER! IT'S A DEVICE THAT WOULD HAVE OPENED THE PHANTOM ZONE AND ENABLED THESE VILLAINS TO COME OUT AND TRY TO DESTROY ME!
BWAMMM!
PLAN "A" FAILED!
QUICK! WE'LL USE... PLAN "B"!!
6

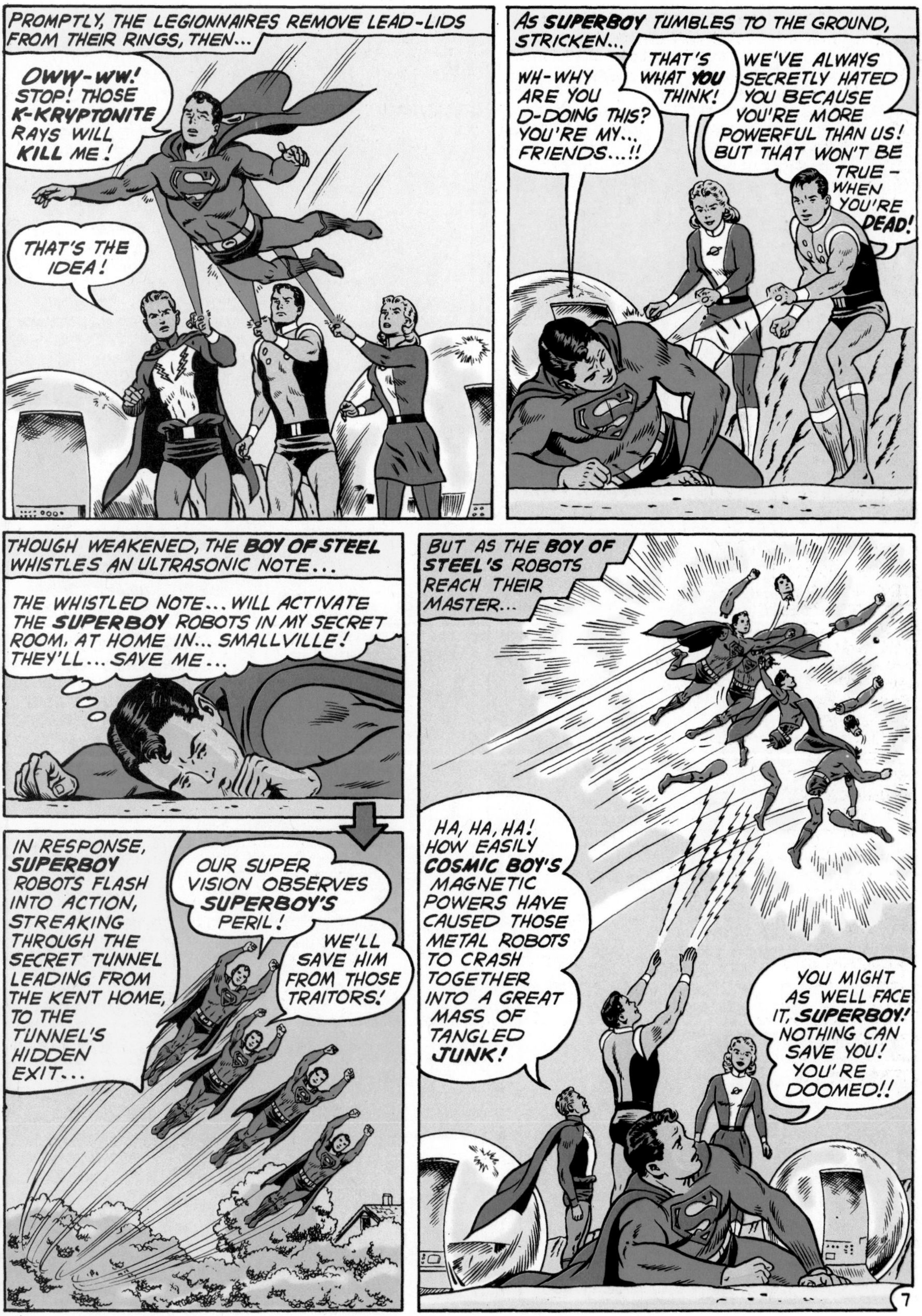
PROMPTLY, THE LEGIONNAIRES REMOVE LEAD-LIDS FROM THEIR RINGS, THEN...
OWW-WW! STOP! THOSE K-KRYPTONITE RAYS WILL KILL ME!
THAT'S THE IDEA!
AS SUPERBOY TUMBLES TO THE GROUND, STRICKEN...
WH-WHY ARE YOU D-DOING THIS? YOU'RE MY... FRIENDS...!!
THAT'S WHAT YOU THINK!
WE'VE ALWAYS SECRETLY HATED YOU BECAUSE YOU'RE MORE POWERFUL THAN US! BUT THAT WON'T BE TRUE -- WHEN YOU'RE DEAD!
THOUGH WEAKENED, THE BOY OF STEEL WHISTLES AN ULTRASONIC NOTE...
THE WHISTLED NOTE... WILL ACTIVATE THE SUPERBOY ROBOTS IN MY SECRET ROOM, AT HOME IN... SMALLVILLE! THEY'LL... SAVE ME...
IN RESPONSE, SUPERBOY ROBOTS FLASH INTO ACTION, STREAKING THROUGH THE SECRET TUNNEL LEADING FROM THE KENT HOME, TO THE TUNNEL'S HIDDEN EXIT...
OUR SUPER VISION OBSERVES SUPERBOY'S PERIL!
WE'LL SAVE HIM FROM THOSE TRAITORS!
BUT AS THE BOY OF STEEL'S ROBOTS REACH THEIR MASTER...
HA, HA, HA! HOW EASILY COSMIC BOY'S MAGNETIC POWERS HAVE CAUSED THOSE METAL ROBOTS TO CRASH TOGETHER INTO A GREAT MASS OF TANGLED JUNK!
YOU MIGHT AS WELL FACE IT, SUPERBOY! NOTHING CAN SAVE YOU! YOU'RE DOOMED!!
7

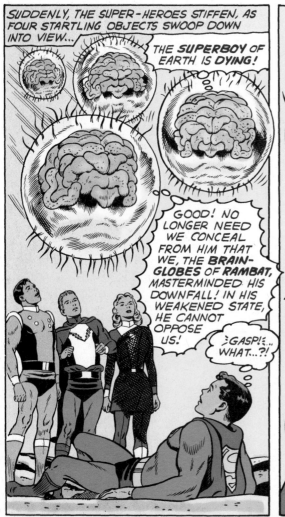

SUDDENLY, THE SUPER-HEROES STIFFEN, AS FOUR STARTLING OBJECTS SWOOP DOWN INTO VIEW...

THE *SUPERBOY* OF EARTH IS *DYING!*

GOOD! NO LONGER NEED WE CONCEAL FROM HIM THAT WE, THE *BRAIN-GLOBES* OF RAMBAT, MASTERMINDED HIS DOWNFALL! IN HIS WEAKENED STATE, HE CANNOT OPPOSE US!

≥GASP!≤... WHAT...?!

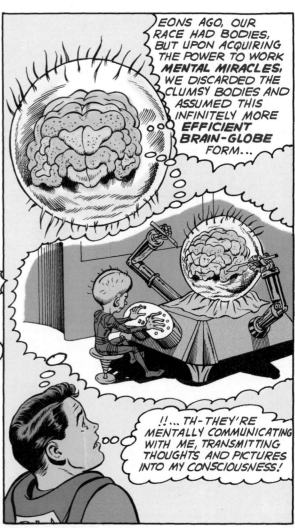

EONS AGO, OUR RACE HAD BODIES, BUT UPON ACQUIRING THE POWER TO WORK *MENTAL MIRACLES,* WE DISCARDED THE CLUMSY BODIES AND ASSUMED THIS INFINITELY MORE *EFFICIENT BRAIN-GLOBE* FORM...

!!... TH-THEY'RE MENTALLY COMMUNICATING WITH ME, TRANSMITTING THOUGHTS AND PICTURES INTO MY CONSCIOUSNESS!

AS *SATURN GIRL'S* MIND POWER TUNES IN ON THE *BRAIN-GLOBES'* THOUGHTS...

ASTOUNDING! THEY'RE TELEPATHICALLY INFORMING *SUPERBOY* HOW THEY LEARNED, THOUSANDS OF YEARS AGO, THAT THEIR PLANET *RAMBAT* WAS DOOMED TO EXPLODE FROM INTERNAL CATACLYSMS!

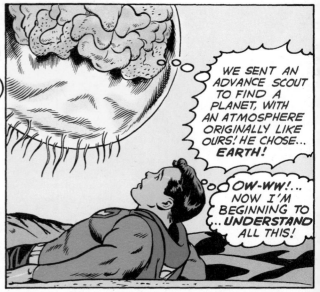

WE SENT AN ADVANCE SCOUT TO FIND A PLANET, WITH AN ATMOSPHERE ORIGINALLY LIKE OURS! HE CHOSE... *EARTH!*

OW-WW!... NOW I'M BEGINNING TO ..*UNDERSTAND* ALL THIS!

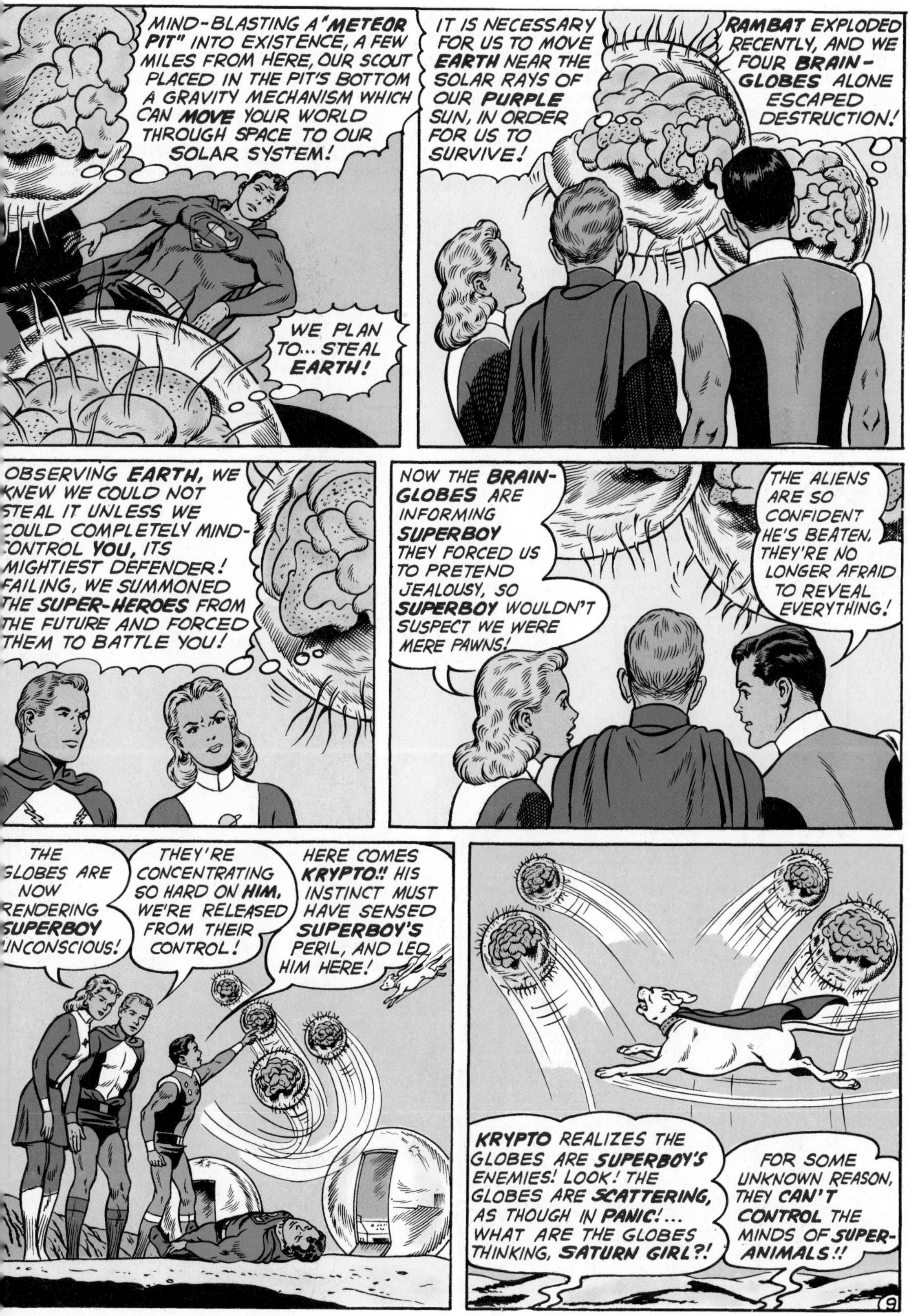

MIND-BLASTING A "METEOR PIT" INTO EXISTENCE, A FEW MILES FROM HERE, OUR SCOUT PLACED IN THE PIT'S BOTTOM A GRAVITY MECHANISM WHICH CAN MOVE YOUR WORLD THROUGH SPACE TO OUR SOLAR SYSTEM!
WE PLAN TO... STEAL EARTH!
IT IS NECESSARY FOR US TO MOVE EARTH NEAR THE SOLAR RAYS OF OUR PURPLE SUN, IN ORDER FOR US TO SURVIVE!
RAMBAT EXPLODED RECENTLY, AND WE FOUR BRAIN-GLOBES ALONE ESCAPED DESTRUCTION!
OBSERVING EARTH, WE KNEW WE COULD NOT STEAL IT UNLESS WE COULD COMPLETELY MIND-CONTROL YOU, ITS MIGHTIEST DEFENDER! FAILING, WE SUMMONED THE SUPER-HEROES FROM THE FUTURE AND FORCED THEM TO BATTLE YOU!
NOW THE BRAIN-GLOBES ARE INFORMING SUPERBOY THEY FORCED US TO PRETEND JEALOUSY, SO SUPERBOY WOULDN'T SUSPECT WE WERE MERE PAWNS!
THE ALIENS ARE SO CONFIDENT HE'S BEATEN, THEY'RE NO LONGER AFRAID TO REVEAL EVERYTHING!
THE GLOBES ARE NOW RENDERING SUPERBOY UNCONSCIOUS!
THEY'RE CONCENTRATING SO HARD ON HIM, WE'RE RELEASED FROM THEIR CONTROL!
HERE COMES KRYPTO!! HIS INSTINCT MUST HAVE SENSED SUPERBOY'S PERIL, AND LED HIM HERE!
KRYPTO REALIZES THE GLOBES ARE SUPERBOY'S ENEMIES! LOOK! THE GLOBES ARE SCATTERING, AS THOUGH IN PANIC!... WHAT ARE THE GLOBES THINKING, SATURN GIRL?!
FOR SOME UNKNOWN REASON, THEY CAN'T CONTROL THE MINDS OF SUPER-ANIMALS!!
9

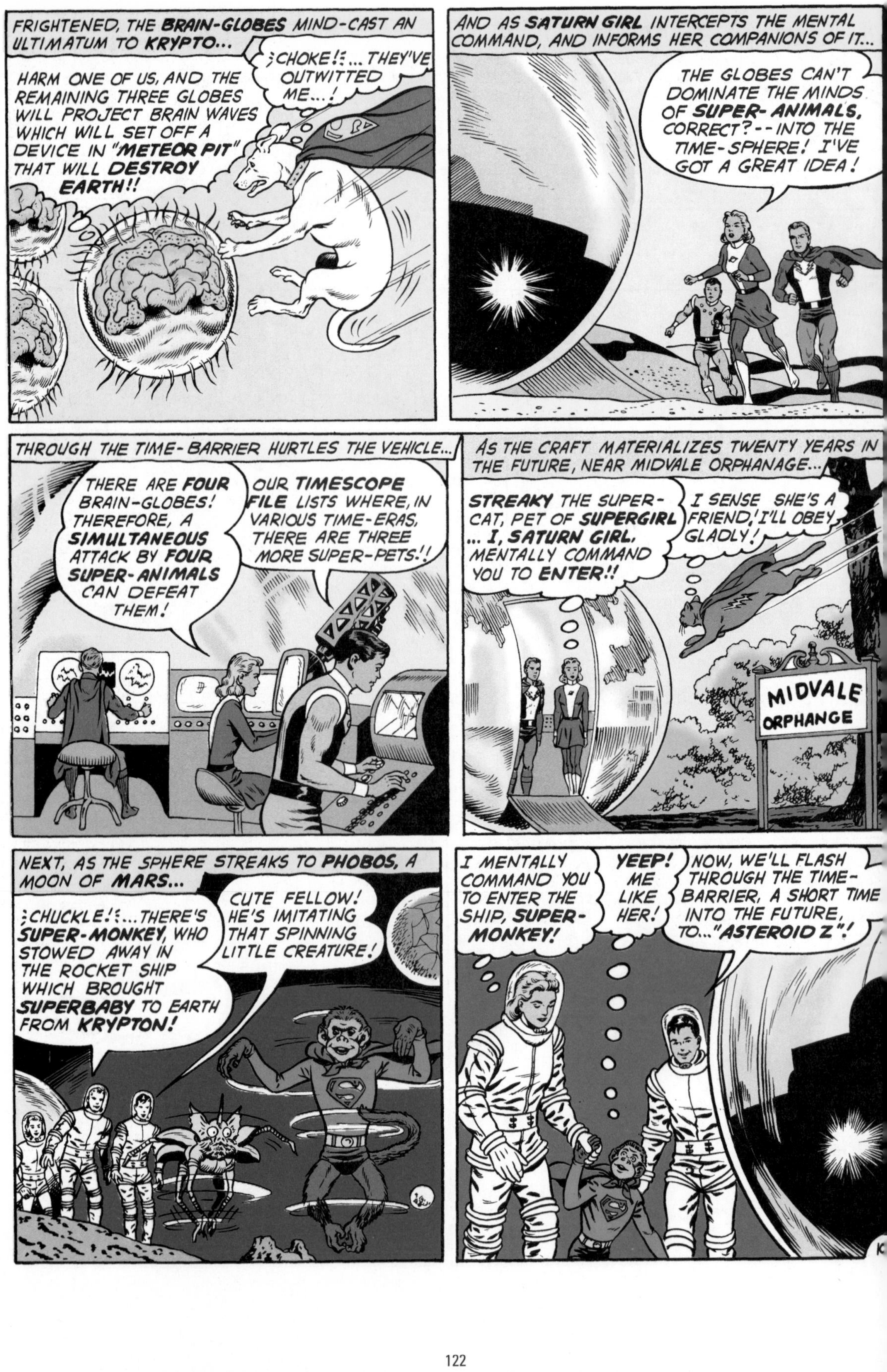
FRIGHTENED, THE BRAIN-GLOBES MIND-CAST AN ULTIMATUM TO KRYPTO...
HARM ONE OF US, AND THE REMAINING THREE GLOBES WILL PROJECT BRAIN WAVES WHICH WILL SET OFF A DEVICE IN "METEOR PIT" THAT WILL DESTROY EARTH!!
;CHOKE!: ...THEY'VE OUTWITTED ME...!
AND AS SATURN GIRL INTERCEPTS THE MENTAL COMMAND, AND INFORMS HER COMPANIONS OF IT...
THE GLOBES CAN'T DOMINATE THE MINDS OF SUPER-ANIMALS, CORRECT?--INTO THE TIME-SPHERE! I'VE GOT A GREAT IDEA!
THROUGH THE TIME-BARRIER HURTLES THE VEHICLE...
THERE ARE FOUR BRAIN-GLOBES! THEREFORE, A SIMULTANEOUS ATTACK BY FOUR SUPER-ANIMALS CAN DEFEAT THEM!
OUR TIMESCOPE FILE LISTS WHERE, IN VARIOUS TIME-ERAS, THERE ARE THREE MORE SUPER-PETS!!
AS THE CRAFT MATERIALIZES TWENTY YEARS IN THE FUTURE, NEAR MIDVALE ORPHANAGE...
STREAKY THE SUPER-CAT, PET OF SUPERGIRL ... I, SATURN GIRL, MENTALLY COMMAND YOU TO ENTER!!
I SENSE SHE'S A FRIEND, I'LL OBEY GLADLY!
MIDVALE ORPHANGE
NEXT, AS THE SPHERE STREAKS TO PHOBOS, A MOON OF MARS...
;CHUCKLE!: ...THERE'S SUPER-MONKEY, WHO STOWED AWAY IN THE ROCKET SHIP WHICH BROUGHT SUPERBABY TO EARTH FROM KRYPTON!
CUTE FELLOW! HE'S IMITATING THAT SPINNING LITTLE CREATURE!
I MENTALLY COMMAND YOU TO ENTER THE SHIP, SUPER-MONKEY!
YEEP! ME LIKE HER!
NOW, WE'LL FLASH THROUGH THE TIME-BARRIER, A SHORT TIME INTO THE FUTURE, TO..."ASTEROID Z"!

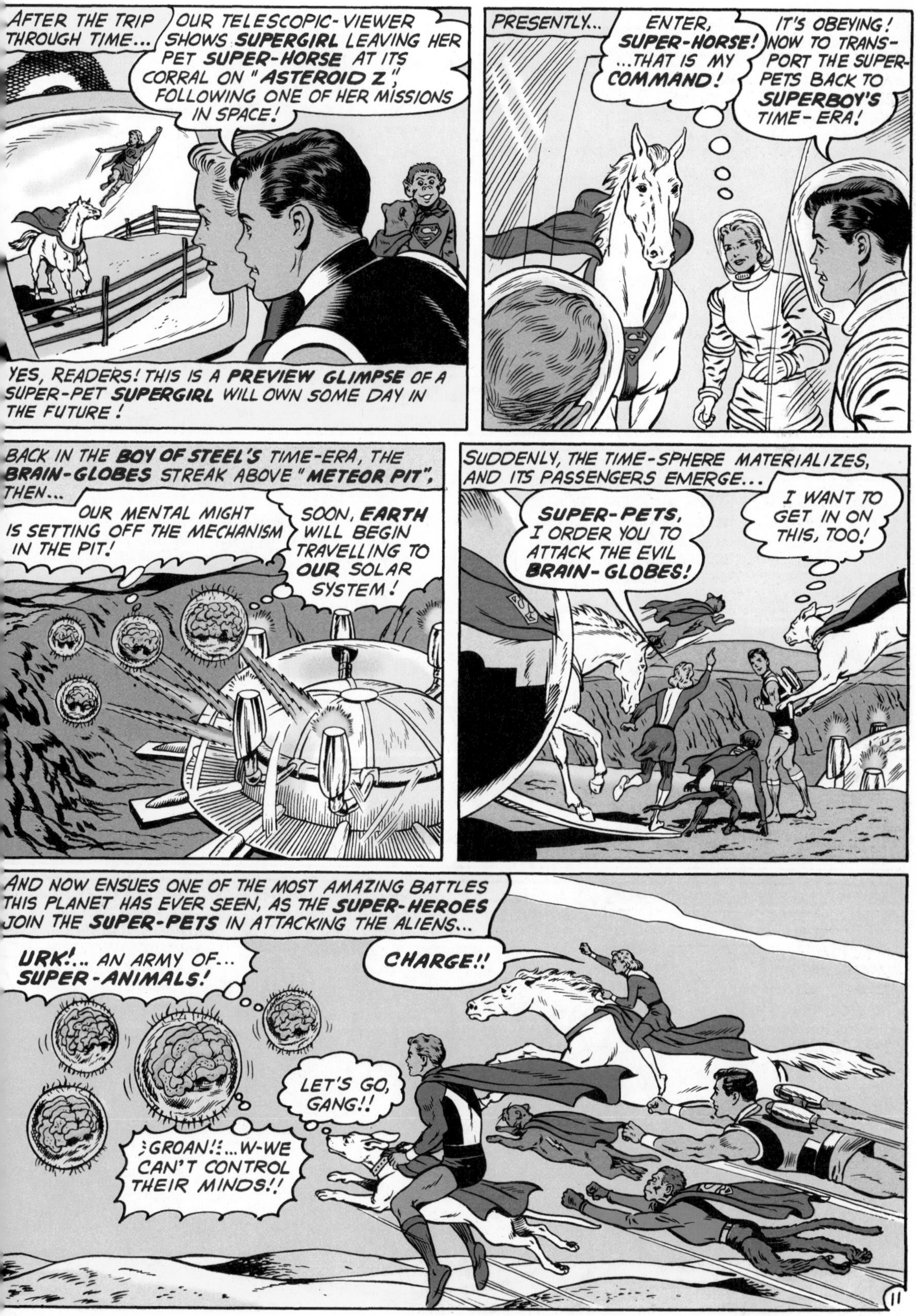
AFTER THE TRIP THROUGH TIME...
OUR TELESCOPIC-VIEWER SHOWS SUPERGIRL LEAVING HER PET SUPER-HORSE AT ITS CORRAL ON "ASTEROID Z", FOLLOWING ONE OF HER MISSIONS IN SPACE!
YES, READERS! THIS IS A PREVIEW GLIMPSE OF A SUPER-PET SUPERGIRL WILL OWN SOME DAY IN THE FUTURE!
PRESENTLY...
ENTER, SUPER-HORSE! ...THAT IS MY COMMAND!
IT'S OBEYING! NOW TO TRANSPORT THE SUPER-PETS BACK TO SUPERBOY'S TIME-ERA!
BACK IN THE BOY OF STEEL'S TIME-ERA, THE BRAIN-GLOBES STREAK ABOVE "METEOR PIT", THEN...
OUR MENTAL MIGHT IS SETTING OFF THE MECHANISM IN THE PIT!
SOON, EARTH WILL BEGIN TRAVELLING TO OUR SOLAR SYSTEM!
SUDDENLY, THE TIME-SPHERE MATERIALIZES, AND ITS PASSENGERS EMERGE...
SUPER-PETS, I ORDER YOU TO ATTACK THE EVIL BRAIN-GLOBES!
I WANT TO GET IN ON THIS, TOO!
AND NOW ENSUES ONE OF THE MOST AMAZING BATTLES THIS PLANET HAS EVER SEEN, AS THE SUPER-HEROES JOIN THE SUPER-PETS IN ATTACKING THE ALIENS...
URK!... AN ARMY OF... SUPER-ANIMALS!
CHARGE!!
LET'S GO, GANG!!
GROAN!... W-WE CAN'T CONTROL THEIR MINDS!!
11

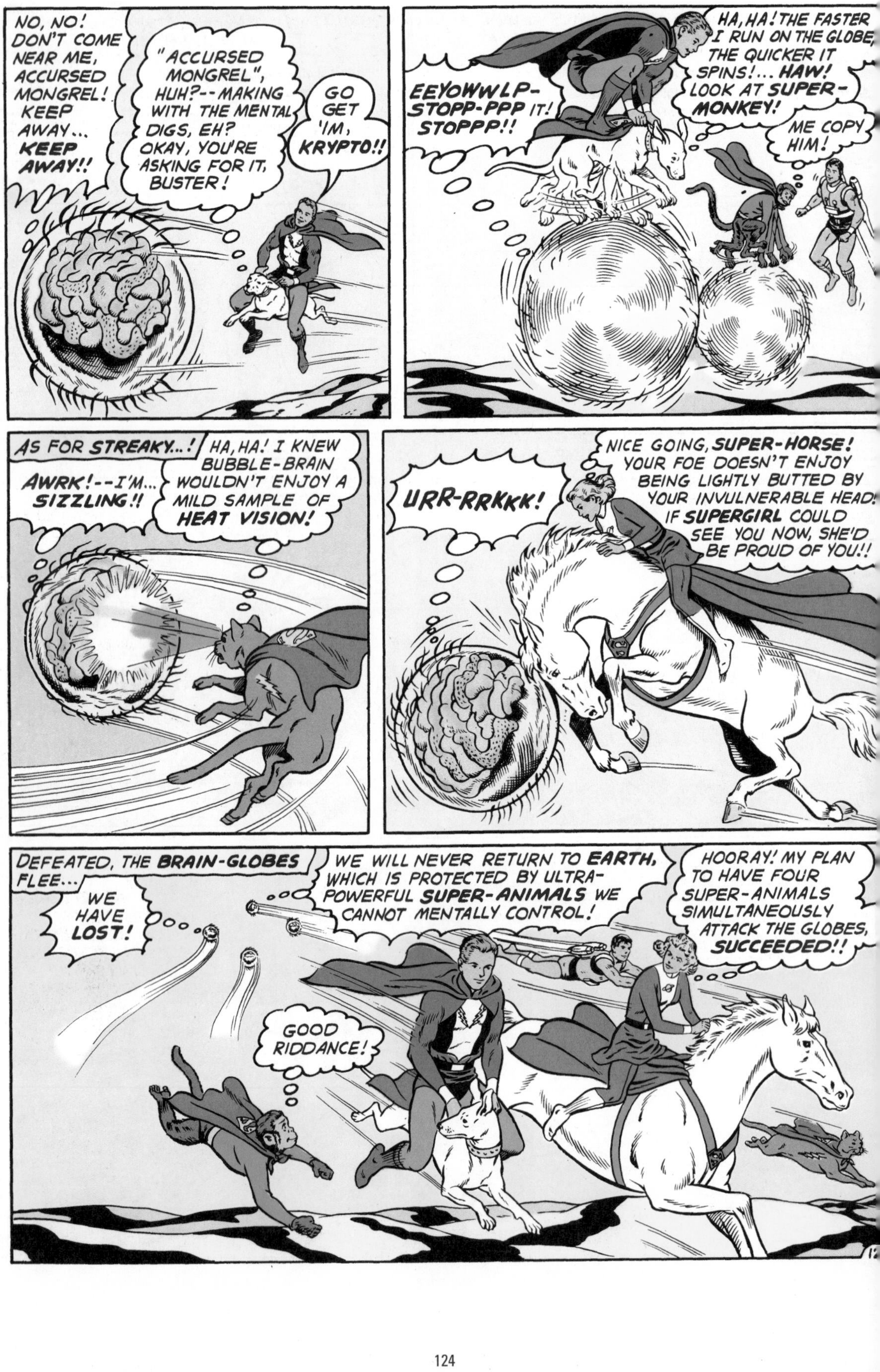
NO, NO! DON'T COME NEAR ME, ACCURSED MONGREL! KEEP AWAY... KEEP AWAY!!
"ACCURSED MONGREL", HUH?--MAKING WITH THE MENTAL DIGS, EH? OKAY, YOU'RE ASKING FOR IT, BUSTER!
GO GET 'IM, KRYPTO!!
EEYOWWLP-STOPP-PPP IT! STOPPP!!
HA, HA! THE FASTER I RUN ON THE GLOBE, THE QUICKER IT SPINS!... HAW! LOOK AT SUPER-MONKEY!
ME COPY HIM!
AS FOR STREAKY...!
AWRK!--I'M... SIZZLING!!
HA, HA! I KNEW BUBBLE-BRAIN WOULDN'T ENJOY A MILD SAMPLE OF HEAT VISION!
URR-RRKKK!
NICE GOING, SUPER-HORSE! YOUR FOE DOESN'T ENJOY BEING LIGHTLY BUTTED BY YOUR INVULNERABLE HEAD! IF SUPERGIRL COULD SEE YOU NOW, SHE'D BE PROUD OF YOU!!
DEFEATED, THE BRAIN-GLOBES FLEE...
WE HAVE LOST!
WE WILL NEVER RETURN TO EARTH, WHICH IS PROTECTED BY ULTRA-POWERFUL SUPER-ANIMALS WE CANNOT MENTALLY CONTROL!
HOORAY! MY PLAN TO HAVE FOUR SUPER-ANIMALS SIMULTANEOUSLY ATTACK THE GLOBES, SUCCEEDED!!
GOOD RIDDANCE!

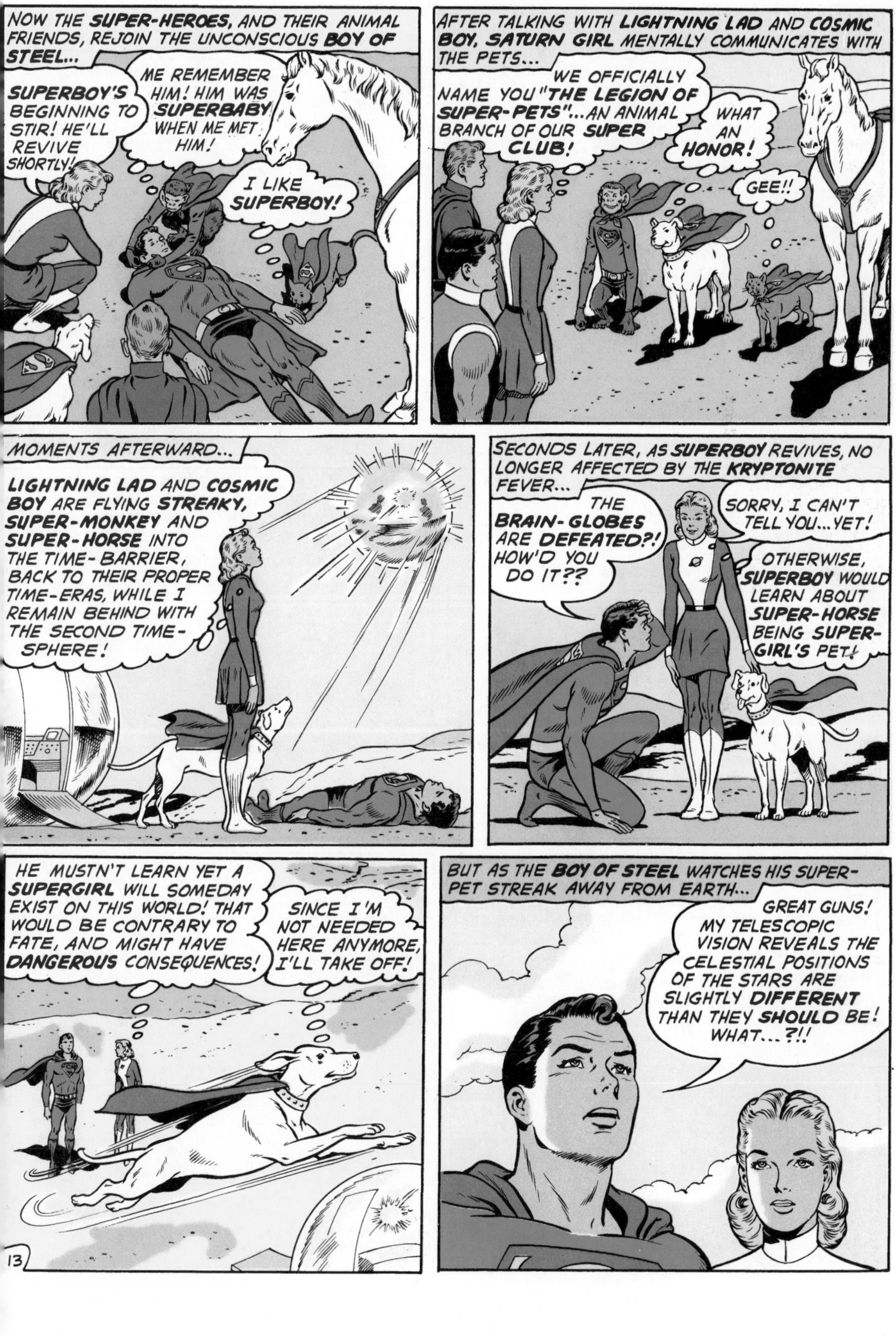
NOW THE SUPER-HEROES, AND THEIR ANIMAL FRIENDS, REJOIN THE UNCONSCIOUS BOY OF STEEL...
SUPERBOY'S BEGINNING TO STIR! HE'LL REVIVE SHORTLY!
ME REMEMBER HIM! HIM WAS SUPERBABY WHEN ME MET HIM!
I LIKE SUPERBOY!
AFTER TALKING WITH LIGHTNING LAD AND COSMIC BOY, SATURN GIRL MENTALLY COMMUNICATES WITH THE PETS...
WE OFFICIALLY NAME YOU "THE LEGION OF SUPER-PETS"...AN ANIMAL BRANCH OF OUR SUPER CLUB!
WHAT AN HONOR!
GEE!!
MOMENTS AFTERWARD...
LIGHTNING LAD AND COSMIC BOY ARE FLYING STREAKY, SUPER-MONKEY AND SUPER-HORSE INTO THE TIME-BARRIER, BACK TO THEIR PROPER TIME-ERAS, WHILE I REMAIN BEHIND WITH THE SECOND TIME-SPHERE!
SECONDS LATER, AS SUPERBOY REVIVES, NO LONGER AFFECTED BY THE KRYPTONITE FEVER...
THE BRAIN-GLOBES ARE DEFEATED?! HOW'D YOU DO IT??
SORRY, I CAN'T TELL YOU...YET!
OTHERWISE, SUPERBOY WOULD LEARN ABOUT SUPER-HORSE BEING SUPERGIRL'S PET!
HE MUSTN'T LEARN YET A SUPERGIRL WILL SOMEDAY EXIST ON THIS WORLD! THAT WOULD BE CONTRARY TO FATE, AND MIGHT HAVE DANGEROUS CONSEQUENCES!
SINCE I'M NOT NEEDED HERE ANYMORE, I'LL TAKE OFF!
13
BUT AS THE BOY OF STEEL WATCHES HIS SUPER-PET STREAK AWAY FROM EARTH...
GREAT GUNS! MY TELESCOPIC VISION REVEALS THE CELESTIAL POSITIONS OF THE STARS ARE SLIGHTLY DIFFERENT THAN THEY SHOULD BE! WHAT...?!!

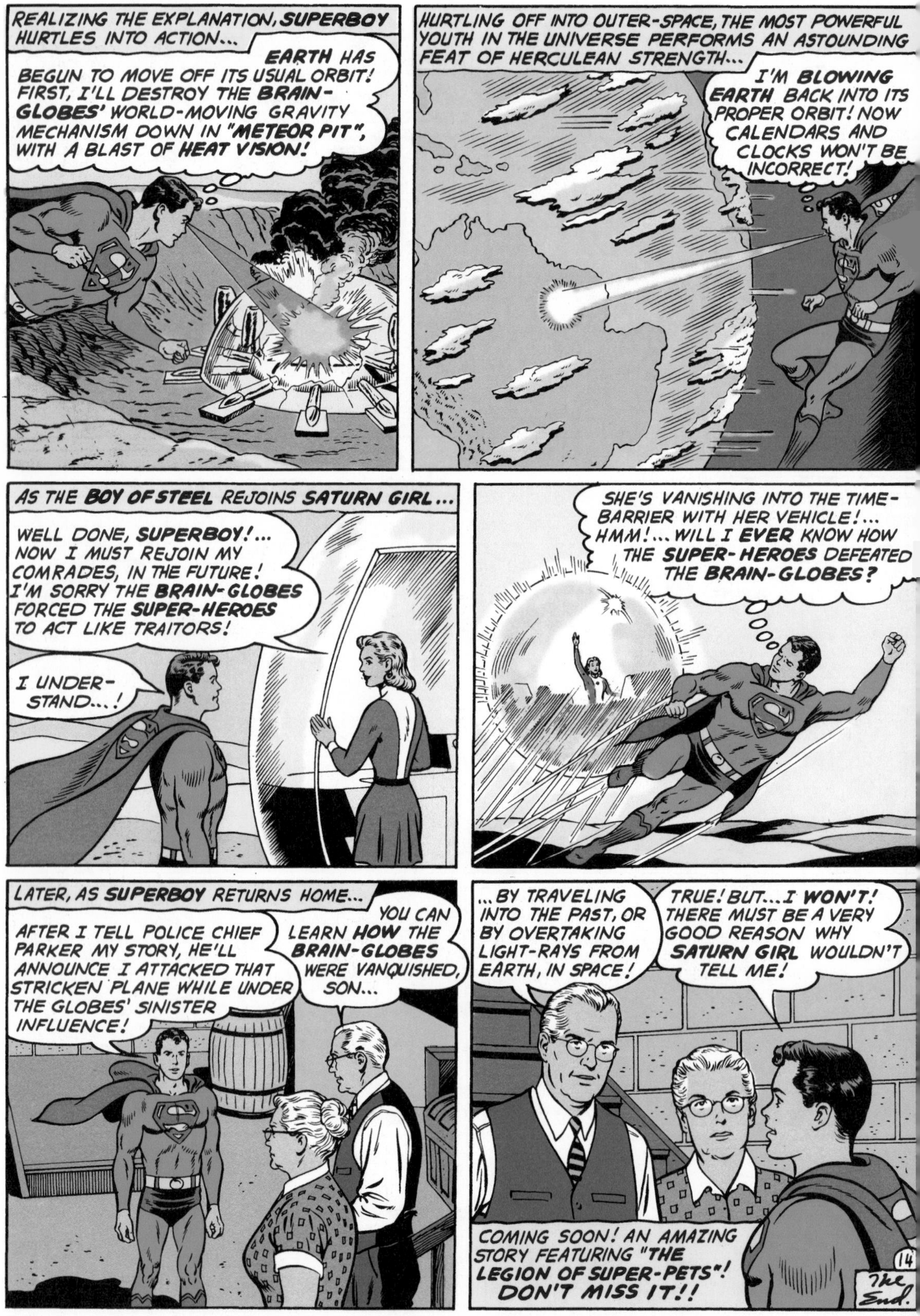
REALIZING THE EXPLANATION, SUPERBOY HURTLES INTO ACTION...
EARTH HAS BEGUN TO MOVE OFF ITS USUAL ORBIT! FIRST, I'LL DESTROY THE BRAIN-GLOBES' WORLD-MOVING GRAVITY MECHANISM DOWN IN "METEOR PIT", WITH A BLAST OF HEAT VISION!
HURTLING OFF INTO OUTER-SPACE, THE MOST POWERFUL YOUTH IN THE UNIVERSE PERFORMS AN ASTOUNDING FEAT OF HERCULEAN STRENGTH...
I'M BLOWING EARTH BACK INTO ITS PROPER ORBIT! NOW CALENDARS AND CLOCKS WON'T BE INCORRECT!
AS THE BOY OF STEEL REJOINS SATURN GIRL...
WELL DONE, SUPERBOY!... NOW I MUST REJOIN MY COMRADES, IN THE FUTURE! I'M SORRY THE BRAIN-GLOBES FORCED THE SUPER-HEROES TO ACT LIKE TRAITORS!
I UNDERSTAND...!
SHE'S VANISHING INTO THE TIME-BARRIER WITH HER VEHICLE!... HMM!... WILL I EVER KNOW HOW THE SUPER-HEROES DEFEATED THE BRAIN-GLOBES?
LATER, AS SUPERBOY RETURNS HOME...
AFTER I TELL POLICE CHIEF PARKER MY STORY, HE'LL ANNOUNCE I ATTACKED THAT STRICKEN PLANE WHILE UNDER THE GLOBES' SINISTER INFLUENCE!
YOU CAN LEARN HOW THE BRAIN-GLOBES WERE VANQUISHED, SON...
...BY TRAVELING INTO THE PAST, OR BY OVERTAKING LIGHT-RAYS FROM EARTH, IN SPACE!
TRUE! BUT... I WON'T! THERE MUST BE A VERY GOOD REASON WHY SATURN GIRL WOULDN'T TELL ME!
COMING SOON! AN AMAZING STORY FEATURING "THE LEGION OF SUPER-PETS"! DON'T MISS IT!!
14
The End.

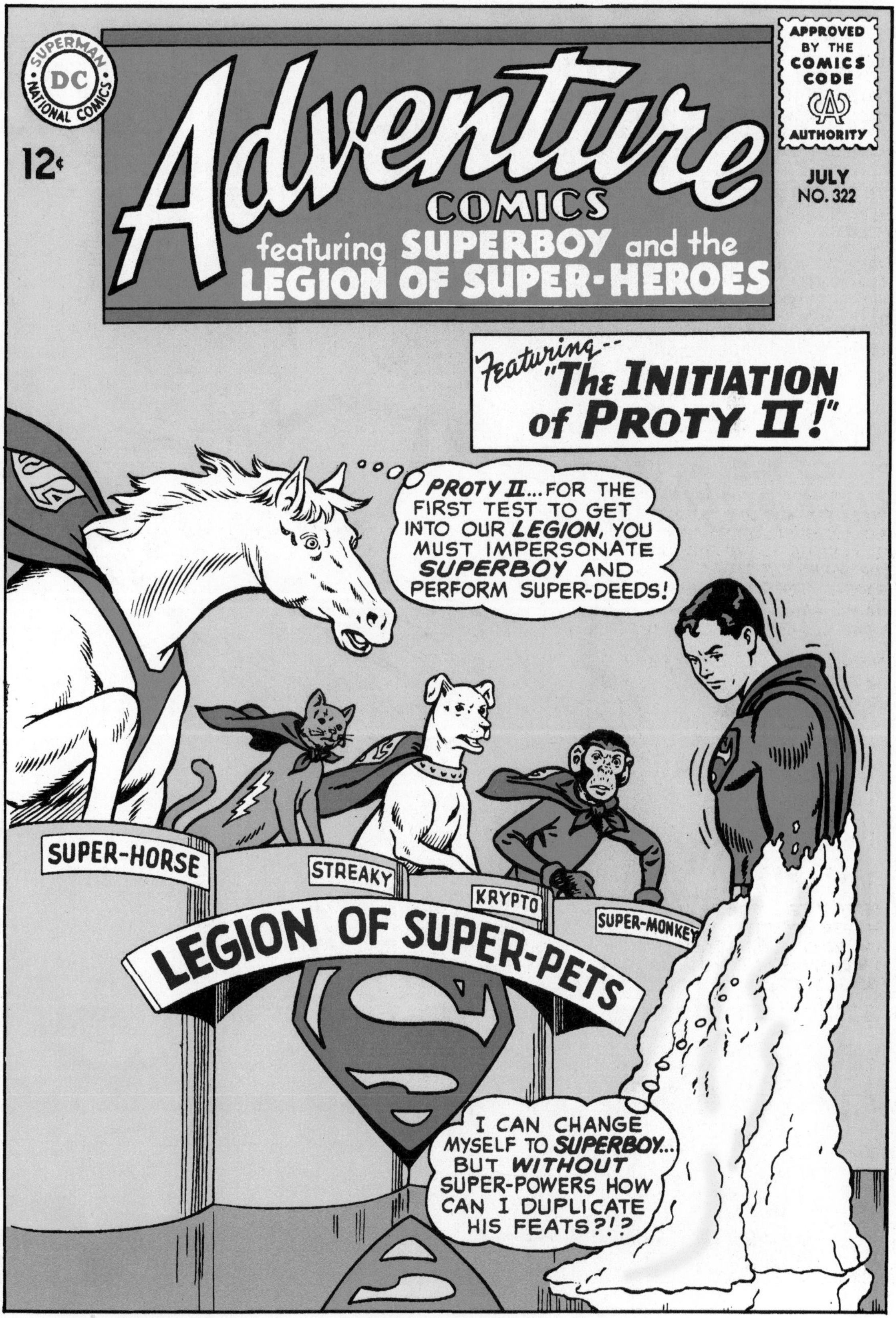
SUPERMAN DC NATIONAL COMICS
12¢
Adventure
COMICS
featuring SUPERBOY and the
LEGION OF SUPER-HEROES
APPROVED BY THE COMICS CODE AUTHORITY
JULY
NO. 322
Featuring-- "The INITIATION of PROTY II!"
PROTY II... FOR THE FIRST TEST TO GET INTO OUR LEGION, YOU MUST IMPERSONATE SUPERBOY AND PERFORM SUPER-DEEDS!
SUPER-HORSE
STREAKY
KRYPTO
SUPER-MONKEY
LEGION OF SUPER-PETS
I CAN CHANGE MYSELF TO SUPERBOY... BUT WITHOUT SUPER-POWERS HOW CAN I DUPLICATE HIS FEATS?!?

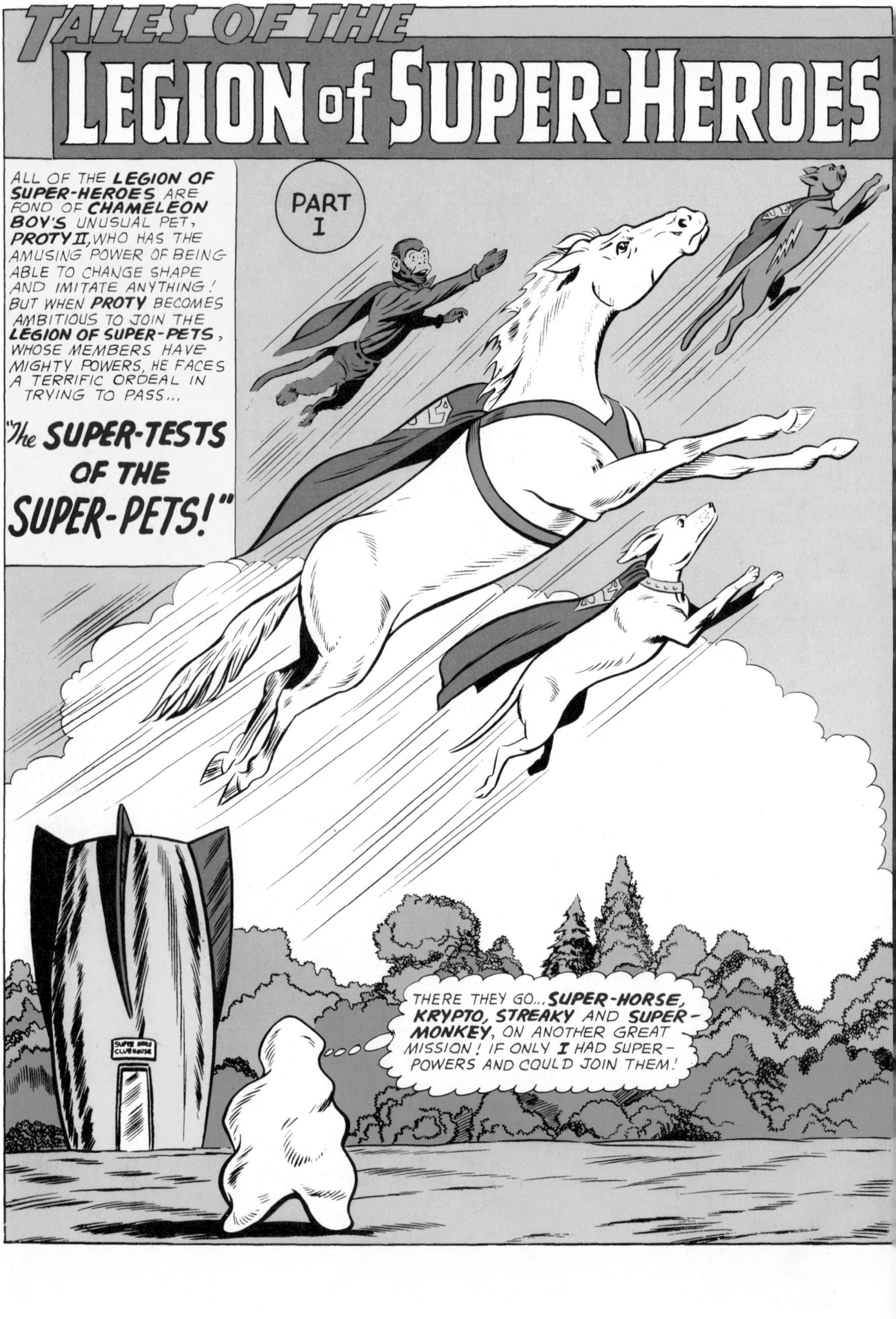
TALES OF THE
LEGION of SUPER-HEROES
ALL OF THE LEGION OF SUPER-HEROES ARE FOND OF CHAMELEON BOY'S UNUSUAL PET, PROTY II, WHO HAS THE AMUSING POWER OF BEING ABLE TO CHANGE SHAPE AND IMITATE ANYTHING! BUT WHEN PROTY BECOMES AMBITIOUS TO JOIN THE LEGION OF SUPER-PETS, WHOSE MEMBERS HAVE MIGHTY POWERS, HE FACES A TERRIFIC ORDEAL IN TRYING TO PASS...
"The SUPER-TESTS OF THE SUPER-PETS!"
PART I
THERE THEY GO... SUPER-HORSE, KRYPTO, STREAKY AND SUPER-MONKEY, ON ANOTHER GREAT MISSION! IF ONLY I HAD SUPER-POWERS AND COULD JOIN THEM!

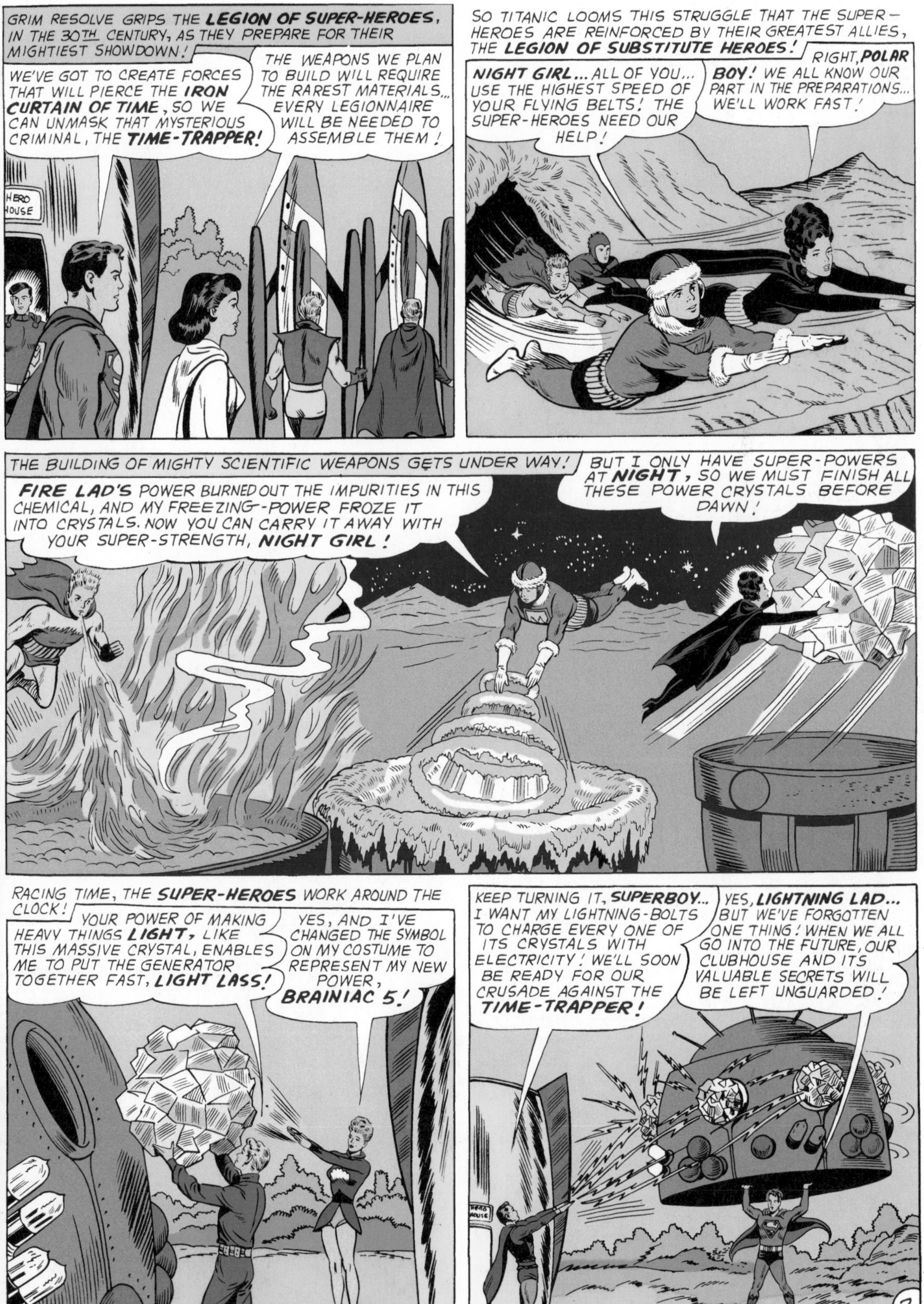
GRIM RESOLVE GRIPS THE LEGION OF SUPER-HEROES, IN THE 30TH CENTURY, AS THEY PREPARE FOR THEIR MIGHTIEST SHOWDOWN!
WE'VE GOT TO CREATE FORCES THAT WILL PIERCE THE IRON CURTAIN OF TIME, SO WE CAN UNMASK THAT MYSTERIOUS CRIMINAL, THE TIME-TRAPPER!
THE WEAPONS WE PLAN TO BUILD WILL REQUIRE THE RAREST MATERIALS... EVERY LEGIONNAIRE WILL BE NEEDED TO ASSEMBLE THEM!
HERO HOUSE
SO TITANIC LOOMS THIS STRUGGLE THAT THE SUPER-HEROES ARE REINFORCED BY THEIR GREATEST ALLIES, THE LEGION OF SUBSTITUTE HEROES!
NIGHT GIRL... ALL OF YOU... USE THE HIGHEST SPEED OF YOUR FLYING BELTS! THE SUPER-HEROES NEED OUR HELP!
RIGHT, POLAR BOY! WE ALL KNOW OUR PART IN THE PREPARATIONS... WE'LL WORK FAST!
THE BUILDING OF MIGHTY SCIENTIFIC WEAPONS GETS UNDER WAY!
FIRE LAD'S POWER BURNED OUT THE IMPURITIES IN THIS CHEMICAL, AND MY FREEZING-POWER FROZE IT INTO CRYSTALS. NOW YOU CAN CARRY IT AWAY WITH YOUR SUPER-STRENGTH, NIGHT GIRL!
BUT I ONLY HAVE SUPER-POWERS AT NIGHT, SO WE MUST FINISH ALL THESE POWER CRYSTALS BEFORE DAWN!
RACING TIME, THE SUPER-HEROES WORK AROUND THE CLOCK!
YOUR POWER OF MAKING HEAVY THINGS LIGHT, LIKE THIS MASSIVE CRYSTAL, ENABLES ME TO PUT THE GENERATOR TOGETHER FAST, LIGHT LASS!
YES, AND I'VE CHANGED THE SYMBOL ON MY COSTUME TO REPRESENT MY NEW POWER, BRAINIAC 5!
KEEP TURNING IT, SUPERBOY... I WANT MY LIGHTNING-BOLTS TO CHARGE EVERY ONE OF ITS CRYSTALS WITH ELECTRICITY! WE'LL SOON BE READY FOR OUR CRUSADE AGAINST THE TIME-TRAPPER!
YES, LIGHTNING LAD... BUT WE'VE FORGOTTEN ONE THING! WHEN WE ALL GO INTO THE FUTURE, OUR CLUBHOUSE AND ITS VALUABLE SECRETS WILL BE LEFT UNGUARDED!
2

SUPERBOY'S RIGHT...WE CAN'T DEPEND ONLY ON OUR BURGLAR ALARMS! BUT MAYBE THE LEGION OF SUPER-PETS COULD STAND GUARD FOR US.

GREAT IDEA! I'LL SUMMON KRYPTO AND STREAKY, SUPER-HORSE AND SUPER-MONKEY, FROM THE PAST!

AS SUPERBOY SPEEDS BACK INTO TIME ON THE MISSION...

CHAMELEON BOY, WITH MY THOUGHT-CASTING POWER, I CAN GET THE TELEPATHIC THOUGHT OF YOUR PET, PROTY II! HE WANTS TO GO WITH US ON THE BIG CRUSADE IN TIME!

NO, PROTY, I CAN'T TAKE YOU WITH ME ON THIS DANGEROUS JOB!

TO PERSUADE HIS MASTER, PROTY USES HIS UNIQUE ABILITY OF INSTANT TRANSFORMATION...

LOOK! PROTY CHANGED HIMSELF INTO AN EXACT DUPLICATE OF A REALLY POWERFUL RAY-GUN, HOPING YOU'LL TAKE HIM!

BUT HE ONLY LOOKS LIKE A RAY-GUN... HE ISN'T REALLY ONE! I TOLD YOU, PROTY, YOU'LL HAVE TO STAY BEHIND!

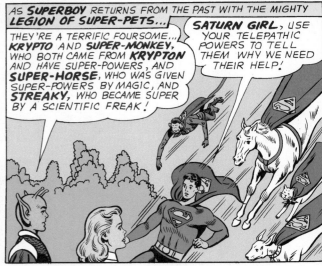

AS SUPERBOY RETURNS FROM THE PAST WITH THE MIGHTY LEGION OF SUPER-PETS...

THEY'RE A TERRIFIC FOURSOME... KRYPTO AND SUPER-MONKEY, WHO BOTH CAME FROM KRYPTON AND HAVE SUPER-POWERS, AND SUPER-HORSE, WHO WAS GIVEN SUPER-POWERS BY MAGIC, AND STREAKY, WHO BECAME SUPER BY A SCIENTIFIC FREAK!

SATURN GIRL, USE YOUR TELEPATHIC POWERS TO TELL THEM WHY WE NEED THEIR HELP!

I'M CONCENTRATING MY THOUGHT-CASTING POWER, NOT ONLY TO EXPLAIN, BUT ALSO TO MAKE THE SUPER-PETS TEMPORARILY TELEPATHIC, SO THEY CAN COMMUNICATE WITH EACH OTHER WHILE THEY GUARD THE CLUBHOUSE!

THEY CAN START THEIR GUARD DUTY NOW, WHILE WE FINISH OUR PREPARATIONS! PROTY, YOU STAY HERE WITH THEM!

AND PROTY II, WHO ALREADY POSSESSES TELEPATHIC POWERS, SEES THE GREAT SUPER-PETS TAKE UP THEIR TASK!

THEY SURELY LOOK IMPRESSIVE, AT THAT SPECIAL TABLE SUPERBOY MADE FOR THEM! I THINK I'LL JOIN THEIR LEGION... AFTER ALL, I'M A SUPER-PET, TOO!

SUPER-HORSE STREAKY SUPER-MONKEY

LEGION OF SUPER-PETS

3

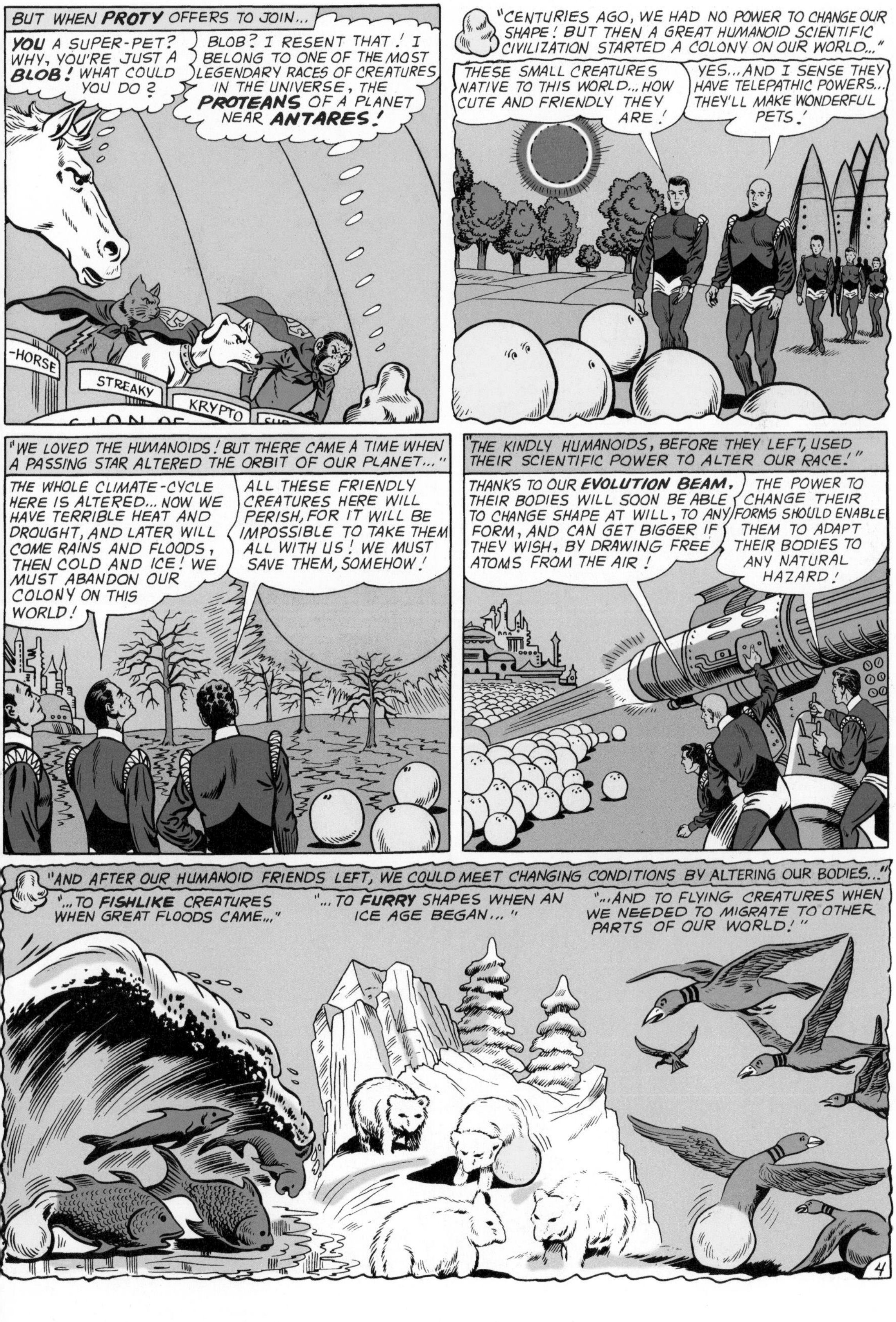

BUT WHEN PROTY OFFERS TO JOIN...
YOU A SUPER-PET? WHY, YOU'RE JUST A BLOB! WHAT COULD YOU DO?
BLOB? I RESENT THAT! I BELONG TO ONE OF THE MOST LEGENDARY RACES OF CREATURES IN THE UNIVERSE, THE PROTEANS OF A PLANET NEAR ANTARES!
-HORSE
STREAKY
KRYPTO
"CENTURIES AGO, WE HAD NO POWER TO CHANGE OUR SHAPE! BUT THEN A GREAT HUMANOID SCIENTIFIC CIVILIZATION STARTED A COLONY ON OUR WORLD..."
THESE SMALL CREATURES NATIVE TO THIS WORLD... HOW CUTE AND FRIENDLY THEY ARE!
YES... AND I SENSE THEY HAVE TELEPATHIC POWERS... THEY'LL MAKE WONDERFUL PETS!
"WE LOVED THE HUMANOIDS! BUT THERE CAME A TIME WHEN A PASSING STAR ALTERED THE ORBIT OF OUR PLANET..."
THE WHOLE CLIMATE-CYCLE HERE IS ALTERED... NOW WE HAVE TERRIBLE HEAT AND DROUGHT, AND LATER WILL COME RAINS AND FLOODS, THEN COLD AND ICE! WE MUST ABANDON OUR COLONY ON THIS WORLD!
ALL THESE FRIENDLY CREATURES HERE WILL PERISH, FOR IT WILL BE IMPOSSIBLE TO TAKE THEM ALL WITH US! WE MUST SAVE THEM, SOMEHOW!
"THE KINDLY HUMANOIDS, BEFORE THEY LEFT, USED THEIR SCIENTIFIC POWER TO ALTER OUR RACE!"
THANKS TO OUR EVOLUTION BEAM, THEIR BODIES WILL SOON BE ABLE TO CHANGE SHAPE AT WILL, TO ANY FORM, AND CAN GET BIGGER IF THEY WISH, BY DRAWING FREE ATOMS FROM THE AIR!
THE POWER TO CHANGE THEIR FORMS SHOULD ENABLE THEM TO ADAPT THEIR BODIES TO ANY NATURAL HAZARD!
"AND AFTER OUR HUMANOID FRIENDS LEFT, WE COULD MEET CHANGING CONDITIONS BY ALTERING OUR BODIES..."
"...TO FISHLIKE CREATURES WHEN GREAT FLOODS CAME..."
"...TO FURRY SHAPES WHEN AN ICE AGE BEGAN..."
"...AND TO FLYING CREATURES WHEN WE NEEDED TO MIGRATE TO OTHER PARTS OF OUR WORLD!"
4

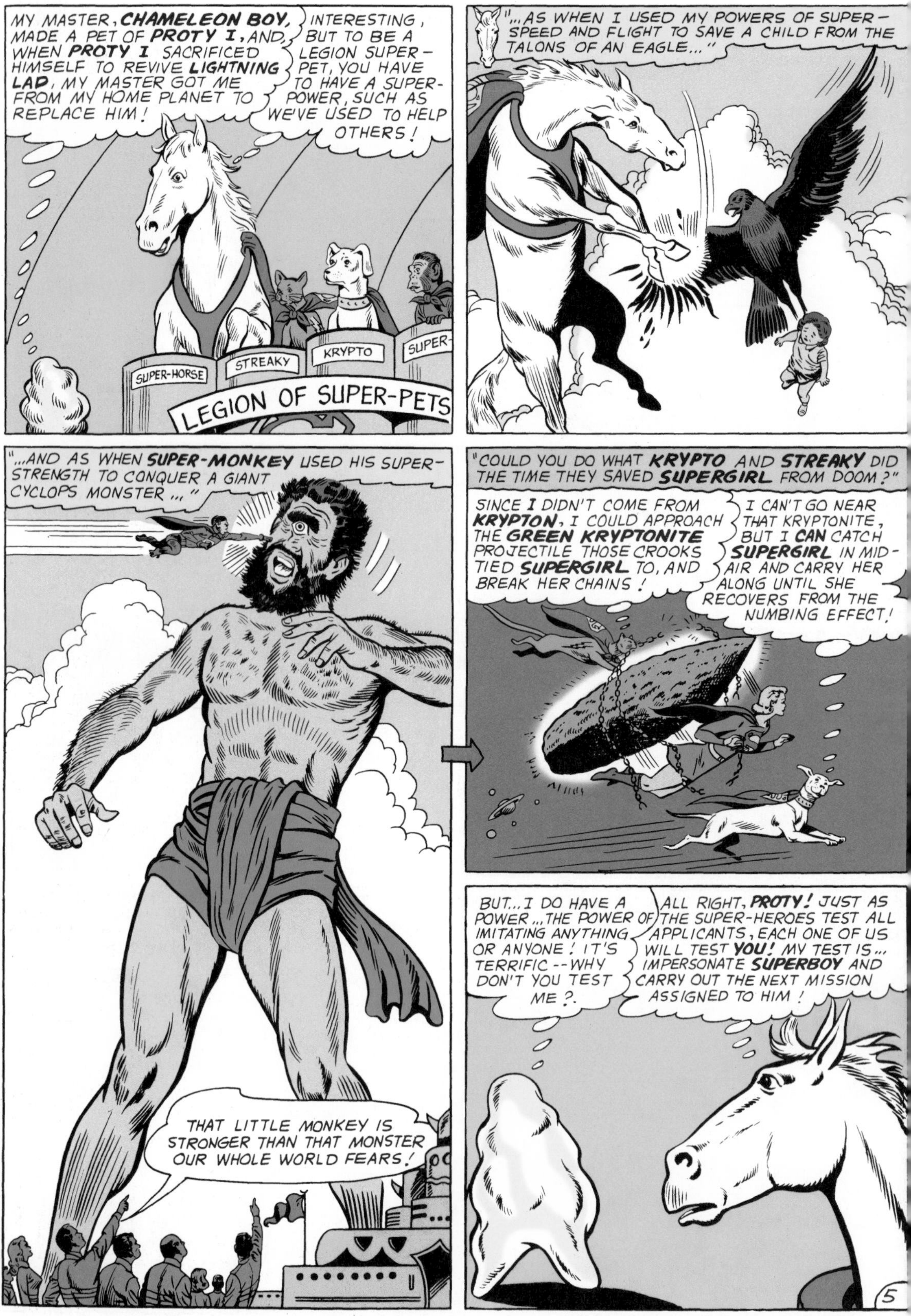
MY MASTER, CHAMELEON BOY, MADE A PET OF PROTY I, AND, WHEN PROTY I SACRIFICED HIMSELF TO REVIVE LIGHTNING LAD, MY MASTER GOT ME FROM MY HOME PLANET TO REPLACE HIM!
INTERESTING, BUT TO BE A LEGION SUPER-PET, YOU HAVE TO HAVE A SUPER-POWER, SUCH AS WE'VE USED TO HELP OTHERS!
SUPER-HORSE
STREAKY
KRYPTO
SUPER-
LEGION OF SUPER-PETS
"...AS WHEN I USED MY POWERS OF SUPER-SPEED AND FLIGHT TO SAVE A CHILD FROM THE TALONS OF AN EAGLE..."
"...AND AS WHEN SUPER-MONKEY USED HIS SUPER-STRENGTH TO CONQUER A GIANT CYCLOPS MONSTER..."
THAT LITTLE MONKEY IS STRONGER THAN THAT MONSTER OUR WHOLE WORLD FEARS!
"COULD YOU DO WHAT KRYPTO AND STREAKY DID THE TIME THEY SAVED SUPERGIRL FROM DOOM?"
SINCE I DIDN'T COME FROM KRYPTON, I COULD APPROACH THE GREEN KRYPTONITE PROJECTILE THOSE CROOKS TIED SUPERGIRL TO, AND BREAK HER CHAINS!
I CAN'T GO NEAR THAT KRYPTONITE, BUT I CAN CATCH SUPERGIRL IN MID-AIR AND CARRY HER ALONG UNTIL SHE RECOVERS FROM THE NUMBING EFFECT!
BUT... I DO HAVE A POWER... THE POWER OF IMITATING ANYTHING OR ANYONE! IT'S TERRIFIC -- WHY DON'T YOU TEST ME?
ALL RIGHT, PROTY! JUST AS THE SUPER-HEROES TEST ALL APPLICANTS, EACH ONE OF US WILL TEST YOU! MY TEST IS... IMPERSONATE SUPERBOY AND CARRY OUT THE NEXT MISSION ASSIGNED TO HIM!
5

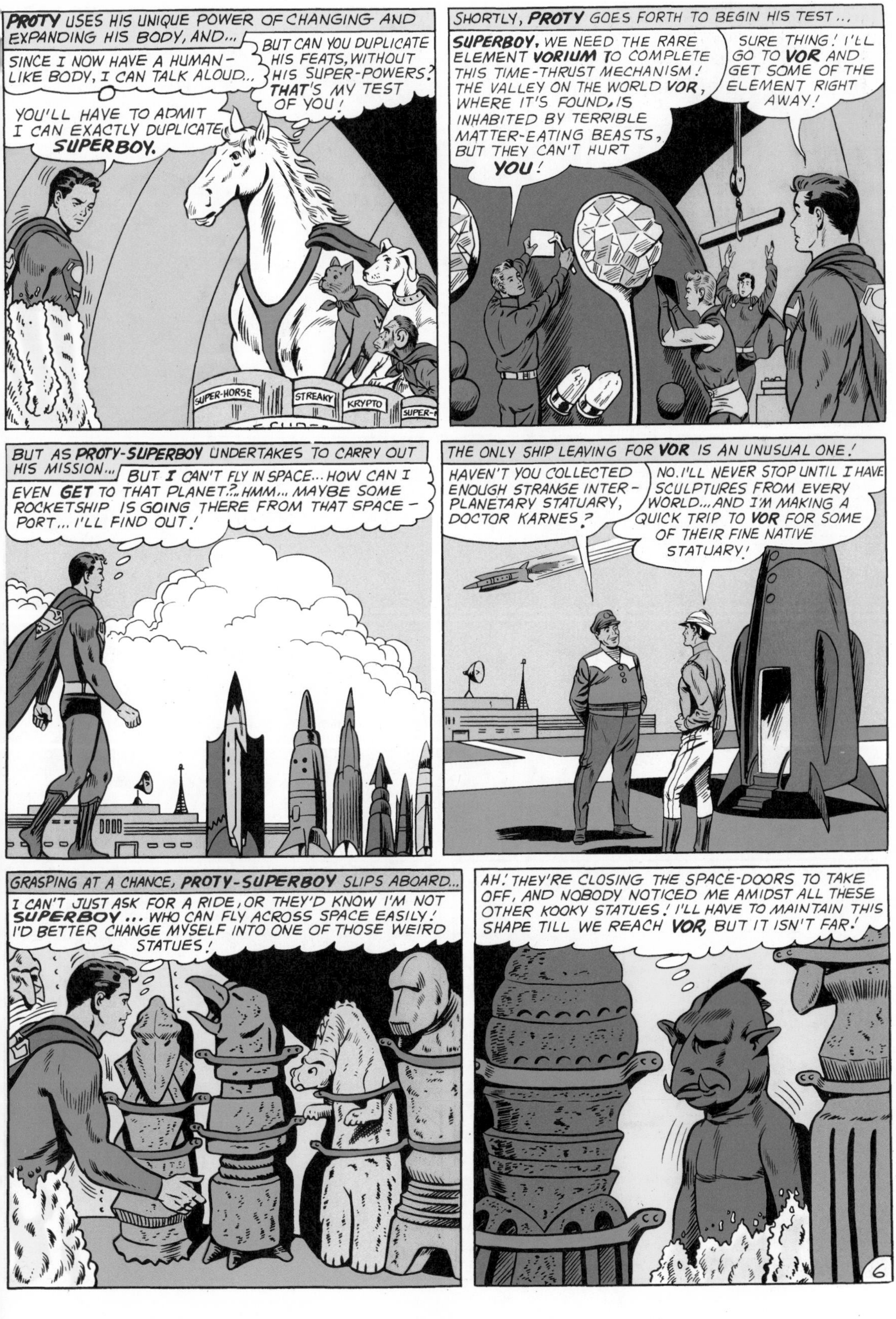
PROTY USES HIS UNIQUE POWER OF CHANGING AND EXPANDING HIS BODY, AND...
SINCE I NOW HAVE A HUMAN-LIKE BODY, I CAN TALK ALOUD...
BUT CAN YOU DUPLICATE HIS FEATS, WITHOUT HIS SUPER-POWERS? THAT'S MY TEST OF YOU!
YOU'LL HAVE TO ADMIT I CAN EXACTLY DUPLICATE SUPERBOY.
SUPER-HORSE
STREAKY
KRYPTO
SHORTLY, PROTY GOES FORTH TO BEGIN HIS TEST...
SUPERBOY, WE NEED THE RARE ELEMENT VORIUM TO COMPLETE THIS TIME-THRUST MECHANISM! THE VALLEY ON THE WORLD VOR, WHERE IT'S FOUND, IS INHABITED BY TERRIBLE MATTER-EATING BEASTS, BUT THEY CAN'T HURT YOU!
SURE THING! I'LL GO TO VOR AND GET SOME OF THE ELEMENT RIGHT AWAY!
BUT AS PROTY-SUPERBOY UNDERTAKES TO CARRY OUT HIS MISSION...
BUT I CAN'T FLY IN SPACE... HOW CAN I EVEN GET TO THAT PLANET?... HMM... MAYBE SOME ROCKETSHIP IS GOING THERE FROM THAT SPACE-PORT... I'LL FIND OUT!
THE ONLY SHIP LEAVING FOR VOR IS AN UNUSUAL ONE!
HAVEN'T YOU COLLECTED ENOUGH STRANGE INTER-PLANETARY STATUARY, DOCTOR KARNES?
NO. I'LL NEVER STOP UNTIL I HAVE SCULPTURES FROM EVERY WORLD... AND I'M MAKING A QUICK TRIP TO VOR FOR SOME OF THEIR FINE NATIVE STATUARY!
GRASPING AT A CHANCE, PROTY-SUPERBOY SLIPS ABOARD...
I CAN'T JUST ASK FOR A RIDE, OR THEY'D KNOW I'M NOT SUPERBOY... WHO CAN FLY ACROSS SPACE EASILY! I'D BETTER CHANGE MYSELF INTO ONE OF THOSE WEIRD STATUES!
AH! THEY'RE CLOSING THE SPACE-DOORS TO TAKE OFF, AND NOBODY NOTICED ME AMIDST ALL THESE OTHER KOOKY STATUES! I'LL HAVE TO MAINTAIN THIS SHAPE TILL WE REACH VOR, BUT IT ISN'T FAR!
6

LATER, WHEN THE SHIP HAS LANDED ON **VOR**...

HEY! ONE OF THOSE WEIRD STATUES JUST WALKED OUT OF DR. KARNES' SHIP!

YOU'D BETTER GET OUT OF THE SUN... YOU'RE DELIRIOUS IF YOU'RE SEEING THINGS LIKE THAT!

RESUMING HIS IMPERSONATION OF THE **BOY OF STEEL**, **PROTY** REACHES A VALLEY OF FANTASTIC CREATURES!

THESE ARE THE ANIMALS THEY TOLD ME ABOUT, THAT DIG UP THE RARE ELEMENT **VORIUM** AND **EAT** IT! THEY'D ATTACK ME AT ONCE... AND THOUGH I LOOK LIKE **SUPERBOY**, I HAVEN'T HIS INVULNERABILITY!

AGAIN **PROTY** CALLS ON HIS TRANSFORMATION POWER TO HELP HIM...

I HAVE AN IDEA! IF I CHANGE MYSELF TO LOOK LIKE ONE OF THEM, THEY WON'T BOTHER ME WHEN I GO DOWN THERE!

ABRUPTLY, A NEW PROBLEM FOR **PROTY**...

OUCH! I MAY **LOOK** LIKE THEM, BUT I CAN'T DIG INTO ROCK, AS THEY DO! I'M STYMIED... AND IF I FAIL THIS TEST **SUPER-HORSE** GAVE ME, I'LL NEVER GET INTO THE LEGION!

WHAT SAVAGE BEASTS! THEY **FIGHT** WITH THEIR HORNLIKE HEADS! BUT WAIT... THERE'S SOME OF THE **VORIUM** MINERAL LYING ON THE GROUND! I CAN TAKE THAT, AND WON'T HAVE TO DIG!

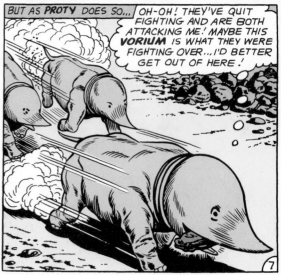

BUT AS **PROTY** DOES SO...

OH-OH! THEY'VE QUIT FIGHTING AND ARE BOTH ATTACKING ME! MAYBE THIS **VORIUM** IS WHAT THEY WERE FIGHTING OVER... I'D BETTER GET OUT OF HERE!

7

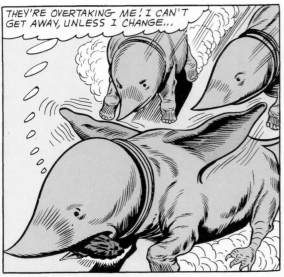

THEY'RE OVERTAKING ME! I CAN'T GET AWAY, UNLESS I CHANGE...

...INTO A BIRD! WHEW! THAT WAS JUST IN TIME! NOW TO GET BACK TO THE SPACEPORT AND STOW AWAY AS ANOTHER "STATUE" ON THAT COLLECTOR'S SHIP, FOR THE RETURN TRIP!

WHEN THE SHIP REACHES EARTH, AND **PROTY** HAS CHANGED TO "**SUPERBOY**" AGAIN...

SUPERBOY! I DIDN'T KNOW YOU'D VISITED MY SHIP...THIS IS AN HONOR!

ANOTHER MOMENT, AND HE'D HAVE CAUGHT ME CHANGING!

I WAS...ER...ADMIRING YOUR COLLECTION, DOCTOR. MUST GO NOW...

AND SOON, IN THE LEGION CLUBHOUSE, **PROTY** HAS A MOMENT OF TRIUMPH...

HERE'S THE **VORIUM!** I GUESS I PASS YOUR TEST, **SUPER-HORSE!**

I HAVE TO ADMIT YOU PASS...THOUGH I CAN'T IMAGINE HOW YOU DID IT, WITHOUT ANY SUPER-POWERS!

BUT THAT MOMENT OF TRIUMPH IS SHORT!

NOW IT'S TIME FOR YOU TO TAKE MY TEST! **SATURN GIRL** IS GOING ON AN IMPORTANT MISSION...YOU MUST AGAIN DISGUISE YOURSELF AS A LEGIONNAIRE AND ACCOMPANY HER ON THAT MISSION, WITHOUT LETTING HER KNOW YOUR IDENTITY!

BUT, **STREAKY, SATURN GIRL** HAS TERRIFIC TELEPATHIC POWERS THAT WILL EASILY READ MY MIND AND PENETRATE MY IMPOSTURE!

FELLOWS...GIVE ME A BREAK! THIS TEST IS AN **IMPOSSIBLE** ONE TO PASS!

SORRY, **PROTY**, BUT IF YOU FAIL IT, YOU CAN'T EVER ENTER THE **LEGION OF SUPER-PETS!**

8

END OF PART I

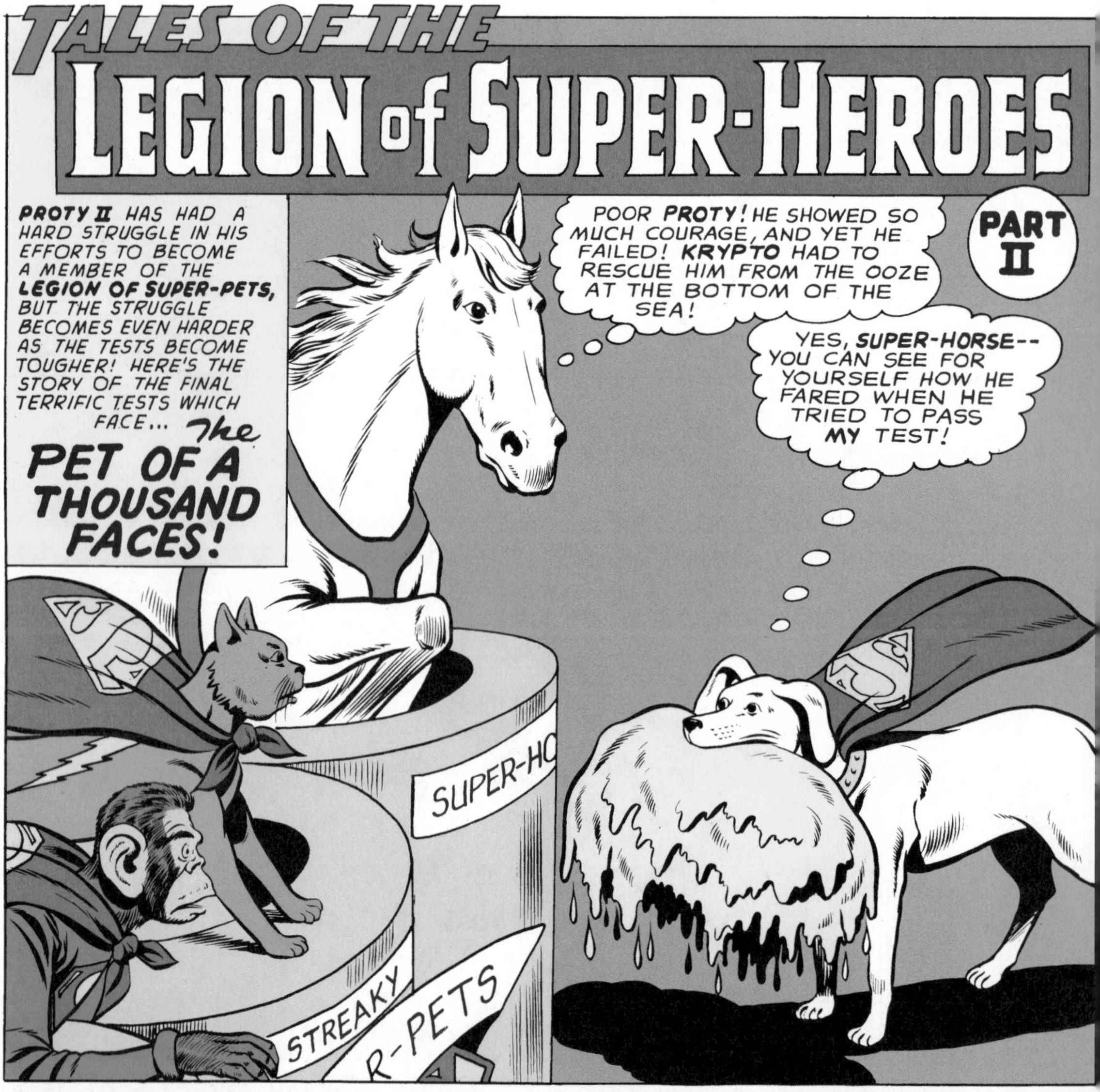
TALES OF THE
LEGION of SUPER-HEROES
PART II
PROTY II HAS HAD A HARD STRUGGLE IN HIS EFFORTS TO BECOME A MEMBER OF THE LEGION OF SUPER-PETS, BUT THE STRUGGLE BECOMES EVEN HARDER AS THE TESTS BECOME TOUGHER! HERE'S THE STORY OF THE FINAL TERRIFIC TESTS WHICH FACE... The PET OF A THOUSAND FACES!
POOR PROTY! HE SHOWED SO MUCH COURAGE, AND YET HE FAILED! KRYPTO HAD TO RESCUE HIM FROM THE OOZE AT THE BOTTOM OF THE SEA!
YES, SUPER-HORSE-- YOU CAN SEE FOR YOURSELF HOW HE FARED WHEN HE TRIED TO PASS MY TEST!
SUPER-HO
STREAKY
R-PETS

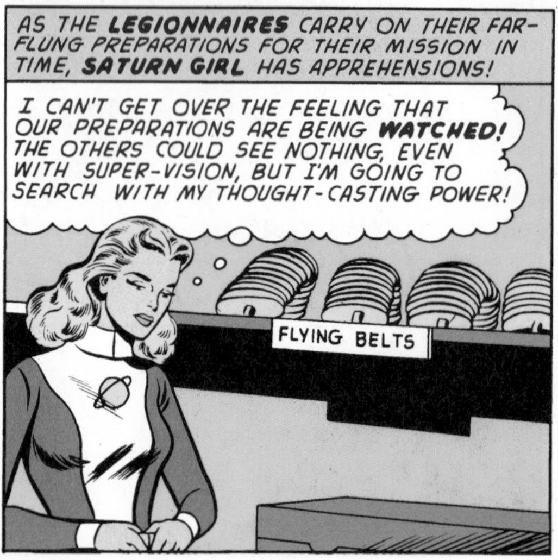
AS THE LEGIONNAIRES CARRY ON THEIR FAR-FLUNG PREPARATIONS FOR THEIR MISSION IN TIME, SATURN GIRL HAS APPREHENSIONS!
I CAN'T GET OVER THE FEELING THAT OUR PREPARATIONS ARE BEING WATCHED! THE OTHERS COULD SEE NOTHING, EVEN WITH SUPER-VISION, BUT I'M GOING TO SEARCH WITH MY THOUGHT-CASTING POWER!
FLYING BELTS

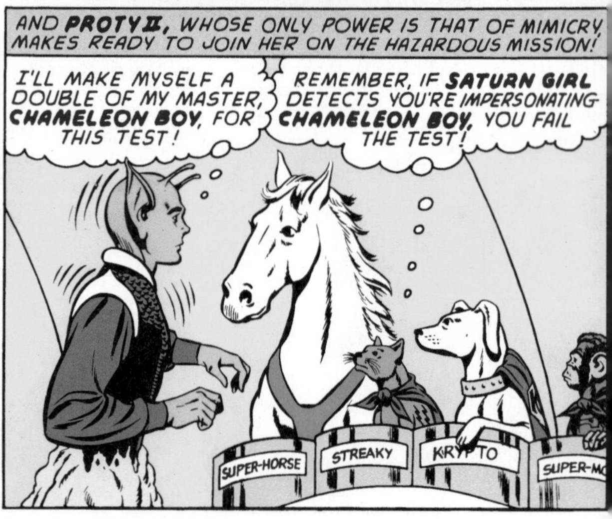
AND PROTY II, WHOSE ONLY POWER IS THAT OF MIMICRY MAKES READY TO JOIN HER ON THE HAZARDOUS MISSION!
I'LL MAKE MYSELF A DOUBLE OF MY MASTER, CHAMELEON BOY, FOR THIS TEST!
REMEMBER, IF SATURN GIRL DETECTS YOU'RE IMPERSONATING CHAMELEON BOY, YOU FAIL THE TEST!
SUPER-HORSE
STREAKY
KRYPTO
SUPER-MO

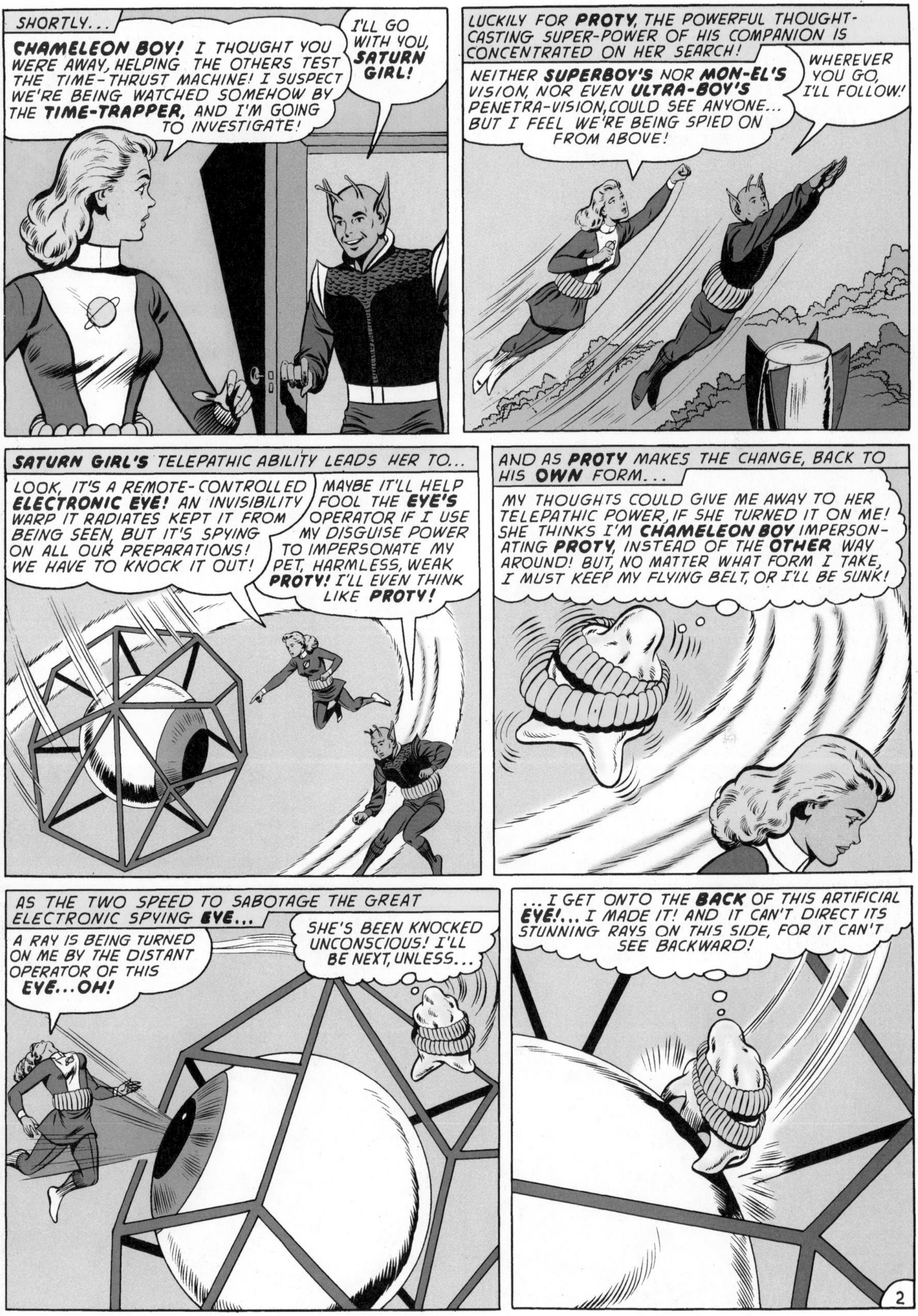
SHORTLY...
CHAMELEON BOY! I THOUGHT YOU WERE AWAY, HELPING THE OTHERS TEST THE TIME-THRUST MACHINE! I SUSPECT WE'RE BEING WATCHED SOMEHOW BY THE TIME-TRAPPER, AND I'M GOING TO INVESTIGATE!
I'LL GO WITH YOU, SATURN GIRL!
LUCKILY FOR PROTY, THE POWERFUL THOUGHT-CASTING SUPER-POWER OF HIS COMPANION IS CONCENTRATED ON HER SEARCH!
NEITHER SUPERBOY'S NOR MON-EL'S VISION, NOR EVEN ULTRA-BOY'S PENETRA-VISION, COULD SEE ANYONE... BUT I FEEL WE'RE BEING SPIED ON FROM ABOVE!
WHEREVER YOU GO, I'LL FOLLOW!
SATURN GIRL'S TELEPATHIC ABILITY LEADS HER TO...
LOOK, IT'S A REMOTE-CONTROLLED ELECTRONIC EYE! AN INVISIBILITY WARP IT RADIATES KEPT IT FROM BEING SEEN, BUT IT'S SPYING ON ALL OUR PREPARATIONS! WE HAVE TO KNOCK IT OUT!
MAYBE IT'LL HELP FOOL THE EYE'S OPERATOR IF I USE MY DISGUISE POWER TO IMPERSONATE MY PET, HARMLESS, WEAK PROTY! I'LL EVEN THINK LIKE PROTY!
AND AS PROTY MAKES THE CHANGE, BACK TO HIS OWN FORM...
MY THOUGHTS COULD GIVE ME AWAY TO HER TELEPATHIC POWER, IF SHE TURNED IT ON ME! SHE THINKS I'M CHAMELEON BOY IMPERSONATING PROTY, INSTEAD OF THE OTHER WAY AROUND! BUT, NO MATTER WHAT FORM I TAKE, I MUST KEEP MY FLYING BELT, OR I'LL BE SUNK!
AS THE TWO SPEED TO SABOTAGE THE GREAT ELECTRONIC SPYING EYE...
A RAY IS BEING TURNED ON ME BY THE DISTANT OPERATOR OF THIS EYE...OH!
SHE'S BEEN KNOCKED UNCONSCIOUS! I'LL BE NEXT, UNLESS...
...I GET ONTO THE BACK OF THIS ARTIFICIAL EYE!... I MADE IT! AND IT CAN'T DIRECT ITS STUNNING RAYS ON THIS SIDE, FOR IT CAN'T SEE BACKWARD!
2

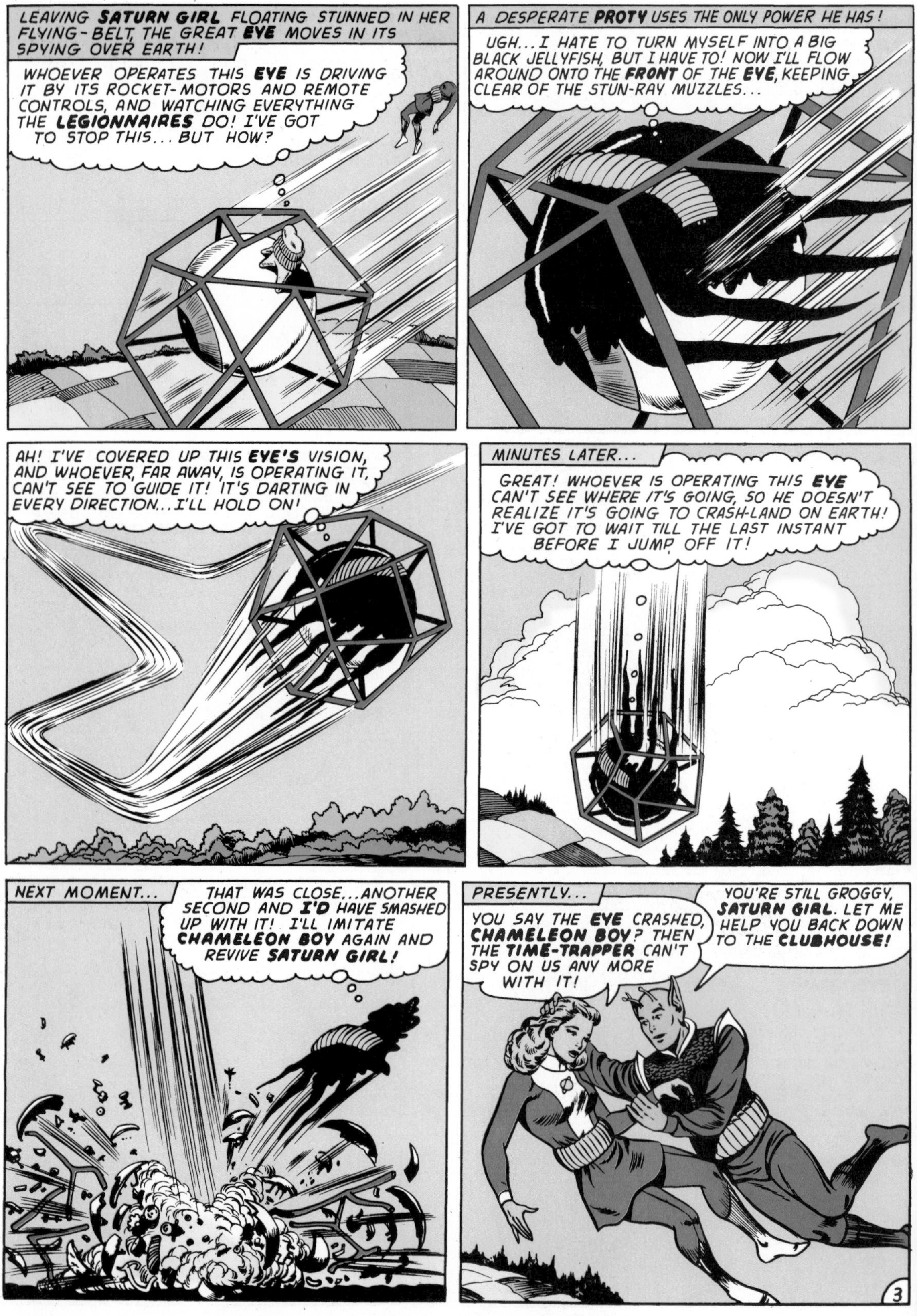
LEAVING SATURN GIRL FLOATING STUNNED IN HER FLYING-BELT, THE GREAT EYE MOVES IN ITS SPYING OVER EARTH!
WHOEVER OPERATES THIS EYE IS DRIVING IT BY ITS ROCKET-MOTORS AND REMOTE CONTROLS, AND WATCHING EVERYTHING THE LEGIONNAIRES DO! I'VE GOT TO STOP THIS... BUT HOW?
A DESPERATE PROTY USES THE ONLY POWER HE HAS!
UGH... I HATE TO TURN MYSELF INTO A BIG BLACK JELLYFISH, BUT I HAVE TO! NOW I'LL FLOW AROUND ONTO THE FRONT OF THE EYE, KEEPING CLEAR OF THE STUN-RAY MUZZLES...
AH! I'VE COVERED UP THIS EYE'S VISION, AND WHOEVER, FAR AWAY, IS OPERATING IT, CAN'T SEE TO GUIDE IT! IT'S DARTING IN EVERY DIRECTION... I'LL HOLD ON!
MINUTES LATER...
GREAT! WHOEVER IS OPERATING THIS EYE CAN'T SEE WHERE IT'S GOING, SO HE DOESN'T REALIZE IT'S GOING TO CRASH-LAND ON EARTH! I'VE GOT TO WAIT TILL THE LAST INSTANT BEFORE I JUMP OFF IT!
NEXT MOMENT...
THAT WAS CLOSE... ANOTHER SECOND AND I'D HAVE SMASHED UP WITH IT! I'LL IMITATE CHAMELEON BOY AGAIN AND REVIVE SATURN GIRL!
PRESENTLY...
YOU SAY THE EYE CRASHED, CHAMELEON BOY? THEN THE TIME-TRAPPER CAN'T SPY ON US ANY MORE WITH IT!
YOU'RE STILL GROGGY, SATURN GIRL. LET ME HELP YOU BACK DOWN TO THE CLUBHOUSE!
3

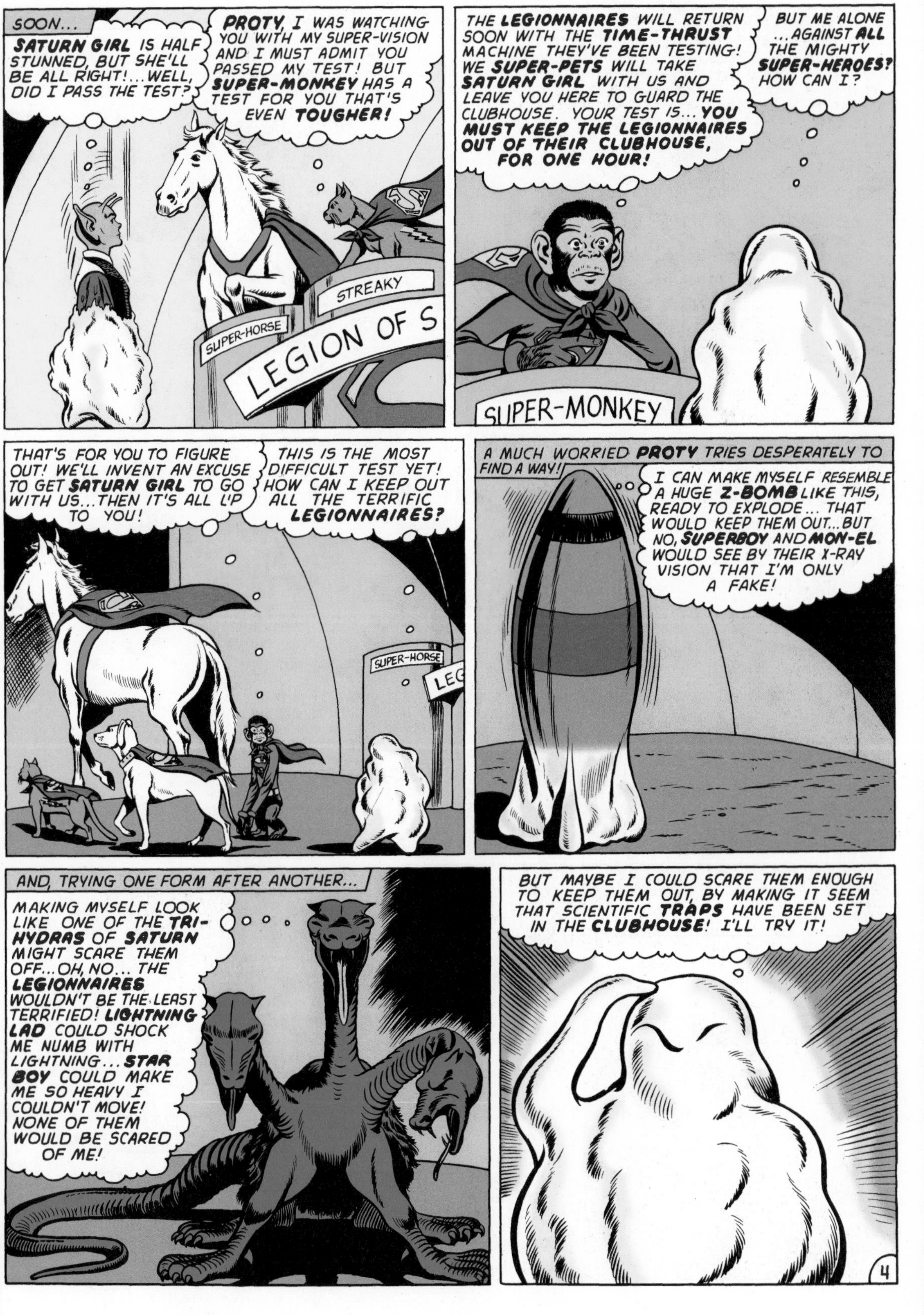
SOON...
SATURN GIRL IS HALF STUNNED, BUT SHE'LL BE ALL RIGHT!... WELL, DID I PASS THE TEST?
PROTY, I WAS WATCHING YOU WITH MY SUPER-VISION AND I MUST ADMIT YOU PASSED MY TEST! BUT SUPER-MONKEY HAS A TEST FOR YOU THAT'S EVEN TOUGHER!
STREAKY
SUPER-HORSE
LEGION OF S
THE LEGIONNAIRES WILL RETURN SOON WITH THE TIME-THRUST MACHINE THEY'VE BEEN TESTING! WE SUPER-PETS WILL TAKE SATURN GIRL WITH US AND LEAVE YOU HERE TO GUARD THE CLUBHOUSE. YOUR TEST IS... YOU MUST KEEP THE LEGIONNAIRES OUT OF THEIR CLUBHOUSE, FOR ONE HOUR!
BUT ME ALONE ...AGAINST ALL THE MIGHTY SUPER-HEROES? HOW CAN I?
SUPER-MONKEY
THAT'S FOR YOU TO FIGURE OUT! WE'LL INVENT AN EXCUSE TO GET SATURN GIRL TO GO WITH US...THEN IT'S ALL UP TO YOU!
THIS IS THE MOST DIFFICULT TEST YET! HOW CAN I KEEP OUT ALL THE TERRIFIC LEGIONNAIRES?
SUPER-HORSE
LEG
A MUCH WORRIED PROTY TRIES DESPERATELY TO FIND A WAY!
I CAN MAKE MYSELF RESEMBLE A HUGE Z-BOMB LIKE THIS, READY TO EXPLODE... THAT WOULD KEEP THEM OUT...BUT NO, SUPERBOY AND MON-EL WOULD SEE BY THEIR X-RAY VISION THAT I'M ONLY A FAKE!
AND, TRYING ONE FORM AFTER ANOTHER...
MAKING MYSELF LOOK LIKE ONE OF THE TRI-HYDRAS OF SATURN MIGHT SCARE THEM OFF...OH, NO... THE LEGIONNAIRES WOULDN'T BE THE LEAST TERRIFIED! LIGHTNING LAD COULD SHOCK ME NUMB WITH LIGHTNING... STAR BOY COULD MAKE ME SO HEAVY I COULDN'T MOVE! NONE OF THEM WOULD BE SCARED OF ME!
BUT MAYBE I COULD SCARE THEM ENOUGH TO KEEP THEM OUT, BY MAKING IT SEEM THAT SCIENTIFIC TRAPS HAVE BEEN SET IN THE CLUBHOUSE! I'LL TRY IT!
4

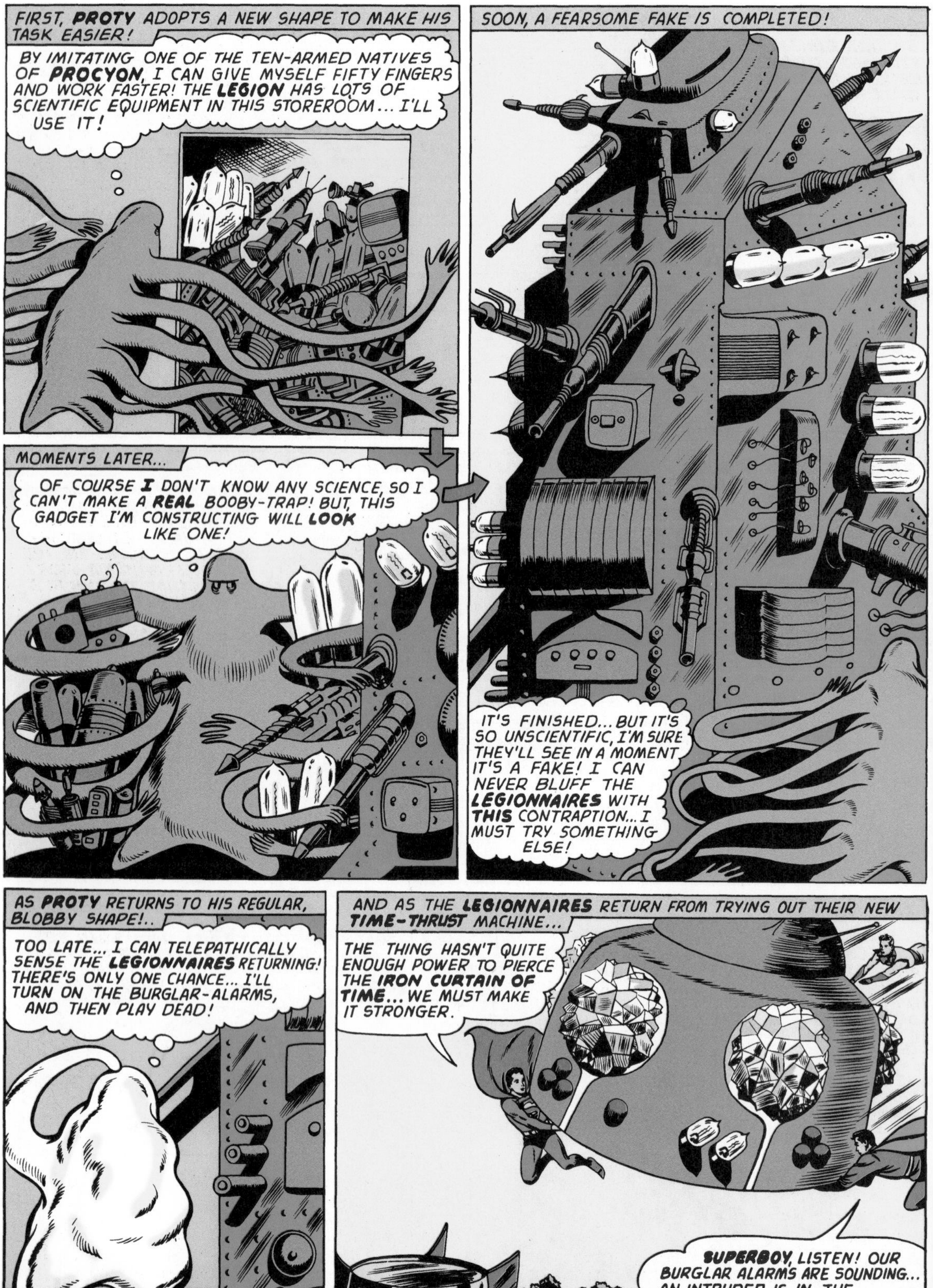

FIRST, PROTY ADOPTS A NEW SHAPE TO MAKE HIS TASK EASIER!
BY IMITATING ONE OF THE TEN-ARMED NATIVES OF PROCYON, I CAN GIVE MYSELF FIFTY FINGERS AND WORK FASTER! THE LEGION HAS LOTS OF SCIENTIFIC EQUIPMENT IN THIS STOREROOM... I'LL USE IT!
MOMENTS LATER...
OF COURSE I DON'T KNOW ANY SCIENCE, SO I CAN'T MAKE A REAL BOOBY-TRAP! BUT, THIS GADGET I'M CONSTRUCTING WILL LOOK LIKE ONE!
SOON, A FEARSOME FAKE IS COMPLETED!
IT'S FINISHED... BUT IT'S SO UNSCIENTIFIC, I'M SURE THEY'LL SEE IN A MOMENT IT'S A FAKE! I CAN NEVER BLUFF THE LEGIONNAIRES WITH THIS CONTRAPTION... I MUST TRY SOMETHING ELSE!
AS PROTY RETURNS TO HIS REGULAR, BLOBBY SHAPE!..
TOO LATE... I CAN TELEPATHICALLY SENSE THE LEGIONNAIRES RETURNING! THERE'S ONLY ONE CHANCE... I'LL TURN ON THE BURGLAR-ALARMS, AND THEN PLAY DEAD!
AND AS THE LEGIONNAIRES RETURN FROM TRYING OUT THEIR NEW TIME-THRUST MACHINE...
THE THING HASN'T QUITE ENOUGH POWER TO PIERCE THE IRON CURTAIN OF TIME... WE MUST MAKE IT STRONGER.
SUPERBOY, LISTEN! OUR BURGLAR ALARMS ARE SOUNDING... AN INTRUDER IS IN THE CLUBHOUSE!
5

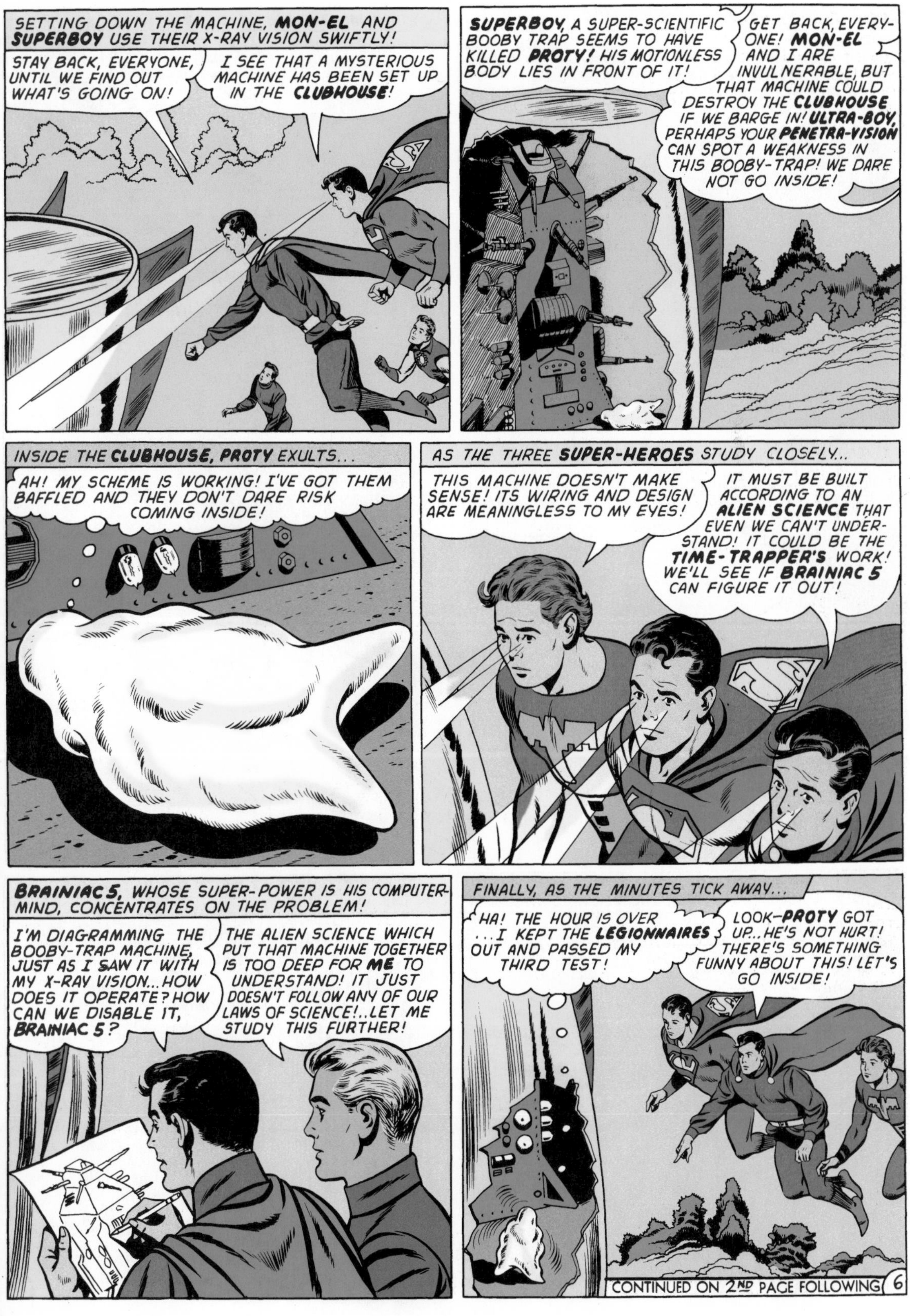
SETTING DOWN THE MACHINE, MON-EL AND SUPERBOY USE THEIR X-RAY VISION SWIFTLY!
STAY BACK, EVERYONE, UNTIL WE FIND OUT WHAT'S GOING ON!
I SEE THAT A MYSTERIOUS MACHINE HAS BEEN SET UP IN THE CLUBHOUSE!
SUPERBOY, A SUPER-SCIENTIFIC BOOBY TRAP SEEMS TO HAVE KILLED PROTY! HIS MOTIONLESS BODY LIES IN FRONT OF IT!
GET BACK, EVERYONE! MON-EL AND I ARE INVULNERABLE, BUT THAT MACHINE COULD DESTROY THE CLUBHOUSE IF WE BARGE IN! ULTRA-BOY, PERHAPS YOUR PENETRA-VISION CAN SPOT A WEAKNESS IN THIS BOOBY-TRAP! WE DARE NOT GO INSIDE!
INSIDE THE CLUBHOUSE, PROTY EXULTS...
AH! MY SCHEME IS WORKING! I'VE GOT THEM BAFFLED AND THEY DON'T DARE RISK COMING INSIDE!
AS THE THREE SUPER-HEROES STUDY CLOSELY...
THIS MACHINE DOESN'T MAKE SENSE! ITS WIRING AND DESIGN ARE MEANINGLESS TO MY EYES!
IT MUST BE BUILT ACCORDING TO AN ALIEN SCIENCE THAT EVEN WE CAN'T UNDERSTAND! IT COULD BE THE TIME-TRAPPER'S WORK! WE'LL SEE IF BRAINIAC 5 CAN FIGURE IT OUT!
BRAINIAC 5, WHOSE SUPER-POWER IS HIS COMPUTER-MIND, CONCENTRATES ON THE PROBLEM!
I'M DIAGRAMMING THE BOOBY-TRAP MACHINE, JUST AS I SAW IT WITH MY X-RAY VISION... HOW DOES IT OPERATE? HOW CAN WE DISABLE IT, BRAINIAC 5?
THE ALIEN SCIENCE WHICH PUT THAT MACHINE TOGETHER IS TOO DEEP FOR ME TO UNDERSTAND! IT JUST DOESN'T FOLLOW ANY OF OUR LAWS OF SCIENCE!..LET ME STUDY THIS FURTHER!
FINALLY, AS THE MINUTES TICK AWAY...
HA! THE HOUR IS OVER ...I KEPT THE LEGIONNAIRES OUT AND PASSED MY THIRD TEST!
LOOK—PROTY GOT UP...HE'S NOT HURT! THERE'S SOMETHING FUNNY ABOUT THIS! LET'S GO INSIDE!
CONTINUED ON 2ND PAGE FOLLOWING
6

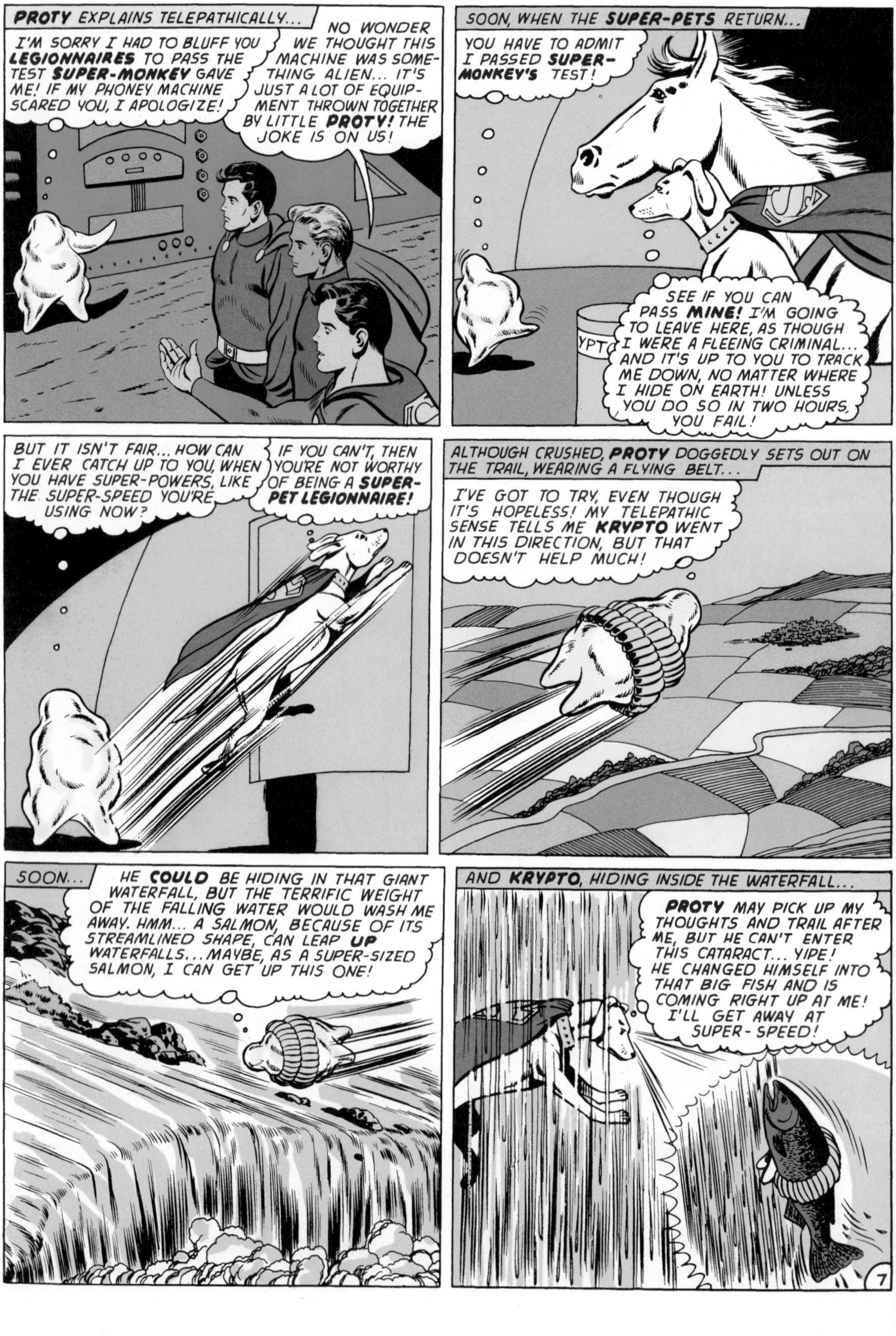

PROTY EXPLAINS TELEPATHICALLY...
I'M SORRY I HAD TO BLUFF YOU LEGIONNAIRES TO PASS THE TEST SUPER-MONKEY GAVE ME! IF MY PHONEY MACHINE SCARED YOU, I APOLOGIZE!
NO WONDER WE THOUGHT THIS MACHINE WAS SOMETHING ALIEN... IT'S JUST A LOT OF EQUIPMENT THROWN TOGETHER BY LITTLE PROTY! THE JOKE IS ON US!
SOON, WHEN THE SUPER-PETS RETURN...
YOU HAVE TO ADMIT I PASSED SUPER-MONKEY'S TEST!
SEE IF YOU CAN PASS MINE! I'M GOING TO LEAVE HERE, AS THOUGH I WERE A FLEEING CRIMINAL... AND IT'S UP TO YOU TO TRACK ME DOWN, NO MATTER WHERE I HIDE ON EARTH! UNLESS YOU DO SO IN TWO HOURS, YOU FAIL!
BUT IT ISN'T FAIR... HOW CAN I EVER CATCH UP TO YOU, WHEN YOU HAVE SUPER-POWERS, LIKE THE SUPER-SPEED YOU'RE USING NOW?
IF YOU CAN'T, THEN YOU'RE NOT WORTHY OF BEING A SUPER-PET LEGIONNAIRE!
ALTHOUGH CRUSHED, PROTY DOGGEDLY SETS OUT ON THE TRAIL, WEARING A FLYING BELT...
I'VE GOT TO TRY, EVEN THOUGH IT'S HOPELESS! MY TELEPATHIC SENSE TELLS ME KRYPTO WENT IN THIS DIRECTION, BUT THAT DOESN'T HELP MUCH!
SOON...
HE COULD BE HIDING IN THAT GIANT WATERFALL, BUT THE TERRIFIC WEIGHT OF THE FALLING WATER WOULD WASH ME AWAY. HMM... A SALMON, BECAUSE OF ITS STREAMLINED SHAPE, CAN LEAP UP WATERFALLS... MAYBE, AS A SUPER-SIZED SALMON, I CAN GET UP THIS ONE!
AND KRYPTO, HIDING INSIDE THE WATERFALL...
PROTY MAY PICK UP MY THOUGHTS AND TRAIL AFTER ME, BUT HE CAN'T ENTER THIS CATARACT... YIPE! HE CHANGED HIMSELF INTO THAT BIG FISH AND IS COMING RIGHT UP AT ME! I'LL GET AWAY AT SUPER-SPEED!
7

KRYPTO GAVE ME THE SLIP! BUT I'LL CHANGE BACK TO MY OWN FORM AND KEEP AFTER HIM!

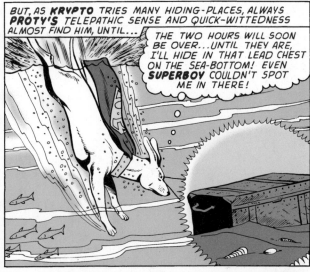

BUT, AS KRYPTO TRIES MANY HIDING-PLACES, ALWAYS PROTY'S TELEPATHIC SENSE AND QUICK-WITTEDNESS ALMOST FIND HIM, UNTIL...

THE TWO HOURS WILL SOON BE OVER...UNTIL THEY ARE, I'LL HIDE IN THAT LEAD CHEST ON THE SEA-BOTTOM! EVEN SUPERBOY COULDN'T SPOT ME IN THERE!

YIPE; GREEN KRYPTONITE! IT MUST HAVE BEEN PUT INTO THIS CHEST FOR SAFETY AND DROPPED INTO THE SEA BY A FRIEND OF SUPERBOY... AND I RASHLY OPENED IT! IT'S PARALYZING ME... CAN'T MOVE...

A LITTLE LATER...AS PROTY FOLLOWS THE TRAIL...

I GOT A TERRIFIC THOUGHT OF FEAR FROM KRYPTO'S MIND THAT LED ME HERE...BUT...HE'S PARALYZED BY GREEN KRYPTONITE! I'VE GOT TO SAVE HIM...BUT THAT KILLER SHARK LOOKS AS IF HE WANTS TO DEVOUR ME!

THIS SHAPE SCARED THE CRITTER AWAY... IF IT ONLY KNEW, IT COULD HAVE FINISHED THE REAL ME WITH ONE GULP! NOW I MUST GET KRYPTO TO SAFETY...

THIS IS HARD WORK...DON'T KNOW IF I CAN MAKE IT...AND KRYPTO HASN'T RECOVERED FULLY YET, THOUGH HE SOON WILL...

8

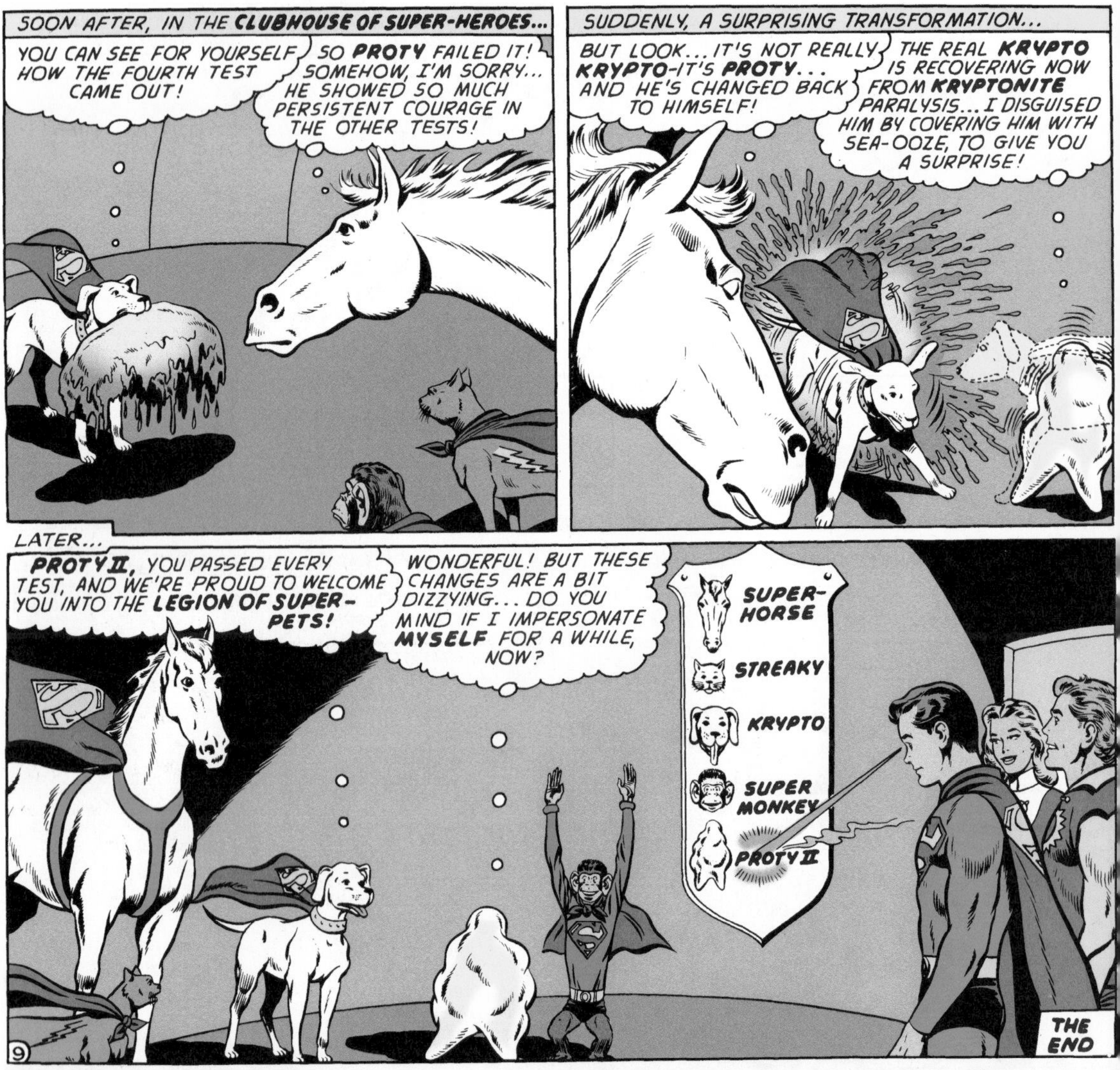
SOON AFTER, IN THE CLUBHOUSE OF SUPER-HEROES...
YOU CAN SEE FOR YOURSELF HOW THE FOURTH TEST CAME OUT!
SO PROTY FAILED IT! SOMEHOW, I'M SORRY... HE SHOWED SO MUCH PERSISTENT COURAGE IN THE OTHER TESTS!
SUDDENLY, A SURPRISING TRANSFORMATION...
BUT LOOK... IT'S NOT REALLY KRYPTO-IT'S PROTY... AND HE'S CHANGED BACK TO HIMSELF!
THE REAL KRYPTO IS RECOVERING NOW FROM KRYPTONITE PARALYSIS... I DISGUISED HIM BY COVERING HIM WITH SEA-OOZE, TO GIVE YOU A SURPRISE!
LATER...
PROTY II, YOU PASSED EVERY TEST, AND WE'RE PROUD TO WELCOME YOU INTO THE LEGION OF SUPER-PETS!
WONDERFUL! BUT THESE CHANGES ARE A BIT DIZZYING... DO YOU MIND IF I IMPERSONATE MYSELF FOR A WHILE, NOW?
SUPER-HORSE
STREAKY
KRYPTO
SUPER MONKEY
PROTY II
9
THE END

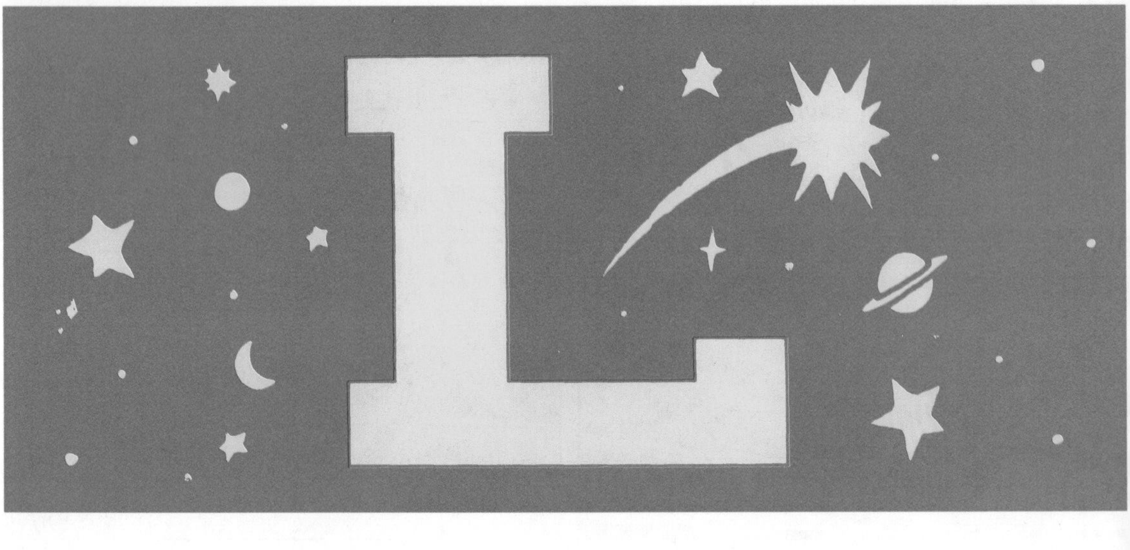

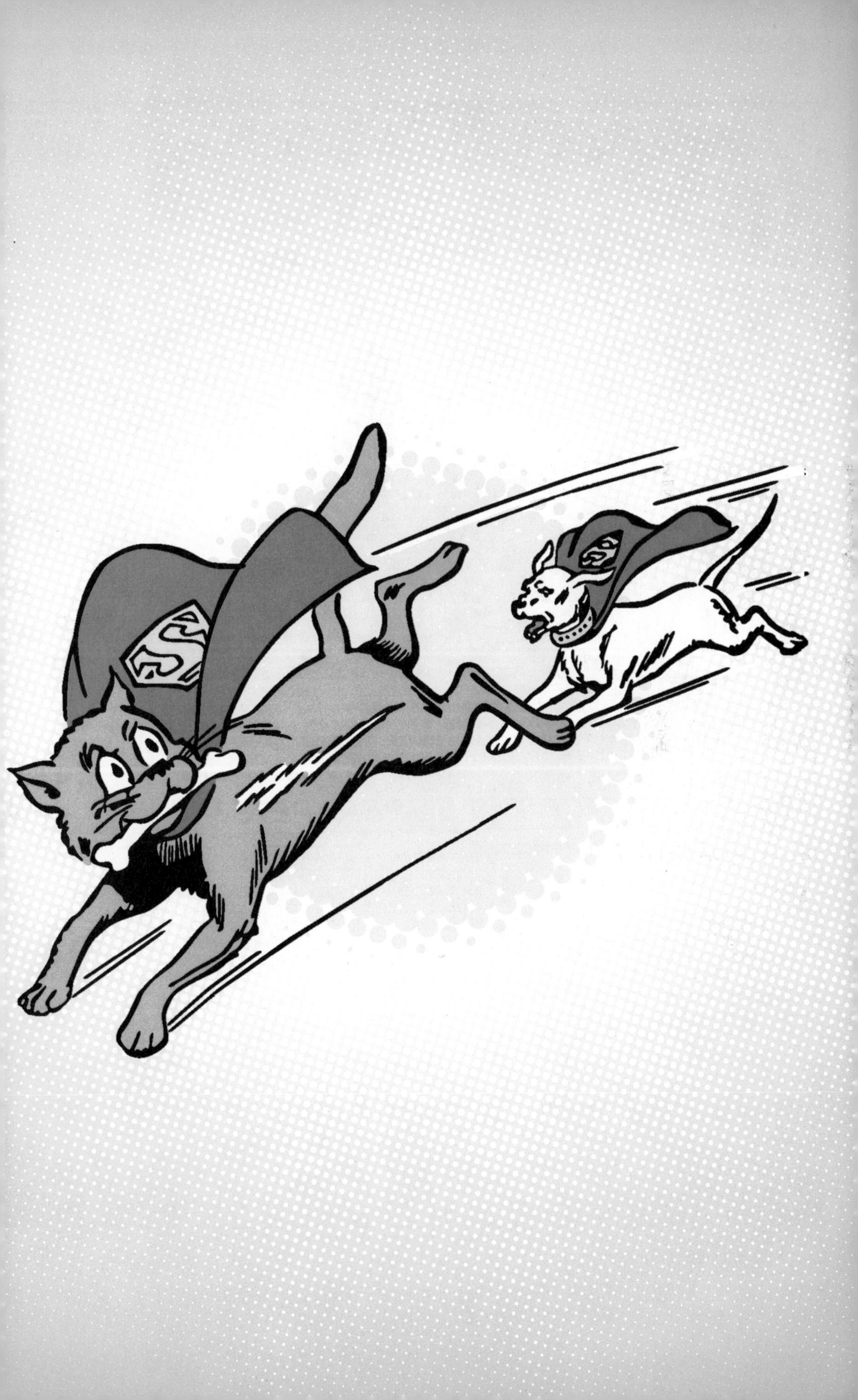

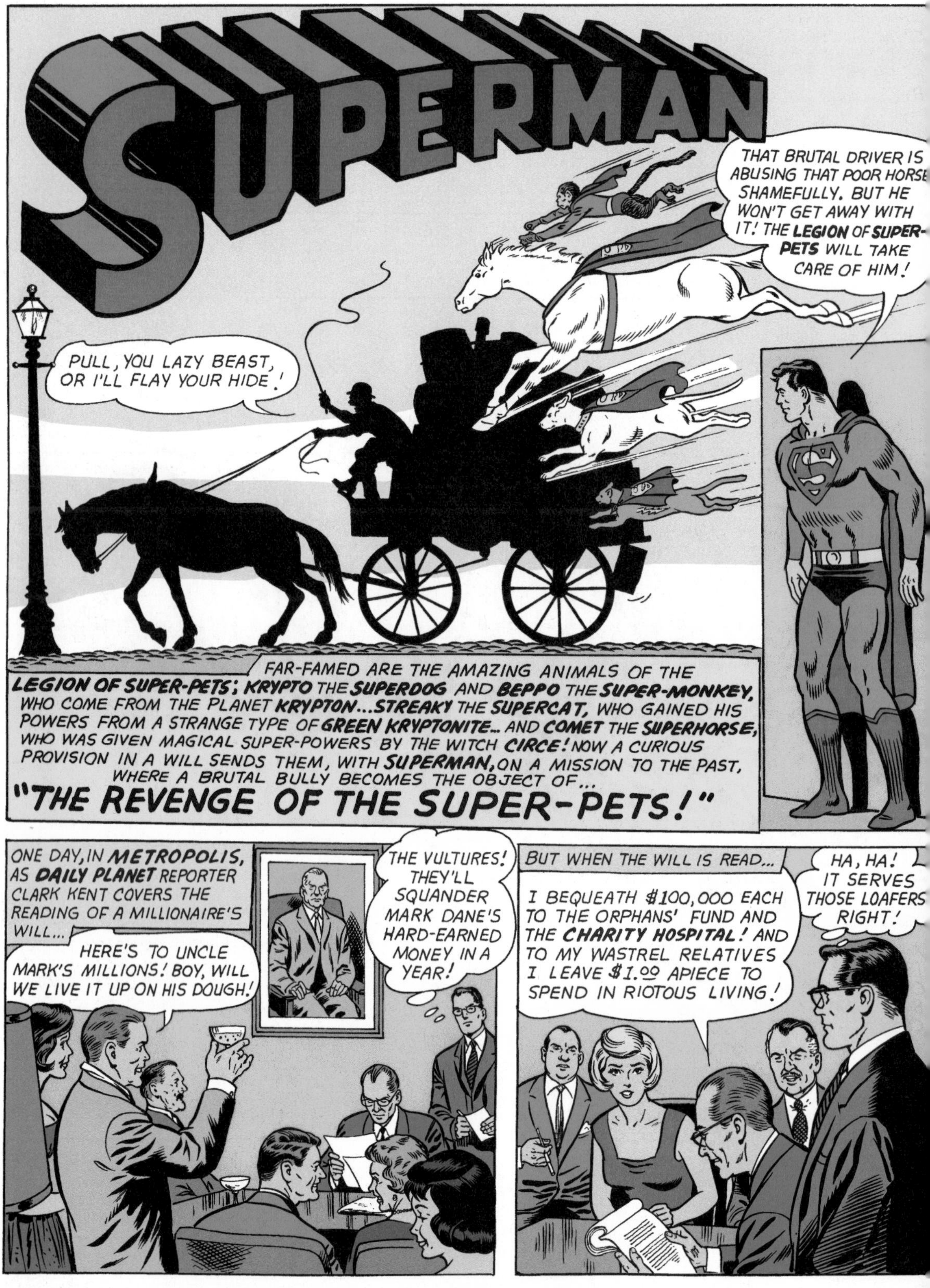
SUPERMAN
THAT BRUTAL DRIVER IS ABUSING THAT POOR HORSE SHAMEFULLY. BUT HE WON'T GET AWAY WITH IT! THE LEGION OF SUPER-PETS WILL TAKE CARE OF HIM!
PULL, YOU LAZY BEAST, OR I'LL FLAY YOUR HIDE!
FAR-FAMED ARE THE AMAZING ANIMALS OF THE LEGION OF SUPER-PETS; KRYPTO THE SUPERDOG AND BEPPO THE SUPER-MONKEY, WHO COME FROM THE PLANET KRYPTON...STREAKY THE SUPERCAT, WHO GAINED HIS POWERS FROM A STRANGE TYPE OF GREEN KRYPTONITE... AND COMET THE SUPERHORSE, WHO WAS GIVEN MAGICAL SUPER-POWERS BY THE WITCH CIRCE! NOW A CURIOUS PROVISION IN A WILL SENDS THEM, WITH SUPERMAN, ON A MISSION TO THE PAST, WHERE A BRUTAL BULLY BECOMES THE OBJECT OF...
"THE REVENGE OF THE SUPER-PETS!"
ONE DAY, IN METROPOLIS, AS DAILY PLANET REPORTER CLARK KENT COVERS THE READING OF A MILLIONAIRE'S WILL...
HERE'S TO UNCLE MARK'S MILLIONS! BOY, WILL WE LIVE IT UP ON HIS DOUGH!
THE VULTURES! THEY'LL SQUANDER MARK DANE'S HARD-EARNED MONEY IN A YEAR!
BUT WHEN THE WILL IS READ...
I BEQUEATH $100,000 EACH TO THE ORPHANS' FUND AND THE CHARITY HOSPITAL! AND TO MY WASTREL RELATIVES I LEAVE $1.00 APIECE TO SPEND IN RIOTOUS LIVING!
HA, HA! IT SERVES THOSE LOAFERS RIGHT!

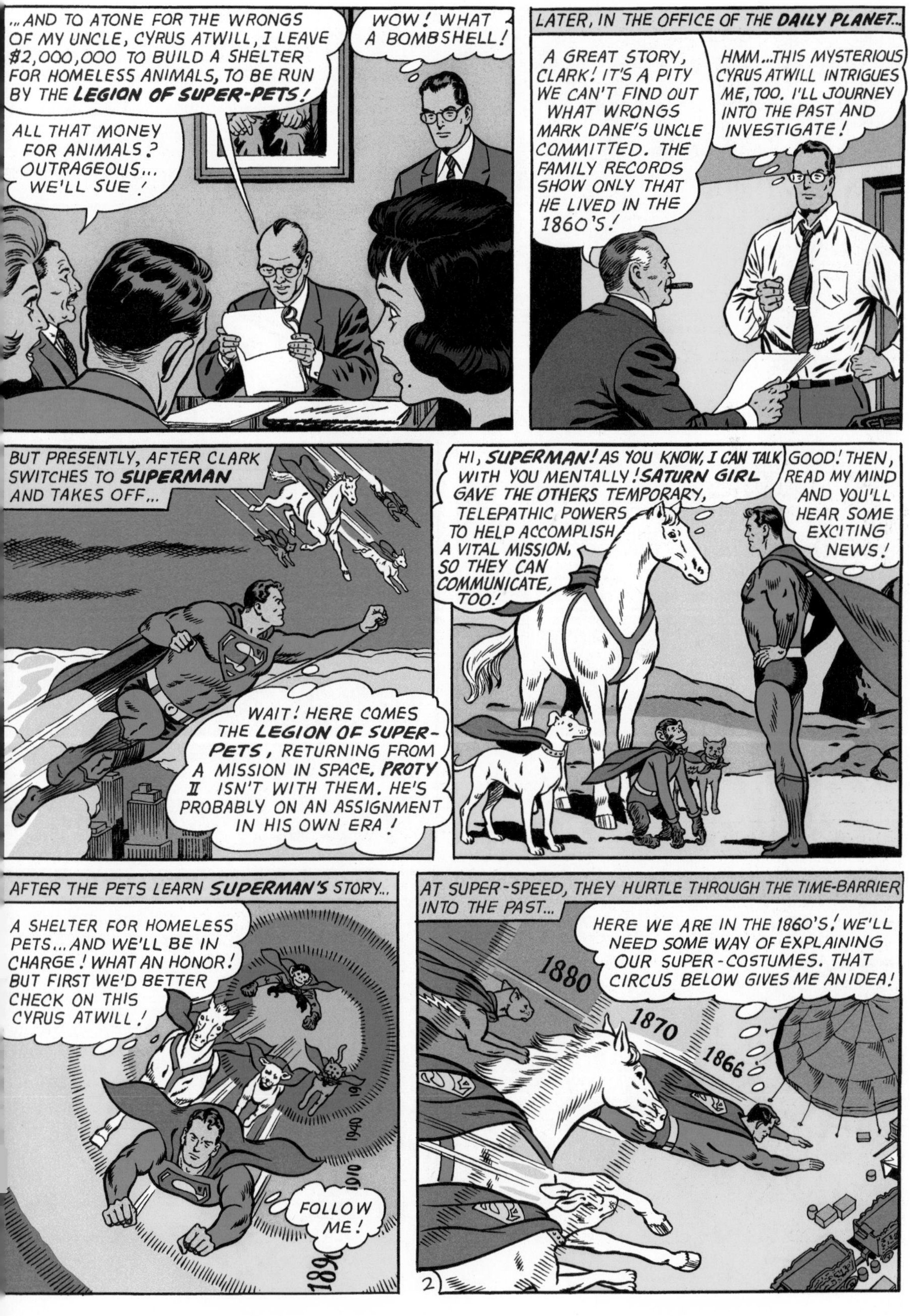
...AND TO ATONE FOR THE WRONGS OF MY UNCLE, CYRUS ATWILL, I LEAVE $2,000,000 TO BUILD A SHELTER FOR HOMELESS ANIMALS, TO BE RUN BY THE LEGION OF SUPER-PETS!
WOW! WHAT A BOMBSHELL!
ALL THAT MONEY FOR ANIMALS? OUTRAGEOUS... WE'LL SUE!
LATER, IN THE OFFICE OF THE DAILY PLANET...
A GREAT STORY, CLARK! IT'S A PITY WE CAN'T FIND OUT WHAT WRONGS MARK DANE'S UNCLE COMMITTED. THE FAMILY RECORDS SHOW ONLY THAT HE LIVED IN THE 1860'S!
HMM...THIS MYSTERIOUS CYRUS ATWILL INTRIGUES ME, TOO. I'LL JOURNEY INTO THE PAST AND INVESTIGATE!
BUT PRESENTLY, AFTER CLARK SWITCHES TO SUPERMAN AND TAKES OFF...
WAIT! HERE COMES THE LEGION OF SUPER-PETS, RETURNING FROM A MISSION IN SPACE. PROTY II ISN'T WITH THEM. HE'S PROBABLY ON AN ASSIGNMENT IN HIS OWN ERA!
HI, SUPERMAN! AS YOU KNOW, I CAN TALK WITH YOU MENTALLY! SATURN GIRL GAVE THE OTHERS TEMPORARY, TELEPATHIC POWERS TO HELP ACCOMPLISH A VITAL MISSION, SO THEY CAN COMMUNICATE, TOO!
GOOD! THEN, READ MY MIND AND YOU'LL HEAR SOME EXCITING NEWS!
AFTER THE PETS LEARN SUPERMAN'S STORY...
A SHELTER FOR HOMELESS PETS...AND WE'LL BE IN CHARGE! WHAT AN HONOR! BUT FIRST WE'D BETTER CHECK ON THIS CYRUS ATWILL!
1940
1890
FOLLOW ME!
AT SUPER-SPEED, THEY HURTLE THROUGH THE TIME-BARRIER INTO THE PAST...
HERE WE ARE IN THE 1860'S! WE'LL NEED SOME WAY OF EXPLAINING OUR SUPER-COSTUMES. THAT CIRCUS BELOW GIVES ME AN IDEA!
1880
1870
1866
2

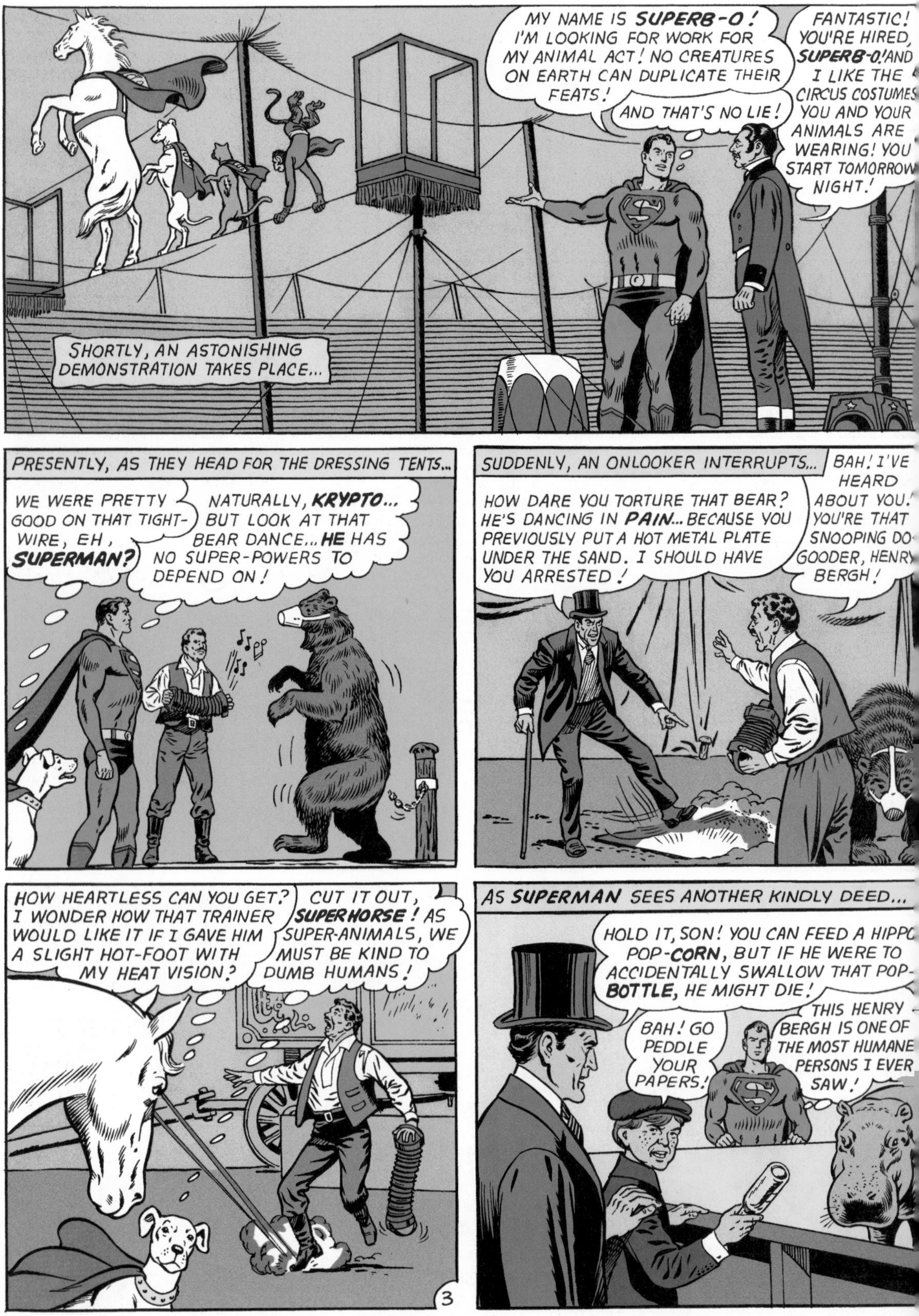

MY NAME IS SUPERB-O! I'M LOOKING FOR WORK FOR MY ANIMAL ACT! NO CREATURES ON EARTH CAN DUPLICATE THEIR FEATS!
AND THAT'S NO LIE!
FANTASTIC! YOU'RE HIRED, SUPERB-O! AND I LIKE THE CIRCUS COSTUMES YOU AND YOUR ANIMALS ARE WEARING! YOU START TOMORROW NIGHT!
SHORTLY, AN ASTONISHING DEMONSTRATION TAKES PLACE...
PRESENTLY, AS THEY HEAD FOR THE DRESSING TENTS...
WE WERE PRETTY GOOD ON THAT TIGHT-WIRE, EH, SUPERMAN?
NATURALLY, KRYPTO... BUT LOOK AT THAT BEAR DANCE... HE HAS NO SUPER-POWERS TO DEPEND ON!
SUDDENLY, AN ONLOOKER INTERRUPTS...
HOW DARE YOU TORTURE THAT BEAR? HE'S DANCING IN PAIN... BECAUSE YOU PREVIOUSLY PUT A HOT METAL PLATE UNDER THE SAND. I SHOULD HAVE YOU ARRESTED!
BAH! I'VE HEARD ABOUT YOU. YOU'RE THAT SNOOPING DO-GOODER, HENRY BERGH!
HOW HEARTLESS CAN YOU GET? I WONDER HOW THAT TRAINER WOULD LIKE IT IF I GAVE HIM A SLIGHT HOT-FOOT WITH MY HEAT VISION?
CUT IT OUT, SUPERHORSE! AS SUPER-ANIMALS, WE MUST BE KIND TO DUMB HUMANS!
3
AS SUPERMAN SEES ANOTHER KINDLY DEED...
HOLD IT, SON! YOU CAN FEED A HIPPO POP-CORN, BUT IF HE WERE TO ACCIDENTALLY SWALLOW THAT POP-BOTTLE, HE MIGHT DIE!
BAH! GO PEDDLE YOUR PAPERS!
THIS HENRY BERGH IS ONE OF THE MOST HUMANE PERSONS I EVER SAW!

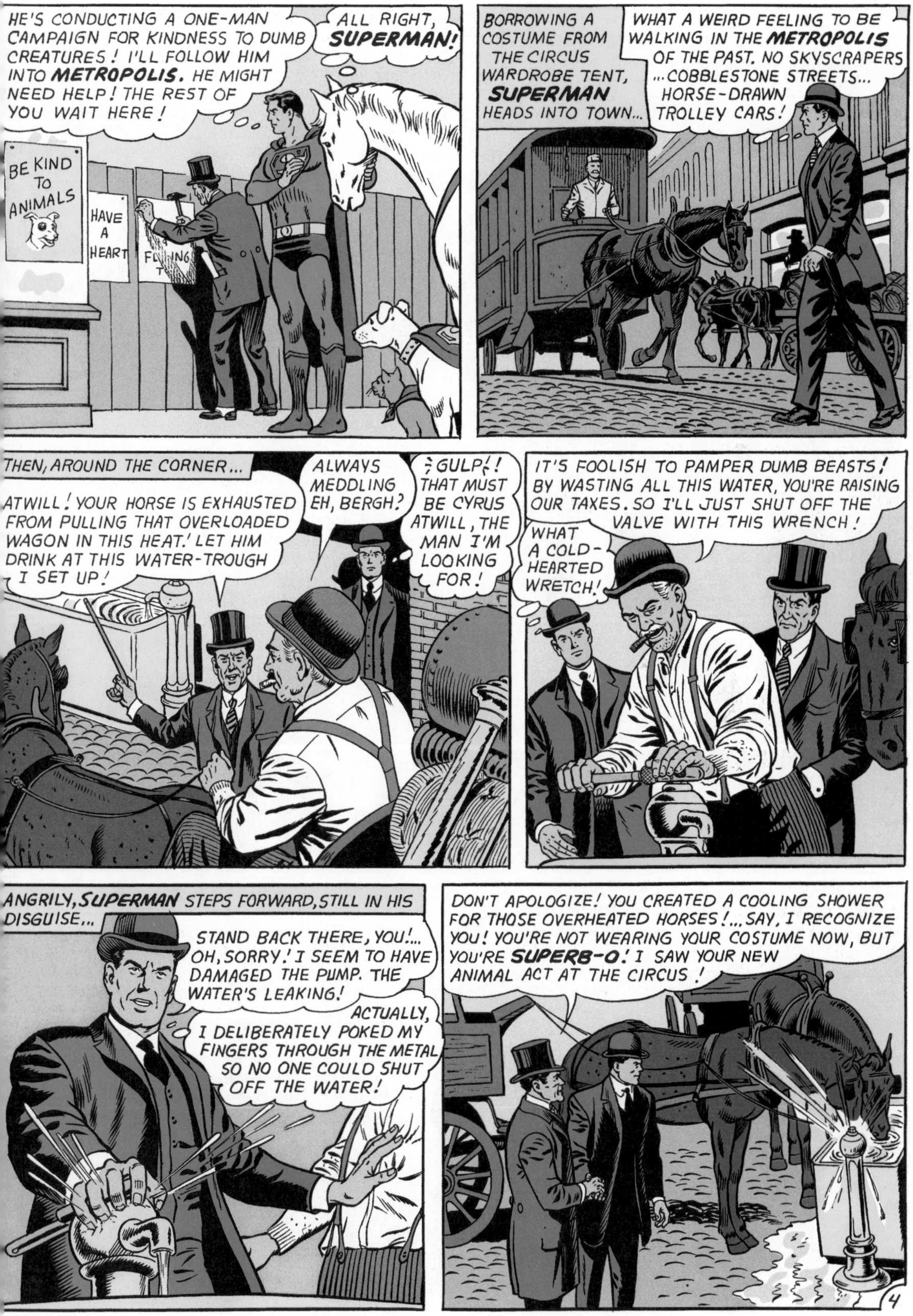

HE'S CONDUCTING A ONE-MAN CAMPAIGN FOR KINDNESS TO DUMB CREATURES! I'LL FOLLOW HIM INTO METROPOLIS. HE MIGHT NEED HELP! THE REST OF YOU WAIT HERE!
ALL RIGHT, SUPERMAN!
BE KIND TO ANIMALS
HAVE A HEART
BORROWING A COSTUME FROM THE CIRCUS WARDROBE TENT, SUPERMAN HEADS INTO TOWN...
WHAT A WEIRD FEELING TO BE WALKING IN THE METROPOLIS OF THE PAST. NO SKYSCRAPERS ...COBBLESTONE STREETS... HORSE-DRAWN TROLLEY CARS!
THEN, AROUND THE CORNER...
ATWILL! YOUR HORSE IS EXHAUSTED FROM PULLING THAT OVERLOADED WAGON IN THIS HEAT! LET HIM DRINK AT THIS WATER-TROUGH I SET UP!
ALWAYS MEDDLING EH, BERGH?
GULP! THAT MUST BE CYRUS ATWILL, THE MAN I'M LOOKING FOR!
IT'S FOOLISH TO PAMPER DUMB BEASTS! BY WASTING ALL THIS WATER, YOU'RE RAISING OUR TAXES. SO I'LL JUST SHUT OFF THE VALVE WITH THIS WRENCH!
WHAT A COLD-HEARTED WRETCH!
ANGRILY, SUPERMAN STEPS FORWARD, STILL IN HIS DISGUISE...
STAND BACK THERE, YOU!... OH, SORRY! I SEEM TO HAVE DAMAGED THE PUMP. THE WATER'S LEAKING!
ACTUALLY, I DELIBERATELY POKED MY FINGERS THROUGH THE METAL SO NO ONE COULD SHUT OFF THE WATER!
DON'T APOLOGIZE! YOU CREATED A COOLING SHOWER FOR THOSE OVERHEATED HORSES!... SAY, I RECOGNIZE YOU! YOU'RE NOT WEARING YOUR COSTUME NOW, BUT YOU'RE SUPERB-O! I SAW YOUR NEW ANIMAL ACT AT THE CIRCUS!
4

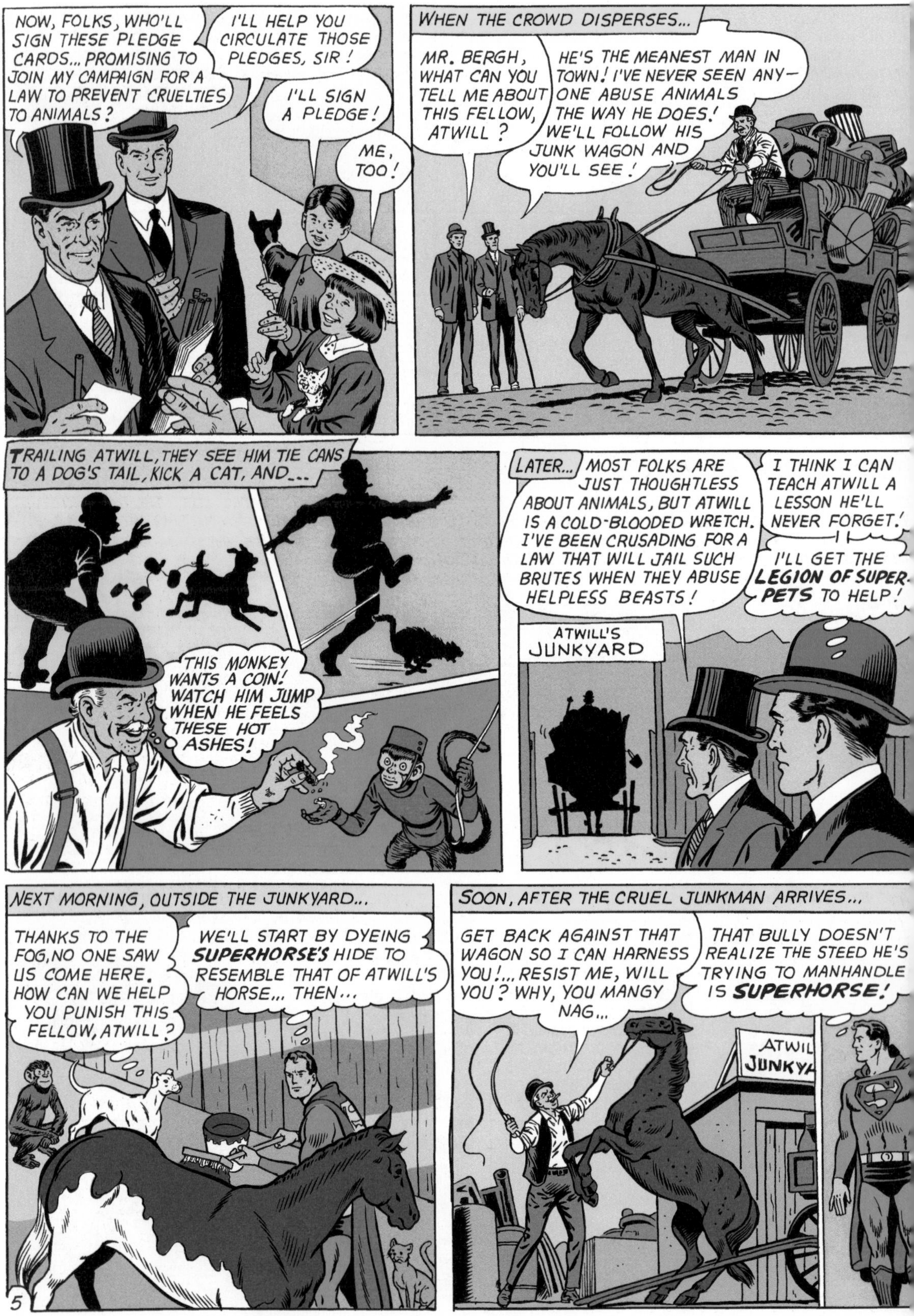
NOW, FOLKS, WHO'LL SIGN THESE PLEDGE CARDS... PROMISING TO JOIN MY CAMPAIGN FOR A LAW TO PREVENT CRUELTIES TO ANIMALS?
I'LL HELP YOU CIRCULATE THOSE PLEDGES, SIR!
I'LL SIGN A PLEDGE!
ME, TOO!
WHEN THE CROWD DISPERSES...
MR. BERGH, WHAT CAN YOU TELL ME ABOUT THIS FELLOW, ATWILL?
HE'S THE MEANEST MAN IN TOWN! I'VE NEVER SEEN ANY-ONE ABUSE ANIMALS THE WAY HE DOES! WE'LL FOLLOW HIS JUNK WAGON AND YOU'LL SEE!
TRAILING ATWILL, THEY SEE HIM TIE CANS TO A DOG'S TAIL, KICK A CAT, AND...
THIS MONKEY WANTS A COIN! WATCH HIM JUMP WHEN HE FEELS THESE HOT ASHES!
LATER...
MOST FOLKS ARE JUST THOUGHTLESS ABOUT ANIMALS, BUT ATWILL IS A COLD-BLOODED WRETCH. I'VE BEEN CRUSADING FOR A LAW THAT WILL JAIL SUCH BRUTES WHEN THEY ABUSE HELPLESS BEASTS!
I THINK I CAN TEACH ATWILL A LESSON HE'LL NEVER FORGET!
I'LL GET THE LEGION OF SUPER-PETS TO HELP!
ATWILL'S JUNKYARD
NEXT MORNING, OUTSIDE THE JUNKYARD...
THANKS TO THE FOG, NO ONE SAW US COME HERE. HOW CAN WE HELP YOU PUNISH THIS FELLOW, ATWILL?
WE'LL START BY DYEING SUPERHORSE'S HIDE TO RESEMBLE THAT OF ATWILL'S HORSE... THEN...
SOON, AFTER THE CRUEL JUNKMAN ARRIVES...
GET BACK AGAINST THAT WAGON SO I CAN HARNESS YOU!... RESIST ME, WILL YOU? WHY, YOU MANGY NAG...
THAT BULLY DOESN'T REALIZE THE STEED HE'S TRYING TO MANHANDLE IS SUPERHORSE!
5

ABRUPTLY, **SUPERHORSE** STREAKS SKYWARD --WITH A PASSENGER!...

TRY TO ABUSE **ME**, WILL YOU?

WHEE-HEE-HAW!

YiiiiiiiI!

THIS CRAZY BEAST IS DRAGGING ME UP THROUGH THE CLOUDS! HOW IS IT POSSIBLE?

SECONDS LATER, **SUPERHORSE** PLUNGES BACK TO EARTH...

I WONDER HOW HE ENJOYED HIS RIDE? HA, HA! SERVES ATWILL RIGHT!

THUMP

AS ATWILL RECOVERS HIS SENSES...

I MUST HAVE BEEN SEEING THINGS! THAT NAG SHOOK ME UP SO BADLY, I MISTOOK THE FOG FOR CLOUDS. I'D BETTER LEAVE THAT CRAZY BEAST HERE AND USE MY PUSHCART TODAY!

HURRY! WE HAVE TO PREPARE HIS NEXT LESSON IN KINDNESS TO ANIMALS!

SOON, AT A "CONSTRUCTION SITE" PREPARED BY **SUPERMAN** AT SUPER-SPEED...

HEY, JUNKMAN, YOU CAN HAVE THAT PILE OF SCRAP-IRON AND PIPE!

THANKS! I'LL JUST CHASE THAT MUTT AWAY AND...;ULP.;

THAT HEAVY DUMBBELL I TOOK FROM MY CART BROKE ON THE DOG'S BODY!

KLANK!

IT MUST BE MY IMAGINATION. I'LL JUST KICK THIS MONGREL OUT OF THE WAY, AND...

EEEYOWWW!

HA, HA! HE MASHED HIS TOE ON **KRYPTO'S** INVULNERABLE BODY! THAT SKUNK HAD IT COMING!

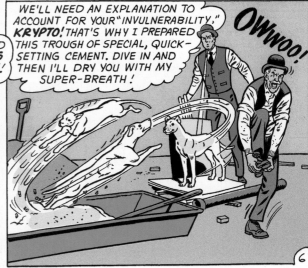

WE'LL NEED AN EXPLANATION TO ACCOUNT FOR YOUR "INVULNERABILITY," **KRYPTO!** THAT'S WHY I PREPARED THIS TROUGH OF SPECIAL, QUICK-SETTING CEMENT. DIVE IN AND THEN I'LL DRY YOU WITH MY SUPER-BREATH!

OWWOO!

6

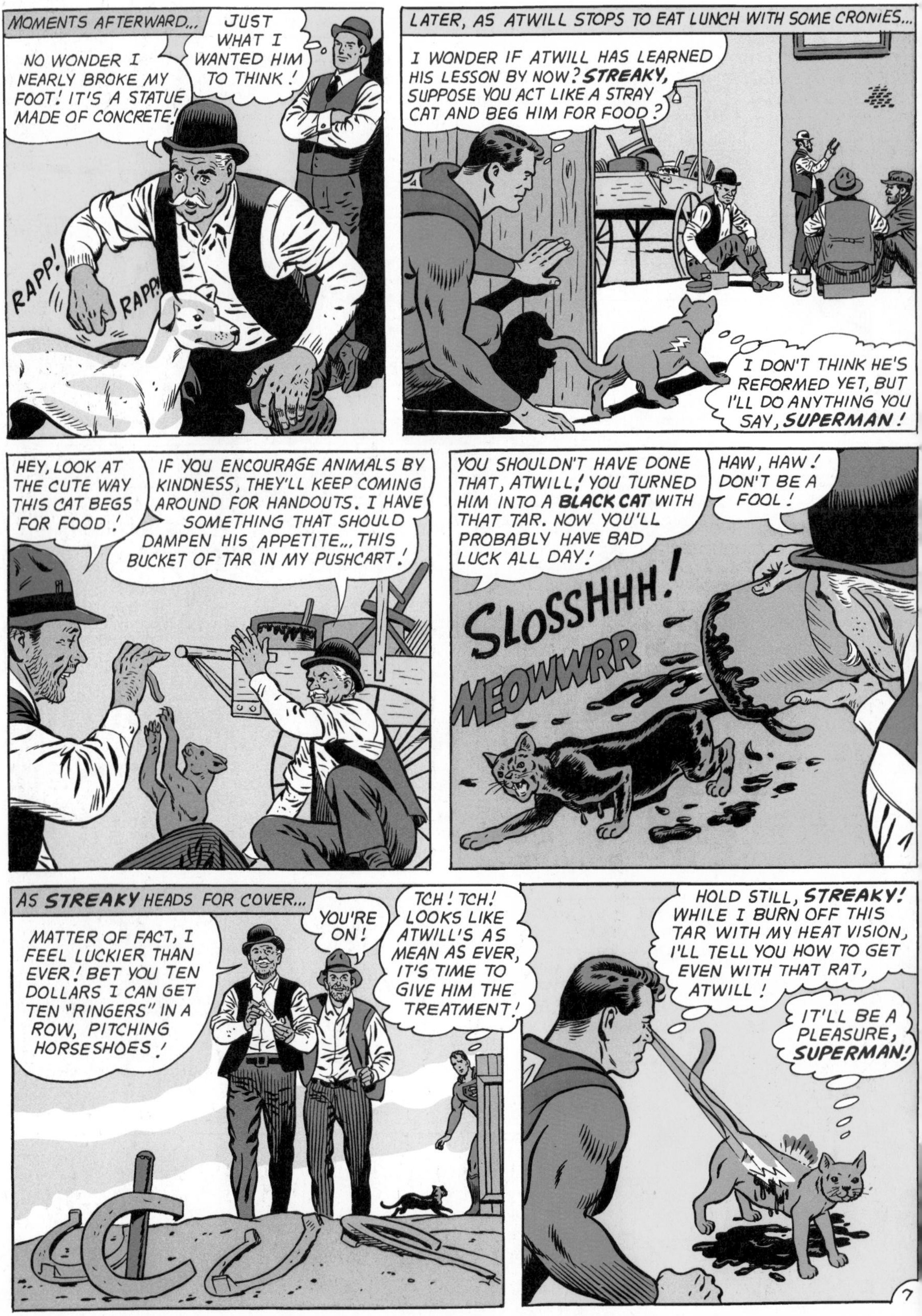
MOMENTS AFTERWARD...
NO WONDER I NEARLY BROKE MY FOOT! IT'S A STATUE MADE OF CONCRETE!
JUST WHAT I WANTED HIM TO THINK!
RAPP! RAPP!
LATER, AS ATWILL STOPS TO EAT LUNCH WITH SOME CRONIES...
I WONDER IF ATWILL HAS LEARNED HIS LESSON BY NOW? STREAKY, SUPPOSE YOU ACT LIKE A STRAY CAT AND BEG HIM FOR FOOD?
I DON'T THINK HE'S REFORMED YET, BUT I'LL DO ANYTHING YOU SAY, SUPERMAN!
HEY, LOOK AT THE CUTE WAY THIS CAT BEGS FOR FOOD!
IF YOU ENCOURAGE ANIMALS BY KINDNESS, THEY'LL KEEP COMING AROUND FOR HANDOUTS. I HAVE SOMETHING THAT SHOULD DAMPEN HIS APPETITE... THIS BUCKET OF TAR IN MY PUSHCART!
YOU SHOULDN'T HAVE DONE THAT, ATWILL! YOU TURNED HIM INTO A BLACK CAT WITH THAT TAR. NOW YOU'LL PROBABLY HAVE BAD LUCK ALL DAY!
HAW, HAW! DON'T BE A FOOL!
SLOSSHHH!
MEOWWRR
AS STREAKY HEADS FOR COVER...
MATTER OF FACT, I FEEL LUCKIER THAN EVER! BET YOU TEN DOLLARS I CAN GET TEN "RINGERS" IN A ROW, PITCHING HORSESHOES!
YOU'RE ON!
TCH! TCH! LOOKS LIKE ATWILL'S AS MEAN AS EVER, IT'S TIME TO GIVE HIM THE TREATMENT!
HOLD STILL, STREAKY! WHILE I BURN OFF THIS TAR WITH MY HEAT VISION, I'LL TELL YOU HOW TO GET EVEN WITH THAT RAT, ATWILL!
IT'LL BE A PLEASURE, SUPERMAN!
7

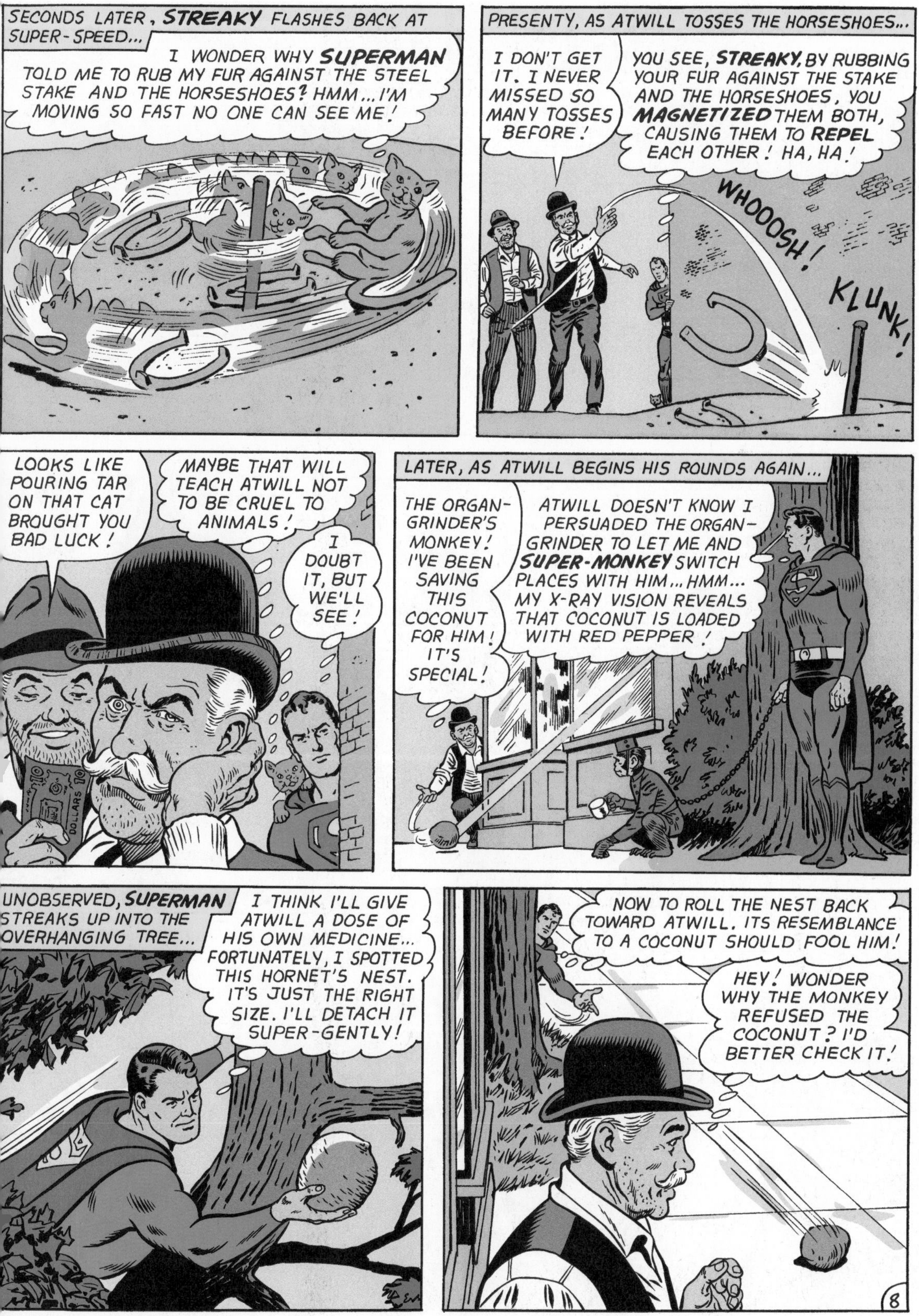

SECONDS LATER, STREAKY FLASHES BACK AT SUPER-SPEED...
I WONDER WHY SUPERMAN TOLD ME TO RUB MY FUR AGAINST THE STEEL STAKE AND THE HORSESHOES? HMM... I'M MOVING SO FAST NO ONE CAN SEE ME!
PRESENTY, AS ATWILL TOSSES THE HORSESHOES...
I DON'T GET IT. I NEVER MISSED SO MANY TOSSES BEFORE!
YOU SEE, STREAKY, BY RUBBING YOUR FUR AGAINST THE STAKE AND THE HORSESHOES, YOU MAGNETIZED THEM BOTH, CAUSING THEM TO REPEL EACH OTHER! HA, HA!
WHOOOSH!
KLUNK!
LOOKS LIKE POURING TAR ON THAT CAT BROUGHT YOU BAD LUCK!
MAYBE THAT WILL TEACH ATWILL NOT TO BE CRUEL TO ANIMALS!
I DOUBT IT, BUT WE'LL SEE!
DOLLARS
LATER, AS ATWILL BEGINS HIS ROUNDS AGAIN...
THE ORGAN-GRINDER'S MONKEY! I'VE BEEN SAVING THIS COCONUT FOR HIM! IT'S SPECIAL!
ATWILL DOESN'T KNOW I PERSUADED THE ORGAN-GRINDER TO LET ME AND SUPER-MONKEY SWITCH PLACES WITH HIM... HMM... MY X-RAY VISION REVEALS THAT COCONUT IS LOADED WITH RED PEPPER!
UNOBSERVED, SUPERMAN STREAKS UP INTO THE OVERHANGING TREE...
I THINK I'LL GIVE ATWILL A DOSE OF HIS OWN MEDICINE... FORTUNATELY, I SPOTTED THIS HORNET'S NEST. IT'S JUST THE RIGHT SIZE. I'LL DETACH IT SUPER-GENTLY!
NOW TO ROLL THE NEST BACK TOWARD ATWILL. ITS RESEMBLANCE TO A COCONUT SHOULD FOOL HIM!
HEY! WONDER WHY THE MONKEY REFUSED THE COCONUT? I'D BETTER CHECK IT!
8

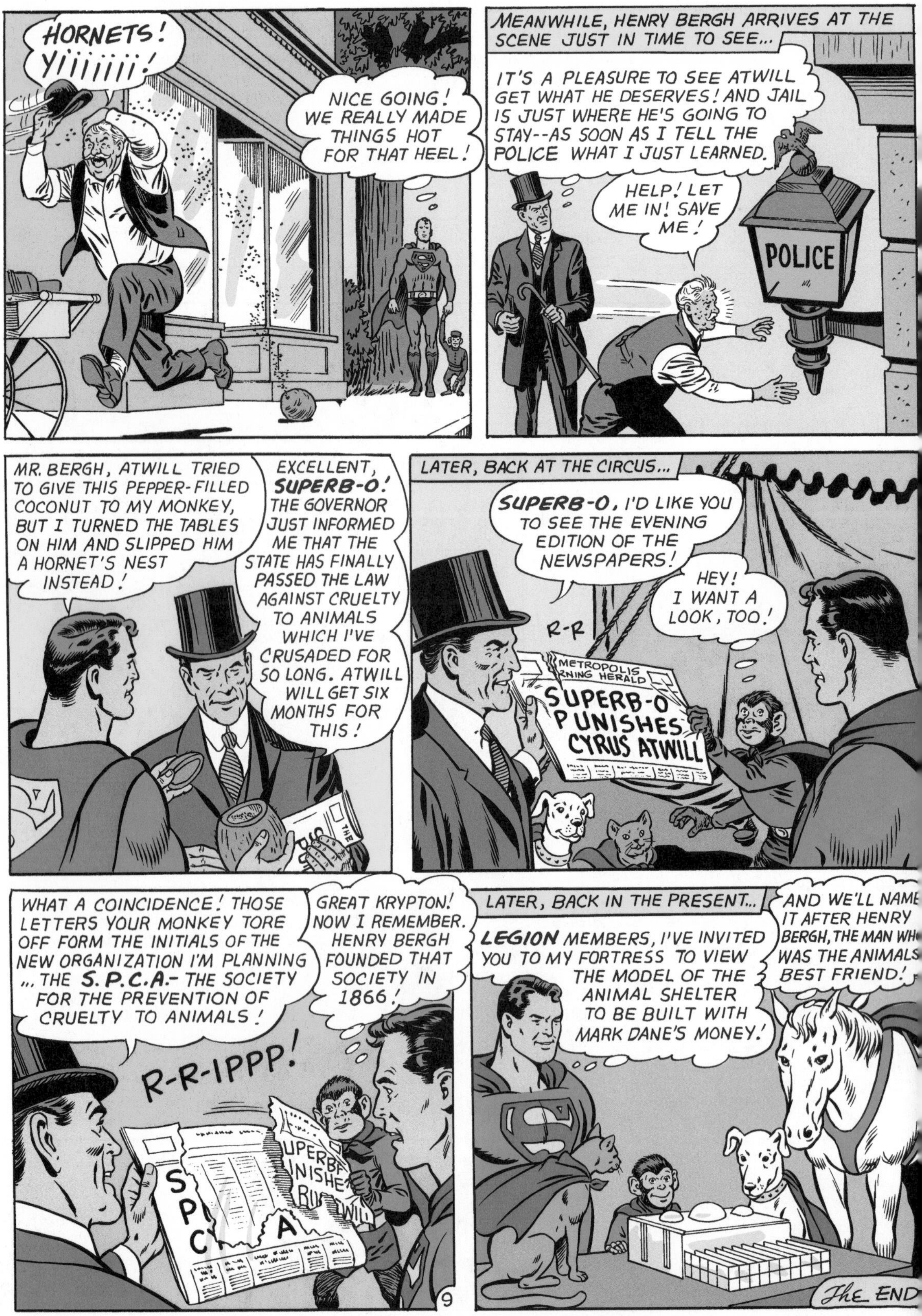
HORNETS! YIIIIIII!
NICE GOING! WE REALLY MADE THINGS HOT FOR THAT HEEL!
MEANWHILE, HENRY BERGH ARRIVES AT THE SCENE JUST IN TIME TO SEE...
IT'S A PLEASURE TO SEE ATWILL GET WHAT HE DESERVES! AND JAIL IS JUST WHERE HE'S GOING TO STAY--AS SOON AS I TELL THE POLICE WHAT I JUST LEARNED.
HELP! LET ME IN! SAVE ME!
POLICE
MR. BERGH, ATWILL TRIED TO GIVE THIS PEPPER-FILLED COCONUT TO MY MONKEY, BUT I TURNED THE TABLES ON HIM AND SLIPPED HIM A HORNET'S NEST INSTEAD!
EXCELLENT, SUPERB-O! THE GOVERNOR JUST INFORMED ME THAT THE STATE HAS FINALLY PASSED THE LAW AGAINST CRUELTY TO ANIMALS WHICH I'VE CRUSADED FOR SO LONG. ATWILL WILL GET SIX MONTHS FOR THIS!
LATER, BACK AT THE CIRCUS...
SUPERB-O, I'D LIKE YOU TO SEE THE EVENING EDITION OF THE NEWSPAPERS!
HEY! I WANT A LOOK, TOO!
R-R
METROPOLIS
RNING HERALD
SUPERB-O PUNISHES CYRUS ATWILL
WHAT A COINCIDENCE! THOSE LETTERS YOUR MONKEY TORE OFF FORM THE INITIALS OF THE NEW ORGANIZATION I'M PLANNING ... THE S.P.C.A.- THE SOCIETY FOR THE PREVENTION OF CRUELTY TO ANIMALS!
GREAT KRYPTON! NOW I REMEMBER. HENRY BERGH FOUNDED THAT SOCIETY IN 1866!
R-R-IPPP!
S P C A
9
LATER, BACK IN THE PRESENT...
LEGION MEMBERS, I'VE INVITED YOU TO MY FORTRESS TO VIEW THE MODEL OF THE ANIMAL SHELTER TO BE BUILT WITH MARK DANE'S MONEY!
AND WE'LL NAME IT AFTER HENRY BERGH, THE MAN WH WAS THE ANIMALS BEST FRIEND!
THE END

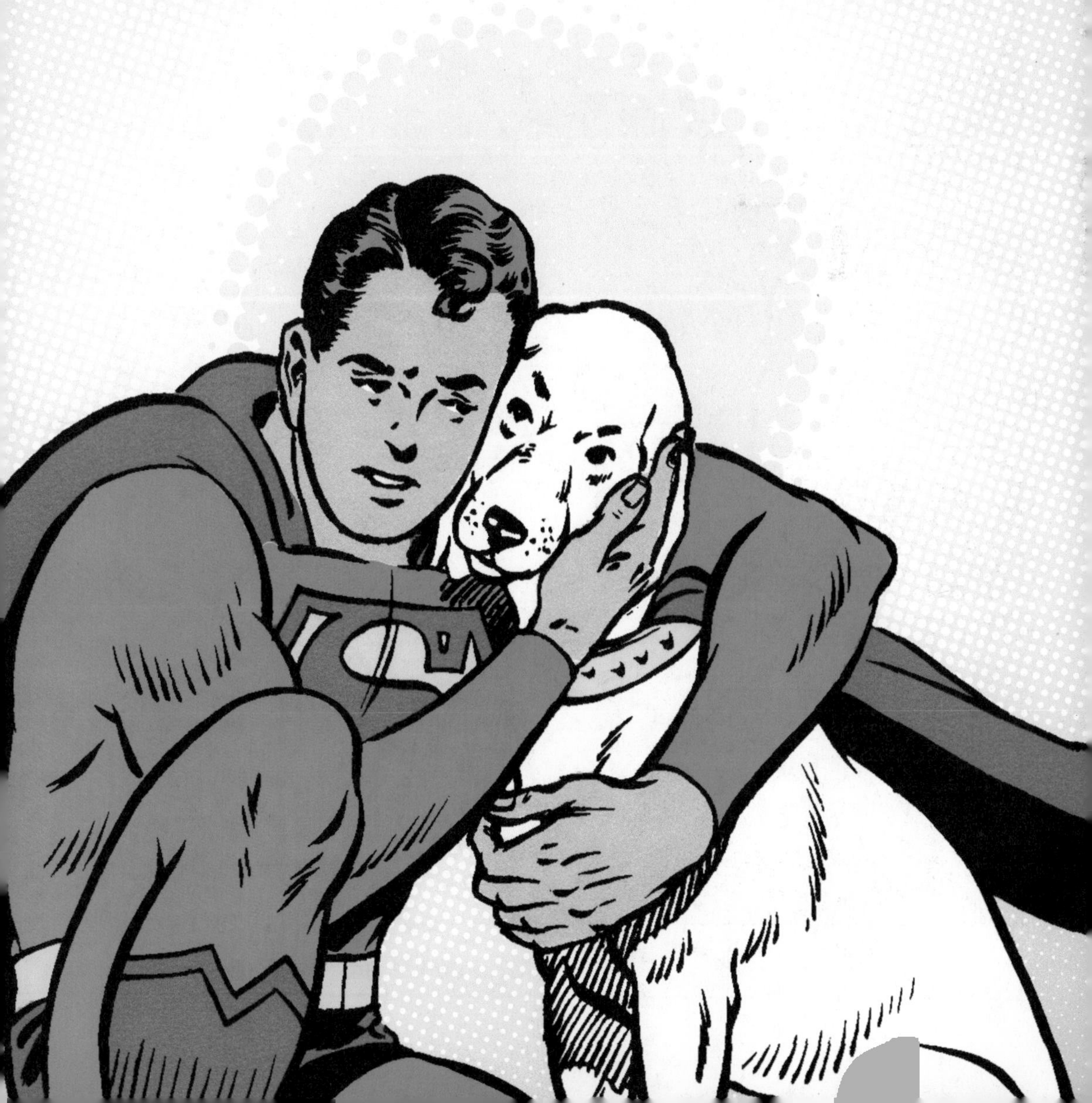

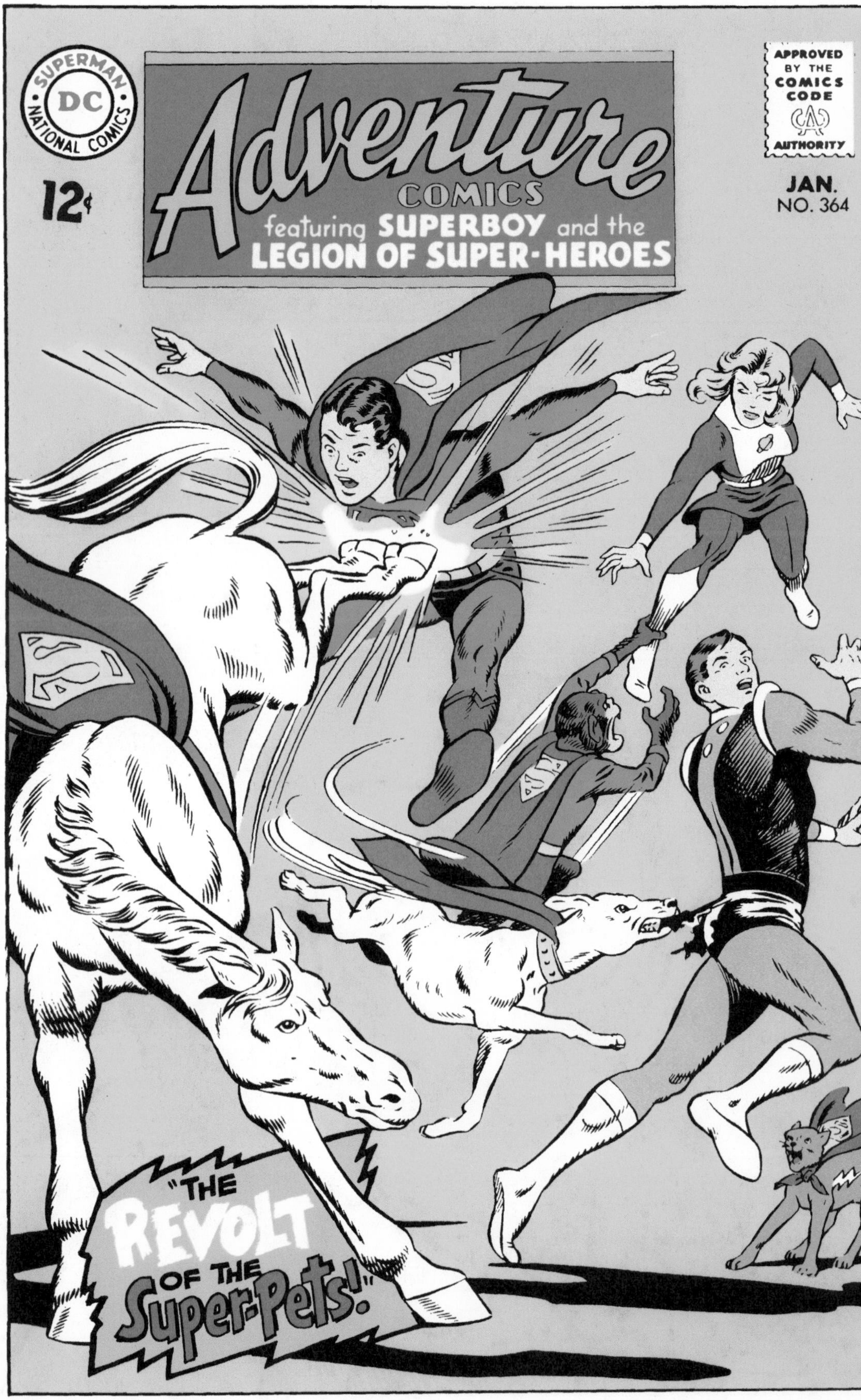
SUPERMAN
DC
NATIONAL COMICS
12¢
Adventure
COMICS
featuring SUPERBOY and the
LEGION OF SUPER-HEROES
APPROVED
BY THE
COMICS
CODE
AUTHORITY
JAN.
NO. 364
"THE
REVOLT
OF THE
Super-Pets!"

TALES OF THE
LEGION of SUPER-HEROES
SUPER-PETS
WE MAY AS WELL LEAVE, LEGIONNAIRES! HERE WE'RE ONLY HAS-BEEN HEROES!
...AND SO, PEOPLE OF THANL, I HEREBY DEDICATE THIS NEW HEADQUARTERS TO OUR BRAVE DEFENDERS, THE ANIMAL HEROES!
HOORAY!!
WHO IS OUSTING THE MIGHTY LEGION AS UNIVERSAL DEFENDERS OF LAW AND ORDER?... WOULD YOU BELIEVE... THE SUPER-PETS? YOU'D BETTER BELIEVE IT, BECAUSE YOU ARE ABOUT TO WITNESS...
"The REVOLT OF THE SUPER-PETS!"
COSTANZA

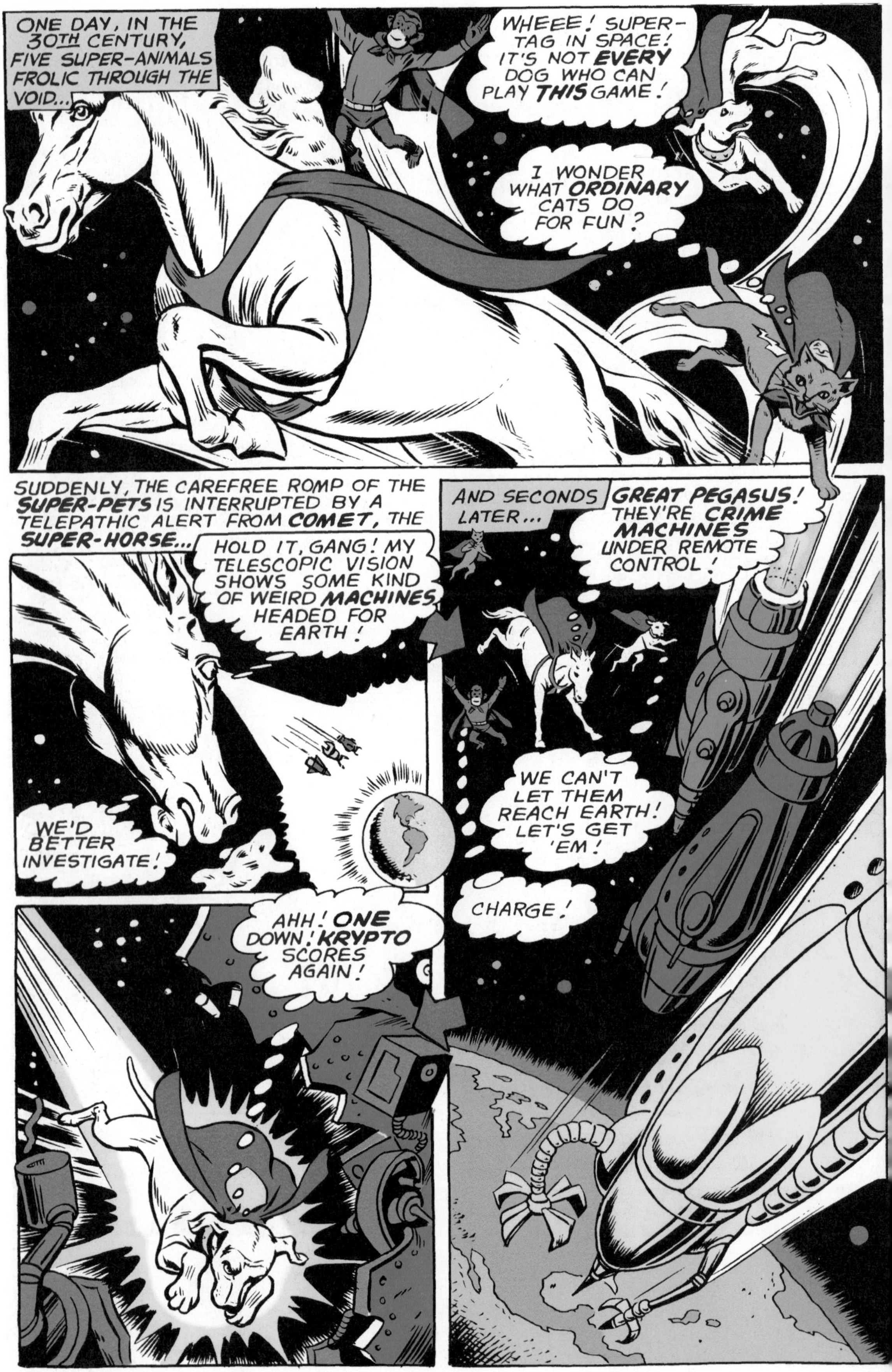
ONE DAY, IN THE 30TH CENTURY, FIVE SUPER-ANIMALS FROLIC THROUGH THE VOID...
WHEEEE! SUPER-TAG IN SPACE! IT'S NOT EVERY DOG WHO CAN PLAY THIS GAME!
I WONDER WHAT ORDINARY CATS DO FOR FUN?
SUDDENLY, THE CAREFREE ROMP OF THE SUPER-PETS IS INTERRUPTED BY A TELEPATHIC ALERT FROM COMET, THE SUPER-HORSE...
HOLD IT, GANG! MY TELESCOPIC VISION SHOWS SOME KIND OF WEIRD MACHINES HEADED FOR EARTH!
WE'D BETTER INVESTIGATE!
AND SECONDS LATER...
GREAT PEGASUS! THEY'RE CRIME MACHINES UNDER REMOTE CONTROL!
WE CAN'T LET THEM REACH EARTH! LET'S GET 'EM!
CHARGE!
AHH! ONE DOWN! KRYPTO SCORES AGAIN!

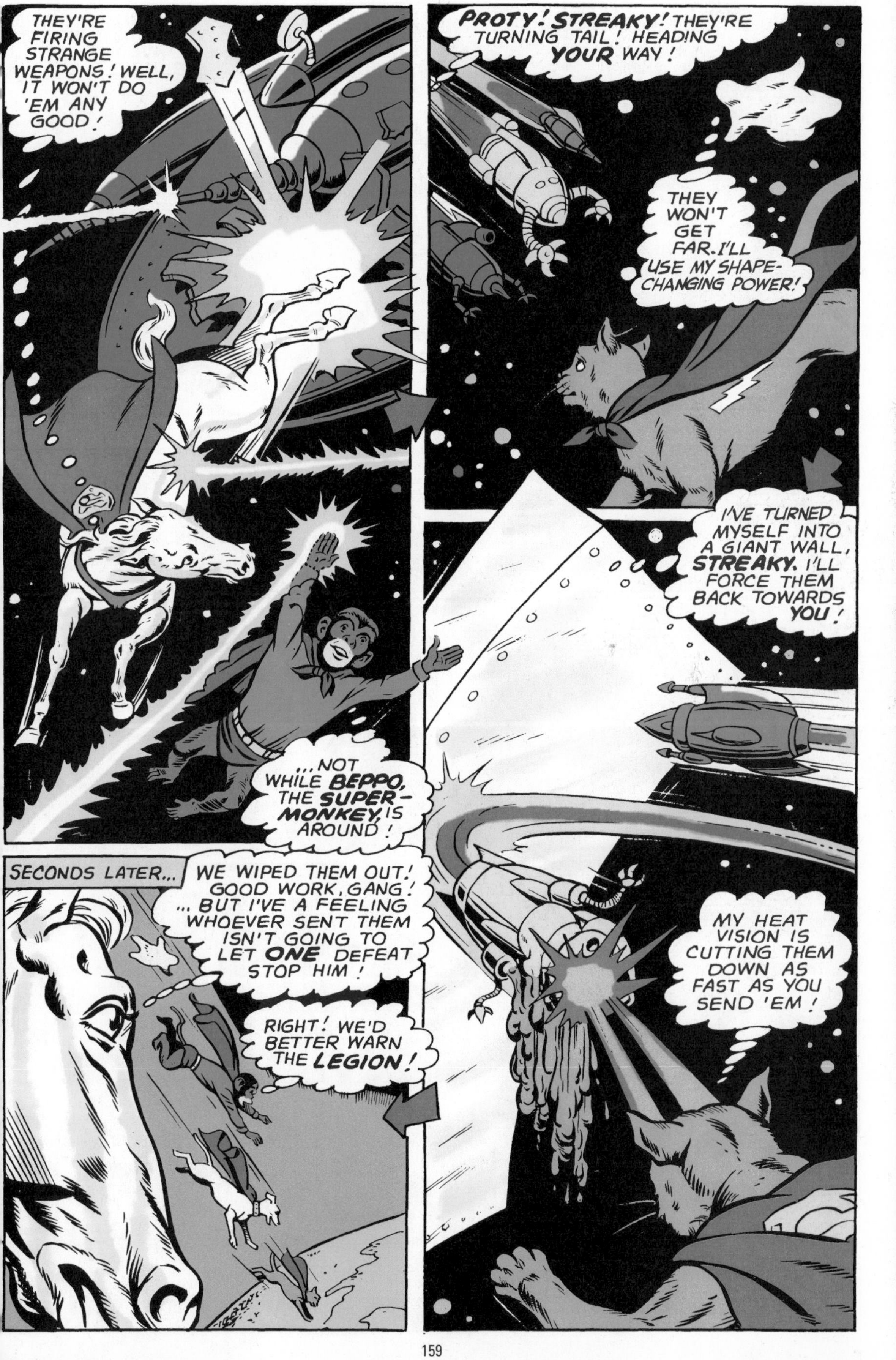
THEY'RE FIRING STRANGE WEAPONS! WELL, IT WON'T DO 'EM ANY GOOD!
...NOT WHILE BEPPO, THE SUPER-MONKEY, IS AROUND!
PROTY! STREAKY! THEY'RE TURNING TAIL! HEADING YOUR WAY!
THEY WON'T GET FAR. I'LL USE MY SHAPE-CHANGING POWER!
I'VE TURNED MYSELF INTO A GIANT WALL, STREAKY. I'LL FORCE THEM BACK TOWARDS YOU!
MY HEAT VISION IS CUTTING THEM DOWN AS FAST AS YOU SEND 'EM!
SECONDS LATER...
WE WIPED THEM OUT! GOOD WORK, GANG! ...BUT I'VE A FEELING WHOEVER SENT THEM ISN'T GOING TO LET ONE DEFEAT STOP HIM!
RIGHT! WE'D BETTER WARN THE LEGION!

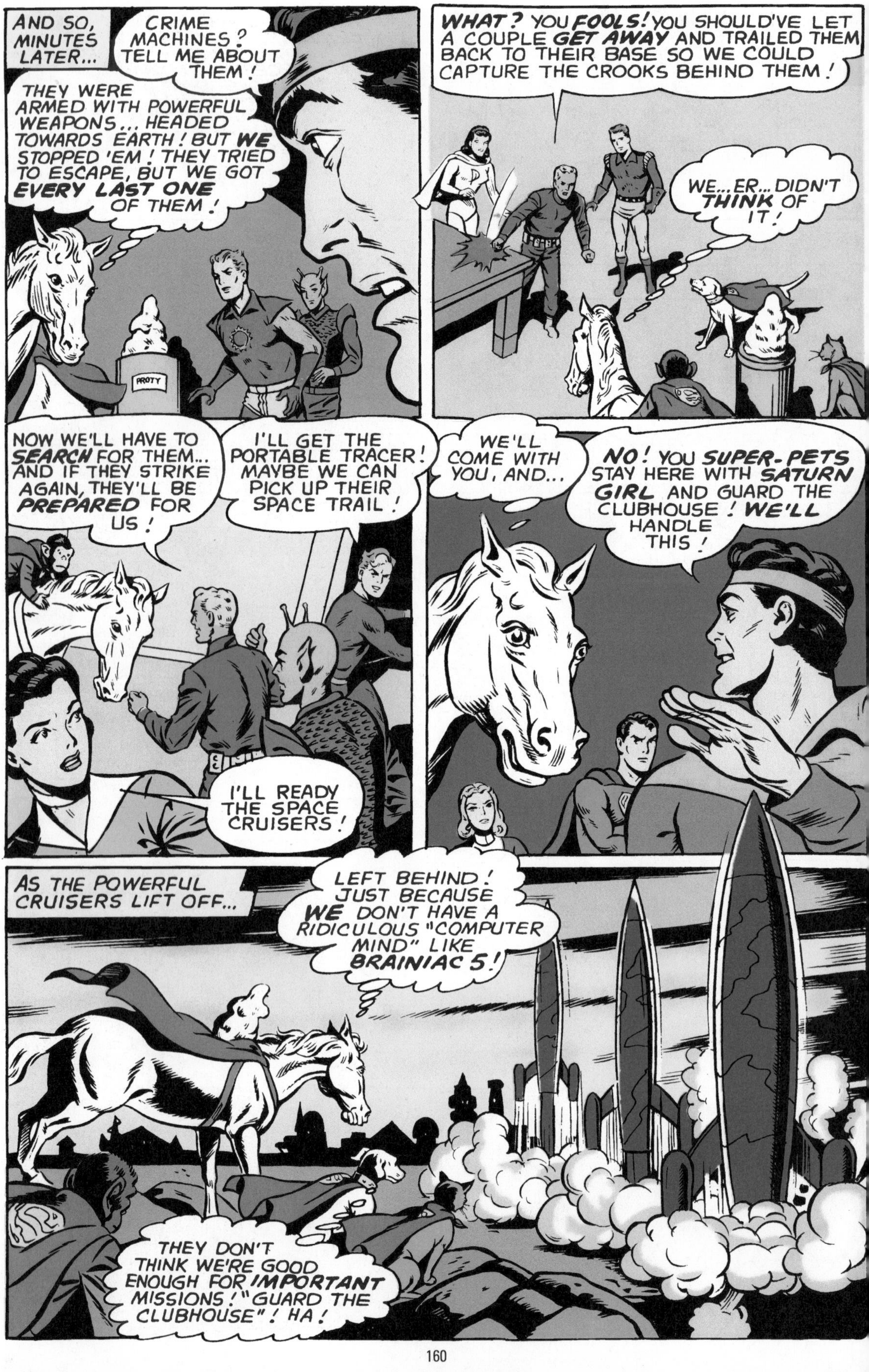
AND SO, MINUTES LATER...
CRIME MACHINES? TELL ME ABOUT THEM!
THEY WERE ARMED WITH POWERFUL WEAPONS... HEADED TOWARDS EARTH! BUT WE STOPPED 'EM! THEY TRIED TO ESCAPE, BUT WE GOT EVERY LAST ONE OF THEM!
PROTY
WHAT? YOU FOOLS! YOU SHOULD'VE LET A COUPLE GET AWAY AND TRAILED THEM BACK TO THEIR BASE SO WE COULD CAPTURE THE CROOKS BEHIND THEM!
WE... ER... DIDN'T THINK OF IT!
NOW WE'LL HAVE TO SEARCH FOR THEM... AND IF THEY STRIKE AGAIN, THEY'LL BE PREPARED FOR US!
I'LL GET THE PORTABLE TRACER! MAYBE WE CAN PICK UP THEIR SPACE TRAIL!
I'LL READY THE SPACE CRUISERS!
WE'LL COME WITH YOU, AND...
NO! YOU SUPER-PETS STAY HERE WITH SATURN GIRL AND GUARD THE CLUBHOUSE! WE'LL HANDLE THIS!
AS THE POWERFUL CRUISERS LIFT OFF...
LEFT BEHIND! JUST BECAUSE WE DON'T HAVE A RIDICULOUS "COMPUTER MIND" LIKE BRAINIAC 5!
THEY DON'T THINK WE'RE GOOD ENOUGH FOR IMPORTANT MISSIONS! "GUARD THE CLUBHOUSE"! HA!

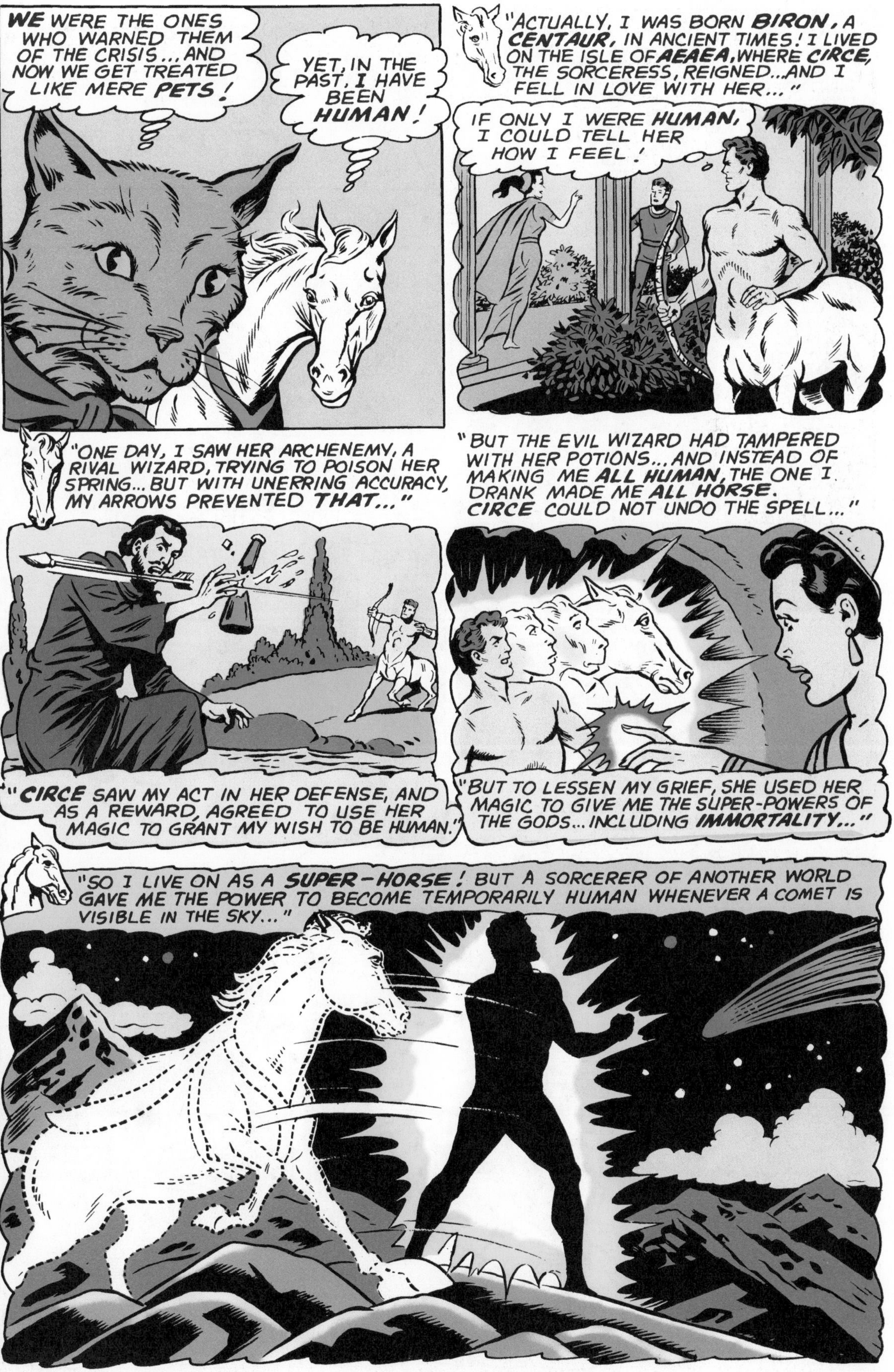
WE WERE THE ONES WHO WARNED THEM OF THE CRISIS... AND NOW WE GET TREATED LIKE MERE PETS!
YET, IN THE PAST, I HAVE BEEN HUMAN!
"ACTUALLY, I WAS BORN BIRON, A CENTAUR, IN ANCIENT TIMES! I LIVED ON THE ISLE OF AEAEA, WHERE CIRCE, THE SORCERESS, REIGNED...AND I FELL IN LOVE WITH HER..."
IF ONLY I WERE HUMAN, I COULD TELL HER HOW I FEEL!
"ONE DAY, I SAW HER ARCHENEMY, A RIVAL WIZARD, TRYING TO POISON HER SPRING... BUT WITH UNERRING ACCURACY, MY ARROWS PREVENTED THAT..."
"CIRCE SAW MY ACT IN HER DEFENSE, AND AS A REWARD, AGREED TO USE HER MAGIC TO GRANT MY WISH TO BE HUMAN."
"BUT THE EVIL WIZARD HAD TAMPERED WITH HER POTIONS... AND INSTEAD OF MAKING ME ALL HUMAN, THE ONE I DRANK MADE ME ALL HORSE. CIRCE COULD NOT UNDO THE SPELL..."
"BUT TO LESSEN MY GRIEF, SHE USED HER MAGIC TO GIVE ME THE SUPER-POWERS OF THE GODS... INCLUDING IMMORTALITY..."
"SO I LIVE ON AS A SUPER-HORSE! BUT A SORCERER OF ANOTHER WORLD GAVE ME THE POWER TO BECOME TEMPORARILY HUMAN WHENEVER A COMET IS VISIBLE IN THE SKY..."

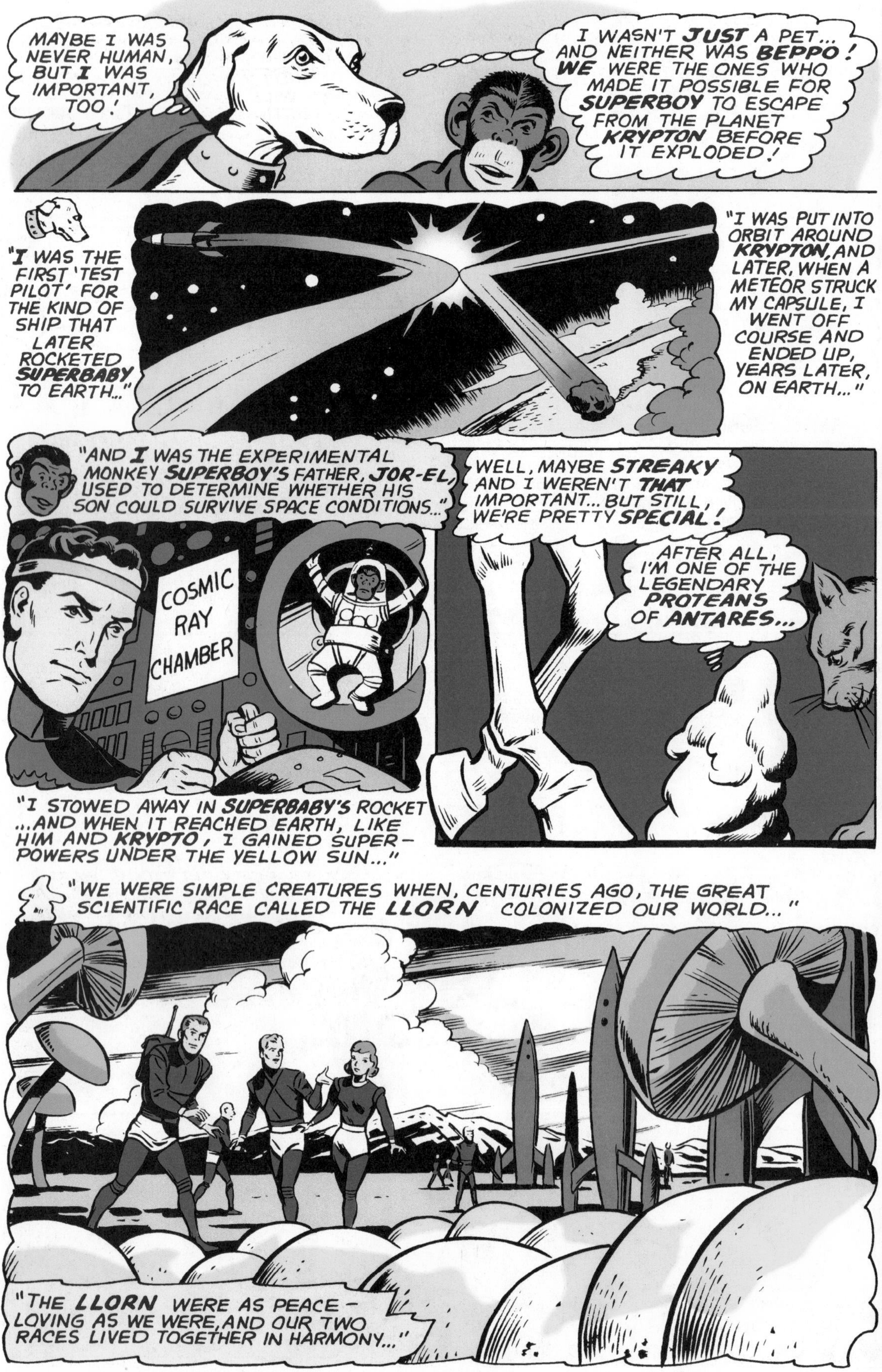
MAYBE I WAS NEVER HUMAN, BUT I WAS IMPORTANT, TOO!
I WASN'T JUST A PET... AND NEITHER WAS BEPPO! WE WERE THE ONES WHO MADE IT POSSIBLE FOR SUPERBOY TO ESCAPE FROM THE PLANET KRYPTON BEFORE IT EXPLODED!
"I WAS THE FIRST 'TEST PILOT' FOR THE KIND OF SHIP THAT LATER ROCKETED SUPERBABY TO EARTH..."
"I WAS PUT INTO ORBIT AROUND KRYPTON, AND LATER, WHEN A METEOR STRUCK MY CAPSULE, I WENT OFF COURSE AND ENDED UP, YEARS LATER, ON EARTH..."
"AND I WAS THE EXPERIMENTAL MONKEY SUPERBOY'S FATHER, JOR-EL, USED TO DETERMINE WHETHER HIS SON COULD SURVIVE SPACE CONDITIONS..."
COSMIC RAY CHAMBER
"I STOWED AWAY IN SUPERBABY'S ROCKET ...AND WHEN IT REACHED EARTH, LIKE HIM AND KRYPTO, I GAINED SUPER-POWERS UNDER THE YELLOW SUN..."
WELL, MAYBE STREAKY AND I WEREN'T THAT IMPORTANT... BUT STILL, WE'RE PRETTY SPECIAL!
AFTER ALL, I'M ONE OF THE LEGENDARY PROTEANS OF ANTARES...
"WE WERE SIMPLE CREATURES WHEN, CENTURIES AGO, THE GREAT SCIENTIFIC RACE CALLED THE LLORN COLONIZED OUR WORLD..."
"THE LLORN WERE AS PEACE-LOVING AS WE WERE, AND OUR TWO RACES LIVED TOGETHER IN HARMONY..."

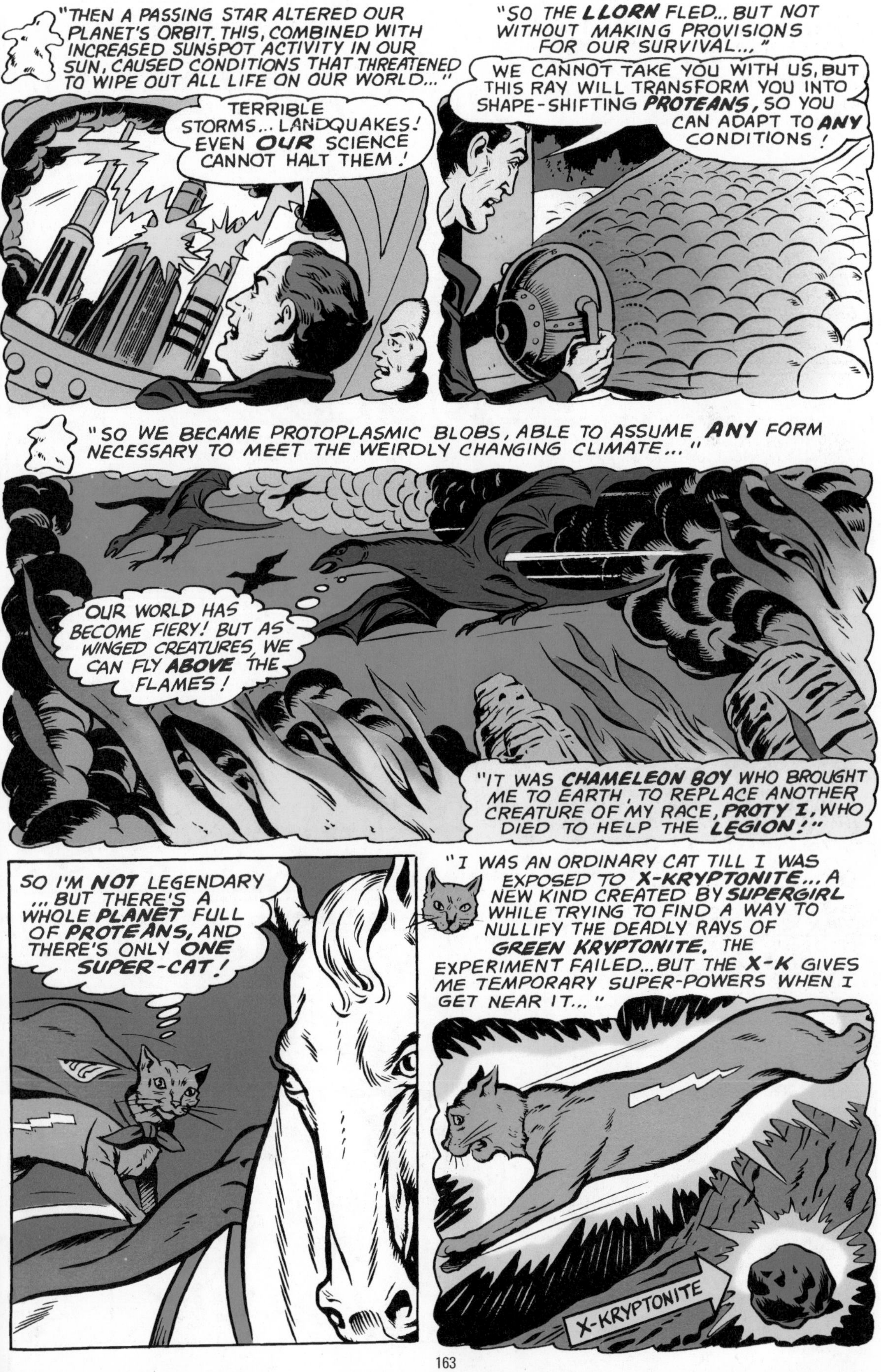
"THEN A PASSING STAR ALTERED OUR PLANET'S ORBIT. THIS, COMBINED WITH INCREASED SUNSPOT ACTIVITY IN OUR SUN, CAUSED CONDITIONS THAT THREATENED TO WIPE OUT ALL LIFE ON OUR WORLD..."
TERRIBLE STORMS... LANDQUAKES! EVEN OUR SCIENCE CANNOT HALT THEM!
"SO THE LLORN FLED... BUT NOT WITHOUT MAKING PROVISIONS FOR OUR SURVIVAL..."
WE CANNOT TAKE YOU WITH US, BUT THIS RAY WILL TRANSFORM YOU INTO SHAPE-SHIFTING PROTEANS, SO YOU CAN ADAPT TO ANY CONDITIONS!
"SO WE BECAME PROTOPLASMIC BLOBS, ABLE TO ASSUME ANY FORM NECESSARY TO MEET THE WEIRDLY CHANGING CLIMATE..."
OUR WORLD HAS BECOME FIERY! BUT AS WINGED CREATURES, WE CAN FLY ABOVE THE FLAMES!
"IT WAS CHAMELEON BOY WHO BROUGHT ME TO EARTH, TO REPLACE ANOTHER CREATURE OF MY RACE, PROTY I, WHO DIED TO HELP THE LEGION!"
SO I'M NOT LEGENDARY ... BUT THERE'S A WHOLE PLANET FULL OF PROTEANS, AND THERE'S ONLY ONE SUPER-CAT!
"I WAS AN ORDINARY CAT TILL I WAS EXPOSED TO X-KRYPTONITE... A NEW KIND CREATED BY SUPERGIRL WHILE TRYING TO FIND A WAY TO NULLIFY THE DEADLY RAYS OF GREEN KRYPTONITE. THE EXPERIMENT FAILED... BUT THE X-K GIVES ME TEMPORARY SUPER-POWERS WHEN I GET NEAR IT..."
X-KRYPTONITE

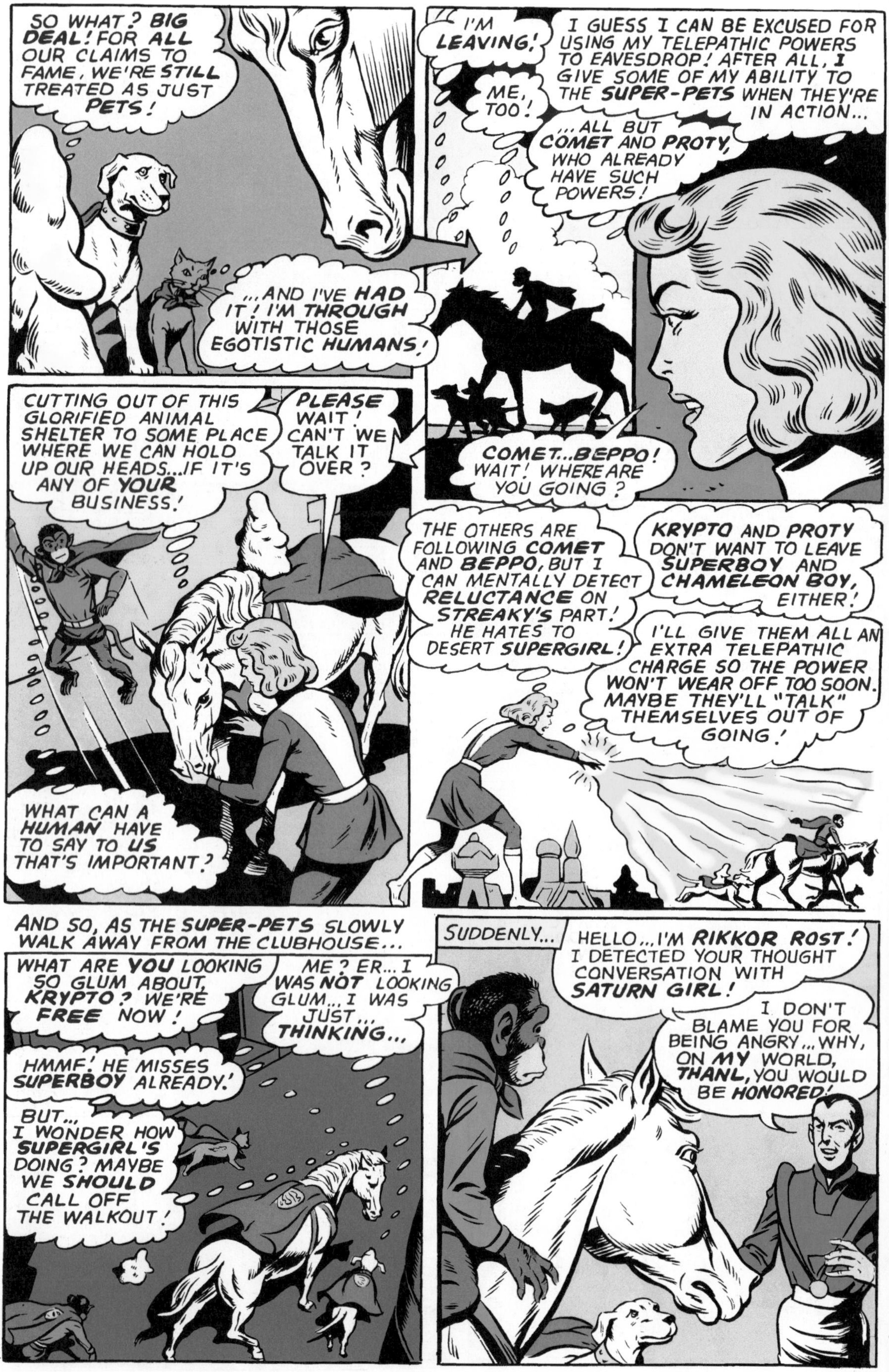
SO WHAT? BIG DEAL! FOR ALL OUR CLAIMS TO FAME, WE'RE STILL TREATED AS JUST PETS!
...AND I'VE HAD IT! I'M THROUGH WITH THOSE EGOTISTIC HUMANS!
I'M LEAVING!
ME, TOO!
I GUESS I CAN BE EXCUSED FOR USING MY TELEPATHIC POWERS TO EAVESDROP! AFTER ALL, I GIVE SOME OF MY ABILITY TO THE SUPER-PETS WHEN THEY'RE IN ACTION...
...ALL BUT COMET AND PROTY, WHO ALREADY HAVE SUCH POWERS!
COMET...BEPPO! WAIT! WHERE ARE YOU GOING?
CUTTING OUT OF THIS GLORIFIED ANIMAL SHELTER TO SOME PLACE WHERE WE CAN HOLD UP OUR HEADS...IF IT'S ANY OF YOUR BUSINESS!
PLEASE WAIT! CAN'T WE TALK IT OVER?
WHAT CAN A HUMAN HAVE TO SAY TO US THAT'S IMPORTANT?
THE OTHERS ARE FOLLOWING COMET AND BEPPO, BUT I CAN MENTALLY DETECT RELUCTANCE ON STREAKY'S PART! HE HATES TO DESERT SUPERGIRL!
KRYPTO AND PROTY DON'T WANT TO LEAVE SUPERBOY AND CHAMELEON BOY, EITHER!
I'LL GIVE THEM ALL AN EXTRA TELEPATHIC CHARGE SO THE POWER WON'T WEAR OFF TOO SOON. MAYBE THEY'LL "TALK" THEMSELVES OUT OF GOING!
AND SO, AS THE SUPER-PETS SLOWLY WALK AWAY FROM THE CLUBHOUSE...
WHAT ARE YOU LOOKING SO GLUM ABOUT, KRYPTO? WE'RE FREE NOW!
ME? ER...I WAS NOT LOOKING GLUM...I WAS JUST... THINKING...
HMMF! HE MISSES SUPERBOY ALREADY!
BUT... I WONDER HOW SUPERGIRL'S DOING? MAYBE WE SHOULD CALL OFF THE WALKOUT!
SUDDENLY...
HELLO...I'M RIKKOR ROST! I DETECTED YOUR THOUGHT CONVERSATION WITH SATURN GIRL!
I DON'T BLAME YOU FOR BEING ANGRY...WHY, ON MY WORLD, THANL, YOU WOULD BE HONORED!

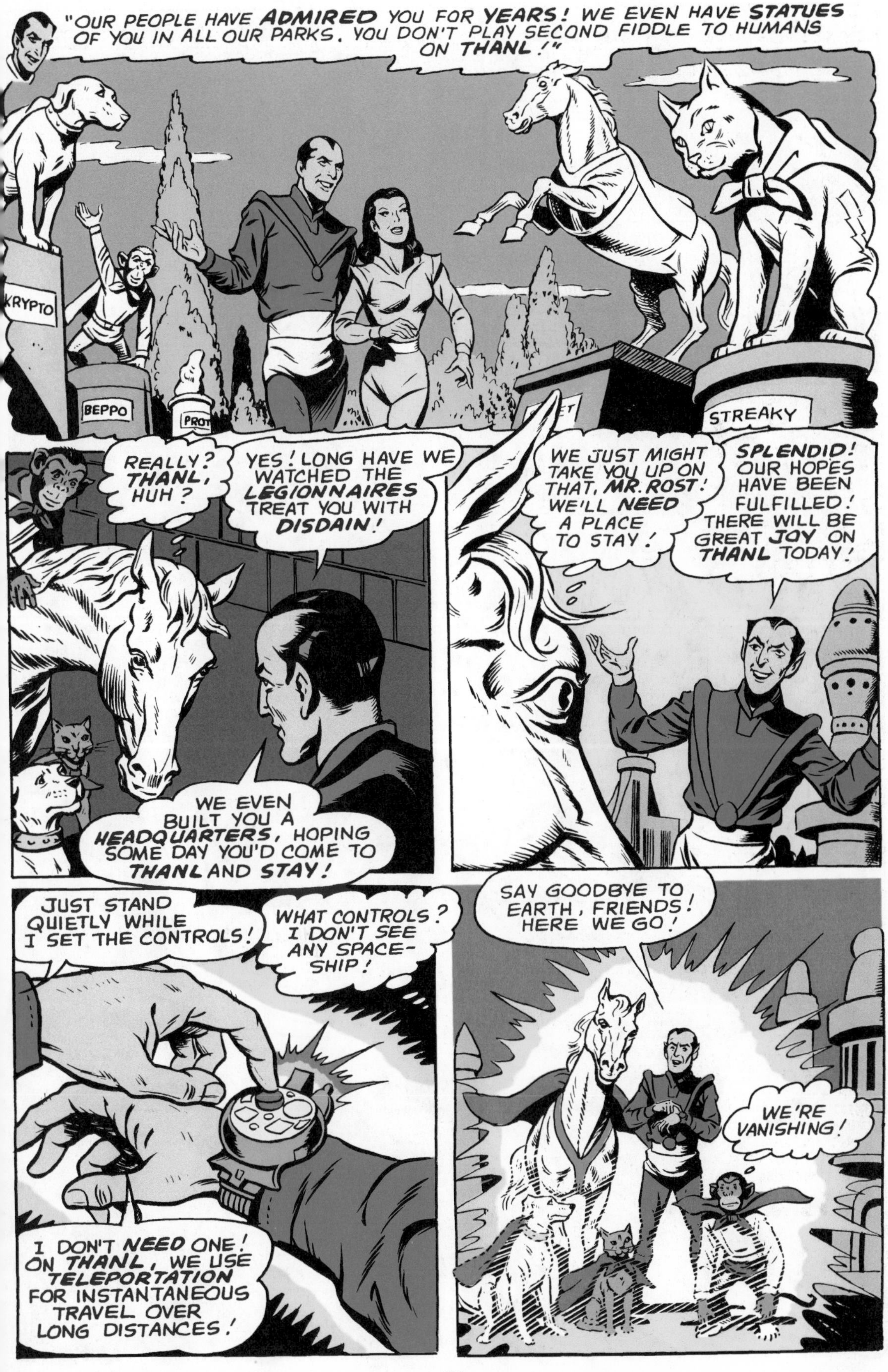

"OUR PEOPLE HAVE ADMIRED YOU FOR YEARS! WE EVEN HAVE STATUES OF YOU IN ALL OUR PARKS. YOU DON'T PLAY SECOND FIDDLE TO HUMANS ON THANL!"
KRYPTO
BEPPO
STREAKY
REALLY? THANL, HUH?
YES! LONG HAVE WE WATCHED THE LEGIONNAIRES TREAT YOU WITH DISDAIN!
WE EVEN BUILT YOU A HEADQUARTERS, HOPING SOME DAY YOU'D COME TO THANL AND STAY!
WE JUST MIGHT TAKE YOU UP ON THAT, MR. ROST! WE'LL NEED A PLACE TO STAY!
SPLENDID! OUR HOPES HAVE BEEN FULFILLED! THERE WILL BE GREAT JOY ON THANL TODAY!
JUST STAND QUIETLY WHILE I SET THE CONTROLS!
WHAT CONTROLS? I DON'T SEE ANY SPACE-SHIP!
I DON'T NEED ONE! ON THANL, WE USE TELEPORTATION FOR INSTANTANEOUS TRAVEL OVER LONG DISTANCES!
SAY GOODBYE TO EARTH, FRIENDS! HERE WE GO!
WE'RE VANISHING!

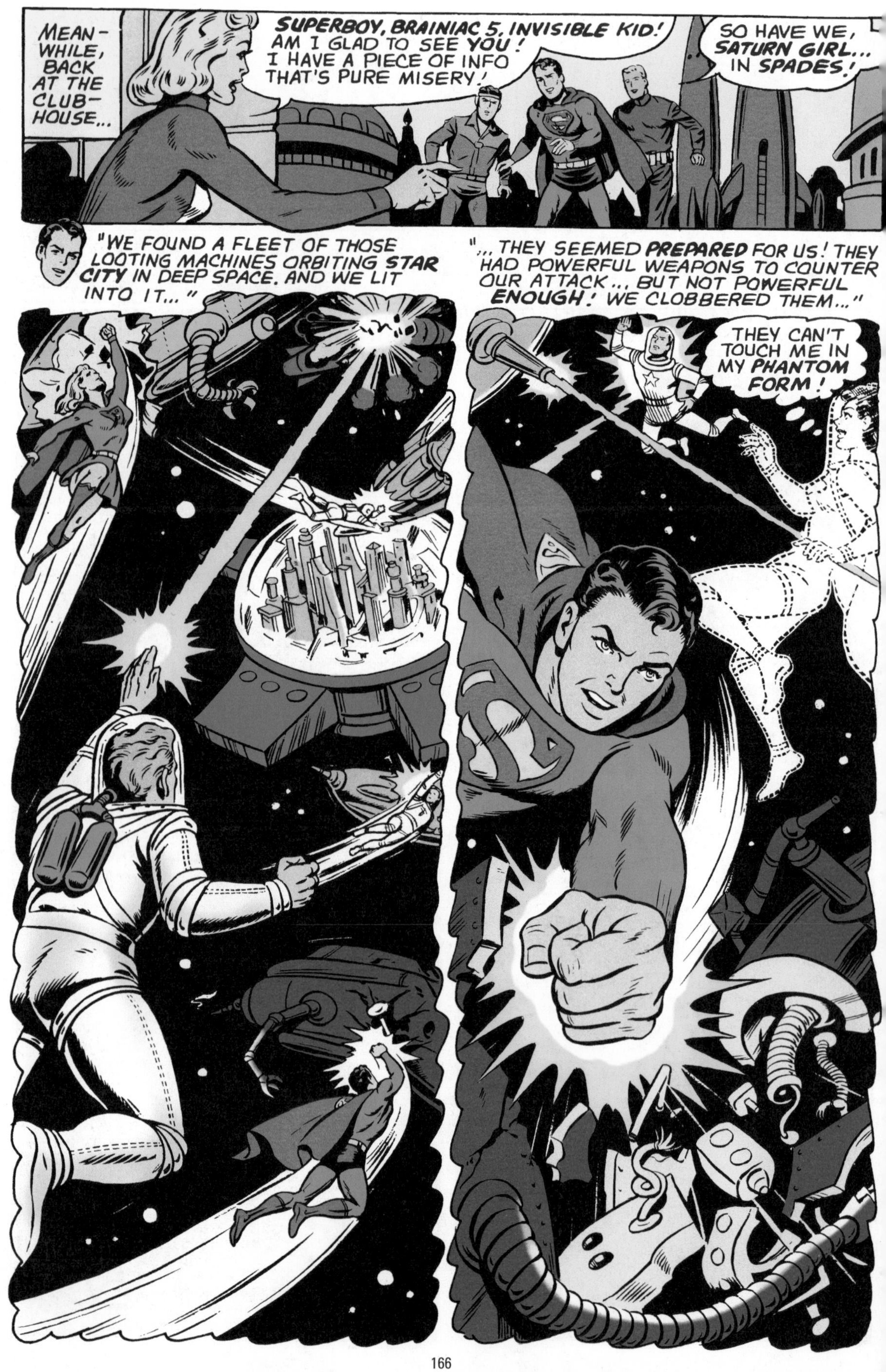

MEAN-WHILE, BACK AT THE CLUB-HOUSE...
SUPERBOY, BRAINIAC 5, INVISIBLE KID! AM I GLAD TO SEE YOU! I HAVE A PIECE OF INFO THAT'S PURE MISERY!
SO HAVE WE, SATURN GIRL... IN SPADES!
"WE FOUND A FLEET OF THOSE LOOTING MACHINES ORBITING STAR CITY IN DEEP SPACE. AND WE LIT INTO IT..."
"... THEY SEEMED PREPARED FOR US! THEY HAD POWERFUL WEAPONS TO COUNTER OUR ATTACK... BUT NOT POWERFUL ENOUGH! WE CLOBBERED THEM..."
THEY CAN'T TOUCH ME IN MY PHANTOM FORM!

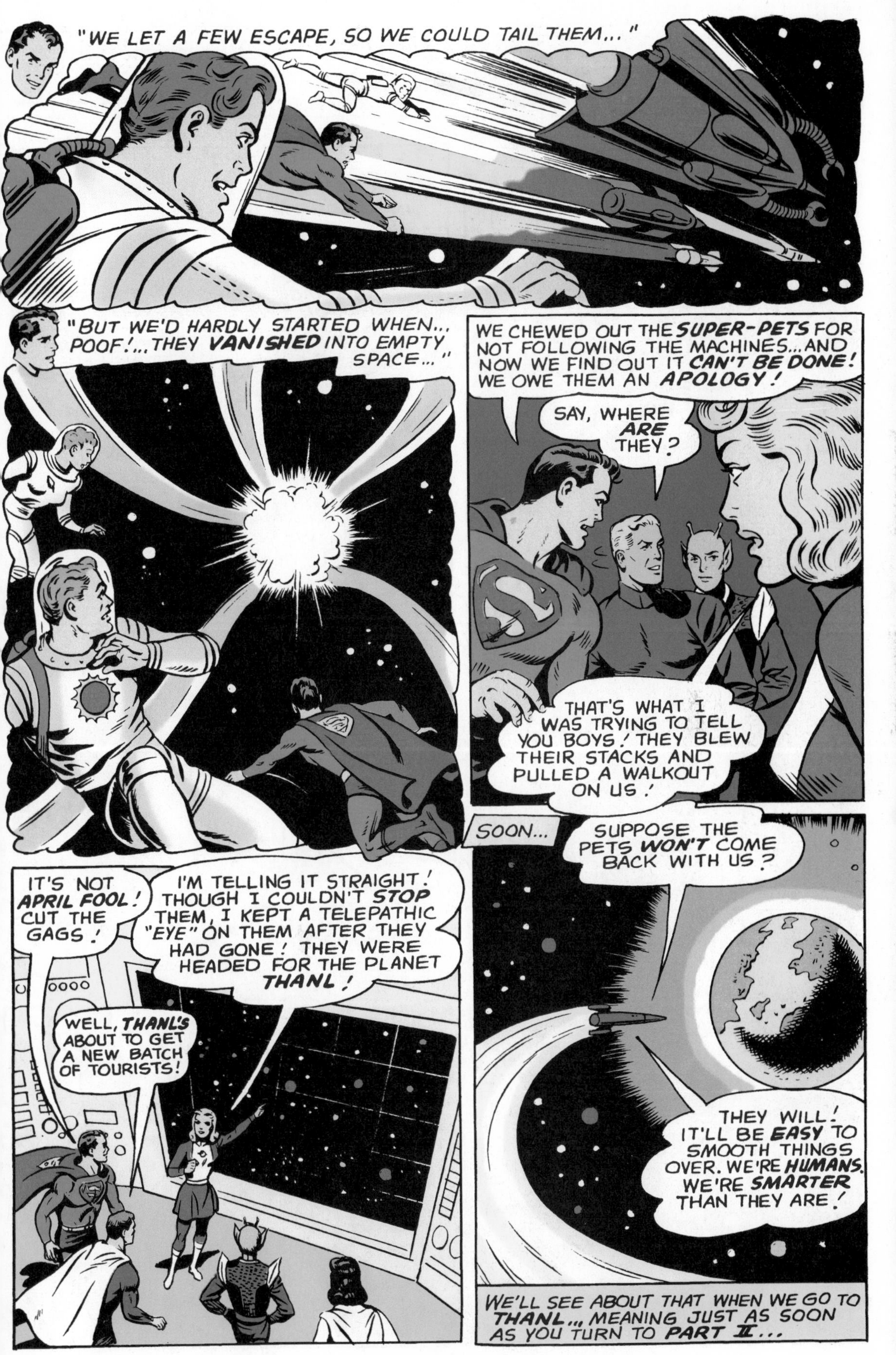
"WE LET A FEW ESCAPE, SO WE COULD TAIL THEM..."
"BUT WE'D HARDLY STARTED WHEN... POOF!...THEY VANISHED INTO EMPTY SPACE..."
WE CHEWED OUT THE SUPER-PETS FOR NOT FOLLOWING THE MACHINES...AND NOW WE FIND OUT IT CAN'T BE DONE! WE OWE THEM AN APOLOGY!
SAY, WHERE ARE THEY?
THAT'S WHAT I WAS TRYING TO TELL YOU BOYS! THEY BLEW THEIR STACKS AND PULLED A WALKOUT ON US!
IT'S NOT APRIL FOOL! CUT THE GAGS!
I'M TELLING IT STRAIGHT! THOUGH I COULDN'T STOP THEM, I KEPT A TELEPATHIC "EYE" ON THEM AFTER THEY HAD GONE! THEY WERE HEADED FOR THE PLANET THANL!
WELL, THANL'S ABOUT TO GET A NEW BATCH OF TOURISTS!
SOON...
SUPPOSE THE PETS WON'T COME BACK WITH US?
THEY WILL! IT'LL BE EASY TO SMOOTH THINGS OVER. WE'RE HUMANS. WE'RE SMARTER THAN THEY ARE!
WE'LL SEE ABOUT THAT WHEN WE GO TO THANL... MEANING JUST AS SOON AS YOU TURN TO PART II...

PART II "FANG, CLAW and HOOF"

WHEN THE GREAT SHIP SETS DOWN ON *THANL*...

SO THIS IS *THANL*! IT LOOKS VERY ADVANCED AND CIVILIZED!

HOW ARE WE GOING TO *FIND* THE *SUPER-PETS*? WE HAVE A WHOLE *WORLD* TO SEARCH!

I DON'T THINK WE'LL HAVE TO DO *MUCH* SEARCHING! LOOK THERE!

AND AS THE *LEGIONNAIRES* APPROACH...

GREAT CYRANUS! IT'S A *CELEBRATION*...IN HONOR OF THE *SUPER-PETS*!

LET'S GO TAKE A CLOSER GANDER!

HEROE'S HEADQUARTERS

THE *SUPER-HEROES* LAND IN THE PARK...

LOOK AT THIS! *STATUES* OF *KRYPTO*, *STREAKY*, AND THE OTHERS...*PLAQUES* COMMEMORATING THEIR ADVENTURES!

A WHOLE PARK FOR THE PETS! WHAT DO THE *THANLIANS* HAVE AGAINST HUMAN HEROES?

SUPER ANIMALS
6LM USPJ112.
SMQPLITE
JRILSI NWII
SMAT CYILS
BBEMISLIE
SOGUIWEA

CHUCK THE CHATTER! LISTEN TO THAT GUY'S SPIEL!

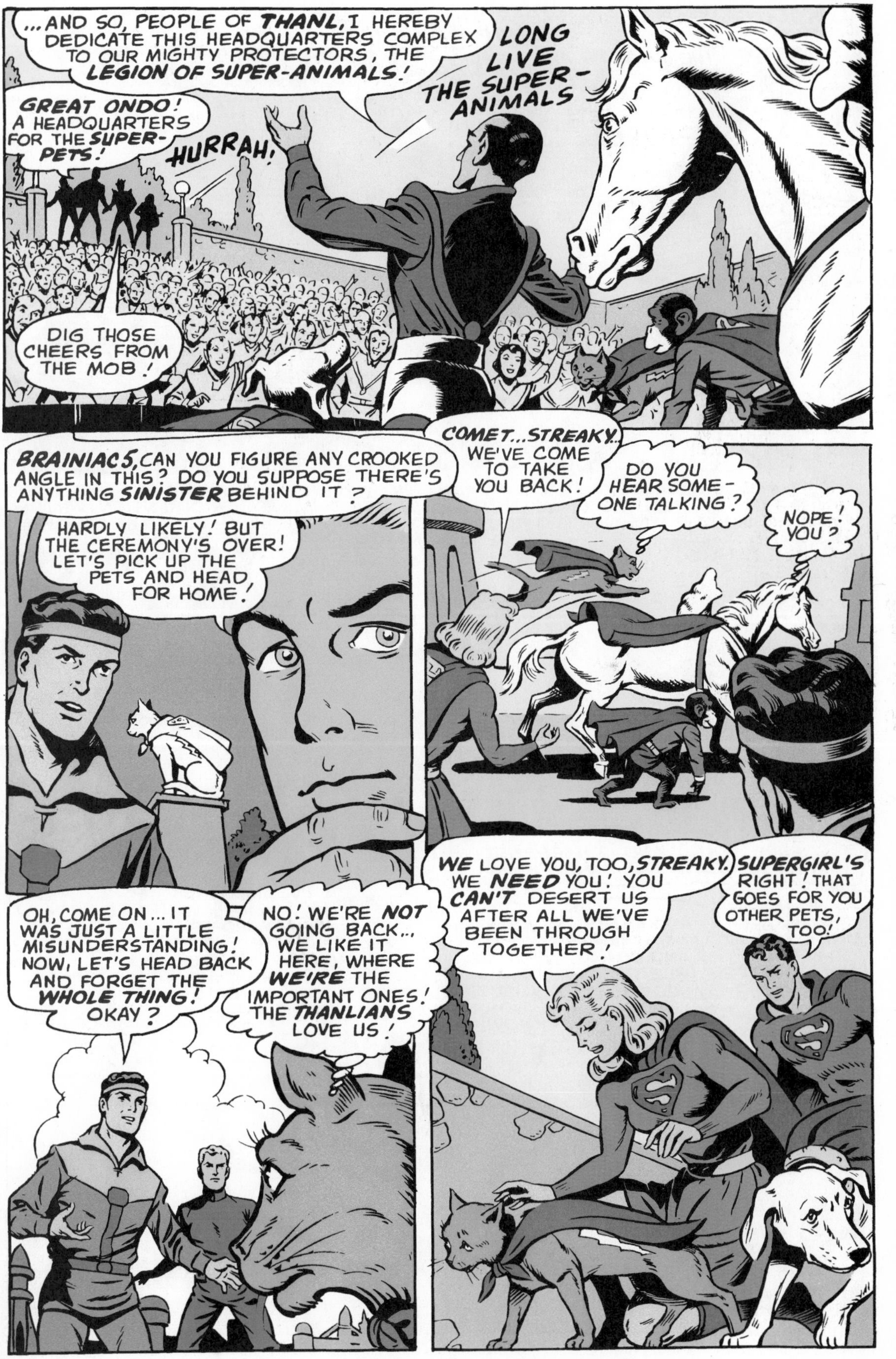
...AND SO, PEOPLE OF THANL, I HEREBY DEDICATE THIS HEADQUARTERS COMPLEX TO OUR MIGHTY PROTECTORS, THE LEGION OF SUPER-ANIMALS!
LONG LIVE THE SUPER-ANIMALS
GREAT ONDO! A HEADQUARTERS FOR THE SUPER-PETS!
HURRAH!
DIG THOSE CHEERS FROM THE MOB!
BRAINIAC 5, CAN YOU FIGURE ANY CROOKED ANGLE IN THIS? DO YOU SUPPOSE THERE'S ANYTHING SINISTER BEHIND IT?
HARDLY LIKELY! BUT THE CEREMONY'S OVER! LET'S PICK UP THE PETS AND HEAD FOR HOME!
COMET...STREAKY... WE'VE COME TO TAKE YOU BACK!
DO YOU HEAR SOME-ONE TALKING?
NOPE! YOU?
OH, COME ON... IT WAS JUST A LITTLE MISUNDERSTANDING! NOW, LET'S HEAD BACK AND FORGET THE WHOLE THING! OKAY?
NO! WE'RE NOT GOING BACK... WE LIKE IT HERE, WHERE WE'RE THE IMPORTANT ONES! THE THANLIANS LOVE US!
WE LOVE YOU, TOO, STREAKY. WE NEED YOU! YOU CAN'T DESERT US AFTER ALL WE'VE BEEN THROUGH TOGETHER!
SUPERGIRL'S RIGHT! THAT GOES FOR YOU OTHER PETS, TOO!

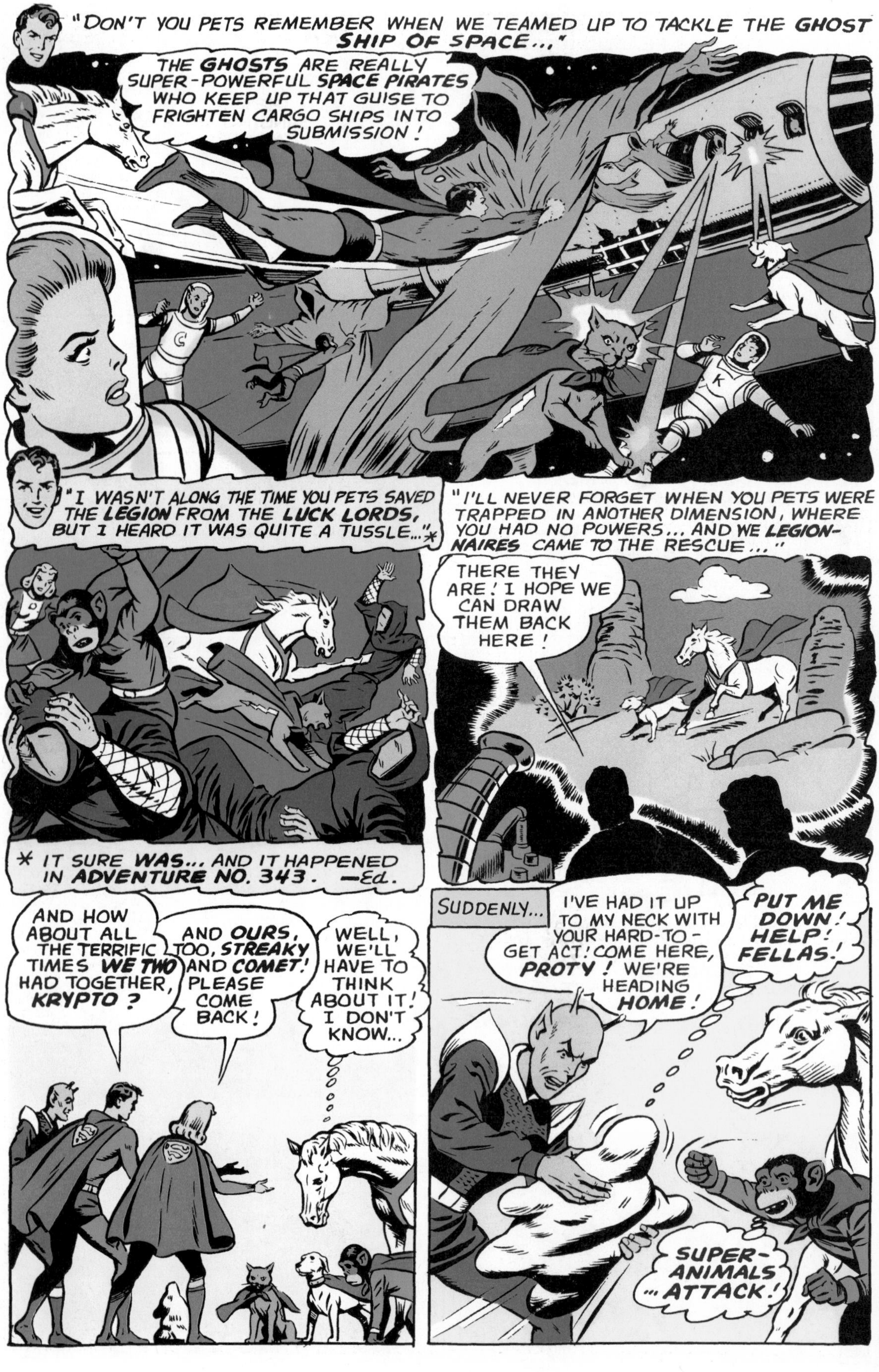
"DON'T YOU PETS REMEMBER WHEN WE TEAMED UP TO TACKLE THE GHOST SHIP OF SPACE..."
THE GHOSTS ARE REALLY SUPER-POWERFUL SPACE PIRATES WHO KEEP UP THAT GUISE TO FRIGHTEN CARGO SHIPS INTO SUBMISSION!
"I WASN'T ALONG THE TIME YOU PETS SAVED THE LEGION FROM THE LUCK LORDS, BUT I HEARD IT WAS QUITE A TUSSLE..."*
* IT SURE WAS... AND IT HAPPENED IN ADVENTURE NO. 343. —Ed.
"I'LL NEVER FORGET WHEN YOU PETS WERE TRAPPED IN ANOTHER DIMENSION, WHERE YOU HAD NO POWERS... AND WE LEGIONNAIRES CAME TO THE RESCUE..."
THERE THEY ARE! I HOPE WE CAN DRAW THEM BACK HERE!
AND HOW ABOUT ALL THE TERRIFIC TIMES WE TWO HAD TOGETHER, KRYPTO?
AND OURS, TOO, STREAKY AND COMET! PLEASE COME BACK!
WELL, WE'LL HAVE TO THINK ABOUT IT! I DON'T KNOW...
SUDDENLY...
I'VE HAD IT UP TO MY NECK WITH YOUR HARD-TO-GET ACT! COME HERE, PROTY! WE'RE HEADING HOME!
PUT ME DOWN! HELP! FELLAS!
SUPER-ANIMALS ...ATTACK!

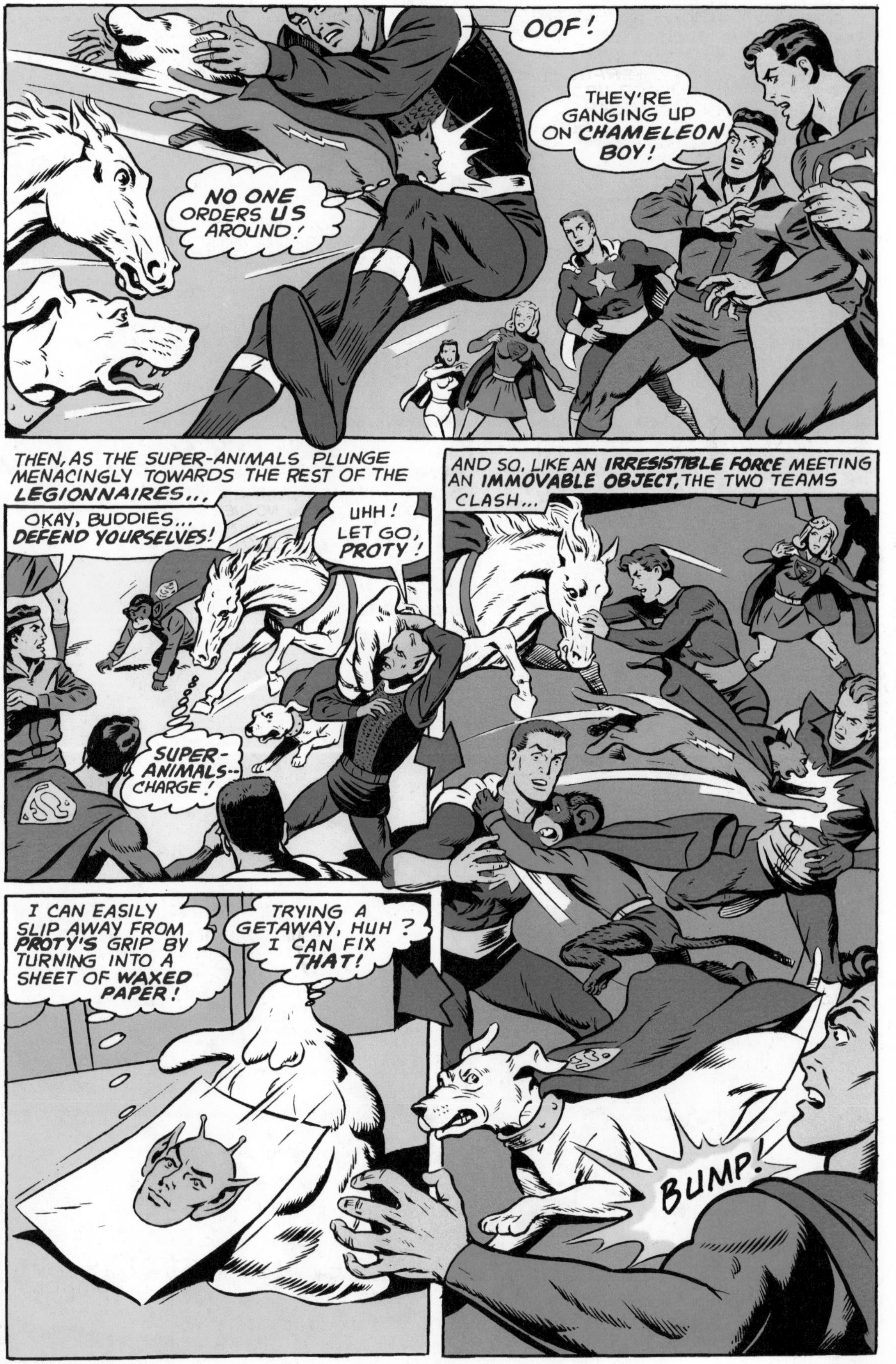

OOF!
THEY'RE GANGING UP ON CHAMELEON BOY!
NO ONE ORDERS US AROUND!
THEN, AS THE SUPER-ANIMALS PLUNGE MENACINGLY TOWARDS THE REST OF THE LEGIONNAIRES...
OKAY, BUDDIES... DEFEND YOURSELVES!
UHH! LET GO, PROTY!
SUPER-ANIMALS-- CHARGE!
AND SO, LIKE AN IRRESISTIBLE FORCE MEETING AN IMMOVABLE OBJECT, THE TWO TEAMS CLASH...
I CAN EASILY SLIP AWAY FROM PROTY'S GRIP BY TURNING INTO A SHEET OF WAXED PAPER!
TRYING A GETAWAY, HUH? I CAN FIX THAT!
BUMP!

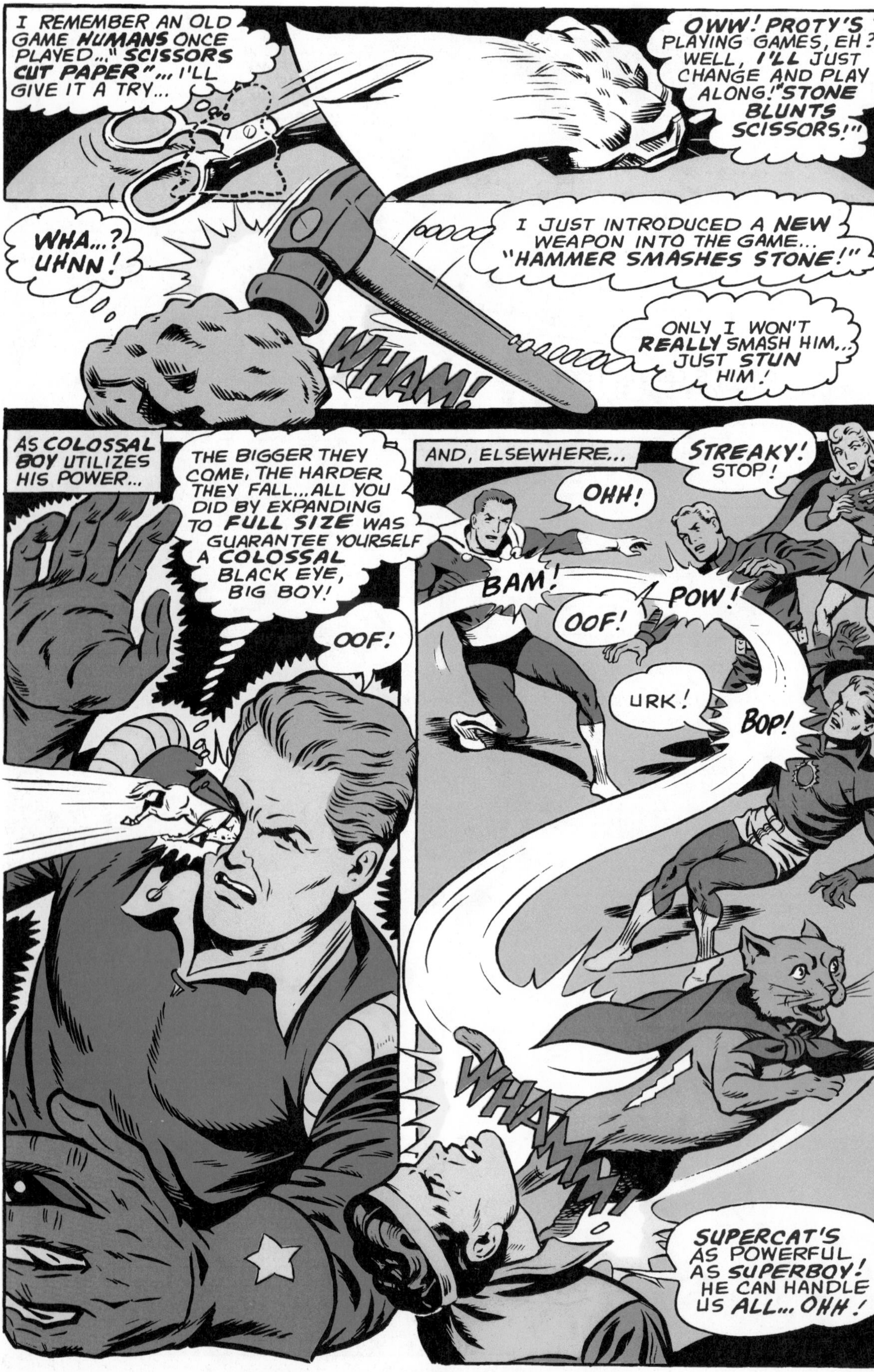
I REMEMBER AN OLD GAME HUMANS ONCE PLAYED..."SCISSORS CUT PAPER"... I'LL GIVE IT A TRY...
OWW! PROTY'S PLAYING GAMES, EH? WELL, I'LL JUST CHANGE AND PLAY ALONG! "STONE BLUNTS SCISSORS!"
WHA...? UHNN!
I JUST INTRODUCED A NEW WEAPON INTO THE GAME... "HAMMER SMASHES STONE!"
ONLY I WON'T REALLY SMASH HIM... JUST STUN HIM!
WHAM!
AS COLOSSAL BOY UTILIZES HIS POWER...
THE BIGGER THEY COME, THE HARDER THEY FALL... ALL YOU DID BY EXPANDING TO FULL SIZE WAS GUARANTEE YOURSELF A COLOSSAL BLACK EYE, BIG BOY!
OOF!
AND, ELSEWHERE...
STREAKY! STOP!
OHH!
BAM!
OOF!
POW!
URK!
BOP!
WHAMM!
SUPERCAT'S AS POWERFUL AS SUPERBOY! HE CAN HANDLE US ALL... OHH!

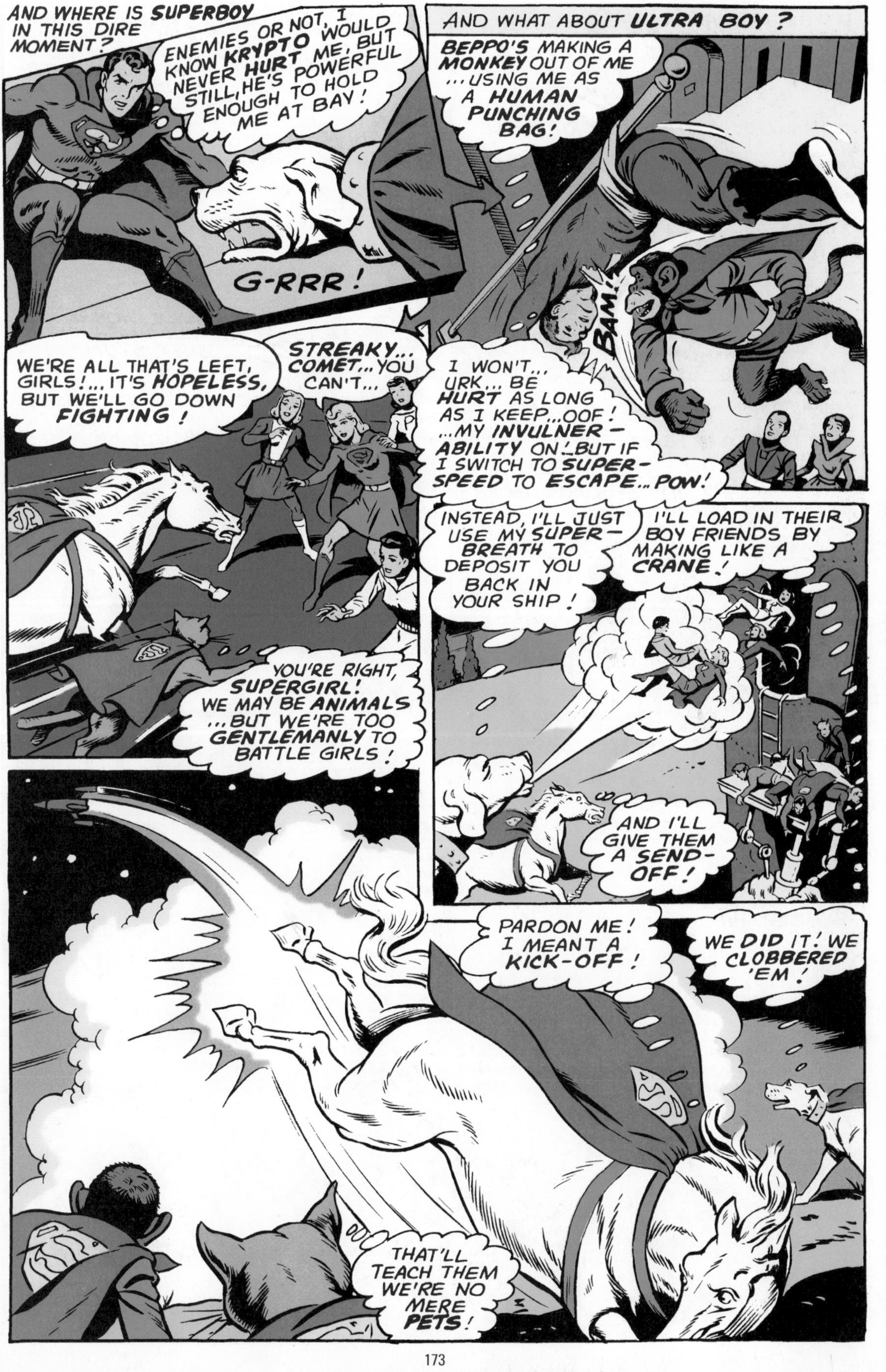
AND WHERE IS SUPERBOY IN THIS DIRE MOMENT?
ENEMIES OR NOT, I KNOW KRYPTO WOULD NEVER HURT ME, BUT STILL, HE'S POWERFUL ENOUGH TO HOLD ME AT BAY!
G-RRR!
AND WHAT ABOUT ULTRA BOY?
BEPPO'S MAKING A MONKEY OUT OF ME ...USING ME AS A HUMAN PUNCHING BAG!
BAM!
I WON'T... URK... BE HURT AS LONG AS I KEEP...OOF! ...MY INVULNER-ABILITY ON!...BUT IF I SWITCH TO SUPER-SPEED TO ESCAPE...POW!
WE'RE ALL THAT'S LEFT, GIRLS!... IT'S HOPELESS, BUT WE'LL GO DOWN FIGHTING!
STREAKY... COMET... YOU CAN'T...
YOU'RE RIGHT, SUPERGIRL! WE MAY BE ANIMALS ...BUT WE'RE TOO GENTLEMANLY TO BATTLE GIRLS!
INSTEAD, I'LL JUST USE MY SUPER-BREATH TO DEPOSIT YOU BACK IN YOUR SHIP!
I'LL LOAD IN THEIR BOY FRIENDS BY MAKING LIKE A CRANE!
AND I'LL GIVE THEM A SEND-OFF!
PARDON ME! I MEANT A KICK-OFF!
WE DID IT! WE CLOBBERED 'EM!
THAT'LL TEACH THEM WE'RE NO MERE PETS!

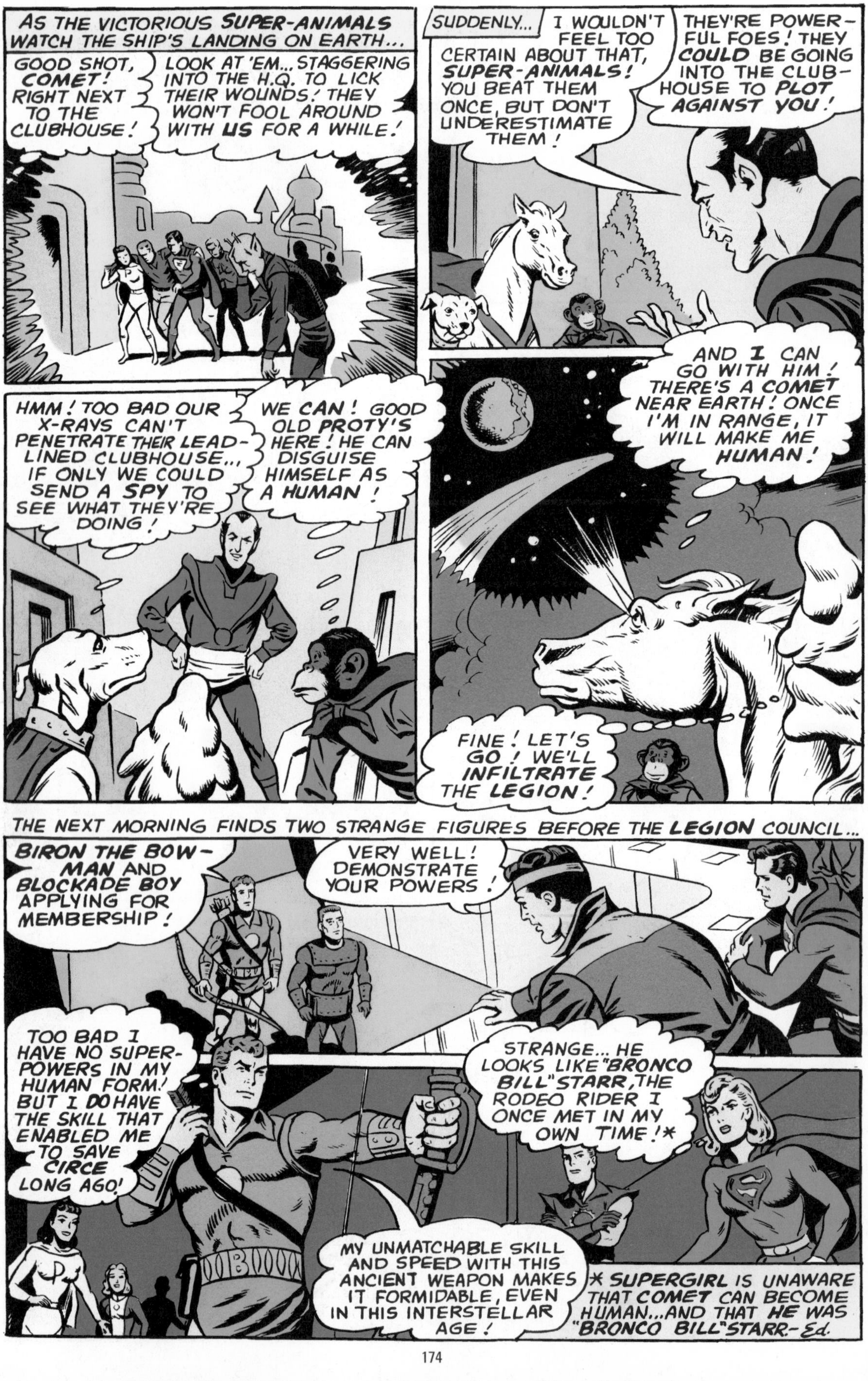

AS THE VICTORIOUS SUPER-ANIMALS WATCH THE SHIP'S LANDING ON EARTH...
GOOD SHOT, COMET! RIGHT NEXT TO THE CLUBHOUSE!
LOOK AT 'EM... STAGGERING INTO THE H.Q. TO LICK THEIR WOUNDS! THEY WON'T FOOL AROUND WITH US FOR A WHILE!
SUDDENLY...
I WOULDN'T FEEL TOO CERTAIN ABOUT THAT, SUPER-ANIMALS! YOU BEAT THEM ONCE, BUT DON'T UNDERESTIMATE THEM!
THEY'RE POWER-FUL FOES! THEY COULD BE GOING INTO THE CLUB-HOUSE TO PLOT AGAINST YOU!
HMM! TOO BAD OUR X-RAYS CAN'T PENETRATE THEIR LEAD-LINED CLUBHOUSE... IF ONLY WE COULD SEND A SPY TO SEE WHAT THEY'RE DOING!
WE CAN! GOOD OLD PROTY'S HERE! HE CAN DISGUISE HIMSELF AS A HUMAN!
AND I CAN GO WITH HIM! THERE'S A COMET NEAR EARTH! ONCE I'M IN RANGE, IT WILL MAKE ME HUMAN!
FINE! LET'S GO! WE'LL INFILTRATE THE LEGION!
THE NEXT MORNING FINDS TWO STRANGE FIGURES BEFORE THE LEGION COUNCIL...
BIRON THE BOW-MAN AND BLOCKADE BOY APPLYING FOR MEMBERSHIP!
VERY WELL! DEMONSTRATE YOUR POWERS!
TOO BAD I HAVE NO SUPER-POWERS IN MY HUMAN FORM! BUT I DO HAVE THE SKILL THAT ENABLED ME TO SAVE CIRCE LONG AGO!
STRANGE... HE LOOKS LIKE "BRONCO BILL" STARR, THE RODEO RIDER I ONCE MET IN MY OWN TIME!*
MY UNMATCHABLE SKILL AND SPEED WITH THIS ANCIENT WEAPON MAKES IT FORMIDABLE, EVEN IN THIS INTERSTELLAR AGE!
* SUPERGIRL IS UNAWARE THAT COMET CAN BECOME HUMAN... AND THAT HE WAS "BRONCO BILL" STARR. - Ed.

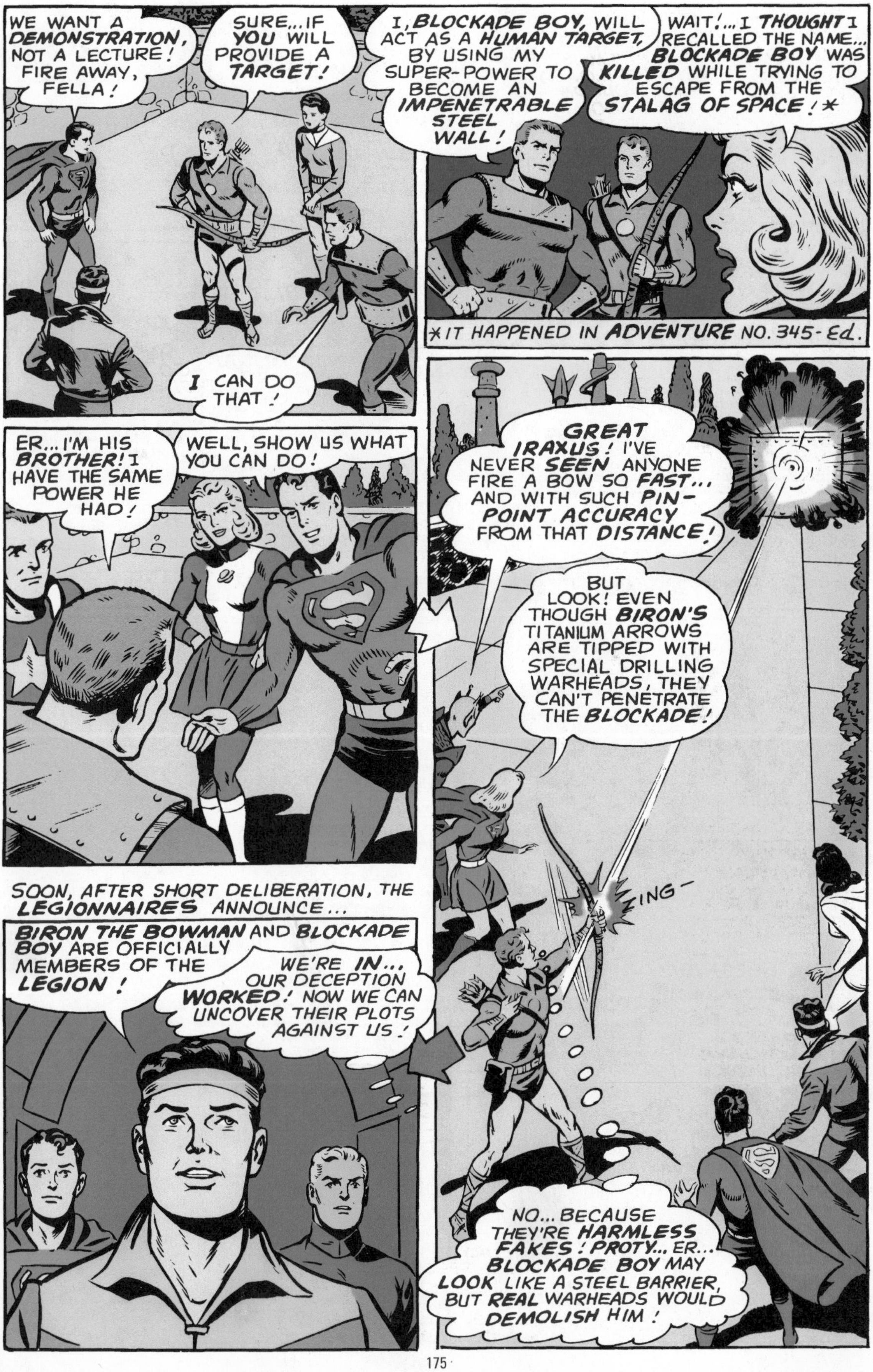

WE WANT A DEMONSTRATION, NOT A LECTURE! FIRE AWAY, FELLA!
SURE...IF YOU WILL PROVIDE A TARGET!
I CAN DO THAT!
I, BLOCKADE BOY, WILL ACT AS A HUMAN TARGET, BY USING MY SUPER-POWER TO BECOME AN IMPENETRABLE STEEL WALL!
WAIT!...I THOUGHT I RECALLED THE NAME... BLOCKADE BOY WAS KILLED WHILE TRYING TO ESCAPE FROM THE STALAG OF SPACE!*
*IT HAPPENED IN ADVENTURE NO. 345-Ed.
ER...I'M HIS BROTHER! I HAVE THE SAME POWER HE HAD!
WELL, SHOW US WHAT YOU CAN DO!
SOON, AFTER SHORT DELIBERATION, THE LEGIONNAIRES ANNOUNCE...
BIRON THE BOWMAN AND BLOCKADE BOY ARE OFFICIALLY MEMBERS OF THE LEGION!
WE'RE IN..., OUR DECEPTION WORKED! NOW WE CAN UNCOVER THEIR PLOTS AGAINST US!
GREAT IRAXUS! I'VE NEVER SEEN ANYONE FIRE A BOW SO FAST... AND WITH SUCH PIN-POINT ACCURACY FROM THAT DISTANCE!
BUT LOOK! EVEN THOUGH BIRON'S TITANIUM ARROWS ARE TIPPED WITH SPECIAL DRILLING WARHEADS, THEY CAN'T PENETRATE THE BLOCKADE!
ZING-
NO... BECAUSE THEY'RE HARMLESS FAKES! PROTY... ER... BLOCKADE BOY MAY LOOK LIKE A STEEL BARRIER, BUT REAL WARHEADS WOULD DEMOLISH HIM!

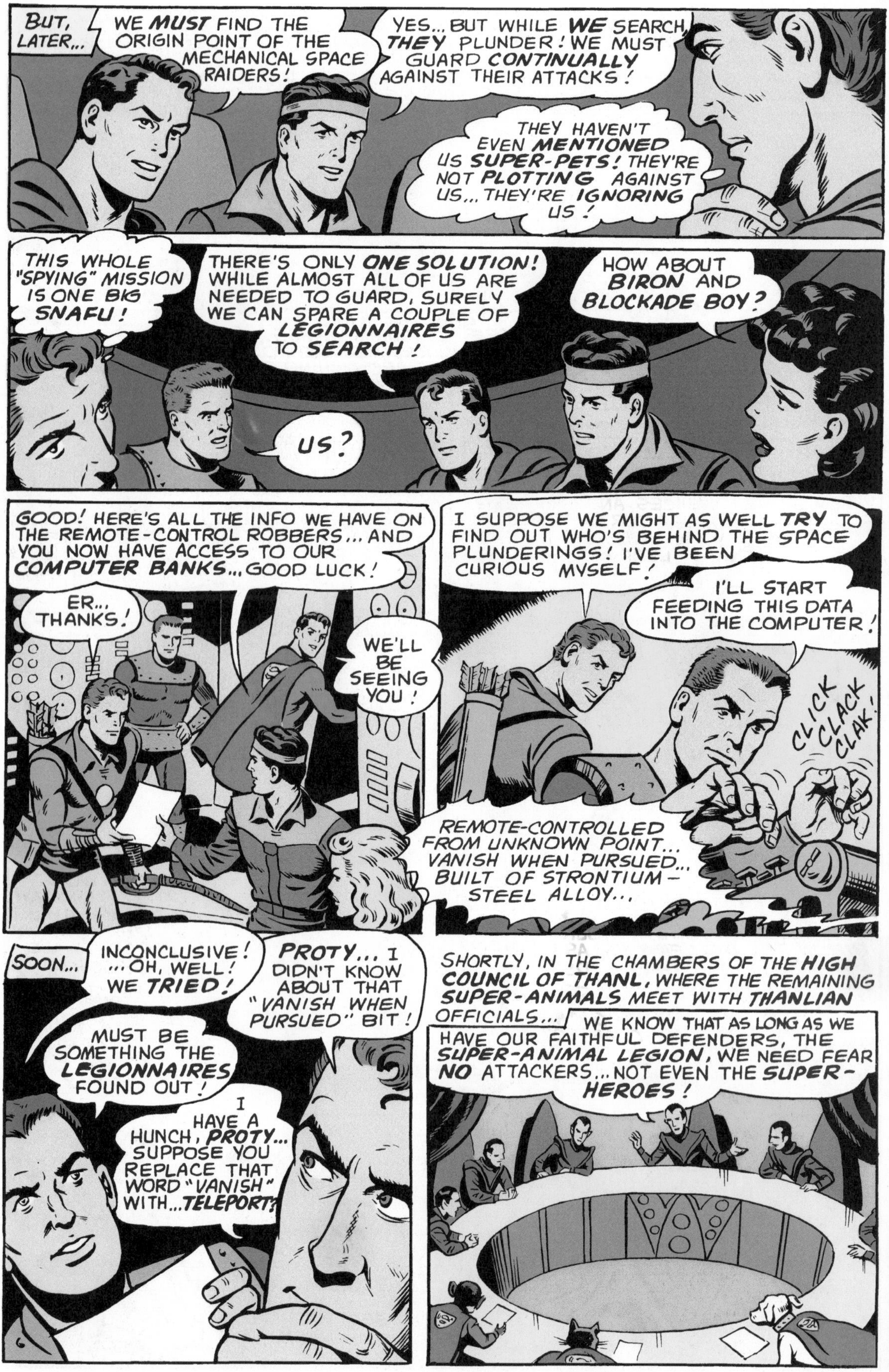
BUT, LATER...
WE MUST FIND THE ORIGIN POINT OF THE MECHANICAL SPACE RAIDERS!
YES... BUT WHILE WE SEARCH, THEY PLUNDER! WE MUST GUARD CONTINUALLY AGAINST THEIR ATTACKS!
THEY HAVEN'T EVEN MENTIONED US SUPER-PETS! THEY'RE NOT PLOTTING AGAINST US... THEY'RE IGNORING US!
THIS WHOLE "SPYING" MISSION IS ONE BIG SNAFU!
THERE'S ONLY ONE SOLUTION! WHILE ALMOST ALL OF US ARE NEEDED TO GUARD, SURELY WE CAN SPARE A COUPLE OF LEGIONNAIRES TO SEARCH!
HOW ABOUT BIRON AND BLOCKADE BOY?
US?
GOOD! HERE'S ALL THE INFO WE HAVE ON THE REMOTE-CONTROL ROBBERS... AND YOU NOW HAVE ACCESS TO OUR COMPUTER BANKS... GOOD LUCK!
ER... THANKS!
WE'LL BE SEEING YOU!
I SUPPOSE WE MIGHT AS WELL TRY TO FIND OUT WHO'S BEHIND THE SPACE PLUNDERINGS! I'VE BEEN CURIOUS MYSELF!
I'LL START FEEDING THIS DATA INTO THE COMPUTER!
CLICK CLACK CLAK!
REMOTE-CONTROLLED FROM UNKNOWN POINT... VANISH WHEN PURSUED... BUILT OF STRONTIUM-STEEL ALLOY...
SOON...
INCONCLUSIVE! ...OH, WELL! WE TRIED!
PROTY... I DIDN'T KNOW ABOUT THAT "VANISH WHEN PURSUED" BIT!
MUST BE SOMETHING THE LEGIONNAIRES FOUND OUT!
I HAVE A HUNCH, PROTY... SUPPOSE YOU REPLACE THAT WORD "VANISH" WITH... TELEPORT?
SHORTLY, IN THE CHAMBERS OF THE HIGH COUNCIL OF THANL, WHERE THE REMAINING SUPER-ANIMALS MEET WITH THANLIAN OFFICIALS...
WE KNOW THAT AS LONG AS WE HAVE OUR FAITHFUL DEFENDERS, THE SUPER-ANIMAL LEGION, WE NEED FEAR NO ATTACKERS... NOT EVEN THE SUPER-HEROES!

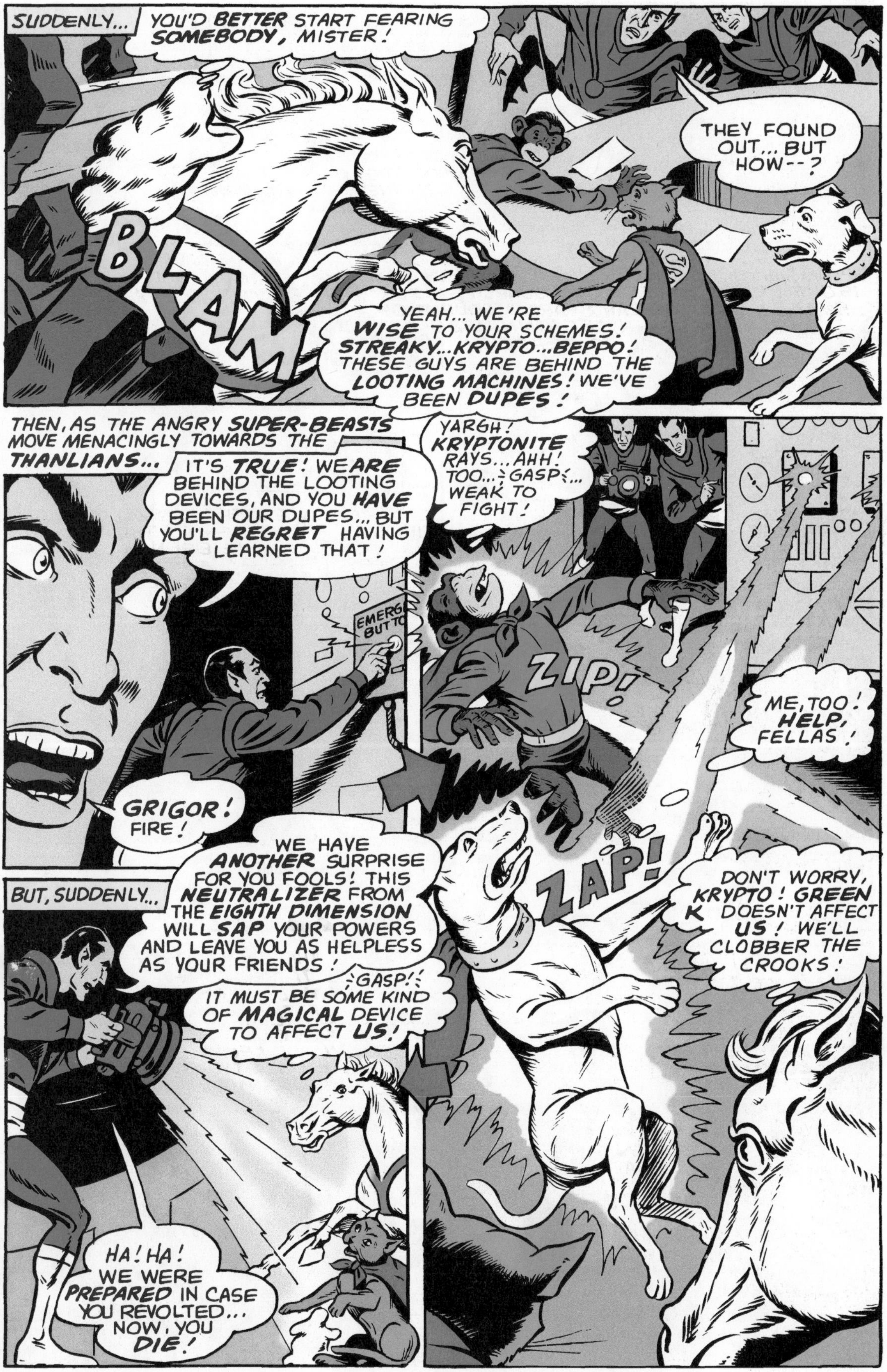
SUDDENLY...
YOU'D BETTER START FEARING SOMEBODY, MISTER!
THEY FOUND OUT... BUT HOW--?
BLAM
YEAH... WE'RE WISE TO YOUR SCHEMES! STREAKY...KRYPTO...BEPPO! THESE GUYS ARE BEHIND THE LOOTING MACHINES! WE'VE BEEN DUPES!
THEN, AS THE ANGRY SUPER-BEASTS MOVE MENACINGLY TOWARDS THE THANLIANS...
IT'S TRUE! WE ARE BEHIND THE LOOTING DEVICES, AND YOU HAVE BEEN OUR DUPES... BUT YOU'LL REGRET HAVING LEARNED THAT!
GRIGOR! FIRE!
YARGH! KRYPTONITE RAYS... AHH! TOO... GASP... WEAK TO FIGHT!
ZIP!
ME, TOO! HELP, FELLAS!
ZAP!
BUT, SUDDENLY...
WE HAVE ANOTHER SURPRISE FOR YOU FOOLS! THIS NEUTRALIZER FROM THE EIGHTH DIMENSION WILL SAP YOUR POWERS AND LEAVE YOU AS HELPLESS AS YOUR FRIENDS!
GASP! IT MUST BE SOME KIND OF MAGICAL DEVICE TO AFFECT US!
DON'T WORRY, KRYPTO! GREEN K DOESN'T AFFECT US! WE'LL CLOBBER THE CROOKS!
HA! HA! WE WERE PREPARED IN CASE YOU REVOLTED... NOW, YOU DIE!

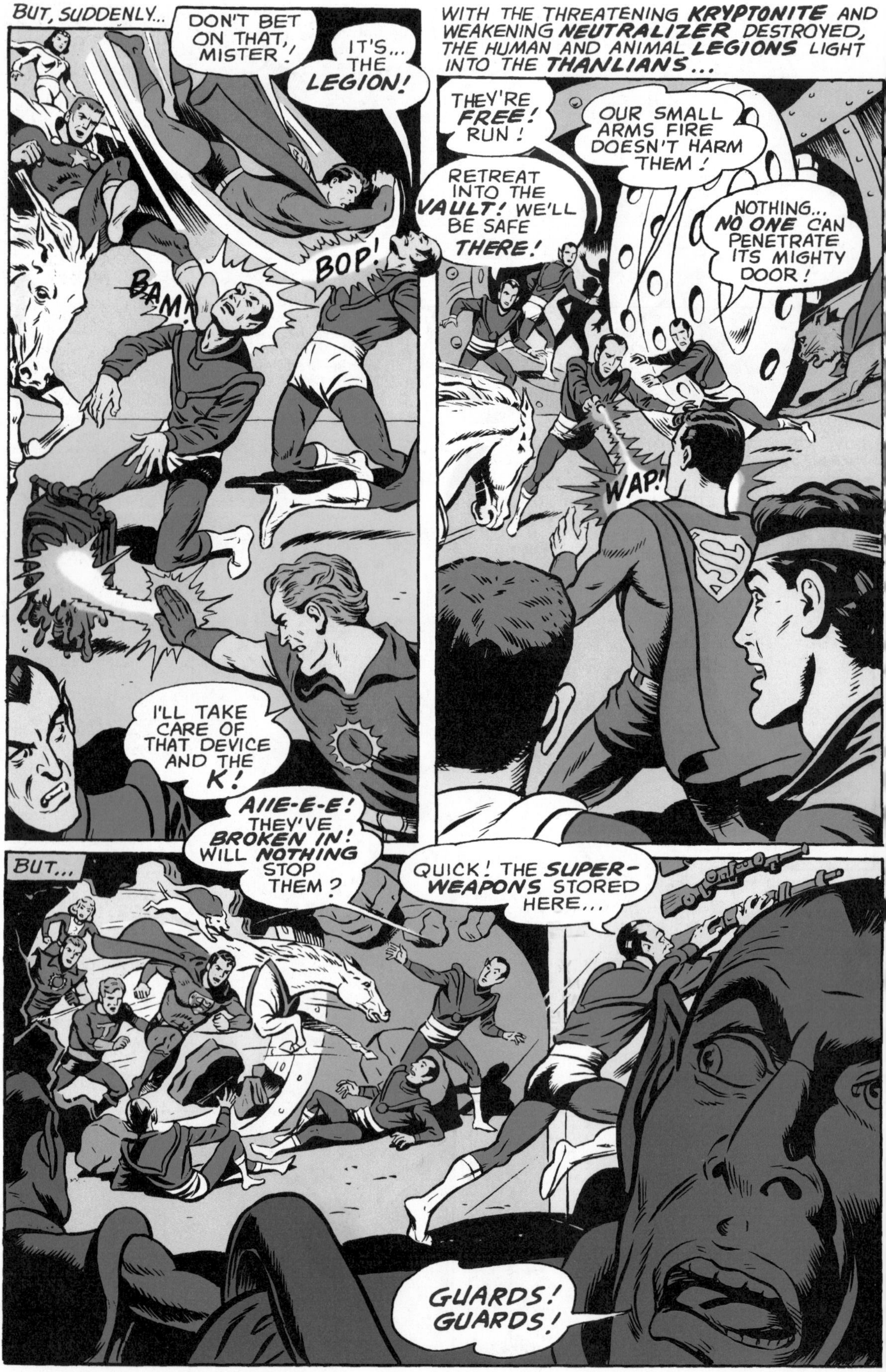

BUT, SUDDENLY...
DON'T BET ON THAT, MISTER!
IT'S... THE LEGION!
BOP!
BAM!
I'LL TAKE CARE OF THAT DEVICE AND THE K!
WITH THE THREATENING KRYPTONITE AND WEAKENING NEUTRALIZER DESTROYED, THE HUMAN AND ANIMAL LEGIONS LIGHT INTO THE THANLIANS...
THEY'RE FREE! RUN!
OUR SMALL ARMS FIRE DOESN'T HARM THEM!
RETREAT INTO THE VAULT! WE'LL BE SAFE THERE!
NOTHING... NO ONE CAN PENETRATE ITS MIGHTY DOOR!
WAP!
BUT...
AIIE-E-E! THEY'VE BROKEN IN! WILL NOTHING STOP THEM?
QUICK! THE SUPER-WEAPONS STORED HERE...
GUARDS! GUARDS!

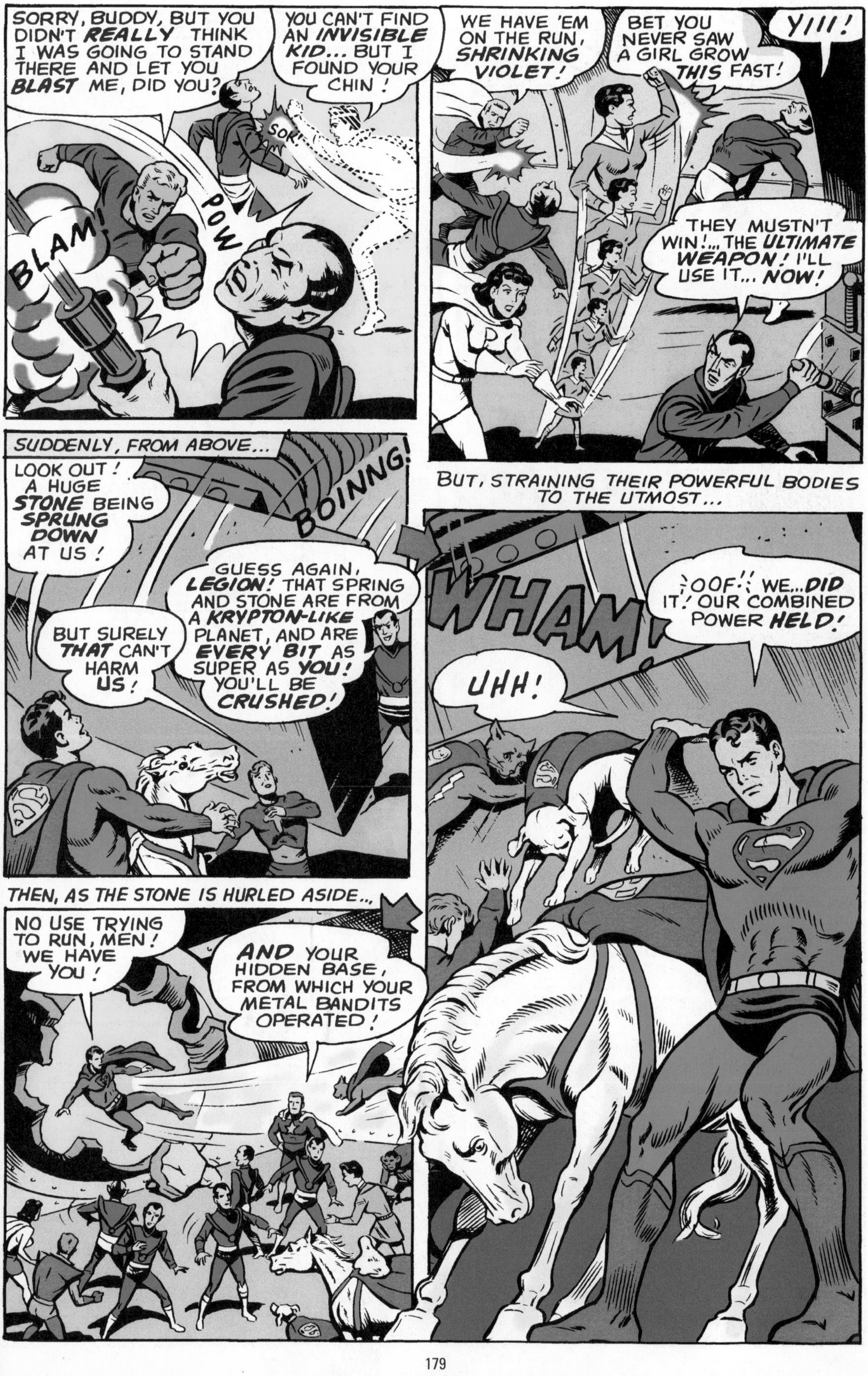
SORRY, BUDDY, BUT YOU DIDN'T REALLY THINK I WAS GOING TO STAND THERE AND LET YOU BLAST ME, DID YOU?
BLAM!
POW
YOU CAN'T FIND AN INVISIBLE KID... BUT I FOUND YOUR CHIN!
SOK!
WE HAVE 'EM ON THE RUN, SHRINKING VIOLET!
BET YOU NEVER SAW A GIRL GROW THIS FAST!
YIII!
THEY MUSTN'T WIN!... THE ULTIMATE WEAPON! I'LL USE IT... NOW!
SUDDENLY, FROM ABOVE...
LOOK OUT! A HUGE STONE BEING SPRUNG DOWN AT US!
BOINNG!
BUT SURELY THAT CAN'T HARM US!
GUESS AGAIN, LEGION! THAT SPRING AND STONE ARE FROM A KRYPTON-LIKE PLANET, AND ARE EVERY BIT AS SUPER AS YOU! YOU'LL BE CRUSHED!
BUT, STRAINING THEIR POWERFUL BODIES TO THE UTMOST...
WHAM!
OOF! WE... DID IT! OUR COMBINED POWER HELD!
UHH!
THEN, AS THE STONE IS HURLED ASIDE...
NO USE TRYING TO RUN, MEN! WE HAVE YOU!
AND YOUR HIDDEN BASE, FROM WHICH YOUR METAL BANDITS OPERATED!

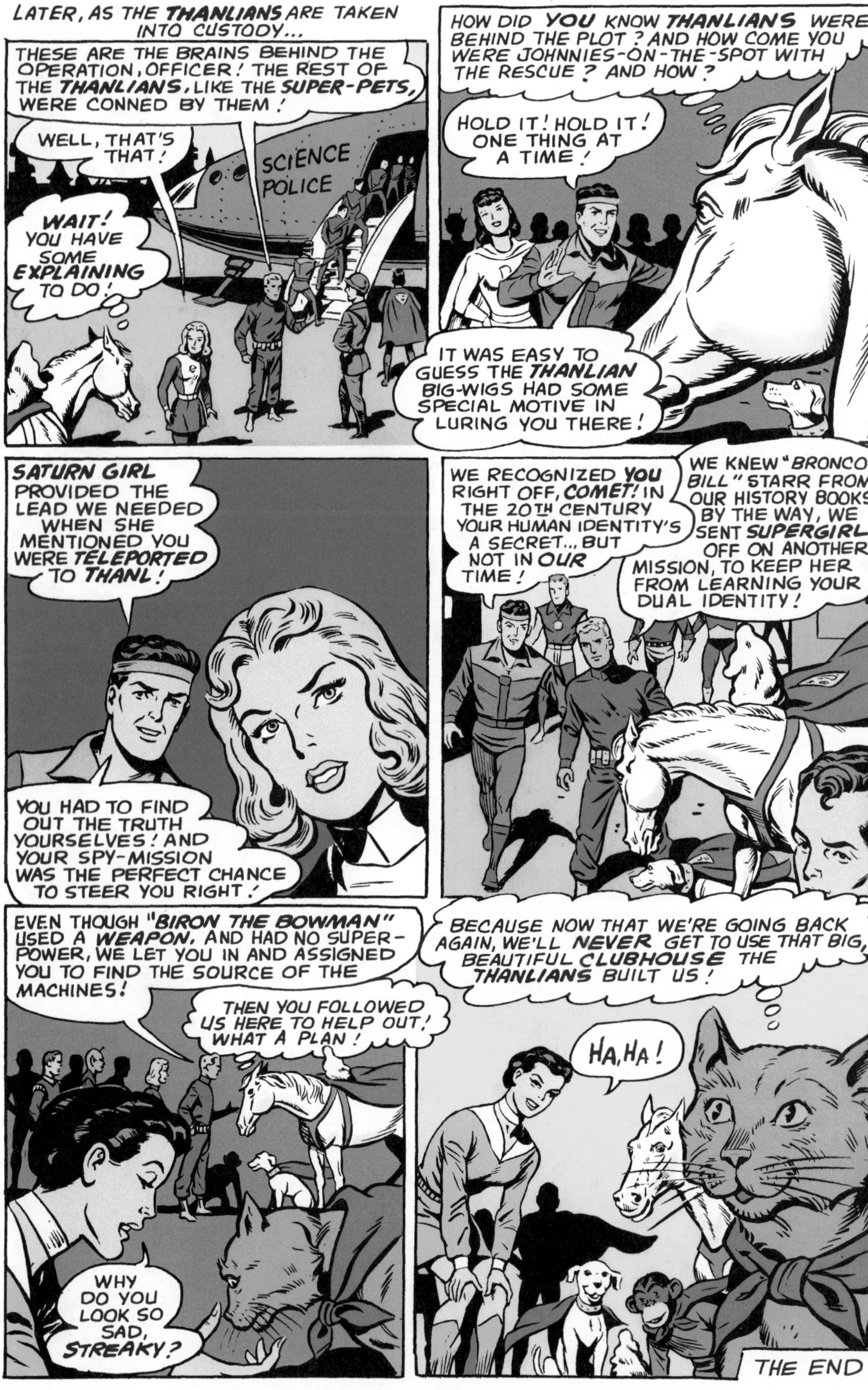
LATER, AS THE THANLIANS ARE TAKEN INTO CUSTODY...
THESE ARE THE BRAINS BEHIND THE OPERATION, OFFICER! THE REST OF THE THANLIANS, LIKE THE SUPER-PETS, WERE CONNED BY THEM!
WELL, THAT'S THAT!
SCIENCE POLICE
WAIT! YOU HAVE SOME EXPLAINING TO DO!
HOW DID YOU KNOW THANLIANS WERE BEHIND THE PLOT? AND HOW COME YOU WERE JOHNNIES-ON-THE-SPOT WITH THE RESCUE? AND HOW?
HOLD IT! HOLD IT! ONE THING AT A TIME!
IT WAS EASY TO GUESS THE THANLIAN BIG-WIGS HAD SOME SPECIAL MOTIVE IN LURING YOU THERE!
SATURN GIRL PROVIDED THE LEAD WE NEEDED WHEN SHE MENTIONED YOU WERE TELEPORTED TO THANL!
YOU HAD TO FIND OUT THE TRUTH YOURSELVES! AND YOUR SPY-MISSION WAS THE PERFECT CHANCE TO STEER YOU RIGHT!
WE RECOGNIZED YOU RIGHT OFF, COMET! IN THE 20TH CENTURY YOUR HUMAN IDENTITY'S A SECRET... BUT NOT IN OUR TIME!
WE KNEW "BRONCO BILL" STARR FROM OUR HISTORY BOOKS! BY THE WAY, WE SENT SUPERGIRL OFF ON ANOTHER MISSION, TO KEEP HER FROM LEARNING YOUR DUAL IDENTITY!
EVEN THOUGH "BIRON THE BOWMAN" USED A WEAPON, AND HAD NO SUPER-POWER, WE LET YOU IN AND ASSIGNED YOU TO FIND THE SOURCE OF THE MACHINES!
THEN YOU FOLLOWED US HERE TO HELP OUT! WHAT A PLAN!
WHY DO YOU LOOK SO SAD, STREAKY?
BECAUSE NOW THAT WE'RE GOING BACK AGAIN, WE'LL NEVER GET TO USE THAT BIG, BEAUTIFUL CLUBHOUSE THE THANLIANS BUILT US!
HA, HA!
THE END

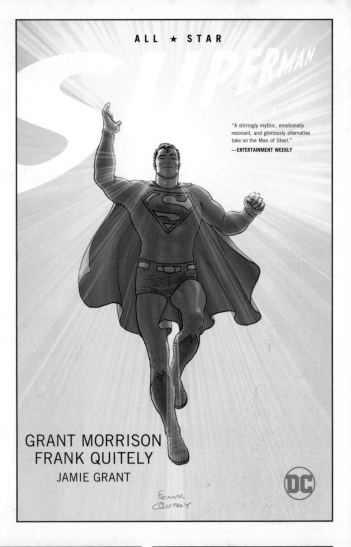

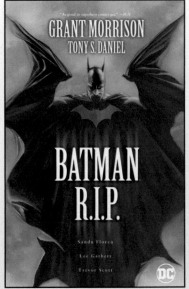

"Jack Kirby created much of the language of superhero comics. He took vaudeville and made it opera. He took a static medium and gave it motion."

–Neil Gaiman

JACK KIRBY
NEW GODS

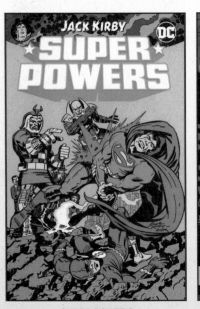

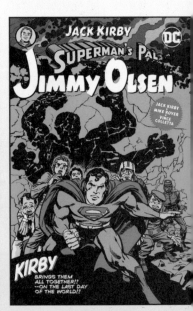

**SUPER POWERS
BY JACK KIRBY**

**DC UNIVERSE
THE BRONZE AGE OMNIBUS
BY JACK KIRBY**

**SUPERMAN'S PAL
JIMMY OLSEN
BY JACK KIRBY**